COYOTE HUNGER

THE COMPLETE SERIES

RHIAN CAHILL

Coyote Hunger
By Rhian Cahill

For more information visit:
www.rhiancahill.com

For what's coming next, latest releases, sales and more, join
Rhian's Royal Readers
http://www.rhiancahill.com/contact/newsletter/

COYOTE HOME

COYOTE HUNGER

For the man who rocks my world. Together forever.

1

RUN

The thump of paws hitting hard ground echoed off the valley walls, twigs snapped and leaves were crushed in the mad dash through the forest. Adrenaline pumped through veins pounding with the exhilaration of running free. Rowan loved to run in coyote form but tonight wasn't any old frolic in the woods. Tonight was about escape.

Quinn raced beside her, his beating heart and heavy breaths a welcome comfort. They ran together, darting between trees and through the underbrush as they made their way over the mountains. Speed was important. Quinn needed to be back in Whispering Springs before morning or questions would be asked too soon. Rowan needed to be far from home before anyone discovered her missing.

Her injuries from Marcus' attack were quickly repairing but she still felt dull aches rippling through her muscles. She leapt over a fallen log and the pack strapped to her back shifted to the side, throwing her off balance. Rowan stumbled, her front paws losing their grip in the slippery debris of rotting leaves littering the forest floor. The ground rushed up to meet her and pain exploded in her head. With a yelp, she crumpled to the dirt.

"Rowan!"

Quinn had shifted back to human form and was on his knees beside her, the strap of his pack digging into his bare chest. He ran his hands along her fur-covered limbs, her side and over her skull. His fingers gently probed for any injury. Rowan panted for breath and waited for the dizziness to fade before she changed from coyote to human.

"I'm okay," she gasped. "Just winded."

He reached for the snap on her pack and flicked it open. The tightness in Rowan's chest eased slightly and she drew in a deeper breath as the bag fell to the ground behind her.

"Thanks."

"We'll rest here for a bit." Quinn removed his own pack and placed it beside them.

Rowan pushed off the ground and sat cross-legged, her uncovered ass connecting with the cold floor. Her body protested the move but she didn't have the luxury of being a wimp tonight or ever again for that matter. She dragged her bag closer, unzipped it and pulled out a water bottle. With a flick of her wrist, she popped the top and took a couple of gulps before handing it to Quinn.

His hand wrapped around hers but he didn't take the container. Rowan looked up to find him staring at her. The naked longing swirling in his gaze heated her blood and called to her coyote. Already close to the surface, her beast answered with a call of her own. Need and want zapped through her. Quinn's hand shook, the fine tremors vibrating along her skin in an electric wave that made every instinct she had scream with desire.

He squeezed her fingers before he removed his hand with a growl. "Damn, I want you."

Rowan watched the struggle he waged inside, every emotion crossed his face as he fought to gain control. She knew Quinn was trying to hold back for her benefit but she didn't need his protection. She needed him.

Before she could second-guess the move, Rowan crossed the distance between them. She wrapped her arms around Quinn's neck and slammed her mouth to his. Her tongue slipped out to trace the seam of his lips. For what seemed like hours he remained motionless, unresponsive to her demanding kiss. On the verge of pulling back, Rowan found herself toppling forward instead.

Quinn fell back, his arms clamped around her waist to hold her close as he took them to the forest floor. He took control, his mouth eating at hers with need and desperation. Rowan could feel the raw emotions rolling off him, or maybe they were hers bouncing back. Tonight might be the only night they'd ever share and she intended to make the most of it.

Years of waiting collided with fear of what was to come and drove them both quickly to the edge. Her nipples pebbled, poked into the hard muscle of Quinn's chest, the contact taking the hunger deeper. Undone by the arousal swamping her, Rowan rocked her hips and rubbed her pussy on the hard length pressing against her. He sucked her tongue into his mouth as his hips thrust up.

His cock slid along her slick folds, bumping her clit and delivering sparks of fire into her core. Her womb clenched and moisture flowed from her body to coat them both. The scent of her cream surrounded them and Rowan's body rippled with the orgasm just out of reach. She tore her mouth from his, gasped for breath as she braced her hands on his shoulders and pushed up.

"Not here. Not like this."

Quinn's plea went unheeded as Rowan sought the one thing that would calm the frenzy taking her over. She had to have him inside her. Take him until they were one. Her hand slipped between them and her fingers encircled his erection. She squeezed his flesh, stroked him from root to tip. Using her legs, she rose up and guided the head to her opening.

"Rowan."

Their gazes met and as she lowered her body they held their breath. Resistance to the invasion clenched her muscles and sent fear trickling through her.

"You're not ready."

Rowan threw her head back and laughed. The idea that she

wasn't ready for this moment was ludicrous when she'd waited the last five years for this very minute. She leaned forward, brushed her lips on his and whispered, "I'm more ready than I've ever been."

She pushed down and a little more of his cock breached her resisting body. The pain was minimal and no doubt would get worse before the sheer pleasure of being with Quinn surpassed it. With small gyrations, Rowan slowly took him deeper. Each inch stretched her walls to the point of pain but not enough for her to stop.

"Jeez, you're killing me here," he ground out through clenched teeth.

Quinn's face and chest were coated in sweat, his muscles straining as he held still beneath her. With one final lunge she buried his length to the hilt. Any pain was quickly gone as sensations she'd never experienced registered. The fullness of having him inside, the way his cock brushed her tender walls, the cradle of his hips supporting hers, all unfamiliar but so right.

A moan slipped from her throat, mixed with the pleasure of being joined to Quinn and the vagueness of when they would be together again after tonight, and rumbled with a ragged edge. She slumped forward, laid her cheek on his chest and absorbed the truth of them together. Now.

"Take your time." His hand caressed her hair, his fingers combing through the strands. "We can stop if it hurts."

Rowan smiled. Quinn always thought of her first. Sadness flooded her as the certainty of being without him in the future clutched her heart. She took a deep breath. Determination to not allow Marcus or his father to take this beautiful moment from them straightened her spine and gave her the courage to take what joy she could from the darkness that surrounded them.

His hand stroked down her spine, a tender touch meant to soothe, not inflame. But when it came to Quinn everything he did had her body on hyper-alert. A shiver trailed his fingers, the gentle shudder not stopping until it reached her curling toes. Heat spiraled in her belly and dripped lower. Her pussy clenched and his shaft pulsed as her walls gripped him tighter.

As her body adjusted to being joined with Quinn the world disappeared. Her mind focused on the pleasure streaking its way toward a peak she'd never reached before. Bombarded, Rowan knew only one thing. Move. She had to move.

"Rowan, do you want to stop?"

Quinn's words came the second she put action to thought. He growled when she swiveled her hips and he slid out until only the head of his cock remained inside her. They both moaned as she reversed the motion. Experimenting, Rowan arched her back and cantered her pelvis. The angle changed and more of her tender flesh burst into flame at the new contact. Her clit throbbed, her sheath quivered and more cream lubricated her swollen folds.

"God, that feels good."

Rowan had to agree. A smile curled her lips and she pushed back to sit, straddling him. Quinn's hands grasped her waist, helped her lift and drop as she found a rhythm that excited them both.

"Damn." His fingers tightened, dug into her sides. "I'm not gonna last long."

Good. She wouldn't be far behind him if she didn't go over the edge first. They'd always stopped before either of them reached the point of no return. An orgasm would mark them and they couldn't afford to risk it until they were ready to be mated and before now that wasn't an option.

She rocked her hips, drove down hard and pulled back slow. Her clit grazed the base of his shaft on every plunge. Muscles coiled, her walls sucking at his length with each pass. Quinn's hand left her side and delved between her legs. His fingers zeroed in on the tight bundle of nerves. Pleasure sharpened and Rowan's movements turned frantic.

Quinn finally moved under her. He'd given her control until now but he took it from her with lightning speed. He thrust up, driving his cock impossibly deep. His hands splayed on her hips and he held her still while he fucked her. She rode the razor edge of her orgasm, almost, but not quite going over. A growl filled the air and Rowan's world tilted.

He spun them, had her on her hands and knees before her next heartbeat. Her fingers curled into the dirt and leaves as Quinn's thighs met hers. His hot length probed between her legs and with one hard thrust he sank back inside her welcoming pussy. Rowan's back arched and she pushed her ass against him, taking him deeper. Quinn curled his front over her, their hot, slick skin sliding together.

The slap and squelch of flesh meeting flesh filled the air, mixed with the scent of sex and teased and tantalized until Rowan's breath became jagged rasps of fire lancing her lungs. His fingers found her clit, he circled the wet bud, pinched it—tugged. Sensation splintered and stars flashed before her eyes. Her womb clenched, her pussy clamping around the hot rod impaled in her depths.

A scream ripped from her throat as her orgasm tore through her. Quinn continued to pound into her from behind, his hands gripping her waist to hold her still. Her head and shoulders dropped to the ground, leaves mashed into the side of her face but nothing mattered but the delirious bliss rolling over her.

The growl that rumbled in the air made her jump, the snarl quickly followed by a howl made her coyote lie down and open for her mate completely. Quinn's chest connected with her back and Rowan raised herself up and arched into him. She turned and dropped her head, offered him the tender slope of her neck to sink his teeth into.

Sharp canines scraped her skin, the sting more tingle than pain. Quinn's fingers continued to strum her clit. Her orgasm had receded only to be driven back up again by his caress. He growled against her neck, the sound vibrating down her spine and into the heat simmering in her belly. His thrusts turned into erratic, frenzied pumps of his cock into her convulsing pussy.

Quinn jerked and buried himself to the hilt. Hot spurts of cum bathed her cervix as he sank his teeth into the side of her throat. There was no pain, a slight sting before fiery tingles raced out in a game of chase. Ribbons of delight connected erogenous zones and pulled tight. Spasms started low and deep, spiraling out until they dropped her off the edge again.

Spent, they slumped forward, crumpling to the floor in a tangled mess of bodies and limbs. Quinn rolled to his side and took her with him. He cradled her in his arms, his ragged breath bathing her neck and shoulder. Rowan's breathing was just as harsh, as was the pounding of her heart against her ribs. Her bones felt as solid as cooked noodles and Rowan wondered if she'd ever be able to walk again.

Reality started to return with the night sounds of the forest around them. She knew they had to get up and keep going. If they were going to make the rendezvous site and give Quinn plenty of time to get back to Whispering Creek before daybreak they needed to go now.

Rowan turned in his embrace. "We need to go."

"A minute more won't hurt." He dropped a kiss on her nose. "Rest for a second and then we'll head out again."

By the time their bodies cooled they'd regained their breath. Rowan was the first to move, Quinn gave her one last squeeze before letting go. Neither spoke as they retrieved their bags. Rowan stashed the water bottle inside before stretching the elastic strap and locking the clip into place. The band pinched but once she shifted to coyote form it would be a perfect fit.

"Ready?"

"No, but do we have a choice?" Quinn asked.

Rowan didn't answer him. They both knew this was their only option now that Marcus had attacked her. With the senior Connelly as sovereign, Quinn and Brogan had no way of protecting her against Marcus' advances. No matter how violent he'd become, his father refused to stop him. And with Connelly's supporters firmly in place, Rowan's only hope was to leave and return when it was safe.

The question was, how long would it take to rid the pack of the evil that had taken hold after her and Brogan's parents had died?

2

————————

Quinn slowed, turned to sniff the air and waited for Rowan to catch up. They'd taken the last thirty minutes at a walk, the steep descent needed concentration and careful steps. Even in their coyote forms, this ridge was treacherous. She caught up and stopped beside him, her head tilted to the side, she waited for his lead. He wanted her again. Once wasn't enough and before dawn she'd be gone.

They were less than fifty feet from the valley floor and he knew of a small secluded section of rock face that almost formed a cave. He'd head there and they could take a break before moving on. Quinn was satisfied the only other person in this area of the mountains was Brogan and he, about an hour behind, was trailing them at a discreet distance. Rowan didn't know her brother followed, it was just a precaution but they couldn't risk going without him.

He nodded for her to follow and made his way down the last few feet of mountainside. There had been plenty of time to think after their mad dash through the forest. Once they'd cleared the second ridge the chance of anyone seeing them had been unlikely. Only a few pack members lived beyond the town center and those that did chose the eastern side, not the west.

Getting Rowan off the mountains and away from Marcus quickly and with as much stealth as possible meant their best bet was going west. It had taken less than ten minutes to make their plan and put it into action. It had taken twice that for Rowan and Brogan to talk him out of going after Marcus the second Rowan had told them what had happened. He stumbled on a loose rock when the image of her bruised and bleeding as she staggered through the back door flashed through his mind.

His animal had come roaring to life, ready to rip apart the threat to his mate. It didn't matter that they hadn't completed their mating. For years they were forced to wait, first Rowan's age and then the death of her parents had stopped them. And since that fateful day no one in the pack made a move without the sovereign's okay and there was no way in the world the current sovereign would okay their joining.

Malcolm Connelly ruled by brute strength and intimidation. The once prosperous pack now floundered under his leadership. Quinn and Brogan were working to improve the stability of the pack but the younger members were leaving in droves, there was nothing here but fear and a nonexistent community. Without the next generation, the pack didn't stand a chance of surviving.

They had a plan, were steadily working toward it but with the assault on Rowan he knew things would only get worse from here on. Neither he nor Brogan could protect her from what both Connellys wanted. Standing and support within the pack was what they needed and didn't have. It was only a matter of time before the violence escalated and Quinn wanted her safe. *Needed* her to be safe. And that meant sending her away.

Quinn moved more quickly, Rowan close behind. Not far now and they could rest again. He'd take every extra second with her he could get. The moon, high in the sky, illuminated the rocky section of the valley they headed toward. Small bushes filled this area of the basin, which meant there wasn't as much cover but his senses told him no one else was around to see as they made their way to the darkness of the outcrop.

He shifted back to human form and quickly checked for any animals—dead or alive. His nose told him there weren't any but he wanted to be sure. With the wall of rocks the ground was clear of rotting vegetation and it didn't look like any creature had made this place home since he'd last been here. Quinn stepped back and motioned for Rowan to go first.

She'd shifted and removed her backpack. His body tightened. The sight of Rowan always jangled his nerves but a naked Rowan could jumble his brain in a nanosecond. He blanked out their trek across the mountain and forgot all about the danger she was in. The only thing on his mind was tackling her to the ground and taking her again. With his hands clenched at his side so he didn't reach for her, Quinn followed Rowan into the dark shelter.

"Are we staying here long?"

Her question startled him but it was her naked body suddenly plastered to the front of him that shocked him speechless. She wove her fingers into his hair and pulled his mouth to hers. His cock sprang to life, hardening between them. Their tongues dueled as they each demanded the other give. Rowan's flavor intoxicated—drove him dizzy with lust. The scent of her arousal mixed with the smell of their earlier lovemaking surrounded them in a lush cocoon.

Quinn's hands slid down the curve of her spine to cup her ass. He squeezed and lifted her against him. Rowan wrapped her legs around his waist and ground her sex against his hard-on. Slick heat coated his swollen flesh and he flexed his hips, rubbing his length over her clit. She bucked into him and threw her head back with a moan. Her breasts rose up and he leaned forward to suck one pointy peak between his lips.

He pulled the delicate morsel deeper, pushed it to the roof of his mouth before retreating and dragging his teeth lightly over the hard tip. Her back bowed and he almost lost his footing. Quinn regained his balance and bent his knees, taking them to the floor quickly. She straddled his hips, her legs crossed behind him to wrap around his torso like a pair of arms.

Rowan held him tight, her breasts pressed to his face and Quinn wasted no time in letting his lips explore her. He licked, kissed and sucked his way across her smooth skin. His beard stubble would leave red marks but he didn't care, he knew by her little cries of delight he wasn't hurting and he wanted to mark her. Wanted her to remember him after she'd left.

The thought of Rowan leaving clenched his heart. It went against everything claiming a mate should be. His coyote howled at the injustice of losing his mate after finally taking her but Quinn's human side knew the only way to truly protect her was to remove her from danger. Until he and Brogan were able to take a stronger standing in the Whispering Mountains pack Rowan would need to remain hidden. He didn't want to think about how long that could take.

Instead he concentrated on the now, and the hot woman in his arms. Quinn nibbled his way up her chest to the slender column of her throat. He nipped with his teeth until she tilted her head giving him better access to the delicate slope. He laved the shallow dip where her pulse beat frantically. A fine film of sweat covered her skin and he lapped at it as he made his way to her mouth.

When he reached her full lower lip he tugged it with his teeth, urging her to open for him. She complied on a moan and he slipped his tongue out to taste her, just a quick lash to tempt her to come play. He tickled the corners of her mouth before caressing the curve of her smile. Quinn kept his actions slow, teasing them both until it wasn't enough. Their breathing grew harsh, the sound amplified by the cavern walls. Their movements got faster, frantic for just the right friction.

Rowan tore her mouth from his and they both gasped for breath. She rocked her pelvis and his cock slid between her slick folds to rest at her opening. He gripped her hips and thrust into her heat. Sunk to the hilt, her flesh scorched him from tip to root. His sac tightened, her sheath like a hot silk cloth draped around his shaft. She began to ride him, up and down, in a slow slide of rippling muscle that threatened to milk the cum from his balls. He wouldn't last long.

Quinn had spent years imagining getting inside Rowan and the reality far outweighed anything his limited imagination could conjure up. Being his mate she was guaranteed to send his hormones into overload but now that they'd joined he struggled to think past burying himself inside her over and over again. If anything this second time felt better than the first.

Her backside slapped on his thighs on each down stroke, the noise echoing around them. She rode him. Took them both up to the peak as if they hadn't sated themselves an hour ago. Quinn leaned forward and clamped his teeth on her tender flesh where shoulder met neck. His tongue licked at the soft tissue caught between his teeth and he bit a little harder. She moaned and dropped her head, nibbling on him the same way.

The orgasm stole his breath but nothing could steal the coyote instinct to claim what was his. Sharp canines pierced delicate skin with the first blast of cum through his cock. A second spurt coincided with an intense burning at his throat where Rowan bit him but he was too far down the magical path of ecstasy to register what it meant. Rowan's pussy clenched, her convulsing walls pulling every drop of cum from the bottom of his balls.

As his heart rate slowed and his lungs started to fill with life-giving oxygen Quinn's body sent out a protest. Pain radiated from his knees and shins, the hard rocky ground unforgiving on his weight-bearing limbs. Rowan lay limp on his chest, her heavy breathing fanning out over his pecs. She'd slumped in his lap as the final wave of her climax subsided. He needed to move her, get them both cleaned up and comfortable.

How he would do that in a dirt-covered, cave-like grotto he didn't know. They had limited supplies in their packs. Just a few essentials for Rowan to take with her in her flight to safety and their water bottles. She had two sets of clothes but nothing else. Even if time had permitted, she couldn't afford to run with much more than what she had. The one thing she did have plenty of was money.

Quinn and Brogan had given her all the cash they had in the house. Quinn had also asked Dale to get her some more, he'd told his friend he'd replace it once the bank opened on Monday. He wanted more than anything to go with her but if they ever hoped to return the pack to a prosperous one, he and Brogan needed to work together to make it happen. It was up to the younger generation, those that were left, to see to the future stability of Whispering Springs.

Rowan understood what they wanted to do, *needed* to do. She was the first to say the only way for her to stay safe was to leave the pack. With Marcus intent on having Rowan and his father willing to back him in his quest, no one could protect her well enough to keep her alive. And Quinn feared it would come to that. If she didn't bow to Marcus, and she never would, he'd kill her.

As much as it went against every need and want inside him, Quinn would rather Rowan be alive and away from him than the alternative. He'd just have to work extra hard to make the mountains a safe haven once more. Somewhere that she could return, a place she'd want to come back to. He squeezed her closer, soaked in the warmth and smell of her. If he was going to let her go he wanted to burn the memory of her in his arms, the way she smelled and the feel of being joined with her on his soul.

"I love you."

Her words floated on the quiet night, a balm to the heart that was tearing in two inside his chest.

"I know." He kissed the top of her head. "I love you too."

"I don't want to let you go."

Quinn squeezed his eyes tight, the pain in her voice sliced at his gut. "If for one second I thought we could do this another way, we would." He eased away to look in her eyes. "I want you alive, whether it's by my side or a thousand miles away I don't care. I'll do everything I can to make it safe for you to return. I promise."

He brushed his lips over hers, a light touch to seal his promise. Rowan's mouth opened on a sigh and Quinn took advantage and slipped his tongue into the dark warmth beyond. The kiss was easy, a delicate exploration that stole his breath. Unhurried, he took the time to savor, to memorize every taste, every texture. After she left tonight Quinn had no idea how long it would be before he saw her again— had her again, and he'd be damned if she'd leave without him having all of her.

His cock hardened. They remained joined and he bucked his hips to slide against her slick heat. Her pussy fluttered along his length and more blood pumped into his shaft. Rowan groaned into his mouth. The sound echoed through his head and sent his pulse pounding in his ears. She rolled her pelvis, rocked them together in a slow rhythm that drove his arousal higher. Quinn wanted to slam into her, his coyote wanted hard and fast but the man wanted, *needed* soft and slow.

Rowan broke their kiss, trailed her lips down his jaw and continued until she nibbled on his throat. Her hands inched over his shoulders, down his back. When her fingers connected with his pack they both froze. Quinn was stunned to realize he still wore the bag. They both reached to undo the clasp, their hands tangling and making the task difficult. Laughter spilled from Rowan and he soaked in the sound, added it to his store of memories.

"How did we manage to not notice this before?" She nudged his hands away and quickly snapped the clip free.

He smiled. "More important things to notice I guess."

Quinn cupped her breasts, flicked her nipples with his thumbs and Rowan sucked in a breath. Her chest rose and filled his hands with her warm flesh. He leaned forward, drew a taut peak into his mouth and the pack hit the ground behind him. Her fingers curled around his head and held him close. Not wanting to disappoint, he did as her action suggested and sucked harder.

Her nipple puckered hard as a rock against his tongue and Quinn clamped the small bud between his teeth. Rowan's back arched and her breast pulled from his mouth with a small pop. His cock pulsed as her muscles rippled in a wave from root to tip. He groaned. The sound turned into a growl as she rose up and plunged back down. She dug her fingers into his shoulders, her nails biting into his skin.

Together they rocked, thrusting in counterpoint until Quinn's groin burned with the orgasm building. The first spasms of Rowan's climax sent fire shooting up his spine and bursting from his balls. Cum surged up his length and spewed from the tip to bathe her core.

Her cry of release bounced off the rock walls, the sound like music in his ears.

She sat in his lap, her head resting on his shoulder and he wrapped his arms around her to hold her closer. Their skin, hot and sticky, clung, binding them together just as their souls now were.

3

Rowan waited, crouched behind a tree, making no sound. She could hear Quinn moving around behind her but nothing else moved. Her sense of smell had never been that good, she got by but in no way did she compare to Quinn. Then again no one compared to him when it came to scenting the air.

They arrived at the designated meeting point about fifteen minutes ahead of time. Quinn wanted to be in place down the road from the lookout parking lot to make sure nobody followed Dale. Rowan didn't think they had anything to worry about. Dale Turner was a big city cop, he knew what he was doing. Dale's skills were the reason Quinn had called him.

A low hum filled the air, growing into a roar as the vehicle moved up the mountain road toward them. Headlights flashed off the trees around her but the car kept going. She heard the brakes squeal and finally silence. Rowan waited. Quinn wouldn't move up to meet Dale until he was sure they were alone so she held still and ignored the numbness in her feet.

She wore jeans, a t-shirt and sweater. Sneakers without socks. Quinn, on the other hand, was barely covered by a pair of shorts. He'd left both bags at her feet and once he gave her the all clear she'd move everything left into one pack to take with her. The money Quinn and Brogan had given her was in her pocket. Rowan hated the idea of carrying so much on her but she couldn't afford to access her bank account if she wanted to remain undiscovered.

Quinn appeared before her, sucking the breath from her lungs. It wasn't just his near naked state that left her breathless. He'd moved without a sound, she'd had no clue he was there until he popped up in front of her eyes.

"It's clear." He reached a hand out to her. "Come on, we'll fix the bags at the truck."

Dale Turner was bigger than she remembered, then again he was only a boy when he'd left Whispering Springs. Now he was every inch a man. Her fingers tightened around Quinn's. She didn't fear Dale so much as leaving Quinn. Her instincts were screaming to hold on and never let go but the rational part of her knew she had to leave. If she didn't it wouldn't just be her life in jeopardy.

Marcus would stop at nothing to get at her and she knew because he'd told her, he'd go after Quinn and Brogan to get his way. To protect her mate and her brother she had to leave and let them do what was necessary to rid their pack of the evil festering inside. Neither of them could do that if they were worried about her. For the first time in her life she would be on her own and Rowan had no doubt the next few weeks would be the hardest she'd ever experienced.

Even harder than the day they buried her parents.

She walked beside Quinn, head held high like she had all the courage in the world. If it wasn't for her shaking insides she might even fool herself into believing it.

"Dale." Quinn extended his hand to his old friend. "Long time."

Dale grabbed Quinn's hand, his grip strong. "Too long, but then I don't make it a habit of visiting the mountain now that I've got no family left."

"Sorry about your mom."

"Thanks but it was past time. She'd been sick so long it was a blessing for her to find peace."

Quinn turned to Rowan. "You remember Rowan?"

"I'd like to say it's nice to see you again, Rowan, but under the circumstances I don't think it quite fits."

Rowan smiled, but she didn't look happy, more like she was in pain. "No, the circumstances are not the nicest."

He squeezed her hand and tugged her under his arm before turning back to Dale. "Did you do everything I asked?"

"Yeah, it's all sorted. She'll be out of the state before anyone knows she's left the mountains. After that Rowan can decide where she goes."

"Thanks. I owe you."

"No you don't. This is what friends are for."

Rowan had pulled free of his arms and was busy stuffing everything into one of the packs. There was a slight tremor in her hands but other than that it could be any normal day. Except it wasn't and getting it over with quickly wouldn't make it hurt any less.

Quinn knew he was dragging this out but he couldn't bring himself to let Rowan go yet. A few more minutes wouldn't matter.

"Are you ready? We need to get on the road." Dale directed his question to Rowan and Quinn felt her stiffen beside him.

"No, but I don't have a choice do I?"

Dale shrugged. "Not if you want to stay alive."

His friend knew all that was going on in the pack, Quinn had made sure he'd filled him in on enough detail to ensure he understood the danger Rowan was in. He trusted Dale to see to her safety. The man was one of the few he would consider asking for help. Of the other two, one was at this moment heading back to Whispering Creek and the other was in town keeping a close eye on their mutual enemy.

This was it. He had to let her go and hope like mad it wasn't the last time he saw her. Quinn grabbed Rowan's elbow, spun her into his arms and slammed his mouth to hers. His tongue invaded her mouth and conquered any protest she might have. There was no fight, she gave and took in the same breath. They stood there on the moonlit road and devoured each other. The not-so-gentle clearing of a throat brought them back to earth with a jerk.

Dale had turned his back while they kissed. His discreet action proving Quinn's trust was well placed. He could breathe easy knowing Rowan was in good hands. She stepped out of his embrace and took a deep breath before handing him the spare pack.

"I'm ready. Let's go."

With one final look at him she turned and walked away. Quinn clenched his fists, his jaw, every muscle in his body, fought to keep himself in place and not run after her. They were making the right decision. And if it wasn't right he'd move heaven and earth to fix it.

Rowan stared straight ahead. She didn't want to look at Quinn. Didn't want to watch him disappear from view as they drove away. Tears dripped down her cheeks and off her chin to land on her hands clasped tightly together in her lap. Dale started the pickup and she couldn't stop herself. Her gaze darted to the side mirror. He stood at the edge of the forest, a solitary figure in the darkness of pre-dawn hours.

Dale put the vehicle in gear and began to drive. The crunch of gravel under heavy tires grew louder as the car picked up speed. The man watching them leave got smaller with every inch they drove. A sob rattled her chest, the sound a desperate cry from a heart splintering in two. Emotions swelled, bubbling up and over as Rowan's coyote howled for the mate she was leaving behind.

Unable to control the urge, she spun in her seat to look through the rear window. Darkness hid his expression but Rowan knew from Quinn's stance that he hurt as much as she did. Her chest ached and her stomach cramped. The pain almost caused her to double over but she wouldn't turn away, wouldn't deny herself this final glimpse of him. As the truck took a bend in the road Quinn was taken from her field of vision and lowering her forehead to the back of the seat Rowan cried for all they were being denied.

The silence in the cab was broken by Dale's deep voice. "I won't tell you everything will work out." He ran his hand over her back but it was little comfort. "I will tell you that I know Quinn and Brogan well enough to know that if anyone can fix what's wrong with the pack it's those two."

Rowan knew he spoke the truth. Each had the determination and strength to get the job done but the two of them together would be a formidable force. She turned around to face forward and put her seat belt on. Her tears had stopped but the pain hadn't. The ache wouldn't go away until she was home. Back in Quinn's arms.

As the drone of tires rolling over tarmac filled the air Rowan used the mundane sound and the miles they traveled to collect herself. She put her love for Quinn and all she'd left behind in a corner of her heart and closed it off. With each new breath she took, she vowed to do all in her power to help them and if that meant living away she would. She'd be as strong as they needed her to be and when she finally returned she'd take her place in the pack and make her mate and brother proud.

Quinn's paws pounded across the damp earth. He drove his body hard, the need to numb his senses overwhelming as he fought against his coyote to keep heading home. The animal wanted to turn around, follow the truck that had taken his mate but Quinn knew to do so would mean denying them any future at all. The sound of an approaching coyote didn't slow him down.

His coat hung limp, weighed down by the sweat pouring from his body as he pushed it to the limit. Brogan joined him, each running to assuage the ache inside them. Quinn wouldn't use his own pain to diminish his friends. They'd both given up a hell of a lot tonight. Before he knew it they were in the trees behind the house. Slowing, he brought himself to a stop at the tree line.

He didn't want to go forward and he couldn't go back. With a shudder that traveled from his head to his tail he took the first step toward his life without Rowan by his side. Brogan stayed back, allowed him to lead them across the field that was their backyard. Quinn would have to thank him for that consideration later. They reached the front porch and he shifted from coyote to human.

Naked as the day he was born, Quinn sat on the cold front step and stared off into the distance. Silently, his best friend joined him. Lost in his own thoughts he didn't acknowledge Brogan's presence. Didn't think he could speak yet even if he had something to say. It was Brogan who broke the quiet.

"We'll bring her home." His words were a vow, one they both shared.

Quinn tried to talk but all that came out was a croak worthy of a frog. He swallowed, cleared his throat and tried again.

"Yes, we will."

"I can live with her not being here as long as she's safe from Marcus."

"She'd be safe if you let me go after him now," Quinn growled.

"You know you can't do that. Connelly would set one of his henchmen on you in a heartbeat, he just needs an excuse. Don't give him one, Quinn."

"How can you sit back and not want to rip Marcus to pieces for what he did to Rowan?"

"I never said I didn't want to." Brogan sighed. "Truth is it took every ounce of control I have to *not* go after him. I'd love nothing more than to kill him with my bare hands but we both know that isn't going to help any of us."

Quinn let out a breath. He knew Brogan was right. They needed to gain support from the pack, needed to prove to the Council the sovereign should be removed from his position. And the only way to do that was to outsmart him. The senior Connelly would be tricky to trip up, he'd spent years cementing his brand of leadership on the pack and no one was willing to go against him.

Violence would probably be involved but it wouldn't be the way they won this fight. They needed the support of as many councilmen as they could get and they needed to stop the younger generation from leaving the mountains too. Without the future to fight for, the older pack members wouldn't see any point in throwing their allegiance behind Brogan.

"You're right. I just need to get past tonight and then I'll be fine." Quinn hoped he spoke the truth. Living without Rowan would not be easy but he would do what he had to so he could secure their future and that of the pack.

Brogan stood and clapped his hand on Quinn's shoulder. "I'm going inside for coffee. Are you coming?"

"No. I think I need to be outside a bit longer. Maybe go for another run." Energy vibrated through his body, his coyote stirring with renewed hunger. He wanted to break free and run. But Quinn was in control. The animal urges would not get the best of him. Standing abruptly, he knocked Brogan's hand off. "I'll be back soon."

He jumped off the steps and without thought he shifted to coyote form and ran. He headed for the ridge that would give him a clear view of his home and remind him of everything he stood to lose if he didn't pull himself together and fight with all he had. As he darted through the underbrush he disturbed creatures just waking from a night of sleep. The forest stirred to life around him, another reminder of all that was at stake.

With speed and agility he made his way up the mountain and to the outcrop that overlooked the house he shared with the Wilder siblings. Pain lanced his chest as he thought of how empty the house would be without Rowan in it. How empty he would be without her.

Brogan Wilder stood at his bedroom window with coffee in hand. He'd known where Quinn was headed, he didn't think his friend should be alone but he gave him the space he seemed to need. He had a clear view of the mountainside and the ridge behind the house. From there, he knew you could see for miles. Raising his mug he took a sip of rich dark liquid.

The sun was almost up and Brogan knew today would be the beginning of a long road. One he wouldn't travel alone but only the toughest would survive it. He wasn't sure how exactly they were going to remove Malcolm Connelly from his position as sovereign but he knew they would. All he had to do was think about what his sister and his best friend were being forced to endure to know he'd do whatever it took to put the pack back to rights.

A small flock of birds burst from the trees near the top of the ridge and Brogan knew Quinn was close to reaching the summit. He understood the need to run, the need to feel in control that was coursing through his friend's veins. Brogan's own blood pumped with the yen to run and never stop but he couldn't afford to give in. Not today and not ever. If he was going to lead the pack into a prosperous future he couldn't give in to the emotion.

His shoulders slumped with all that rested on them. Brogan knew he'd done the right thing sending Rowan away, knew how much easier it would be for them to wrestle control of the pack from Connelly with her safely stashed away. But all the logical arguments in the world couldn't take away the pain of losing his sister. Not even knowing she'd be able to come home one day helped to ease the ache in his heart.

He could only imagine the pain his best friend and sister were suffering. If nothing else he'd make sure both Connellys paid for that. Brogan wasn't a vengeful person but where the Connellys were concerned he'd make an exception. Determination straightened his spine, they would see this through. Satisfied they'd made the right decision, Brogan watched and waited for the new day.

And as dawn broke, a lone coyote stood on Whispering Ridge. In the solitude of the first morning light he threw back his head and howled.

4

———————

HOME

Timber crashed against timber. Windows rattled in their frames and the hardwood floor vibrated beneath her bare feet.

Time to face the music.

Rowan turned toward the door. She knew what she would see but knowing and seeing were two different things. Silhouetted by the sun, the six-foot-four wall of solid muscle standing in the doorway was menacing in appearance and attitude. She should be terrified but she'd never been afraid of Quinn. She knew to the depth of her soul that he'd never hurt her no matter what she'd done.

"Hello, Quinn."

"Get your things, you're coming home."

Rowan rolled her eyes. He hadn't changed. Six years hadn't tempered his demanding personality. Then again it had done little to curb her rebellious nature and need to provoke him. In fact, it had increased her need to make her own decisions. Her independence had come at a cost. Being separated from her family, her home—her mate. It had almost cost her sanity.

"No." She wasn't going to allow Quinn or her brother to tell her what to do anymore. She'd finally come home to face her destiny and her mate but she was here on her terms, best to get everyone used to the new Rowan from the start.

"No?" Quinn's brow creased and the confusion swirling in his caramel brown eyes almost made her back down. Almost.

She sucked in a deep breath, stiffened her spine and straightened her shoulders.

"I'm not coming to Whispering Creek yet. I need time."

"Time? For what? And why the hell didn't you tell me you were on an earlier flight?" Anger and hurt simmered in his voice.

"I need to adjust to being home, Quinn."

"You're not home. Your home is Whispering Creek—by my side."

"I am home. Whispering Mountains is home."

"You're not staying here. Get your things or I will."

"No."

"Rowan," he growled.

"Quinn, please try to understand. I've been gone six years—"

"Exactly. You've spent too long away from me already. Get your stuff."

"No. I'm not leaving the cabin until I'm ready."

He took a step toward her, a growl rumbling deep in his bare chest and his eyes flared amber with the anger her disobedience raised. She put up a hand and stood her ground.

"Don't you dare come any closer." To her surprise, he stopped. She swallowed over the lump in her throat. "Please, Quinn. You have to understand. I've ignored my coyote for six years. I can't even remember what she looks like. I need to reconnect, need to be comfortable in both my skins. I can't do that if I have to deal with the pack."

Commotion behind Quinn drew both their gazes. Brogan stood at the door stomping snow and mud from his boots. He stepped into the room and threw a bag at Quinn.

"Get dressed," Brogan barked at Quinn but his eyes were on Rowan. "What the hell do you think you're doing?" he demanded.

Great. Two alpha males to deal with. On their own she knew she could handle them but together, batting for the same cause...

Rowan closed her eyes, tried to focus on what she knew she wanted. What she needed. Dragging in more oxygen, she steeled her determination to get them to see it from her side. The swish of cloth and the metallic hiss of a zipper closing snapped her eyes open.

She breathed easier. Now that Quinn had some clothes on she wouldn't have to deal with the distraction of his naked body. And what a gorgeous body it was, all sculpted muscle and smooth male skin. Memories of exploring his hard male flesh with her hands sent a shiver down her spine. She curled her fingers, clenched them tight to stop her hands from reaching out to touch.

How she hadn't jumped him the second he slammed through the door stark naked was beyond her. There was not one day, one night over the last six years where her body hadn't craved his and all the pleasure tangling with him gave her. She licked her dry lips before speaking to her brother.

"Hello to you too, Brogan."

He looked sheepish for all of two seconds before his face drew into an angry scowl. Rowan sighed. She really didn't want their first meeting to be clouded with anger. But then what she wanted and what she got were rarely the same.

"When did you get in? And why didn't you tell us you were coming early?"

The coffee machine dinged, signaling it was ready. A shot of caffeine was just what this occasion needed. At least she needed it. She turned, reached into the cupboard for two more cups and poured each of them full to the brim. None of them took milk and she'd given up sugar a few years ago.

Quinn moved up beside her, close but not touching. Heat radiated off him and his scent flowed around her, through her. Breathing deeply she pulled him in, filled her lungs with the smell she'd gone so long without.

"Here." He held the sugar bowl out to her.

Raising her gaze to his, she said, "I don't take sugar anymore."

Shock bloomed in his eyes, then confusion.

"It's just one of many things that have changed, Quinn." She tried not to squirm when he leaned in close, sniffed at her neck, her breasts. She knew he was scenting for another male. He wouldn't find one. "That hasn't."

A low rumble was Rowan's only warning. He turned quickly, slanting his mouth over hers. Crushing pressure and his probing tongue had her opening to him. Need slammed into her. Quinn wrapped his arms around her waist, lifting her off the floor and against his body. His hard length trapped between them. Her hands gripped his shoulder, slid into the hair at his nape and over his scalp. She tugged his head closer. Their teeth bumped and scraped and the kiss turned volcanic.

Heat blazed through her blood, pumping into her breasts and pussy, throbbing to a tribal beat only Quinn could drum up. She bent her legs, curled them around his hips and ground her pounding clit on his cock. A snarl vibrated in her chest, her coyote snapped at her control and threatened to break free. Twisting her head, she ripped her mouth from his. It was too much. She felt her grip weaken, knew the beast would spring forward at any second.

"Stop," she panted.

He didn't hear her. His mouth traveled along her jaw and down her neck. Rowan's muscles stretched, her teeth lengthened and her claws popped out and dug into Quinn's scalp.

"Quinn!" Brogan's shout penetrated the hammering in her ears.

Her legs dropped to the floor as Quinn pushed her away to look at her. It was too little too late.

"Fuck!" The word exploded from his mouth.

The animal she'd denied for so long broke free and she shifted before he let her go.

Q uinn stared at Rowan.

What the hell just happened?

One minute she was in his arms the next she was shifting. He let go, allowed her to slide to the floor as she changed to coyote. If he wasn't so freaked out he'd laugh at the sight of her in T-shirt and shorts. Brogan made it across the room as Quinn dropped to his knees beside her.

"What the hell happened?" Brogan's words echoed his own thoughts.

"I don't know."

Quinn stroked the fur along her neck. Rowan's eyes drifted closed and she lowered to her belly on a sigh. Her movements were lethargic—listless, as she settled into a comfortable position. A shudder rippled down her canine body and her breathing evened out, slowed, deepened. He knew she'd taken a run earlier, that's how he knew she was here. Brogan had asked him to check on the group of naturals living up on Whispering Ridge—make sure they had a food source. He'd been heading back when he smelled her. Rowan's scent was imprinted on his soul, he'd know it anywhere.

He had run the rest of the way back to the house as fast as his human legs would take him, only to discover she wasn't there. His nose never failed him, he had known she was close. He'd yelled for Brogan to follow, stripped out of his clothes and taken to the forest in coyote form. Excitement and fear in equal measures had swamped him. What was she doing up the mountain? Why hadn't she told him she was arriving today?

Rowan's warmth and scent soaked into him. His fingers tangled in her coat, trailed down her neck and over her side. She whined softly, snuffled and settled back down when he petted her head and murmured soothing words. It didn't matter how she'd gotten here or why she'd come without telling him or Brogan. What mattered was the years of waiting were over.

Rowan was finally home.

"Is she asleep?" Brogan's whispered words were laced with concern.

"Yeah, I think so." Quinn scooped her up in his arms, bundled her against his chest as best he could. Brogan steadied him as he got to his feet. "I'll put her on the sofa, closer to the fire."

"Is she sick?"

"I don't think so. Her temperature feels normal and she talked and looked fine before…" He didn't want to think about the scorching kiss they'd shared before she'd changed in his arms.

He placed her on the sofa and settled on the floor in front of her, continued to stroke her coat, more to soothe himself than Rowan. Brogan brought the cups of coffee she'd poured them. He passed Quinn his before he sat in the chair opposite. They remained silent, each lost in their own thoughts. Neither voiced their concern about Rowan's sudden appearance. Quinn had no idea how long they sat there while she slept, all he knew was he'd finished the coffee long before her eyes opened.

A sigh of relief huffed from his chest and he smiled.

"Shift back, Rowan," he murmured.

She took a long time to change back and Quinn wondered if Brogan's concern about illness had merit. She looked tired. The dark circles under her eyes were a deep purple and sunken into the tender flesh of her face. He ran his fingertips over her cheek, along her jaw, around her neck and into her hair. Leaning forward, he brushed his lips over hers. Quinn pulled back an inch and kept his eyes focused on hers.

"Hey. How do you feel?"

"I'm okay, just need to rest."

"What happened, Rowan?"

"I've ignored my coyote too long. I can't control the shift anymore." She swallowed hard, licked her lips. "And changing drains my strength."

"What do you mean you can't control it?" Quinn asked.

"It just happens. Like just now, my coyote took over and I couldn't hold her back. I couldn't earlier either."

"Here, drink some water." Brogan offered her a glass. "When did this start?"

Quinn helped Rowan sit up and she leaned back into the sofa, squeezed her eyes shut and took a deep trembling breath. Her eyelids lifted and the tears pooling in the brown orbs tore at

Quinn's heart like claws. "Today's the first day I've shifted in six years."

Rowan watched the two most important men in her life absorb her words. Quinn was the first to speak.

"Not once?"

"No. I couldn't afford to give myself away. I've used everything I could to mask my scent and done whatever it took to go unnoticed."

"Not even when you were alone?" Brogan asked.

"No. You know shifting releases more of your scent."

"So what you're saying is that you need to learn to control your coyote again, like you did at puberty?" Quinn asked.

"Yes, but in the meantime I don't want anyone in the pack to know I'm unstable. You saw what happened when we kissed. I can't control the urges anymore than I can the coyote." She sighed. "All it took earlier was stepping outside and seeing the forest."

"She wanted to run," Brogan said.

"Yes, she did." Rowan looked at her brother. There were signs of aging but other than a few little wrinkles around his eyes and mouth he hadn't changed much. "I got in last night. Drove up in the dark, and with the jet lag, I didn't take much notice of the mountains around me. I just dragged myself inside and crashed. When I went out this morning to get my bags...well let's say things got a little hairy." She laughed at her own joke. Neither one of them found it amusing.

Quinn pushed to his feet. "You're coming home."

He was back to ordering her around. Well too bad. She knew she needed to stay here, away from everyone and everything that would distract her from reacquainting herself with her wild side. She wouldn't let him or Brogan change her plans. All she needed was a couple of days, maybe a week to get her bearings and then she'd be ready to face the pack and all that coming home meant.

"No. I'm staying here." Pleased with the strength in her voice she stared at Quinn. He'd have to carry her out of here to get his way and she doubted he'd resort to that.

"You can't stay here alone," Brogan said.

She turned to him. "Why not? I've been alone for the last six years, Brogan. A couple more days won't hurt."

"You're not going to budge on this, are you?" Quinn's question drew her gaze back to him.

"No."

"Brogan's right, you can't stay here alone. I'll stay with you."

"You can't," she blurted. "Look what happened before. I need to concentrate on gaining control. How am I supposed to do that if you're here? The slightest touch could set me off."

"I won't touch you."

"Right," she scoffed. "We haven't been able to keep our hands off each other since we were teenagers. I don't see us managing it now."

"I won't touch you until you think you're ready. But I'll be here when you can't control your coyote. I'll make sure nothing happens to you when you shift, Rowan." He bent at the waist, leaned in until their faces were so close his breath fanned over her lips. "And when you think you've got control, I'll push you. I'll touch you until you forget your name, never mind your coyote."

Desire blazed in his eyes and she sucked in a breath as her arousal spiked in response.

"But-but..." She struggled to remember what they were arguing over.

"You want to stay here. This is the way we do it. If you don't like it get your things and I'll take you home."

She turned to Brogan, pleaded with him silently to intervene but one look told her she wouldn't be getting any help from him. She didn't need him to voice his opinion but he did anyway.

"Quinn's way or no way, Rowan. I'll tie you up and carry you down the mountain myself if you don't agree."

She blew out a breath and fell back against the soft leather cushion. Alpha males and their demanding ways. At least she knew they ordered her around out of concern and not meanness. Other members of the pack used their size and strength to intimidate, enjoyed the fear they instilled in those they tormented. Even with all their faults and bossy alpha ways, Quinn and Brogan loved her. And she loved them. She'd give in on this, but only because it kept her away from the pack and the one person she hoped never to see again.

5

Rowan retreated to the bedroom, leaving Quinn and Brogan to talk about pack business and how they'd account for Quinn not being around if anyone questioned where he was. They'd gone out to her rental car to retrieve her bags earlier and she busied herself removing her toiletries and a couple of outfits. The rest she'd send with Brogan when he went back to Whispering Creek.

Home.

So close and yet so far. How many times had she dreamed of this moment? For years her nightmares were filled with never being able to return and now to be this close...

"Hey."

She turned to find Brogan lounging against the door jam. He studied her and she tried not to fidget under his close scrutiny.

"Hey, yourself." She smiled and stepped toward him.

He pushed off the wall and met her halfway. When he opened his arms she leapt into his embrace, soaking up his warmth and the love he'd always given her.

"I missed you so much." Her words were muffled against his neck as she drew in his familiar scent.

"I missed you too, Rowan." He squeezed her tight before putting her back on her feet. "But I wish you'd told us what was going on. You wouldn't have had to face this alone."

"I didn't want you to see me like this." She shrugged a shoulder and turned away. "I want you to see me as the strong independent woman I am and not the needy teenager you had to hide away."

"You may have been a teenager, but you were never needy." His hands skimmed down her arms, comforting in their movements.

"I'm sorry."

"No need for sorry. Are those to go home?" He pointed at her still-packed bags.

"Yes, I don't need much while I'm here. I'm not planning on venturing out before I return home." She followed him when he went to pick up her bags. "Oh, and in the next few days there'll be some more of my stuff arriving. I'd planned to be back by the time everything arrived but I didn't bank on having such a hard time with my coyote."

Brogan stroked a hand over her hair. "It's okay, Rowan. Take all the time you need. There's no rush."

Tears flooded her eyes and she blinked rapidly to stop them from spilling. How had she ever survived without Brogan's unconditional love and support?

"Hey, none of that." He cupped her face and brushed at her tears with his thumbs. "It'll be okay, you're home now."

A sob broke free. Her heart hurt with all she'd missed by not being here. She still believed leaving the pack had been the right decision. They didn't stand a chance against a corrupt sovereign and his equally immoral son. Brogan pulled her to his chest, wrapped her in his warm embrace and held her tight while she cried out all the grief she hadn't allowed herself to feel until now.

Quinn sat back and soaked up the sight of Rowan making dinner. Brogan left earlier, choosing not to eat with them. Quinn knew why. The quicker Rowan was able to get control of her coyote, the quicker she'd be going home. Brogan knew the sooner he let her get on with it, the better. Neither wanted her to suffer and they would gladly take any pain or frustration on her behalf but this was something she had to do on her own. He had no clue how he'd be able to sit back and watch her struggle through it. It had almost done him in when she'd been a teenager and he'd had no idea they were mates then. The next few days were going to be tough. For both of them.

Even now his fists were clenched around his knees in a white-knuckled grip. The urge to go to her and fold her in his arms was razor sharp. He knew she'd cried on Brogan's shoulder. He hadn't needed his friend to tell him. Her eyes were red and puffy from her tears and it cut him up inside that he hadn't been able to stop them from falling. That he hadn't been the one to soothe her when they had. Her emotions bashed against his, tugged and pulled until her pain was his. He should be able to protect his mate from everything.

"You can't do this for me." Rowan's quietly spoken words snapped him from his thoughts. He hadn't realized she'd stopped what she was doing and turned to watch him.

"I know, but it won't stop me from wanting to."

"After dinner I'd like to practice shifting but I'm not sure it's a good idea to get naked in front of you just yet."

He grinned. Yep, if she got naked he'd be all but crawling out of his skin to jump her. Kind of like he was now, even with all her curves hidden beneath her T-shirt and shorts, his body pulsed with the need to possess her.

"You could just wear what you've got on. They were loose on you earlier when you shifted."

She scrunched up her pert nose and thought about his suggestion. "Okay. That'll work for now."

Satisfied, Rowan turned back to her dinner preparations giving him a view that made his mouth water. The shorts might not be tight but they were cut high exposing her long lean legs. His tongue tingled with the need to taste those sculpted calf muscles, toned thighs and the slope of her ass. He didn't even want to think about the dimple above the heart shaped cheeks, or the crease between them.

He stifled a low groan. The ache in his rock-hard cock wasn't going to be taken care of anytime soon. Not unless he wanted to do it himself and he knew jacking off wouldn't begin to slake the lust now that Rowan was back. He'd never been with anyone else. He knew that wasn't normal but he'd always been weary of his coyote genes and by the time he'd been ready to take the step into manhood Rowan had hit puberty and everything had changed.

He remembered being at the lodge the night she'd shifted the first time. Remembered the gut slam of need and knowledge that blindsided him the second she'd stepped through the door. It had taken her months to make a full change, the skill taking time to master for all born coyotes. At the onset of adulthood each of them struggled to connect with their dormant animal. She'd been fourteen. Way too young for him to do anything about them being mates. Brogan had almost gone ballistic on him. No, he had. It was the one and only time they'd fought. Once Quinn had made it clear he would wait for Rowan, his friend had calmed down.

The night of Rowan's attack had changed everything. With Connelly firmly in control of the pack, they couldn't begin to protect her and getting her out had been the only way to ensure her safety. Sending her out into the world without him was the hardest thing Quinn had ever done. She'd been eager to complete their mating ritual and with the added protection of being mated, Rowan didn't have to worry about the attention of other male coyotes. It had been the only time they'd had sex. Until then they'd settled for a lot of making out.

How they'd managed to stop on any of those occasions was a mystery. The taste and scent of Rowan filled him. He didn't need to remember. It was part of him, mixed with his own essence. They were combined forever in a way no one could ever undo. The sizzle in his veins turned to a boil and his jeans threatened to strangle his dick. The damn things were choking the life out of the erection trying to break free of the unforgiving denim. He needed to get out of them. Now. Good thing they kept a supply of clothes here at the cabin.

His chair scraped over the timber floor as he pushed away from the table. Rowan spun around, eyes wide, legs braced. It shocked him to see her fear. Surely she knew he'd never hurt her.

"I'm just going to get cleaned up and changed." He watched, waited for her muscles to relax. When she took a deep breath and smiled, he said, "I'll be about ten minutes."

"It's okay. Dinner won't be ready for about thirty minutes."

He walked over, brushed his fingers over her cheek. "You know I'd never hurt you, right?"

Her eyes closed and she nodded. "Yes."

"Look at me." He waited for her gaze to meet his. "I love you with everything I am. You are all I am. We'll see this through. Together."

Eyes swimming with tears, she stood on tiptoes and brushed her lips over his. A light caress, nothing worthy of racing hearts or raging hormones, but with Rowan there was never anything else. The fire ignited, scorched him from the inside until he all but melted. Stepping back, he put distance between them. It would be so easy to reach out, pick her up and carry her off to bed. His jaw clenched hard enough to take a layer of enamel off his teeth. He took another step away from temptation and damn if she didn't work out what he was doing.

The Rowan he knew peaked out, sparkled in her eyes and tipped her mouth into a saucy little grin. An answering smile teased his lips.

This is what he wanted to see. His Rowan, not the one who jumped at the slightest noise. The one who teased and laughed and wasn't afraid of him or what he made her feel. And until this moment he hadn't realized how hurt he was by her fear of all they were to each other. That would change. He'd make sure it changed. Before long he'd be able to hold his mate in his arms without either of them worrying about her losing control of her coyote.

"I'll be back," he said in his best Terminator impersonation.

She threw back her head and laughed. A belly deep, carefree gale that fizzed in his blood and brought light to his heart as the echo of it followed him out of the kitchen.

Ten minutes in a cold shower and he still had a hard-on to rival the Eiffel Tower. The sweat pants didn't hide it either but there was no way he was putting another pair of jeans on. He wanted to be able to use his cock when Rowan was ready and he risked permanent damage if he stuffed himself into what amounted to a denim torture device. He walked out into the living room, his erection pointing the way.

Rowan was setting the small dining table with plates when he came up next to her. Her gasp and wide eyes had him covering himself with his hands.

"Sorry. You've always had that effect on me and it's not going to go away until after…" He didn't want to voice what would help the problem. "Just ignore it. I'm going to. Well I'll try at least."

"This isn't going to work. I can't expect you to put up with—" she stalled, waved her hand in the direction of his tented pants. "It's got to hurt."

"See now, the hurt isn't what I'd call pain and if I left I'd be in the same state. I can live with it. It's less than what you'll be going through and I've already told you I'm not going anywhere. We do this together."

She blew out a puff of breath, her bangs fluttering out of her eyes. "Fine. But don't complain when you've got blue balls." Turning, she stomped off into the kitchen to retrieve dinner.

"What can I do to help?" he asked, following her.

"Grab the green salad from the fridge and put it on the table. What do you want to drink? Coffee or soda?"

"I'll grab a soda. What are you having?"

"I'll have one too."

They said nothing more until their plates were full and they'd made inroads into filling empty stomachs. The silence was comfortable and neither felt the need to fill it with mundane chatter. It had always surprised Quinn, their ease with each other. Even before Rowan had hit puberty and they realized they were mates, the relationship between them had been more than her being his best friend's little sister. For as long as he could remember she was a part of him. Long before they'd crossed into physical intimacy, they'd been emotionally intimate.

He'd never balked at telling her anything. She was his past, his present and his future. And he'd see her through this, help anyway he could so she could take her place in the pack and finally come home.

Rowan leaned away from the table. She was stuffed so full of food, moving was impossible without rupturing something. Eyes half closed in post pig-out lethargy, she watched Quinn through her lashes. He continued to devour mouthfuls of the stew she'd made. His utter enjoyment was displayed with little moans as he chewed and swallowed every bite. She'd missed his enthusiasm. Nothing was ever done with less than full gusto.

Her gaze followed his hands, the bob of his Adam's apple, the flick of his tongue as it reached out to catch a drop of sauce from the corner of his mouth. She wanted to lean over, slip her tongue out and catch that escaping morsel for him. He was completely absorbed in the task of eating. The meal wasn't anything special, just a basic stew with meat and veggies but he ate it like it was a meal served in a five-star restaurant. Using a piece of crusty bread, he soaked up the last of the gravy, popped it into his mouth and looked up at her.

Smoldering, sated eyes met hers. Bedroom eyes. He'd always had them and they could turn her inside out with a look. Nothing had changed. Her coyote stirred, pulled and pushed to be let free. Rowan held on, stopped the change from happening. She gulped in air, tried to slow her breathing down by closing her eyes and thinking of anything but Quinn. He remained perfectly still, didn't draw a breath and still she felt his presence. Every nerve tingled with desire, need. Muscles stretched, skin pulled and teeth lengthened.

Shudders racked her body and sweat slicked her skin, quickly absorbed by the fur thickening all over her body. It was too hard to hold back and she was too tired to fight her coyote anymore. With a whimper she slid from her chair to the floor and let go.

A chair scraped the floor and then Quinn was next to her, murmuring words of comfort and stroking his fingers through her coat. Her shuddering eased and a sigh escaped her chest. She wanted to sleep. Curl up and sleep, but she couldn't. She needed to muster enough strength to change back. He lifted her head, placed it in his lap while he continued to soothe her with the caress of his hand. It took a few minutes but she didn't drop into oblivion like she had before.

She barked once, pulled away and sat back on her haunches. Her muscles shook, her bones popped, like knuckles being cracked, and then she was human again. She slumped forward, Quinn catching her before she face-planted into the floor. Scooping her up, he rose to his feet as if she weighed nothing and headed for the bedroom.

"Where are you taking me?" she murmured.

"Bed. The circles under your eyes just got darker and after the effort to control and change you just put in I'd say it's time for you to sleep."

"I don't want to sleep. I've got to clean up after dinner."

"Nope. I'll do that. You'll go to bed. I don't care if you just lie there; you're not getting up until morning. I'll take care of the kitchen."

"Quinn." Her protest was weak but she made the effort anyway.

"Rowan," he mimicked her tone.

She smiled as her eyes drifted shut. He laid her on the soft mattress, pulled the quilt up over her and tucked her in as if she were a child. With no energy left to complain, she admitted defeat and snuggled into the comfy bed, her mind sinking into sleep in seconds.

Quinn waited until her breathing evened out. Sure she'd dropped into a deep sleep, he left the room to tackle the clean up. It didn't take long to cover the leftovers, rinse the plates and stack the dishwasher. He checked to be certain he hadn't missed any dirty plates before filling the powder holder and switching it on, the electrical hum the only noise in the quiet room. He'd locked up earlier but he went around and double-checked the door and all the windows.

He switched off the lights and made his way back to the bedroom. The fact Rowan hadn't mentioned sleeping arrangements told him how exhausted she was. She'd probably go to town on him in the morning but he wasn't sleeping anywhere but next to her from now on. He was never allowing her away from him again.

She was still curled on her side, the quilt tucked up under her chin. Even in the darkened room the shadows under her eyes stood out. He'd make her get plenty of rest. She could practice shifting as much as she wanted but he would do everything else. From now on, he'd take care of her, feed her and put some weight on her bones. That had to be part of her problem. She couldn't weigh more than a ten year old. He'd soon fix that. Plenty of food and plenty of rest and he'd be taking her home in no time.

Stripping out of his clothes, he climbed in beside her. For her sake, he left his boxers on but he wouldn't be making any other concessions. He reached over, curled an arm around her waist and snuggled her back against his chest. Her warmth seeped into him. Her scent surrounded him. Her ass fit into the cradle of his hips and his erection pressed into the crease between her soft, squeezable cheeks. It would be so easy to slip inside her in this position.

How they would make it until she gained control was anyone's guess. Holding her while she slept had his heart racing, his groin pounding and his coyote howling to take, to possess. She was his mate, he should be able to have her any way he wanted. Anytime he wanted. He might just end up with those blue balls she predicted earlier. If touching her set off a shift then he'd change as well and there wouldn't be a problem. They'd not mated in their coyote forms and he couldn't deny the thrill the thought delivered.

Quinn smiled into the dark. Maybe they were going about this all wrong. Maybe she needed to connect with her coyote and its base animal needs. She'd held off the change at dinner, he'd watched her struggle before her exhaustion had won out. And then, when she'd shifted back, it hadn't taken as long as earlier in the day. She was already making progress at controlling her coyote.

He pulled her closer, nuzzled the nape of her neck and tasted her skin. She was warm and soft, sliding under his tongue like the sweetest dessert. He shuddered with the need to take what he wanted. To fuck her until they both lay sated. Until they satisfied the mutual cries screaming at them from within.

As much as he wanted to do things her way, Quinn didn't think their coyotes would let them for long. Already he could feel the pull. His beast had its mate within reach and wouldn't be happy to wait. Hell, he wasn't happy to wait but he had to give Rowan her chance. If he didn't she'd fight him and he couldn't risk losing her again. He'd let her go once, there was no way he'd do it a second time.

6

Rowan came awake slowly. Surrounded in warmth, she wanted to stay asleep but something nagged at her mind, made her think she needed to get up now. Stretching, she arched her back and rolled over onto a warm body.

"Ah..." She leapt from the bed, got tangled in the covers and went down on her ass, hard. As pain radiated from her squashed rear end her senses kicked in and a familiar scent filled her nostrils. She groaned with embarrassment. Flopping back on the floor, she hoped Quinn had slept through her drama queen moment. When a chuckle came from above she knew she was out of luck.

Quinn's head popped over the side of the mattress. "Morning, Rowan. You're one of those leap-out-of-bed types I see." His smothered laughter made her want to strangle him. He knew full well she hated mornings.

"You've just scared ten years off my life and you think it's funny?" Rowan tugged the sheet away from her legs and with as much dignity as she could manage, got to her feet and straightened her clothes. She wished she'd stayed on the floor when she looked at Quinn. Lying across the bed on his stomach with nothing but a strip of cloth covering his ass, he was every woman's wet dream come to life. Her slumbering coyote sat up, and Rowan breathed deep, only to suck in another lungful of Quinn's scent.

She fought to hold her beast back and remembered how hard it was when she'd learned to shift as a teenager. Using every trick she'd ever been taught, Rowan soothed the animal and held tight. Quinn needed to get dressed. In reality, it probably wouldn't make that much difference but every little bit helped.

"Get dressed," she growled between clenched teeth.

He scrambled out of bed, snatched his clothes from the floor and pulled them on without a protest. With all those muscles covered she would at least be able to look at him and pretend she was in control. Rowan eased back, unclenched her jaw and relaxed her arms and legs. Each small win over her coyote built her confidence, gained trust between her human and animal sides. But she needed to reward her coyote for behaving.

"I need to shift now. I'm in control, well as much as I can be at the moment, but I need to let her go."

"Okay, change. I'll be right here."

His unconditional support went a long way to soothing both her and her beast. Taking a deep breath, Rowan made her first intentional shift in six years.

The snap and pop of bones moving filled the room, the last of the changes not as loud or as painful as the first ones. It still took her longer than it should for a coyote her age but the time had shortened since yesterday. Then again, they'd changed together. The first three times had been the beast inside breaking free. Rowan felt more comfortable, more connected to her wild side than she had before and with one leap, her coyote bounded onto the bed.

Standing on four legs, she surveyed the room around her, absorbed the differences between now and when she was last here. Other than the bigger bed, the furniture was the same, even the quilt was the one handmade by her grandmother. Her gaze landed on Quinn. He'd changed, broadened across the chest a little. The lines beside his mouth and eyes could be from stress or laughter but they didn't detract from his appeal. They showed character and life. A life she hadn't been there to share.

The need for him to hold her surged through her, to feel the heart beating beneath his chest and his strong arms wrapped tightly around her. Shifting back came easier, the speed with which she took human form sucked the breath from her lungs and she fell forward only to be caught before she toppled off the bed. A wall of muscle lay against her cheek, the drumbeat on the other side soothed Rowan's need for closeness. The warm bands of muscle circling her back were like steel but she didn't feel restrained. Quinn's embrace was exactly what she needed.

They went from holding each other to devouring in seconds. Rowan had no idea who made the first move but when their lips connected it was like being struck by lightning. Every nerve sprang to attention and her blood rushed through her body, filling sensitive tissue to the point of bursting. Quinn's tongue lashed out, darted into her mouth to collide with hers. Rowan took all he offered and asked for more.

Teeth bumped and scraped along lips and tongues, and breath became secondary to taking in the man holding her. Lack of oxygen forced them apart but didn't stop the urge to take or the consuming need roaring to life inside her. They tumbled to the bed, legs entwined as hands pushed and pulled at clothing. From one breath to the next, Rowan's only goal was to get Quinn naked. To feel his skin against hers—to taste every inch of him.

Bare flesh met fingertips and she sighed with relief but craved more. Her hands molded every slope, every muscle, as they explored the changes in Quinn's body. So much was the same yet different. Hungry for more, Rowan followed her hands with her mouth. She skimmed his chest, stopped at one pebbled nipple to draw it in between her lips. She sucked hard and Quinn's hips thrust against her, his erection cradled by the softness of her stomach. Her hand traveled down his hard abs to delve inside his pants.

She wrapped her fingers around Quinn's cock, the hard length hot within her grasp. She stroked down to the root and cupped his balls before squeezing lightly. Mutual groans broke free as his sac pulled tight. Regaining her grip, she pulled her hand up to the tip, sweeping her thumb over the bead of moisture leaking from the slit. He pumped his hips and Rowan worked her hand up and down his rigid flesh, squeezing tighter with every thrust.

Desperation clawed at her. The passion neither of them had ever been able to deny exploded. She needed to taste him. To feel him inside her. Tugging at his remaining clothes, Rowan freed his cock and fought to move down his body. Quinn's hands circled her arms stopping her descent.

"No. Christ. You do that and I'm a goner," he panted.

"I don't care." She twisted to get free but his grip was strong and he flipped her beneath him to stop her struggles.

"Not this time."

He shoved her top under her arms with one hand and lunged for her breasts. All protests died in her throat as he sucked a nipple into his mouth, swirled his tongue around the tip and scraped lightly with his teeth. Her back arched, more of her sensitive mound filling his mouth. He let her go, sat back and reached for the hem of her top. In a quick tug he had it up and off and flung across the room. Her pants followed.

Quinn proceeded to drive her wild. Touching and tasting her everywhere. No part of her was left out of his assault. Her nipples grew impossibly tight and her clit throbbed with arousal long ignored. The ecstasy bombarding her electrified her senses and aroused her coyote. Her beast stretched Rowan's control and forced her to clamp down on the delicious sensations Quinn's hands and mouth stirred. He pushed his leg between hers and spread her wide, exposing her for his wandering hand.

Fingers probed her slick folds. Sliding deeper, they teased her. Two fingers circled her opening before plunging deep. Her hips left the bed, propelled up with the decadent pleasure his invasion brought. His tongue continued to lavish attention on her breasts, swapping between them to give equal care. Quinn pressed down on her clit at the same time he stroked inside her core and Rowan's world shattered. With a scream she came. Her body thrashed as wave after wave of bliss rolled through her.

And her coyote broke free.

Quinn felt Rowan's climax a second before she shifted. He threw himself to the side but wasn't quick enough to stop her claws from slicing into his scalp. The lacerations weren't deep and would heal without much bother but it would be one more reason for her to push him away. He knew her. She'd be devastated that she'd hurt him. Neither of them would come out of this unscathed and a few little scratches weren't anything he hadn't suffered before. Besides, he'd be damned if he'd let her do this alone.

Quinn's breath stalled in his throat as Rowan's coyote pounced on his chest. She licked his face and neck, nipped at his shoulder with her teeth. Her canines would leave welts but didn't break the skin. Frozen in place, he waited for the right moment to push her away. He didn't have a problem with getting it on in coyote form but they both had to be that way. Gently he placed a hand on her head, entwined his fingers in her fur and gave a small tug. When she turned to look at him Quinn took the opportunity to move out from under her and shift.

In his coyote form he nudged her with his snout and she quickly yielded to him. She rolled to her back, baring her stomach and throat, submitting to his alpha position. He was hard as granite and wanted desperately to claim his mate, but he fought his animal needs as he nuzzled her, using his tongue and teeth to soothe instead of arouse. If he gave in and took her now it would be a step backward in the path to control for Rowan. She needed his support and if that meant going without for now he'd do it.

It took some time and he had a few bite marks to show for it but she did settle, allowing him to take the time to look at her. Six years had changed her. The color of her coat was different—darker. Her physique was more muscular than it had been. Instead of a girl's body blossoming into womanhood, Rowan now had the curves of a mature woman and that change was evident in coyote form. Quinn longed to be able to explore every inch of her. He hadn't been able to do it before when they'd mated, but he'd do it now she was home. He'd learn all the parts of his mate.

Curled up together, they lay quietly, the occasional nip or lick their only movements. Minutes passed and finally Rowan dozed. He waited a few more minutes before carefully removing himself from their tangle of limbs. Jumping from the bed he shifted back to his human body and scrambled back into his clothes, the more barriers between him and Rowan the better. Any extra time his common sense had to kick his brain into gear was a bonus.

He thought about waking her and then decided to leave her while he grabbed a shower. He could also take care of the not-so-little problem that was tenting his sweats. Quinn shook his head. Who was he kidding? Jerking off would only add to his troubles. Nothing would ease his condition but Rowan and there was no chance of that anytime soon. Sliding a drawer out slowly to minimize the noise, he searched out another pair of sweats and T-shirt. The jeans he'd had on yesterday could stay where they were in the bathroom until they went home.

Home.

Quinn didn't attempt to hold back the smile spreading across his face. To finally take Rowan home, as his mate, had been a dream he'd held close to his heart for over six long years. And now it was so close he could taste it. Stepping back over to the bed, he checked on the sleeping beauty who had held his heart for over a decade. A decade of pain and absence. What would the next ten years give them?

With Brogan as sovereign and Quinn by his side as regal, they stood to have it all. Once Rowan gained control of her animal side and they went home to Whispering Creek, there would be nothing standing in the way. They could live as mates the way they should have been from the start. He felt sure the pack would embrace her with open arms when she made her arrival home known. Until then he'd be the one with open arms.

. . .

Like last night, the cold water did nothing to cool his arousal. He stepped from the shower the same way he'd entered it—his cock pointing the way. Dried and dressed, he checked on Rowan again before heading to the kitchen and food. They kept the cabin stocked with staples but he couldn't remember the last time they topped those supplies up. He found a packet of bacon in the freezer but no eggs in the fridge. The pantry did have a pancake mix though. He could whip those up while the bacon fried.

Quinn busied himself with breakfast preparations and a glance at the clock told him it was more like brunch but he wasn't getting into technicalities. The scent of bacon frying and coffee brewing filled the room. He lifted the last of the cooked bacon from the pan onto the plate and stashed it in the oven to keep warm while he made the pancakes. With fresh coffee now filling his cup, there wasn't much more he could ask for.

"Morning."

Ah...maybe one thing. He turned to find Rowan standing just inside the kitchen, barefoot and wearing another outfit similar to yesterday's. Her apprehension brought a flash of anger and he tamped it down quickly so he didn't worry her anymore. Why she'd be afraid of him now Quinn didn't have a clue. For the moment he'd ignore it and act as though this was any other normal day.

"Morning, Rowan. Breakfast is almost ready. Do you want a cup of coffee before we eat?" He moved to the pot, ready to pour her a cup when she stepped next to him.

"I can finish breakfast." She lifted the bowl of pancake batter from the counter.

"Oh no you don't." He snatched the bowl out of her hands and put it back down. "I'm cooking breakfast. You get to sit on that cute butt and watch." He steered her toward the table in the corner. Before she could protest, he had her in a chair.

Surprised by her easy acceptance, Quinn used it to his advantage and went back to fixing their meal. He poured Rowan a coffee, and remembering her comment about not taking sugar anymore, he left the brew black. Placing the mug on the table in front of her, he bent to brush his lips over hers. Ignoring the small jerk away his actions caused, he slid his tongue out and traced her lips from corner to corner. With a small amount of pressure she opened for him and he dipped inside to taste. A few quick licks and he pulled back, ending the kiss.

"Mmm...now that's a good morning."

"I'm sorry."

"For what?" He looked down at her, puzzled by her apology.

"For this morning when we were...well you know. I could have hurt you badly. I had no control over—."

He placed a finger on her lips, stopping any further words from spilling out. "Rowan, you did nothing wrong. Your coyote wanted her mate and I understand that. I'm fighting the same conflict inside, only I have more control at the moment. You have nothing to apologize for." He had no intention of telling her about the claw marks on his scalp but now he understood her timid behavior when she first came in. He didn't wait for her to comment. Turning back to the counter, he set about getting the pancakes cooked.

Rowan sat sipping her coffee. Watching Quinn move around the kitchen with such ease was one more reminder of what she'd missed. When she'd left he couldn't tell the difference between a fry pan and a spatula. Now he not only knew the difference but how to use them and if the aroma filling the room was an indication, he used them well. He dropped batter into the pan, testing if it was ready before he turned it over. It looked easy but she knew from experience one had to judge the timing just right or you wrecked the pancake.

His sure competent movements spoke of familiarity and she supposed he'd gotten a lot of practice over the last six years. The muscles in his arms rippled with motion and the shirt molded to his back revealed more movement across his shoulder blades as he flipped another pancake. Her body heated, each nerve tingling with awareness as she absorbed the sight of Quinn. After this morning Rowan couldn't believe just looking at him had her turned on again.

The orgasm that had exploded through her had destroyed every bit of her control and let loose the animal who wanted only one thing. Her mate. She was shocked at what she'd done after shifting. They were lucky she hadn't hurt him with the way she'd been nipping at him with her sharp coyote teeth. When he'd managed to move her away and shift, she'd wanted nothing more than to turn her back and let him mount her but he hadn't let her. He'd kept her on her back and after she'd calmed down, let her roll to her side—curled beneath him. If she'd ever been unsure of his love, she was in no doubt now.

Quinn's behavior from the minute he'd slammed through the door yesterday had been nothing but loving and supportive. He may have tried to throw his weight around but he hadn't forced her to do anything but accept his presence and that wasn't such a hardship. The man was definitely worth looking at. And being taken care of wasn't so hard to stomach either. To have that after being without for so long brought tears to her eyes and a lump to her throat. The only person to give her that kind of support since she'd left home was El.

The move to Australia six years ago had been the best thing she'd done in her attempt to stay hidden. Not only had she remained safe but she'd met El. God, she'd only left her two days ago and she missed her friend so much it was a physical ache. Quinn and Brogan would go a long way to soothing that pain but Rowan knew she and El would be friends forever. They were sisters of the heart and if it hadn't been for their friendship she knew without a qualm she never would have lasted this long away from home.

Quinn's hand on her chin startled her out of her thoughts. He tipped her face up and used his thumbs to wipe the tears from her cheek. Tears she hadn't known were falling.

"What's wrong? Why the silent tears?" The concern in his voice matched the emotion swirling in his eyes.

She shrugged. "It's all too much. I was thinking about us and how I've missed so much of your life."

"I've missed yours too, Rowan. We both lost a lot over the time you've been away but I plan to make up for it every day for the rest of our lives." He leaned forward, brushed a kiss on her temple, her cheek, her lips. "If you'll let me."

"Oh, Quinn." She wrapped her arms around his neck and pulled him close. She wanted to hold and be held. No, she needed it. Required the reassurance this was real and that she was in his arms and finally home.

"Shh…it's okay. Everything will be fine now you're home."

Rowan wanted to believe him. With all her heart she hoped he was right but there were still hurdles to overcome. She had to face the pack and explain her absence. Would they believe her when she told them of the threat to her safety? And what of the man hell-bent on having her to use her in his quest to become sovereign? Had he given up on his thirst to possess her now that Brogan had taken his rightful place in the pack or would she have another battle to fight after she'd gained control of her coyote?

If Marcus still wanted her as his mate, regardless of the fact they weren't destined to be together or that she and Quinn had mated, the battle wouldn't just be over her possession.

It would be for her life and Quinn's.

7

Quinn admired the way Rowan continued to face the challenges before her. He knew once she made herself known to the pack there would be more trouble. The council would want to know where she'd been and why she now wanted to return but they were the least of his concerns. She could handle the council and the rest of the pack for that matter, but he didn't know how she'd deal with facing Marcus after all these years.

Just thinking of him and what he'd done to Rowan had Quinn ready to kill. To rip the bastard to pieces.

He wished he and Brogan had been able to convince the council the man shouldn't be allowed to stay in the pack after they'd removed the senior Connelly, but until he did something worthy of exile they were stuck with him and all the problems he caused. If only Brogan had been sovereign at the time of Rowan's attack, it would have been easy to persuade the council then. They'd just have to be careful because if Quinn knew one thing it was that Marcus would do his best to stir up more trouble.

For now he'd concentrate on helping Rowan gain enough control to be comfortable with returning home. She might be on the mountain but this wasn't home. It was a safe harbor that could only last for so long. Anyone could discover she was back if they were in the forest for long. They needed to finish this so she could finally return to where she belonged. Judging by the speed with which she just shifted, it wouldn't be long before she'd be ready.

The late afternoon sun filtered through the trees surrounding the cabin, the dappled rays bouncing off the snow and sparkling in the puddles the warmth of the day had made. They'd been out here practicing for over two hours, Rowan shifting between coyote and human with ease now. As far as Quinn was concerned there was just one test left. They had to know if she could control the shift with him in close proximity because he had every intention of being by her side every minute of every day.

No time like the present to test her but they needed to be inside before he pushed. As much as he didn't think they were in any danger, he wanted them both safely locked indoors in case Rowan couldn't control the shift. He wouldn't think about his own control. The hard-on in his pants was a constant, one he'd managed to ignore for the most part. Tonight things would change. Once the sun went down he'd have her where he wanted her, under him.

He'd let her lead today, followed and allowed her to do things her way but now it was his turn. They both needed to know that she could control her coyote in any situation and seeing how he was responsible for three uncontrolled changes it would be a good test of her strength. The only problem was he was tested just as much with each minute he spent near her. Every second he didn't claim her, his body strained against his will to give her what she wanted and not take what he craved.

Rowan moved with a sensuality that had Quinn's insides humming. Each stretch of muscle, shift of skin to fur and back again, every smile she offered when she changed form with ease, had his coyote pulling to be let free. His nerves, as well as his control, were stretched tight. He wouldn't last much longer without having her. It was a good thing he wouldn't have to. If she shifted when she came tonight he'd change and claim her coyote.

Tonight would be the end of this torture he was enduring. Rowan wasn't fairing much better. He knew by the way she looked at him her arousal was high. He didn't need the taut nipples showing through her tank top or the way her breath hitched and she licked her lips when he caught her looking at him as confirmation. The flush on her cheeks wasn't just from exertion either. He might not be able to see because of the shirt she wore but he'd bet anything her breasts glowed with the same rosy hue as her cheeks.

Aching with need, his cock throbbed in his pants. Eager to see Rowan's flushed skin beneath him, Quinn jumped to his feet and stalked toward her. She froze in place, wide eyed as she watched him approach. Her sharp intake of air and labored breathing told him she knew his intentions. He stopped two feet away, afraid to get any closer for fear he'd take her here and now.

"Enough for today," he growled, his voice gravelly with the lust riding his back. "We're moving inside. It's time to take this one step further."

Rowan's eyes widened farther and her nostrils flared as she sucked in a breath. With only a nod, she stepped around him and raced toward the house. Quinn closed his eyes and took a deep breath, giving her time to lock him out if she wanted. He knew she wouldn't but he'd give her that option anyway. It also gave him a moment to regain control of the beast currently howling to take what was his. If they came together right now he wouldn't be gentle and he wanted their first time after so long to be about their love, not their animal need to mate.

He sighed. Was there even a difference? He didn't know if he could separate the two but he'd be damned if he'd take her like an animal this first time.

R owan closed the bathroom door but didn't turn the lock. Shutting it would keep Quinn out. She trusted him to respect her need for privacy. Not that she wanted to stay away from him. A few minutes to freshen up and calm down were all she sought. Her nerves tingled with expectation and her coyote howled with excitement. To finally be in Quinn's arms after all this time seemed surreal. On the one hand, it was as natural as breathing, but on the other, she was terrified.

Terrified of all he made her feel, all they were to each other. Time and distance hadn't dulled what was between them and she hoped she'd managed to master her coyote and merged her two sides completely. Relief at reaching this point flowed through her. Tense shoulders relaxed and the ache in her heart eased. That told her how much being with him but not *being* with him affected her. The strain of holding back, of not touching even when all she wanted was to brush her fingers along his arm in passing. The fear of hurting him if her coyote broke free was enough to have her taking a wide berth around him at all times. After tonight there would be no need for such care.

Today had proven she had the ability to control her coyote with ease now they'd gotten reacquainted. While she'd concentrated on perfecting her shift, Quinn had sat and watched. Never once did he interfere or approach her. She knew what he planned now that she'd gained confidence and she anticipated it with an eagerness that thrummed through her. The sooner they got started the better. But first she wanted a shower. Shifting back and forth had worked up a sweat that clung to her skin.

She stripped off her clothes and stepped into the shower cubicle. The large space allowed her room to stand back out of the water as she waited for the hot to come through. Goose bumps covered her flesh but quickly vanished as the steam rose and she slipped beneath the showerhead. Her shoulder-length hair stuck to her neck in strands, rivulets of water trailing from each end. Eyes closed tight, she turned her face under the spray and allowed the warmth to cascade over her.

Not wanting to take too long, she shampooed her hair and washed her body in record time. Showering had always been an indulgence but now she had other decadent treats to pursue. Or treat. The giggle that bubbled up her throat both surprised and thrilled her. Pleasure had been a rare event in the past few years. Always the nagging fact that she couldn't return home weighed on her mind and stopped her from enjoying the simplest of things.

She had stayed away not only to protect herself but Quinn. Rowan worried not enough time had passed for Marcus to have moved on. Still, she refused to remain apart from Quinn any longer. Doing so had worn her down, torn her apart. Marcus had stolen so much from them. No more would she allow her sorrow to cloud her days—or nights. Now she would embrace all that life had to offer with an open heart and mind.

Starting with Quinn.

Rowan shut off the water and reached for a towel. Brisk movements had her body dry so she wouldn't drip all over the floor. She used a second towel to wrap around her head, squeezing hard to soak up the excess water from her hair. Satisfied, she removed the towel and slid it over the hanging rail. It was then Rowan realized she hadn't brought clean clothes in with her. There were two options. Use a towel to cover herself or walk out naked and hope Quinn wasn't waiting on the other side of the bathroom door. It wasn't like he hadn't seen her naked before anyway.

She took a deep breath and cracked open the door to peer through the gap. There was no sign of Quinn but she could hear him in the kitchen. Flinging the door wide, she raced across the small hall to the bedroom. About four feet by four feet square, the hall basically comprised of three doors and an opening that led to the living area. The bathroom door stood between the two bedrooms so she only had to dash half the distance before making it to the relative safety of the bedroom.

The curse that met her ears as she crossed the threshold told her she hadn't been quick enough. Heavy footsteps and a growl followed her into the room. With a lightness she hadn't felt in far too long, she darted to the far side of the bed and turned to face her mate. Quinn's chest rose and fell in sharp, ragged breaths, his nostrils flared and his eyes blazed with desire. A shiver traveled the length of her spine and ripples of pleasure skittered over her skin.

He looked at her with such need it took her breath and tightened her insides. Her instincts made her yearn to lie on the bed and give him whatever he wanted, but it warred with her own needs and wants. Nerve endings pulsed, sending sensation throughout her body, no part of her left unaffected. Her breasts grew heavy and the nipples puckered into hard nubs. The heat building between her legs beat with the rhythm pounding in her ears. Liquid arousal pooled in her pussy, coating her slit and inner thighs.

Quinn moved and her heart jumped. Like earlier in the yard, he stalked her, hunted her down like prey. Far from being scared, Rowan reveled in the excitement his actions brought. Held in place by his hypnotizing stare, she waited. He reached her before her next breath and the thrill of standing before him naked while he remained fully clothed shot aching need into her core. A stuttered breath caught in her chest and left her breathless.

Caught between the urge to act and the wish to submit to his every whim, Rowan stood transfixed, mesmerized. Her body trembled with longing when Quinn raised one hand to trail his fingertips lightly over her stomach, up between her breasts and under her chin. Tilting her face until their gazes met, he studied her with such intent that her insides quaked. His head lowered, bringing his mouth to hers. Lips brushed, pulled back, moved forward. Her eyes fluttered closed.

"Are you ready for me, Rowan?" Quinn spoke against her mouth.

Her eyes popped open and staring into his, she gave the slightest of nods.

Her world spun as Quinn lifted her from the floor and turned. Her stomach dropped as he threw them both on the bed. His weight pressed into her, trapping her between his hard body and the soft bedding. Rowan didn't get a chance to catch the breath that flew from her lungs. Quinn's mouth took hers in a savage kiss that burned all thought of breathing away.

Their tongues dueled, each forcing their way inside the other to taste and take. Yielding, she allowed him to control the kiss. Aching with want, her hands began to roam his body. Frustration at finding the barrier between his skin and her fingers brought a growl to her throat. She tugged at his clothes, bit his lip to get his attention. Quinn surged back, separating their mouths, each of them left gasping for breath.

"Clothes. Off. Now." Each word was spoken on a ragged puff of air.

He pushed to his knees, straddling her hips. As she shoved his shirt up, he gripped the hem and yanked it over his head, tossing it aside. Her hands were already working on removing his pants without much luck. Another frustrated growl rent the air but this time it was Quinn's. A quick roll to the side and he had his pants past his hips and off. Before she could take advantage of his exposed position, he flipped back over on top of her.

Hot skin met hot skin. Rowan moaned in delight. Quinn's answering groan filled her mouth as he thrust his tongue between her lips. Taking the kiss deep, he took her on a carnal ride that ignited fire in her veins. Lust exploded between them. Hands searched and found sensitive flesh, delivering spikes of pleasure throughout her body. Mouths meshed, tongues stroked and teeth nipped. Cream flowed from her core, spreading slick heat between her legs.

She parted her thighs allowing Quinn's hips to slip between them. His erection nestled along her sex and ground against her clit. Her pussy clenched. Rowan bent her knees and wrapped her legs around his waist. Heals digging into his ass, she pulled him down as she surged up, their pelvises locked together. Ecstasy burst through her and she began to rock against him. Coated in her juices, his cock slid across her swollen folds and pushed her closer to the orgasm just out of reach.

Quinn's lips left hers to trace a line of kisses over her jaw and down her neck. He licked and nibbled his way toward her breasts. His tongue swirled around one sensitive nub before sucking it between his lips. Drawing hard, he pressed the taut peak to the roof of his mouth. Her hips rocked faster and more fluid seeped from her convulsing channel. It wasn't enough. The climax she needed taunted her with its closeness. Her head thrashed on the bed and her body undulated beneath his, trying to grab hold of what she craved.

Raw desire flooded her body, made her frantic to get what she wanted. Quinn continued to work her breasts, feasting on each nipple in turn. His teeth scraped the inflamed points. Electric darts exploded from the slight pain, delivering yet more fragmented need to the tender tissues lining her pussy. Rowan grabbed Quinn's hips, tilted her own until the head of his cock was lined up with her opening, arching up she forced his flesh into hers. His mouth left her breast and she cried out at the loss.

"God, Rowan, stop," he panted.

Her answer was to push higher, take a little more of him inside.

"Slow down." His words were harsh on each jagged breath. "Want it to last."

Slow down? Was he insane? She'd die if she didn't feel him embedded in her fully. Rowan rolled her hips, slid her slick heat farther onto his shaft. His cock jerked against her as the tight fit gave them both immense pleasure. Quinn growled.

"Damn it, Rowan."

He tried to withdraw but with her hands on his hips and her legs hugging his waist she followed.

"I wanted slow and easy this first time."

"No," she gasped. "Hard and fast. Now."

Using her arms and legs she thrust up, lifted off the bed and impaled herself on his cock.

Quinn's control snapped.

Like the crack of a whip, it echoed in his mind and his body moved. Thought fled and instinct took over. Arms curled under her back, he wrapped his hands around her shoulders. His fingers dug into her soft skin in a death grip that left his knuckles white. Flexing his hips he withdrew from her clasping sheath and slammed back in. Withdraw. Advance. Withdraw. Advance. The rhythm hard and fast, exactly what she'd asked for. What his body craved.

Wet slapping noises filled the air, mingled with the scent of arousal to make a potent aphrodisiac to their already over-stimulated senses. She met him thrust for thrust. Pounding in and out of the tight vise of her body, Quinn knew only one thing. Rowan. His coyote howled as he claimed his mate and Quinn grunted with every lunge forward. With each pass along her rippling channel her body jerked beneath his, restricted by his weight, her movements minimal. The hot slide of his cock on her moist flesh sent fire shooting into his balls and up his spine.

Quickening his pace, Quinn powered his hips, the soft curves of her ass cushioning each blow his thighs made when they connected. He tucked his head to latch his mouth around a nipple. Suckling the hard tip, he used his teeth to scrape the tender bud. Rowan bucked and thrashed, her pussy contracting around his cock. Her quivering walls milked him, made his balls squeeze tight. He drove into her, ground his pubic bone against her clit and set off an explosion.

She erupted under him. Her pussy clamped hard, held tight to his shaft. He dragged his length out and surged back in. He rode her, pistoned in and out of her pulsing flesh until the fireball in his groin took him. Molten lava roared through him and burst free to spill in Rowan's core. No part of him went unscorched. Every muscle rigid as he strained against her, buried to the hilt in her writhing body. Exhausted, Quinn collapsed on top of her.

Sweat dripped down his forehead, coated his skin and pooled between them. Their chests slid as they pulled in great gulps of air in an attempt to satisfy oxygen-starved lungs. He tingled from head to toe and was sure he'd see stars if he opened his eyes. Rowan squirmed beneath him and his cock twitched with renewed life. Still locked inside her depths, Quinn felt the last of her orgasm subside. Each squeeze of muscle a tantalizing reminder of the peak they'd just ascended.

With the little energy he had left, Quinn rolled to the side. He took Rowan with him until they lay in reverse. Her splayed on top of him. His erection, still semi-hard in spite of the climax he'd just had, slid to leave only the head breaching her opening. Rowan moaned and her pussy fluttered, the grip on the sensitive gland at the crown hardened his shaft further. Her nipples prodded his ribs as she rocked her hips, the roll allowing his cock to slide in then out of her. He groaned. She moved again.

Hands on her hips, Quinn turned her rock into a thrust. Stroke after stroke, he bucked up into her willing body. Slow and steady, he moved within her, drawing it out, taking his time to love her. Her walls held him like a glove. Warm and wet, he slid along rippling muscles, their combined cum lubricating the way. His fingers pressed into the flesh of her ass, kneading the cheeks, he pulled her up and down his erection faster. She spread her palms on his chest and bracing her arms, sat astride him.

The angle of penetration changed, rubbing sensitive spots, eliciting moans from both of them. Rising to her knees, Rowan began to ride him. Slow slide up, fast drop down. She set a rhythm that teased. The pace remained unhurried, and Quinn enjoyed the vision before him. Back arched, head thrown back, she rode him. She took them both on a leisurely journey to paradise. Unlike the frenzied, breathless rush of their first coupling, this unhurried pace satisfied his initial intention of a slow, thorough loving.

Rowan's breasts bounced with her movements and he couldn't resist cupping them in his palms. He curled his fingers and molded her supple flesh, testing the weight and brushing her nipples with a sweep of his thumbs. The little cries of delight slipping from her throat spurred him on and he pinched the buds until they puckered tight. Their dark brown color looked like drops of chocolate on her creamy skin. Surging up, he sucked first one and then the other between his lips.

Coated in his saliva, they sparkled. With finger and thumb he pulled and pinched one while his mouth went to work on its twin. He opened his jaw wide, sucked in as much as he could and flicked his tongue across the peak. She thrust her chest into his face, forced more of her mound past his lips. Greedy, he took what she offered.

Pulling back, he scraped his teeth gently along her skin. When he got to her nipple he bit harder and tugged. Her pussy tightened around his cock and she rode him faster.

He reached between them, used his fingers to locate the bundle of nerves at the top of her slit. The bud, already popped from its protective hood, was covered in slick cream. Circling the nub, he kept his tempo in time with hers. If she sped up so did he. When she slowed down, he did too. Rowan soon worked out his actions and took advantage. With a skill that came from her sensual nature, she used him to take her over the edge. She bucked and rolled her pelvis, drawing him with her on her way to the top.

It started with tiny quivers and turned into clasping spasms. Her climax rushed through her. Her muscles convulsed in a rolling motion, from the base of his cock to the tip, they surrounded him. He felt the burn in his balls as he hit the peak and went over. His sac pulled up tight and shot cum through his shaft like a bullet from a gun, the recoil jolting his hips. A grunt escaped around the breast in his mouth and he let it go to pull Rowan's face to his, claiming her lips in a breath stealing kiss as the last of his seed spilled deep inside her.

Quinn cupped her head in his hands and staring into her eyes, he said the words he'd waited what seemed like a lifetime to say.

"Welcome home, Rowan."

8

Home.

Rowan's exhausted body sprang to life. She could go home to Whispering Creek.

Now.

A smile stretched her lips and laughter bubbled in her chest. Excitement fizzed in her veins and her head spun with the thrill of finally getting her most precious wish. Home. She was going home.

She smacked her lips to Quinn's, kissed him hard before raising her hips and letting his spent cock slip from her body. The friction sent a delicious shiver along her pussy walls, adding to the happiness bombarding her. Bounding off the bed, she danced around the room, laughing and cheering. And crying. Tears streamed down her face and dripped from her chin but she didn't care. Nothing mattered right now. She could leave the cabin. *They* could leave.

Rowan spun around and rummaged in a drawer for something to wear. She threw on the first sweatshirt she found. Quinn's scent surrounded her and her libido jumped. Damn it was good to be with him. Smiling, she dragged on a pair of shorts. Pulling another set of pants and shirt from the drawer she tossed them over her shoulder and toward the bed. A muffled curse met her ears. Twirling in circles, she continued to laugh and cry, only stopping when she got too dizzy to spin anymore.

"What are you doing?"

"I can go home!" Her words came out as a high-pitched squeal.

"What, now?" He arched an eyebrow.

"Yes, now!" Arms out wide, she whirled around once more.

"God, Rowan, can't we wait until morning?"

"No. I've waited six years, Quinn. With every breath, every thought, I've wished for this moment and now it's here." Breathless with excitement, she jumped on the bed beside him. Grabbing his hand, she wove her fingers with his. "Don't you see? We can go home. Together."

Quinn brought their joined hands to his lips. He feathered light kisses on each knuckle before turning her hand over and kissing her palm. Tiny shockwaves of electricity fired up her wrist and into her arm. The tingle of arousal darted off in all directions when the sensation met her shoulder. She trembled.

"If that's what you want, we'll go." He squeezed her hand and let it go. "But we better hurry up. If we're going I don't want to leave too late. We're supposed to get a snowstorm overnight."

"Really? I love snowstorms. I can't remember the last one I saw." Rowan's mind ticked back through the years, all the way back to her last winter in the mountains. For a moment, sadness descended but she soon snapped out of it when Quinn rolled off the bed. She'd vowed not to let the past cloud her future and she was damn well going to be sure she didn't.

"I'll grab our dirty laundry while you dress, it won't take a second and we'll be ready to leave."

Rowan left the bedroom and picked up the clothes hamper in the bathroom before making her way to the living area. Quinn was already pulling on his boots. A shiver traveled up her spine at the sight of muscle flexing in his arms as he tugged the work boots over bare feet. Her skin prickled with awareness and her heart rate increased. You'd think they hadn't gone at it like animals ten minutes ago. The man turned her on just being in the room. She tried to swallow, her mouth and throat suddenly dry as dirt making it difficult.

"Ready?" she croaked.

He reached for the laundry as he stood. "Yep, let's get going."

They made their way out to Rowan's rental car. It was a good thing they were leaving now. There was no way the little hatchback would make it down the mountain if the predicted snowfall was a heavy one. Quinn pulled the keys from his pocket and she wondered when he collected them. For that matter she couldn't remember when she'd last had them, lucky he was on the ball. Early evening chill surrounded them and they quickly got in the car, Quinn starting it and cranking the heater up. Rowan shuddered as the first blast of air came out cold.

"Give it a second and it'll warm up. It won't take long to get to the house and Brogan will have the furnace going."

The ride along the mountain road took about fifteen minutes. With each passing second Rowan became more and more excited and by the time they turned up the drive to the house she was bouncing on her seat. She soon stopped when the log structure came into view. The long sweeping front porch, the wide double-entry doors, the second-floor windows and the shingled roof looked exactly how she remembered them. She held her breath, afraid it was all a dream and she'd wake up to find it all a lie.

"Fuck."

Quinn's curse jarred her out of her thoughts. Turning to look at him, she found his fingers gripped the wheel so tight his knuckles had turned white. A muscle ticked in his jaw and he stared at the house with anger. Rowan looked back at the house but couldn't work out what was wrong other than the big four-wheel drive parked right in the middle of the driveway.

"Does Brogan have visitors?"

"An unwelcome one, yes," Quinn forced out between clenched teeth.

"Well that's okay, we can just leave him—"

"No. It's not okay." He turned to face her and Rowan's heart pounded. "The owner of that truck is someone I don't want you near. Ever. We'll drive around for a while and come back."

"Don't be silly, Quinn. Why can't we go inside and what do you mean by you don't want me near them?" Sweat broke out on her skin and she wished with all she was he didn't say the one name she knew would come out of his mouth.

"Marcus."

She sucked in a breath, held it tight and tried to calm her galloping heart. Marcus couldn't hurt her. Not like last time. She wouldn't let him get close enough ever again. With effort, she willed her muscles to relax, her pulse to slow. Each labored draw of air into her lungs eased as she looked at Quinn.

"I won't let him touch you. I'll kill him if he does."

His vow was one she could see in his eyes. Without doubt she knew he'd back up his words with actions. As they sat in the dark of the car, the motor vibrating under the hood and the heater blasting warm air onto their faces, Rowan made a personal vow. She would not allow Marcus to take any more from her. Wouldn't let him destroy what had taken years to rebuild. She was stronger now, no longer a scared teenager but a grown woman prepared to fight for what was hers. Quinn. Her home. Her destiny.

Rowan reached over and cupped his cheek. "You won't need to kill anyone, Quinn. He wouldn't hurt me again. I wouldn't let him." She stroked her fingers along his stubble-covered jaw. "As much as I don't want to see him, I'm going in. That's my home and I have a right to be there. He won't keep me from it, or you, ever again."

Taking a deep breath, she wrapped her fingers around the door handle and waited for Quinn to turn off the engine. This was where it really began. Coming home and gaining control of her coyote had been the easy part. Facing her demons would take everything she'd learned over the past six years. It would also take courage and strength. She'd had neither as a teenager, both attributes had developed over time and she was more than ready to use them to claim what was hers.

Quinn couldn't believe their luck. Of all the bad timing, he had to go and pick this one to drive into. Rowan had to face Marcus at some point but he'd hoped to put it off as long as possible. The reality was they were getting the first meeting over with now. He hated to see the happiness fade from her eyes and be replaced by fear. She'd been so excited before they pulled into the driveway. With spine straight, shoulders back and chin thrust forward she sat waiting for him to turn the car off and get out.

The fear had been replaced by a stubborn, determined glint. He knew that look, it was the one she had when she was prepared to get what she wanted. And right now she wanted to go home and he would make sure she got her wish with the least amount of trouble. Even if it meant he had to toss Marcus out of the house on his ear.

A flick of his wrist and the engine died. Sudden silence filled the car. Quinn hopped out and jogged around to help Rowan get her footing. The sight of her bare feet had him laughing.

"Forget something?" he asked as he slid one arm behind her back and the other under her knees.

"Put me down, Quinn. I can walk."

"You'll freeze your toes off on the snow. I'll put you down on the porch."

Why hadn't he noticed she'd left the cabin without shoes? His long strides ate up the ground, he took the steps two at a time and had just put her on her feet when the front door flew open and Brogan charged out to pull her into a hug, her toes dangling off the ground. He was about to suggest going inside when a voice broke the quiet.

"Well, well, well, if it isn't the return of the prodigal bitch, alive and well."

The snarl Quinn issued through his teeth was matched by

Brogan. Taking a step forward, he was stopped by a gentle touch on his arm.

"Hello, Marcus, I didn't see you there." Rowan's voice held no trace of animosity toward the man who'd destroyed so much of her life.

Marcus ignored her, turned his attention to Quinn. "Finally managed to leash the bitch I see."

Quinn saw red. He'd rip the man's throat out for referring to her in such a derogatory manner. The hand on his arm gripped harder, fingers and nails digging in to stop him. Rowan was right to stop him. He couldn't afford to do anything stupid, not before or after she made herself known to the council and the pack members. Reining in his anger, Quinn tried to remember who the better man was but with his coyote howling to take down the threat to his mate, it proved a difficult task. The sneer that curled Marcus's lips was almost his undoing.

"Or is it the big bad regal who's been leashed?"

Marcus didn't know when his life was in jeopardy but then Quinn had never believed the man had more than one active brain cell. And right now his mouth was using it.

"Weren't you leaving?" Brogan asked.

"Yes, I have better places to be than at a sickly sweet family reunion." Marcus pushed past, shouldering Quinn in the chest as he went.

Rowan's nails dug into his skin. "Don't," she whispered. "He's not worth it."

She was right of course but damn if he wouldn't enjoy taking the bastard out. No one said a word as they watched Marcus jump in his truck and rev the engine. He peeled out of there, sprayed the drive and the far end of the porch with snow and slush as he swung the back end around and headed down the drive. Quinn breathed easy when the truck was out of sight. He didn't for one minute think that would be the end of it but for now Rowan was safe.

He draped his arm over Rowan's shoulders and turned them back to the door. "Come on, let's get in out of the cold and welcome you home properly."

Brogan closed the door behind them, taking his time to lock all the deadbolts. Something they didn't do very often. That alone told Quinn how concerned for Rowan's safety her brother was. Catching Brogan's eye, they let Rowan go ahead of them. When Quinn felt she was out of earshot he asked the question he'd wanted to ask the second he'd seen Marcus's truck.

"What did Marcus want?"

"He came to inform me of an official complaint he filed with the council."

"What the hell has he cooked up against you this time?" Quinn kept an eye on the door Rowan had disappeared through.

"Actually this time he's gone for you."

His gaze jerked back to Brogan. "What?"

"He's claiming you killed Rowan in a lovers rage and buried her in the mountains somewhere."

Quinn's jaw dropped—his mind blank. This latest challenge to their positions as sovereign and regal left him speechless.

"You know I'm just going to make you two repeat whatever it is you're saying once you get in here so you may as well come in and start over now before you get too far into it," Rowan yelled from the living room.

Brogan rolled his eyes. "Damn, it's good to have her back." He slapped Quinn on the back. "Come on, let's go satisfy her curiosity."

Rowan knew whatever Marcus was here for hadn't been good. Brogan had worry lines creasing his brow and Quinn looked like he'd been punched in the stomach. Apprehension skittered down her spine and she waited for one of them to start talking.

In the end, she had to ask. Neither of them was forthcoming with the information and the longer they delayed the less time they had to work out how to deal with the problem.

"Okay, enough with the silent treatment. One of you needs to start talking now." She gave them both her best intimidating stare.

"Marcus has gone to the council with the accusation that Quinn killed you in a lover's argument and buried your remains in the mountains." Brogan looked from her to Quinn and back again. "He says he knows where you're buried too."

The quaking started low in her belly, vibrated up into her chest until it forced its way up her throat and burst from her mouth. Arms wrapped around her waist, Rowan doubled over and laughed herself stupid.

"Why the hell are you laughing? He's accused Quinn of murder." Brogan's voice rose above her hilarity.

When she couldn't catch her breath to form a word she gave up and flopped back on the couch to let the mirth die a natural death. Unlike her. She hadn't died at all. More giggles spilled out and Quinn sat next to her patting her on the back as if she was choking. By the time she'd calmed down, Brogan had sat in the seat opposite.

"Can't either of you see how funny this is?" Her head swiveled back and forth, taking in both their troubled expressions. "For a start he'd have to produce a body and he's gonna look pretty stupid when that body shows up breathing."

Her revelation didn't appease them. Sighing, she slumped back into the cushion. Rowan really couldn't see why they were so concerned. All she had to do was turn up in town tomorrow morning and prove Marcus wrong.

Quinn's quiet words broke the silence. "You showing up only proves I didn't kill you, it doesn't prove we didn't fight or that I didn't hurt you seriously enough to warrant your disappearance. The council will still want to investigate the allegations fully and while they're doing that and occupying my time and energy, Marcus will be trying something else."

"If we've learned one thing about Marcus in the last few years, it's that he's predictable. He always starts something and uses it as a smoke screen for what he's really after," Brogan said.

"But why would he accuse Quinn now, after all this time?"

"I don't know, but the more I think about it the more I realize Marcus wasn't at all surprised to see you. Which makes me think he knew you were here."

"He could have picked up her scent in the forest the same as I did," Quinn said.

"Hmm. You might be right. He was looking around like he expected someone else to come into the room the whole time he was here." Brogan rubbed his hand across the back of his neck, a sign Rowan remembered from her youth. He was frustrated at not knowing all the answers.

She stifled a yawn. The warmth of the room seeped into her bones and muscles and made her drowsy. Cuddling into Quinn's side, she relaxed and let her eyelids drift shut. Continuing their discussion on Marcus, Rowan listened with half an ear, only adding the odd word here or there. Her knowledge of Marcus was limited by the time she'd spent away from the pack and before that she'd had very little to do with him.

Quinn had pulled her in under his arm and gave her a squeeze when she yawned for about the tenth time.

"I think we should call it a night and start fresh in the morning. Rowan's tired and needs to rest," Quinn said.

"There isn't really that much we can do anyway. We've been talking in circles for a while and still haven't come up with a decent idea." Brogan pushed from his chair. "I'll check everything is locked up tight before going to bed."

Brogan leaned down and brushed a kiss across her forehead. "It's great to have you home, Sis. Sleep well and I'll see you both in the morning."

Rowan watched him leave the room. Another yawn split her mouth wide and cracked her jaw.

Quinn chuckled. "Come on sleepyhead, let's get you into bed." Like he had out at the car, he picked her up and carried her. He stopped near the door. "Flick the light off for me, my hands are full."

Doing his bidding, Rowan snuggled in to enjoy the ride up to her room. Only they didn't go to her old room, they went to the bigger one at the back of the house. Depositing her on the king-size bed, Quinn switched on a bedside lamp, illuminating the room. It was clearly stamped with his personality and hers. All the mementos she'd left behind had been moved in here.

The photo of her parents on their wedding day sat on the dresser. The gold frame that held her cherished picture of Quinn sat next to it. Her jewelry box, a gift from her mother, held prime position on the tallboy in the corner and when he opened a drawer of the dresser and removed one of her favorite sleeping shirts, Rowan couldn't hold back the tears.

9

Now that her crying jag had calmed to the odd hiccup, Rowan nestled into Quinn's side. He hadn't said a word when the dam burst. He'd wrapped her in his arms and let the storm blow over. Drained, both physically and mentally, she soaked up his warmth—basked in the glory of being loved by this man. If she put everything aside, her destiny to hold the position of royal, his role in pack leadership and them being mates, she would still love him. Before she ever knew what romantic love was she'd been in love with Quinn.

He'd been a part of her for so long—longer than she could remember. Leaving him behind had left a hole in her that gaped and oozed like an open wound. From the moment he'd crashed back into her life the gash began to heal. Each second that passed eased the pain a little more. Surrounded by all she'd known and loved in her youth, and with her future stretched out in front of her, Rowan felt at peace for the first time in her adult life.

She didn't think her worries were over but she wouldn't let them stand in her way again. Maturity and absence had made her heart and mind stronger and she planned to take charge of her world one step at a time. She'd made headway with her coyote, she'd faced her fear of Marcus with surprising ease and when it came time to front the council, Rowan would be more than ready.

Quinn's hand traveled in lazy circles on her lower back. The soothing motion sent conflicting sensations throughout her body. The light, comforting strokes lulled her into sleep but the tingle of skin on skin when his fingers grazed beneath her shirt sent darts of awareness to every nerve ending. A shiver skipped along her spine and trembled to the tips of her fingers and toes. Arousal swirled low in her belly, hardened her nipples and wet her core.

Rowan slung a leg over his and pushed her throbbing center against his hip in the hope of relief. A spark of electricity shot into her clit and her inner muscles clenched. Cream soaked her panties. Quinn's arm tightened and his hand stopped. For a moment not a breath was taken. Time froze and the world stilled as they lay there. One heartbeat. Two. Then Quinn moved and nothing else mattered.

His tongue invaded her mouth and conquered. He stole her breath and gave it back again. The hand on her back had moved to her ass, splayed fingers cupping one cheek. Other clever digits teased her breast, plying a nipple until it beaded tight. Rowan's hands weren't idle either. They pulled and tugged at clothing. Groped at muscles rippling under smooth skin and teased sensitive flesh. Moans, muffled by their joined mouths, filled the air.

The heady scent of desire cloaked them, pushed them higher. Quinn tore his mouth from hers, dragged his lips over her chin and down her throat. His teeth scraped across her skin, goose bumps trailing in their wake. He sucked at her neck, hard enough to leave a mark. The tinge of pain mixed with pleasure fizzed in her veins, pumped through her to pound in her core. Rowan's pussy convulsed, moisture seeping from within to heat folds slick with need. Surging up, she ground her sex against his side.

Quinn growled and yanked free of her hold. In one quick move, he ripped his shirt over his head and dropped it on the floor beside the bed. Rowan scrambled to do the same. When he reached for her pants, sliding his fingers in the waistband she didn't protest. Lifting her hips to help, she was soon stripped bare. With greedy hands, she helped him remove the rest of his clothes before reaching to envelop his cock in her fist.

Hard and hot, it jerked in her grasp. Long, firm strokes from root to tip and back again had him groaning. Pre-cum beaded at the slit and Rowan leaned forward to swipe it off with her tongue. His hand cupped the side of her head, fingers tangled in her hair and tugged her closer. She took the hint and opened her mouth to suck the mushroom tip inside. Swirling her tongue, she teased the sensitive gland. He growled in approval and his fingers curled—dug into her scalp.

Flavor exploded on her tongue. The scent of musky male arousal filled her nostrils, saturated her senses. Hungry for more of his taste, Rowan slid his shaft between her lips. She closed her mouth around him and sucked hard. Cheeks hollowing, she pulled him deeper, flicking her tongue along his length as she did. He thrust his hips, driving into her mouth. The plump head nudged the back of her throat and she swallowed around it, fought the urge to gag.

Quinn loosened his hold on her head and withdrew from her mouth. Rowan greedily slurped at his cock as it slipped free. He pushed her to her back, put his hands on her thighs and spread her legs wide. Dipping his head, he took a deep breath before blowing a stream of warm air over her clit. Her body jolted, electrified by the sudden stimulation. With a sweep of his tongue, he laved her from back to front.

He devoured her. With teeth, tongue and lips, he ate at her, sent her rocketing toward orgasm and over the edge in minutes. Spasms racked her from head to toe, her hips bucking beneath his ravishing mouth. There was no time to come down. Quinn took her back up to the peak before surging over her and penetrating her in one hard thrust. Her walls clamped, held tight to his cock. Buried to the hilt, he stilled, pelvis locked to pelvis.

Frustrated with need, Rowan contracted her muscles, squeezing along his length. He flexed his hips; the base of his shaft brushed her clit and sent a barrage of intense craving to her core. She wrapped her legs around his thighs, dug her hands into his ass and arched her back to urge him to move. When that didn't work she sank her teeth into his shoulder.

"Move, dammit!"

"Not yet. Don't want to come too soon," he panted.

Rowan growled and thrashed under him. His cock slid from her pussy, hitting her G-spot and sending sparks of delight into her belly. She drove her hips up off the bed and plunged onto his erection again, her muscles quaking with lust. Quinn's cock pulsed as he rammed into her, slamming home hard. Every inch of delicate tissue was stimulated beyond measure. He withdrew, plunged forward, withdrew. In and out, he took them both to new heights.

Back and forth, they rocked together, each movement harsher than the last. Frantic, savage actions brought them closer to release. Nails and teeth bit into flesh, dragged across sweat slick skin. Grunts and groans rebounded off walls, echoed in her ears and competed with the slap of wet bodies colliding. Quinn's hands curled over her hips, his fingers dug in and pinned her in place as he pumped into her. Clawing at his back, Rowan dug her heels into the bed and tried to meet him thrust for thrust.

Caught in his strong grip, she strained against him. Head thrown back, Rowan pushed her breasts into Quinn's chest. Taut nipples prodded hard muscle. Coarse hair abraded the tender buds, they puckered tighter and electric pulses of need beat through her to center in her core. She bent her knees, flung her legs around his waist to lock her ankles together and pull him closer. Her pelvis titled, her ass lifted off the bed and his cock stroked in deeper. Pounding in and out, the mushroom head brushed her G-spot with each slide.

Quinn's teeth clamped down on her nipple at the exact moment he drove balls deep and ground his pubic bone hard against her clit. Fire burst inside her and stars exploded in front of her eyes. Her body went rigid, every muscle frozen in that split second before she shattered into a million pieces. The world narrowed to nothing but the ecstasy flooding her senses. She called his name, a rasp of sound that was barely heard over Quinn's cry of release.

Clutched within her, his cock jerked and spilled a pool of warmth as he emptied his seed. Her walls continued to convulse with her orgasm, milking him of every last drop of cum. What seemed like hours but probably only seconds later, Rowan's body relaxed. Her limbs felt like jelly and they slipped from around Quinn to fall to the bed. He'd slumped on top of her, his breath hot and fast, bathed her neck. She couldn't raise more than a grunt when he spoke.

"Too heavy." Quinn levered up on his elbows but didn't get off.

His fingers swept the hair from her face. Cupping her jaw, he tipped her face up and placed a butterfly light kiss on her mouth. Rowan forced her eyelids open and found herself staring into Quinn's caramel brown eyes.

"It's so good to have you in this bed."

Rowan laughed.

"You know what I mean." He smiled and gave her another kiss. "But *having* you in this bed is pretty damn good too."

He rolled to the side and got off the bed. With his arms stretched over his head, Quinn's back and ass were on perfect display. She watched, mesmerized by the shift and flex of muscle and sinew under smooth tan skin. Licking her lips, she imagined running her tongue down his spine and dipping into the crack of his ass. Nibbling her way across the curve to the crease where leg met butt. He was one fine specimen of mankind standing naked for her enjoyment.

"If you're not careful you'll drool all over the bed," he said.

Slowly she brought her gaze up past his rear end, up the line of his back and to his face. He looked at her over his shoulder with a grin. Rowan smiled, not worried about getting caught ogling him.

"A little drool can't hurt. It's only water." He turned and gave her an eyeful. She swallowed. "Besides, I find my mouth suddenly dry."

Quinn threw back his head and laughed. The deep rumble shook his chest and made his cock bob. At half-mast, his erection stood out from his torso, the base was surrounded by dark hair and his large balls swung free below. She turned on her side and reached out to skim one finger from sac to tip and back again. Quinn shook and his cock grew harder. Palming the length, she gripped tight and pumped her hand up and down.

"Enough." He stepped back, pulling away. "You need rest." He scooped up the discarded sleep shirt and tossed it at her before stalking off to the bathroom, naked butt jiggling all the way.

Flopping back on the bed, she debated showering but gave up on the idea when the comfort of the bed proved too enticing. The temperature in the room was warm in spite of the cold wind howling outside the window. The storm blowing up would likely dump snow overnight and turn the weather below freezing. But here in the comfort of the home she'd been born in she could rely on the furnace to do its job and keep the sub-zero temp at bay.

Listening to Quinn run the water in the bathroom, Rowan closed her eyes. The rattling pipes, the wind whistling under the eaves and the creaking of timber settling were a welcome reminder of everything this house meant to her. Comfort, safety, home.

Quinn washed up quickly. He grabbed a clean towel and washcloth and headed back to Rowan. She looked so peaceful lying sprawled on the bed and as he got closer her soft snoring reached his ears over the storm outside. Sound asleep and more beautiful than he remembered, she took his breath. To see her here, in their bed, the one he'd carved himself, made his heart whole for the first time in six years.

He sat on the edge of the bed, admiring the changes in her lithe body. She'd always been slim, but now that was tempered by sleek muscles and womanly curves. Her black hair was damp and plastered to her forehead, her face still flushed from their earlier exertion. Soot-colored eyelashes fanned over her cheeks and her pink lips, slightly parted, invited him to kiss.

Nothing else would please him more than to lean over and lick her pouty mouth but it was late already and they had so much to face in the next few days that he couldn't bring himself to disturb her slumber. He used the warm washcloth to clean her up, trying not to wake her. A few times she stirred but she remained asleep while he wiped and dried her. Wadding the cloth and towel together, he threw them in the general direction of the bathroom.

Quinn folded back the bedding on one side and gently rolled Rowan over onto the sheet. Covering her with the quilt, he walked around the bed and climbed in on the other side. Putting an arm around her waist, he pulled her back until her spine nestled against his chest and her ass cradled his cock. The crease between her cheeks made the perfect resting place for his erection.

The wind howled outside as the storm picked up force. The legendary whistle that had given the mountains their name grew louder. Older members of the pack talked of the mountains whispering to those who chose to listen. It was a tale told for generations and even though Quinn didn't believe most of what was said, he knew from experience that once the mountain whispered it was best to find shelter. The predicted snowfall was going to be a big one.

He pulled her body closer to his, her murmured protest reminding him not to squeeze the life out of her, but he could help it. He wanted to hold her and never let go. The next few days would be busy and if the snowstorm brewing dumped too much of the white stuff they'd be stuck at the house. There was no way he'd risk the mountain road if there was more than a foot of snow on the ground.

No doubt by now Marcus would have spread the word of Rowan's return. He wouldn't let an opportunity like that pass without using it. Quinn could only image what crap he'd make up this time. The man lived to cause trouble and did so every chance he got. But unlike in their youth, when Marcus's father was regal and later sovereign, he wouldn't be able to cover up any attempt he made to get at Rowan so easily.

Quinn would need to keep his wits about him too. He'd wanted nothing more than to squeeze the life out of Marcus for calling Rowan a bitch and if she hadn't been there he probably would have. Her steady calm had spread over him and kept him from doing something stupid and playing right into Marcus' hands. Before they went anywhere, they needed to sit down with Brogan and work out a strategy.

Without knowing what Marcus had planned, they wouldn't be able to do much in the way of prevention but they could certainly be prepared for the worst. Quinn didn't think Rowan would have difficulty being accepted back into the pack and the Council had been questioning Brogan on her possible return since the moment he became sovereign. They were more than ready for her to come home and take her place as royal.

He was being selfish but he wished there was a good dump of snow between now and morning. It would allow him to keep her to himself for a little longer. They had a lot of catching up to do. He wanted to know everything she'd done, everywhere she'd been. He wanted to tell her all that he and Brogan had done for the pack in her absence and he wanted to roll between the sheets until neither of them could stand.

Nuzzling the side of her neck, Quinn breathed in deep and sucked in a lungful of her scent. Wrapped in his arms, she was all he wanted and he'd do anything to protect her. If push came to shove, he'd take Marcus out and worry about the consequences later. Nothing and nobody would hurt her or force her to leave her home again. He cuddled into her back and let the comfort of having her here sink in. Rowan continued to snore softly and he let the warmth of holding her and the sound of the raging weather lull him to sleep.

Quinn jolted awake, reaching for Rowan as he sat up. Already up and moving off the bed, she grabbed for a shirt.

"What the hell was that?"

He didn't get a chance to answer her, the door flung open and Brogan burst into the room. "Are you two all right?" He scanned the room for some perceived menace.

"We're fine. What was it?" Quinn asked while he pulled on pants.

"I think we've got a broken window. I thought it came from in here." Brogan turned and left as quickly as he'd come in.

"I think it was my old room," Rowan said as she followed her brother out the door, Quinn right on her heels.

Brogan stood three feet inside the doorway of Rowan's old room staring at the mess of broken glass and snow littering the floor and furniture. They hadn't left much in this room, a queen bed and dresser the only large items. There was a small writing desk and chair in one corner and a plush recliner in another. The desk and dresser remained unmarked but the bed and recliner had a layer of snow and glass glittering on them. The wind howled through the window and filled the room, dropping the temperature a good thirty degrees. Rowan shivered and Quinn moved around her to block the worst of the cold.

"How would the wind pick up a rock and hurl it through the window?"

"What rock?" Quinn surveyed the debris for what she was talking about.

Brogan stepped forward and Rowan's hand shot out and stopped him in his tracks.

"You've got no shoes on, Brogan."

Her reminder came just in time. They were all barefoot and not exactly dressed to tackle the clean up and repair of the window. Walking backward, Quinn pulled Rowan with him as he moved into the hall.

"Close the door to stop the chill from getting into the rest of the house, Brogan. We'll get dressed and clean this up now. I'm not leaving it until morning, if the snow gets any worse the room will be soaked by then." Rowan spun away from them and went back to their room.

"The weather didn't do this," Brogan said.

Quinn thought the same but remained quiet on the subject for now. "Let's fix the window first and worry about the rest later."

He found Rowan not getting dressed but standing by the window peering out into the darkness. The rollers on the timber door of the wardrobe squeaked as he pushed it open. He grabbed jeans and a flannel shirt to throw over his T-shirt. She hadn't moved when he turned back and he walked over to see what she was looking at.

"Why would someone be out on a snowmobile in near blizzard conditions?"

"What?" Quinn cupped his hand on the glass and scrutinized the darkness. "I can't see a damn thing."

"Over by the trees on the left, see the tracks? They're not covered because of the tree canopy."

She was right. Once he knew where to look, his keen coyote vision picked up the distinct trails of a snowmobile leading off into the forest. It appeared he'd be going out in the storm to scout around. He wouldn't follow the path cut into the snow but he'd be sure to find anything that might have been left behind. If the person had sat watching the house for long there could be a clue as to their identity. Not that he needed one. His gut told him it was Marcus but what was he playing at throwing rocks?

Quinn was of the opinion the man was impulsive and stupid but sitting in a snowstorm in the dead of winter was downright insane. And if Marcus had crossed over that fine line into the mentally unstable they were in for far more trouble than he ever could have imagined or expected.

10

———

"You are not going out there in this weather. I don't care who was skulking around the house, I'm not letting you put your-self in danger when the culprit is long gone," Rowan yelled at him.

She'd been yelling at him since he'd told Brogan he'd go out and take a look around while they secured the window and cleaned up. He understood her concern but it was misplaced, there would be no taking chances with the storm and darkness awaiting him. Quinn wanted to catch the person but he wouldn't risk his own neck to do it.

"Stop yelling at him, Rowan. He's doing his job and you know it. The quicker he's out there, the quicker he's back." Brogan thrust hammer and nails into her hands. "You can watch from the damn window if you want."

It was a wonder Brogan didn't crumple to the floor with the look his sister gave him. Before she could open her mouth and start yelling again Quinn tried to reassure her he'd be safe and calm her down. That temper of hers was mixing with her stubborn streak and he didn't want any more mess to clean up tonight. He remembered the arguments the siblings used to have. Nothing was safe unless it was nailed down, which worried him more now that Brogan had given her the timber and steel tool.

"I'm going to walk around the house and then out to the tree line, no farther. I promise." He planted a kiss on her lips and scooted out the front door before she could stop him.

Snow slapped his face and the wind cut through the layers of clothes he wore. The weather had eased up a little but there was already a good ten inches of ground cover. Slowly he combed the area around the house, the snowfall had covered any evidence of an intruder but then they might not have gotten that close. The rock could have been lobbed from a fair distance, if the thrower had a good arm, and he recalled Marcus being a damn good baseball player in their youth, the star of their high school team.

Quinn headed over to the tree line, his boots sinking into the drifts of snow. It made for slow going and with the wind threatening to blow him away he struggled to stay on his feet. The area between the house and trees yielded no more than his initial search. Quinn could see where the machine had been parked. A trough beneath a tree about six feet in gave it away. He examined the immediate vicinity, coming up empty. Frustrated, he sighed and looked up, color catching his gaze.

Caught in a low branch were strips of fabric. Standing still, he studied the small pieces of material. They were ripped from a snow jacket, a black and red one. He stepped over to get a better look. On closer inspection, Quinn determined they were from the sleeve of a well-worn parka. He had one very similar in his closet. Anyone who'd attended Whispering Springs High School had one. There were no distinct markings, so unless they could locate the rest of the coat, their chances of proving who was out here were nil.

Irritated at yet another dead end, Quinn made his way back inside. The wind had died down making the slog across the yard easier. As he rounded the corner of the house the door flew open and Rowan stood there waiting for him. It certainly beat any welcome he'd ever received from Brogan. Stomping the snow from his boots on each step, he took his time. He wanted to savor this homecoming. The first of many ahead in the future but this one would always be special. He cleared the threshold and stepped into the welcoming warmth.

Rowan closed the door and latched the deadbolts behind him. He stumbled back into the wall when she launched into his arms, her lips landing on his. It took a moment for him to act but once his brain engaged he swept his tongue into her mouth. In an instant he went from cold to hot. Her flavor seeped into him, spread out and teased his senses until all he could think of—could feel—was Rowan. She took over, turned his thoughts to one thing only. Getting naked and claiming her.

"Ahem."

Quinn untangled their tongues and pulled free. Dazed, they stared at each other, breathing hard.

"When you two are ready, I'll be in the living room." Brogan's footfalls echoed in the foyer.

"Damn." Quinn let her unwind her arms and lowered her to the floor, when he'd picked her up he hadn't a clue. "Hold that thought, we'll get back to it after I tell you both what I found."

Rowan nodded and reached for his hand. Fingers curled together they went to join Brogan. Someone had stoked the fire and Quinn unzipped his jacket and draped it over the back of a chair to dry. He shucked his boots and placed them on the hearth before he sat on the floor so his soaked jeans didn't wet the sofa.

"Well? Did you find anything?"

Quinn smiled at Rowan's impatience. He was surprised she'd waited this long before grilling him for information.

"Nothing other than you're right, there was someone out there. They were in the tree line for a while but I couldn't tell if they'd gotten close to the house or not. Too much snow."

"So do you have a theory?" Brogan asked.

"Yeah. They were in the trees watching the house for a long time. The depression from the snowmobile was still there. I found part of a jacket sleeve caught in a low branch, whether it happened before the rock was thrown or after, I can't say. But what I can say is there's no way to prove who did it. The material is from a Whispering Springs High parka, could have been anyone."

"But you think it was someone," Brogan stated.

"Marcus." Rowan spoke before Quinn could voice his thoughts.

He turned to stare at her. "Why would you think that?"

"Because the rock was thrown into my old room. It's not the first time he's tossed rocks at that window. Only last time they were pebbles and he only wanted my attention, not to hurt me." She shrugged. "That didn't come until later."

"Why don't I know about this? You've never mentioned him doing that." Brogan's words rang with shock at this new revelation.

"Mom and Dad knew. It was when I was about thirteen I think. He only did it a couple of times and then stopped. I don't know if Dad said something to him or if he got the hint that I wasn't interested."

One more reason for Quinn to hate the man, not that he needed more than Marcus' attack on Rowan as grounds for hatred. His jaw clamped and he ground his teeth together at the memory of her coming home bruised and bleeding. If she hadn't begged him not to leave her he would have gone out and hunted Marcus down that night. Brogan had stopped him from going after the bastard when they'd gotten her off the mountain, but he could still feel the boiling anger, still taste the need to kill.

"Quinn?"

He turned to Rowan, saw the concern on her face and cursed himself for not being able to hide his feelings. She had enough to worry about without him adding to the pile, he needed to remember that. One way to take her mind, and his, off things was to lose themselves in each other. In a few hours it would be daylight and they would have to think about the outside world but for now he'd make sure the only thing she thought about was him and the mind numbing pleasure he gave.

· · ·

owan watched the emotions flicker across Quinn's face. He
went from pissed off to aroused in record time. The sad part,
or maybe it was a good thing, she found every one of his expressions
appealing. He turned her on just by breathing but when he really set
out to push her hot buttons he proved lethal. And if she was any
judge, Quinn had decided it was time for bed.

He got to his feet and stalked toward her. Wrapping a hand
around her upper arm, he hauled her off the sofa to her feet and
marched her out of the room.

"Yep. No worries. See you both in the morning." Brogan's words
and laughter followed them into the hall.

"Quinn?"

He ignored her. This take-charge man all but dragging her to his
cave had her blood pumping and her juices flowing. Why was she so
ready to submit to his forceful nature when it came to sex? In everything else she challenged him but in this she turned into a swooning
female eager to surrender to his command. A shudder moved over
her. Her breasts grew heavy and her nipples puckered tight. The ache
in her clit pounded in time with her galloping heart.

The toe of her sneaker caught the edge of a step, her knee missed
the tread by a hair when Quinn picked her up and tossed her over his
shoulder in a fireman's hold. Her head bounced and bumped into his
back. Rowan wound her arms around his middle and hugged his
spine. He took the rest of the stairs two at a time and slammed the
door closed with his foot as he entered their room. Wasting no time,
he dropped her on the bed and came down on top of her.

His mouth took hers in a hungry kiss. He thrust his tongue inside,
savagely taking hers prisoner and delivering a delightful blend of give
and take. Hands fumbled with clothing, each attempting to remove
whatever fabric was within their grasp. Limbs tangled and frustration
mounted. The desire for skin on skin slashed with a razor's edge,
tearing at nerves with wicked need.

Their lips separated, breaths mingling as they gasped for air in
the vacuum of sexual demand. Trapped by Quinn's burning gaze,

Rowan stared at hunger so great she feared being devoured whole. Answering want filled her, clawed at her insides and stirred her coyote. The snarl and snap of a beast greedy for its mate echoed in her soul. Quinn's caramel eyes turned yellow as his coyote answered the call from hers.

A growl rumbled in his chest and vibrated up his throat, the sound muffled by his clenched jaw. Natural instinct had her whimpering and exposing her neck, offering herself to him. His nostrils flared and he bent down to lick the vulnerable column. With gentle laps, he bathed her tender skin. He kissed and nibbled his way to the sensitive hollow beneath her ear. Tickled and teased until she squirmed beneath him.

The frenzied need abated. Her surrender to him soothed the raw need to claim. Now the urge was to savor, enjoy the spoils of the gift given. Slow, deliberate moves weaved their spell and turned her body pliant under his fingertips. He removed her clothing piece by piece, exploring each inch of skin revealed. Lulled into a sexual stupor, Rowan wallowed in the bliss flowing through her.

His magic hands and mouth worshiped her, made her world a kaleidoscope of heavenly pleasures. When he parted her legs to delve between her folds, Rowan arched off the bed, sensation saturating senses and mind. The peak came quickly and took her by surprise. Hurtling over the edge, she clawed his scalp as she held on to the center of her universe.

As her orgasm ebbed he rose above her, stripped off the remainder of his clothes and covered her body with his. Skin on skin from chest to knees, lean muscle met willowy curves. Her spread thighs cradled his hips and his cock pressed on her engorged pussy, hurling electric jolts of want into her womb. Coated in her cream, Quinn slid his erection back and forth, probing her entrance before moving back to bump her clit. He reached for her hands, held them beside her head and entwined their fingers.

Eyes locked on his, Rowan saw love and lust swirl together in a potent mix of longing. Holding her gaze, he lowered his face and sealed his mouth to hers. The kiss soft—gentle. He flexed his hips and lined his shaft up with her opening. His girth stretched her as he entered. With a long drawn out thrust, Quinn drove home, filling her completely. Her groan of relief was swallowed by his hungry lips. His tongue caressed her mouth the way his length stroked her pussy.

A slow, easy rhythm took them up the path to satisfaction. Each pass of his cock a carnal glide on their ride to heaven. Every brush of his tongue a slick lash of sinful delight. Lured into his world of leisurely passions, Rowan followed where he led. Seduced and tantalized by Quinn's languid movements, she relished the sensation of total abandonment of control. Fingers curled in his, she held on as he took them higher into the bliss of promised ecstasy.

When her climax broke, it swept her up and flung her to the winds. The shattering of body and mind so absolute she felt nothing but the man above her, driving into her faster. Harder. One final lunge and Quinn jerked before he buried himself to the hilt and stayed there. Warmth bathed her core as his cum spilled inside her. Fingers and toes tingled, arms and legs heavy as lead weights, Rowan sank into the mattress.

Quinn shifted to the side, his cock slipped free and her walls clenched in regret. Flutters traveled the length of her channel to her womb, squeezed her tummy tight. Breath after breath rasped in her ears, accompanied by the beating of her heart. Blood rushed in her veins, the echoes of lust tainting the flow. Drained of energy, she let her eyelids close and floated off to sleep.

By the time Quinn found the strength to move Rowan was asleep. On her back, arms and legs sprawled, she looked dead to the world. Sweat stuck her bangs to the side of her face and he smoothed them back with his fingers. Her rosy cheeks had a sheen of moisture and her scent drifted in the air to tease him. She looked so peaceful in her slumber, he tried to shake the bed as little as possible when he climbed out and headed for the bathroom.

Business taken care of, he washed up and went back to bed. Lying next to Rowan, he pulled the covers up and tucked them both in.

Predawn light could be seen through the window and Quinn glanced at the clock. Less than two hours until sun-up. Today would be a long one. Flakes still fell from the sky but the wind had slowed to a breeze. If it stopped snowing soon they'd be able to head into town after lunch.

He heard Brogan moving around downstairs and figured his friend had decided not to bother going back to bed. If it wasn't for the warm woman sharing his bed, Quinn would be staying up too. But he'd rather be awake next to a sleeping Rowan than wandering the house in the early hours of the morning. Turning on his side, he lifted the blanket and watched Rowan's breasts rise and fall with each breath.

Her creamy skin, marked in places from his teeth and beard stubble, tempted him to taste. Large nipples stood at attention like soldiers guarding a fort. He ran a finger around one pouty tip, it puckered into a tight little bead and the normally pink flesh darkened. She stirred, snorted a choked breath and turned over presenting him with her back. The notches of her spine protruding in a long line of follow the dots.

Resisting the urge to trace the delicate row of bones, Quinn moved closer and spooned his body around hers, gratified when she snuggled back against him. He slid one arm beneath her and cupped her breast with his hand. The other, he draped over her side and splayed his fingers across her stomach. Her ass nestled into his groin, his cock slipping snug between her cheeks.

He'd had more sex in the last twenty-four hours than he'd had in his entire life. He should be exhausted and totally sated but he still had a hard-on and his coyote would be more than happy to claim his mate again. The need no longer held the raw edge of starvation, the long abstinence satisfied by the feast of the last day. He burrowed his nose into the hair at her nape, breathed deeply and filled his lungs with her scent.

The house creaked around them and the wind rattled the windowpanes. Rowan continued to sleep, her soft snore and even breathing something Quinn cherished. For the second night in a row she slept in his arms. The reality far better than any dream he'd ever had in the years without her. Until yesterday he'd been clueless to the joy of holding her through the night. When she'd staggered into the house that fateful night long ago neither of them knew there were only hours left before circumstances would tear them apart.

He suppressed a shudder as the memory of Rowan's bloody and bruised body collapsing on the kitchen floor flashed in his mind. By the time he and Brogan had managed to tend to her wounds she'd roused enough to tell them what happened to her. Quinn's blood ran cold even thinking about what she'd survived at the hands of Marcus. It soon boiled when he imagined getting hold of the asshole and ripping him to pieces. One small bit at a time.

Quinn's wandering mind strained more than his heart. Muscles tensed and ready to fight squeezed hard, involuntarily, banding around her like a straight jacket. Rowan squirmed in his embrace, squeaked a protest. She settled quickly once he loosened his hold. He waited for her breathing to even out again and then gradually worked her out of his arms. Turning to his back, he stared at the ceiling. Deep breaths and the knowledge she lay beside him unharmed helped to rein in his anger.

Calm, Quinn gave up on sleep and slipped from the bed. Careful to make no noise, he grabbed some sweats and a shirt from the dresser. He dressed and checked she was covered up before he left the room and headed downstairs. None of the chill remained from the broken window and he descended the stairs in sockless feet. The smell of fresh coffee pulled him in the direction of the kitchen. Brogan sat at the island bench, a steaming mug clasped in his hands. Quinn helped himself to a cup of the dark liquid.

A sip to test the temperature preceded a mouthful of the rich wake-me-up elixir. Strong and black, just the way he liked it. The stool legs scraped when he pulled out the seat opposite Brogan. They sat in silence, sipped at their cups of caffeine and waited for dawn to arrive. Light came flooding in through the big glass windows in the back wall and as the sun rose to blanket the mountains, the blue sky showed its cloud-free expanse.

"How is she?"

Quinn didn't answer Brogan's question right away. He thought about Rowan and how she'd dealt with the obstacles so far. Her biggest freak-out moment had come when he'd gone out to investigate their rock thrower.

"She's ready."

"Good. We'll need her to be."

Quinn raised a brow. "Oh?"

Brogan shrugged. "A gut feeling." He sipped his coffee. "I think Marcus has gone over the edge. The rock was juvenile and not something a focused man would do. An obsessed one, yes, but one who's rational and methodical would never use such immature tactics."

He had to agree with Brogan's assessment. At some point Marcus had crossed a line. Quinn only hoped it wasn't Rowan's return that made him snap but knew it was a fruitless wish. With the pack's royal now back, Brogan's position as sovereign strengthened and so did Quinn's as regal. There had never really been a threat to their appointed status, but the trouble Marcus caused while they guided the pack made it harder to move forward and cement all their futures.

If he let himself be honest he'd have to admit the only sure way to see the pack prosper for generations to come would be to remove Marcus. The council would never vote to exile any pack member without a valid reason and hard evidence to back it up.

Until Marcus slipped up they were stuck with him.

11

Rowan woke to bright sunshine and an empty bed. Curled under the quilt, she took her time stretching the kinks of sleep from her body. A glimpse of the clock told her it was well past time to get up. Muffled noises from below could be heard over the twitter of a bird outside the window. She rolled over and stretched her arms above her head, arched her back and popped bones stiff from slumber.

Sleep encrusted eyes squinted at the blaze of light through the open blind. She had to remember to close that before going to bed tonight. Mornings weren't her favorite time of the day. She'd go so far as saying she hated them and with her usual reluctance she threw back the covers and crawled out of bed. Her fists scrubbed at her eyelids as she made her way to the bathroom to attend to the need suddenly making its presence known low in her belly.

The house may have been kept a comfortable temperature but the warmth hadn't extended as far as the toilet seat. The shock of cold to her ass and thighs sucked the breath from her lungs. She couldn't get done quick enough and shivered from top to toe while her bladder emptied out. Finished, she debated a shower but decided to find out where Quinn was first. Walking through the bedroom, she picked up last night's clothes a piece at a time, like a treasure hunt she collected articles and threw them on.

Her teeth felt furry and she was sure to have morning breath but before she could return to the bathroom to fix either the smell of coffee filtered into the room. Closely followed by Quinn. She growled and lunged for the mug in his hand. He handed it over readily and she gulped down the lukewarm contents, the strong, dark blend well on its way to improving her day.

Quinn's chuckle skipped over her nerves and danced down her spine. He leaned in to place a kiss on her nose. "You're cute all sleep rumpled and grumpy."

"Grumpy? Who's grumpy? I'm too brain dead to manage grumpy yet."

He took the empty cup from her and, gripping her shoulder in one large hand, turned her toward the bathroom. A little nudge and he pushed her a step away. "Go get showered, you need to get ready to face the day."

About to protest about getting another coffee, it wasn't words that left her mouth. With a yelp, she jumped when Quinn slapped her ass to get her moving. Peering over her shoulder with narrowed eyes, she mumbled about rough treatment and missed coffee but did as he'd suggested and went to take a shower. His laughter echoed around the room. The only thing stopping her from smacking him back was his promise of more coffee when she was done.

Rowan kept her shower short. The enticement of fresh brewed coffee and a rumbling stomach too much to ignore. Wrapped in a towel, she went in search of clean clothes. The dresser produced underwear and T-shirts; in the wardrobe she found jeans and jackets. Everything she'd sent home with Brogan had been laundered and put away. Either someone came in and cleaned house for her brother and Quinn or they'd become very domesticated over the years. She imaged the two alpha males in aprons and gloves scrubbing bathrooms and mopping floors.

Laughing, she left the room and went downstairs. Her sock covered feet made no sound as she descended the stairs and followed her nose to the kitchen. The deep tones of Quinn's voice could be heard through the door and Rowan's nerves did a little happy dance in response. But the second she pushed the door open every part of her centered on the coffee pot in the corner. Zeroing in on the machine, she grabbed a cup off the counter and was sipping on liquid good-morning in seconds. Eyes closed, she savored the hot brew.

"I see you've grown to love mornings, Rowan." Brogan's voice spoke in her ear just before he kissed the top of her head.

Opening her eyes, she met his gaze, his laughing, hers narrowed with mock anger. "Aren't we the jokester this morning?"

Quinn chuckled. "Told you she was the same sunny Rowan."

"Humph." She turned back to refill her mug and ignored both of them.

Brogan ruffled her damp hair like he used to do when they were younger. Emotion choked her. Tears stung her eyes and clogged her throat. She sucked in a breath, chewed on her bottom lip and willed the tears away. Concentrating on the view out the window, Rowan swallowed past the lump in her throat. A couple of deep breaths and she was under control again, the urge to bawl her eyes out gone.

With a smile on her face, she turned away from the window. Mug full of coffee, Rowan walked over and pulled out a stool. Perched on the seat, she watched as her brother went back to cooking bacon and Quinn popped bread into the toaster. They worked together efficiently to get breakfast on the table. It didn't take long before she found herself with a plate load of bacon, scrambled eggs and toast.

Timber scraped on tile as Quinn and Brogan sat down next to her. Stomach rumbling, Rowan forked up a mouthful of eggs. Flavor exploded on her tongue. Cheese, egg, garlic and onion combined in a fluffy delicious mixture of breakfast heaven. Her tummy gurgled in delight as the first bite hit. Another scoop and her taste buds tingled. Suddenly ravenous, she couldn't shovel it in fast enough. The crispy bacon soon followed the eggs. With her plate scraped clean, she pushed it away.

Washing the wonderful meal down with some coffee, Rowan looked up to find both men staring at her.

"What?"

Neither of them said a word.

"Well, what?" This silence was a little unnerving. She felt like a bug under a microscope.

"Do you want more?" Quinn asked, pushing his still full plate toward her.

"No. I want to talk about what's going on today." Rowan pushed back from the counter. "But first I want a refill."

Mug in hand, she headed for the pot and topped off her cup with the last of the strong blend. "That's the last of it. Should I make another pot?"

"I'm fine." Brogan held up his hand.

"I'll pass and you should slow down too. What's that? Your fourth?" Quinn asked.

"I wasn't keeping count but I can tell you I'm nowhere near my limit yet."

Rowan sat back down, warm mug cradled between her hands and started the conversation she knew they had to have. "So, when are we going into town?"

"We're not. William called this morning. He'll be coming out to see us after lunch," Brogan informed her.

"Why would he do that?"

"Because he agrees with us that you shouldn't meet the rest of the pack yet," Quinn said. "And he'd like to talk to you away from everyone else first."

"Oh." Rowan could guess what William would ask her about. She wasn't sure if she was up to talking about why she'd left but ready or not the time had come to tell all.

"In the meantime I thought I'd take a walk in the forest and see if our late night visitor left any other clues to their identity. Want to come with me?" Quinn asked.

"Definitely." She gulped down the last of her coffee. "Just let me get some warmer clothes on and I'll be ready."

Rowan dumped her dirty dishes in the sink and rushed from the room. The thrill of getting out in the forest again energizing her more than the bucket-load of caffeine she'd consumed. Maybe they could shift and go for a run after they'd scouted around. Smiling, she charged up the stairs two at a time.

"Do you think it's wise to take her out with you?"

Brogan's question wasn't unexpected. Quinn had thought about taking her with him all morning but in the end he knew Rowan was more than ready to face her life here. He planned for them to share this life, and that meant the good and the bad.

"She'll be fine." He picked up his plate and took it to the sink. "I doubt she would let me go out without her anyway, and we both know I'm the best tracker out of the two of us so it would be me going out there." Dish rinsed and stacked in the sink, he went back to where Brogan sat.

"She does look better than the first time I saw her," Brogan said.

Reminded of how fragile she'd looked, Quinn frowned. "Yeah, she's always been tough, but watching her these last two days..." He shook his head. "Rowan has an inner strength that she hasn't even begun to tap into."

"Well let's hope she won't need to. But, knowing Marcus the way I do, I'm sure she will."

"Yes, but this time we'll be there to back her up."

Brogan stood. "Yes."

They cleared the rest of the dishes and loaded the dishwasher. With the kitchen spotless, they headed to the living room to wait for Rowan. Brogan stoked the fire while Quinn shoved his feet into his boots. The heat had done its job and dried his jacket since the wee hours of the morning. Lacing up his left shoe, he heard footsteps on the stairs and hastened to tie the right one. The crash that echoed from the hall had him on his feet and running from the room with Brogan on his heels.

Skidding to a halt, he stared at Rowan buried beneath a pile of boxes, shoes and jackets. The wide-open closet doors and her colorful choice of language revealed where the crash had come from. He'd been meaning to clear that cupboard out for months, looked like she'd done his job for him.

Quinn reached down and pulled her off the floor. She came up with a pair of boots, one in each hand. He recognized them; they normally sat on the top shelf out of the way. How had she managed to cause the avalanche when they'd been right in front?

"Damn. You pulled the whole shelf down, Rowan." Brogan had his head in the closet, inspecting the damage.

"If you didn't have all that junk up there it wouldn't have happened." Rowan pouted.

The look on her face made him laugh. He remembered her attempting to use that look on them when she was a teenager and needed to keep out of trouble. Some things hadn't changed at all. Quinn pulled her close and hugged her. Kissing the top of her head, he set her aside and helped Brogan put everything back in the cupboard. They'd go through it all later and throw out what they didn't need.

Behind him, Rowan pulled on her snow boots. He tossed a jacket at her, what she had on wouldn't keep the cold out for long. With the last shoe thrown back in, Quinn slammed the doors and hoped they all remembered to be careful next time they went in the closet. Brogan turned to him and slapped him on the shoulder.

"Watch your backs. I've got a feeling we haven't seen the last of our midnight guest and I want you both prepared for anything."

"No worries. We'll stick to the tracks if they're still visible and head back in as soon as we lose the trail."

"Stop acting like a big brother and best friend and start thinking like a sovereign," Rowan said.

"As sovereign I should be going out there."

"No, you should be sending out your best tracker. You might think I'm not ready to be Quinn's backup but I'm all you've got right now and I am capable of defending myself if there's trouble."

Before Brogan could change his mind, Quinn ushered Rowan out the door. "I'm not expecting anyone to still be out there, Brogan. We'll be careful."

"Don't take unnecessary risks." Brogan turned to point at Rowan. "Especially you."

Rowan rolled her eyes and leaped off the porch. He gave Brogan a reassuring smile and followed her. The snow level hadn't risen since he was out here earlier. With any luck the snowmobile tracks would be nice and clear. As she lead the way across the yard, Quinn scanned the tree line to make sure he was right and there wasn't someone hanging around.

The sun had a bit of warmth to it. Soft snow squished under his boots and by the end of the day a lot of what had fallen last night would have melted away. They stopped at the tree line. With daylight it proved easy to see the trench from the snowmobile and the strips of cloth flapping in the gentle breeze. Rowan walked over to where the fabric hung in the tree and examined it closely.

"It was ripped free when he was leaving."

"How can you tell that?"

"The branch it's snagged on is facing toward the house, if he brushed past on the way to throw the rock nothing would have caught."

Quinn stepped over and looked at what she was talking about. "You're right. So after throwing the rock our friendly visitor made a run for it but before that he sat here watching the house."

They both stood near the dent in the snow bank and turned to look at the house. Quinn crouched to where he thought he'd be if he were astride a snowmobile. He had a clear line of vision straight into Rowan's old room. In fact the view was so good he'd be able to see her if she were standing at the window.

"Fuck," he cursed under his breath.

"Come on. Let's see where these tracks go." She tugged on his sleeve.

He needed to punch something. The thought of someone watching her boiled his blood. His suspicion of who their spy was made it worse. Rowan entwined her fingers with his and pulled him hard to get him moving. Before they took two steps, Quinn yanked her back into his arms. He buried his face in the side of her neck, breathed deep and held her tight. The comfort of holding her close and knowing she was safe eased his anger and focused his mind.

Twin grooves led them through the forest in the direction of the mountain road that led to Whispering Ridge. A thirty-minute trek had Quinn sweating and he turned to see how Rowan was doing. He needn't have worried. She'd proven herself more than fit in the last two days and this little stroll in the woods didn't bother her. When they reached the gravel road the trail stopped. Another set of tracks took up on the road. Someone had driven a four-wheel drive up here recently.

One that had been parked right where the snowmobile disappeared.

With no way of telling the type of vehicle or owner, they'd reached a dead end. Again. A game of cat and mouse was the last thing Quinn wanted to play but as usual Marcus led them on a merry chase. He sighed, turned back to head the way they'd come. Rowan stood off to the side, her face all scrunched up in concentration.

"What?"

"I'm not sure." She took a deep breath. "Can you smell that?"

Quinn sucked in a breath. Slowly. The air was scented with coyote. Not natural but shifter. Two different individuals. Neither of them familiar to him. And if he wasn't mistaken, newly turned. It didn't make any sense but he wasn't going to hang around to work it out.

"Let's go."

He grabbed Rowan's hand and started jogging. There was no time to waste; he wanted her back at the house, safe from possible danger. It was rare for new coyotes to show up in Whispering Springs, even rarer for a human to show up and be turned. Scenting two on the air couldn't be good news. Quinn pushed her in front of him, let her hand go as she took the hint and ran.

They could run the distance in less than half the time it took them to walk. He could hear Rowan's labored breath ahead of him. Her long legs ate up the ground and he had to stretch to keep up with her. It wasn't enough. About half a mile from the clearing, two coyotes came at them from the side. Quinn went down hard as one of them slammed into his ribs. He rolled, pushed to his feet and ran. Thankful to see Rowan hadn't stopped, he followed.

Flashes of red flickered through the trees in front of him and he knew Rowan was on her feet and running as hard as she could. A glimpse of gray to the right was the only warning before one of the animals crashed into his legs, taking him to the ground again. The second coyote landed on his back stopping him from somersaulting to his feet but the momentum took them tumbling over the snow. He used his legs and arms to lash out and stop teeth from connecting with flesh.

Two on one wasn't a fair fight but Quinn couldn't worry about that now. He had to get free of these two. His fist smashed into the side of a head, bones crunched and pain seared up his arm. A boot connected with ribs, a nauseating crack and yelp of pain followed. Given a reprieve, Quinn jumped to his feet and sprinted after Rowan. No longer able to see her, he used his ears to listen but couldn't hear anything over his own harsh breathing and pounding heart.

Leg muscles burned. Pushing hard, he leaped over a fallen log. Between the trees, he made out the clearing, a blaze of red streaking across the white snow. He cleared the tree line only to be tackled again. Pain sliced into his knee and hip when he crashed to the ground. Air exploded from his chest and he could do nothing but gasp in agony. Jaws snapped, tore at fabric and ripped at skin. Stunned, he curled up and protected his neck with his arms.

"Quinn!"

Rowan's scream echoed over the yard, the blood-curdling shriek froze the blood in his veins. Sheer terror lanced his heart. Were there more than two of them? Adrenalin and coyote kicked in. He struck out, hit flesh and bone and kept going. Blow after blow landed with a sickening thud, each one stronger than the last. Unable to shift with the two animals attacking him, he had no choice except to fight in human form but a partial shift would give him strength—teeth and claws to do more damage. To hold the half shift took skill and concentration but Quinn was determined to win and save Rowan.

Nothing short of death would stop him reaching her.

Protecting her.

12

———

Her lungs burned with each choppy breath. Her legs screamed in pain and the stitch in her side threatened to double her over but she kept running. Every second counted. The house was in sight now, so close, just across the clearing. Pounding feet and paws echoed behind her and she fought the urge to turn around. She couldn't waste the time. Getting to the house and Brogan could be their only hope.

Flesh and bone collided behind her. Rowan glanced over her shoulder and stumbled at the vision of human and animals rolling in the snow. The blows, grunts and snarls a strange musical note on the air. A yowl of pain and her insides went cold.

"Quinn!"

Forced to turn away and continue went against everything her coyote wanted to do. Her mate was in trouble and she needed to help him. But her human side knew the best way to do that was to get to the house. Get Brogan and a gun. Her legs pumped harder, her chest ached and her eyes filled with tears she refused to let free.

Brogan came through the door, rifle in hand, and raced to meet her. He grabbed her arm, shoved her behind his back and braced the gun on his shoulder. The loud boom ricocheted around them. Aimed into the air, the shot was meant as a warning but it did no good. Three bodies—one human, two coyote—continued to wrestle. Brogan fired again.

Nothing happened. Among the rustling and tearing of cloth Rowan could hear the groans and yelps of pain as teeth and claws and fists found their mark. Firing over their heads wouldn't do it, these animals were in a frenzy and they wouldn't stop unless someone or something stopped them. She yanked the weapon from Brogan's hands. Before he could turn around and stop her, she lined up the sight and fired.

No thought. No breath.

One shot.

Her aim was true and the bullet went dead center between the eyes of one coyote. He fell to the ground, pushed aside by the still fighting bodies. The second shot was harder. With only the two of them, the risk of hitting Quinn grew higher. Brogan stood beside her. His calm steady presence gave her the composed nerves to pull the trigger. This time her line was accurate but a twist of torsos as she squeezed her finger sent the slug into the coyote's shoulder and not the back of his head.

Yelping, he backed away from Quinn. The animal's head thrashed from side to side as he limped toward the tree line. Brogan stripped off his clothes, but the coyote sensed danger and bolted into the forest. Rowan sped across the distance to Quinn. He'd rolled to the side but didn't move to get up and she feared they'd been too late. She dropped to her knees and put the rifle within easy reach. The blur of fur and legs sailed past them.

Brogan was on the hunt.

Quinn moaned and Rowan breathed a sigh of relief. His clothes were torn, the legs and arms suffering the worst damage. Blood from numerous scratches soaked the fabric but the amount wasn't life threatening. Gently she examined him for broken bones. Nothing stood out but he'd need an x-ray to determine if his ribs were cracked. His groan when she pressed on his side indicated they were at least bruised.

"I'm okay."

Rowan's heart skipped and a sigh of relief slipped from her throat. "Dammit, Quinn, you scared the life out of me." She stopped herself from hugging him for fear of hurting him.

"Just need to catch my breath."

Gasps of pain accompanied every shift of position. His injuries made his progress to sit slow and awkward. Rowan grabbed his shoulder to steady him when he swayed. As soon as he seemed stable she let go but didn't move away to check the coyote. She didn't need to, death would have been instantaneous.

"Nice shooting." Quinn tipped his head in the direction of the carcass.

"Not good enough to get two."

"You got him and I sliced through his neck before you fired. I doubt he'll get far."

"Even if he gets far, Brogan will catch him."

"Help me up."

"Do you think you should move yet?"

"Rowan, if I don't get my ass off this snow the damn thing will be frozen solid and any scratches I have will be the least of my worries."

"Oh."

She wrapped an arm around his waist and together they stumbled to their feet. Steady, Quinn pulled away and began to walk to the house. Rowan stayed close but his steps were measured and sure. When they got to Brogan's clothing she realized she'd left the rifle with the dead coyote.

"Damn. Wait here." She jogged back but before she picked up the gun Rowan checked the dead coyote. There were no familiar markings on the animal and she didn't recognize his scent, but then, she'd been away so long he could be a newcomer to the pack.

"He's not one of ours."

Quinn's voice startled her. "I told you to wait."

"I'm fine, besides we need to move the body closer to the house."

He used Brogan's pants to tie around the torso of the coyote. It made a crude rope but would do to drag the corpse to the house.

Quinn moved with ease and other than the ripped jeans and jacket there was no evidence of his recent fight for life. His shifter genes worked quickly to repair the wounds inflicted and return his strength.

Together they made the slow trek across the snow. With the adrenaline wearing off, Rowan started to shiver. When they reached the back of the house her whole body shook and her teeth chattered.

"Get inside where it's warm." Quinn nudged her toward the door.

"No. I'm not cold. It's reaction. I've never killed anyone before."

Quinn pulled her against his chest and held her tight. "You did what you had to."

"I know but still it's not something I want to do again in a hurry."

"Thank you."

"For what?"

"Saving my life."

"I don't think it would have gotten to that point." Rowan's stomach somersaulted thinking about what might have happened.

"Maybe not, but it would have been worse if you hadn't taken action."

"Brogan would have made the kill if I hadn't."

"Speaking of him, here he comes now." He loosened his hold. "Looks like he caught the other guy."

Rowan turned in Quinn's arms. Brogan strode toward them on two legs, the limp body of the coyote slung around his shoulders like a wet towel. It struck her as odd to see her brother stroll naked in such an easy manner. Before she'd lived outside of the pack she never would have thought about it but after spending several years with humans who hide themselves in public she felt the urge to turn away and give him privacy. She'd have to get used to seeing nude bodies again.

Hands wrapped around the animals legs, Brogan shrugged his shoulders and flipped the carcass over his head. It landed with a plop in the rapidly melting snow.

"He bled out before I got to him." Brogan bent to retrieve his pants from where Quinn dropped them. "I think you sliced through his jugular. The blood trail was thick and short."

"Rowan's shot was off because he pulled back when I clawed him."

"So, any idea how we have two newly turned coyotes wandering around in the mountains?" Brogan asked.

"No. I'm not familiar with the human scent either. They've never been in town," Quinn said.

"We need to get them in to Doc. She'll be able to do a DNA test to determine if they were turned by one of the pack." Brogan zipped his jacket before turning to Rowan. "I see you haven't lost your shooting skills."

"I haven't fired a gun since I left. Not sure if it's a good or bad thing I didn't need to think about what I was doing."

"Considering you saved Quinn, I'd say good." Brogan pulled her in for a quick hug. "Okay, let's get these loaded in the back of the truck."

"Hey, wait a second, you said she. Is Doc Monroe gone?"

"Gordie's taken over the practice. Doc and Mrs. Monroe are touring around in a RV he bought and did up."

Rowan turned to Quinn. "Gordie came back?" Excitement bubbled in her veins at the thought of seeing her childhood best friend again.

"Yep." Quinn tapped Rowan on the nose. "And as soon as we get these coyotes loaded I'll drive you to town to see her."

She refrained from jumping up and down like a toddler but there was no way to contain the smile that stretched across her face. Five years apart, Rowan and Gordie had struck up a close friendship during their teenage years. They'd gone through their first shift together, she as a maturing coyote and Gordie as a newly turned one. When Gordie's mate and unborn baby were killed in a car accident, she'd left Whispering Springs and not returned before Rowan had made her escape.

The last time she'd seen Gordie was eight years ago. After leaving for college the summer after the accident, Gordie had only come home for short visits and didn't see anyone but her family. Rowan had missed the closeness the two shared, and until El, she'd gone without a close female friend. Of course El knew nothing about Rowan's heritage so there were parts of herself she had never shared with anyone but Gordie. The idea of reconnecting their friendship thrilled Rowan and spurred her into action.

Between the three of them, they moved the coyotes around to the driveway. Brogan must have shoveled the snow while Rowan and Quinn were out in the forest because the packed gravel drive was cleared off ready to use. How he'd managed to do it all alone she couldn't say. Quinn had parked her small rental behind his truck so she dashed inside to get her keys while the men loaded the bodies in the truck bed.

As she rushed down the drive her foot slipped on a patch of ice. Arms flailing, Rowan skidded about ten feet before going down. Flat on her back, the air sucked from her lungs, she stared up at the blue sky and fought for breath. The crunch of running feet as they sloshed through the snow and gravel came from the opposite side of the vehicle to where she landed. Quinn's face popped into view.

"Are you all right?"

Unable to speak, she nodded.

"Then talk to me." Panic was written all over Quinn's face.

"Can't." Pain filled her chest. "Yet."

Color drained from his face and he reached for her.

"No," she panted. "Give me a minute."

Lying on the hard-packed drive, Rowan took her time catching her breath and cataloging the aches and pains now racking her from head to toe. Other than a few bruises, she'd missed out on serious injury. She rolled to her side and sat up. Quinn's arm slipped around her shoulders. With her breathing back to a normal rate, she looked around for the keys that were flung from her hand when she hit the ground.

"Did you see where the keys went?"

"No."

They both looked around but the keys were nowhere in sight.

Getting to her feet, Rowan turned around slowly. She couldn't see any holes in the snow so they hadn't sunk beneath the surface. Confused by their disappearance, she tried to remember the exact sequence of her fall and the moment her grip on the keys was lost. She'd slid a few feet on her back and the keys had left her hand as she landed, which meant they had to be near Quinn's truck.

Rowan stepped the few feet with care, she didn't want to risk losing her footing again. The obvious place would be under the truck. The four-wheel drive sat a good two feet off the ground. The keys could have easily flown beneath it. She got down on her knees to peer below the chassis. A quick glance revealed the keys but they weren't the only thing she found. Next to the front right-side tire sat a large puddle of liquid. She might not know that much about cars but any idiot would know that amount of oily fluid spelled trouble.

"Ah, Quinn?" She reached out and retrieved her keys.

"Yeah." He crouched down beside her.

"When did you last drive the truck?"

"The day you arrived. Why?"

"There's a pool of oil or something under there." She pointed to the front wheel. "Way too much for just a small leak."

Quinn dropped to his stomach and shimmied underneath the cab. Rowan bent down again and joined him. He dipped a fingertip into the mass and brought it to his nose. One sniff and he pulled his hand away to rub the slick goo between his fingertips before wiping the excess off with a clump of snow. The space didn't allow for Quinn to turn over but he twisted his neck and began poking at the under-carriage.

"Fuck."

The curse echoed in the confined area and Rowan watched him yank a section of hose to get a closer look.

"Brogan, get under here and look at this," Quinn yelled.

"What is it?" she asked.

"Someone cut the brake line. This puddle is brake fluid."

"What's wrong?" Brogan's face appeared on the opposite side of the car.

"Did you take the truck out while we were at the cabin?" Quinn asked.

"No, I haven't used it since I drove back here the day Rowan arrived." Brogan maneuvered his way under to get a better look. "Is that the brake line?"

"Yep. Sliced clean through."

"No way it was an accident. The cut is too precise." Brogan examined the hose in Quinn's hand.

"Looks like our midnight visitor got closer to the house than we thought," Quinn said.

The cold began to seep into Rowan's clothes so she left the men to their inspection and wiggled her way out from under the truck. A glance at her watch showed it to be after midday and the grumble of her tummy told her well past lunchtime. She brushed the snow from her clothes and decided a change of outfit was needed before they drove in to see Gordie. Quinn stood up beside her and Brogan strode around the hood to join them.

"William is due to arrive any minute. I suggest we lock up the back of the truck to keep our cargo safe and head indoors to get warm and dry before he gets here," Brogan said.

"Rowan, you go on in. We'll clear up out here and be in when we're done." Quinn nudged her toward the house.

"I can help." She got the feeling he was trying to get rid of her but couldn't think why.

"It'll only take us a minute and there's nothing for you to do anyway so you might as well go in and get changed."

He gave her another push and having no further argument, she went. She walked slowly, hoping to catch any conversation they may have without her there but neither of them said a word before she reached the front steps and out of earshot. Rowan took her time but once she had the door open and a blast of warm air surrounded her, she slipped inside and forgot about eavesdropping.

· · · ·

Quinn waited until Rowan closed the door behind her. "I don't think Rowan's the target."

"What makes you say that?"

"The attack earlier and now the cut brake line." Quinn held up a hand to stop Brogan from objecting before he finished explaining. "I agree the rock through the window of her old room looks like she's the target but the other two incidents point to me. Neither of those coyotes went after her when they could have and the truck is mine."

Brogan remained quiet. Quinn knew he was right. Rowan's involvement was pure luck. Marcus had been planning his latest attempt to disrupt their positions in the pack for a while, the claim he made to the Council the first of his moves to destabilize his and Brogan's leadership. His senses told him Gordie would find Connelly genes when she looked at the two dead coyotes. Their scent had a faint trace of Marcus but Quinn couldn't be sure if the bastard had anything to do with turning them.

"You think Marcus is trying to get rid of you?"

"Yeah, with me out of the picture it would be easier to remove you as sovereign."

"He might think so but you aren't my only support in the pack."

"I don't think that matters. He's crossed a line somewhere and isn't thinking rationally, not that he ever really did but now the end goal is to be sovereign and he'll do whatever it takes to get it."

"William will be here soon. He's one of the few who understand the danger Marcus represents. We'll explain what's happened and then take the bodies to Doc."

"It would be good to have it on record with the whole council. Do you think William could call a meeting for this afternoon?" Quinn slammed the tailgate shut. "It might be a good idea to call one anyway so Rowan can make her presence known."

"Good idea. Let's get inside and change so we're ready to go right we speak to William." Brogan turned and headed toward the house.

Quinn clicked the canopy lid on the truck bed in place and checked it was locked before following his best friend. He continued to run the events of the last twenty-four hours through his mind. The more he thought about it the more he was sure Marcus was coming after him directly this time. In the past he'd only caused general mischief but for some reason the ante had been upped. He just hoped they could stop anyone else from getting hurt.

13

———

Quinn sat in the front of Brogan's truck. The three of them were following William into Whispering Springs. After they'd explained everything the older man had insisted they take the strays to Doc's office right away. The men had moved the bodies from Quinn's truck to the back of William's before starting out. Rowan sat beside him, equal parts excitement and nervousness coming off her. He knew she was worried about fronting the council but the prospect of seeing Gordie again put a smile on her face.

Both women had changed over the years but he hoped they would be able to reestablish their close friendship. It would be good for Rowan to have someone to connect with in the pack. A lot of her friends had moved away from the mountains and only returned for brief visits. One more thing they needed to change, too many of the younger coyotes were leaving the pack to live among humans in the big cities. They were changing that slowly and in time they planned to build a tourist industry around the mountains the pack called home.

The plans were going well, but to make sure their secret remained safe they were building a resort farther down the mountain. The humans who came to enjoy what Whispering Mountains offered should have no need to venture into the town. Brogan's vision for the pack's future would breathe new life into an old world. Hopefully in time, some of the younger generations would return to build their lives here. A couple, like Gordie, had already returned and more of the younger ones were talking of staying instead of leaving.

No one spoke, each of them lost in their own thoughts, but it wasn't an uncomfortable silence. Instead it comforted, having his mate and best friend with him made Quinn feel all was right with his world. But it was a false comfort and until they removed Marcus as a threat, he couldn't be complacent. He would need to be on alert, they all did. Dirty tricks were to be expected at every turn and now it would seem that Marcus had gone a step further. Nothing would stop him getting what he wanted. Not even murder.

Whispering Springs came into view and Rowan sucked in a breath. Quinn turned to find her eyes sparkling with tears. He reached for her hand and entwining their fingers, he brought it to his mouth and kissed her palm.

"Welcome home," he said.

"I've missed so much. There are new buildings everywhere." Rowan sniffled between words.

"Not that many but a lot have had facelifts and last summer saw most of the pack out slapping new paint on anything that stood still long enough," Quinn joked.

"We took a big hit the winter before. Four bad blizzards in a row did major damage to most of the older buildings. While we rebuilt those, we spruced up the rest," Brogan added.

"And Doc got a state of the art clinic to work in." Quinn let go of her hand and wrapped his arm around her shoulders. "We're heading there first."

She snuggled into his side, her head resting on his chest. He caught Brogan's look of concern and tried to reassure him with a smile. Rowan would be fine. Coming home had to be an emotional roller coaster for her and she was bound to have some shaky moments.

William took the street leading to the back of the clinic. With any luck no one would see them unloading the dead coyotes and they could keep the strays a secret from the rest of the pack until they knew where they'd come from and why they were wandering around in the forest. Brogan pulled in behind William, the back door of the clinic opened and Gordie stepped out. She shook hands with the councilman as they got out of the truck, then she turned to greet them.

"Morning, Brogan, Quinn..." Her eyes widened and her mouth dropped open. "Rowan?"

"Hi Gordie." Rowan stepped around him.

"Oh my God. It really is you." Gordie leaped forward, enveloping Rowan in a hug.

Quinn gave them some privacy and went to help the others with the coyotes. He didn't like tears in Rowan's eyes.

Not even happy ones.

Rowan held on tight. The familiar scent and feel of Gordie soaked in and welcomed her home a little bit more. Memories bombarded her. Times when things were simple and life stretched before her without a worry teased Rowan, her innocence and naïveté had cost her dearly. In one violent act, her world had been destroyed by someone she thought she could trust. She would not let it happen again.

"I can't believe you're here." Gordie's voice was choked with tears.

"It's me. And you have no idea how glad I am to see you." Rowan spoke over the lump in her throat.

They pulled apart. Rowan took in the woman Gordie had become. Other than the tears on her cheeks, she looked every bit the professional doctor. From her white coat, open to reveal the tailored slacks and cream blouse beneath, the stethoscope draped around her neck to dangle against her chest to the glasses perched on her nose, her attire screamed "trust me". The heavy snow boots on her feet the only contradiction but she even managed to make them look good.

"Gosh, Gordie, you're as beautiful as ever."

A light flush filled her friend's face. "Stop it. Have you looked in the mirror at all? You'd get a dead man's pulse racing."

"Speaking of dead men." Rowan turned to watch the men take the second coyote into the clinic. "Let's get inside so you can hear what happened."

The smile left Gordie's face and she wiped the moisture from her cheeks. "Come on, we can talk after this is over."

Arm in arm, they followed the men into the clinic. Rowan waited for Gordie to secure the door before they walked down the hall and into an examination room. She took in the tables, cupboards and equipment and realized they were standing in a morgue. The two coyotes were laid out on steel trolleys and Gordie flicked a switch on the wall beside them. Lights suspended above each table blazed to life, illuminating the bodies.

"So, what have we got?" Gordie slid into doctor mode. She scrubbed her hands and pulled on gloves before she moved toward the closest corpse.

"They're newly turned and not from around here," Quinn said.

Gordie's gaze lifted and met briefly with William's before she turned to face Quinn. "Where'd you find them?"

"I didn't. They found me. Tried their best to take me down but Rowan fired the single shot that killed that one." He indicated the coyote Gordie stood next to. "The other one took a bullet to the shoulder and a slice to the neck before running off. He bled out before Brogan got to him."

"Where was this?" Gordie began examining the animal in front of her.

"In the forest behind the house."

"Any strange behavior before they attacked?" She peeled back the coyote's lips to reveal his teeth.

"We didn't see them until they attacked."

Again, Gordie glanced at William. There was something going on and Rowan wanted to know what.

"Why do you two keep looking at each other like that? What aren't you telling us?" she asked.

William gave a slight nod and Gordie turned to Brogan. "These aren't the first coyotes to be found. Last month I found one beside the road up near Steve's place. He'd been hit by a car and left for dead. I called William, who met me here, but there wasn't anything I could do, his internal injuries were too great and he'd lost a lot of blood. He died on the operating table."

"Why wasn't I told about this?" Brogan looked to William.

"Because we still don't know where he came from or who turned him. I didn't want to start any unnecessary panic by informing the council," William explained.

"I would have kept your confidence, William." He turned back to Gordie. "Can you see if these two are connected to the other one?"

"Yes, I'll do a DNA profile but I'll tell you now I don't expect to find any more than I did last time. I can pin down the genetic line but not the direct link."

"You know what line?" Quinn asked.

"Yes."

"Who?" Brogan spoke through gritted teeth.

"Connelly." William said.

"What?" Brogan roared. "I'll kill him."

"That's the exact reason I didn't tell you before now. We have no proof that Marcus is involved and until we have hard evidence our hands are tied. You know the council will never exile him unless there are irrefutable facts linking him to any of his crimes."

"Fuck!" Brogan paced, his frustration clear.

Rowan looked at Quinn, the tension thrumming in the room could be cut with one of Gordie's scalpels. Seconds passed without a word. Gordie broke the silence by moving over to the second coyote. She snapped on a new set of gloves and got to work examining the animal. Rowan stood out of the way and watched as hair, organs and tissue samples were taken for testing. Not being squeamish around blood had its advantages.

Quinn and Brogan were talking in hushed tones with William on the other side of the room. She wanted to know what they were discussing but the body being dissected reminded her she'd killed. She'd hunted before but in coyote form, and only small vermin. Even though she'd had no choice, she should have shot to maim, not kill. The deaths of these two strangers would stay with her for life and though she had to come to terms with it, she refused to feel guilty for saving Quinn.

Gordie moved with precision and skill, and Rowan stared in awe at her childhood friend. The age difference had never worried either of them. They'd clicked on a deeper level than most teenage friends except the strain Gordie had been under after the accident made it hard to keep the friendship together. Rowan had cherished any time spent with her but had known things would be harder once Gordie left for college. The brief visits had been few and far between and even then she hadn't gotten more than a glimpse of Gordie. Distance and time had eventually seen them drift apart.

Now, with them both back in Whispering Springs, they could reestablish their bond as mature adults. She couldn't wait to hear all about Gordie's time living among humans, not that she would have found it as hard as Rowan had at first. Gordie had the advantage of being born human, Rowan only had the stories her friend told her to go on when she'd left town. Without those, she was sure someone would have found out what she really was. She wanted to tell Gordie all about El and Australia. The places she'd been and people she'd met. After the meeting with the council she would invite Gordie over for dinner.

"It'll take a while for the results but as soon as I know something I'll ring you."

Gordie's words snapped Rowan out of her thoughts. The men had moved to stand around the table and were listening to Gordie talk about similarities between these coyotes and the one from last month. If someone was turning humans and leaving them to fend for themselves they had bigger problems than rocks through windows and cut brake lines. Those misdeeds could hurt someone but turning humans and abandoning them could hurt the entire pack.

"This is worse than rocks through windows and cut brake lines, isn't it?" Rowan couldn't help voice her concern.

Quinn walked over and cradled her jaw in his hand. "If this isn't an isolated case we definitely have a bigger problem. But we'll find out who's responsible and stop them. I promise." He bent down and brushed his lips across hers. "For now, it's time to go meet with the council."

Rowan noticed William had left and Brogan waited at the door for her and Quinn. "Will you still be here after I've met with the council, Gordie?"

"I'm here until five. Come back after your meeting and have coffee with me. I don't have anyone booked but I can't guarantee I won't get a walk in."

Rowan smiled. "That would be great. See you in a while." She led the way outside, the heavy silence behind her spoke of how serious their troubles were.

Quinn admired the way Rowan worked the room. She had each of the council members eating out of the palm of her hand and didn't even know it. With concise explanations, she told them why she'd left and stayed away for so long. Her honesty and lack of hesitation in answering any question they threw at her won their respect and convinced them she only did what was right for her safety.

There were still a couple of the older men who refused to believe Marcus would do such a thing but they accepted her recount of the events and overlooked his involvement. If Quinn didn't know better he'd say Marcus was a cat shifter, the bastard certainly had nine lives. He continued to get away with every horrible thing he did. Unless they caught him red-handed there was little hope of the council voting to exile him from the pack.

He and Brogan sat quietly while Rowan and the council talked. Once they accepted her return, William opened the meeting to discuss the recent events and the turned strays that had shown up.

The meeting went from calm to chaotic in seconds. Everyone had their own opinion of who could be responsible and no one could agree on how to handle the situation. With things going nowhere fast, William told each person in the room to go home and think seriously about what would be the best way to deal with the problem.

Quinn, Brogan and Rowan waited as the council members filed out. William remained seated and Quinn suddenly realized how old he was. Their coyote genes allowed them to live longer than non-shifters but they still aged. William had to be around one hundred. He didn't look older than fifty by human standards, but the last few years of instability had taken their toll on a number of the elder pack members. He knew Doc had put Vincent on bed rest the other month because of exhaustion and with their quick-healing genes it was a worry.

"Brogan, you need to find out who's behind this and stop them." William shoved his chair back and stood. "I don't care how. I don't want to know how, but you and Quinn need to eliminate the problem. Now."

"Are you telling me to...?" Brogan didn't bother to continue. The look William gave him before leaving the room was enough.

"Did he just tell us to do whatever it takes?" Quinn asked.

"Yeah, I think so." Brogan looked as stunned as Quinn felt.

As sovereign and regal they were supposed to be beyond reproach. One step out of line and the council would remove them and vote in another coyote. He didn't think William would set them up for a fall but they still weren't sure where everyone's loyalties lay and couldn't risk putting themselves in the firing line. They would need to be careful and watch their backs to be sure they weren't being set up to fail. Not that he really thought William would do that to them.

Rowan had remained quiet but he could tell by the look on her face she had something to say. "Out with it. What are you thinking?"

"I don't think you should step out of line like William alluded. I know I don't have any recent experience with the pack or the council but I'm telling you both now, crossing the line would destroy everything you've done in the last few years."

"I have no intention of crossing the line, Rowan. I'm concerned that William would even suggest it. Either he knows more than he's saying or he's afraid we'll be exposed if humans continue to be turned," Brogan said.

"So what do we do? We could ask Doc what she thinks. She's been doing that genetic study of coyotes. She's bound to have a theory." Quinn slipped his arm around Rowan's waist and led her out of the room.

"We can grab some coffee from the diner and head over there now. She's expecting me anyway," Rowan said.

They left the lodge and walked along the footpath. It was a quiet afternoon, the snowfall the night before kept most people at home but those who were out stared as they went past. Rowan grew tenser with every step and he tried to comfort her by tucking her tighter to his side.

"It's okay. They'll stop once word gets out but for now it's a shock to see me." She shrugged. "I guess I'll be fodder for the town gossip for a while yet."

They reached the clinic just as it started to snow again. Light flurries fell from clouds that threatened a heavier fall. "Go in and sit with Doc while we go grab the coffee." He steered Rowan toward the door.

"Okay, but I don't think we should stay in town too long. Those clouds look ominous."

He waited until she was safely inside out of the cold and snow. Steve McKenna called out to Brogan and Quinn left the two of them talking to duck across the road to the diner. He just stepped off the curb when an engine roared and tires squealed. A shout from behind came a second too late. He turned to jump clear but his boot slipped on a patch of ice and he couldn't get enough grip to move quickly. The screech of tires and the scent of burning rubber filled the air and Quinn knew that only a miracle would save him from being hit.

The vehicle clipped his thigh and spun him around as it lifted him into the air. The weightless motion of flying rolled his stomach.

He landed with a thud, the impact jarred every bone and rattled his head. Pain lanced his chest and shoulder. His vision blurred as his mind whirled. Shouts faded into the background as the agony rolled over him. One voice stood out among the others and he tried to hold onto it but his body couldn't take anymore and he slipped into the blackness creeping in.

14

———————

Rowan and Gordie ran from the clinic at the first screech of tires. They burst through the door and onto the footpath in time to see Quinn be catapulted into the air as the old truck connected with his side.

"Quinn!"

Her stomach dropped to her toes and her heart lodged in her throat as she raced the short distance to his inert body. Ignoring the shouts of warning and squealing of tires, Rowan fell to her knees next to him. He was twisted in an awkward position but she didn't dare risk moving him yet. She reached out and placed her fingers on his neck, his pulse beat steady beneath his skin. Eyes closed, he remained motionless.

"Rowan, get out of the way." Brogan's shout barely heard over the engine roar, rubber skidding on pavement and yelling.

She glanced over her shoulder for Gordie. The car speeding down the road chilled her blood and froze her limbs. Staring in horror, she watched it draw closer. The man behind the wheel stared back, an evil smile on his face as he aimed the vehicle straight at them. A huge black SUV sped past her and headed for the truck.

With a crunch of metal, the two cars collided in a bone rattling crash. Glass exploded and showered the road around them. Rowan ducked her head and covered Quinn's face with her body.

Rowan's ears rang. The creak and groan of metal coming to rest made a strange symphony with the tinkle of glass on concrete. Her hands stung like hundreds of pins were stabbed into the back of them. Carefully, she lowered them from around her head and brought them down to look at. Tiny slivers of glass peppered her skin and the arms of her jacket. So small they sparkled like fairy dust. Drops of blood began to form around some of the larger pieces.

Feet pounded across the ground, shoes crunched on debris as people began to move. Voices yelled for others to help and sirens could be heard coming closer. Mercifully the snow had stopped falling at some point but it wouldn't be long before it started again.

Brogan scrambled over to her side. "Are you okay?"

"I think so. But Quinn hasn't woken yet. Where's Gordie?"

"Checking on the drivers." He looked past her at the mangled wreckage. "Steve's all right, he's climbing out now but the other guy doesn't look good. His head is at a weird angle."

"Steve was driving?" Rowan cleared an area next to Quinn and sat.

"He used his truck to stop the other guy from mowing you both down."

"Not soon enough for Quinn."

"How is he?" Gordie crouched down and started to check for injuries.

"He hasn't come to at all." Rowan brushed some hair from his face.

"God, Rowan, let me see those hands."

"They're okay, a few scratches, some glass still imbedded but nothing life threatening. Tend to Quinn first."

"We need to get him inside. Brogan, can you go in and get the spinal board? It's in the first exam room."

"Sure, did you check Steve?"

"Yeah, just bruising, the airbag saved him from serious injury."

"And the other driver?" Brogan asked.

Gordie shook her head.

"Another stray?"

"No. William and Steve are getting the area cleared so we can remove him from the truck and get him into the clinic as quickly as possible. As soon as we get Quinn inside I can deal with the other problem."

Rowan turned to see the crowd gathered on the street. A number of them pointed at the crashed vehicles and the dead driver. Steve removed a rug from the back of his SUV and used it to cover the body. Recognition struck her and she sucked in a breath.

"Malcolm Connelly."

"What?" Brogan asked.

"The driver. It's Malcolm Connelly."

"It can't be. He's been dead for two years."

"Brogan, go get the spine board. We need to get Quinn inside and Connelly out of sight before anyone else works out who the dead man is." Gordie felt down each of Quinn's legs without moving him. She looked up at Brogan who stood there with his mouth open. "Go."

Brogan spun and sprinted to the clinic. He returned in no time, the board under one arm. He placed it on the ground next to Quinn before going to talk to William. Steve came to help Gordie get Quinn ready. He stirred when they wrapped the collar around his neck to immobilize his head but he didn't come around until they lifted him.

"Fuck." The curse came out strained.

"Easy, big guy," Steve said.

"Don't call me names, shrimp."

Relief filled her. Quinn's injuries couldn't be too serious if he could joke with Steve. The three of them rolled him onto the spine board and Gordie secured the straps.

"I don't need this stupid thing." Quinn tugged on the bindings. "I took a bump to the shoulder, that's all."

"Then why were you out cold for so long?" Gordie asked.

"Sleeping on the job, big guy?" Steve pulled the straps tighter.

"Hey, not so tight, I'm not going anywhere."

Gordie reached for Rowan's hands and began picking out some of the larger pieces of glass. Blood welled up to bead on her skin and each tug was followed by a mild sting. Rowan breathed deep and tried not to focus on what Gordie was doing.

"I'll need tweezers for the rest." Gordie turned to Steve. "And you'll let me look at you when I've seen to Quinn and Rowan."

"Sure, Doc, you can touch me all you want." He grinned in an exaggerated leer.

Gordie gave him a dirty look and got to her feet. Steve watched her walk away, naked yearning in his eyes. Rowan didn't know what was going on between them and wouldn't ask but she'd have to remember to question Quinn later.

"Ready to go?" Brogan stepped over, Gordie and William close behind him.

"What's going on over there?" Quinn asked.

"Nothing you can help with at the moment." Brogan gripped one end of the stretcher while Steve grabbed the other. "Let's get you inside and I'll tell you everything you missed."

"I can walk, you know. I'm not an invalid," Quinn grumbled.

"Just lie there and behave. I'm getting tired of seeing you on the wrong end of trouble, Quinn MacClellan," Rowan said.

"Yeah, listen to your mate or we might drop you on your head," Steve said. "Oh wait. You did get dropped on your head."

"Ha ha, very funny."

Rowan laughed at Quinn. He looked hilarious strapped to the stretcher with the sullen look on his face. The banter between him and Steve had dissolved most of her tension. As soon as Gordie told her Quinn was fine, the rest of her anxiety would be gone too.

Quinn let Doc poke and prod and he allowed her to take x-rays, the whole time keeping quiet. He knew what she'd find. His head was hard as rock and there was no permanent damage from the whack it took. The other injuries were minor as well. He jarred his shoulder and landed on his already bruised ribs but with Rowan hovering over him every step of the way he let Doc do what she had to.

He refused the painkillers she offered. The fall had made his mind fuzzy enough. His shoulder would be stiff and sore, but already his ribs felt better. By morning he'd be good as new. Nothing beat coyote genes when it came to healing. Finally finished, they made their way to the room where Brogan, Steve and William waited with the corpse of the madman who'd tried to run him down. He needed to thank Steve for stopping the second attempt on his life.

Quinn walked into the room and stopped dead.

"Fuck. Is that who I think it is?" Had the bump on his head damaged his vision?

"Yes. Malcolm Connelly," Brogan said.

"Shit. I thought he was dead."

"So did the rest of us," William added.

"Christ. Dead man walking."

"We're trying to piece things together. But I think we've found our mystery turner of humans," Brogan said.

"I'll need to match the DNA samples but it's likely you're right." Doc went to the sink, scrubbed her hands and snapped on a pair of latex gloves.

"Where the hell has he been all this time?" Quinn didn't think anyone would be able to answer but he asked anyway.

"Maybe Marcus can help us out with the answer to that." Rowan stepped up beside him. "Why did you all think he was dead?"

Quinn looked at Brogan. There were so many things Rowan had yet to learn and he wasn't sure what Brogan wanted her to know. The fighting between pack members had lasted for years. When Brogan won the fight against Malcolm and the older man had fallen into the Canyon, everyone had assumed he'd died. Odds were Marcus not only knew his father was alive, but he'd been harboring him all these years.

"There's a lot you need to know but now isn't the time or the place. Any objections to me taking Quinn and Rowan home now, Doc?"

"No, but keep an eye on Quinn. I didn't see any hemorrhaging on the scan but you can never be too careful."

"I'll be fine. Let's go before the storm hits full force."

"There's not much we can do with the storm coming. Best if everyone gets home safe and sound and we'll meet as soon as the weather allows," William said.

"William, I want the council informed of Malcolm's sudden appearance and I want it made clear that Marcus is a threat until proven otherwise."

"I'll go and ring everyone now. Not sure it'll get us what we want but at least he'll be watched more closely."

"I'll stay and help Doc clean up and secure the body. You guys get on home," Steve offered.

"Thanks, Steve. If you hear anything on the gossip line, let me know." Brogan fished his keys from his pocket.

Quinn slid his arm around Rowan. "We'll see you both later."

"I'll keep you up to date as the results come in," Gordie said.

"See ya," Steve helped Doc put Malcolm's body in the special cooler.

"I'll call you later to arrange catching up, Gordie," Rowan said before they left the room.

They made their way to the back door. Quinn checked that the lock engaged when he closed it behind them. Brogan had the truck running and the heater on full blast. Quinn ushered Rowan in first and she slid across the bench seat to make room for him. The door slammed, shutting out the cold and cocooning them in a bubble of warmth.

Storm clouds darkened the day long before sunset and the small amount of snow on the ground made the drive home treacherous. Brogan took extra care as he weaved his way along the mountain road. By the time they reached the house, the wind had picked up. Leaves and branches were flying around the yard—it made the dash to the front door like a game of dodge ball. The sky opened up the second they got inside.

Rowan removed her jacket and boots but he stopped her before she could open the closet doors. They still hadn't tidied up after the last time she used it and there was no way he was opening it up tonight. He didn't have the energy to clean out the junk, all he wanted to do was crawl into bed and hold her. It had been a long day and he was more than ready for it to be over.

"We'll put our stuff by the fire to dry. I'm not risking the exploding closet again today." Quinn tugged Rowan toward the living room.

"I'll be in my office. I want to make sure William made those phone calls to the council. I'll see you two in the morning." Brogan strode down the hall and out of sight.

"Night." Rowan handed him her bundled jacket and boots. "I'm having a shower and falling into bed."

The protest on Quinn's tongue stopped when he noticed the dark circles under her eyes were back. He bent and kissed her forehead before walking into the living room to stoke the fire and lay out their gear. Rowan's sock-covered feet made no sound going up the stairs but he knew where she was by every creak of timber. Dumping the clothes on the floor by the hearth, he pulled off his boots and went to grab a couple of logs from the wood box in the corner.

It didn't take him long to get a roaring fire going and their jackets and boots spread out in front of it. He stood for a moment staring into the dancing flames, his mind on the last few days. How could so much have happen in less than a week? Pipes groaned overhead and he was reminded of the best part of the recent events. Rowan. He could picture her as she stepped into the shower. The water would stream over her shoulders and cascade down her lithe body until every naked inch of her glistened.

His cock hardened and pressed against the fly of his jeans. The denim cupped his arousal in a tight pleasure-pain grip. Damn. What was he doing downstairs fantasizing when he could be upstairs with the real thing? Quinn turned quickly, the lump on his head pounded but he ignored it. Nothing could distract him from his goal. Rowan, naked and plastered against him. Under him. Over him.

Rowan slid the bar of soap along her arm and coated her skin in a slippery trail of white bubbles. The wounds on the back of her hand had already begun to heal and only the largest ones stung as she cleaned away the grime left behind by the day's events. She shuddered, the danger of losing Quinn still fresh in her mind. He was safe, the danger still existed but for now they'd escaped and had a direction to go in to neutralize the threat for good.

She didn't doubt they'd find themselves a target again in the future. Marcus was involved in some way but proving it would be the challenge. Once Gordie determined the connection to the strays they would make their move. The Council would have to look at exiling him from the pack. Until they did, she would be on guard. Expect the unexpected and hope no one else got hurt in a madman's attempt to gain control.

Behind her the glass door swung open and Quinn stepped in. She looked over her shoulder to find him staring at her ass. A little wiggle produced a groan from his throat. Smiling, she tilted her hips and thrust her butt toward him. He grabbed her thighs and pulled her back. His cock pressed between her cheeks, cradled in the warm crevice. Rowan's sex clenched and grew moist with desire.

The water and soap on her body made a lubricant that allowed them to move against each other with ease. She leaned back into his embrace. His hands slid around her ribcage and up to cup her breasts. Talented fingers plucked at hardened nipples, arousing her further. Quinn nibbled along her neck, sharp bites and soft licks, he teased and tormented her. Her hips bucked, dragged his erection across sensitive flesh burning with the need to be taken.

"Can't wait," he growled in her ear.

He sucked her earlobe into his mouth, he swirled his tongue and nipped with his teeth. Hands dug into her hips, held her still as he pulled back and drove forward. She arched her back, pushed her pussy higher as the need to feel him imbedded to the hilt sliced into her. The head of his cock probed her opening and her muscles squeezed, tried to pull him in deeper. He rocked slightly, teasing them both with the promise of what was to come.

Urgency filled her. With a frustrated growl, Rowan thrust backward. His length breached her pussy and plunged deep. Stretched around hard flesh, her muscles convulsed, gripping him tight. Quinn's hand skimmed along her hipbone and zeroed in on the bundle of nerves vibrating at the top of her slit. One finger circled her clit before dipping into the cream flowing from her channel. Slick with moisture, he brought the digit back to stroke the bud protruding from its hood.

He withdrew from her heat only to plow back in at the same moment he pressed on her clit. Lightning struck. Rowan's orgasm burst out in white-hot pleasure. Her body vibrated as every nerve was lit with pure ecstasy. Quinn drove in and out of her quivering core. With blinding speed, he took her up and over another peak, shattering the last of her control. She bucked against him, his hold the only thing keeping her from collapsing to the ground.

Quinn held her in place, taking what he needed. Time after time, he rammed into her. Their legs slapped together as he continued to ride her. With her hands braced on the wall, she pushed back and tightened her muscles around his cock. He surged forward. Buried to the hilt, he flexed his pelvis and came.

Panting for breath, Rowan wobbled on her feet. Quinn slipped from her body and she slid to the floor at his feet, all energy gone. He turned off the water and opened the shower door. Large hands wrapped around her arms and pulled her up. The towel he wrapped her in was warm and soft and she snuggled into it as he dried her. Tender care and a loving touch had been missing for so long, to experience them again with Quinn was a dream come true.

Emotion swelled. Tears stung her eyes and clogged her throat. Deep breaths couldn't stop the tide. Droplets leaked to slide down her cheeks. Sniffling, she buried her face in the terrycloth to hide them from Quinn.

"Hey, are you okay? Did I hurt you?" He raised her face to his.

She smiled through watery eyes. "No. It's just so good to finally be home."

EPILOGUE

"So you're telling us there's no way to prove Marcus was involved in anything that his father did?" Brogan's voice rang with frustration.

"I can prove without doubt that Malcolm Connelly turned the strays we've found in recent weeks. I can't give you anything on Marcus," Gordie's words sounded like an apology.

"Damn."

"And we have no evidence that he was involved in the cutting of Quinn's brake cable either." Rowan's heart sank. "With what we've learned about Malcolm it would be reasonable to assume he was responsible for that too."

Growls emanated from all three men in the room. Steve and Gordie had arrived ten minutes ago with news none of them wanted to hear. The council would be happy to pin all on the senior Connelly, and they'd be right to do so. It pissed her off to know Marcus would get away with what he'd done. She knew he'd been involved.

"So now what?" Steve asked.

"We watch him. He's bound to lay low for a while but we need to keep our eyes and ears open." Brogan stood. "I'll go ring William and let him know what you found, Doc."

Quiet descended after Brogan left. No one wanted to see Marcus get off scot-free but for now their hands were tied.

"Don't worry. He's bound to slip up sooner or later and when he does we'll be there to catch him," Quinn vowed.

COYOTE WILD

COYOTE HUNGER

For those of you who love the coyotes as much as I do.
For Shannon for taking a chance on the first book and keeping her head up when life threw a curve ball.
For Grace, because I find your enthusiasm inspiring and your support unconditional.
For Mari and Nic because without you girls I wouldn't be where I am in this crazy business.
And, as always, for the boy who promised me the world and the man who gave it to me. I love you, Babe. Together Forever.

1

Need slammed into Brogan Wilder like a two-by-four to the gut. He knew lust, dealt with it when it rose, but this...

This was unlike anything he'd ever experienced. The beast inside chafed at the chains of restraint, snarled and snapped to be let free.

Brogan searched the room but nothing he could see should have him ready to shift. His sister Rowan sat on the sofa, his best friend and her fiancé, Quinn, beside her. They were the only others in the room. The fine hairs on the back of his neck stood at attention and the blood in his veins heated and pumped harder. Whatever had his instincts screaming to take, to possess, had moved closer.

Skin grew tight and hot as he fought with his inner beast. Shifting wasn't an option. Not yet. First he needed all his human skills to determine what had the power to do this to him. Then he'd have to decide if it was friend or foe. He sniffed the air, tried to place the feminine scent teasing his senses. It wasn't Rowan or any other female he knew.

"For pity's sake, Brogan, sit down. You're making *me* nervous and I know you're all bark and no bite. If you don't relax you'll scare El right back to Australia." Rowan's words broke into his agitated thoughts.

"What?" He tried to focus on his sister and what she was saying.

"Eloise. Remember? She'll be coming down from her room any minute and I want you to be on your best behavior. It took months of nagging and pleading to get her to agree to come out for the wedding. I want her to enjoy herself and not regret saying yes."

Rowan pushed off the lounge and came to stand beside him. Placing her hand on his arm she said, "Please, Brogan. She's the best friend I've had since Gordie, the only friend. She likes *me*. Not Brogan's sister."

Brogan looked at her. She was all grown up, ready to face her destiny but not without scars. They all had them but Rowan would have more if it wasn't for Eloise Crawford. He knew their friendship had been what kept his sister from going mad the few years she'd been forced to live away from home. He sucked in a deep breath and let it out slowly.

"Okay, I'll try. But something's got the beast's hackles up and I can't figure out what." He'd never hidden any of the ugly side of who or what he was from Rowan and he wouldn't do it now.

"Rowan?"

A musical voice with a strange sultry accent came at the instant his beast went on red alert and yanked at Brogan's control.

He couldn't keep the growl inside, or stop the change in his eyes that Rowan wouldn't miss. If Brogan's instincts were right, his mate had just stepped into the room.

Rowan's eyes went wide and her face drained of color. Shaking her head, she whispered, "No. Brogan, no."

Brogan squeezed his eyes shut, dragged the beast back under control. It wouldn't do to scare Eloise before they'd even met. When he opened his eyes again it was to find Rowan watching him warily. A rush of breath left her when she saw he had command of his coyote.

"It's not my choice, Rowan. The fates have spoken." He tried to ease her with a hug. Drawing her close he murmured, "You'll need to help guide her."

"No."

"Yes, Rowan. Remember, what's done is done, we move on from here."

She pulled from his arms and stood with hands on hips. "You hurt her and I'll tear you to pieces," she snarled.

Brogan smiled. He had no doubt she'd follow through on her threat. He'd seen her go to battle for someone she cared about. Her loyalty to those she loved was unquestionable, but if those she loved were pitted against each other she always sided with the weaker one.

Rowan looked past him to the woman who stood twenty feet away and had his body reacting as if she were plastered to his side. He could smell her, almost taste her. If he didn't get a hold of himself he had no doubt Eloise Crawford would run screaming into the hills or to the nearest airport and first plane out of there.

"El, you've unpacked?" Rowan asked as she stepped around him.

Brogan looked at Quinn, who'd remained suspiciously quiet during the little demo of his animal behavior. Their gazes connected and he could see the laughter in his best friend's eyes. The bastard knew this wouldn't be easy and if Quinn knew anything about him, he knew everything. As he knew Quinn. He wouldn't fool himself into thinking Quinn felt sorry for him. Oh, no. To Brogan's way of thinking, Quinn was looking forward to the inevitable fight to come.

El watched her best friend pull away from the man built like the side of a house. He was huge. She'd be lucky to come up to his shoulder, not that she'd get too close, something about him made her stomach churn and her heart pound.

The air in the room crackled with tension, thick with energy, the kind that spikes before a lightning strike. The skin that had tightened moments before she left her room now tingled, stretched, pulled tighter. Her hair stood on end and goose bumps broke out all over. She felt the need to strip off her clothes and rub herself all over the big man who still hadn't turned to face her.

Her eyes bored into the back of his head, even when Rowan reached her side and grabbed her up in another hug of welcome.

Distractedly, El returned Rowan's affection and tried to ignore the slight desperation in it. She'd always been able to judge Rowan's moods and right now anxiety rolled off her in waves.

"I'm so glad you're finally here," Rowan said as she gave one final squeeze and let go.

El dragged her gaze away from the rigid man across the room and looked at her friend. Nothing could detract from the happiness etched all over the beautiful face in front of her. Rowan glowed and it went far deeper than the smile spreading her lips. Her eyes sparkled and she no longer had the pinched expression El had come to expect.

"I'm glad I came, too. Although if you'd mentioned how damn cold it would be I might have reconsidered," she joked. El gripped both of Rowan's hands and pulled her arms out wide. "Being home must really agree with you. I didn't say it earlier but you look gorgeous. But then you always do."

"Stop. You'll make me blush." Rowan let go of one hand and tugged her farther into the room. "Come and meet Quinn and Brogan, they just got home."

El hadn't noticed the second man earlier and as they got closer to the two men on the other side of the room her heart rate accelerated. A layer of sweat coated her skin and her breasts grew heavy, her nipples impossibly hard. Between her legs throbbed and went slick. With each shortened breath her nostrils were filled with the scents of open air, the rich, earthy aroma of the forest, and man. It was the last smell that had her nerves in overdrive.

The numbing cold she'd felt from the moment she stepped off the plane no longer existed. Instead her body burned with a heat unlike anything in living memory. Fire burst and consumed, leaving behind an arousal so great each step, each rub of her thighs took her closer to an orgasm that would be shattering.

What was going on? Sure she hadn't had sex in months but then she hadn't wanted to. Until now. Now she wanted to get down and dirty with the guy who still had his back to her. El's feet faltered and she stumbled. Rowan turned to glance at her, her eyes going wide when she caught sight of El.

Great. It was painfully obvious that her friend knew what had made El trip over her own toes. She felt her cheeks blush. She was already so hot with arousal they were probably day-glow red.

"Jeez, Brogan, turn it down." Rowan's words made no sense. "Here, let's go into the kitchen while my brother gets himself sorted out."

Doing an about-face, Rowan marched them back the way they'd come. "Quinn, get him calmed down or make him leave," Rowan said over her shoulder as they cleared the doorway.

Dazed and confused, El let herself be led past the stairs and down a long hallway toward the rear of the house. Picture frames covered the walls, a perfect mixture of people, nature and animals. All the photographs showed Rowan's distinct style. One large photo caught El's attention. A lone coyote stood on a snow-covered hill, his body facing away, his head turned to look straight into the camera. He appeared to be posing for the person taking the shot.

A chill raced down El's spine. He seemed to stare straight at her as though he could see her. His gaze held her captive and she swung her head to keep him in her sights as Rowan pulled her past. Those yellow eyes followed her, and caught in some sort of trance, she twisted her neck to the point of pain, her eyes ensnared by his.

A door swished open and she was forced to turn, to watch where she walked or risk an injury. The second they stepped into the kitchen El was swamped with warmth. The room, large and bright, welcomed her with its cozy feel. Big windows covered the back wall, the view of the yard, forest and mountains in the background unobstructed. The winter sun reflected off the snow and lit up the huge room.

The big, granite-topped island in the center of the room held a sink and work area with four stools lined up on one side. Rowan pushed her onto one before heading to the wall of cupboards.

"Sit. I'll get us a drink, something warm, and we'll catch up."

El watched Rowan open a glass-paneled door, pull out two tall mugs and make her way to the coffeepot. She changed filters, scooped in coffee and flipped a switch, all her movements smooth and confident, so different from the woman El had first met. Oh, she'd seen an improvement in Rowan over the years they'd spent together but now she saw the woman that had been hidden inside. Strong, sure of herself, Rowan had finally grown comfortable with who she was and the world around her.

Something El wished she could be again.

Brogan let his muscles relax and his coyote subside. The beast was still wide awake but no longer threatening to pull free. Knowing what he was dealing with made things easier. He couldn't just take El and expect her to fall into line. If she was a shifter it would be easy but she wasn't. He wasn't even sure she knew what they were, never mind that he was one.

"You need to back off some."

Quinn's quiet voice pulled Brogan's gaze across to where his friend stood beside the fireplace. When had Quinn moved from the lounge? Normally he was aware of everything around him. Had El messed up his instincts so much that he failed to notice what went on next to him?

"I know. I just didn't expect it. I've never struggled to hold my control like that before. Was it like that for you?"

"Yeah. You get used to it and once you join it's not as bad."

"Jeez, no wonder you drove me insane all those years ago. Good thing you and Rowan finally sorted everything out."

"There was never any doubt as there isn't with you and El. But it'll be an interesting time between now and then."

Quinn's smirk had his hackles rising but Brogan knew he deserved everything the other man dished out. He'd given Rowan and Quinn plenty of crap while they had danced around each other before she'd been forced to leave home. Brogan sighed. Obviously it was his turn at the mating waltz.

"The problems won't just be between you and El," Quinn said.

"I know. But since I can't change who my mate is I'll just have to deal with what comes."

"The Council will have to be informed and there are those who will use El's non-blood status to undermine your position."

"I don't care about any of that. What I care about is making sure El doesn't freak out when she discovers we aren't exactly human."

"That might prove to be the easy part yet."

"I doubt any of this will be easy."

"Probably not, but we'll have to keep her from the pack until she understands, Brogan."

"Yeah, I'm more than glad you and Rowan decided on a small ceremony. El won't have to face anyone until after." Brogan didn't say after what, they both knew that until he turned El she couldn't be left alone or come in contact with any members of the pack.

"She'll be safe here but after the wedding we were supposed to take her up to the cabin. She wants to take wilderness photos for her next book. That gives you a week to convince her to stay and do what's necessary so she can."

"And if I can't convince her?"

Quinn shrugged. "You don't have a choice and you know it."

Brogan had no idea where to start when it came to wooing El. He'd never wooed a woman before. All he had to do was open his bedroom door and they fought each other to get inside. El would be different. For starters he had to tell her what he was without scaring her half to death and then convince her that he wasn't an animal when in essence he was.

The first step would be to actually meet her. The sooner they got used to each other the sooner they could get on with what had to be done. Hopefully Rowan was telling her who and what they were, but if not, he'd have to. He swallowed over the lump in his throat and rubbed the back of his neck. His muscles were tight—hard—but not from the beast wanting to break free.

No, now he was tense with nerves. If he didn't do this right he stood to lose more than his mate. He stood to lose his position as sovereign of the pack.

2

———————

El listened to all Rowan had done since they'd parted almost a year ago. It was plain to see Quinn made her happy. She glowed from within. While Rowan talked, El said nothing. She wasn't ready to tell her friend what happened after she'd left. Wasn't ready to reveal the betrayal, the hurt, or her own stupidity. Trusting Ken had been the single dumbest thing she'd ever done. The price of that mistake had been high and Eloise had paid the price.

"I've babbled enough, what's been happening with you?" Rowan asked.

"Same old, same old. You know how it is," El hedged.

"What about the guy you'd started seeing? Ken? Are you two still going out?"

"Um, no. Things didn't work out the way I expected."

"Oh, come on, tell me all the details."

"Maybe later. For now I want to hear about what you've planned for your honeymoon." She changed the subject before Rowan could dig too deep into a wound that hadn't healed. Her heart hadn't been broken in the Ken debacle, she'd been ashamed of how little the nasty break-up had affected her heart. Finding him in bed with her assistant had hurt but finding her business accounts cleaned out of their funds had been far more devastating. El had come to the conclusion she'd never really loved Ken, it had been more of an in love with love thing. No, her heart hadn't been broken but her pride and self-confidence had.

El allowed Rowan's plans to fill her mind. With images of tropical beaches dancing in her head she almost forgot the hormones doing a two-step through her body. She even fooled herself into thinking she imagined the level of arousal she'd been caught in.

They'd finished their first cup of coffee when her temperature suddenly spiked and the air around her crackled. Her skin pulled tight, her nipples drew up into rock-hard nubs and moisture filled her panties. The pounding of her heart echoed in her ears and she swayed on her stool, lightheaded with the rush of blood through her body.

Rowan grabbed her arm and stopped her from toppling to the floor. Gripping the counter edge, El tried to take deep breaths. Her head cleared but blood roared in her ears, making her dizzy all over again. She knew before the door opened that he was coming. The hunk of testosterone from the front room. She knew with every quiver of her flesh he was the reason she turned into a boiling pot of lust.

"Are you all right?" Rowan asked.

She concentrated on the mug in front of her, tried to block out everything else and focus on the cup. El felt him enter the room, felt him back off but not leave. What the hell was with that? Rowan still had her by the arm, talking to her but she couldn't make out the words over the pounding in her ears.

With great effort El managed to speak. "I'll be all right. Just give me a second. Jet lag, I think."

"You need to go lie down, have a rest before lunch." Rowan slipped from her stool, pulling El up with her.

"I think you're right. A nap will do me good." El didn't think a nap would help anything but she needed out of the room and away from the man who crowded her without coming near.

She stood on wobbly legs, got her balance but wondered how the hell she was going to get upstairs without falling flat on her face. A cautious step had her knees shaking and her hand flying out to catch the edge of the counter again.

She caught something all right, something solid and warm but it wasn't the counter.

Fire streaked up her arm from her hand. She'd connected with his hip. Her fingers curled into the denim and held on. If she thought he generated heat at a distance it was nothing compared to the furnace he was up close. Every muscle grew soft. The air in her lungs evaporated and her mind went blank seconds before the world went black.

Brogan had never been more thankful for his quick reflexes than now. El had barely begun the slide to the floor before he had his arm around her waist and her body snug against his. He looked over her head at Rowan.

"She fainted," he said.

The astonishment on Rowan's face mirrored his. Her mouth opened and closed, but no words came out.

"Did that ever happen with you and Quinn?" he asked.

"Once, but that was during a joining, not from just a touch." Quinn's quiet words came from behind him.

Brogan looked over his shoulder. "Is this normal?"

"Probably. You had some serious vibes going on before, but when her hand connected with you the heat just about singed *my* eyebrows." Quinn reached over and checked El's pulse.

Brogan knew her heart raced but it had slowed since she fainted. He altered his grip, scooted his arm behind her knees and swung her up against his chest. She couldn't weigh a hundred pounds, her bones were slight and there was a small amount of padding in all the right places. She was such a little thing. How could she possibly hold up against him?

The fear of what his strength could do to her sliced through him. How could he possibly hope not to hurt her? His needs were wild, and his need for her was greater than any he'd known. Arms trembling, he turned to face Quinn.

"She's so tiny." His words quaked with the anxiety exploding in his mind.

"Don't underestimate her, Brogan. El is tiny in stature but huge in courage," Rowan said.

"Rowan's right. Her inner strength is what you need to worry about and she's more than proven herself over the years they spent together."

He stared at Quinn, hoping he was right. Needing him to be right.

"Did you give her the back room? I'll take her up and sit with her until she comes around." At Quinn's nod Brogan stepped toward the door.

"No. I'll sit with her. I don't think her waking up with you in the room is a good idea." Rowan's soft footsteps followed him.

He knew she was right but he wanted to stay with El. No, what he really wanted was to take her to his room, lock the door and not let her out until she'd accepted who he was. Rushing things wouldn't get him anywhere, but the need to get there now warred with his need to protect her.

Rowan scooted around him and led the way upstairs. Entering the bedroom had his senses tingling. Every part of the room felt touched by El. Her scent lingered in the air and her warmth filled all the corners. In less than two hours she'd stamped her claim on more than just him.

When Rowan pulled the covers back he lowered El's inert body to the bed, together they removed her shoes. She'd be more comfortable with her clothes off but he doubted she'd be happy waking up naked, especially with him in the room. There was no way he was leaving her no matter how much his sister protested.

He sat on the bed at El's hip and brushed the hair from her face. They didn't pull the covers over her as the central heating kept the room warm and he didn't want her to overheat. Her face still looked flushed but her forehead was cool to his touch.

"You can go now, Brogan. I'll sit with her," Rowan murmured.

"I'm staying."

His sister chose not to argue, whether from the tone of his voice or the distraction of worrying about El, he didn't care. He wasn't leaving until she woke.

El rubbed her cheek against the fluffy pillow beneath her head. *Pillow?* She was in bed? The last thing she remembered was standing in the kitchen, telling Rowan she'd lie down for a while. She didn't remember coming up here.

Warm fingers smoothed her hair back. Startled, her eyes flew open and she pulled away. Two gold orbs stared back. They made her think of animals hiding in the bushes in the dead of night, but these eyes belonged to a very real, very large man. One who sat on her bed as if he had every right to be there.

"Easy, I won't hurt you." He continued to stroke her hair with steady, even sweeps.

"What...what happened?" Her whispered words had him leaning closer.

"You fainted, but you're okay. I didn't let you hit the floor." His gaze was hypnotic and strangely reassuring.

Warm breath fanned her face, filled her with the need to draw it in, take part of him inside her. She wanted to rub against the hand stroking her head. She didn't even know who he was.

"Who are you?"

"Brogan."

Rowan's brother.

The man who'd become an image in her mind. Strong, solid. Rowan had talked so much about him and Quinn over the years that El felt she knew Brogan even though they'd never met or spoken. He looked nothing like what her imagination had conjured up. This man was huge for a start and those eyes... She'd never seen that color in a human. Molten gold—simmering and swirling as if in constant flow.

She licked her dry lips, swallowed over the rawness in her throat. She'd been freezing since she arrived in the country but now her body was acting as if she were on Bondi beach in the middle of a heat wave.

"Do you want a drink?" Rowan's head popped up behind Brogan's shoulder. El hadn't realized there was anyone else in the room.

"Just a glass of water." Her tongue stuck to the roof of her mouth and her words came out as if the damn thing were four times its normal size.

"Be right back." Rowan disappeared, her footsteps echoing softly.

"Do you still feel dizzy?" Brogan asked.

Did she? No, not anymore, but she remembered the flash of heat just before everything went black. Her parched throat and tacky skin were signs that she hadn't imagined the burn she got from touching him. Where was that burn now?

"No, I'm feeling much better." She tried to sit up.

"Don't get up yet." With a hand on her shoulder, he pushed her back down.

"I was just going to sit," she protested.

"Oh, okay, hang on then."

He leaned over her and his chest brushed across her breasts, trailed over the tips, bringing them to instant attention. He grabbed a pillow from the other side of the bed and lifted her to tuck it behind her head, pressing her sensitized flesh into him. A shiver traveled down her spine.

"Now there's something I never expected to see. Brogan Wilder playing nursemaid." Rowan's laughter filled the room.

El's gaze fell on his face. Was he blushing?

Yes, his cheeks and neck had a tinge of pink in them. He pulled away and allowed his sister to pass her the glass of water. El couldn't help it; in great big gulps she tried to quench her arid throat and douse the fire springing to life inside her.

"Hey, hey, slow down." Brogan snatched the glass from her. "You'll choke if you're not careful. Just take small sips."

He held the drink to her lips and she tried to take it back but he wrapped his fingers around her wrist and pulled her hand away.

"I can do it myself," she huffed.

"Yes, you can, but I'm doing it for you and you're going to let me." His stern tone invited no further argument.

"Best to let him have his way, El, since he'll just make things harder if you don't," Rowan said as she headed to the door. "I'll be downstairs if you need anything."

El watched her friend go. She didn't want to be left alone with Brogan but she couldn't think of a reason that she could voice and Rowan wouldn't leave her if he posed any real threat. She slowly turned to look at Brogan. The heat was still there but somehow not as scorching, not as frightening. The effect he had on her confused her more than anything. He was such a big man who exuded strength from every pore and yet somehow at the moment he seemed vulnerable.

Her gaze met his and he smiled. If she hadn't been turned-on before, she was now. That smile wasn't just toe-curling, it was panty-wetting. It held all sorts of naughty intentions and El wanted to strip herself bare and let him have at it. She'd never been overly sexual. Sex was nice but she didn't crave it. No other man had ever wiped her mind of everything but the need to consume and be consumed.

Brogan had her body coursing with sensations foreign to her, needs she had no idea she was capable of. Caught between common sense and baser urges, she wondered which way she'd go. She devoured him with her gaze, watched his eyes blaze with heat, heard his ragged breath grow shallow. He leaned forward, his lips inches from hers. Would he kiss her? Did she want him to?

Yes!

In the next breath Brogan closed the distance.

Heat lightning streaked through her, electrified every nerve, every cell. Her whole body screamed to be touched, stroked—possessed. Arching up, she slammed her breasts into his chest. Crushed against the wall of muscle, her nipples tingled and hardened, a line of fire darting from each straight to her throbbing core.

His tongue pushed against her lips and opening, she invited him in. The tangy taste of Brogan filled her mouth, her soul and she groped for his head, pulled him closer. Their tongues dueled—

clashed—ought for control of a kiss that was all about greed. Teeth scraped against lips as each tried to get farther inside the other.

She pulled him down until the length of his body pressed into hers. She spread her legs wide, wrapped them around his hips and ground her sex on his. The hard ridge rubbed her clit, sent flames through her pussy and drew moisture from her core. Their hips pumped, mimicking the act their bodies craved. Over and over, his cock thrust against her clit, pushing her closer to the edge.

His hand slid between them and cupped a breast, lifting it. Fingers tweaked her nipple, tugged to the point of pain. Sensations splintered and El's arousal detonated. With blinding intensity she shattered into a thousand pieces. The one thing keeping her from flying away, keeping it all tied together was him. A hoarse cry tore from her throat.

"Brogan."

3

———

What the hell was he doing?

Brogan held El in his arms as she came. Her body arched and bucked, shook with every spasm that rolled through her. They'd barely touched but she was so sensitive to his every move. Was that because they were mated?

He wanted to think it was him, wanted to think he was the only man to give her intense, instant pleasure.

With a final shudder, her body went soft beneath him. When had he moved on top of her, his body pinning hers beneath him?

Their mouths had pulled apart when El's orgasm broke and now they both dragged in great gulps of air. The harsh rasp of breath pumping in and out was the only noise in the room. Reality crashed in on him and he pulled back to look at her.

Her face, flushed with blood and slick with sweat, glowed with satisfaction. Her eyes fluttered open, unfocused and dreamy, they stared up at him. He shouldn't have touched her. She didn't know who he was, *what* he was, and before he had her she would have to know. He wouldn't be happy until he knew she came to him freely, knowing what she was getting.

"This shouldn't have happened. I'm sorry." Brogan scrambled up, got off the bed completely.

She stared at him, the dreamy expression gone, replaced with confusion. He knew the second it turned to anger. Her blue eyes turned glacial, slicing into him with their piercing stare. He swallowed the words bubbling in his throat, the ones that would soothe her and explain. The ones that would land him right back in bed when she wasn't ready for that yet.

"Why you—"

Her words cut off when she picked up a pillow and threw it at him. He ducked but it brushed his shoulder. "Eloise, please." A second pillow connected with his skull.

"Get out!" she screamed.

He held his hands up in surrender and backed toward the door. "Calm down, I'm going, but I'm warning you, this isn't over. I will be back."

She launched from the bed, picked up one of her missiles and charged at him.

"Calm down? Why you miserable, bloody—"

Thump!

Her weapon slammed into the back of his head as he turned. "Dammit, El, you'll pay for that later."

"And stay out!" Her shout was promptly followed by the slamming of the door.

He stared down at the raging hard-on in his pants. My God, she was magnificent angry. Her eyes shot fire and her cheeks flushed red. She wanted to beat him senseless and he wanted to *fuck* her senseless. If the whole thing wasn't so serious it'd be funny.

Footsteps echoed behind him.

"Off to a good start I see." Quinn chuckled, his eyes dropping to Brogan's groin.

"Don't say it. I screwed up. She probably won't talk to me for the rest of my life but I didn't fuck her. Not quite anyway."

"How can you not quite fuck her?"

"We kissed. Fooled around a bit," Brogan said before mumbling, "It's what happened after that got me in trouble."

"What happened?"

"Knock it off, Quinn. I'm not giving you the details of my sex life." What was with Quinn anyway? They hadn't had sex. He'd come crashing back to reality before things had gone that far.

"Did she orgasm?"

"What the fuck? What kind of question is that? And why the hell are you asking?" Brogan yelled.

"Because, dipshit, if she did by your hand, you marked her."

"I know that."

Quinn took a deep breath. "I'll ask a different way, is she marked?"

"Fuck!"

"I'll take that as a yes."

"Fuck!"

"You said that already."

"I know but... Fuck!" Brogan paced two strides away, two strides back.

"She can't leave the house. And she has to be told. The sooner the better."

Brogan knew Quinn spoke the truth. He ran his hand over his face. Why did it have to be so easy to mark your mate? "We tell her today. It can't wait."

"You can't just dump it on her. Not after she fainted and..." Quinn waved his hand in the direction of her door.

"Dammit, she has to know. And you said it yourself, the sooner the better."

"Fine, do it your way."

"Don't I always?"

"Yes, but somehow I think this time might be different."

"I may have marked her and placed her in danger but I'm here to protect her. Nothing will happen."

Quinn snorted. "It's not her I'm worried about. Get yourself sorted." He pointed at Brogan's still-hard cock. "I'll get Rowan to come up and check on El."

Brogan gave his friend a nod.

Quinn took two steps before adding, "If you're lucky, I won't tell your sister what happened."

Ah, shit!

Rowan was gonna kill him if she found out. "Don't tell her. It stays between you and me. Once El knows about us it won't matter, she's not going anywhere."

His gut tightened. She no longer had a choice. With one stupid kiss he'd taken it from her and now he'd never know if she stayed because she had to or because she wanted to.

"It'll work out, give her time. She feels what you feel, Brogan, she just doesn't understand it. Go cool down and I'll get Rowan to come check on her."

Quinn's sympathy did nothing to ease the guilt burning a hole in his gut.

The rattle of old pipes in the wall behind him broke the silence. El must have gotten into the shower. Images of her naked, slick with water and soap filled his mind, stirred his blood and made his dick even harder. He squeezed his eyes shut but couldn't stop his mind from picturing the woman on the other side of the wall.

Growling, he stalked to his room. It looked as if he'd be showering too—in cold water. Quinn's laughter followed him down the hall, grating on his already agitated nerves as Brogan stomped away.

He strode into the bedroom, ripping his shirt over his head and tossing it on the floor as he headed toward the bathroom. By the time he hit the cold tap, his pants were undone and halfway down his legs. In less than a minute he had his shoes off and his jeans following.

The pounding of water hitting tile drowned out the groan of frustration he couldn't suppress at the sight of his cock. He'd never had so little control. The beast had remained suspiciously quiet and Brogan had to wonder what that was all about. He hadn't felt it pulling to be free since he'd kissed El, since she'd come apart in his arms.

Damn!

He'd marked her. No wonder the beast had gone back to snoozing, it knew she was his. Stepping under the stinging spray, Brogan closed his eyes and raised his face, let the water stab his skin with its needle-like drops. His mind played over what he'd done, how she'd kissed him back with such demand.

Her need had been as great as his and when she'd shattered at his touch he'd been breathless with awe. She looked so beautiful flushed with arousal. Her eyes all dreamy, her lips plump from their kisses and her nipples hard as diamonds against his chest.

His cock twitched and oozed pre-cum. The cold shower did nothing to cool the blood boiling in his veins or the lust trampling on every nerve. He gave in, leaned back against the wall and grabbed his unruly cock in a tight fist.

Brogan imagined El in the shower, her soapy hands traveling over pink-tinged skin, down over her chest, across her taut stomach and between her legs, slow slides on smooth muscle and supple flesh. With eyes closed and head thrown back, she delved between her thighs. Her lips parted on a moan as she thrust deeper, riding her hand and the pleasure it gave her. With each stroke her hips moved, undulated against the fingers probing inside.

Teeth bared, Brogan increased his grip, moved his hand faster. The image in his mind stilled as her eyes opened wide to stare straight at him as she flew over the edge. He ground his jaw on a growl of satisfaction when she came for him—only him—and he followed.

Cum shot from the tip of his cock, dripped down his hand and onto the shower floor. He kept his movements hard and steady, milking every last drop of seed from his balls. Spent, he slumped against the wall, breathed deep and thought about going to her room and taking her.

No other woman made him lose control. He'd given in to an urge he normally controlled with an iron fist. Instead he had that fist wrapped around his cock as he fantasized about El getting herself off.

He'd come hard and fast but arousal rode his back like he hadn't. His prick, ramrod-straight and steel hard, didn't look as if it was going down anytime soon. She was his weakness, his Achilles' heel and if his enemies worked it out they'd use her to get to him.

He wouldn't allow it. He'd protect her, teach her to protect herself, but first he had to tell her, explain what he was and about the coyote ways. It was going to be a long couple of days. No point putting it off any longer. Brogan ran the soap over muscles still taut with tension. He stepped beneath the spray and rinsed before he flicked the water off and got out.

Ignoring the towels, he headed back into his bedroom. He yanked open drawers, got out a shirt and clean jeans and threw them on the bed behind him. He searched for a clean pair of socks but couldn't find any. Where the hell were they?

A gasp from the doorway had him whipping around and coming face to face with a very shocked—and dressed—Eloise. Her mouth hung open and she didn't take her eyes off his prick, which had its eye pointed her way. Damn thing bobbed as if it was waving hello.

He cleared his throat and her gaze darted up to meet his. He waited to see what she wanted.

"I...um..."

Her neck and face red with embarrassment reminded him of how she looked when she came in his arms. She coughed and tried again.

"I... I wanted to apologize for before. Back in my..." She gestured over her shoulder. Before he could reply she continued. "I know it was as much my fault as yours and I agree that it shouldn't have happened. I can assure you it won't again." Her spine straightened and her shoulders pulled back with her last words.

Well now, wasn't it a shame that he had every intention of it happening again? And again. Time to let her know.

"El, there's no need to apologize and I'm taking back mine. I can also tell you that it will happen again, but not yet. There are things we need to talk about before we find ourselves in the same position."

Her hand flew up to cover her throat, her fingers trembling. He stalked toward her, uncaring of his naked state. Invading her personal space, he breathed deep and could still smell her arousal under the fresh layer of soap and shampoo. She may have tried to wash him off but he was still there, mixed in with the fragrance of her cream.

Oh yeah, she was marked all right. Marked as his. He couldn't wait to have her. All of her.

"Next time you come apart in my arms I'll be buried deep inside your tight body, nothing between us but the pleasure we'll give each other." He ran a finger along her jaw, tilted her head up to see her eyes. "Make no mistake, it *will* happen again."

Eyes wide she let him drag his finger over her lips. So soft. So plump and kissable. He lowered his head, brushed his mouth where his finger had been.

"Next time I won't stop," he breathed against her.

She gasped, her lips parted and a puff of minty-fresh breath filled his nostrils. He took advantage and thrust his tongue out, invading her mouth with hot licks and bold strokes. Her taste intoxicated him, flooded his senses and fueled his lust. He took the kiss deeper, devoured all she had to give.

He swallowed her moan before it left her throat as the urge to take, to possess stole through him. He pulled back and slowed the kiss until it was soft and lush. Breathing hard, she followed him when he broke their bond. Her whimper of protest echoed his.

"Not yet. Soon, but not yet." He breathed hard with renewed need. "There's too much to know, to learn, before I take you."

Her lust-filled eyes drew him in, made him want to break his own decree. He wanted to pick her up, slam the door closed and have her in his bed. The next few days would test his control a thousand times. He'd given it up once, but he wouldn't do it again. He couldn't let this slip of a woman break the one thing he prided himself on most.

The command he had over his needs, desires, and his position as sovereign. He couldn't afford to loosen the reins and show weakness because he could lose El, leadership of the pack and possibly his life.

4

El sat on a stool next to Rowan while Quinn and Brogan stood on the other side of the kitchen. She listened as Brogan issued orders for them to stay inside. Neither she nor Rowan was allowed to leave the house without one of the men. He went on about the weather and snowstorms that blew up unexpectedly, but she didn't think that was why he was forbidding them from venturing out.

She couldn't quite work out what exactly was up but that was the least of her worries. Rowan had just agreed without batting an eyelid. El's mind fought over whether to do as she was told or argue the point that she wasn't stupid and wouldn't get into trouble stepping out into the yard.

The undercurrents running between Brogan and Quinn had her worried. Something was going on beneath the surface and she wanted to know what made these two strangers think they could order her around. She knew whatever it was had to do with her but what could she have done to warrant being a virtual prisoner in this house?

"Okay, now that's settled I've got calls to make. I'll be in my office if you want me." Brogan strode from the room without another word.

Rowan's stool scraped along the floor and over El's nerves. She sat in stunned silence, unable to move or think past what had just happened. Why hadn't she protested? Had the man scrambled her brain so much with one orgasm? Sure it had been mind-blowing, the best she'd ever had to be honest, but she'd never allowed anyone to order her around before. Why start now?

A cup of coffee landed on the counter in front of her. Snapped out of her thoughts, she glanced up to find Rowan looking at her with concern and Quinn nowhere in sight. When had he left the kitchen?

"Are you sure you're okay? You still look a little pale, maybe you should go lie down until dinner." Rowan's forehead creased with worry and El felt bad for causing her friend any anxiety this close to her wedding.

"I'm fine, honest. Still tired but fine. There's nothing to worry about except getting all the final details of your big day finished." El smiled and hoped it reassured Rowan enough for her to stop fretting.

She suffered through a minute of continued scrutiny before Rowan nodded and went to get the folder with all the information for next Saturday. El didn't think there was anything left to do but they agreed to go over it one more time to be sure.

Three cups of coffee and two hours later, they were both satisfied everything was in place and excluding bad weather, the day would go off without a hitch.

She busied herself rinsing their mugs and stacking them in the dishwasher while Rowan puttered about behind her, pulling things from the fridge.

"Why don't you go watch some TV or read while I get dinner started and then we can spend the rest of the afternoon relaxing," Rowan said.

"You don't want help?"

"No, you go on into the lounge room, the fire should be going and I think there are some magazines on the side table."

Rowan bumped El with her hip as she carried vegetables to the island counter. "Go." She made a shooing motion with her elbow. "I'll join you in a few."

El laughed. "Okay, I'm going but if you don't join me soon I'll come get you."

The whole scene reminded El of when they lived together, how easily they fit around each other. How Rowan had always tried to mother her and anyone else she could. Smiling, she entered the lounge room and found the fire roaring in the hearth, the room cozy and welcoming. She plopped down into a recliner and picked up a magazine with one of Hollywood's latest starlets splashed across the cover.

She had no idea how long she sat pretending to read the articles or why she couldn't get her mind off Brogan and his damn orders to stay inside. If he'd said nothing she probably wouldn't have wanted to go out, but because he'd told her she couldn't, her mind had decided she had to.

She felt trapped, suffocated. The house was warm and inviting but it made her itch to breathe fresh air. She wanted to suck the cold winter chill into her lungs and look up at the clear blue sky. Just sitting on the front steps would be enough to relieve the pressure constricting her.

Damn the man for making things difficult.

There was that little scene up in his room to consider too. She'd realized while showering she'd been equally to blame for what happened. At first she'd decided she should leave it alone but then the thought of tiptoeing around each other for the next week made her cringe and she had to apologize.

He'd stood there naked, all sculptured male perfection and her mind had emptied. Completely devoid of anything other than the urge to jump him and finish what they'd started. Even now she hummed with arousal and need. He had her going around in circles. How could she want him so much when she wasn't even sure she liked him?

El hated her indecision, hated the swinging back and forth between lust and loathing. She'd never been this mixed up. She needed to get outside. Needed to walk and think. Action always cleared her mind, gave the answers to her problems. Brogan certainly was turning into a problem. A big one.

Surely she could go out on the porch? She could walk the length of it and clear her head. Would it hurt to sit on the step and watch the world around her? Other than the quick look on the drive in she hadn't seen much of Whispering Springs and Rowan had told her so much about the mountains and her home at Whispering Creek Lodge that El wanted to see it through her own eyes. Just one look, that's all.

Snapping the magazine closed, she dropped it back on the table and pushed from the chair. He couldn't stop her from going outside. Not unless he tied her to her bed. A shiver ran down her spine as an image of Brogan tying her up flashed across her mind's eye.

It wasn't a shiver of fear.

"Grrrr!" Her teeth ground as her frustration built.

Walking down the hall, she put her head in the kitchen door where Rowan was busy washing lettuce. Taking advantage of her distraction El said, "I'm just going to sit on the front step for a bit, get some fresh air."

"Okay." Rowan's acknowledgement came just as El had hoped, without thought.

She backed out of the doorway.

If Brogan found out she'd gone outside he'd flip but what he didn't know couldn't hurt him, or in this case, hurt her. The man might be an "I'm in charge type" but El wasn't about to let him tell her what she could and couldn't do. She marched down the hallway to the front door, building up steam as she went.

Just because he was used to giving orders and people taking them didn't mean she had to. They'd only just met for God's sake. But what really got her mad was that even when he told her what to do or made her angry she was still attracted to him. Her brain might want to argue and tell him to go to hell but her treacherous body wanted to jump his bones.

How could her body betray her like that? And what happened to her spine? Had that bastard Ken done so much damage to her self-esteem? Well, no more. She wasn't about to let any man choose what she could and couldn't do. Or tell her where to go and not go.

El stormed through the front door, breathing hard and mumbling under her breath about tyrants and giving orders. At the last second she swung back, palm out and caught the solid oak panel before it slammed closed. Heaven forbid Mr. High and Mighty *hear* her disobeying one of his rules.

Who did he think he was? Standing there dictating what they could and couldn't do like some maniac despot ruling his subjects with an iron fist. She wasn't even all that pissed off that he'd given the orders. No, she was pissed because both Rowan and Quinn had gone along with him as if he should be obeyed in every way.

Don't do this! Don't do that! Christ, he'd be telling her when to come next.

El stumbled. One foot hit an icy patch of snow and she slipped, her legs separated and wobbled beneath her. Her arms flailed about until she got her feet back under her and caught her balance. Braced with her legs apart and her arms out wide like someone doing jumping jacks, she stood perfectly still and sucked in a breath of frigid air.

Was that what had her so agitated? He aroused her beyond belief and she wanted to do what he said. *Wanted* to please him.

She squeezed her eyes closed, breathed slow and deep and tried to steady her pounding heart and jittery nerves. He'd had her all riled up from the second they met, her body at once screaming for her to get away and get closer. El opened her eyes and continued to walk, taking care not to step on any more slippery patches of snow even though she wanted to stomp about to release the frustration bubbling inside.

A drop of moisture landed on her cheek, distracting her from her troubled thoughts. It was starting to snow. El tilted her face up to let the cold flakes bathe her skin.

It was such a magical scene. The view of the forest and mountains covered in a white blanket that shimmered as more snow fell from the sky was spectacular. The cold didn't just cool her body, it cooled her temper too. Taking the edge off enough for her to think rationally about what Brogan had asked and to see it from his point of view.

She couldn't blame him for being worried about her out here in unfamiliar territory. She'd never been here before and he had a right to be concerned she might get lost or hurt. But she wasn't stupid or incapable and wouldn't put herself at risk.

A sigh exploded from her chest. This was so unlike her, so completely out of character. She prided herself on her level-headed approach to life. Had the last few months done far more damage than she'd believed? Sure, she'd known her pride was dented, and her self-confidence had taken a blow, but this irrational attraction and anger coupled with confusion just wasn't her at all.

The snow sparkled as it floated to the ground, landing on the path and trees, on El. She shuddered and wrapped her arms across her chest. She rubbed her hands from elbow to shoulder, trying to ease the chill and wished she'd grabbed her coat before leaving the house. The storm was getting worse.

Time to head back inside.

She turned and slipped, her hands flying out to stop herself from landing face first. Her fingers sank into the powdery cold slush. Pushing up, El stood and stared at the forest in front of her. The stumble must have turned her around. Gingerly, she spun around. More forest. Sucking in a breath, she twisted back again. Forest.

Oh God!

Slowly she rotated a full three hundred-sixty degree turn.

"Where's the house?" Her whispered words the only sound in the silence of the snowfall.

Oh God! Oh God! Where is it?

She stood still and turned her head to look over her shoulder. She stared straight ahead again, at where she thought the house should be. Was that gray shadow between the trees the house? With her eyes squinted it didn't get any clearer and the curtain of falling snow had grown heavier, causing the scenery to blur further. The shiver that went through her had nothing to do with the cold. Panic lodged in her throat. Fear clutched her heart.

Brogan was going to kill her. She'd done the one thing he'd told her not to and instead of proving she was capable of looking after herself, she'd proven him right.

Her body shook violently. This time it had everything to do with the cold. Her thin sweater was drenched on the shoulders and the sleeves weren't far behind. Her short hair stuck to her scalp, wet with snow that dripped onto her face. Her running shoes were soaking through and her toes had gone numb.

Her teeth chattered sending a jarring rattle through her head. Her fingers and hands were stiff with cold and the knuckles ached. Wrapping her arms around her body, El tucked her hands under her armpits, trying to ease the throb. Now that she stood still and took stock of her body she realized her jeans were wet and getting wetter and she was halfway to frozen.

If she didn't work out which way to go soon Brogan would be the least of her worries. If she couldn't find the house, she'd freeze to death before he got to her.

5

––––––––––

Brogan came up behind Rowan and pinched a slice of the cheese she was cutting for dinner. When he went for a second piece she smacked his hand away with the back of the knife.

"Stop it! You'll spoil your dinner."

"Dinner won't be for a couple of hours and you know nothing could spoil my appetite." He quickly snatched a second piece and darted to the other side of the kitchen.

"Brogan," Rowan warned.

"Okay, no more I promise." He held his hands up. His mood was light since he'd come to a truce of sorts with El. Plus, he'd made it clear she and Rowan were not to leave the house. Between now and the wedding he or his sister would find the right time to tell El about their heritage.

Yes, things were starting to come together.

"Where's El?" he asked.

"Out front."

"*What!*" he yelled.

"She's sitting on the front steps getting some fresh air." Rowan turned to face him, an eyebrow raised.

"Outside?" His voice had lowered but would still have been heard upstairs.

"That's where the front steps were last time I looked."

What the hell was wrong with her? How could she have let El leave the house?

"Jeez, Brogan, lighten up. She's just getting some air, not going on a mountain trek." Rowan shook her head and returned to cutting cheese.

For a second his mouth flapped but no words came out, then adrenaline kicked in and the beast sprang to life.

"Rowan!" he roared.

"What? Why the hell are you yelling at me?" She raised her voice but wasn't yelling.

"How could you let her leave the house? You both promised you wouldn't until after the wedding." He spun on his heel ready to charge through the front door and drag El back inside.

"For Christ's sake Brogan, she's just out front. Nothing's going to happen on our own porch."

Brogan stopped. He didn't want to tell her but he had to now. Had to so she'd understand El couldn't leave the house. He looked at her over his shoulder. "She's marked, Rowan."

"Marked?"

He nodded.

"You had sex with my best friend?" Her soft tone didn't bode well. Any second the explosion would come.

Sure enough, the knife she'd been using sailed past his head and embedded in the wall behind him. Most would say he was lucky she missed but Brogan knew luck had nothing to do with it, she had a true aim. If she'd wanted to hit him she would have, either between the eyes or through the heart. Rowan never missed a target.

"We didn't have sex. It didn't go that far."

"But you marked her!"

"I didn't mean to. It just happened and..."

Rowan flew past him into the hall.

Oh God, Eloise!

He tore out of the kitchen after her. Quinn came down the stairs as they headed for the front door.

"Where's the fire?" Quinn asked.

The door crashed back against the wall.

"El!" Rowan screamed.

"What the hell's going on?" Quinn was right behind him as Brogan hit the porch.

"El came out to get some fresh air," he ground between clenched teeth.

"What? When? Where the hell is she?" Quinn demanded.

"And when the fuck did it start to snow?" Rowan whispered.

"Where is she?" Brogan swung his head, frantically searching for El. There was no sign of her.

"I don't know. She said she'd just be here on the front step."

"Quinn, go in and get some gear." He pulled his sweater and shirt off together.

"Brogan, what are you doing?" Rowan asked.

"I'm going to find her. I'll bring her back if I can. If not I'll keep her in place until Quinn gets to us." He unbuttoned his jeans, pushed them down and yanked his boots off with them.

"Brogan, you can't go to her in your coyote form. You'll scare her to death." Rowan protested.

"I've got no choice. She'll freeze to death if we don't get to her soon."

Quinn came out the door, his jacket on, a pack thrown over one shoulder and El's jacket in his arms. "She didn't take her coat. We need to move now." He picked up Brogan's clothes and shoved them into the pack.

Brogan left the porch at a run as muscles stretched and bones popped. He bent forward and by the time his hands reached the ground they were paws. Shifting for him took no thought, no effort. In seconds he was sniffing the air and following El's scent along the path into the woods.

He heard Quinn running behind him, the distance between them getting greater with each stride. Nose down, he bounded down the trail and quickly disappeared from view. How had she managed to get so far? The storm was rapidly turning into a blizzard and his keen vision was the only thing keeping him from crashing into the trees.

His fur hung limp, wet from the snow and the sweat pouring out of him. He pumped his legs, his heart racing. The strain and pull on his muscles went unnoticed as he ran for all he was worth. The fear of not getting to her soon enough rode his back, made him push harder.

He left the path and was slowed by the density of the trees and thick underbrush. Why had she left the path? Burs caught in his fur. Brogan ignored them. He had to get to El, had to find her before she froze to death. Or worse, someone else found her.

The snow fell into his eyes, blurred his vision. His lungs burned but nothing except finding El would stop him. Her scent grew stronger, the wet conditions didn't hamper his senses but if it got any wetter it would wash her scent away completely. He had to find her before that happened.

Closer now, he slowed. She didn't need him barreling down on her in coyote form. He'd have to approach with care, not frighten her.

Two things hit him at once, the sight of El through the trees about thirty feet in front of him and another coyote between him and her.

El stared at the wild animal in front of her. Teeth bared and hackles raised, he had obviously taken exception to her being in its forest. Well he wasn't the only one. He looked scrawny, his coat ratty and dull but what did she expect? A well groomed canine?

"Nice doggy, good doggy." Hands in front she backed away.

He followed.

The grumble vibrating up his throat stopped her cold. Without moving her head, she searched the area, looking for anything she could use as a weapon to protect herself. He wasn't big, had to weigh less than she did. If she could find something to bash him over the head with there might be a slim chance she'd get to freeze to death after all.

She tried not to think of how else she might die. Those pointy yellow teeth sent icy fear skating through her veins. Saliva dripped from his curled lips and El's flight impulse kicked in. The urge to run, to turn and run, shuddered over muscles rigid with fear, but she didn't move. To do so would mean certain death.

One paw moved forward as a back one followed. With infinite care he walked toward her. He snarled wider, showed more of his menacing jaws. He was stalking her and all she could do was stand there. Wait for him to get closer. She might be able to kick out with her foot if he came within reach without lunging for her throat. How far could he jump?

When he got within twenty feet his snarl turned into a gut-stealing growl, teeth mashing together as he snapped at her. His legs bent and his chest dipped and she knew this was it, he would attack her now and it would be a fight for her life.

She braced her legs apart, bent her knees and bounced on the balls of her feet. All the things she'd been taught in her self-defense class. El figured she could get a good solid kick into his throat if he jumped the right way. If not she'd plant her foot in the first thing it connected with.

The coyote leapt and all her muscles tightened, ready to spring up.

She never got the chance.

With a spine-tingling howl, another coyote pounced. At first she thought it was coming for her as well, but when the newcomer took out the first one in a swift bone-crunching tackle she knew it was time to run. Blood sprayed across the pristine white snow and El's stomach turned.

She would not vomit.

Sprinting to the left, she took off. Trees and bushes slapped at her but she didn't stop. Her heart pounded in time with her feet, her toes squelched in her wet sneakers and her chest burned with each ragged breath. She needed to hide. She'd never outrun the coyote if he gave chase and she was sure he would.

El scanned the area as she ran, looked for anything that might conceal her. There was only one option. The last time she'd climbed a tree hadn't turned out well but if it was the difference between life and death, she'd do it. Spotting one that looked as if it would be easy to climb, she headed straight for it.

Bark dug into her palms as her fingers wrapped around a low branch. It took one tear in her jeans, numerous bruises and two attempts to get her legs over the limb. Her sweater caught as she swung up and she teetered on the verge of falling. The sound of pounding paws gave her renewed strength to throw herself up and out of reach.

The big gray coyote walked between the trees, his coat glossy and thick, his gait regal and confident. El held her breath, prayed he wouldn't see her. He stopped four feet from the base of her tree and without hesitation looked up at her. She gasped as her hold slipped and a gouge ripped in the flesh of her hand.

It was the coyote from the photo.

Casually, as though he hadn't just attacked another animal, he sat on his haunches. His golden eyes watched her and, like with the photo, El was mesmerized, helpless to look away. From one heartbeat to the next she relaxed and knew without a doubt that he wouldn't hurt her.

Why she would think such a thing about a wild animal couldn't be explained but when he lay down on his belly, head on his paws, she felt no threat from him.

Curled on the branch, her numb body began to slide. Her shivering had come back now that the adrenaline was wearing off and her eyes drooped. She was so tired, she wanted to put her head down and sleep. But she knew she couldn't, not in the tree anyway. Falling was not an option. She'd break something for sure.

She climbed down from her perch. Careful not to startle the coyote with any quick movements, she eased to the ground and sat with her back against the trunk. With the danger passed, her body came alive with pain, cold and fatigue. Keeping an eye on the coyote, El waited for an attack in case she'd misjudged him. It never came. He watched her with unblinking eyes.

Feeling safe but tired, she bent her legs and hugged them to her chest. Closing her eyes she lowered her forehead to her knees as bone-rattling shakes swamped her. Her arms and legs went numb and her teeth chattered. She didn't flinch when the coyote sat next to her. Too exhausted, El had no strength left to move more than her head, she opened her eyes to look at him.

He was warm. His fur so soft she wanted to burrow into him and sleep. In the back of her mind she knew what she was doing was insane. She sat with a wild animal at her side but she wouldn't move. *Couldn't* move. His actions spoke of care and protection. He'd stopped the other coyote from attacking her and now he was keeping her warm, standing guard. And she was so sleepy.

The cold had her thinking and doing things she wouldn't under normal circumstances. Obviously she was hallucinating, in the throes of hypothermia or something. He rubbed his head back and forth on her arm. The motion soothed and reassured her he didn't intend to hurt her. If she died out here in this frozen wonderland at least she wouldn't be alone.

Lethargic with cold, she slumped against him. His coat encouraged snuggling and she buried her hands in his fur. Her cheek lay on his neck and she closed her eyes and enjoyed the heat he gave off. His heartbeat set a steady rhythm beneath her ear and lulled by his warmth and comfort, El draped her body over his.

She must have dozed because she didn't hear anything until Quinn stood in front of her. He dropped to his knees beside her, tossing a bag at her feet.

"Here, get changed. We need to get her back fast."

Confused by his words, El tried to get up.

"Not you, El. Let's get your coat on." Quinn gently eased one arm into the thermal garment.

Cold air flowed over her side as the coyote stood. She turned to watch him walk away, expected him to leave now there was another person here. But he didn't. With grace he walked a few feet away and before she could understand what she saw, Brogan stood before her. Naked.

Oh, my God! She was hallucinating. She did not just see that gorgeous animal turn into Rowan's brother. He reached for the bag Quinn had brought and pulled clothes out. Dressing quickly, he returned to her side just as Quinn got her zipped up.

"Brogan?" she whispered, the word full of the confusion swirling in her head.

"Shh... It's all right. I've got you now. We'll get you home and warm." He pulled her close and hugged her tight before he picked her up and started walking through the falling snow. El curled into his body and gave up the fight to stay awake.

6

Her face tucked into his neck sent shivers down his spine. She was cold as ice. The shaking had stopped while he lay against her in coyote form and now as he held her against his human body he knew there was no time to waste. He'd have to send Quinn to clean up.

"Quinn, over on Whispering Ridge is a coyote." He wouldn't need to explain further.

"Is he dead?"

"I don't know. El took off and I had to go after her."

"Okay, I'll see you back at the house."

As his best friend, Quinn could be trusted to do what needed to be done. As regal, Quinn held the position of Brogan's second and his loyalty was expected.

In the two years he'd held sovereign nothing had been easy. There were members of the pack who thought as a half-blood he had no right to the position. He'd like to think his skills and progress with pack finances and the more stable community proved them wrong.

The human in his arms could destroy all he'd achieved. No one liked outsiders, especially non-bloods. Even after he turned El, gave her the ability to shift, she'd always be a non-blood. Could he expect her to go through life being looked down at? Did he have a choice?

Could he let her walk away if that was what she wanted? She was his mate, for him there would be no other. Could he live without her? Let her leave him and go on with her life, unprotected and maybe with someone else? She was marked as his and no matter where she went other shifters would know it.

No. If she couldn't live here with him, he'd leave with her. He'd walk away from all he'd known for her. Convince her they were meant to be together. But there was no point thinking about it now. They'd cross that bridge when and if they came to it. For now he had to concentrate on getting her back to the house.

He had no idea how long he trudged through the falling snow when the house came into view. The storm had almost reached whiteout and it was no wonder El had lost her way. Even he'd struggle without his natural coyote senses.

Rowan opened the door as Brogan came up the path.

"Upstairs. I've got blankets warmed and hot drinks ready."

"She's unconscious, the drinks can wait." He angled through the door, careful not to bump El's head on the frame.

Two at a time, he raced up the stairs. Rowan had turned up the heat because it got hotter with every step he took. At the top he turned toward his room.

"Brogan, you're going the wrong way," Rowan said.

He ignored her.

By the time he reached his bedroom sweat was beading on his skin but El needed the warmth so he wasn't about to complain.

He placed her on her feet. With one arm wrapped around her waist he started to pull her out of her wet clothes.

"Help me get her undressed," he barked.

"Okay, then I'll get the blankets from her room."

Between them they got El stripped naked. With one hand he ripped the covers off his bed and waited for Rowan to bring the blankets.

"Lay one on the bed," he ordered.

He was being blunt to the point of rudeness but his first priority was getting El warm. He'd apologize later.

When Rowan got the first blanket down, he laid El on it. *Christ!* Her skin was blue. He let Rowan cover her while he stripped out of his wet clothes. Body heat would be the best way to bring her temperature back up and he had every intention of sharing his.

"What are you doing?"

"I'm getting in with her. Body heat, Rowan, it's the best way." Lifting the blanket edge he climbed in and pulled El against him.

"She's so still. Maybe we should take her to the hospital."

"The storm is getting worse. We can't take her or we'd be risking all our lives. We just need to get her warmed up." Brogan hoped he was making the right decision.

"Where's Quinn?" Rowan asked.

"He'll be here soon."

"That's not what I asked, Brogan. Why didn't he come in with you?"

"He had to do something for me."

"What?" Tension laced her voice.

"Not now. After we get El warm I'll explain everything."

"But—"

"Later." He still wasn't sure what—if anything—they'd tell Rowan or El. It would all depend on what Quinn found on Whispering Ridge.

El lay motionless beside him. He covered her and tucked the blanket around them to keep their body heat trapped. Her breathing was so shallow he couldn't feel her chest rising but he kept his fingers on her pulse point to assure himself she was still alive. He willed her to warm up.

Curled around her as best he could without crushing her, he clenched his teeth against the chill of her flesh. He may as well be hugging a snowman.

By scant degrees her temperature rose. She remained still in his embrace even as her skin lost the blue tinge that had scared him into thinking he'd been too late getting her home.

Sweat broke out on his back, his chest. The cocoon he'd made slowly turned into a furnace. He wouldn't last much longer in here with her. A few more minutes and then he'd get out and dress. The blanket, damp along his back from his sweat would have to be changed, too.

Rowan had disposed of their wet clothing before returning to sit in the chair near the window. Her gaze darted between watching for Quinn and checking El. Brogan knew she was torn between her dual worries. Her mate hadn't returned and the storm had finally become full whiteout conditions.

"He's back!" Rowan sprang from her perch and raced from the room.

Brogan's cue to get up and dressed. He wanted to know what Quinn had found. He hoped it wasn't what he thought it had been. Gently, he slipped his arm out from under El. She moaned and rolled over to follow him. Her hand reached out and grazed his chest, a nail scraping his nipple. The small bud hardened and his cock throbbed with arousal.

He'd managed to keep his desire for El at bay while he held her naked body, but in the back of his mind it was there. Waiting for the slightest move to bring it bounding out of the corner to take over his every thought, his every breath. He hated himself for wanting her when she was so sick and hated that they were in this situation at all.

She curled into a ball as a moan slipped from her lips and tormented his sensitized nerves. He grabbed a new blanket from the pile Rowan had left on the end of the bed. Draping it over her, he tucked the sides in. He pushed her hair from her face and ran his fingers through the damp strands. She settled at his touch, murmured and snuggled deeper into his bed.

Happy to see her face had lost its gray-blue tinge and her skin felt warmer beneath his fingers, he turned to get dressed. Pulling jeans and a shirt out, he quickly put them on. He could hear Rowan and Quinn coming up the stairs and from the tone of their hushed voices they were arguing. He smiled. Quinn was not giving up any more information than Brogan had.

"How is she?" Quinn asked as he came into the room.

"Warmer. She hasn't woken yet. Stirred a little when I got out of the bed just now, but that's all." Brogan walked over and placed the back of his hand on her forehead. Definitely warmer.

"Is someone going to tell me what happened out there?" Rowan demanded.

His sister wouldn't give up until she knew every detail. "I'm not sure yet. Let Quinn tell us what he found first and then I'll have a better picture."

"He was a natural. Old and starved half to death. I don't think he would have had the strength to do El much damage. He certainly didn't have enough to fight you."

"Damn."

"Yeah. There's more."

Brogan's head snapped around to look at Quinn. He didn't need to hear the words. He knew what Quinn would say.

"Marcus turned up while I was burying the body. He's reporting you to the Council." Quinn didn't look happy about his run-in with Marcus.

Marcus was full-blood and thought he should hold sovereign but the man was an idiot of the first order and his leadership skills started and ended with intimidation and scare tactics. Not the type of leader any pack would want—or need.

"He can report me. I've done nothing wrong. I took the threat away with as little force as possible. The only thing I'm guilty of is leaving him there and going after El. But under the circumstances, that's acceptable," Brogan said.

"Yes, but we all know Marcus will put a spin on it," Rowan chimed in.

"He can, and I can front Council, explain what happened and if they still think I should step down as sovereign I will. But I think Marcus might be forgetting one thing. If I step down, Quinn, you take over." Brogan was thankful for that little bit of pack law.

"Does that mean we can expect him to try to kill Quinn again?" Rowan's voice quivered with fear.

"He can try but he won't succeed." Steely determination filled Quinn's words.

"He won't get away with it like last time, Rowan. We might not have been able to prove his involvement before but this time we know what and who we're dealing with," Brogan said.

It had cost them all to let Marcus get away with his involvement in the attempt on Quinn's life but as sovereign and regal their hands were tied by pack law. Next time Marcus did something, they'd make sure they had proof to take to the Council.

Or Brogan would ignore the law and go after him anyway. He'd keep that to himself though. No point worrying Rowan any more than she already was.

"Quinn, go get out of those wet clothes. We'll work out what to do about Marcus after El wakes. There's not much we can do with the storm anyway," Brogan said.

"I'll get dinner in the oven. I think we could all use something warm to eat." Rowan leaned over El and checked the warmth of her skin with her palm. "She should wake soon, shouldn't she?" she asked.

"I think so. But she'll be tired as well as hypothermic. She's warmer now and that's what counts." Brogan sat on the edge of the bed, brushing his fingers lightly over El's cheek and pushing the hair off her face.

He waited for Rowan to leave the room. "Do you think Marcus was behind the natural's attack on El?"

"Hard to say but I wouldn't put it past him."

Brogan wouldn't be surprised to find Marcus had somehow been involved but how would he know El had gone wondering off unless he was watching the house? There would be no room for secrets now, with Marcus prowling around and stirring up trouble they would all need to be careful. Especially El.

"We can't afford to wait any longer. We'll have to tell her everything when she wakes. With Marcus causing trouble with the Council she'll need to know what's going on." Quinn voiced what Brogan had already decided.

When El woke, they'd tell her everything. What they were and what danger they were in from a man bent on gaining sovereign.

E l woke with a start and a cry of pain. Every muscle and bone ached.

"Easy. You're safe now." The deep voice rolled over her.

Brogan.

She opened her eyes, the low light of the room sending prickles of pain into her skull. Tears formed, blurring her already limited vision.

"Where..." Her throat felt dry and scratchy.

"Here, drink some warm tea."

Brogan lifted her head, held a mug to her lips and she sipped at the sweet liquid. He kept her from drinking too fast, tilting the cup away after each sip. For the second time today she found herself on the receiving end of this hard man's gentle care.

After a few sips he took the cup away and placed it on the bedside table. Her eyes had adjusted to the low light and El could see that she was in Brogan's room. In his bed. He propped a pillow behind her back and she leaned into it, letting the softness cushion her sore body.

"I hurt," she whispered.

"You will for a while. You were awfully cold when I found you." The low soothing rumble of Brogan's voice shivered over her skin.

She wasn't feeling cold now. Her body was heating quickly as she began to wake further. She could smell snow and forest and Brogan. For someone who could describe a photograph with vivid words, she was at a loss as to which ones to use for his scent. It was hot and male, all Brogan.

"Are you still cold?" he asked.

"No."

No, she certainly wasn't. If anything she was rather hot. She pushed the blanket down in the hope of cooling off a bit. Brogan's drawn-in breath had her gaze darting to his face. He was staring at her chest. Looking down she found out why. She was naked. Where had her clothes gone? Who'd taken them off?

Scrabbling for the cover, she pulled it back up but the damage was done. He'd seen her breasts and her pointy nipples. He had to know they weren't hard from being cold.

"What happened to my clothes?"

"They were soaked. We had to get you warm quickly. We took them off and used body heat to warm you up," he explained.

"Body heat?" Oh God, please no.

Brogan's devilish smile was all she needed to know the body heat had been his. Never mind seeing her naked, he'd been wrapped around her.

Her face flushed with arousal—or was it embarrassment? She couldn't decide which. The thought of being in Brogan's arms with not a stitch on had her hard nipples throbbing and her pussy watering. She closed her eyes and groaned. Would she always be in a state of confusion with this man?

"Don't worry, El. I behaved myself. Besides, when I don't behave I want you fully aware of everything I'm doing to you. No offense, but you brought new meaning to the words *cold fish in bed*." His deep chuckle had goose bumps rising on her skin.

"How did I get here?" She tried to remember what had happened but her mind wouldn't clear and the only thing she could remember was losing sight of the house.

"I found you and brought you home." He was back to brushing her hair off her face, the motion soothing and arousing. Everything the man did seemed to turn her on.

"But I couldn't see the house. The snow..."

"I know, I warned you that the storms could blow up quickly out here."

She'd been standing in the snow looking around at nothing but forest when she'd heard heavy breathing behind her.

"The coyote!" she gasped.

"It's okay, he can't hurt you now," Brogan reassured.

"No. Not the wild one, the one from the photo downstairs." Her gaze met Brogan's and she knew before he said anything that what her mind was now remembering was real. It hadn't been a vision.

"Oh, God," she whispered, pulling away.

"I'll never hurt you." Brogan's words were gentle but full of conviction.

"You...you..." El couldn't say it, couldn't voice what she was thinking.

"I need to explain but I want Rowan and Quinn here when I do. What we have to tell you will be a shock but you have to know that none of us would ever hurt you or put you in danger." Brogan got off the bed and went to the door. "I'll be back in a second. I'll just get them so you can know the truth."

The truth? What truth? That he'd somehow turned from a coyote into a human? Human? Jeez, if he'd turned into a coyote he wasn't human. What did you call someone that was an animal one second and a human the next?

El laughed out loud, the slightly hysterical sound bouncing around the room. What had she gotten herself into?

7

"You're awake." Rowan ran into the room and plopped on the bed next to her.

El looked at her and tried to decide if she could change form like Brogan. Her friend didn't look any different than she always had and nothing about her pointed to her not being human. Of course Brogan looked completely normal too.

"I was so worried. You scared us all half to death. Don't ever do that again," Rowan admonished.

"Can you..." Again the words stuck in El's throat.

Rowan grabbed both her hands and squeezed her fingers. "I'm sorry I never told you, but it's not exactly something that comes up in everyday conversation." She shrugged.

El had to agree with her. In fact she couldn't think of how it would ever come up in a conversation.

"El, I need you to hear me out. When I'm finished you can ask any questions you want and I'll answer them," Brogan said as he sat back on the bed.

Quinn stood behind Rowan. She scrutinized both of them closely but couldn't see anything to raise her suspicions. She turned back to look at Brogan. Nothing made her think they were anything but human.

With a nod she said, "Okay, I'll listen."

"We're what are called shapeshifters. We can change from human form to coyote. We're not the only kind of shifter but for now I'll just explain about us." His hand waved to indicate Rowan, Quinn and himself, which answered her earlier question. They could all change shape.

"There are two ways to become one. You're either born with the ability to shift or turned by a shifter. We were all born shifters but there are those in our community that have been turned. Once a human is turned they are able to shift form with practice but they're still considered non-bloods by our pack and inferior by some.

"Some shifters are referred to as half-bloods and others full-bloods. Some believe that half-bloods are as inferior as non-bloods, but those are feelings I aim to change. As sovereign, I'm working toward bringing our people together and forming a stronger connection that will enable us to continue to live among humans without detection." Brogan's last words held the strength of his will to achieve his goal.

"In every way that counts, we're human, El. We think and feel exactly the same, but we can change into coyote form when we want to," Rowan explained.

"There's one other significant difference between us and humans." Quinn's words drew El's gaze to him. "We mate for life. It's not a choice we logically make. When we meet our mate our bodies know and the result is a strong physical attraction that can be unbearable until we join for the first time."

"Once you meet your mate there is never anyone else. It's not something we can change," Brogan continued. "When mates are together they're marked, meaning all other coyotes know who you belong to. The mark works both ways, for the male and female.

"This can cause problems when the mate isn't a shifter." Brogan took her hand in his. "A human must learn about us and our ways before being turned and the choice should be theirs, not the shifters. Once a mark is made, it cannot be removed."

"This can be dangerous in a number of ways. As a human if you don't know you're marked and go into another shifter community you risk being physically attacked but you're also at risk from natural coyotes." Rowan's gaze was sympathetic. "Brogan marked you this morning."

El's gaze snapped to Brogan and her mouth hung open in shock.

"I have no excuse to offer for what I did, El." His Adam's apple bobbed as he swallowed hard. "Because of my lack of control I've taken your choice from you. You have no option now. You have to accept me as your mate."

"But...you said a human mate could choose whether or not they wanted to be turned."

"Yes, and you still have that choice but you have to take me as your mate. I can't allow you to go unprotected. If you don't want to be turned I won't turn you but I can't let you go. I'll leave Whispering Springs if that's what you want," he offered.

"I don't understand."

"I think what Brogan is trying to say is that he's prepared to leave Whispering Springs with you to live in Australia. You still have choices but he's taken away your option of not being tied to him," Rowan said.

"Okay, so I can choose to be turned or not but I can't choose to deny my mate? Is that right?"

"Yes."

"Yes."

Brogan and Quinn spoke at once.

El squeezed her eyes shut and laid back on the bed. This was so unreal. There were so many things to take in and she knew whatever happened her life would never be the same. Taking a deep breath, she opened her eyes and looked at Brogan.

"Will you do something for me?"

"Anything."

"Show me."

"Now?"

"Yes." As an afterthought she added, "Please."

She watched as he stood and began removing his clothes. Without a sign of discomfort at getting nude in front of Quinn and Rowan, he stepped back from the bed and as he bent to the floor, he changed from Brogan to coyote. It happened so fast she barely saw the change. One second he was Brogan the next he wasn't.

"Does it hurt to change?" she asked.

"No, but the first few times drain you of energy," Quinn explained.

"Does he understand what I'm saying?" El watched Brogan but continued to ask Quinn her questions.

"Yes, we still think as we do in human form but we have the added instincts and skills of the coyote body. We're exactly the same just in a different physical shape."

"How do you turn a human?"

Brogan growled but the sound didn't frighten her. Smiling she held out her hand for him to lick. He came closer, running his tongue over her outstretched palm before leaping onto the bed to stand over her and nuzzle the side of her face.

"I think I'll let Brogan explain about turning a human. You might want to ask him to change back now. He won't until you do." Quinn pulled Rowan to her feet. "We'll leave you alone for a while. You need to make a decision so we can deal with the pack Council."

"What Council?" El asked.

"We'll explain about it later. For now you need to talk to Brogan and make your choice," Quinn closed the door behind them as they left.

Brogan's coyote form lay next to her on the bed, his head resting on her stomach. Beneath the blanket El remained naked and the tickle of his warm breath fanned out over her belly. She remembered Quinn's comment about mates having an unbearable attraction until they joined. It explained why she'd been a bundle of lust since meeting Brogan.

"Oh, Brogan. What are we going to do?"

He whined, reminding her she hadn't asked him to change back yet.

"Change back, please."

She expected him to get off the bed but he didn't. He simply changed to human form and remained with his head on her stomach.

"I can't tell you what to do, El. I know what I want you to do but I also know what I've forced you to accept. I'm not sorry you're mine." He ran a finger along her jaw, up and across her lips.

Fire ignited from his touch and streaked through her body, leaving her in no doubt that they had an incredible attraction.

"Why aren't you freaking out about what I am?" he asked.

El smiled. "I guess my lifetime love affair with all things mythical helps me to accept it. Of course it doesn't hurt to have seen it with my own eyes." She laughed. "You know I've dreamed about creatures of myth and legend for most of my life and devoured every written text about them I could get my hands on. Maybe I knew I'd need it one day."

"Maybe." He toyed with a strand of hair.

"How do you turn a human, Brogan?"

"There are a couple of ways to do it."

"A couple?"

"Yes, but the most successful way is by joining." He tugged lightly before tucking the lock he held behind her ear.

"Meaning?" She thought she knew but wanted to hear him say it.

"Sex, El. I'll be able to turn you when we have sex." Surely there was a little more to it than that. After all, he'd said they could be mated without her being turned.

"So how did you mark me?" she asked.

"I wasn't thinking clearly and you kind of took me by surprise with how responsive you are. When I made you come earlier I marked you as mine." He trailed a finger around the shell of her ear.

"I didn't make you come so you're not marked."

"No. But I don't need to be marked to know I'm yours."

"You don't want me to mark you?" Had she misunderstood him?

"More than my next breath but it isn't my choice to make."

"I'm getting tired of all these choices, Brogan. Do you want to be mated with me or not?" Her frustration with him and the situation grew.

"Yes."

"Then turn me," she said.

"I don't need to turn you to be your mate, El. It's two different things."

"Okay, so what happens if we mate but you don't turn me? Am I able to live here with you without being able to shift?" She needed to be clear on this because once the decision was made there would be no turning back. Not that there was any going back now but she still wanted to understand.

"No. The shifter community would never accept you and I would be forced to give up my position as sovereign. If you choose not to be turned we would have to leave here."

"So if I choose to be your mate but not a shifter we leave. If I choose not to be either, we leave. Is that right?"

"Yes."

"And you would do that, even if I don't accept you as my mate?"

"Yes."

"Why?"

"Because you're my mate and without you I'm not whole."

"Even if we aren't mated?" El struggled to understand what he was saying. He couldn't love her—he didn't know her. But he would sacrifice everything for her regardless of her decision. He said he'd taken away her choice but he'd also taken away his own. By being her mate he was forced to go along with what she chose, forced to leave his home and life to follow her. They were both out of choices.

"Brogan, what you've just told me shows that we both no longer have a choice in what we do. No matter what I decide you will be affected and so will I." She reached out and ran her fingers through his thick black hair, the silky curls twisting over her skin. "Are you a good sovereign?"

"I've made some improvements and stopped all of the fighting between the shifters living in and around Whispering Springs." Pride over his accomplishments shone bright in his eyes.

"Would they suffer if you left?" He turned toward her hand when she stroked down the side of his face.

"No. Not if Quinn stayed but I don't know if he and Rowan would stay without me here."

"What do you want to do? Do you want to stay in Whispering Springs?" El watched his eyes, wanted to be sure he told her the truth.

"I want to be with you. Wherever that is," he said.

"That's not what I asked, Brogan."

"This is my home. I was born in this house, in this room. I wouldn't leave it for anything but you."

"Then our choice is made. And it is our choice. It will have an impact on both of us." She covered his mouth with her fingers when he started to speak. "For me, moving here wouldn't be that big a deal. I have no family ties in Australia and I can work on my nature books anywhere that has internet access and a phone. For you to leave here you would be letting the shifter community down and walking away from the only life you've ever known. I couldn't live with you giving all that up. The guilt would eat at me. I can't ask you to make that sacrifice and I won't. My choice is made. Turn me, Brogan."

8

Conflicting emotions bombarded Brogan. Relief at El's acceptance of who he was, *what* he was, lifted the weight he'd been carrying in his chest. Elation at being able to claim his mate flowed through him, sparking his arousal and need to possess. And fear. Knowing what was involved in turning a human and actually doing it were two different things.

A coyote should only turn a human once—if at all—and never outside a mated pair. Icy tingles traveled his spine and the muscles in his stomach clenched tight. He knew how to turn El. Knew the instinct to do so would come naturally when they joined but fear of causing her pain had him breathing hard and sweat popping out on his forehead.

He wanted to flip her over onto her knees and take her. Claim her as his forever. He'd never been nervous about taking a woman to bed but El was different. Having sex had nothing to do with claiming your mate.

"Brogan?" El's voice drew him out of his thoughts.

He had to tell her there was more to being turned than just fucking. She needed to know that he'd have to bite her, allow his coyote teeth to extend and sink into the soft flesh of her neck.

"El." He gulped over the hard ball lodged in his throat. "I, um..." Stammering like an idiot, Brogan searched his mind for the best way to explain what he had to do. "To turn you I have to bite you at the exact moment we both climax."

"Bite me?"

She hadn't backed away from his touch and still ran her fingers through his hair. He took that as a good sign.

"Yes, I need to use my coyote teeth to pierce your neck. I'm told it doesn't hurt because of the endorphins and hormones produced by our mating but I've never turned a human so I can't be sure. I don't want to hurt you." His blood ran cold and pain sliced into his heart at the idea of El suffering in any way.

"Brogan, I know we don't really know each other but I trust you. I know you'd never intentionally hurt me."

"I don't want to unintentionally hurt you either," he said. He'd never been this nervous or fearful.

"We don't have to do this now do we? Can't we spend some time getting to know each other? I want to know about Whispering Springs and your life. Will you tell me?"

Brogan took a deep breath. He could do that. He could tell her about his life and what he saw that life becoming now that she would be a part of it. There was just one problem. He wanted to fuck her and make her his before he did anything else. He might be as nervous as hell about turning her but he didn't feel one bit of anxiety about joining with her.

He moved to sit up and caught the blanket with his elbow. It slid down to reveal the top half of a cream-colored breast. In her effort to grab the cover El pushed it off farther, revealing the top of her other breast and one beaded nipple.

A growl rumbled up his throat and past his lips. His dick went rock hard as need took hold and his coyote sprang to life. All thoughts of going slow fled his mind, along with the blood now flowing like boiling lava through his veins and into his cock.

He crawled up the bed and buried his face between her exposed breasts, breathing deep and filling his lungs with her scent. He brought a hand up to cup one firm mound and tweak the already hard nipple between his fingertips. Lashing with his tongue he laved the tight bud, circled it before sucking it into his mouth.

El moaned and arched into him, pushing her breasts higher for his feasting. He used his other hand to lavish attention on the breast not in his mouth, pulling at the pointed peak with gentle tugs of his fingers. With each tug his blood beat faster, hotter. Burning him from the inside out as it flowed through his body and centered in his cock.

It wasn't enough. He wanted all of her. Wanted to touch, taste and devour every inch of her. Leave no part of her unmarked by him. When he was finished, no one—least of all El—would doubt she belonged to him.

He let go of her breasts and ripped the blanket from between them, her gasp of surprise swallowed when he slammed his mouth to hers. With savage intent he took, thrust his tongue into her warm depths and plundered all he found. Teeth, tongue and lips melded in a frenzy so hot it stole his breath.

There was no time to think of gentling the kiss. El took him deeper with demands of her own. Her hands skimmed over his skin, touching everywhere they could reach. She tried to pull him down, urged him to lie on top of her. Tremors shook his arms and he dropped to his elbows, keeping his full weight off her.

Their bodies lined up, soft to hard. Hollows met ridges and hot skin fused. Her breasts and hard nipples pressed into his chest, the peaks catching in his hair. His own nipples hardened at the contact. He ground his hips into hers, while his cock throbbed against the silky soft skin of her stomach.

Her fingernails grazed his back and sent electric shards of pleasure shooting down his spine into his balls. Heat lightning streaked to the tip of his dick where a bead of pre-cum told how close he was to exploding. Much more of this delicious torture and Brogan would disgrace himself like a randy teenager.

He pulled free of her mouth, both of them gasping for breath. Chests heaved and hearts pounded between them. If they didn't slow down it would be all over in seconds. Then again once wouldn't satisfy him and it wouldn't be long before he was ready to go again. He doubted he'd ever get enough of her.

Through hooded eyes he gazed at her swollen lips—red and puffy from his kiss—they issued an invitation to lick and nibble. But he wanted to snack on more than her mouth. He needed to feed on all of her. The slope of her neck, the arch of her shoulder, the sweep of her breast, the plane of her stomach and the valley of her sex. He planned to sample every inch of her luscious body.

He dipped his head, nibbled along her jaw and up to the soft spot below her ear. His tongue flicked out and lapped at her lobe before tracing the outer shell of her ear. El shuddered beneath him, tilted her head to give him better access to her neck. With open lips he latched on to the flesh under her ear and suckled hard, leaving his mark on her creamy skin.

Her scent and taste exploded through him, obliterating everything from his mind but El and the consuming need she dragged out of him. Need, want, desire and hunger clawed at him. His coyote urged him to take as his human side compelled him to savor. Coyote instincts pushed to the fore and his teeth lengthened.

Canines scraped but didn't break the skin on her neck as he drew his mouth down her throat to the curve beneath her chin. The flutter of her fast beating pulse vibrated on his lips. He nudged her head back with his cheek, nipped her lightly before running his tongue over the pounding hollow.

He trailed his mouth lower, headed for the breasts he'd barely spent time on. He planned to spend a lot of time on them in the future. Her skin, dewy and flushed a beautiful shade of rose, fed his need to taste. Little nips, open-mouthed kisses and sweeping licks took him to his prize. El whimpered and moaned under him, the sounds fanning the flames lashing at his reins of control.

As he moved over her plump mounds he took care to avoid the sensitive tips, heightening her arousal by teasing close, then backing away. Her hips left the bed, pushing into his and grinding his cock against her pubic bone. His balls tightened, tucked up closer to his body and pre-cum dripped from his slit.

The slick liquid coated the head and—thrusting forward—he slid his dick over her heated skin. Fire erupted, destroying the last of his control and he latched on to a taut nipple, sucked hard and thrust again and again.

El went wild, thrashing beneath him. Her orgasm took them both by surprise. Cream and heat from her pussy covered his balls. He pulled his hips back, grabbed hers in his hands and tilted her pelvis. In one hard thrust he sank into her core.

Mindless of anything but El and the hot glove surrounding his cock, he slammed into her repeatedly, rode her like the animal he was. Control and finesse long gone, he took them both on a frenzied give and take.

He pulled her legs over his hips, opened her wider, drove in deeper. His shaft hit the spot inside her slick walls that sent her crashing headfirst into another orgasm before the last one was over. Muscles with vise-like strength gripped his cock and held him tight. Buried to the hilt he had no choice but to follow her over the edge.

Fiery bursts of cum spilled from his body, took his breath with each spurt. Three, four, five times—his balls squeezed and sent his seed into the heart of El. On the last surge Brogan collapsed, managing to fall to the side and not crush her under his weight. With the little energy he had left, he wrapped his arm around her back and rolled them, his cock still buried deep inside her body.

Her toes were numb—her fingers too. In fact her whole body was numb and except for the fire dragging in and out of her lungs, El couldn't feel a thing. Last thing she remembered was going up in flames. Spontaneous combustion. Every time Brogan made her come it was more intense, took longer to stop and far more time to return to reality.

The man was a pleasure machine. Each stroke, every brush of his fingers or lips sent her careening into bliss. She'd never lost control the way she did with him. She didn't lose it exactly, more like handed it over for him to do whatever he wanted. Not that she would complain anytime soon. Oh no, not one word of complaint would leave her lips.

Sweat clung to her skin, tacky and warm. The moisture between her legs resembled a hot bath and Brogan's hard cock, still clamped within her pussy walls, throbbed. Little sparks of pleasure shot into her clit with each beat. Renewed arousal simmered and stirred, built in a slow, steady warmth that centered in the pit of her tummy.

Like a cat, El rubbed her face on the hard muscles of his chest. The small bud of his nipple peaked against her cheek and she turned to lick it, curled her tongue around the tip and sucked until it puckered tighter. His chest rumbled, the growl vibrating along her jaw. She gave his other nipple attention, used her fingers and nails on the one still wet from her mouth.

He stirred under her and she pinched one peak between finger and thumb while trapping the other in her teeth. Brogan bucked beneath her and his cock twitched, bumping her G-spot. Sensation burst out, making her clit pound and her pussy weep. She rotated her hips, moving up and down his erection. The pool of warmth in her belly boiled and she lifted to get more friction, deepen her lunges.

Wrapping his hands over her shoulders he pushed her up. She used her legs to lift and drop her pelvis, rolling and twisting her hips for added stimulation. Liquid flowed from her. The combination of her cream and his cum filled the air with the scent of sex.

Flesh slapped together and moans of pleasure floated around them. Their breathing grew harsh, rasped in and out as they climbed toward another peak. His fingers dug into her hips, guiding her movements, urging her to go faster. Thrusting up, he drove himself deeper on each of her down strokes.

She lost the rhythm and her balance but he held them in position, drilling her with his cock. Unrelentingly he drove them both, taking them up and over with devastating speed. Muscles lax, she fell on top of him and waited for him to stop but he continued to pump into her, building another orgasm from the ashes of the last.

A growl pierced the air. For a second she thought he'd shifted to coyote but he remained human. In a move too quick to register he changed their position until she was on her hands and knees.

Slamming forward hard, he entered her from behind. Each thrust sent him deeper and her arousal higher. With ease he had her teetering on the edge, ready to fly off. His hands cupped her breasts, his chest flush along her spine and still he powered into her. Her legs shook, from weakness or desire it didn't matter.

Being taken with a greed that bordered on savage should have been frightening, but instead of being scared she felt safe, protected, cherished. Surrounded by Brogan, she let go and gave herself over to his need. He licked her shoulder, nipped at her nape and kissed her sweat-slicked back, his mouth was as devastating to her senses as his cock.

She arched her back, pushed her hips out to take more of him. With each slide over her G-spot he pulled on her nipples and the combined sensations thrilled her, made her shake with lust. Arms braced on the headboard, she met each forward thrust. Head thrown back, she shoved backward each time he drove into her. His balls slapped her clit and she erupted.

Hot lava filled her pussy and sent her clit into spasms that bordered on pain. Every part of her electrified with the molten heat they generated. Curled over her, Brogan sank his teeth into her neck. There was no pain. The sensation at her throat was as intense as the one in her crotch and she exploded in another orgasm.

They collapsed together, legs and arms tangled. He reached for her hands, loosened her grip on the headboard and entwined their fingers. His harsh breath warmed her ear, sent tingles of delight skittering down her back. Her body lay boneless beneath him with barely the energy to breathe and yet he managed to pull desire from the depths of her soul.

He licked at her neck, little laps of his wet tongue. The spot was tender beneath his ministrations at first. With each pass the soreness lessened and El relaxed and sighed into the bedding. Brogan continued to nuzzle at her neck, calming her body and clearing her mind.

He'd bitten her.

With no warning he'd plunged his teeth into her. It hadn't hurt. If anything it had been one of the most pleasurable experiences she'd ever had. Did this mean she could shift now?

She lay still, catalogued each part of her body, tried to find any difference. Other than complete satiation she couldn't find any abnormality, any sign her body had been altered.

"El? Are you okay?" His breath puffed in her ear, fanned over her face.

"You bit me," she murmured.

"I know. I didn't mean to, it just happened. Did I hurt you?" He squeezed her fingers and rolled to his side.

"No. It didn't hurt." He snaked an arm around her stomach, pulling her back to his front, spoon fashion.

"I'm sorry. I did it on instinct. By the time I thought about it I'd already sunk my fangs into you. There was no stopping." He drew circles over her stomach with a finger.

"Am I turned now? Can I change form?" A shudder of fear at the unknown flowed through her.

"I think so, I'm not sure. I've never done this before, remember? I just know what I've been told." Pulling her hair aside, he kissed the spot where his teeth had pierced her skin.

El snuggled farther into his embrace. Her eyes grew heavy with the need for rest after their strenuous physical activity. Their heart rates had slowed, their breathing eased and cuddled against his large body she lost the will to stay awake.

9

———

Brogan watched El as she talked with Rowan, their heads bent close together. The serious looks on their faces told him not to interrupt. Instead he took his time to absorb every detail of his mate as she focused intently on what Rowan was saying. He knew she had questions, she'd asked him a few earlier.

When he'd woken with El in his arms, their bodies flush together and covered with the smell of sex, he'd known all was right with his world. His fear of hurting her had eased with their mating. She matched his needs with demands of her own. Life together would be a ride worth taking.

Bringing up the fact he'd neglected to use any form of protection had turned out better than he'd hoped. She'd assured him she was committed to staying and while unplanned, a pregnancy wouldn't be a bad thing. He wondered what she'd say when she found out she was already pregnant.

It didn't matter whether it was the right time to conceive or not, their mating released hormones that brought on ovulation. One more part of being turned he hadn't mentioned. He couldn't bring himself to feel guilty, the image of a very pregnant El had fused itself to his mind and he couldn't shake it. She would be beautiful full with child. His child.

He left the room with a smile that wouldn't quit and returned to his study where he waited to hear from the Council. The storm had passed hours ago and the phone lines were back on so he expected to hear from William soon. It would all depend on how quickly Marcus had informed the Council of his supposed wrongdoing.

Quinn had questioned the wisdom of waiting for the summons and suggested contacting the Council first but Brogan thought that would make him look guilty of whatever charge Marcus brought against him. The thrill of going up against his enemy raced through his veins. It had been a while since they'd bumped heads.

Heading for the window, he stared out at the snow-covered yard. Six o'clock at night and it was darker than midnight. The storm may have passed but the remaining clouds blocked out what was left of the day. He wouldn't be fronting the Council tonight. They'd have to wait for morning, if they called him in at all.

It was taking too long for them to contact him. Something was up and Brogan could only wonder what went through the mind of a man bent on getting even for an injustice that never happened. Marcus had accused him and Quinn of numerous things, the least of which being they'd stolen leadership of the pack from him.

Sovereign wasn't something one could take. It was given by the Council in accordance with the laws that governed their pack. He hadn't even wanted it at first, knew a lot of their people looked down at him because his mother was non-blood. His father might have been able to trace his lineage back to the first full-bloods to populate the area but that made no difference to those prejudiced against anyone without pure coyote parents.

"I'm worried they haven't called yet," Quinn spoke behind him.

Brogan turned to face him, leaned back on the windowsill.

"Me too. Marcus is up to something. The niggle in my gut tells me it's not going to be good. We need to be ready for anything."

"I'm worried he'll attack you this time. He wants sovereign, so getting to you would be the ultimate goal for him," Quinn reasoned.

"Well we can't do anything until the Council calls, if they call."

As if on cue, a shrill ring cut off Quinn's reply.

Brogan pushed off the window and walked the ten feet to his desk. The phone rang once more before he snatched it up.

"Hello."

"Brogan, this is William. I won't bother with the pleasantries. We'd like you and your regal to front the Council and explain some things that have been brought to our attention." Always one for getting straight to the point, William wasted no time now.

"Sure, we'll be there in the morning," he said.

"We'd like you to come into town now."

"No. The snow is still thick on the ground and I'm not risking the drive in when it's already dark. We'll be there at nine in the morning." He wouldn't budge on this. Driving in these conditions with full visibility would be bad enough. He wasn't about to do it at night.

"Fine. We'll be waiting."

The phone clicked in his ear. He placed it back on the desk and faced Quinn. "They wanted us to come in now."

"I heard. Marcus is definitely up to something if he's got them convinced they need to see you this late." Quinn sat in the chair in front of the desk, legs stretched out.

"We knew he'd exaggerate, if not outright lie about what happened. Obviously he's spun a mighty tall yarn." Brogan skirted the desk and took his own chair. "And William asked for you to attend."

"As regal, I would be there anyway."

"Yes, but he said *you and your regal*, which for me means Marcus has concocted some tale where we're both involved." He steepled his fingers beneath his chin and thought about what William asking for the regal to attend meant.

"I guess me burying the body would have them asking to see me," Quinn conceded.

"Probably. We'll find out tomorrow."

"Was that the Council?" Rowan asked from the doorway.

"Yes, we've been summoned for tomorrow morning."

"Did they say what Marcus accused you of this time?" Rowan's frustration at Marcus and his continued campaign to have Brogan removed as sovereign rang in her voice.

"No. William didn't even mention him, just asked that my regal and I front the Council." He shrugged.

"Great. So you can't even go in there prepared. Ring them back and ask what's going on," she ordered.

Quinn chuckled and Brogan lifted an eyebrow in question.

Rowan's face flushed red but she didn't back down. "You might be sovereign, Brogan, but I'm royal and that gives me just as much right to be informed by the Council as it does for them to summon you both."

"Rowan, I know you see your position as important and it is. You're the heart of our people but when it comes to things like this the Council still functions in the old ways. Women aren't included in the management of the pack." Brogan hated to remind her of the narrow mindset of their people. He didn't much care for the reminder himself.

"Fine." She turned on her heel and left.

Brilliant. Now he had to worry about his sister's nose being out of joint.

Quinn rose from his chair. "I'll go unruffle some feathers, shall I?"

He laughed. "Yes, that would be good. I know your kind of unruffling has her in a daze for hours."

Quinn shot him a lecherous grin. "Duty calls and I must do my part as regal." He bowed low before they both burst into laughter.

With Quinn gone he finished up some paperwork. El found him as he filed the last sheets away.

"Are you busy?"

"Never too busy for you." He got up and came around the desk to meet her.

"Can we talk?"

"Sure, what's on your mind?" He hoped she wasn't upset with him over Rowan's snit.

"You turned me, right?"

He nodded.

"How do I change?"

Brogan sucked in a breath. She wanted to shift? He'd told her earlier there was no rush and she'd agreed to learn all she could before trying for the first time but she'd obviously changed her mind in the last few hours.

"Now?"

"Yes, I know I said I'd wait but I want to feel what it's like and I think it might help me to understand the new senses I've developed in the last few hours." She sniffed the air. "I didn't need to look for you with my eyes, I just followed my nose."

Ah, the increased sense of smell. Being able to smell him clearly would be a bit weird for her.

"What else have you noticed?"

"I think my vision is sharper but I'm not one hundred percent sure of that, and my hearing is better. I could hear you on the phone earlier and when you were talking with Rowan. I could have been in the room with you it was that clear."

"Those are the most prominent improvements you'll have, but there are a few others. For instance you'll have extreme sexual arousal during your time of heat." It was a shame she wouldn't be in heat for a few months, he was looking forward to the experience.

"Extreme? More than what I have been since I got here?" Her astonished tone made him laugh.

"Oh, yeah. You won't be able to go more than a couple of hours without mating." He stopped laughing when her eyes almost bugged out of her head and her mouth fell open. "It'll be fine, El. You won't ovulate like a human, it's not as frequent."

She snapped her jaw closed. "Still...*hours?*"

"Let's worry about that another time." Taking her hand he led her from the room.

"Where are we going?"

"Upstairs. You'll want the privacy of our room to shift."

"Isn't your office private enough?"

"El, you'll need to get naked to change, remember?"

She stumbled beside him and he cupped her elbow to steady her.

"Um, no. I forgot that part. I guess it wouldn't be nice for Rowan or Quinn to walk in on us."

"You'll learn that getting naked in front of other shifters is a natural and frequent thing. No one will be looking at you." He would, but that was fine since she was his to look at.

"I doubt I'll ever be able to get naked and shift in front of anyone," she mumbled under her breath.

He smiled as he led her upstairs to their room. Funny how it had changed to theirs the second he'd taken her. Whether she noticed him calling it theirs or chose to ignore it he didn't care. She'd soon learn that when coyotes mated, they shared everything.

El followed Brogan into his bedroom. The first thing she noticed was all her things had been moved in there. And second, he was already taking off his clothes. Staring slack-jawed, she watched the magnificent specimen he revealed inch by inch.

When he finished undressing he closed the distance between them and grabbed the hem of her shirt.

"Come on, let's get naked," he teased.

She let him strip the top over her head. When he went for the snap on her jeans she reached for his cock. Satin on steel, the hard length pulsed against her fingers. She tightened her grip, stroked down to the base and back to the head where a drop of cum beaded on the tip.

"El...keep that up and I won't be teaching you how to shift," he growled as she repeated the movement.

Smiling, she looked at him from under her lashes and used a seductive tone of voice. "Would that be so bad? We could get back to the shifting thing after we—"

She didn't get to finish. Her jeans were shoved down her legs as he put a foot on the bunched up denim and lifted her off her feet. The fabric slipped off, leaving her in her panties and socks. Not exactly a sexy look but Brogan didn't seem to care. He had her pinned to the bed with his body before she could take a breath. His mouth crushed hers as his tongue invaded and conquered any objection she might have. He stole her breath, gave her his and drew her down a path of carnal needs and wants she gladly followed him.

Their hips thrust up and down, grinding their heated flesh together. The silk barrier of her panties was no match for the fire burning between them. He reached down, grabbed the elastic edges and ripped the flimsy covering from her body.

El gasped as a growl issued from Brogan's throat. He pushed a knee between hers, shoved her legs apart to make room for his hips. His mouth ate at hers and his tongue thrust deep, laying claim to all that he touched. All thought fled when he gripped her thighs and pushed them wider and probed the slick channel at her core.

One thrust and he drove himself deep, impaling her on his throbbing flesh. His balls pulsed against her ass and the stinging hot globes branded her skin. Brogan ripped their mouths apart, dragged in a breath and stared at her from lust-filled eyes. His dilated pupils were rimmed with molten gold.

"You burn my cock with your pussy. You're so tight and hot I lose myself inside you every time."

He jerked back, slammed forward, withdrew again until the head of his cock rested at her opening.

"I want this to last forever but each time my cock touches your wet folds I'm lost in the rush." He slid in, slow and steady until pelvis met pelvis.

Matching moans of pleasure spilled past their lips. With frustrating slowness he continued to fill her over and over with deep, smooth strokes. Each lunge sent her higher but not enough to push her over the edge she frantically gripped at. Desperate nails clawed at his back, tried to urge him faster.

Lifting her legs, El curled them around his hips and dug her heels into the back of his thighs. She arched into him, used her legs to pull him down, force him deeper. Harder. Faster. She tilted her head, her mouth grazed his neck and she bit down on the corded muscle under her lips.

He reared back, sent his cock driving into her, hitting her G-spot and clit. The results were explosive. The orgasm rolled through her, tossed her into a kaleidoscope of color and light before scattering her to the ends of the earth.

Her pussy filled with Brogan's seed. Hot bursts slashed into her as he pounded his length in and out. She licked his neck, the metallic taste of blood flowed across her tongue. Heavy lids lifted and she stared at where she'd bitten him. Shocked at her actions, she gasped. "Oh, God!"

"It's okay, El. Lick the broken skin, your saliva will help it heal," he panted.

"But…"

"Shh. I'm fine, it didn't hurt, doesn't hurt. It's what we do when we mate, a natural part of the process." Each word exploded on a puff of air as he struggled to catch his breath.

Crushed beneath Brogan's dead weight and the wound she'd inflicted staring her in the face, El fought back tears and lost. Emotions tumbled inside her, tangled up and flowed over. A sob filled her chest, shook her shoulders and slipped past her throat.

"El?" Brogan rolled them to the side. "Baby, what's wrong?" He brushed the hair from her face, the tears from her lashes.

"I…I…" She hiccupped.

"Are you hurt?"

She shook her head.

"Then what is it? Was it something I did?"

Another shake of her head.

"Baby, you're killing me here. Tell me what's wrong."

"I…bit you," she cried.

"Ah, baby, it's okay. Honest. I told you, it's normal. Please, stop crying," he pleaded.

She sniffed and buried her head into his chest. The storm of emotions receded, bringing relief from the crying she couldn't begin to explain. It wasn't just the bite. Over the last forty-eight hours so much had happened. She'd flown halfway around the world, reunited with a dear friend she'd missed terribly, almost froze to death through her own stupidity and met a man who rocked the world she lived in.

She'd made a life changing decision, one that turned her life upside down and inside out while altering her physically as well as emotionally and leaving her struggling to find her feet in a world she didn't understand. She clung to the one lifeline, the one constant, in a world that had spun out of control.

Brogan.

10

Morning arrived cold and sunny. It was just past dawn and Brogan lay awake, watching El sleep. When she'd finally settled down after her crying jag he'd gotten to the heart of the issue. There wasn't only one. There were many.

With all the things that had happened since her arrival he wasn't surprised she'd had a meltdown. She deserved one. They'd talked for hours. He'd explained some of the coyote law and things she could expect now that she was a shifter. She'd asked about his life and he'd done the same. There wasn't much left to discover about each other.

Now he had to get through this morning's meeting with the Council. Marcus had been a thorn in his side for so long Brogan wasn't sure what he'd do without him around to stir up trouble. They'd soon find out because he had every intention of this being the last time Marcus caused anyone problems.

He hated to leave the bed and El but it was past time to get up. It would take an hour by road to get into town. Over land in coyote form would be less than half that but arriving naked wouldn't be a good start to the meeting.

El didn't stir when he slipped from the bed and tucked the covers around her. Even covered, the sight of her had his libido soaring. It didn't help to have her scent all over him or the smell of sex filling the room. His cock twitched and he shook his head at the damn thing. It had a mind of its own and all it wanted was El.

It looked as if he'd be suffering through another cold shower. He swore under his breath. Cold showers and holding back his wild impulses were becoming a regular thing. Something he'd have to fix when he got the problem of Marcus out of the way.

He left the door to the bathroom open. He wanted El to know where he was if she woke to find him gone. Soap in hand, he made quick work of scrubbing down and rinsing. A squirt of shampoo later he was clean from head to toe and all the bits in between. Still sporting a semi-erection, he shut the water off and stepped out.

Peeking through the door, he saw El slept. She was curled on her side facing him and he soaked up the thrill of having her in his bed.

The towel was rough against his skin and he dragged it over his body in quick swipes, doing a rush job of drying off. Satisfied, he made his way back to the bed.

"El, baby." Hand on her shoulder, he gave her a nudge. "Come on sleepy-head, time to rise and shine."

She murmured something sounding suspiciously like a swear word and he chuckled. Not a morning person.

"Come on, El." He yanked the blanket off her. "I've got to go soon and I want to eat breakfast with you before I leave."

"Go away," she murmured as she curled up tighter.

She looked like a child. Petite as she was, the position made her look smaller, more vulnerable. He didn't like the idea of her being exposed. This afternoon he'd teach her to protect herself. Not that she'd need to since he wasn't planning on letting her out of his sight when he returned from town.

He reached down and scooped her into his arms, her squeal of surprise delighting him.

"Time for sleeping beauty to get in the shower," he said.

"No! Coffee! Need coffee." She struggled in his grip but she was no match for his size or strength.

With one hand he turned the water on and stepped beneath the spray. She sputtered and protested but it was too late. They were both drenched.

"Jeez, Brogan," she gurgled. "If this is how you plan to wake me every morning I might re-think staying."

His arms tightened around her and bands of steel constricted his heart. She'd leave him? His heart stopped for several beats, then it took off at an alarming pace, pounding in his head and ears. Fear sliced into his soul before common sense took hold and he realized she was joking.

"You'll never leave," he breathed. "If you did I'd hunt you down and bring you back. You're mine." His final words erupted on a growl.

"What?" She turned her face to his.

"You're never leaving."

"No, I'll never leave." She placed her hands on either side of his face, pulled him closer. "I couldn't leave you if the devil himself tried to chase me away."

El kissed him. Not with the passion they'd burned with before but tenderness he'd never experienced from a woman. She poured what he hoped was her soul into that one locking of lips. Gently, he plied her mouth open, dipped inside and handed over everything he was in return.

By the time they made it out of the shower, Brogan had ten minutes to gulp down the bacon and eggs Rowan had made. At the dining table they rarely used, he talked with Quinn about the meeting and reminded both Rowan and El to stay inside. His gut was telling him not to leave the house but as sovereign he had no choice. He pushed back from the table and picked up his plate.

"Leave that. You and Quinn get going. The quicker you get there the quicker you can sort it out and come home," Rowan said.

"Okay." He put the plate back down. "Remember what I said. We have no idea what Marcus is up to so don't leave the house, not even to go on the front steps." He threw El a pointed look. "Either of you."

He headed for the door, his mind already switching gears to what lay ahead.

"Ahem," Rowan cleared her throat in an exaggerated fashion. "Aren't you forgetting something, Quinn?"

Brogan stopped and turned to see what his sister was talking about. Quinn, who'd been a step behind him, hightailed it across the room to Rowan and bent over to kiss her goodbye. With a sheepish grin on his face, he apologized before scuttling back to Brogan.

Because El hadn't made a point of asking or even commenting, he made sure she knew how much he'd miss her while he was gone. Striding over, he pulled her from her seat and plastered his mouth to hers. When he came up for air they were both breathless and her eyes held that dreamy look he was coming to love.

The trouble was he now sported a hard-on in his jeans. Good thing they had an hour before they hit Whispering Springs.

Brogan's hands were wrapped around the leather steering wheel in a white-knuckled grip. The mountain road was treacherous at the best of times but after a snowfall it turned deadly. With care, he kept the speed as fast as possible without risking losing control on the slippery surface. Each mile he put between him and El made his gut tighten.

It was more than the need to be with his mate. All his coyote instincts were screaming and his beast pulled at its restraints. The hair on his nape stood on end, his heart pounded as if he'd run ten miles and his palms, slick with sweat, slid on the wheel. Disaster loomed up ahead but what it could be eluded him.

On the approach to town the road was littered with branches and snowdrifts from the plows that would have been through first thing this morning. No large trees had fallen that he'd seen and he hoped the destruction was minimal everywhere. Some pack members had suffered considerable damage in the last blizzard but he didn't think yesterday's had been as bad.

They hit the end of Spring Road and were brought to a standstill.

Traffic backed up the whole length as far as the eye could see. Four-wheel drives lined the street bumper to bumper. More off-road vehicles filled the parking spots along the side. Either everyone in Whispering Springs had come to town for supplies to make repairs or word had spread about the sovereign being summoned.

Quinn whistled low, the sound piercing in the cab of the truck. "Looks like we've got an audience."

"It'll take hours to drive through this lot." Making a snap decision, Brogan spun the wheel and made a u-turn. He turned onto School Road and parked in front of the two-story high school building.

"I guess we're walking," Quinn said as he undid his seatbelt and opened the door.

"Yep, we'll get there a hell of a lot faster. Besides, being seen in the open will give the impression I've got nothing to hide, which I don't." Brogan got out and walked around the hood to the curb. He pushed the lock button on his key as he met Quinn on the path.

The rumble of a diesel engine vibrated the ground beneath their feet. Pivoting, he saw Steven McKenna pull the town's big snow plow onto the street. Huge wheels rolled over tarmac and brought the machine closer. Steve had the plow scoop up, there was no snow on the road now. The main streets would have been plowed first thing and there hadn't been a drop of snow since the evening before.

Parking behind Brogan's truck, the big engine rattled and shook the hunk of metal in its final breath of life as Steve cut the power. The scent of diesel hung heavy in the air, coating Brogan's nose and throat.

Steve flung the heavy door open and jumped down from the cab.

"Hey, Brogan, Quinn." Steve nodded at them as he strode around to where they waited on the footpath. He slapped Brogan on the back in greeting. "So I hear you're forcing humans to turn now."

About to take a step, Brogan faltered and turned to look at his friend and fellow shifter with his mouth hanging open.

"Well, now we know what kind of shit Marcus is spreading," Quinn said.

Steve's smile spread from ear to ear. "And don't forget he's going around killing off the naturals in some underhanded attempt to rule the coyote world." Steve laughed.

Brogan didn't see the funny side. "What other venom is he spewing?"

"What? That's not enough?" Steve continued to chuckle. "He claims to have seen you attack a natural to impress some human woman who you then forced to turn into a shifter. Just the usual bull-shit that spills every time Marcus opens his mouth."

"You obviously aren't buying into it. What's the rest of the pack saying?" Quinn asked.

Steve was the closest thing to a gossip columnist the pack had. He outdid the old biddies with his knowledge of what went on in and around Whispering Springs. If anyone could get Brogan the information he needed, it was Steve.

"Most are inclined to think it's bullshit but it's the human in the equation that has everyone curious. The entire pack knows a human arrived at your place the other day." Steve aimed a questioning look at Brogan.

Brogan knew his friend didn't really think he'd force the change on El. His interest was more in El herself. It wasn't often a human came through town, never mind a single female. A bolt of jealousy and possessiveness speared his gut.

"Mine," he growled, the beast rearing its head in defense of its mate.

Hands up, Steve took a step back. "Whoa! Stand down, Brogan. I'm not planning on poaching."

He shook himself, tried to remember this was his childhood friend who would never stab him in the back.

"Sorry. I'm still coming to grips with everything."

"No worries. So you found your mate then." It was a statement, not a question.

"Yes, El's the woman Rowan lived with in Australia for all those years. She's here for the wedding."

Quinn laughed. "And she'll be staying for one of her own."

Steve stuck out his hand. "Congratulations! For what it's worth, I think this may cement your standing as sovereign. Producing the next generation will put you in good stead with the Council."

Brogan shook the offered hand. "Thanks. After this latest Marcus-emitted bullshit is cleared up why don't you come out to the house and meet her?"

"I'd love to, but I've got a date." Steve waggled his eyebrows.

"Anyone we know?" Quinn asked.

"Nah, she's from the city, visiting over in Mountain Pass. Friend of a friend kind of thing." He shrugged. "Doubt anything will come of it. Come on, let's get to this shindig and see what happens."

They headed in the direction of Spring Street. Brogan nodded hello to those they passed. He even stopped to talk to a few but he tried to make the stops short. That niggling sensation in his gut was getting bigger. It was more like a nudge now. Two blocks from the community center he remembered what he'd wanted to ask Steve.

"Hey, Steve, do you know what Marcus is up to? Other than spreading garbage around."

"Nothing I would consider unusual. I know he's been in town less and less over the last few weeks. Could be the weather, though. We've had some mean storms rolling in recently." Steve turned to look at him. "Why? Got something you want me to look at?"

"No. Nothing I can put a finger on. Just keep your eyes and ears open for me."

"Sure. If I see or hear anything, I'll let you know."

No one spoke again until they reached the community center where Steve bade them farewell to go get himself some breakfast at The Den Café. Brogan and Quinn made their way to the closed-door meeting and the Council members waiting for them.

11

El came downstairs after taking up Brogan's clean laundry. Not even one day as his mate and already waiting on him hand and foot. Shaking her head, she smiled. She wasn't really waiting on him but helping Rowan out. After they'd cleared away the breakfast dishes Rowan had started in on the dirty clothes.

El had never seen a mountain of laundry before. The pile started on the floor and stood higher than her waist. Load after load went from washer to dryer. The process took half the morning but there was finally nothing left to wash. Just pile after pile of folded clothes to be put away.

Rowan was upstairs still and El decided to get a start on dinner. She could throw a pot of spaghetti sauce on to simmer and then they'd just have to put the pasta in to boil when they were ready to eat. It also freed up the rest of the day for her and Rowan to talk. Brogan hadn't been much help with learning to shift. His less than helpful instructions were "Just think about your inner coyote and it'll happen."

How was she supposed to think of her inner coyote when she'd never had one? He'd promised to help her later but she wanted to try before he got home. If she could manage the change with Rowan's help she could surprise him when he got here and maybe they could go for a run in the woods. The idea of running wild in the forest with Brogan at her side sent a shiver down her spine and warmth through her chest.

Another question she wanted to ask Rowan was whether or not they mated in coyote form. El wasn't sure she was ready for that if they did, but she needed to know everything about living as a shapeshifter. Brogan had said her cycle would be different too. Did that mean pregnancy would also be different?

Oh God. Would she give birth to a pup? Or worse! A litter of puppies?

Shuddering at the mental image, she searched the pantry for ingredients. Her great grandmother's sauce recipe had been passed down through the females of her family, like a rite of passage.

Rowan burst through the door. "Hey, what are you doing?"

"Making spaghetti sauce for dinner."

"Grandma's sauce?" Rowan licked her lips.

"Yep."

"Oh God." She dropped on a stool at the island counter. "I haven't indulged in that particular brand of heaven since I left Australia."

"I promise to make enough for you to freeze some for another night." El laughed. Every time she made enough for more than one meal, Rowan managed to empty the saucepan, even going as far as trying to lick the bottom of the pot.

"You won't have to. Now that you're mated with Brogan you can make it fresh for me whenever I want it." Rowan sat with a smug look on her face.

"I should teach you to make it yourself," El said, knowing it would never happen. They'd shared a house for nearly three years and she hadn't managed it.

"That would spoil the 'handed-down-through-the-family' feel to it."

Rowan was right. It wouldn't be the same without a Crawford woman stirring the pot.

"Can I ask you something, El?"

"Sure."

"Did Brogan turn you?"

Her gaze jerked up to meet Rowan's. "Why?"

"Well, there's a change in your scent that you might not be aware of."

"What sort of change?"

"Um, I'm not sure I should be the one telling you this. Just answer my question. Did Brogan turn you?"

"Yes."

"Did he explain what happens when a female human is turned?"

"About the increased sex drive when I'm in heat?"

"No. Well, yes, there is that, but there's something else I'm sure my brother conveniently forgot to tell you." Rowan chewed her lip.

"What? We talked last night about a lot of things so maybe he did tell me."

"When a female human is turned during mating, the hormones and chemicals released into her system by the act of joining and by the bite increase the chances of getting pregnant."

"Oh, that's okay. We talked about an unplanned pregnancy. It's not the right time of the month for me, Rowan so I'm not worried about it. And truthfully if it happened I wouldn't be upset."

"Maybe I didn't say that right. El, the chance of you getting pregnant is very high. As I said the hormones released push your system, kind of prodding it so that you are ready to conceive," Rowan explained.

"Okay." El wasn't worried about getting pregnant. It was extremely unlikely, she was at the very beginning of her cycle and she'd always been as regular as clockwork.

"El?"

Rowan waited until she looked up.

"What?"

"You're pregnant."

El burst out laughing. She couldn't be pregnant. Well, she could but it wasn't likely and even if she was, a doctor couldn't tell yet. God, an egg wouldn't have even made it to her uterus yet.

When Rowan didn't laugh and there was no hint of a smile on her lips, El sobered. "But…"

"What Brogan forgot to mention, and I've botched up completely explaining, is the act of turning a human female forces her system into overdrive and stimulates her ovaries making them produce eggs. I've never known any woman who hasn't conceived when being turned."

Rowan got up, came around the island and wrapped her arm around El's shoulders.

"Last night your scent was different but I put it down to mating with Brogan. This morning when you came down for breakfast I thought I could smell the change again. After spending all morning together I know what I smell, you're definitely pregnant."

"Pregnant?" El's hand covered her lower stomach. Surely she would know if she'd conceived a child? Wouldn't she feel it?

"I didn't tell you when you first got here because we've kept it just between Quinn, me and Brogan but I'm two months pregnant. I haven't been to town in all that time because the minute I step out on one of those streets the whole shifter community will know. We want to wait until after the wedding to tell people."

El absorbed what Rowan said. Inside both of them grew new life. Their children would be almost the same age. They could grow up together. Cousins. A little numb from what she'd learned, she still couldn't stop the thrill that started to grow inside her heart.

She'd grow up an only child of only children and her parents had been older so El had lost them both early. Both had died within weeks of each other when El was twenty.

The idea of being part of a family again. Of her child having a cousin to play with on a daily basis sent a surge of pleasure through her. She'd be experiencing all the joys of having her first child with her best friend. It was mindboggling.

"I should say congratulations," El uttered.

A child.

Brogan's child.

"El, you're looking a bit pale, maybe we should sit down for a minute." Rowan's concern touched a soft spot in El and tears sprang to her eyes.

She reached her arms around her best friend, pulling her close for a hug. Rowan hugged her back and they stood in the bright kitchen and cried. Not sad tears but happy, emotional tears.

When they stopped, they both dried their eyes and finished putting the ingredients for the sauce together in silence, each lost in thought. After mulling over everything, El was more determined to learn how to shift before Brogan got home. She wanted to surprise him with both the ability to change and her pregnancy.

He probably already knew she was pregnant but she wanted to tell him. And then she wanted to show him.

"Teach me to shift."

"What?"

"I haven't changed yet and Brogan wasn't very helpful when I asked him how to do it. I want to be able to shift before he comes home. I want to surprise him and I'm sure he already knows he got me pregnant."

Rowan smiled. "Oh, yeah, he'd know."

"So will you help me?"

"Of course. Let's get this all cleared away and we can get started."

Together they put the last of the ingredients into the pan and put it on to simmer. They cleared away the garbage and stacked the dirty dishes in the dishwasher. When the last counter was wiped and the kitchen was filled with the smell of tomato and spices, they made their way into the lounge room to discuss the fine art of shifting.

"Brogan said he thinks about his inner coyote and he shifts but I've never had a coyote so how can I think of it?"

"Until I came home last year, I hadn't shifted since before I left. I couldn't remember what my coyote looked like so I just pictured Quinn and Brogan. It might be harder for you. I've only ever been with one turned human for their first time and that was over ten years ago. But Gordie grew up in the pack so that wouldn't really help anyway."

Rowan walked over to the fireplace, picked up a couple of photo frames and made her way back to El.

"Here, if we put these pictures of Brogan in front of you they might help. Sit on the floor next to the coffee table, that way you won't have to drop down as you change."

"Should I take my clothes off?" El asked.

"Oh yeah, sorry. Do you want me to close the curtains?"

"Would you mind?" El wasn't concerned with Rowan seeing her naked but didn't want to give anyone else coming around a free show.

Going to each of the windows, Rowan pulled the curtains closed. Returning to El, she began removing her clothes.

"Why are you taking your clothes off?"

"I thought you might be more comfortable if we did it together. It might help you to shift if I'm doing it too," Rowan said.

"Thank you," El choked out. Her eyes stung with the emotions bubbling inside her. "Sorry, I'm turning into an emotional wreck."

Laughing, Rowan said, "Get used to it. I cry at the drop of a leaf these days. Everything I've read about being pregnant says it's normal and part of the joy of carrying a new life."

"I can't believe the things I've done since getting here. There's been a whole load of firsts for me in the last few days," El sniffled.

"You don't regret coming, do you?"

They were both naked now.

"No. I don't regret anything, least of all coming to see you."

Rowan sat on the floor and El followed. Sitting next to each other with the photos of Brogan in coyote form in front of them, El looked at the beautiful animal and tried to picture herself as one. Her muscles stretched, pulled and her skin tightened but nothing else happened. She closed her eyes and concentrated.

She pulled her bottom lip between her teeth and bit into the soft flesh. The sharp sting sucked the breath from her lungs as she gasped in pain.

"What? Are you all right?" Rowan asked.

Rowan gasped when El opened her mouth to answer.

"Your teeth have changed and I think you've bitten your lip," she said. Reaching over with a tissue she'd grabbed from the table, Rowan dabbed gently on the wound.

El ran her tongue over canine teeth, the long sharp fangs strange to touch. A wicked grin split her mouth.

"I did it! I changed!"

"Not quite." Rowan chuckled.

"Well sure, but it's a start. Don't take my victory from me." She pouted.

"Okay, let's try again. Did you feel anything else changing?"

"Yes, my muscles and skin pulled tight first and then my teeth changed."

"Your eyes have changed color too. They're not as light. The blue has gone a couple of shades darker."

"Really? I want to see them, but I want to try again first."

She closed her eyes, thought about the changes she'd managed so far and the next thing she knew she was looking at things from a different angle. The smell of the room filled her nose and made her sneeze. She sniffed the air. A bark next to her had her turning to Rowan.

Damn!

They'd done it. Rowan's coyote form wasn't as big as Brogan's and her coloring not as light, she had white mixed in with dark gray. Looking down at her paws, El tried to decide if she liked the color of her coat.

Rowan's ears twitched and she looked toward the door. El titled her head, tried to hear what had drawn her friend's attention. It took less than a second for Rowan to shift back to human.

"Change back, El," she commanded as she dragged her clothes on. "Quick, change back. Get dressed."

Panic seized her. She sat frozen in coyote form as Rowan pulled the last of her clothes on and ran from the room. Shattering glass and timber echoed through the house and El stood on two legs in human form without knowing how she'd done it. Scrabbling into her clothes she heard Rowan scream and footsteps pounded down the hall.

She'd just gotten her sweater on when a man dressed in black burst into the room and charged toward her. The scream caught in her throat as he tackled her to the floor. She kicked out, tried to free herself from his grasp but he pinned her to the ground with his weight. He outweighed her by at least a hundred pounds.

His forearm pressed into her throat, cutting off her air. Clawing at his arm with her hands, she couldn't get a hold of the slick, skin-like black clothing. Her heart pounded in her ears, her lungs burned with the need for air and stars exploded across her vision. The last thing El heard before everything went black was his malicious laughter.

12

———————

Brogan paced the meeting room. The seven other members of the pack sat in silence. No one had spoken a word since he and Quinn had arrived. William was the one to break the quiet.

"There's no point getting agitated, Sovereign. Marcus should be here soon."

Brogan glared at him without breaking stride. Every instinct he had screamed at him to return to El. Something wasn't right. Marcus took every opportunity to undermine his leadership with the eagerness of a teenager getting his first taste of pussy. So where the hell was he?

Something was definitely wrong.

"Five more minutes and we're leaving," he growled.

He had to get back to El. He'd left her at the house with Rowan. She should be safe and the time together would be good for El, she could learn a lot from his sister but he wanted to be close by. Needed to be close to her.

There was a ruckus outside the room before the door crashed open. Expecting Marcus to have arrived Brogan turned to find Rowan, red-faced and covered in sweat. Naked as the day she was born, Rowan stood, her chest heaving for breath. Steve slipped into the room behind her.

Quinn was out of his chair, stripping off his jacket and across the room in a second. Like a gunshot, the echo of his chair hitting the floor thundered in the quiet room.

"He took her!" Rowan gasped out.

Every muscle went taut. Every nerve sprang to life and Brogan's coyote fought to be free.

"What the hell?" Quinn struggled to get Rowan covered. "Let me get my jacket on you."

"No. He took her," she repeated taking a step toward Brogan.

"When?" He didn't need to ask who, it was obvious by his conspicuous absence at this meeting he'd prompted.

Marcus.

I'll kill him!

"I don't know how long." Rowan's breathing had eased and Quinn lowered her into a chair William pulled over.

"Oh my God! You're hurt!" Quinn pulled her from the seat, took her place and cradled Rowan in his lap. "You're bleeding, Rowan." Color drained from Quinn's face.

Brogan strode over, pushed William out of the way to get to his sister. "What the hell happened, Rowan? Who hurt you?"

"It's okay." Her words were laced with exhaustion. "Just a bump."

"Like fuck it's 'just a bump.' The damn thing is bleeding down your back." Quinn's barely suppressed anger vibrated in his voice.

Brogan lifted the hair from the back of Rowan's neck and saw the trail of red running from her scalp. Examining the cut on the back of her head, he decided she'd probably need stitches.

"Get Doc," Brogan barked.

One of the Council members scuttled off to do his bidding and he turned Rowan's head gently to look at her eyes.

"How long were you out, Rowan?"

"Don't know," she murmured.

"Do you know where he took El?" Fear for El clawed at his gut and gave him a harsh tone.

"No, I lost them. They were gone when I came to. I followed their scent through the woods but he had a vehicle waiting about halfway down the drive. I just know he took the road north. He went up the mountain, not down." Her words were starting to slur and her eyelids drooped then finally closed as she used the last of her energy.

The room around them came to life with the councilmen talking over one another. Doc Munroe hustled in closely followed by two guys pushing a gurney.

"Lay her on the bed, Quinn," Gordie Munroe ordered.

Indecision flashed in Quinn's eyes. Brogan knew he'd be torn between getting Rowan the care she needed and not wanting to let her go. Brogan could relate. He'd felt the same when El had been caught in the snowstorm.

Steve stepped close beside him. "Brogan, I think I know where he's gone." He kept his voice low so only Brogan would hear.

"Where?"

"I overheard some of the old-timers at the Café. They were talking about Marcus and something he'd said. It rang some bells and with what Rowan just said about him going up the mountain, I think he's taking her to the canyon. He's luring you there."

Rowan moaned as Doc probed her head wound, diverting Brogan's attention for a minute. Moving to her side, he stood next to Quinn and waited to hear what Gordie found.

"How far along is she?" Gordie asked.

"Two months." He and Quinn spoke together.

Gordie looked at them and smiled. "I don't think there's anything to worry about but I want to do an MRI of her head and an ultrasound for the baby just to be sure. We need to get her over to the clinic."

"Go with her, Quinn. I'll take Steve and go after El," Brogan said.

Rowan's hand shot out and grabbed his forearm. Her nails, not yet fully retracted from coyote form, dug into his flesh.

"No, take Quinn. He's the best tracker in the pack." Her eyes pleaded with him. "Bring her back."

"Rowan—" Brogan began.

"Don't you dare treat me like a delicate female. I just ran all the way from the house after being bashed over the head. I think I can manage to get a couple of scans done. Gordie knows what she's doing. I couldn't be in better hands."

"She's right. We need Quinn to get us close without being heard and there are no better hands than Gordie's." Steve directed a challenging look at Gordie and she visibly bristled.

"Please, Brogan," Rowan begged.

"Brogan, we need to go get your mate now, we have no idea how long he's had her or what he's got planned," Steve said.

He squeezed his eyes closed, tried to think beyond the need to get his mate and act like sovereign. Rowan was right, she was in the best hands and they did need Quinn to find El. Opening his eyes, he looked at his regal.

"I won't pull rank, it's up to you but I will say she's right. You are the best tracker we have. Doc is more than capable of looking after Rowan and the baby until we get back and it's unlikely Marcus will try anything in town. I doubt he'd even show his face now that he's snatched El."

"Rowan, honey, are you sure?" Quinn leaned in close, brushed his lips over Rowan's.

"Yes. Go get her and this time he doesn't get away with it, Quinn."

Brogan didn't think there was any worry on that score. Marcus had finally done something he couldn't cover up. He turned to face William.

"Marcus will be exiled from the pack if he makes it out alive." As sovereign he could decree the removal of a member with the support of the Council and he had no doubt they would support him on this one.

No coyote messed with another's mate, least of all the sovereign's.

The first thing El noticed was the pain lancing her side. She was lying on hard ground, sharp jagged edges digging through her clothes into her ribs and hipbone. The second thing she reacted to was the cold. She shivered as her senses came more awake. Moaning, she tried to move her legs and couldn't. Something held them together.

Her eyes popped open, her vision unfocused at first but as it cleared she took note of her surroundings. She also took note of the fact her ankles and wrists were tied together with rope. The quiet indicated no one was near and remaining perfectly still, she concentrated on listening for any clue she wasn't alone.

Nothing.

Not even the raspy sound of breathing.

She had no idea where he'd taken her or where he'd gone. The ground around her had been cleared of snow, small mounds of white sat in front of her and it covered all the trees and shrubs in sight. A rock or stick dug into her thigh as she twisted to look behind her. The view was the same. He'd left her outside, in the forest somewhere.

Urgency grabbed hold. She needed to get away before whoever had taken her came back. El had no idea who the man was or what he wanted but the thought of him returning sent ice rushing through her veins and fear exploding in her gut. If he'd left her here, he'd meant for her to die alone. If not, he planned to come back. El didn't like either of those ideas.

Clouds covered the sky, blocking out the sun so she couldn't make out what time it was or which direction he'd taken her. The freezing temperature made her numb, but the rope around her limbs added to the sensation by cutting off her circulation. She wouldn't be able to get away with her hands and feet tied. How could she get free? The nylon cords were biting into her flesh and she hadn't tried to loosen them yet.

She needed to think, clear her mind of the panic and fear then work out a way to get untied and back to Rowan. El didn't know what had happened at the house but she was pretty sure the guy who'd taken her had hurt her friend. Had Brogan and Quinn come back from their meeting and found Rowan hurt and El missing? Were they out here looking for her?

Pain streaked up her arms and pulling them in front of her for a closer look took effort. Biting her lip to stop from crying out, El studied the knots at her wrists. It didn't look as if she'd be able to undo them. Her abductor hadn't been kind enough to leave her with a neat bow to loosen them. She pulled the ropes to her mouth and used her teeth to tug at dirt-covered fibers.

They didn't give and the movement rubbed the raw skin already circling both her arms. She needed something sharp. There was no hope of getting through the thick rope with her teeth. Frustration bubbled and a growl slid up her throat. Muscle and skin stretched and her teeth lengthened.

Her teeth.

With renewed hope, she brought her hands to her mouth and sank her coyote teeth into the knots. El gnawed at the ropes, felt them give a little. She could do this. Wiggling her hands and fingers to bring back the circulation, she bit down harder. One strand snapped, fell from her wrist. It gave her room to move and soon a second and third piece of rope fell away.

El breathed through the pain as blood surged back into her fingers. She shook her hands, clenched and unclenched her fists to try and ease the throb. She gritted her teeth and used her stiff arms to push herself up. The agony in her ribs eased but there would be bruises. The dull ache was manageable and she didn't appear to have suffered any other injuries. Her legs, numb and weak from lack of blood, hurt but she drew them up to examine her ankle restraints.

She was greeted with bigger and more complicated knots than the ones on her wrists. She growled and bent double, thanking her lucky stars for years of gymnastics and yoga. Flexibility had always been her strong point. Her back and shoulders ached as she stretched to reach the knots with her teeth. Sensing victory within her grasp, El ripped at the ropes with teeth as sharp as a knife.

The last tie gave way and slipped to the ground and El checked her sore, bleeding ankles. The abrasions were covered in dirt but there was no time to tend them. She scanned the area and saw no sign of her attacker. Sniffing the air, she could only pick up a faint trace of him. There hadn't been time to take note of him when he'd grabbed her at the house but one thing she did know from his scent, he was a coyote shifter.

What he hoped to gain by bringing her out here and leaving her she couldn't guess but she would not let him win. Logic told her the man Brogan had told her about was behind this. Whether he'd been the one to take her or someone else it didn't matter, she'd fight for everything she cared about. Rowan, Brogan and the baby she carried inside. She wouldn't let Marcus take what she'd only just discovered. Whatever his game, she'd do all she could to get back to the house and Rowan.

Or had he left Rowan out here too? Was she bound somewhere nearby?

El struggled to her feet and her knees wobbled before holding firm. On shaky legs, she turned to check for any sign of life. She couldn't smell anyone else. Felt sure she was out here on her own. There was no trace of Rowan.

The only sign of life was a set of footprints in the snow leading away through the trees. Drawing in a deep breath, El took a tentative step, her stride shaky at first but with each tread her legs grew steadier and she followed the trail in the hope of finding her way out of the forest.

With each footstep El knew she was in trouble. Bare feet and snow didn't mix. She'd been taken without a coat and her jeans and sweater weren't enough to keep the cold from sinking all the way down to her bones, their dampness wasn't helping either. Gingerly she walked through the slush, her toes growing colder by the second. Numbness moved up from her feet and dulled the pain of her abused ankles but that was little comfort when she found herself lost in the middle of an unknown forest for the second time in as many days.

Her best option was to shift. She'd only managed the complete change once but if she wanted to survive she had no choice. Taking coyote form would give her a few important advantages, the best one being her attacker didn't know she could shift.

El stripped out of her clothes and buried them under a snow drift. No point leaving clues. Her first attempt gave her claws, teeth and a coating of fur. Shivering she tried again but with her body racked by cold she found it hard to concentrate. Sucking in a deep breath she gave the last of her energy to shifting.

This time she slid into it with ease. A pleased rumble filled her chest but she knew not to let it out. She needed to be silent. Using her heightened sense of smell, she followed the trail of human prints, listening for signs she was close to another form of life. Moving off to the side of the tracks, she walked slowly, padding lightly through the snow to make as little noise as possible.

The trail weaved its way through the forest and she was starting to wonder if he was walking in circles to confuse anyone that might follow. Who, other than her, might want to track her kidnapper was easy to work out. If Brogan had discovered her abduction he'd be out looking for her, she knew to the depth of her soul that he'd search until he found her and the man responsible for attacking her.

She hoped the man had left some sort of clue as to where he'd taken her or Brogan could search the Whispering Mountains for days and not find her. Not that she was going to wait around to be rescued. The thought of sitting in the cold snow didn't appeal even if she was the type to expect someone else to solve her problems.

With renewed determination, El continued to move forward, being careful to listen and smell for any danger that may be lurking nearby. The forest was quiet around her and it felt like she was the only person alive in the whole world. If the situation wasn't so deadly it would be beautiful. She was quickly learning that looks could be very deceiving. Just look at what she'd become. A mythical creature she'd only ever dreamed of before now.

A shapeshifter.

13

Brogan tossed his phone onto the dashboard.

"Who was that?" Steve asked.

"Doc. She said Rowan and the baby are fine. And she wanted to let me know that word of El's abduction has spread. More than half the town is moving out into the mountainside to help search for her and Marcus."

"It might be better if someone else finds him." Quinn's quiet words sent chills down Brogan's spine. He knew his friend wanted to kill Marcus with his bare hands for hurting Rowan. Hell, he felt the same way.

"We'll find him. And Steve, you're our safety net. You'll be the one to take him down."

Steve chuckled wryly. "What makes you think I don't want to kill him as much as you two?"

"Your devotion to our friendship is admirable," Brogan said.

"It has nothing to do with our friendship. I promised not to say anything and I won't but I can tell you he's done some damage to a mutual friend that should have gotten him exiled months ago." Steve's cryptic words had Brogan seething.

Quinn growled beside him. "Does this have to do with Doc?"

"You know?" Steve's astonishment was clear.

"No. All I know is Rowan helped her and refused to tell me what went on," Quinn clarified.

"I want to know the full story when we get back to town," Brogan demanded.

"She won't tell you. She doesn't want anyone to know. Ever," Steve said.

Whispering Mountain lookout was around the next bend and the four-wheel drive parked on the side of the road proved Steve's hunch right. Pulling in behind they jumped from Brogan's truck, Steve and Quinn each heading to a different corner of Marcus's vehicle to deflate the tires. The bastard would not be getting away by car if he managed to elude them.

Tinted windows made seeing inside difficult but there were no bulky shadows big enough to be El. Besides, Marcus might be an idiot but he wouldn't leave her in the car and go off. No, he'd take her into the forest and make sure she couldn't get away.

Quinn finished disabling the car and stood. Scanning the area, he moved off the embankment and into the tree line, tracking their prey. Brogan and Steve moved in behind, letting Quinn lead the way through the trees. They'd trekked for about ten minutes when Quinn stopped abruptly. He took a deep breath and analyzed the air.

"Marcus isn't far ahead of us, his scent is stronger." Quinn turned and sniffed again. "There's another coyote near."

A dark blur of motion drew Brogan's attention to the left. A coyote he'd never seen before pounced on him, taking his legs out from under him and knocking the wind from his lungs as they crashed to the ground together. He struggled to keep the sharp teeth and powerful jaws from closing over his throat.

He lost his grip on the damp fur and the coyote lunged for his head. Braced for the pain of teeth piercing skin, he was shocked when the animal licked his face from jawbone to forehead. The second swipe finished in his ear, drool leaving a sticky trail.

Fingers twined in the fur around the animal's neck, Brogan held the beast still and stared into a pair of eyes he knew well. Seeing the familiar gaze coming from a coyote stunned him.

"Shit! *El?*"

Her exuberant barks made him laugh. Jeez, she'd shifted. He pushed her off, wanting to get to his feet and look at all of her. A snarl had them all turning. Not fifteen feet away stood Marcus in coyote form and before any of them could react, the animal sprang forward.

In human form, Brogan would sustain a lot of damage before getting the upper hand against a coyote as large as Marcus but his enemy never got the chance to hurt him. With a bark so fierce at first he hadn't thought it came from her, El attacked. She plowed into Marcus's side, taking him to the ground.

Her agility and fast movement surprised all of them. She had the other coyote pinned to the snow, her razor sharp teeth poised around its vulnerable neck. One bite and it would all be over.

He couldn't let her do that.

Marcus whined and his eyes bulged. Brogan knew she'd broken skin.

"El, let him go. We won't let him get away but you have to let go." He inched closer to where they were, Quinn coming around the other side. "Eloise, you don't want to do this," he coaxed. "Come on, let him go. Quinn and Steve will make sure he doesn't get away. He'll answer to the Council for what he's done and be exiled from the pack."

She didn't move, frozen in place with Marcus quivering beneath her. In coyote form her every instinct would be screaming to finish off the other animal, eliminate the threat.

Quinn moved into her line of sight and she growled a low warning in her throat. Marcus flinched and whimpered.

"El, please, baby. For me, let him go," Brogan pleaded. He'd get down on his knees and beg if he had to. If she killed Marcus she'd have to live with the guilt. He didn't wish that on her no matter how much he wanted Marcus dead.

She finally let go of Marcus' throat but didn't get off him. El held him down with bared teeth and her weight. After Quinn got him by the scruff she got up, trotted to Brogan and sat on her haunches like a domesticated pet instead of the wild coyote she'd just been.

He reached down, ran his fingers through her gray coat. She was damp and cold. For the second day she'd been caught out in the snow. He hoped this wouldn't become a habit.

"You can change back now, El."

Quinn coughed, cleared his throat. "That might not be such a good idea."

"Why not? I want to check she's okay, that he didn't hurt her," Brogan argued.

"Brogan," Steve interjected. "As much as I'm a guy and getting a look at a naked woman is one of my constant aims in life, I don't think she'd be comfortable being naked in front of us."

"Oh, right. I guess I'm so used to that part I just don't think about it." He was never this thoughtless. She scrambled his brains so much he was forgetting the basics. "But she can't go to town in coyote form."

"You've got a blanket in your truck don't you?" Steve asked. "She can shift back and wrap it around her. She needs to see Doc."

"We'll wait here, give you a head start so she can change without an audience," Quinn added.

Brogan looked at his two friends, thought about warning them against doing anything to Marcus but decided not to. He trusted them to bring him back safely to face the Council.

"Come on, El, let's go to the truck."

She padded along beside him, comfortable in her coyote form. She was a beautiful animal. Her coat, though damp, looked healthy and the colors were a mixture of different shades of gray. A little gold around the ears and neck gave her a warm glow. She was an average size and considering how small she was in human form, Brogan found that strange.

It wouldn't matter what she looked like, he'd still want her. His coyote clawed to be let free. He wanted to run through the forest with her by his side, but that pleasure would wait for later. First they had to get her to Doc's clinic.

And Marcus back to town.

. . .

With Marcus restrained in the back of Brogan's truck, the drive down the mountain was made in silence. El was too exhausted to talk and lay quietly in Brogan's arms while Quinn drove and Steve rode up front. The men had been very careful not to crowd her when they'd emerged from the woods. No one would look her in the eye and they let Brogan bundle her into the back without comment.

El had kept her gaze away from Marcus. While she didn't fear him, knew after their little wrestle she could take him if she had to, she didn't want to look at the coyote who threatened to take so much from them all. Brogan had told her Rowan was injured but okay and he continued to reassure her that everything would be fine now, but the reality of what she'd been through was beginning to sink in.

Her own injuries were minor but she would see the doctor just to be sure. The warmth seeping into her from Brogan lulled her to a light doze and she snuggled closer. With her arms wrapped around his neck, El held on, not wanting to let go of him ever again.

Jolted from sleep, El grabbed Brogan tighter. Silence reigned for a second before pandemonium broke free. People called out, their voices muffled by the car until Quinn opened his door and the noise became a roar. Faces crowded against the windows, staring in at her and El shrank back into Brogan.

"Get them away from the truck," Brogan bellowed.

Steve jumped from the cab, pushing bodies away from the vehicle as he did. Quinn came around to the curb and opened the door, reaching in to offer her his hand but El refused to take it and burrowed in closer to Brogan.

"Get them all away."

Brogan's voice rumbled in his chest against her cheek and rang in her ears. Feet scuffed on concrete as Quinn and Steve did their best to make a clear path through the sea of gawkers. And that's what they were, not one of them pretended to be doing anything but staring at her. A couple of burly men made their way through the throng, pushing people aside willy-nilly as they headed for the back of the truck and Marcus.

"Come on. It's okay, I won't let anyone hurt you." Brogan cradled her against his chest and sidled along the seat to the door.

She couldn't help flinching as he stepped from the cab, she knew she was safe in his arms but the men had chosen the same moment to lift Marcus from the truck bed, leaving them within two feet of each other.

"Get him locked up." Brogan's booming voice quieted the crowd, a hushed silence descending.

One of the men collared and leashed Marcus, pulling him away through the crowd. El breathed easy but the small comfort was short-lived when the crowd surged forward and surrounded Brogan.

"Jesus, give him room would you?" Quinn formed a barricade in front of them as Brogan moved forward.

People fell in step behind them as they made their way to the building and the door Steve held open. Questions flew around them but no one uttered a word until they were safely inside with the door closed.

"Steve, go over to the sheriff's office and tell William what happened."

"Shouldn't you do that?" Quinn asked.

"Later. First I want to make sure El's all right."

El leaned back and looked up at Brogan. "I'm okay, go do what you have to."

"No. Not until Doc checks you out and says you're fine. Plus I want to see Rowan before I leave the clinic."

"Quinn?" Rowan could be heard yelling from down the hall.

"Rowan's here?" El watched Quinn head across the room at a run.

"Yep, let me take you to say hi and then Doc can get a good look at you before I take you home." Brogan walked toward the hall on the other side of the waiting room.

"She's really okay?" The thought of Marcus hurting Rowan sent fear and guilt rolling in El's stomach.

"She'll be fine with a little rest and a few days to heal." A woman in a white coat met them in the hallway. "Take her into the room next to Rowan's, Brogan."

"Can she see Rowan first, Doc?"

"Let's leave that until after I get a look at her. Besides, I think Quinn will want to spend time alone with Rowan first."

Brogan followed the doctor into an exam room that looked anything but sterile. The walls were painted with murals of animals and colorful mobiles hung from the ceiling. A closer look revealed all the animals were coyotes, young cubs at various stages of development prancing around the walls and leaping from the roof. Obviously this was the room they used for children.

"Sorry about the room but Rowan's in one and the other is full of supplies that arrived earlier today that I didn't get a chance to put away because of the emergency." She went straight to the sink in the corner, scrubbed her hands and pulled on a pair of latex gloves. "You can put her on the bed, Brogan."

"Right."

Brogan gently placed El on the exam table, making sure the blanket stayed wrapped around her. Not much point when the doctor would want to remove it to check her over. The discomfort swirling in El's stomach had nothing to do with her nudity beneath the blanket and everything to do with the events of the last few hours. Having Brogan at her side helped keep her from freaking out.

"Brogan you need to move so I can get at my patient."

Muttering what sounded like sorry, he stepped to the side, closer to El's head. He wove his fingers through her hair, brushing it away from her face, the soothing motion enough to distract her from what the doctor was doing until she touched a particularly raw spot on her ankle.

"Ouch."

"Sorry, this section has no skin left at all. I'm afraid it's going to hurt a bit more when I clean the dirt from your wounds."

El ground her teeth through the rest of the exam. While her ankles and wrists hurt she'd escaped any further injuries. The doctor still wanted to do a scan of her head to be sure she hadn't suffered any head trauma while unconscious but all signs pointed to nothing more than the minor abrasions on her arms and legs.

"I'm going to do a couple more tests, check your blood and get that scan organized but it won't be too much longer and you can go home." The doctor opened a cupboard and pulled out a bundle of cloth. "Here, you might be more comfortable in a gown."

"Thanks, Doc." Brogan helped her sit up and slip into the stiff garment.

"You're welcome." The doctor removed her gloves and held out a hand to El. "And it's a pleasure to meet you. Rowan's told me a lot about you, although I wish it were under different circumstances."

"Thank you, Doctor." El shook the offered hand.

"Please, call me Doc or Gordie."

"I'm Eloise but everyone calls me El."

"Okay, let me get you out of here." With a smile Gordie left the room.

She returned a few minutes later with a tray of implements El didn't like the look of. Seeing the vials to hold blood made her stomach roll and she quickly turned away to examine the mural opposite her.

Brogan held her hand while Gordie inserted the needle to take her blood for the tests. At the prick of pain El turned. The sight of her blood filling the plastic tube undid her. Lightheaded, she swayed and if Brogan hadn't been next to her she would have toppled from the bed to the floor. Again. She was getting tired of playing the swooning female. Never in her life had she fainted but she seemed to be passing out at regular intervals since coming to Whispering Springs.

14

Brogan knew he needed to go and face the Council about Marcus but he couldn't bring himself to leave the woman sleeping on the bed. He wanted nothing more than to take her home and forget the last few hours ever happened.

Rowan and Quinn quietly slipped into the room.

"How is she?" Rowan whispered.

"She'll be fine physically, not sure about her mental state though, the last few hours, hell the last couple of days have been rough." Brogan stood and pulled Rowan into a hug. "How about you? Baby doing okay?"

"I'm fine, we're fine. Twelve stitches in my head and a little sore but I'll live." Rowan pulled from Brogan's embrace and stepped up to the bed. "She looks exhausted."

"Yeah. I'm just waiting for Doc to give the all clear and then I'm getting her out of here." Brogan turned to Quinn. "You ready to face Council?"

"Whenever you are."

"Rowan, can you sit with El until we get back? I won't be long but if I don't show my face now they'll come looking for me and once I get El out of here I want no one and nothing disturbing her."

"Sure, you and Quinn go and get things sorted out because we all know William will be on our doorstep if you don't." Rowan settled in the chair Brogan had vacated.

"We'll be as quick as we can. Hopefully El won't wake until I get back."

"I'll be here if she does."

Brogan leaned over and kissed El's forehead. She didn't stir. Vowing to get back before she woke, he turned and headed for the door leaving Quinn to follow.

They found William and the rest of the Council members at the sheriff's office. The crowd on the street had dispersed to a degree but there were still more people than a normal day in downtown Whispering Springs. Brogan ignored all but his target, he didn't want this to take longer than necessary and if he allowed himself to be waylaid by a pack member it would be like issuing an open invitation.

"William, Councilmen." He nodded at the others briefly before turning back to the older man.

"Brogan, Quinn. Shall we take this indoors?" William's voice vibrated with tension.

Quinn was ahead of them, he stood with the door to the sheriff's department held open, waiting. Brogan ushered the councilmen in ahead of him. Dale Turner, the town's newly elected sheriff, met them in the foyer. Brogan had been glad when Dale returned to the mountains to take up a position with the local law enforcement a year ago. He was especially thrilled when the community had elected him to the position of sheriff six months later.

"Brogan, I've cleared the conference room for you." The sheriff extended his hand toward Brogan.

He shook the other man's hand. "Marcus?"

"Holding cell downstairs."

"Good." Brogan turned to the others. "Let's get this meeting done, shall we gentlemen?"

As at the front door, he allowed the older men to precede him. Each one gave him a wide berth as they passed. Brogan wouldn't hold it against them or bring up the fact they'd refused to listen to him or anyone else before now where Marcus was concerned. All he wanted was for them to declare him exiled and be done with it. He waited for them all to take a seat around the large table before closing the door and leaning against it.

One could hear a pin drop, no one spoke and each member of the Council found something other than him to look at.

"Do it." Brogan directed his words at William.

With a sigh the old man got to his feet, the legs of his chair scraping on the linoleum flooring.

"I, William Brant, declare Marcus Connelly exiled from Whispering Mountains pack and the area in which we reside. All in favor raise your hand."

One by one, the members' hands came up.

"Done." On a sigh, William sagged back into his chair, weariness etched in every line on his face.

"Sheriff, see that Marcus is escorted to his house. I want him guarded until he packs up and leaves. Anything else, William?"

"No, Sovereign. I expect to be kept up to date on Marcus until he's gone." Exhaustion laced the councilman's words and Brogan was struck but how old William was.

"I'll keep you both informed of all movements," Dale said.

"Good." Brogan pushed off the door. "Now if you'll excuse me, gentlemen, I have a mate that needs my attention." He opened the door and strode from the room.

Quinn followed a few minutes later. He and the sheriff were deep in discussion as they made their way over to where Brogan waited in the foyer.

"Dale's going to personally oversee Marcus' departure," Quinn said.

"Thank you. I know we still have a couple of issues with one or two of your deputies and their continued support of the Connellys. I know I can trust you to see this through correctly."

"My pleasure, Brogan. It may have taken a while but we finally have just cause to exile Marcus. I'll make sure it's done."

Brogan reached over to shake hands. "I know I've said it before but I'm glad you returned home. You're just what the pack needs to continue on our path to a brighter future."

"Somehow I think that's more you than me but thanks for your praise. I'll be in touch later." Dale turned and headed to the back of the station.

Brogan and Quinn left the building in silence. He figured Quinn's mind was exactly where his was. On his mate. The sidewalk appeared to be empty but Brogan could see the pack members looking through shop windows, waiting in their cars and in small groups all looking in their direction. The whole town seemed to hold its breath as they made their way back to the clinic. He wouldn't be making any announcements himself but someone would have to tell them soon.

El liked Gordie. In the last thirty minutes she'd learned a lot from her. Waking to discover Brogan gone had frightened her but Rowan's presence had quickly put her mind at ease. When the doctor had joined them it was obvious the two women knew each other well and it wasn't long before the three of them were chatting like old friends.

She'd been shocked to find out Gordie had grown up here as a human, only being turned in her late teens. El didn't know the circumstances of Gordie's past but she did know she'd left the mountains for a few years before returning home to take over from her stepfather as the pack doctor. El planned to ask Rowan more questions later but she did manage to get several of her questions about the changes she was experiencing answered.

Gordie had also prescribed vitamins for the baby and strict instructions for complete bed rest until next week when she wanted to see both El and Rowan again. If anything showed up in the blood tests she'd give them a call, but that was unlikely. Rowan would need her stitches removed before then because of her coyote metabolism. The gash on Rowan's scalp would heal quickly and the doctor wanted to pull the sutures out before the skin attached to it and made it more difficult.

The phone rang in another room and Gordie excused herself to go answer it. El leaned back into the pillows and yawned. Fatigue stole through her and she closed her eyes. Rowan sat quietly in the chair next to the bed and El turned her head to look at her friend. Long lashes fanned out over pale cheeks and soft snores issued from between slightly parted lips. The day had taken its toll on both of them and she hoped Brogan and Quinn would return soon so they could all go home.

It was amazing how quickly she'd accepted Whispering Springs as home. The beautiful log house and the surrounding mountains had a history and warmth El felt to her very soul. She couldn't wait to go back and begin her life with Brogan. Smiling, she closed her eyes and snuggled into the pillows. Thoughts of a future with her mate filled with love and happiness eased her into sleep.

Brogan stopped in the doorway to El's room, the sight of the two sleeping women held him in place. El lay curled on her side facing Rowan, her back to him. Her tangled hair and the bruises and raw skin around her wrists and ankles a reminder of what she'd endured earlier. She'd proven her strength twice over in the last few hours. His anxiety over her size had all been for nothing, El would handle herself well when it came time to meet the pack.

His sister sat with her neck at an awkward angle in the armchair beside the bed, the white bandage around her head a stark reminder of the injury she'd sustained at the hands of Marcus. Anger stirred in his gut but he tamped it down. Knowing the man would never touch either of them again pleased him.

Breathing deeply, he stepped into the room. Three steps put him beside the bed where he pulled the blanket over El, covering the gape in the back of her hospital gown. He hoped not to wake her but she turned slumberous eyes in his direction. The smile that stretched her lips when she focused on him had his stomach flopping and his heart squeezing.

"Can we go home now?" Her sleep-slurred voice flowed over him. Her acceptance of his home as hers warmed him deep inside.

"Soon as Doc gives you the all clear." Brogan smoothed a hand down El's cheek and cupping her jaw, tilted her head so he could lower his mouth to hers. He brushed her lips lightly with his.

"Where's Quinn?"

He'd forgotten his sister sat next to the bed. Brogan looked over El to Rowan. "He's just finding Doc."

"She went to answer the phone." Rowan stood and stretched her back.

"Quinn will find her." Brogan straightened. "How are you both feeling?"

"Tired," El murmured.

"I feel like going home." Rowan sat back down. "Did you get everything sorted out?"

"Yes. The Council exiled Marcus and the sheriff is escorting him from the mountains as I speak."

"Good."

"Are we ready?" Quinn strode into the room followed by Doc.

"Ladies, it's been lovely chatting with you but I do believe it's time for you both to leave." Doc smiled at Brogan. "Did they exile him?"

"Yes."

She nodded before turning to El and Rowan. "I've given Quinn the bag with both your pregnancy vitamins and the cream for your abrasions, El. Rowan, I want to see you in a couple of days to remove your stitches and I'll see both of you in here in one week for a checkup."

Brogan helped El sit before scooping her up in his arms. Her arms slid around his neck and she snuggled in close to his chest. Warm breath fanned out over his neck and he placed a kiss on top of her head. He turned to find Rowan giving Quinn a stern look and pointing her finger at him.

"Don't even think about it, Quinn MacClellan."

Quinn raised his arms, paper bag hanging from one hand, and stepped back. "Didn't even cross my mind."

Rowan stared at him a few more seconds before walking from the room. Quinn chuckled and followed her through the door.

Brogan shook his head. He had no idea how Quinn was so in sync with his sister. She'd always been a complete mystery to him and nothing had changed in the months she'd been home. El squirmed in his arms, snapping his thoughts back to her and the need to take her home.

"See you in a week, Doc."

"If you're worried at all just give me a ring." Gordie followed him to the front door. "Here, let me get that for you."

Brogan stepped through the opened door to find his truck at the curb. Steve held the back door open and he slid El onto the seat before turning back to Steve and Doc.

"Thanks for everything today. I appreciate your help."

"I didn't do anything out of the normal, Brogan," Gordie said.

"No need for thanks. I've got your back whenever you need." Steve stepped back to stand next to Gordie.

"I'm still grateful for all you've both done." He climbed in beside El and closed the door.

Brogan pulled El into his lap. He stretched the seatbelt as far as it would go and snapped it in around both of them.

From the driver's seat Quinn asked, "Ready to go?"

"Yes." He squeezed El a little tighter. "Time to go home."

15

El listened to the steady thump of Brogan's heart beneath her cheek. Warmth radiated off him and flowed over her, soaking in to help shield her from the chill in the air. The drone of rubber rolling on tar, the murmur of Quinn and Rowan's voices and Brogan's words of reassurance that everything was okay, melded together in a soothing rhythm that comforted. Winding mountain roads swayed the truck in a rocking motion that lulled her to sleep as she lay in Brogan's arms.

Brogan held her close, stroked his hand up and down her back and dropped the occasional kiss on her head. When they pulled into the driveway it seemed like only five minutes since they'd left town, not an hour. Quinn parked as close to the house as the snow drifts would allow. The engine died and everyone moved quickly, cold air bursting into the cab of the truck as the doors opened.

El slid from Brogan's lap to the seat and waited for him to hop out. She climbed down, only to be lifted off her feet before they touched the ground. Holding on, she let Brogan carry her to the porch. Rowan opened the front door as they came up the stairs. A blast of hot air flew through the opening and surrounded them. The warmth smelled of spaghetti sauce and spices, everything that reminded her of home. El's tummy rumbled, the scent of her Grandma's special recipe sparking her hunger. Brogan laughed and continued into the house.

"Hungry, are we?"

"I guess so. I hadn't thought about it before now."

"Well, once I get you tucked up in bed I'll bring you some dinner."

"I can eat downstairs, Brogan."

"Nope. Doc said complete bed rest until she sees you again next week."

"I don't think she meant I couldn't get up to eat."

"Complete bed rest is complete bed rest, Eloise. That means no getting up for anything, including food."

They made it to the top of the stairs before El realized he was serious. "I think the idea was to take it easy but I'm sure I'm okay to get up for the essentials, like eating and bathing."

"There will be no getting out of bed for the next week. I want to make sure your body recovers from the traumas of the last two days." Anxiety and fear laced Brogan's words.

El sighed, she didn't want to upset him and if she was honest the thought of spending a week in bed with Brogan held an appeal all its own. He strode into the bedroom, kicked the door closed with his boot as he passed and placed her on her feet next to the bed.

"Do you need to use the bathroom before you get into bed?"

She shook her head.

"Okay, let's get you out of that ugly gown first."

He reached behind her to undo the ties of the horrible green garment the Gordie had given her. The material wasn't the best, it was new and still held the stiff, rough feel all new clothes have before they've been washed several times. Once the ties were free, Brogan peeled the loose fabric from her shoulders and let it fall to the floor. Her nipples pebbled as the scratchy material brushed over them.

El shivered.

Being naked while Brogan was fully clothed sent an erotic jolt through her. After the day she'd had, sex should be the last thing on her mind but when it came to Brogan it seemed to be the only thing she thought about. He reached around her to yank the covers back before easing her onto the cool sheets. The idea of getting into bed alone held no appeal and El grabbed his hand to pull him in with her.

"Hey, none of that. You need to rest and if I get in there with you there'll be no resting anytime soon." He tugged to free his hand.

"I don't need rest right now, Brogan." She tightened her grip. "I need you to hold me. Need to know this is real and that we're both okay."

Brogan didn't say a word. He shook off her hold and began stripping out of his clothes. El scooted back in the bed and made room for him to climb under the covers with her. Warmth came off him in waves, banishing the chill in the bedding and the icy fear that had remained in her heart. They were safe, maybe not unhurt but safe from the man determined to do them harm.

El wrapped her arms around Brogan and pulled their bodies together until skin touched skin. Heat lashed out, zipping along nerve endings to set them alight with desire. Arousal swirled in the pit of her stomach, spreading out ribbons of warmth to drive her need for closeness higher. She smoothed her hands over his hot flesh until being held wasn't enough. She wanted to consume him—be consumed. Taken to the place where only Brogan could lead.

She covered his chest with open-mouthed kisses. Her tongue and lips teased each of his nipples until he moaned in pleasure. Sliding her hand between them, El circled his hard length with her fingers. The hot, pulsing flesh burned her skin and sent a shudder of delight into her core. With a firm grip, she worked her hand up and down his cock, smoothing her thumb through the bead of moisture that formed on the head.

"Jeez, El. You need to rest."

"No. I need this. I need to be as close to you as I can get." She stroked him harder.

"Christ."

Brogan's breath came in ragged puffs that blew at her hair and his hips jerked into her as he grew harder in her grasp.

"Dammit, El, we shouldn't do this," he ground out between clenched teeth as he grabbed her hand to stop her movements.

"Yes we should." El tilted her head back to look into his eyes. "Please."

He stared at her, the swirl of emotions in his eyes mesmerizing. Whatever he searched for he found, because in a heartbeat he pulled her hand free and rolled them until she lay pinned beneath him. Air rushed from her lungs, sucked out by the molten desire flashing in his gaze.

"Fine, but we do it my way, my pace."

Breathless, El nodded.

In slow motion he lowered his mouth to hers. The agonizing wait both excited and frustrated her. Brogan's tongue swept between her lips, delving inside to tangle with hers. She tried to take the kiss deeper but he pulled back.

"No." He spoke against her mouth. "My way."

His lips traveled across her cheek, butterfly kisses that soothed and seduced. Reaching her ear, he sucked the lobe into his mouth, nipped it with his teeth before his tongue traced the delicate shell. Warm air rushed over her skin leaving tingles in its wake. Brogan nudged her jaw with his cheek as he kissed his way down her neck and El turned her head to give him room to explore the sensitive flesh along her throat.

Brogan continued at his leisure. The unhurried pace tormented and teased El's senses until urgency filled her. Clawing at his back, she arched beneath him, tried to drag him closer.

"More."

"Soon." His hot breath bathed her nipple seconds before the tight bud was engulfed in wet heat.

El cried out. Pleasure rippled over her to center in her core. Her clit throbbed and moisture dripped from her pussy to coat her thighs. Brogan switched to her other nipple, one hand cupping her breast to lift it to his mouth. He sucked hard, drawing more of the tip between his lips. His tongue swirled around the tender peak and jolts of electricity fired off in all directions.

Her head thrashed on the pillow. The sensations bombarding her drove her closer to the orgasm threatening to crash over her. Brogan's hand left her breast, brushed over stomach muscles that quivered at his touch before sliding lower to cup her mound. Cream-slicked folds pulsed as he stroked her clit and El's hips bucked as the first wave of her climax gripped her.

A sob of desperation caught in her throat as Brogan removed his hand. He pushed a knee between her legs, shoved them wide and placed the head of his cock at her entrance.

"Not without me, El." He dropped to his elbows and cupped her face in his hands so she was forced to look at him. "Don't close your eyes. Watch me while I love you."

Through heavy eyelids, El focused on the emotions swimming in the golden glow of Brogan's gaze. Love, desire and need, with just a trace of fear swirled in a mesmerizing mix that she couldn't look away from even if she wanted to. He rocked his hips and entered her slowly. Her drenched sheath welcomed him, clasping his length as each inch pushed inside.

Buried to the hilt, Brogan held still. His gaze dropped to look between them and El raised her head to glance down at where their bodies joined. While they both watched, he pulled out. Her pussy walls clamped hard around him in an attempt to keep him from leaving. His erection, glistening with her cream, caused her muscles to flutter around the head, dragging a groan from Brogan and a shudder from her.

In long, drawn-out strokes, he made love to her. In and out. Push and pull. Brogan took them on a slow ride to the top. El wanted to feel his mouth on hers. Needed to taste him. Raking her fingers through his hair she urged his head toward hers. She captured his lips. Spice and warmth exploded across her tongue as they deepened the kiss. Urgency built—in the probing of his tongue and the thrusting of his cock—until their movements became frenzied with the need for more.

Brogan plunged into her body, strumming sensitized tissues and setting off El's orgasm. Wave after wave broke over her. His hips slammed forward, ramming his pulsing shaft to the hilt time and again. He sank his teeth into the side of her neck as he thrust deep one final time. With a guttural growl he came. Hot cum bathed her cervix, triggering a second climax. Her body bowed under him as breath stealing pleasure consumed her.

The rasp of harsh breathing filled her ears to compete with the pounding of her heart. Her nostrils were coated in the scent of sex and Brogan with every inhalation. His dead weight pressed her into the bed but El welcomed the burden. Their sweat-slicked skin grew tacky and cool as they came back to earth. He pushed up on his arms and withdrew from her body. Muscles gone lax with satisfaction clutched at his retreating flesh.

Brogan dropped to the mattress beside her—one arm draped across her chest and sighed. His eyes remained closed and El reached over to brush the hair from his forehead. He murmured something unintelligible but didn't move. She smiled, had he fallen asleep?

"I love you." The words left her lips before she realized she was even thinking them.

"Love you, too." Brogan's usual deep rumble was muffled by his face being squashed against the bed. His eyes opened, the beautiful gold color full of the emotion they'd just spoken. "Come here."

Turning on his side, he pulled her close so they lay face to face. He dipped his head and kissed her, just a light peck on the lips. Leaning back, he studied her face for a few seconds. "We haven't talked about it but are you okay with being pregnant?"

She smiled. "More than okay. I can't explain it but everything just feels so right."

Brogan's hand slipped between them to rest over her still flat stomach. "I hope she's just like her mother."

El laughed. "And I hope *he's* just like his father."

"Maybe we'll both get our wish."

Her laughter stopped cold. *Two?* The thought of one terrified her in an exciting way, but two? She shook her head. "No thanks. One at a time will be just fine thank you."

Laughter rumbled in Brogan's chest.

"Are you still hungry? Want me to go get you some dinner?"

"No, I'm too tired to eat now, maybe later." She cuddled in close, tucking her head on his shoulder. "Just hold me until I go to sleep."

"I'll hold you longer than that, El. I'm not planning on letting you go ever again."

Her lips curved against his neck. He wasn't the only one who wasn't planning on letting go. She'd found the place she was supposed to be, the man she was meant to be with. There was no way in the world she was letting either go without a fight.

EPILOGUE

The sun shone bright and El couldn't wish for a better wedding day. After everything that had happened since she arrived in Whispering Springs, today was a welcome relief. Glancing in the mirror, she checked her appearance one more time. Pleased with what she saw, she took a deep breath and walked from the room.

Rowan met her at the top of the stairs, decked out in a beautiful wedding gown that was her mother's. Her best friend radiated with happiness. Getting to share this day with Rowan as more than a bridesmaid thrilled El just as much as the idea of being Mrs. Brogan Wilder in a few short minutes.

"Ready?"

"As I'll ever be."

"No second thoughts?" Rowan studied her carefully. "You've made some huge changes already, I'm sure Brogan would understand if you wanted to wait to get married."

"Are you kidding? That's probably the one thing I'm most sure of." El reached for Rowan's hand and tugging lightly she pulled her toward the first step. "Come on, our men are waiting."

Rowan laughed. "Yeah, and if we're more than a few seconds late they'll be charging up the stairs to come get us."

Together they took the steps a little quicker than normal, both excited to get the day underway. By the time they reached the bottom El knew this would be the best day of her life. Sharing it with her best friend added to the occasion but the best part was pledging her love to Brogan in front of the gorgeous mountains she now called home.

The yard was filled with people, most El had never seen before but Gordie met them at the door looking lovely in a pantsuit with snow boots.

"What can I say?" Gordie shrugged. "I'm a practical girl at heart."

El and Rowan both grabbed a handful of lacy white fabric and raised their skirts. Gordie looked down and burst out laughing.

"No one wants to deal with frostbitten toes on their wedding night," El said around her own laughter.

"I can think of plenty of other things to be dealing with that's for sure," Rowan added.

"Come on, everyone's waiting, two men in particular are getting a little impatient."

Over Gordie's shoulder El could see Brogan make his way through the crowd toward them with Quinn right on his heels.

"Speak of the devils," Rowan murmured.

As the men reached them a car pulled up the driveway. All talk stopped as everyone waited to see what the sheriff wanted.

Brogan slipped his arm around her shoulders and held her tight to his side as they waited for the new arrival to approach them. El didn't recognize the man who got out of the car but the vehicle and uniform told her he was head of the local law enforcement. When he smiled and offered his hand to Brogan she let out the breath she hadn't realized she was holding.

"Sovereign."

"Sheriff." Brogan reached over and shook the outstretched hand. "What brings you here today?"

"Thought you'd want to know Marcus Connelly drove his four-wheel drive off Stattler Bridge earlier this morning. We're working to retrieve the vehicle and the body now."

"He's dead? Are you sure?" Gordie asked.

"We believe so but we haven't found the body yet, it's not in the vehicle."

Brogan tensed next to her, Quinn stood straighter and Rowan sucked in a hash breath. Fear slid down El's spine. She didn't know why the three people closest to her would react in this way but when Gordie gasped and stumbled forward El knew Marcus driving off a bridge wasn't good news.

"He's not dead." Rowan turned to Quinn. "Until they find a body I won't believe he's dead."

"Sheriff, Rowan's right. Unless you recover his body we'll assume Marcus survived the crash. Which means the fight isn't over." Brogan squeezed El closer.

"We'll need to be on our guard until we know for sure." Quinn motioned Steve McKenna over. "Steve can you take Doc and the sheriff inside, we'll join you all in a minute."

"Quinn, I think we should go ahead with the wedding. Everyone will be leaving after the ceremony and we can deal with this then. We don't want people getting curious yet," Rowan said.

"I agree." Brogan said. "Are you all able to hang around for about thirty minutes? We don't have anything elaborate planned so it'll just be a matter of clearing everyone out of here."

"I'll need to get back to the search as quickly as possible but I've left a good man in charge so I can give you one hour before I have to leave," the sheriff said.

"No problem, Brogan. Doc and I rode up together. We'll wait as long as you need." Steve moved to take Gordie's elbow but she avoided his touch by moving closer to Rowan.

"Okay, let's get you four married." Gordie pointed to Brogan and Quinn. "You two go to where you're supposed to be waiting patiently for your brides-to-be."

Both men did as they were told and headed for the pergola where the wedding was to take place.

"Let's get this show on the road." Rowan followed the men.

El feared what this latest news would mean but with Brogan by her side she was prepared to face any trouble that may come their way. She took a deep breath to calm her nerves and took the first step toward the man she'd come to love with all her heart.

BONUS EPILOGUE
FEBRUARY 14

Brogan stared through the frosty glass at the delicate flakes of snow drifting from the gloomy gray sky. The storm had been and gone leaving behind a snowfall that looked like glitter being tossed around inside a snow globe. Barely more than specks, each flake floated on the air going every which way as they descended to the ground.

So fragile yet so resilient.

Like his Eloise.

El slept in the big bed behind him; he should be snuggled beneath the warm blanket with her. Instead, he stood naked, gazing at the mountains behind his house. His mind was plagued with doubts and uncertainties but it was the guilt that had driven him from a warm bed before daybreak.

No matter how many times he ran recent events through his head he couldn't reason away the regret that continued to churn in his gut all these weeks later.

He'd listened to her time and time again tell him she was happy, that the decision to stay had been hers, except Brogan couldn't rid himself of the notion that his choices had robbed El of hers.

"Brogan?" Her sleep slurred voice drifted through the room, tickled over his skin.

He closed his eyes and savored the sound of his name on her tongue. That sexy accent he hoped she never lost flowed through his veins, settled low in his gut, and stirred heat in his groin, thickening his cock.

She'd said his name many times over the previous months and Brogan came to the conclusion that it was something he couldn't live without. No matter how much blame he heaped on his own shoulders.

"Mmm," he hummed without turning, waiting for the inevitable.

The covers rustled in the quiet of their room and he held his breath. "Come back to bed, Brogan."

Ah, there it was. Brogan recognized the tone of her voice—she knew what he was thinking about, knew he was likely beating himself up about something neither of them could change. It wasn't the first time they'd found themselves in this position.

El had been able to gauge his moods from the start but now they'd spent so much time together, he thought she might know him better than he knew himself.

"Playing it over and over in your mind won't change or help," she murmured, the covers rustling once more.

A sigh left his chest as his eyes opened. Snow still fell, a sparkling curtain of glittering white but the clouds had brightened some, the morning fast approaching. Winter might still have its icy grip on Whispering Springs but Mother Nature managed to show beauty in her cold brutality.

Spring was coming. Even now, green foliage poked out from under the colorless wet blanket that had covered everything around them for months, and the sun's rays kissed bare skin with warmth when the clouds parted long enough for it to show its bright yellow face.

As the sky lightened with dawn, a thin strip of blue licked the top of the mountains. Brogan smiled; the idea of seeing a clear sky later in the day pleased him. He had plans that didn't include freezing their asses off in a snowstorm. He'd barely gotten over finding El half frozen in one earlier in the season; he wasn't risking that again.

Turning, he leaned against the windowsill and folded his arms over his chest. El had rolled on her side and propped her head up on her hand. She studied him, her blue eyes taking in every naked inch of him—including the ones rapidly growing under her scrutiny. Brogan's chest tightened, the love and lust shining in her gaze pulling on the ribbons she'd wrapped around his heart.

She'd owned him from the moment his coyote had recognized her as his mate but since he'd gotten to know her, that ownership went deeper. He couldn't have picked a more perfect woman if he'd had a thousand years to search.

"We can say *what if* everyday but it doesn't matter. What is important is you and me. What we have is real and I refuse to allow you to question it any longer, Brogan."

He opened his mouth to protest but she cut him off before he made the smallest sound.

"No. I don't want to hear any more about choices taken away. I made the decision to stay, to be turned, and you know what?"

Brogan shook his head and pressed his lips together; she was on a roll, he didn't want to interrupt.

"I'd do it all again. Yesterday. Today. Tomorrow." She reached out the hand not under her head, leaned forward, and stretched it toward him, palm up. "Please, Brogan, put it aside and come back to bed."

How did he refuse a request like that?

El was his everything. Every thought, every breath, every beat of his heart, they all belonged to her.

His wife.

He still couldn't believe she'd married him days after meeting. But he couldn't deny the click, the rightness of them together. In spite of the guilt, he knew the fates had given him the perfect partner.

Pushing off the windowsill he made his way to the bed. "I love you," he said as he leaned over to brush his lips on hers. "I'll live with the any guilt if it means having you beside me for the rest of my life."

"Done." She threw the covers back and scooted toward the

middle of the bed to make room for him. "Now get in here and let me warm you up."

He was rock hard now. The sight of El stretched out without a stitch of clothing on heated him up, it was a guarantee he'd be burning up once he climbed in beside her.

Smiling, he slid onto the bed and reached for her. "Come here; let's see how hot we can get."

E l hated the regret Brogan felt over the circumstances that brought them together. In spite of the events that led to them mating, she knew she was where she was meant to be. With the person she was meant to be with.

He'd saved her. And not just from the storm that almost killed her when she'd first arrived in Whispering Springs.

He'd saved her from a lonely life and a bleak future. He gave her the bright, joyful future she'd once looked forward to but lost sight of when someone she'd trusted broke that trust and cut her self-confidence off at the knees.

She'd told Brogan all about Ken. How she'd realized she'd allowed him close because she'd been missing her best friend, Rowan.

It might have been Rowan's invitation to visit that had El boarding the plane all those months ago but it was the aching loneliness that had made the decision easy. And staying? Well, that was the easiest decision of all.

She got to live with her best friend again and who wouldn't be grateful to a friend who welcomed you with open arms and a hot brother.

Honesty made her admit it was the brother who had her staying. He might think he'd forced her decision, and he had, just not in the way he believed.

"I would have stayed regardless."

"What?" Brogan murmured as his lips brushed hers.

"If you hadn't marked me. I would have wanted to stay."

He pulled away, his gaze searching hers.

"I know you think you forced my hand but you didn't. I came here knowing things in my life were going to change. I was adrift in my old life. Rowan had left and then my business and confidence took a hit and I lost my way. Lost sight of what I'd been working toward. Hell, I'm not sure I hadn't already lost that long before Ken pulled the rug out from under me."

"I'd prefer it if you didn't mention another man while you're naked in my arms," Brogan growled.

"You can't be jealous."

"No. I have no need. You're mine and I know it. You know it. But the thought of how he treated you makes me want to hurt him. A lot."

"Ah, my hero." Smiling, she smacked her lips on his then said, "Is it bad that I like that you feel that way?"

"No. I'd expect you to feel the same if someone hurt me."

El frowned. "I wanted to kill Marcus."

"You almost did."

"Why did you stop me?" She'd never asked, he'd never explained, and she still regretted not taking Marcus out when she could have.

Brogan sighed. Brushed hair back behind her ear. "You were newly turned and while your coyote would have been comfortable with the kill, your human half wouldn't have been as easy with it."

"Yes, it would." She gripped his face in her hands, her gaze locked with his. "That man hurt Rowan, did terrible things to her long before the day he took me, but what makes me the most angry, the reason I'd rip his throat out if I could get my teeth into it, is that he hurt you by using me. That a coward's move."

"He saw you as a soft target."

"I'm not soft."

Brogan chuckled. "No. You've proven that more than once."

"You should have let me kill him."

"It doesn't matter now. He will never hurt either of us again. And again we seem to be talking about another man when you're naked in my arms." Brogan's hand slid down her side and around her waist.

Pulling her closer, he said, "We've got better things to concern ourselves with right now."

Smiling, El wiggled closer. "Oh?"

"Hmm..." He lips brushed hers, once, twice. "Yeah, someone said something about warming me up."

"I did." Grinning she said, "What's the best way to do that, do you think?"

"Body heat." He slipped a knee between hers as he rolled them over until El lay beneath him. "Friction works best. You know"—his legs parted hers, his thighs spreading hers wide, his cock pressing into the open cradle of her sex—"rubbing bodies together generates the best heat."

El faked a shiver. "I'm really cold."

Smiling, Brogan rocked against her, his thick shaft sliding over her clit pulling a moan from each of them. "We should get as close as we can then."

She spread her legs further, bent her knees to open her pussy more. "How close?"

"This close." Tilting his hips, he thrust forward and entered her in one stroke.

With a gasp, El curled her spine, lifted her hips up, took him deeper. "Closer works."

"Closer always works."

"Enough talking. Get busy."

"Yes, ma'am."

As he withdrew, she locked her ankles behind his back and sank her fingers into the taut globes of his ass, tugging him forward. "Don't hold back. I want it all. I want all of you, Brogan. No more guilt, no more second guessing. I'm here because I want to be. Because you're it for me. You fit me in a way I've never felt before. A way I never want to live without."

"El..."

"I love you. Make love to me."

"I don't think I deserve you but I'm taking you anyway." He drove back in, ground his pelvis against her so his shaft pressed into her clit the way he'd discovered she liked. "You're mine," he gasped between thrusts as he picked up the pace.

"Yes. Take me."

Plunging deep he held still. "I love you."

Smiling, El gave his ass a squeeze. "Then love me."

"With pleasure." He started a push-pull rhythm that had his cock touching every sensitive nerve in her sex, sending pulses of electricity deep in her core.

"Oh there's nothing but pleasure with you."

"*Us*. There's nothing but pleasure with *us*."

El drew in a deep breath, relishing the cold filling her chest. The day had turned out sunny and warm. Well, warm compared to what it had been since she'd arrived. She still wore three layers, scarf, gloves, and a thick jacket.

"It's crazy how warm today feels."

Brogan chuckled. "The first sighting of the sun usually brings everyone out of hiding. If we went to town I'm sure the streets would be full of pack members venturing out for the first time in months."

"Is that normal? For everyone to hibernate through winter?" she asked, dodging around a rock on the path that wasn't really a path.

"Yes, and no. Some for sure, they lock down early winter and don't come out until after spring. Others like to get out between snow-ins."

"Should we go to town while the weather is good? You haven't been there for weeks and I'm sure you have sovereign responsibilities you should be taking care of." She hated the thought of him neglecting his people to spend time with her.

"No." He reached back to help her up a rocky section of slope. "If tomorrow's the same, and the prediction is it will be, then we'll go to town, have lunch at the Den, and I'll do whatever it is I might need to do and you can go shopping. I know Rowan keeps things well stocked but I'm sure there are some things we're running low on by now. We'll drag her and Quinn with us."

"Oh, I'd love to have lunch or at least chat with Doc, Tatum, and Kat. We haven't all been together since Doc's wedding."

"Whatever my lady wants," Brogan said with an exaggerated bow.

"Knock it off." She slapped his arm lightly. "Do we need to do anything for Wild Encounters? It's not long before you're up and running again."

"No. Everything is ready to go and having Brady on board means I can spend less time in the mountains and more time on expanding the business."

"You really think building a ski lodge lower down the mountain will be good? You're not worried about non-shifters finding their way up here?"

"Quinn and I have gone back and forth on this point for months. We've got safeguards in place. Plus they won't want or need to leave Whispering Slopes. You helped make sure of that with all your suggestions about shops and making the resort more like a town than just a hotel with ski fields."

"And you're staffing it with shifters only, right? Less chance of someone who shouldn't be directed up here being sent this way."

"We are."

"How long before you open doors do you think? Next winter?" She'd enjoyed being in on the discussions about expanding Wild Encounters and couldn't wait to see the company in action. Brogan had promised to take her on a couple of treks when he went out and she'd already thought about which of her cameras she wanted to take.

"No. We want to do this right, so we're not rushing things. The plan is winter after next and I'm not inclined to push that forward even if we are on track to do so."

"Oh," El gasped as she slipped on wet rock.

Brogan swung around and grabbed her arm, pulling her close against his chest and saving her from planting on her ass. "Whoa. Careful."

"Okay, this is getting harder and I haven't asked until now but where the hell are we going?"

"Not much longer. Up the top of this ridge is what we've come for."

Glancing up the slope, El decided she could make the next twenty feet or so. They'd been trekking for a half hour. Brogan had led her into the forest behind the house and urged her up the mountain. She wasn't against the trek, but after weeks of inactivity she was feeling every step of it.

Her thighs ached and her feet hurt where the new boots Brogan had bought her rubbed her heels and toes. It was a good thing it really wasn't that warm; without the slight numbing effect of the cold she was positive she'd be feeling it a lot worse.

"You go up first," Brogan directed as he moved her in front of him.

He kept his hands on her waist as they moved up the last of the slope and came over the top.

"Oh," El breathed. "It's... I don't have words."

The vista in front of them stretched for miles. Miles and miles of forest dusted in white. This was what people meant when they talked about a winter wonderland. It was magical.

"Dammit! Why didn't you let me bring a camera?" she asked as she spun around to face Brogan. If the view had taken her breath, the sight of Brogan sucked every molecule from her body. "What...?"

"Eloise, I know you come from a different world than mine and I wanted for us to truly combine our lives," he said from where he knelt at her feet. In his outstretched hand lay a ring. "Will you marry me?"

"Brogan." She sighed. "You didn't have to—"

"I know. I wanted to. So..." He lifted his hand higher. "Will you marry me?"

"I already wear your ring." She held up her left hand. "But my answer hasn't changed, won't change. Yes, I'll marry you every day for the rest of our lives if you want me to."

Slipping the beautiful sapphire ring on her finger beside her wedding band, he said, "The blue sapphire is for your eyes and the surrounding ring of smaller yellow sapphires are for mine."

"Brogan," she gasped. "It's gorgeous but what I love most is that you thought about this so deeply."

"I wanted you to wear a reminder of us together so whenever I'm not with you, all you have to do is look at this ring and know that I am in fact with you. Always."

Throwing her arms around his neck, she grabbed handfuls of his hair and pulled his lips to hers. Speaking against his mouth, she said, "You're already with me always. You live in my heart, Brogan. Forever."

COYOTE WHISPERS

COYOTE HUNGER

*Alan, I know they're not kangaroo shifters but this one's for you.
Billi and her invaluable snow info and the Heat Wave readers for the
drywall.
Fedora, thank you for keeping me in line.
Mr. C, I love you more with every day. Together Forever.*

*I'd like to give a special thank you to all the readers of the Coyote Hunger
series. Without you and your demands for more I wouldn't have written
Doc and Steve's story so soon. Thank you from the bottom of my heart for
loving the members of the Whispering Mountains coyote pack as much as
I do.*

1

MAY 18

Steve sat enclosed by darkness and listened to the sounds of the forest as it settled into the coming night. The sun had gone down hours ago thanks to the mountains he called home, but true sunset still had a few minutes. He'd lived in Whispering Springs or the surrounding mountain range his whole life.

Never once had he felt the urge to leave it behind and explore the world. He took the occasional trip down the mountainside to visit one of the big cities, but there was no appeal in staying away longer than a day or two, a week at most.

He breathed deep, pulling the chilled, late-spring air into his lungs, the accompanying sting of cold meeting warm, a welcome twinge. His house had been finished for two months, but he hadn't moved everything in until this past weekend.

A grin curled his lips as he thought about why it had taken so long. Having his two best friends somewhat occupied with Rowan's return had slowed down both the finishing of the house and the moving in. Not that he'd complain. Steve was more than happy Rowan had finally come home and even happier to see her reunited with her mate, Quinn.

The night around him grew still, quiet in a way that pricked his instincts, caused his hair to stand on end, and drew his coyote's attention. Steve slowly sat forward, leaned over to put his beer bottle on the deck beside his chair, before closing his eyes and honing his senses to listen—to smell. The crush of undergrowth beneath running feet hit him first, followed by a body-slamming gust of fear. He scented two shifters but he couldn't place them. Tried harder to separate them and connect either essence to the memory of its owner.

A howl of agony echoed up the ridge, sliced into his gut and pulled his coyote out with amazing speed. On his feet, Steve was glad he'd forgone shirt and shoes after his shower as he removed his sweats. Free of the restrictive garment, he shifted as he leapt over the deck railing to the ground one story below. He landed with a jolt to every bone but ignored it as he ran through the forest in the direction of the horrific screams of distress.

As he drew closer he could hear the struggles, smell the fear—the blood. *The enjoyment.* The attacker, in coyote form if he wasn't mistaken, was thrilled with his catch. A catch Steve had every intention of setting free. His muscles shuddered and it wasn't just from the exertion of running all out. He thought about stealth but a bloodcurdling cry and bark of triumph changed his mind. Low branches and shrubs slapped into him, tangled with his fur, as he powered his bulk toward the fight up ahead he glimpsed through the trees.

The other animal's head whipped up, yellow eyes and white teeth glowed in the dusk as he turned in Steve's direction. A frustrated howl rent the air as the coyote turned from his prey and bolted in the opposite direction. Torn between going after the retreating coyote and tending to the victim, Steve hesitated enough to have the decision made for him. Whoever the coyote was, he had too much head start and the metallic stench of blood told Steve his first concern should be the wounded human crumpled on the ground.

Ripped, blood-splattered clothes covered the too-still body, but there was no mistaking the feminine shape or perfume. He reached her side and shifted back to human form. Uncaring of his naked state, he knelt beside her head and felt for a pulse. The steady beat reassured him but how long would it stay that way? The overpowering aroma of spilled blood masked her scent, but he knew she was one of the pack, her scent was familiar. Too familiar.

No!

His fingers trembled as he brushed away hair to reveal the face he saw in his dreams and Steve's heart stopped.

"Doc?" The hoarse whisper ached in his throat.

His heart kicked back in with a thud. Adrenaline pumped through his veins and the urge to cradle her in his arms took hold but Steve knew he couldn't. Not yet. He had to check her injuries, stop the bleeding if he could. He ran his hands down her limbs to check for broken bones. In his limited knowledge he held back a howl of frustration. She was the one who should be doing this. She was the doctor. The person who stitched the cuts, set the broken bones and soothed the bruises.

Hands and fingers sticky with blood, Steve rolled her to her back and breathed a sigh of relief when she moaned.

"Doc? Can you hear me?"

She shuddered under his touch but didn't answer as he tried to find where she bled from the most. Her jeans and shirt were wet with blood but he couldn't find anything too deep or gushing enough to take the time to stop the flow. He needed to get her to the house. There he could remove what was left of her clothes and see how bad the damage was under light. He could also clean her up and decide if she required medical attention better than he could give.

They were about three hundred feet below his house but with the slope and thick vegetation, that distance may as well be three miles. It would take him longer to get up the hill than it had coming down with the burden of carrying Doc, and Steve knew every second counted. He tried to be as gentle as possible, but she whimpered when he worked his arms under her and pulled her against his naked chest.

In all the fantasies he'd had of Doc cradled against his naked body, this wasn't one of them. The woman set his blood on fire but carrying her now froze that same blood in his veins. Knowing someone had set out to hurt her—*had hurt her*—made Steve's coyote want to hunt down her attacker and do some hurting of his own. He turned and headed for home, careful not to let any branches scrape against her battered body. By the time he reached halfway, shivers raked her from head to toe and he knew shock had set in.

He lengthened his stride. The urgency to get her home giving him the strength to move over the ground quickly. When the large, dark shadow of his house came into view he breathed a sigh of relief and went toward the basement door. Once inside, Steve did something he'd never done before. He closed the solid timber panel and threw the deadbolt home.

The house was dark—quiet, but he stopped to listen in case they weren't alone. There was nothing different from when he'd left. No new scents and Steve's instincts told him no one was inside—or had been. He took the stairs to the main floor, Doc held tight in his embrace. It never entered his mind to take her to a guest room. Instead he headed straight for his bedroom, laid her on his bed and switched the bedside light on to get his first good look at her.

Steve sucked in a breath. Her delicate face was bruised and bloody, one eye swollen and the shiner already showing. The split in her bottom lip looked bad, it gaped open and blood flowed in a thin line down her chin. The dark shadow along the right side of her jaw worried him. She'd obviously taken one to the chin at some point, whether a direct strike or glancing blow he couldn't say. Doc reminded him of a prize fighter after ten rounds in the ring.

As gently as he could, he removed her clothes. He started at her feet, tossing her boots to the floor behind him. Her jeans were torn in places and the patches of blood, while concerning, didn't seem to be life threatening. Steve popped the button and tugged the zipper down. Lucky for him, Doc chose to wear clothes too big for her petite frame and the pants slid down over her hips with little resistance. With her legs bare he could see the scratches and knew the heavy denim had saved her from worse harm.

When only her bra and panties covered her, Steve ducked into his bathroom for the first-aid kit. He filled a small bowl with warm water and grabbed a washcloth and towel. The dirt and blood needed to be cleaned away before he could treat her wounds and assess the damage.

She hadn't moved or made more than the occasional whimper since they came inside and the worry of her lack of response played on Steve's mind. Should he have taken her straight to town? No point second-guessing now. He had to take care of her as best he could.

Most of the lacerations were minor except one across her left breast had him more than a little concerned. He had to remove her bra to see the entire wound. It went from the top curve below her collarbone to just under her nipple and the two shallow scratches either side of the deep cut told him a paw had caught the tender flesh and sliced it.

His back teeth would be ground to stumps by the time he finished. The need to hunt down her attacker burned in his gut and his coyote yanked to be let free but Steve couldn't do anything yet. Doc needed him and he wouldn't go off and leave her. He couldn't no matter how much his animal side wanted to.

Doc whimpered and moaned while he cleaned the lesser scrapes but jerked awake as he swiped the large gash on her breast. Her body stiffened and he waited for the panic, for her to fight him but her instincts were good, she just opened the eye that wasn't swollen shut and watched him as he cleaned, then treated the wound with disinfectant lotion.

"You're safe now, Gordie, I won't let anyone hurt you again." His words did little to soothe his agitated nerves but she relaxed into the bed.

Steve rolled her to the side, took care of the cuts on her back before easing her over again. The marks on her face were the only ones left to deal with and he wasn't at all sure what to do about her lip, but first he'd get her one of his shirts. He didn't want her to get cold and he didn't think Doc would be too happy when she came to her senses a bit more and found herself all but naked in his bed.

He'd been trying to get her there for years but no matter what he did, Steve could never convince her that's where she belonged. Having her here now, like this, tore him up inside.

He had what he'd always wanted but at what cost?

——————

Gordie watched Steve. The barest of tremors shook his hands as he tended to her injuries. Her focus was off, one eye blurry and the other refused to open. Dizziness made her nauseated and the churning of her stomach warned of possible rebellion. Taking slow, deep breaths she catalogued the damage. Nothing felt broken, but she was pretty sure she had a mild concussion.

She hadn't seen it coming. One second she was walking through the forest and the next she received a punch in the face. The blow snapped her head back and slammed her into a tree. For a moment Gordie was stunned, and her attacker managed a few more good hits before shock wore off and she began to fight back. A kick to the balls had given her precious seconds to run. She hadn't counted on him shifting.

Fear sliced through Gordie as Steve stood.

"Don't leave me." The words came out garbled and the pain that lanced her lip made her cry out.

"Easy. I'm not going anywhere." He was back beside her, brushing her cheek with his fingertips. "I'm just getting a shirt for you to put on."

She squeezed her eye shut and breathed deep. Pain radiated out through her chest, the side she'd landed on when the coyote had pounced on her burned and Gordie knew the fact she was bruised and not broken was a miracle. The sting of tears scalded her eyes and scratched the back of her throat. She wouldn't cry. *She wouldn't.*

Gordie tried to swallow but her mouth was dry. Her tongue slid out to lick her lip and she jerked on the bed, the pain excruciating, and an agonized shriek left her throat.

"Easy, baby." Warm hands soothed her, skirting around the

numerous aches. "Let's get you covered up so I can take a look at that mouth."

Her body vibrated with the strain of holding the sobs at bay. The bed lifted and Steve's warmth disappeared. Suddenly cold, Gordie shivered, the quaking built in intensity until her teeth chattered. When the mattress dipped and heat brushed against her hip, Gordie shook so violently every part of her screamed in pain.

Groaning, she turned into him as he leaned over to help her sit. With gentleness she'd never expected, Steve tugged a soft flannel shirt up her arm and around her back.

It proved more difficult to get her second arm into the sleeve. Whimpers and moans filled the air. Muscles tense with pain refused to cooperate and Gordie could do little to help. With her arm in at last, Steve lowered her to the bed. Her back spasmed, agony speared up her spine to throb painfully at the base of her skull. Her head swam and her stomach churned. Bile rose in her throat and she turned to the side.

Either Steve had worked out what was about to happen or the man had lightning-fast reflexes. He had the wastepaper basket under her face as she leaned over the edge of the mattress. Abdominal muscles contracted, repelling everything in her stomach up her throat. Acid burned and the metallic taste of blood filled her mouth, making her heave harder. Sweat popped out on her skin, and goose bumps followed by uncontrollable shaking rode alongside the piercing pain of her twisted belly.

He held her hair out of the way, his other hand holding the bin while she emptied the contents of her stomach. Tears streamed down her face and mucus ran from her nose. As the convulsions eased, Gordie slumped forward in exhaustion. The pain receded, her body going numb, and the effort to stay awake grew more difficult. Steve moved her back from the edge, used a pillow to prop her up. Her head drooped and Gordie knew she would be out in seconds but she needed to make something clear first.

"No hospital." Her lip stung and hot fluid trickled down her chin.

"Shit, Doc. I can't stitch that lip and it needs a few. I need to get you to someone who can take care of it."

"No. Hospital." Her words slurred as blackness closed in.

"Gordie."

"Please." The word came out a sob.

"Okay."

"Promise me." She couldn't leave Whispering Springs and she was the only medical personnel on the mountain. She just needed to rest and then she'd be okay to stitch the wound herself.

Steve must have leaned over her because warm, mint-fresh breath fanned out across her face as he sighed. "Okay, Gordie. I promise."

His fingers brushed away the strands of hair stuck to her forehead, his gentle touch again surprising her. Steve was a large man, one she usually avoided touching but not through fear of physical harm. No, he scared her for other reasons she chose to ignore. But as drowsiness pulled at her, the last thing to play across her mind was the big man who treated her with such care.

———

Steve cursed himself a fool as he cleaned Doc's face. He'd given his word and he wouldn't go back on it, but damn, she needed to have her lip tended to. He could stitch it but he knew there would be a horrible scar if he tried. She'd heal quickly with her coyote DNA, but without stitches it would leave her with a visible reminder. The bruising on her face had already gone a deep blue-black, moving through the phases of healing quickly.

The blood and dirt were gone but he hadn't used the disinfectant yet. He wanted to keep his promise but he also needed to know she was okay and he didn't think he possessed enough skill to trust his own judgment. Blowing out a breath, he rummaged through the first-aid kit, hoping to find something that would pull the two sides of her lip together and hold them there. His fingers landed on a box of steri-strips and he ripped it open to examine the small bandages.

They could work. Doc would need to keep her mouth still and

he'd have to watch the wound for infection, but if he used a couple of the strips to pull the sections of lip together it would hold and allow her body to heal. Reading the instructions one more time, Steve laid everything out within easy reach. Once he had the area clean and dry, he pushed the open sides of the cut together and stuck a strip on.

Three more and he'd done the best job he could. He sat back to admire his handiwork and laughed ruefully. Not the best-looking bandage he'd ever seen but it would do for now.

He gathered up the discarded wrappers and went to throw them into the waste bin next to the bed but remembered just in time he'd used it to catch her vomit. Putting them in a pile beside him, he pulled the first-aid kit back together and returned it to the bathroom where he tossed the garbage in the bin.

Back in his room, he cleared away Doc's bloody clothes, the waste basket and the bowl of now-cold water. Steve made sure she was resting before he went to get his pants from the back deck. Detouring past the front door, he locked it. No way would he allow anyone the chance to get near Doc again.

His pants and beer retrieved, he locked the sliding door to the deck and went to the kitchen. He dumped the untouched warm beer down the sink before he threw the bottle in the bin. Forgoing another one, he grabbed a soda instead. He'd need his wits about him from now on.

Not that one beer would get him drunk, but anything that slowed his reflexes was off his agenda until he found the bastard responsible for Doc's attack. Throwing his pants in the laundry as he walked by, Steve made his way back to the bedroom. Happy to see Doc resting easy, he slipped into the bathroom for a quick shower.

With a twist of a tap had the water running. He swallowed the last of the soda and dropped the can in the bin before stepping into the glass enclosure. Water flowed down his body and he tilted his face into the spray to let the hot stream wash the dirt and sweat—the blood from his chest—away.

A shudder traveled through him. The thought of Doc's spilled blood made his own boil with anger and the urge to hunt and destroy the person who'd hurt her. His jaw clenched and he ground his molars hard. They'd pay for touching her, but he needed to focus on Doc before he could take revenge.

Steve soaped himself and rinsed. For the second time tonight, he shut the shower off and stepped out. Brisk movements dragged the towel over his skin, soaking up the moisture and abrading nerve endings already on edge. He tucked the towel over the rail and ran his fingers through his wet hair. Emotions bombarded him. He wanted to hold Doc close and keep her safe but he also wanted to go out and hunt down her attacker.

Frustration tore at him, but Steve knew the only thing he'd be doing tonight would be watching over Doc. He gave himself a shake to loosen his tense muscles before he left the bathroom and returned to Gordie. The scent of blood still tainted the air and his jaw clenched with renewed anger. Pausing, he made a conscious effort to relax. It wouldn't do her any good to feel his rage and for now it had to be all about Doc.

Making his way to the chest of drawers, he pulled out a pair of boxers and stepped into them. Three strides had him beside the bed. Doc was on top of the bedcovers but he didn't want to disturb her so he pulled a blanket from the back of his cupboard and draped it over her. Walking to the other side of the bed he lifted the edge of the cover and crawled in next to her.

He wanted to pull her into his arms but he didn't think he could without hurting her and the last thing he wanted was to add to her pain. Steve reached over to the bedside lamp and switched it off. Moonlight streamed through the window and skylight, bathing the room in a soft glow. Doc lay on her side, facing him, her body curled up as though protecting herself from further harm. His heart ached at how vulnerable she appeared.

Resistance was futile. The woman he wanted to the depth of his soul lay hurting alongside him and he had to touch her. With the tip of one finger he brushed the hair from her eyes. She moved into his caress and he couldn't stop the smile that pulled at his mouth. In her most unguarded moment, she knew him, reached for him. Her actions contradicting every protest she'd made about their attraction.

For three years he'd respected her need to push him away. He knew her denial of their attraction stemmed from the trauma of losing her husband and unborn child, but enough was enough. From now on she wouldn't keep him at arm's length. He'd make sure of it. It was time for her to accept him as her mate. She could object all she wanted, but Steve wasn't about to let things continue the way they had been.

Not after tonight.

He understood her need to protect herself but in doing so she was denying both of them happiness. The fear of being mated had stopped him from pursuing her when they were teenagers, that and her being human. It had terrified him back then and by the time he'd gotten his head around it Anthony had stolen her out from under his nose. Steve didn't plan on letting that happen again and he'd be damned if he would let her fight him any longer.

It was time to claim what was his.

Gordie's first registered thought was pain. Everything hurt. From the tips of her toes to the top of her head, every cell screamed in agony—even her eyelashes as they weighed down her lids. She tried not to move, tried to keep her breathing shallow to stop the vise from crushing her chest. The second thing Gordie registered was the warm body she'd curled herself around. A steady heartbeat drummed beneath the hot flesh pressed to her face. Confusion filled her. Where was she? And who was in her bed?

"Easy, Doc. It's just me." The muscles beneath her cheek vibrated as Steve's voice rumbled through his chest and filled her ears.

The urge to pull away took hold but the slightest movement brought pain. Gordie opened her eyes, one barely more than a crack, and stared at the hard male chest before her. Bits and pieces of the night before started to flit through her mind and she groaned. The walk she'd taken after dinner, the need to be near Steve but not near him.

The attack.

Steve's arms loosened, giving her the freedom to move away if she wanted. But for the first time in three years Gordie wanted to be close to him. She needed him to hold her, to remind her she was alive —safe.

"Do you feel up to talking about what happened?"

Not wanting the ugliness of the night before intruding on the moment, she shook her head. Pain ricocheted around her skull, making her groan.

He didn't comment, just tightened his arms again and pulled her a little closer to his side. Warmth and rightness invaded her. The truth of what she'd been denying since her return to Whispering Springs and the mountains that had been her home from the age of six, slammed into her like never before. It terrified her like never before too, but she couldn't pull away from him. Not after last night. She felt vulnerable—scared, and Steve's steady presence reassured her.

They lay quietly in the predawn light. For long moments Gordie just enjoyed the safety and comfort Steve offered. She knew she'd have to go soon enough, knew she needed to check her wounds and return home. But she didn't want to leave his warm embrace. Wanted to stay wrapped in his arms and let him hold her and make every- thing disappear. But she couldn't expect Steve to take care of her problems for her.

Before last night Gordie hadn't been too concerned by the strange little things that had occurred over the last month. Random things moved at both her house and the clinic. Doors unlocked when she would swear she'd locked them. The creepy, itchy-neck feeling of being watched all the time. None of it had worried her because she'd been so busy she could have forgotten she'd moved that picture or those supplies—or even neglected to lock up after herself.

She couldn't ignore them anymore.

But she dare not tell anyone either. She had no real evidence and nothing but the gut-gnawing instinct that Marcus was behind what had been happening. The only proof anything was actually going on was last night's attack and she hadn't gotten a clear look at her assailant.

She wasn't even sure she'd identified his scent correctly. Even after all the years as a coyote shifter she still couldn't use her senses well. Maybe if she hadn't tried to ignore her wild side she might have had better luck.

Gordie had spent the years since Anthony's death denying her coyote existed whenever possible. She shifted when the pull became too much but other than that, her animal lay slumbering. Unless Steve was around—which was the reason she kept her distance from him. When he was near, her coyote sat up and took notice, wanted to break free and run wild to be with the animal she recognized as her mate. In the last few months staying away from him had become more difficult.

Her need to be close to him had driven her to take walks in the forest below his new home. Before he'd moved into his mountain house they'd lived on the same street and it wasn't until he'd started staying up on the mountain overnight that her true needs had shown themselves.

She'd managed to delude herself for so long. Believed she had her feelings under control. The wild rush of urges and desires had never been a part of her life before. She'd never felt this drawn to Anthony.

Even after he'd turned her, Anthony didn't make her pulse race or her coyote pull to be free. The guilt she'd lived with for years still haunted her. Gordie had hurt Anthony by accepting his love when she hadn't loved him in return. Not the way she should have—the way he deserved.

He'd been her friend and she'd been so desperate to become like everyone else in Whispering Springs she'd gladly taken all he offered. They'd both paid dearly for her mistake. She'd spent the years since his death trying to make up for her decision but the guilt remained.

Gordie closed her eyes tight. Tried to stop her brain from taking her into that dark place she'd locked away the day she left Whispering Springs to attend college. Now was not the time to dwell on the past. She had to think about what to do in the present. Because if she was right in her assumption of who had started a campaign of terror against her, she was in a whole heap of trouble and so was the rest of the pack.

Doc was overthinking again. The woman had a brain that wouldn't quit. While that was good when she was in her doctor role, Steve wished she'd let it rest and just feel for once. Then she might see how right it was for them to be together.

He'd let her push him away, let her rationalize until they were both blue in the face but he wouldn't give her that luxury anymore. From now on they were a couple. He wouldn't push her to mate but in every other area she'd have to accept him by her side.

First he needed to check her wounds and decide whether she should see someone about her lip. He'd dozed on and off since he'd crawled into bed, so he knew Doc had spent a restless night beside him. After he took care of her injuries he'd make them both something to eat, the healing process would require extra nourishment and he planned to make sure she got it. Then they'd talk and she could answer some questions, like what she was doing this far out of town in the forest after dark. Alone.

"I need to have a look at your injuries. I'm not sure I did a good job with your lip but I'm not the doctor here." Steve eased her face up with two fingers under her chin.

He gently cradled her cheek in his palm. The gash looked to be knitting together already. That and the bruising along her jaw and around her eyes made his stomach churn and his coyote wanted to rip apart the person responsible for the damage. It took effort and a bit more enamel ground from his back teeth but he managed to not squeeze her face in his frustration and anger. Steve let his fingertips trail the dark bruise along Doc's chin, the petite angle of her face marred by the ugly mark.

"Damn, Doc. You really got yourself done over. Wanna tell me what happened?"

She stiffened in his arms and fear flashed in her gaze before she looked away. Either she'd been more than physically hurt in the attack or she was attempting to shut him out again.

"Don't try to shut me out. I'm finished with you pushing me away. Dancing around what we are, ends now, Doc." He placed a kiss on top of her head. "I'll wait on the mating, I won't push you on being physically intimate, but I will push you on everything else. From now on we're together whether we have sex or not."

He held her close, rubbed his hand up and down her back until she relaxed against him once more.

"You can't fight what we are forever, Doc. I understand your fear and I'll be patient as best I can but you have to know our mating is inevitable. Neither of us is strong enough to fight these feelings forever."

Warm air whispered over his chest, ruffling his hair and bathing his nipple in a wave of moist heat. Her breasts, concealed by his shirt, pressed into his side as she sucked in a deep breath, their taut peaks poking into his ribcage. The sensations of holding Doc so close bombarded him and his body reacted in typical male fashion. His pulse raced and blood pumped into his cock. He ignored his coyote's call to claim his mate and just held her. She remained quiet for so long Steve thought she would continue to deny their connection but she surprised him.

"I know I can't fight it anymore. I realized that when you moved up here but I'm not ready to take the next step." Her words were barely a murmur but he heard every one as if it were a physical blow to his heart.

"We'll worry about that later. Right now, let's get you all fixed up." Steve gently eased Doc away and turned her onto her back. He leaned up on his elbow and studied her face. "You know, you don't look as bad as I thought you would this morning."

The corners of her mouth tipped up and she winced. "Shoot, that hurt."

"Yeah, your lip is split down the middle. Try not to move your mouth."

"Talking isn't that bad because I can do it without moving my lips too much but smiling is obviously out of the question." She brought her hand up and ran her fingertips over his make-do bandage job.

Steve frowned. "It's not the most professional job, but working with what I have on hand and you extracting that promise you got the best I could offer."

"It feels okay but I should check it."

Doc tried to sit up but he stopped her with a hand on her shoulder. "Stay there. I'll grab the first-aid kit and a mirror." He rolled off the bed and walked around to her side. "Here, let me help you sit."

He pulled the pillows from his side of the bed and, easing her forward, stacked them behind her. Doc closed her eyes as she leaned back. "Do you have any pain pills?"

"Yeah. I'll bring everything I've got." He strode from the room and into his bathroom.

It didn't take long to pull out his supplies, he wasn't exactly overflowing with medical paraphernalia. Steve brought back his haul and dropped it on the bed beside Doc. He walked to his dresser and pulled his mother's hand mirror from the top drawer and headed back to Doc to find her going through his kit.

"This is all you have?"

It was a simple question but there was so much censure in those five words. Sheepishly he said, "Sorry, I'm not as familiar with all this stuff as you are."

Doc looked up, their gazes colliding. "Remind me to make you up a kit, these store-bought jobs are okay but I can give you a better one from the clinic." She barely moved her lips when she spoke but her words were clear.

Steve watched as Doc pulled out bandages, scissors and tape. She held the box of steri-strips before discarding them and searching the small plastic tub for something else. A breath huffed through her nose as she stopped combing the contents and went back to the packet of strips.

"You don't have sutures?"

He shook his head. "No. Only what came in the kit."

She sighed and picked up his mother's mirror. Her eyes widened when she saw her beaten-up face for the first time. The fingers she brought up to brush over the bandage on her lip trembled and her brown eyes filled with moisture. "Damn."

"Yeah, it's not pretty but it's already started to heal."

Doc brushed her fingertips along the bruise on her jaw. "This was the first punch," she murmured.

Steve's gut knotted and his coyote snarled. He managed to keep from voicing his rage. "What were you doing out in the woods?"

Her gaze met his, the dark depths held so much churning emotion the knot in his stomach tightened. "I wanted to be near you."

"You were in the forest to be near me?" He didn't understand how that was near him at all. Why hadn't she just knocked on his door?

"Ever since you moved up here I've been walking in the woods to be close. I needed to feel you."

"Jesus, Doc, you're killing me here." He reached out, ran his fingers down her cheek. "No more. You want to feel me, you come inside."

She turned away and Steve put gentle pressure on her chin to make her look at him. "Promise me, Gordie. I don't want you going anywhere alone again."

His heart stalled while he waited for her answer. When she nodded he released the breath he held and leaned forward. As lightly as he could, Steve pressed his lips to hers. He stilled, savored the heat and feel of her mouth against his. The urge for more rolled over him and he groaned. Before he could take what he so desperately wanted he pulled back and rested his forehead on hers.

"Okay." He breathed deep. "Let's get you fixed up to your standards."

Doc didn't speak while he helped her remove the bandage from her mouth. The wound, like the rest of her injuries, had begun to heal. He held the strips ready for her to apply and by the time she'd finished he was more ashamed of the crappy job he'd done the night before.

"It's not so bad. I doubt I could have done a better job earlier, not without sutures." Her words, he knew, were supposed to reassure him but nothing except an uninjured Doc could do that.

"Feel like eating?" Steve gathered up what was left of the first-aid kit and the trash. "You need to build up your strength. I'm no chef, but I can open a can of soup."

"I'm not sure my stomach is up to eating yet, but you're right. And a bowl of warm soup sounds wonderful." The smile in her voice didn't move her lips or reach her eyes but that wasn't surprising when she had to still be in pain.

"I'll grab those pain pills and a glass of water first." He stood and turned for the door but Doc's voice stopped him before he took a step.

"Steve?"

He turned to face her. "What do you need?"

"Thank you." Her mouth curled slightly on the ends and she couldn't hide the flinch the action caused. "For everything."

Steve sighed. "Gordie you know I'd do anything you asked. The trouble is, until last night you never needed me." He spun around and strode from the room. Emotions collided inside him. Love, desire, rejection, guilt, frustration. One thing about Doc, she made him feel it all.

———

Gordie sank into the soft pillows at her back and closed her eyes. She'd swallowed the pain meds under Steve's watchful eye before he'd gone to the kitchen to heat some soup. It wasn't exactly a nutritional breakfast but at the moment that was the least of her concerns. She needed food while she healed—any food. Her aches had lessened since she'd woken, whether that was the pills starting to work or her own body healing she couldn't say, and really didn't care.

She couldn't bring herself to care about much of anything right now. Having Steve look after her, tending her injuries with such a gentle touch had soothed her in a way she hadn't expected. As much as she'd told him she wasn't ready for the next step in their relationship, Gordie couldn't deny she was closer than ever to giving in to her need for him. The edge of fear that always accompanied her emotions when she thought of Steve and what they could be had disappeared in the space of a few hours.

For years she'd used that fear to keep her distance. Without it, Gordie knew it was only a matter of time before they took the final step. Only one thing stood between them now. She needed to make peace with her past and the guilt she'd lived with for so long. Anthony would be the first person to encourage her to move on, but he wasn't here to nag her into it and as much as it hadn't been on a soul-deep level, she *had* loved him, still mourned his loss as though it happened yesterday.

Letting go of her guilt would be like losing Anthony all over again but it wouldn't be fair to Steve or her to take their attraction further until she had. The attack last night only served to remind her that life was short, too short to not take the happiness offered. Gordie hoped Steve had meant what he said about no pressure. With everything going on in her life right now she didn't think they'd be taking that final step anytime soon.

2

DECEMBER 23

Steve's boots crunched through the fresh layer of snow on the ground as he made his way to the back door. Knocking the slush from his heels, he slipped through the open door and shut it behind him, making sure the deadlock engaged. His gut tightened. It wasn't like Doc to leave the clinic open after hours.

Careful not to make a sound, he turned and listened. Various motors associated with a doctor's office hummed and the tick of a clock beat steadily but Steve couldn't detect any other noise.

Where was Doc? Steve hadn't seen her outside when he pulled up and he'd driven past the front of the building on his way to the back alley. She was expecting him. They'd spoken on the phone not fifteen minutes earlier. So where the hell was she and why was the clinic left unlocked?

Something was wrong. Had been for weeks but Doc refused to talk about it. He cursed her for keeping him at arm's length. Still.

His senses were on full alert as he stepped along the dark corridor. The door to Doc's office was wide open, the chair pushed back from the desk as though she'd gotten up in a hurry. A chill slid down Steve's spine and the hair across his nape stood on end. He went deeper into the building. The next door was closed and he placed his ear against the timber. No sound came from the other side, not that he expected to hear anyone in the storeroom.

Doc kept the room locked unless she was in there but he tried the knob regardless. It didn't budge. Noise farther down the hall had his head snapping around. There was no one in sight and the place had gone quiet as a tomb again but he'd definitely heard something.

Gordie, where the hell are you?

The next room he came to served as the theater and morgue. Steve peered around the door frame. At a glance everything appeared to be in place so he moved on to the first examination room. Bright murals and mobiles made the children's exam room like a playground and other than the gentle sway of the coyotes dangling from the ceiling where the central heating duct blew warm air into the room, there was no movement.

Steve paused, listening for any sign of life. There were two more rooms plus the reception office and waiting area to search. His senses told him he wouldn't find anyone. He could smell Doc's lingering scent, but couldn't tell if she was here or not, the smells associated with any medical facility masked others and that made his instincts howl with frustration. She would never leave the clinic unattended and she certainly wouldn't leave the back door unlocked, never mind open.

He wanted to race through the rest of the building, throwing open doors and yelling Doc's name, but he stayed on the side of caution just in case he'd misjudged the situation. What danger could be lurking he hadn't a clue and he didn't really want to find out. All he wanted was Gordie. To know she was safe. He stepped into the next exam room. Movement to the left in his peripheral vision made him turn and crouch.

A large, silver blur rushed past his temple, ruffling his hair and almost making him miss the other, smaller steel implements flying in his direction. He ducked and rolled to the side. Landing on his stomach, he looked across the room. Gordie stood with her arms raised, an instrument tray in her hands, and the look of fear on her face brought his protective instincts and coyote screaming to the surface.

Steve barely held on to his human side. Something or someone had terrified his mate and he was ready and willing to take that threat apart.

"Gordie!" Steve remained still, strained against the need to go to her, and tried to show the frightened woman he wasn't a danger. "It's me. Steve."

Her face drained of color and her shoulders sagged as she lowered the tray. "Oh God. Steve?" Her words were no more than a breath.

"Yeah, baby, it's me." He slowly pushed off the floor. "The door was open, Doc."

"The door?" Her gaze darted to the doorway behind him.

Her vagueness worried him. Whatever had caused her fear had done a real number on her. She hadn't been this shaken up after the brutal attack months ago. He took a step toward her, his movement made her flinch, the metal tray dropping to the floor at her feet with a spine-rattling crash. Doc's hands clenched into fists at her sides but the action didn't hide the fact she was trembling.

He took another step, kept the motion smooth so as not to startle her again. Steve quickened his pace when she swayed. He'd taken two strides when she began to crumple to the floor. Darting forward, he barely caught her in time and he ended up sitting on the cold linoleum, Doc cradled in his lap. She threw her arms around his neck, buried her face against his chest and burst into tears.

Dumbstruck by this vulnerable Doc in his arms, it took Steve a moment to think straight. Holding her close, he rocked them, ran his hands up and down her back, and whispered words of reassurance he wasn't even sure he believed. He told her it would be all right but he had no idea if his words were true when he had no clue about what had happened.

When her sobbing eased off to the odd hiccup, Steve reached into his pocket for his phone. It took him a couple of tries but he finally got the number he was after and hit call. He listened to two rings before a deep voice answered.

"Dale Turner."

"Come to the clinic."

"What the hell is going on, McKenna?"

"I don't know exactly but you need to come now."

"I'll be there in five."

The line went dead in his ear. He pulled the phone back into view and scrolled through his address book. Hitting call a second time, Steve brought the device back to his ear. It rang five times before Brogan picked up.

"Wilder."

"Where are you?"

"In town, why?"

"You need to come to the clinic."

"I'm not liking the sound of your voice, Steve."

"Neither am I but I'm dealing. Just get here." He hung up before his friend could question him further.

Pocketing the phone, he shifted Doc so he could get them off the floor. She lay limp in his arms as he got to his feet and walked over to the exam table. Placing her on the bed proved difficult when she wouldn't let go of his neck.

"I'm not leaving but I have to let the sheriff in when he gets here." Loud banging echoed down the hallway. "That'll be him now. I'm coming right back."

Steve untangled her arms and settled her back on the pillow. He grabbed the folded blanket from the foot rail, shook it out and spread it over her, tucking in the sides. He brushed a hand over her face, pushing her hair out of her eyes. "Be right back."

Making his way to reception at a jog, he crossed the waiting area and unlocked the front door. Dale, Brogan and Quinn charged in, making Steve jump back or be knocked down by the three men. He started to shut the door when Rowan and El stepped inside.

"Well, the gang's all here."

"Cut the crap, McKenna. What the fuck's going on?" Brogan demanded.

Steve sighed. "I don't know exactly yet. I got here about ten minutes ago and the back door was open with no one in sight."

"Where was Gordie?" Rowan asked.

"In the exam room but I didn't know that then."

"What do you mean by that?" Dale stepped closer.

"I'll explain everything but first I have to get back to Doc." Steve turned, throwing over his shoulder, "Make sure you secure the door."

"Secure the door? Just what the fuck is going on, Steve?" Brogan boomed.

"Stop yelling. Doc's nerves are frayed enough without you adding to it." Steve entered the exam room to find Gordie had turned on her side facing the doorway. Her eyes where huge in her chalk-white face and his gut knotted. He walked over and gathered her into his arms, needing to feel her against him to know she was safe.

Wrapped in the blanket, she curled up on his lap as he took a seat in a chair. She trembled and in spite of the blanket and warm room, her body temperature had gone down as though she'd been outside without her coat.

"Gordie?" Rowan knelt at his feet, brushed her hand over Gordie's head. "Can I get you something? A drink maybe?"

"Tea. Warm, sweet tea will help." El patted Doc's shoulder. "I'll get a cup."

Steve loved that their group of friends were rallying around Doc but hated that she needed them at all. He'd give her another minute to warm up before he asked any questions. The three men stood in the room like a barricade against any further threat, their menacing faces enough to scare off the toughest of adversaries, known or otherwise.

El returned with a mug of tea and Steve held it to Doc's lips. She sipped, her hands wrapping around the cup and his hand. Her fingers interlocked with his and she gave him a gentle squeeze before she pushed the hot drink away and sat up.

"I'm okay." She sighed before lowering her head to rest on his shoulder.

"Wanna tell us what happened?" Steve asked.

"Not really much to tell. Someone was in the clinic. I'd locked up before talking to you so I don't know how they got in. Or how they got out."

"Out's easy. They went through the back door. It was open when I got here." He handed the mug to Rowan. "Did you get a look at who it was? Were they after drugs?"

Doc let out a chest-shaking sigh. "This is going to sound stupid and I won't blame any of you for thinking me crazy."

Dale laughed. "You're the least crazy person on the planet, Doc."

"Besides, in the last year there's been lots of crazy shit going on in this town," Brogan added.

"He was in black from head to foot. A beanie on his head and some sort of scarf over his face but I'd know those eyes anywhere."

Steve tensed. He knew what was coming, felt it in his bones and yet it still hit him like a two-by-four when Doc said the name.

"Marcus." She shuddered and sagged against him. "It was Marcus."

"Son of a bitch." Brogan lunged for El as she slumped to the floor. "Shit."

"I'm okay, Brogan. A little wobbly in the knees, but I'm okay," El said.

"Jesus, woman. Don't *do* that." Brogan held her in his arms.

Steve almost laughed at the terrified tone in his friend's voice but he knew all too well what Marcus was capable of doing. It had only been a few weeks since the maniac had had El at his mercy so her weak knees were understandable.

"Are you sure, Doc?" Dale asked.

"She wouldn't have said it if she wasn't," Steve snapped.

"Whoa." Dale held up his hands. "Just checking. It's my job, remember?"

Steve relaxed his tight grip on Gordie. "Sorry, but Doc doesn't lie."

"Never said she did but adrenaline can do a number on you and so can fear. She wouldn't be the first victim to make a mistake."

"No mistake." Gordie shifted in Steve's arms. "Help me sit up, Steve. It's time we told everyone about last May."

"While you're at it maybe you'll tell us what's been going on for weeks now too?" Steve was over being kept in the dark. If Doc was prepared to reveal what had happened back in spring then she could damn well tell him what the fuck had been going on recently.

***

Gordie knew Steve was right. She hadn't mentioned any of the events leading up to last May's attack or the ones in recent weeks to anyone but today showed her she couldn't deal with Marcus on her own. And there was no doubt in her mind that Marcus was behind everything. A shiver rippled through her. He'd gotten way too close this evening. He wouldn't get a second chance.

"Can we do this back at the house?" She looked at Steve. "I'd prefer to leave here. I'm not avoiding, putting off maybe, but I will tell you everything."

"I don't see why not. Any objections?" Dale asked.

"Yeah, I've got one." Steve's voice cut into her nerves and skated over her skin like ice. "You're not going back to your house."

"What? Of course I am. Where else would I go?"

"My place."

Gordie opened her mouth but didn't get out a sound, never mind a word.

"No arguments, Gordie. I'm done. No more running. No more hiding." His gaze bore into hers, slicing right to her soul. "Understand?"

There was no argument she could put forward. Not with every part of her shrieking for him to stay with her—hold her. In the months since that horrible night in the forest behind his house she'd made every excuse under the sun to keep him at arm's length. He'd pushed but he'd never once stepped over the invisible line she'd drawn between them. Until now.

She nodded.

It surprised Gordie, the relief that washed over her. She would have thought having Steve make the decision would chafe at her independent nature but it felt liberating—right. They stared at each other, testing the new agreement between them. Steve broke the connection and turned to face the others.

"Rowan, can you go over to The Den and ask Kat for some of her famous beef stew to go? Oh, and you better see if she can come out to the house for this too. If not, tell her to come out when she's done for the night." Steve took charge with ease. "Quinn, can I get you to change the locks on the clinic? I'd do it but I want to get Doc home and comfortable before we hash through everything. I have a feeling this is going to take a while."

"Sure thing, I'll meet you out at your place. Brogan, you and El take Rowan with you."

"Gordie, do you want me to ask Kat to get you anything from your place?" Rowan asked.

"We'll deal with that tomorrow. She can make do with what she's got. The clinic is closed now through to New Year so Doc won't need anything in a hurry." Steve finally turned back to her. "Where's your purse?"

"In my office, bottom desk drawer." She still hadn't faced the room but she could hear shuffling and footsteps on the linoleum floor as her friends began to leave.

"Did you walk to work today? Your car wasn't out back," Steve asked.

"No, Kat brought me in. She stayed over last night." Gordie didn't tell him why she'd convinced her sister to spend the night. There was no point starting that conversation yet.

"Okay, let's go." Steve, still holding her in his arms, cradled her close and got to his feet. "Dale, are you following us out to the house now?"

"No, if it's all right with Doc, I'll wait for Quinn to get back with those locks and have a look around in the meantime."

"Do you think you'll find anything?" She tilted her head to look at Dale. "I mean, I didn't hear anything until he was right behind me, no doors opening, no footsteps, nothing." She shivered at the memory of turning around and coming face-to-face with Marcus.

"He's gone, Doc." Steve's quiet words, murmured in her ear,

caused her tense muscles to relax. How he knew what she was thinking, Gordie couldn't begin to explain, and held in his warm embrace
she didn't bother trying. She just snuggled closer.

In no time she found herself strapped into the front seat of
Steve's pickup. The cab still had that new-car smell even though it
was almost a year since he'd had to replace the vehicle. Gordie
pushed away the memories of him using himself and his car as a
barricade between Quinn and a madman. Brogan was right. In the
last year Whispering Springs had seen more than its fair share of
crazy.

They spent the drive out of town in silence. Gordie didn't mind. It
gave her a few minutes to compose herself as the knowledge of what
they'd be before this day was over began to sink in. This time the
shiver that rolled down her spine had nothing to do with fear.

The thought of finally touching Steve like she'd wanted to for so
long sent heat shooting through her veins to pool in delicate flesh.
Her breasts felt heavy, her sex swollen. Moisture soaked her panties
and she had to admit, if only to herself, he made her want things
she'd never imagined.

Steve pulled into his attached garage and switched off the engine.
The silence seemed to echo around them, the air vibrating with the
stillness and Gordie quivered as the power of the moment flowed
over her. Once they stepped from the car nothing would be the same.

No, the change had happened back at the clinic. When she'd
needed Steve with a bone-deep ache that she'd registered even while
consumed with fear. It was that one instant in time where the world
had clicked into place and she'd seen the future as it should be. In a
second she'd gone from terrified and panicked to calm and centered.
She knew what she had to do. Survive at any cost.

Steve turned toward her, his forearm resting on the top of the
steering wheel. He didn't speak, just watched her with that penetrating gaze. The one that read all her innermost thoughts and made
her feel all squirmy inside. No man had ever affected her the way he
did and until today Gordie hadn't thought herself capable of
handling him. Now she knew differently.

"There's no turning back now, Doc." His fingers toyed with the ends of her hair.

She swallowed over the lump in her throat. "I know."

He smiled. "That easy?"

"It's amazing what a little fright can do for the senses." She tried to return his smile but it somehow slipped from her lips before it could form.

"Come here." Steve released her seatbelt and pulled her into his lap, pinning her between his body and the wheel. "You're safe here, Doc."

Gordie figured he meant in his house, but for her, safety was his arms, the security of his embrace and the strength he offered her willingly. She moved closer, nuzzled her face against the warmth of his neck and drew in his scent. It amazed her how just that small action could soothe her nerves and rile them at the same time.

"Gordie." Warm air ruffled her hair before she felt his lips press to her temple. "Come on, let's get inside or everyone will arrive and find us fucking in my truck."

She gasped. His use of strong language didn't bother her, it was the images the words provoked that made her breathless.

"Yeah, I'm that close." He chuckled as he opened the door and maneuvered them out of the cab.

"I can walk."

"I know, but I want to carry you and you're going to let me." His arms tightened around her.

"Okay."

Steve laughed. "All this easy agreement is starting to worry me, Doc."

"Don't worry. I'll be back to my disagreeable self soon enough and then you'll wish you hadn't started this."

"Never."

"You say that now…"

He swung her legs down until her toes barely touched the ground and pressed her against the side of his truck. "I'll say it forever."

She stared into his dark eyes and felt the truth of his words to the depth of her soul. Gordie watched as Steve lowered his head, his lips drawing closer to hers. His breath brushed over her skin in a butter-soft caress, a whisper of contact, a prelude of what would follow. From one heartbeat to the next his mouth was on hers, his tongue thrusting between her lips to delve inside.

Steve stroked his tongue over hers, toyed with her, coaxed her into joining him in his demand for more. She wound her arms around his neck and her legs around his waist, held on to him as hot lashes of lust struck her. Gordie pressed her body to his, crushed her breasts to his chest and ground her clit on the erection trapped between them. Pounding need thumped a beat as old as time as their mouths continued to devour.

On the verge of an orgasm, Gordie whimpered, the small sound swallowed as he drove the kiss deeper. His hands gripped her hips, pulling her tighter against his straining flesh and pressing into her clit with the perfect amount of pressure to send her into orbit. Convulsion after convulsion seized her. Moisture flooded her panties and the aroma of her arousal floated around them.

He eased back, lightened the strokes of his tongue, and slowed the thrust of his hips. As the final waves of her climax ebbed away he pulled his mouth from hers. Breathing hard, Steve tucked her head under his chin and held her. Gordie struggled to catch her breath and her heart beat hard enough to bruise her ribs.

"I think we should take this inside, Doc." With measured steps he made his way to the door leading into the house.

Gordie didn't raise her head, didn't want to see they were in the garage with the door wide open where anyone could see them. She'd always known it would be like this. Knew the minute Steve touched her she'd forget everything and everyone—forget herself.

Steve made it inside and to his room in record time. He was on a hair trigger and Doc wasn't helping with the way she'd wrapped herself around him and kept nibbling on his neck with those sweet lips. Jesus, he couldn't remember why he'd thought this wasn't a good idea yet. There had been a very good reason to wait until after everyone had gone home but for the life of him he couldn't think of it.

They entered his room, a memory of the last time he'd carried her through the doorway intruded and he ruthlessly shoved it back. Steve strode across the room, his gaze locked on the bathroom. He kicked the door shut behind them, the bang echoed off the walls and brought Doc's head up, her gaze connecting with his.

"Shower." Steve ground the word out through clenched teeth as he set her on her feet. "I'll bring you some clothes to wear."

"You're leaving?"

He closed his eyes, his control held by a thread. "If I don't I'm taking you against the wall and I want more time to explore you than a quick fuck in the shower."

"But you made me come."

"Yeah, and I will again, just not yet." Steve opened his eyes to see Doc removing her top. The sexy, white lace bra beneath her blue blouse was made of pure sin. A groan gurgled in his throat. "Christ."

Her hands stilled on the button of her pants and she raised her gaze to his. She studied him with her doctor stare. He knew what she was doing—analyzing, thinking, planning. Damn, that mind of hers was as sexy as her underwear.

He took a step back, reached behind him for the door handle and Doc got right up in his face, her hand pressed to the door behind him as though she could stop him from opening it.

"Get your clothes off now," she demanded.

Steve smiled. "Back to being disagreeable, Doc?"

"You are not leaving this bathroom before I mark you. I don't care if we have sex, I give you a blowjob or a hand job. One way or another you will leave this bathroom mine as I entered it yours."

His cock went rock hard. Her take-charge attitude thrilled him and he couldn't wait to be on the receiving end of any one of those suggestions. "Bossy much, Doc?"

"You like it."

He arched an eyebrow. "Really?"

Doc wrapped her hand around his length through his jeans. "Oh yeah, you like it."

They stared at each other, gauging who would give first. Only the fight was one-sided. Her fingers squeezed and stroked him and even with the denim barrier her touch set his blood on fire. His coyote howled for him to take what she offered while he fought to keep his civility and not rut on her like the beast he was. Control snapped and he glanced at his watch.

"I reckon we have five minutes before anyone shows up and it shames me to say I won't need that long." He gripped her shoulders, pushed her back. "Strip."

She stumbled, caught herself and kicked off her shoes. Her pants came next but he missed the unveiling of her panties as he pulled his shirt over his head. Steve's breath snagged in his chest when he spotted the matching underwear. Dear God, she'd kill him without laying a hand on him. He went to work on his pants, his cock sprang free and Doc dropped to her knees in front of him, her hot breath bathed the head seconds before she swallowed him whole.

"Fuck!"

Doc took him in as deep as she could. The crown bumped against the back of her throat and dragged a groan from his gut. One hand worked his balls, rolling them, tugging, rubbing the sensitive skin beneath. The other gripped the base of his shaft, pumping up and down, matching the rhythm of her mouth. Shit, he wouldn't last a minute, never mind five. She undid him, her lips, her tongue, the grasp of her throat, all designed to drive him out of his mind. He clenched his jaw—his ass cheeks—in his fight not to come.

Damn, he didn't want to do it like this. He wanted inside her cunt, wanted to bathe her womb with his seed and mark her completely as his. With strength he didn't think he had, Steve pulled from Doc's mouth.

"No, not this way the first time." He tugged her to her feet. "Turn around, hold the counter and spread your legs."

She did as asked, even tilted her hips to shove her ass in his direction. Steve toed off his boots and kicked his jeans aside. Stepping between her feet, he bent his knees and lined his cock up with her pussy. The slick evidence of her recent orgasm coated her folds, made the slide inside easy. He rocked forward, pushed deeper and concentrated on not embarrassing himself. Heat engulfed him, her tight walls sucking at his length like her mouth had moments before.

Steve adjusted his feet, brought their bodies more in line and drove his shaft to the hilt. Doc stood on her toes, thrust her hips back and met him stroke for stroke as he began to fuck her in earnest. Deep, hard, long plunges in. Short, sharp retreats. He built the rhythm, pulled her with him as he sought the peak. Curling over her back, he pressed his chest to her spine and slid a hand over her stomach to the juncture of her thighs.

He found her clit, hard and protruding from its protective hood, and circled the wet bundle with a fingertip. Increasing the pressure in small increments, he pushed her toward release. Her inner walls convulsed, a ripple of hot velvet along his probing length like a thousand tongues. His sac tightened, pulled his balls up and Steve knew he was on the verge of coming. Wanting her with him when he went over the edge he doubled his efforts on the nub beneath his finger and sank his teeth into the side of her neck.

Doc bucked against him. Her orgasm slammed into both of them. She squeezed his cock, held it prisoner in her clenching body. Steve's balls burst into flame, shooting hot cum through his shaft and filling her core. Each blast burned his flesh, caused her walls to clamp harder around him, sucking the breath from his lungs. His knees shook, threatened to collapse, and he braced his arm, his palm flat on the counter in front of them.

Their chests heaved with their labored breaths, the harsh sound of rushing air bouncing off the walls around them. He found the strength to lift up, pull his softening cock from her body and step back. Reaching out, he turned the water on so they could clean up. They were running out of time if they wanted to be dressed when the others arrived.

"Come on, Doc, let's get showered and dressed before company arrives."

He wrapped his arm around her waist and picked her up off her feet. She was such a tiny thing compared to him but her size belied her strength. He'd seen her deal with guys almost as big as him. At the moment though, she was as weak as a kitten and allowed him to pull her under the running water without protest.

"It won't matter."

He had to lean over to hear her words above the pounding spray. "What won't?"

"Whether we're dressed or not." She raised her gaze to meet his. "They'll all know."

"Is that a problem?"

She smiled. "No."

Steve bent down, pressed his lips to hers. A chaste kiss by any standard, he moved his mouth against hers, brushing back and forth in light caresses. Their mouths melded, their tongues barely coming into play. Soft and easy, they came together, their bodies, slick from the shower, sliding, skin on skin. Hands roamed in gentle sweeps, sending fire through his veins all over again. Breaking away, he gasped for air and laid his forehead on hers.

"Damn. I'm not gonna get enough of you anytime soon. Good thing it's Christmas and you've got the next week off because once everyone clears out tonight I'm getting you naked and in that bed out there and not letting you up until I've had my fill."

"I'm a little shocked to admit I feel the same." She stepped back, breaking their embrace completely. "Let's get this over with so we can get on with our week."

Doc turned her back and bent under the spray to wet her hair. He reached over her head for the shampoo and handed it to her. Grabbing the soap he made short work of cleaning up before helping her. Steve ran his bubble-lathered hands across every inch of her. By the time they were finished he was sporting a hard-on and wished he didn't have to deal with the people arriving any minute even if they were his friends and he'd called them in.

Steve sighed as he stepped out of the shower and snagged a towel off the rail. He slung it around his hips and picked up a second one for Doc. She shut off the water and walked into his arms.

"It won't be long, you know." She stood on her tiptoes and kissed the end of his nose.

The action was so surprising that Steve stood paralyzed for long seconds.

"What's wrong?" She arched an eyebrow. "Ah. No one's ever kissed you on the nose before."

How did she read him so well? They'd been friends since she'd arrived in the mountains with her mother all those years ago but still, she seemed to understand him on a level no one ever had. Always knew when he'd reached his limit and backed away.

He shrugged. "No actually, they haven't."

"Good." Her lips curled in a smug smile.

"Why is that good?"

"Because it means we get to have a first together."

"Doc, we're going to have lots of firsts before we're done." He slapped her towel-covered butt. "Now get a move on. We've got guests coming."

Steve ushered her out of the bathroom and over to his dresser. Pulling out a drawer, he found her a t-shirt and sweatpants with a drawstring waist so she could cinch it tight to hold them up. She put the shirt on first and the hem came to her knees. If it wasn't for their expected company he'd snatch the pants back and make her wear only his shirt.

"Stop grinning. I'm not leaving the pants off."

There she went again with that mind-reading thing.

"How do you know that's what I'm thinking?"

"It's in your eyes." She glanced up at him as she bent to pull on the sweats. "You get this look of hunger that my mind has no trouble understanding."

"Nice to know I'm so easily read."

"You're not the only one. Everyone's emotions show in their eyes." She shrugged. "I guess I've just learned to look closely over time."

"I don't seem to be able to read you as well."

"Another thing I've learned over the years."

"What?"

"It's called a poker face. I learned early to hide my emotions."

"I know what a poker face is but why would you need one?"

Her fingers twisted in the bow she'd tied the drawstring in. Doc may have perfected a poker face but her actions and body posture gave her away.

"Doc?"

"As a doctor I need to keep my emotions locked away or I'd never survive my job."

"You were unreadable long before you became a doctor." He studied her, tried to see past the shields in her eyes but as usual, failed. "You don't just wear your poker face at work do you, Doc? You have it on all the time. Why is that?"

She laughed, but the brittle sound held no trace of humor. "You think I could grow up in this town without hiding how I felt? It's not easy being the odd man out when you're a kid."

"Gordie, you've never been odd man—"

She held up her hand. "Yes I have. No other person has lived as a human in this town for as long as I did. *Ever.* That alone makes me odd. The fact I married Anthony when I shouldn't have, plus what happened after, just adds to my list of peculiar attributes. I've spent years trying to put all that behind me, there's no way I'll drop my guard and risk starting up another round of whispering for the town to enjoy."

He pulled her into his arms. "You're not odd and no one has ever really looked at you that way. And believe me, you don't need to do anything to become fodder for the rumor mill in Whispering Springs. I've spent years listening to the old-timers chatter at your sister's café and there's plenty that goes on in these mountains for them to talk about besides you. Come to think of it, I don't think they've mentioned you in years."

Doc laughed and shoved away from him. "You idiot. No one is game to talk about me in front of you."

"What? Why?" He crossed his arms over his chest.

"Because you give the evil eye better than the devil himself."

He snarled. "I do not."

This time when she laughed she doubled over and held her ribs. Gasping for breath, she said, "Go look in the mirror, you idiot."

Steve knew what he'd see. There was no controlling the way he reacted whenever he thought of Doc and he hadn't bothered to hide that from anyone since her return to town. And now he'd have the right to show that reaction. He smiled. Oh yeah, the town would soon know whom she belonged to.

"And don't go getting that look."

"What look?"

"That *she's mine, keep away* look."

Damn, she really could read him as easy as a book. "It's the truth and I'm not hiding it ever again." He cupped her cheek in his palm, pleased when she turned into the caress. "I want everyone to know you're mine."

"They already know." She sighed. "They've just been waiting for me to give in."

"And did you give in, Doc?"

"No, I took." She grinned.

"Yes, you sure did. And you did such a good job. I feel all used."

A giggle slipped past her lips, the sound so girlish Steve was reminded of years past when they hung out with the same group in high school.

"I like the sound of that. I want to hear you laugh like that more often," he said.

"Hang around, McKenna and you just might get that wish."

"Oh, I'll be hanging. I'm not planning on going anywhere that isn't with you."

"You're such a sweet talker."

"I can talk lots of ways. After everyone leaves I'll show you my dirty talk." He waggled his eyebrows and licked his lips making a slurping noise.

"Eww... I hope you mean sexy dirty talk or I'm outta here."

Steve wrapped his arm around her neck and dragged her back to his side. "Definitely sexy dirty talk, Doc. Now let's go wait for our company."

He felt her stiffen against him and knew she was thinking about what she'd have to reveal. As much as he wanted to take away her worry he knew she had to do this. He'd stand beside her and support her as best he could but he couldn't fight all her battles no matter how badly he wanted to.

3
____

They'd reached the main area of the house when someone knocked on Steve's front door and continued to knock.

"Let me guess." Steve let her go and walked over to unlock the deadbolt. "This'll be Kat."

As soon as the door opened her sister charged past Steve as if he didn't exist. Kat spanned the gap between them in less than a second and threw her arms around Gordie's neck.

"Thank God, you're okay."

"I'm fine, Kat." Gordie smiled at Steve over her sister's head. "Unless you plan to choke me to death."

Kat eased up on her grip but didn't let go. "Give me a sec. I just need to know you're all right."

Gordie could allow her sister that much. While they hugged in Steve's foyer, Rowan came through the door carrying bags of food. One by one the others came in out of the cold, all of them laden down with groceries. Dale was the last to arrive, murmuring something to Steve as he closed the door behind everyone.

"Come on, Kat. Let your sister go so we can eat all this food you made us drag up here," Rowan said.

"I bought..." Kat sniffled. She leaned back and looked at Gordie with one arched eyebrow. "Well, I'll be." Her sister took a deep breath and smiled. "About damn time, too."

She knew what Kat could smell but this wasn't the time or the place for that conversation. "Not now."

"We've all waited years for you two to get it on. You should be yelling it from the rooftop."

"Shh. I don't want to talk about it at the moment."

"Oh come on, Gordie. You guys have been dancing around each other since you came home years ago. Everyone is going to be thrilled that you finally gave in."

"Kat! I did not—"

"Sure you did, the whole town knows you're the one fighting it."

"Enough, Kat." Steve's quiet words didn't hide the hard edge they were delivered with.

Gordie watched Kat wrestle her need to argue. The girl could argue under wet concrete and she still didn't know why her sister had given up her dream of being a lawyer and taken over The Dec Café from their Granny Roe. She'd probably never find out. Even though Kat was the first to ferret out other people's secrets, she kept her own locked in a vault, not even Gordie was privy to what lay hidden behind that sealed door.

"I brought stew for tonight. I also packed up a heap of groceries, lasagna and a chicken pie. But don't think all this food gives you reason to stay up here Christmas Day. I want to see you both at my place for lunch with presents in hand." Kat marched toward the kitchen.

"She's like this every day isn't she?" Steve asked, shaking his head.

With a sigh, Gordie turned to face him. "Yeah, she is."

"I've seen her take charge of things at the café but have never been subjected to it personally. Did she really bring all that food?"

Gordie laughed. "You saw the bags everyone carted in. Kat's always had this need to feed anything with a mouth. We used to joke when she was little about her finding a mate early and having a truckload of kids to mother." Gordie stared after her sister. "You know I don't think I've seen her date anyone since she was in high school."

"And that's a subject we're not touching." He placed a hand on her lower back and gently nudged her forward. "Come on, we've put it off long enough."

The next few minutes were taken up by Kat giving orders and everyone following them. Bowls were filled with hot stew, and with food in hand they went into the dining room where Steve's hand-carved table and chairs seated all of them with room to spare. Gordie ate a mouthful of food and chewed. Usually her sister's cooking tasted delicious but she could have been eating dirt for all the flavor she could taste tonight.

There was no point putting it off any longer, it wouldn't get any easier. She just had to decide where to start, what was necessary and what she was comfortable disclosing. Pushing her bowl away, Gordie leaned back in her chair and turned her head to catch Steve's gaze. He slipped his hand over hers and gave a gentle squeeze before returning to his meal.

"It started last year when I found the first stray up here. That's the first significant event I can remember, anyway. After that there was all the drama of Rowan's return and the attempt on Quinn's life by the other two strays and of course Malcolm trying to run him down." She reached for her water and took a sip to wet her dry mouth and throat.

"Between January and May there were numerous little things, objects moved in my house and at the clinic, doors unlocked when I was sure I'd locked them, missing papers from my home office, that sort of thing." Gordie took a deep breath and glanced at Steve. He reached for her hand again, entwined their fingers and nodded for her to go on. She kept her gaze locked with his. If she looked away she knew the words wouldn't come.

"May eighteenth I came up here to walk in the forest. I was going to shift, go for a run but decided against it." She swallowed over the lump in her throat. "I didn't hear anything or see anyone before I took a punch to the jaw. The force snapped my head back into a tree. I don't remember a lot of the next few minutes other than I took some hits before I caught my breath and fought back. I never saw who attacked me and whoever it was had masked their scent well enough that I couldn't say for sure who it was."

Gordie trembled. Memories of that night bombarded her, fear churned the food in her stomach and she had to swallow the bile rising in her throat. A chair scraped along the timber floor and Steve pulled her onto his lap, cradling her against his chest. He kissed the top of her head and held her close, warmth seeped from his body into hers, soothing her. She couldn't stop shaking and her fingers and toes were numb from the cold gripping her.

"The details don't matter, Gordie." Steve tucked her head under his chin. "I'll finish this part, okay?"

Gordie nodded. She didn't dare open her mouth to speak for fear a sob would tear free. Or worse, she'd throw up. In the months since the attack she'd done her best to block the whole event out. But in her effort to forget the horrible night she'd pushed the person who saved her and cared for her afterward away as well. It was unfair to Steve but at the time she couldn't cope any other way.

"I heard the attack from the deck so I shifted and ran into the forest. I didn't see who had Doc pinned to the ground but at the time she thought it was Marcus."

Steve's words were met with gasps but it was Brogan's softly spoken words that froze Gordie. The venom in them turned her blood to ice.

"I should have killed him when I had the chance."

"No, Gordie and Steve should have reported the attack," Dale said.

"Probably." She felt Steve's shoulders rise. "But to be honest, I was more concerned with looking after Doc's injuries, and we had no real proof."

"Oh my God, the scar on your lip." Gordie opened her eyes to find Kat kneeling on the floor beside her. "You told me you'd sliced it with a knife while eating fruit."

She tried to smile but the hurt in her sister's eyes stopped her. "I'm sorry. I just wanted to forget. And nothing happened after that."

"Until last month." Warm air ruffled her hair. "What happened,

Doc? And don't tell me nothing because I know you, I know something's been going on for weeks now."

Gordie sighed and sat up to face the others. "The week before El arrived in Whispering Springs my house was broken into but unlike before it was obvious. Whoever it was smashed out the kitchen window." She turned to Dale. "And before you ask, nothing was taken. I don't know what the aim was, to frighten me maybe. They took nothing but went out of their way to let me know they'd been inside by messing with my things."

A growl rumbled behind her. She expected to face an angry Steve at some point, hopefully he'd hold it all in until everyone went home. She knew keeping everything from him was wrong but she couldn't change that now.

"Go on. What else?" Dale asked.

"Nothing until after the wedding." Gordie glanced at Rowan. "It started with little things being moved, food missing, doors unlocked when they shouldn't have been. Clothes that aren't mine laid out on my bed."

"What the fuck?" Steve spun her around on his lap until they were nose to nose. "Some fucking prick was in your bedroom and you never told me!"

"That only happened yesterday. I haven't seen you to tell you." As much as she'd wanted to call him last night, her sister had been with her when she'd arrived home and made the discovery. If she hadn't convinced Kat to stay she would have phoned him. "Kat was with me."

"You found that last night and didn't say anything? Jesus, Gordana, what were you thinking?" Kat gripped Gordie's leg and gave it a shake.

"I didn't want you to worry. If you hadn't stayed I would have called Steve."

"You should have called me regardless."

"Whose clothes were they?"

Gordie turned to Rowan. She could tell by her friend's white face and wide eyes that Rowan knew the answer. "Yours."

"Bullshit! What clothes?" Quinn stood, his chair toppled over, hit the floor with a loud crash. He stared down at Rowan.

Rowan never broke eye contact with Gordie. "My mother's wedding dress."

"Fuck off!" Brogan rose to his feet. "How the hell did that end up in Gordie's house?"

"It wasn't at the cleaners when I went to pick it up last week. They thought it was still out being cleaned but Nancy had phoned to tell me it was ready so I knew something wasn't right. I was hoping they'd just misplaced it."

Brogan turned to El. "And your dress? You put it in with Rowan's."

El licked her lips. Glanced at Gordie and Rowan in turn. "I... I don't know. It's missing too."

"Except Rowan's isn't missing anymore," Dale said.

"No, it's in my closet."

"What I don't get is why leave Rowan's dress at Gordie's? There doesn't seem to be a purpose to it." Kat's head tilted at an angle and she got that look of concentration she wore whenever she thought hard about something. "Do you think this is about getting everyone involved? I mean, before yesterday it all seemed focused on Gordie but add in this dress thing and he's pulling someone else into the equation."

"This isn't math, Kat. Besides, it's Marcus we're talking about, who knows what goes through that twisted head of his," Steve said.

"No, Kat's right. All Marcus' previous actions have targeted individuals, there was no crossover except when Rowan returned and I think that was accidental more than on purpose. This is different. I'm not sure how or why but the game rules have changed," Dale added.

"So what do we do now?" Gordie looked at Dale.

"I want to have a look at your house and I'd like to go back to the clinic in daylight. Do you mind if I do that while you're closed?"

"No, go ahead." Gordie got to her feet. "I'll get you my keys. Quinn do you have the new keys for the clinic?"

"Dale has them."

"Okay." She stifled a yawn. "Sorry, I think it's catching up with me. I'll just go grab those keys."

"Gordie, go on to bed. I'll make sure Dale gets the keys," Steve said.

"I'm fine, just a little tired and my feet are cold."

Steve stood and scooped her up in his arms.

"Hey."

"Hey, yourself."

"Put me down."

"I will." He walked across the room. "Just as soon as I get you in the bedroom. Say goodnight, Gordie."

A chorus of *goodnight Gordie* echoed behind them as Steve strode along the hallway leading to the bedroom.

Gordie yawned again. She really was tired. Maybe she'd just lie down for a few minutes. Steve deposited her on the mattress and stood with hands on hips beside the bed.

"No arguing, you've got dark circles under your eyes. I bet you didn't sleep at all last night, did you?"

She ducked her head. There was no way she could sleep after finding that dress on her bed, not even with her sister in the room down the hall. "No."

"Just as I thought." He reached over and pulled the covers back. "Come on, ditch the pants and climb in."

"Ditch the pants?"

"You can't sleep in those. Leave the shirt on though, it gets chilly even with the heat on."

Before she could move he'd snagged the end of the bow and yanked the drawstring loose. Gripping a bunch of fabric in each fist at her hips he tugged the sweats down her legs and threw them in the general direction of the dresser.

"There. Climb in. I'll go see to our friends and be back before you've missed me."

"Who said I'd miss you?" She smiled around another yawn and her eyelids grew heavy.

"Me." Steve bent over and gave her a smacking kiss on the mouth. "Rest. I'll be right down the hall."

"Rest with me." Her eyes closed.

"Later."

"Okay."

"Back to agreeable Doc, I see."

"Only until I sleep."

Steve chuckled. "Doesn't matter which Doc you are, I'm still glad you're in my bed."

"You just liked the sex."

"Gordie." His fingers brushed her cheek.

"Mmm..."

"Sleep."

"Night."

Steve gazed down at a sleeping Doc and tried not to climb into bed with her. He still had to go out and deal with their friends and he wanted to be sure Dale kept him in the loop about her house and the clinic. Anger still burned in his gut when he thought about her not calling him last night. She wouldn't admit it but she was still holding him at arm's length. A smile stretched his mouth. There would be no holding him off now.

Doc was right, he had enjoyed the sex but it had been far more than a physical act. He'd finally been buried inside her after years of dreaming about it. No fantasy he'd concocted came close to the real thing. Now he wanted a repeat but she needed to rest and he had to sort out a plan of defense because there was no doubt in his mind that Marcus was back on the scene. In fact, Steve was pretty sure the man had never left.

He tiptoed from the room and pulled the door shut, leaving it open a crack so he could hear Doc if she called out. Quiet voices drifted down the hall, they grew louder as he made his way back to the dining room. The table had been cleared and everyone sat with a mug of coffee, at least he thought that's what he smelled. Obviously Kat's talents weren't just with food.

"How is she?" Kat asked.

"Asleep." She eyed him through narrowed lids. He knew what she was really asking but he wasn't getting into that with her. "Later."

Steve spied a spare mug and picked it up. The aroma rose up, teasing his senses with the taste to come. He sipped, the hot liquid filling his mouth, spilling over his tongue. Damn, whoever made this knew what they were doing. Taking a bigger drink he walked out of the room and headed for the garage. They'd left Doc's purse in his truck when they rushed inside earlier. He placed his mug on the table beside the garage door as he walked past.

He retrieved her bag from the truck and headed for the button to shut the roller door and pressed it, but movement at the end of the driveway caught his eye and he quickly aborted the action. Peering into the night, Steve tried to focus but the lack of light outside and the abundance of it inside combined to make it impossible. He stepped to the edge of the garage for a better look when he heard someone behind him. Spinning on his heels, fists raised, he came face-to-face with Dale.

"Sorry, didn't mean to startle you."

"No worries, I'm a little jumpy."

"That's expected. What are you doing?"

Steve pointed down the driveway. "What is that?"

Dale leaned forward. "You got floodlights?"

"Yeah, let me get the switch." Steve strode to the other side of his truck and flicked a couple of levers. Light illuminated the entire front yard.

"Shit!" Dale took off running.

"What the fuck?" Steve dropped Doc's purse and raced after the sheriff.

The new layer of snow on the ground proved difficult to traverse and they slipped and slid their way to the end of the drive. They skidded to a halt as a woman wobbled and lost her footing in the slippery conditions, crumpling beside Dale's car. At least Steve thought it was a female bundled up under all that snow gear.

He crouched down and gripped her shoulder. "Hey, are you all right?"

"C-c-cold." Her voice was muffled by the beanie pulled down low on her forehead and the scarf wrapped around to cover what was left of her face, but neither could hide the chattering of her teeth.

Steve pushed the cold, wet material aside. "Recognize her?" he asked Dale.

His friend sucked in a breath as he squatted beside him. "Tatum. It's Tatum Brant. William's granddaughter. But she hasn't been back in the mountain for years."

"Let's get her inside out of the weather." Steve slid his arm around her as best he could with the bulky jacket she wore. He lifted and Dale steadied them as they got to their feet.

One on either side of her, they headed back to the house. She trembled against him and Steve could feel the damp and cold seeping from her clothes to his. It was awkward, she seemed to be wearing a wardrobe full of clothes beneath her thick coat. They reached the garage and crossed to the connecting door where Brogan and Quinn met them.

"Who the hell is that?" Quinn asked.

"Tatum Brant," Dale answered.

"Where'd she come from?" Brogan asked.

"Bottom of the driveway, she was trying to make it to the house," Steve said. "Can you go shut the garage door and turn off all the lights, Quinn?"

"Sure."

"Oh, and Doc's bag is on the ground near the light switches."

"Got it."

Her trembling had turned into bone-rattling shakes by the time Steve guided them into the living room where he and Dale lowered Tatum to the couch. He began removing her wet outerwear and quickly discovered the reason for her bulky mass. The women came in from the kitchen and immediately rushed over.

"Jesus. Is that...?" Kat asked.

"Tatum Brant," Steve said.

"Is she...?" Doc's sister seemed to be having problems forming complete sentences.

"Pregnant?" Steve finished for her.

"I haven't seen her in years. How'd she get here?"

"No idea and right now my priority is getting her warm," Steve said.

Tatum tried to curl up but her protruding belly hampered her efforts. Dale sat next to her and pulled her against his side. He wrapped his arms around her as best he could and ran his hands up and down her back. "You got a blanket, Steve?"

"Yeah, let me grab one. I'll turn the heat up too."

Steve left the room. After pulling a couple of quilts from the linen cupboard and returning them to the living room, he detoured to his room to check on Doc. She was exactly where he'd left her, sound asleep with one hand tucked under her cheek. The dark circles under her eyes made her face look bruised and he vowed to spend the next week making sure she got plenty of rest so those black smudges disappeared completely. He pulled the covers up over her shoulders and bent down to drop a light kiss on her forehead. Breathing deep, he drew her scent into his lungs.

Memories of earlier flashed through his mind. His cock hardened and a groan rumbled in his chest. There wouldn't be a repeat performance any time soon. Not with everyone still here and Doc in need of sleep. With a sigh, he straightened and forced himself to turn and leave the room. Each step dragged and he wondered at the irony of the moment. He'd waited so long for her to acknowledge their attraction and when she did everything and everyone seemed to be getting in the way of them being together.

As he approached the living room, he could hear raised voices. They got louder the closer he got and he quickened his pace, determined to stop them before it became a yelling match.

"Hey, keep it down, you'll wake Doc."

The sight before him amused and confused him. Dale stood

with the pint-sized Tatum right up in his face. For someone who'd barely functioned a few minutes ago, she'd made a swift recovery. She'd backed the sheriff up against the wall and had a finger prodding him in the chest. Both turned toward him as he entered the room.

"What's going on?" he asked.

"Doc *is* here?" Tatum stepped away from Dale.

Dale grabbed her by the arm. "I told you you weren't seeing her tonight."

"And I told you to stop manhandling me." She tried to pry his fingers from her skin. "I'd hate to see how you treat criminals if this is how law-abiding citizens are handled."

The sheriff dropped her arm like it was a hot rock. "Tatum."

"Sheriff."

Steve watched as they stared each other down and much to his surprise Dale broke away first. He watched the sheriff close his eyes and run a hand down his face. "Tatum, Doc is resting. She had a... scare earlier and isn't up to seeing a patient."

"I'm not a patient. But you haven't given me two seconds to explain myself so it's no wonder you've jumped to the wrong conclusion."

"Tatum, what were you doing out on the road?" Steve asked.

"I came up here after I called in at the café. The woman behind the counter said Doc and Kat were here and she thought Doc might need me," she explained.

"Need you?"

"I'm a nurse. Doc's nurse, actually, but I'm not due to start until after the fifteenth of next month." She walked over to the couch, one hand pressed to the small of her back making her pregnant belly stick out more. Slowly, she lowered to the cushions. "Damn, I must have pulled something trudging through the snow."

"You walked up here?" Dale barked.

"No, stupid. I drove, but I slid on some ice about ten minutes down the road and ended up in a ditch. I walked the rest of the way but then it started to snow and I got colder by the second. I'd just popped the lock on the cop car out front when you two came to my rescue."

"You broke into my car?"

Steve smiled. Tatum didn't seem like such a law-abiding citizen right now. She ignored Dale and kept on with her story.

"Look, I know this is strange but the woman at the café made it sound as if Doc had been hurt and I couldn't just go on over to Gramps' house without checking she was all right." She slumped back against the couch with a sigh. "By the time I reached the end of the driveway my legs were shaking with exhaustion as well as the cold and I was worried I'd collapse in the snow. I thought if I could flip on the siren someone would hear."

"I'm sorry Wendy worried you and put you in danger, but Doc isn't hurt," Steve said.

"Um...Steve?"

"What?" He turned to look behind him at Kat.

"How many bedrooms does this place have?" Kat asked.

"Four. Why?" He glanced past Kat and through the windows running the length of the room. "Oh shit."

"Yeah, that's what I was thinking," Kat said.

He walked over to join her. On the other side of the glass he could see the deck, along with the rapidly accumulating layer of snow covering it. More snow fell in a thick blanket that blocked out the view of the timber railing twenty feet away, never mind the forest beyond.

"Damn. Doesn't look good." Brogan stepped up next to him. "Does anyone know what the weather's supposed to be like?"

"Yeah, we're due for a storm tomorrow. Looks like it moved in early," Dale answered.

"Jesus. I guess I'll go drag out the extra bedding." Steve turned from the window. "How many of us are there?"

"I can share with Kat if she's all right with that and it makes things easier," Tatum said.

"I'm fine with that but don't you dare have that baby in the bed next to me." Kat glared at her.

Tatum laughed. "It's babies and they're not due for another three months."

Dale made a choking sound next to him and Steve turned to see a red-faced sheriff.

"Three months? You look like you're ready to pop now." Rowan sat on the couch next to Tatum. "So you're about four months ahead of me then. And El's pregnant too, but only just. Looks like there'll be lots of new babies next year."

"Tatum, can I have a word please?" Dale walked over and reached for her hand. "In private."

Steve thought he saw her hesitate but then she placed her hand in Dale's and allowed him to pull her to her feet, quickly disengaging their hands when she was steady. His friend seemed lost for a moment and Steve realized he had no idea where to go to have their talk.

"Down the hall, first door on the left is my office. You can use that if you like," Steve offered.

"Thanks. I'll bunk on the couch tonight. Just toss some blankets out and I'll fix it up when I'm ready," Dale said.

"No need. The sofa in the office is a pull-out. Everyone else can take a bedroom."

"Oh, okay. We'll be back in a minute." Dale gripped Tatum's elbow and all but dragged her out of the room.

Steve couldn't help think there was more going on with that pair but he couldn't see how when Tatum hadn't been in the mountains for years and was obviously pregnant with someone's babies.

"Hey, what's up with those two?" Kat asked next to him.

"Don't know and right now I've got more pressing things to think about." He turned to Brogan. "You and El can take the first room on the right down the hall. Quinn and Rowan take the next one and Kat, you and Tatum can share the one across from that. There's extra bedding in the wardrobes. I think I might have spare toothbrushes somewhere too."

Rowan stood and stretched. "I'm beat. Anyone mind if I call it a night?"

"I'm thinking the same thing. Kat, do you need any more help in the kitchen?" El asked.

"No. I just have to load and start the dishwasher. Go on to bed. You've both got baby growing to do."

Steve tuned out the women's conversation and walked back over to the window. He stared out beyond the glass at the wall of white. The snowfall had grown heavier in the last few minutes. If it kept up for long no one would be leaving tomorrow. As long as the storm blew over before morning he could get the plow out and lead them all down the mountain road back to town, but if it continued past sunrise he'd be stuck with his unwanted guests another night.

Warm arms slipped around her waist and Gordie snuggled back against the hard chest pressing in behind her. Soft lips traveled over her exposed neck, sending shivers down her spine.

"Mmm... What time is it?"

"Early. Everyone's gone to bed."

"Everyone?"

Steve sighed, his hot breath bathing her ear. "Yeah, tomorrow's expected snowstorm blew in early. We're stuck with them until morning."

"Oh."

"Don't worry. The minute the snow stops I'll get the plow out and clear the road into town. I guess all that food your sister brought with her will come in handy now."

"Good thing she did bring it, you don't have much in your fridge."

"There's plenty in the chest freezer downstairs." Steve grazed his teeth along her shoulder. "But enough about food. I have a different appetite I want to satisfy."

He trailed his tongue along the shell of her ear before sucking the lobe between his lips and nipping with his teeth. She arched into him and her bottom cradled his erection, the hard length pressing into the crease between her cheeks. Heat pooled in her abdomen and moisture coated her folds. Gordie wriggled around until she faced him. Reaching up, she ran her fingers through his hair.

"Hi."

"Hi, yourself."

She smiled. "Did I miss anything important?"

"Yeah. This." Steve lowered his head and kissed her.

At first he kept the kiss slow and easy but it soon wasn't enough for either of them and he thrust his tongue between her lips to probe inside. She met him stroke for stroke, demand for demand. Sucking hard, Gordie pulled his tongue deeper, used her teeth to scrape the sides as she let go. Steve groaned into her mouth and angled his head for a better fit.

Gordie splayed her fingers on his chest, the hot muscles rippled as she explored his body. Moving her hands lower, she toyed with the washboard abs he'd earned from honest work. She detoured farther south, to his narrow hips and the delicious valleys leading the way to the prize hidden between his legs.

Steve's mouth left hers to graze over her chin and down her throat. He nipped at her collarbone, licked to soothe the slight sting before moving to the other side and repeating his actions, making her gasp. Her fingers curled around his hips, her nails digging in, and his pelvis bucked toward her. His cock rubbed over her clit, the material of her shirt abrading the sensitive nub setting off sparks of delight.

She moaned and moved with him, rocked to find the friction she needed. Her pussy clenched and spasmed with longing and Gordie increased the pace. Steve tugged at her shirt with his teeth, pulled it off her shoulder to lick the skin beneath. Frustrated by the barrier between them, she shoved him away and turned to wiggle out of the top. He helped and in their haste the cloth tore apart at the seam.

He wrenched her free and tossed the shirt over his shoulder. In a second he rolled her under him, slipped his knee between hers and spread her legs wide. His thighs brushed hers, the rough hair tickling her soft skin. Gordie lifted her pelvis to bring her sex in direct contact with his shaft. Hot and hard, the silky length slid along her slick folds, bumping her pulsing clit. She cried out and he covered her mouth with his hand.

"Shh. They'll hear you."

Gordie sucked her lips between her teeth, bit down to hold them in place and nodded. Steve removed his hand and gripped her chin.

"I want to hear you scream. Want to hear my name on your lips when I make you come, but I don't want anyone else hearing that cry of pleasure. That's mine and mine alone."

Steve didn't give her a chance to answer. His mouth covered hers in a punishing kiss meant to claim. He flexed his hips and brought his cock to her opening. Pressing forward, he entered her, breaching her body slowly. She wanted more—all of him. Gordie thrust up and drove his shaft deeper, wrenching a moan from each of them. They moved together, built a rhythm of give and take that quickly grew in speed and strength.

She gnawed on her lips, held them tight between her teeth to muffle the cries of pleasure she couldn't control. Steve's hands circled her hips, his fingers spread over her ass cheeks. He held her still, pinned to the bed, and drove in hard, his length dragging over her swollen clit with every stroke. Her head tossed on the pillow and her nails dug into his shoulders as her orgasm built inside her, tightening with each plunge, every retreat of his cock.

"Please." Gordie hooked her legs over his hips. "Steve."

Her words spurred him on. He pounded into her, pushed them both to the edge as their bodies slammed together—strived for release.

"Touch yourself." His hoarse demand sent a bolt of fire into her core. "Do it."

Gordie slipped her hand between them, her fingers searching for the spot that would bring her relief. She encountered wet heat and probed farther. Cream coated her fingertips as she circled them over her clit, applied a little pressure and brought herself closer to the peak.

Steve leaned on his elbows and lifted up to look at where their bodies were joined. "God, that's so hot. Watching you get yourself off is a huge turn-on, Doc."

He pulled back and Gordie reached lower to graze her fingernails along his length as he withdrew.

"Fuck!" He slammed forward, trapping her hand between them. "Do that again," he growled.

She twisted her hand slightly, used her fingers on his cock and her thumb on her clit, and drove them both insane. Steve jerked, his rhythm erratic for a couple of strokes before he returned to the beat, this time faster. Harder. The first contraction rolled into the second and onto the third, her whole body flowing with the waves of her orgasm as they took her under and dragged him with her.

"Steve."

He continued to drive into her, pushing deeper with each splash of warmth filling her core. Burying his face in the curve of her neck he called her name, the sound more groan than word. Gasping for breath, Gordie held onto him, his weight pressing her into the bedding. Her limbs tingled, whether from lack of circulation or oxygen it didn't matter and she didn't care.

"Too heavy," he murmured against her skin, sending ripples of goose bumps skittering down her neck.

"No. I like feeling your weight crush me."

"Gee, Doc, you say the sweetest things." He grinned against her throat.

"You know what I mean," she sighed.

"Yes I do but you're so fun to tease."

"Really? Well just as long as you can take it as well as dish it."

"Bring it, Doc. I'll take all you've got."

He bucked his hips, his cock, still buried inside her, scraped over tender tissues. Her pussy throbbed, clamped around him.

"Ooh." Steve lifted his head and met her gaze. "Again?"

She arched a brow. "Now?"

His hips rocked, his hardening length pumping in and out. "Yeah. Now."

"Okay, but I'm on top this time." Gordie tried to roll them but he held her beneath him easily.

"You gonna ride me, Doc?"

"Not from dow—"

Her head spun and hair flopped in front of her face. She shoved the strands aside with one hand, gripped his biceps to steady herself with the other and stared down at him. "How the hell did you do that?"

"Be a good girl and I might show you."

"I'm not being a good girl *until* you show me."

"Fine, be a bad one then." Steve grabbed her waist and lifted her. "Ride me." He brought her down.

The new position altered the angle, allowed for deeper penetration. Sensations unfolded, floated out to cover every part of her. Gordie leaned forward, braced her hands on his shoulders and her knees on the bed beside him. She flexed her leg muscles, used them to raise and lower her body on his. On the downward plunge she rotated her hips and ground her clit on his pubic bone.

Gordie took her time. Learned what made him squirm beneath her, what made her gasp above him. There was no frantic rush to reach the top, only a slow, sensual stroll. His hands left her waist, slid up her ribs to cup her breasts. He pinched her nipples between thumb and forefinger and she leaned into the biting touch. Her blood hummed with arousal, rushed to fill tender tissue with molten fire and set her body alight.

Steve used the pressure of his hands to urge her upright and Gordie gasped as his cock slid over new terrain, making her pussy clench and weep. She cupped his hands with hers and together they squeezed her breasts, played with the tips until they were hard knots of need. He tugged his hands from under hers and dragged his fingers over her belly. Her breath caught and her stomach fluttered. Warmth pooled and dripped lower to her sex.

"Don't stop. Keep playing with your breasts. Show me what gives you pleasure."

His words sent a shiver of delight through her and Gordie granted his wish. She tweaked her nipples, pulled them away from her body and twisted. A moan slipped from her throat, the sound deep and gravelly as it vibrated in her ears. She jolted as Steve's finger brushed her clit. The contact sent a dart of fire from the tight bundle of nerves to her core, delivering heat and need.

Her hips rocked, rode his cock in small, sharp thrusts as she concentrated on the wicked swirl of desire skyrocketing inside. Steve continued to ply her clit with skilled fingers. He took her to the edge then backed off only to push her up again. His other hand cupped her ass, his fingers delving between her cheeks to tease the puckered flesh of her anus. She bucked wildly, thrashed back and forth as he pressed harder on the delicate opening.

He touched her in a way no one ever had. Inside and out he knew just what she needed for maximum pleasure. His touch quickened, slowed, sped up again. The varied pace drove her mad. She tried to catch his rhythm but every time she caught on he changed the beat.

"Steve." Gordie gasped for air. "Please. I need."

"Then you shall have." He breached the tight ring of muscle to her back entrance at the same time he applied pressure to her clit and drove his cock up into her. Gordie disintegrated. Stars burst before her eyes as the climax roared through her, dragging every last breath from her lungs and every thought from her mind.

4

———

Gordie woke to sunshine streaming through the skylight above her. Crystal-clear, blue sky without a cloud in sight filled the large, circular glass roof section. Steve stirred next to her and she turned her head to look at him. Dark stubble covered his chin and cheeks, soot-black eyelashes fanned out over his tan skin and the thick slash of his eyebrows curved over his closed eyes.

She wouldn't call him beautiful, he was too rugged, too large for that. But the very thing that kept him from being handsome made him striking. There was an edge to his attraction, a hard one. Gordie had always found him gorgeous. In high school he'd been the one she wanted to date. All the other girls wanted Brogan or Quinn, even Marcus had pulled his share of clamoring females, but Steve was different.

He dated but not like the others. Rarely did she see him out with a girl more than a few times. In fact she couldn't remember him ever having a serious girlfriend. She certainly hadn't seen him date anyone since she'd come home from medical school. It struck her as strange that a man as appealing and manly as Steve wouldn't date.

"You think too hard, Doc."

Her gaze darted to his, those deep-brown orbs studying her. "I didn't know you were awake."

"I noticed. You wouldn't have been checking me out so thoroughly if you'd known I was."

"I wasn't—"

"Uh-uh." He pressed a finger to her mouth. "No more hiding, Doc."

Gordie sighed. "Fine, I was checking you out." She spoke against his skin, the rough texture catching on her lips as they moved.

"And what did you find that was so distasteful?"

"What? Nothing. Why do you ask that?"

"Your nose was all scrunched up and your lips were puckered as though you'd eaten something sour."

"Oh." She tried to think of something to tell him, anything but what she'd actually been thinking.

"Well? And stop trying to come up with a plausible answer."

"Hey. I wasn't."

"Gordie, what were you thinking about?"

She huffed out a breath. "If you really must know, I was thinking how I hadn't seen you date anyone since I came home and that's not normal."

"Ah. So that wonderful mind of yours was about to come up with reasons why you haven't seen me with anyone."

"Well, no. I hadn't gotten that far yet." She smiled sheepishly. He was right. It would have been the next logical step.

"I'm not sure you're ready for the answer to that, Gordie."

"Why?"

Steve brushed his fingers over her temple, pushed a few strands of hair back from her face. "You."

"Me? I don't understand."

"I know you don't." He cupped her chin and tilted her mouth toward his for a quick kiss. "Come on. Let's get going. We'll round up the troops and get them out of here so we can have this conversation in private."

"We are in private, why can't you tell me what you mean now?"

"Because I don't want to explain myself right now." Steve rolled over and climbed out of bed.

"What? Just like that, Steve doesn't want to talk so he gets to stay silent but Gordie can't have the same privilege?"

"*Doc.*"

"No. No more hiding goes both ways. I want to know now."

"Fine." He stomped around the bed until he towered over her. "You want to know why I don't date, I'll tell you. From before you married Anthony I wanted you. No one else. But it scared the shit out of me knowing I'd have to turn you. You were human, Doc, and I wasn't even out of my teens. I never touched you because I knew if I did I wouldn't stop and I wasn't sure either of us could handle that back then."

He took a deep breath, dragged his fingers through his hair, making it stick up at all angles. "And then it didn't matter. You were with Anthony."

Oh God. She hadn't known. Probably wouldn't have accepted Anthony's proposal if she had. "Oh, Steve."

"No." He stepped away. "I don't want your pity."

"Pity's the last thing I'm feeling." She sat up, pulled the covers over her bare breasts. "If I feel anything it's sadness—guilt. I never would have agreed to marry Anthony and let him turn me if I'd known how you felt."

Steve stood staring at her, probing with that intense gaze of his. Gordie couldn't stop the anger bubbling inside her. Not at him, never at Steve. At herself for being selfish enough to accept the offer of a friend when she'd known full well it was a one-sided relationship. She'd used Anthony and he'd let her. They were both to blame for so much, but the majority of shame fell on her.

"He'd still be alive if I hadn't been so selfish." She lowered her head. "Hadn't wanted desperately to be like everyone else."

"No. If we're laying down guilt then I'm to blame for not coming to you with how I felt. If I hadn't been a coward..."

Gordie's head snapped up and she stared at Steve. "That's ridiculous."

"Yes, it is." He reached for her hand, entwined their fingers. "So is blaming yourself for Anthony's death. No one could have stopped the accident. And you and I know that even if you hadn't been married you both would have been going on that trip. The crash would still have happened."

She heard his words, knew he was right but her heart wouldn't believe it. Not when she'd spent years living with the heavy weight of guilt over Anthony's death. Gordie tried to smile, her lips trembling as she made the effort to reassure him. "I know you're right but it's hard to accept when I've made so many life-altering mistakes."

Voices coming from the other side of the door drew their attention. Gordie could hear Kat clear as a bell yelling she'd have breakfast on the table in thirty minutes. She smiled. Her sister might be loud, pushy and a pain in the ass, but Gordie loved her to pieces and had from the minute she'd been born.

"Sounds like everyone is up," Gordie said.

"If they weren't, they are now. Does Kat have a volume switch?"

Gordie laughed. "Not that we've ever found. When she was little, Mom always threatened to gag her if she couldn't be quiet."

"Mmm, that might work." Steve tugged on her hand. "Come on, let's get showered and dressed. We've got a long day ahead of us and the sooner we get started the sooner we'll get finished."

"I've got nothing to wear." Gordie let him pull her to her feet but held onto the sheet. She had to let it go when her feet got tangled up. If it wasn't for Steve's grip she would have fallen on her face.

"You can borrow something of mine and change when we get to your house. You can pack enough clothes to last until you open the clinic back up in the New Year while we're there." He pulled her behind him as he headed for the bathroom. "We'll worry about moving all your stuff later."

Gordie stumbled. "My stuff?"

"Yeah, clothes, furniture, any knickknacks you want to keep, that sort of thing."

"Furniture?"

Steve twisted the tap in the shower and turned to face her. "Doc, did you think you wouldn't be moving in with me now?"

"Moving in?"

He shook his head. "I'm going to assume you're still shaken up after yesterday because I know you're smarter than this, Doc. I want you here, in my house. If you want to wait until your mom and Doctor Monroe can get back to Whispering Springs to get married we can, but that's the only thing we're going to wait for."

"Oh." They were getting married? The words rolled around her head. They felt comfortable and Gordie felt a fluttering in her belly. *Married to Steve.* The idea thrilled her. "Okay."

A sexy smile curled one side of his mouth. "Back to agreeable Doc?"

Gordie couldn't help it. She grinned. "Oh yeah, definitely agreeable."

Pushing up onto her toes, she wrapped her arms around his neck and pulled his mouth down to meet hers. The kiss went on and on. By the time they pulled apart, both were breathless and steam filled the space around them. Hot and wet, inside and out, Gordie tried to remember what they were doing.

"Damn, woman. You trying to scramble my brains?" Steve licked his lips and a shiver snaked down her spine.

She laughed. "If I am, I can't remember why."

Steve's arms tightened around her waist and he lifted her against him. He stepped back, maneuvering them both under the shower. Warm water cascaded down, wetting her hair and splashing into her eyes. She shut her eyelids and tilted her head back to let the water flow over her face. The air surrounding them was charged with heat, the steamy enclosure trapping the sexual energy as easily as Steve clasped her body to his.

He lowered her to her feet. Her skin sliding along his sent sparks of desire shooting through her. His arms loosened and she turned in his embrace to reach for the soap. Gordie lathered her hands before dropping the bar back in the holder and spinning back to run her soapy fingers all over Steve's chest.

She left no area untouched, took extra care to be sure she cleaned every inch of his broad torso. Her insides swirled with desire, touching his muscular physique ramped up her arousal with each stroke of a finger. She moved on to his shoulders.

The wide expanse reminded her of just how big he was. At six feet six inches, Steve was easily the tallest man she'd ever met. It made her feel small and delicate—feminine. She wasn't small for a woman, a little above average at five feet six, but he was a full foot taller than her and yet they fit together so well. Gordie stretched to rake her hands up and around his neck. He bent forward, giving her better access and she curled her fingertips into his muscles, used gentle pressure to work out the knots.

"Man that feels good."

"You're all tense."

Steve chuckled. "I'm in the shower naked with *you*. Believe me when I say the tension you're feeling is the good kind."

"Oh." Gordie stood on her toes and ran her fingers over his scalp. Her body brushed against his, her breasts pressed into his chest and her nipples pebbled as his coarse hair abraded them. She shivered.

"Gordie." Her name was a whispered breath seconds before his head lowered and his mouth took hers.

He thrust his tongue between her lips, probed inside with bold strokes and carnal demands. Heat swirled deep in her belly, her pussy weeping with a demand of its own. She moaned into his mouth, drove her tongue forward to tangle with his. Her fingernails dug into his scalp as she held him to her and took as much as she surrendered.

The kiss was a challenge, a duel. A meshing of mouths designed to bring each of them to their knees. Only it made them stronger. Fueled their desire until the flames threatened to consume them both. His hands cupped her ass, pulled her tighter to him and brought their pelvises together in a lock as old as time. Gordie lifted her legs and wrapped them around his hips. They both moaned when her pussy rubbed against his cock.

He tore his mouth from hers. "Put me inside you," he growled.

"Yes." She reached between them as Steve used his grip on her behind to lift her away from his body. Her fingers encircled his length and held him in place as he pulled her back against him. Slick folds opened, welcomed him with grasping contractions as she sank down his length—each ripple firing nerve endings like a match to a fuse. Gordie buried her face in his neck and moaned.

Steve's grip on her ass tightened and he worked his fingers closer to where his body joined hers, teasing sensitive flesh with skill. He knew just where to touch, when to touch, to drive her crazy. She rocked her hips, tried to get him to move inside her but he continued to tease her while holding her snug against him. Desperate for more, she tangled her fingers in his hair and pulled.

"Move, dammit."

"No." His breath puffed in her ear and he nipped at her lobe with his teeth. "Want. To. Last."

Gordie could hear his teeth grind as he clenched his jaw in an obvious effort for control. But she wanted none of that. She wanted hot and wild. Needed it with razor-sharp edges. With a growl, she sank her teeth into his shoulder. He jerked, his cock sliding over her swollen walls.

"*Yes.*"

She tugged on his hair, licked at the slope of skin that led from his shoulder to his neck and worked her pelvic floor muscles in a punishing wave of catch and release. His control snapped with the click of his jaw. One breath he was still and the next he was powering in and out of her pussy like a man possessed. Gordie let go of his hair to wrap her arms around his neck and hold on.

Over and over he drove into her. Hard. Fast. She bounced against him with the force of his thrusts, her clit grinding on his body with every lunge. Her pussy clenched with the first of many convulsions as her orgasm roared through her and into him. Gordie's hips bucked and thrashed as Steve's name fell from her lips and her name burst from his. They came together in a rush, the ride over before it had barely begun.

Gasping for air, she held on to him as he leaned on the wall behind them and slowly slid to the floor. She straddled his hips, his cock still buried and pulsing inside her. Cold water poured down over them but she didn't care. Nothing could take away the bliss coursing through her veins.

"Water's cold. We have to get out before we turn into icicles." Steve let her go to reach up and switch the shower off. He put his arm back around her and squeezed. "Just need a minute to catch my breath."

"When you're done hunting yours, can you chase down mine?" she murmured into his neck.

His chest vibrated with a chuckle, the tremors tickled her nipples and sent tiny shards of pleasure blasting out in all directions. A shudder raked through her from head to toes.

"You're getting cold."

He surged to his feet, his softened cock slipping from her body as he stood. Her pussy clenched with loss, a hollow ache filling her core where his warmth had been. Steve placed her on her feet and enveloped her in a warm towel. Goose bumps sprang up along her skin as he rubbed her down. The soft terrycloth gently absorbed every last droplet of water. Banging on the bathroom door startled them.

"Come on, you two, breakfast is ready," Kat yelled.

"We'll be right out," Steve answered.

They waited until they heard the bedroom door close behind Kat before venturing out of the bathroom. Steve tossed a clean t-shirt and sweatpants on the bed for her and Gordie quickly pulled them on. The first thing she planned to do when she got to her house was dress in some of her own clothes. She shivered with the thought of what she might find this time when she unlocked her front door.

"Hey." Steve stepped up behind her, ran his hands from her elbows to her shoulders and back again. "It'll be fine. I'll be with you when you go inside so there's nothing to worry about."

She knew he would do his best to protect her from any danger, but he couldn't stop the dread eating at her gut. Her biggest fear was that Dale was right. The game had changed and now no one was safe from Marcus' madness.

———————

Steve turned Doc to face him and bent his knees to bring their eyes level. "I promise he won't hurt you again."

"You can't promise that, Steve. We have no idea what he'll do or when. All we can do is take precautions and be prepared."

"He won't hurt you." Steve's gut churned. The idea of anything happening to Doc burned in his chest and tasted foul on his tongue. He pulled her close, tucked her head under his chin and breathed her in.

She relaxed and cuddled into him. He knew she was right, he couldn't promise Marcus wouldn't hurt her but he'd be damned if he didn't do everything he could to protect her. He'd start with moving her into his house permanently. After they'd had something to eat and plowed their way to town. Steve hoped their trip to her place was uneventful but he didn't discount the buzz of his instincts. There was no way he would let her out of his sight until they'd driven back up the mountain and locked the front door behind them.

"Come on, let's eat." He dropped a kiss on the top of her head and released her. Curling his hand around hers, he pulled her with him out of the room and toward the noise coming from the other end of the house.

When they reached the dining room, everyone was already there and before he could say a word Doc sprinted across the room.

"Tatum."

The two women embraced before Doc pushed Tatum to arm's length and glanced down at her pregnant belly.

"Yeah, we're growing a little bigger than expected."

"A little? What have you got in there, triplets?"

Tatum laughed. "No, just your run-of-the-mill, everyday twins."

"Have you been taking your vitamins? Eating right? Getting plenty of rest?"

"Yes, yes, yes." Tatum laughed.

"Wait. When did you get here? How did you get here?"

"Sit down, my back is killing me." Tatum took her seat again. "We'll catch up while we eat. I'm starving."

Steve pulled out a chair for Doc, sliding it back in as she sat. He took the chair next to her and began loading her plate and his with scrambled eggs, hash browns, sausages and bacon. Kat passed him the coffeepot and he filled both their mugs.

"Hey, I can't eat all this," Doc complained.

"Try to put a dent in it," he said.

"I'll eat whatever you don't." Tatum patted her protruding belly. "Bottomless stomach."

"There's plenty of food, you don't have to eat off Gordie's plate." Kat offered the platter of bacon to Tatum.

"Oh, don't worry." Tatum scooped up a pile of crispy strips. "I'll eat this *and* hers."

"Don't eat too much. I'd hate for you to throw up in my car on the way back to town," Dale said.

"Who said I'm traveling with you?"

Dale stared across the table at Tatum. Steve waited for the sheriff to back down like he had the night before but this time it was Tatum's turn to give in.

"Fine. But I'm eating as much as I want. I haven't chucked since the first month of my pregnancy and I don't plan on starting again now."

He thought it best to deflect any more discussion of vomiting at the breakfast table. "I'll take the plow out as soon as we've eaten. It won't take long to get to town. Anyone take a look this morning to see how deep the snow is?"

"Yeah, we got about a foot. Not much considering how hard it was coming down when we went to bed," Brogan said as he reached for the coffeepot.

"Only a foot?" Steve had expected much more than that.

"If we all follow you down the mountain we shouldn't have any problems. Once you've plowed, our snow tires and chains should handle the road easily." Quinn pushed back his chair and picked up his plate. "Are we heading to the clinic or Doc's house first?"

"Doc's. I want to get in and out of there as quickly as possible and I didn't think we needed to go back to the clinic," Steve said between bites of food.

"Someone will have to pull my car out of the ditch," Tatum mumbled around a mouthful.

"Your car? Why is your car in a ditch?" Gordie asked.

"I slid on some ice down the road a bit last night, had to walk the rest of the way." Tatum shoveled food into her mouth as if she hadn't eaten in months.

"You what?" Gordie pushed her chair back and stood. "Get up. I want to check you over."

"Relax, Doc, I did some checking of my own and I'm good."

"You can't examine yourself." Doc's hands went to her hips.

Steve bit the inside of his cheek to hold in the chuckle at Doc's attempt to give Tatum a stern look. The other woman raised one eyebrow and continued to eat breakfast. He'd come to the conclusion that Tatum did whatever the hell she wanted and you either got in line with her or bashed your head on an invisible brick wall.

"Eat some more and then I'll let you take a look at us, Doc." Tatum aimed her fork at Gordie's plate. "If you wait too long I'll snatch that bacon up."

He watched Doc struggle to decide what to do. That mind of hers was trying to work out whether it was worth arguing. With a sigh, she sat back down and Steve patted her leg. She glanced at him and smiled. Warmth flowed through him, centered in his chest and he leaned over to drop a peck on her lips.

"Eat up. You can check Tatum's okay while I get the plow ready to go."

"Honestly, Doc, I'm fine. I was tired from the walk but no bumps or bruises mar this tub of a body."

"You weren't hurt in the crash?"

"Crash is far too severe a word to use for the slide that put me in the ditch. That old tank of mine just rolled to a stop nose down. It was the best stop I've ever made and I wasn't even in control."

"Maybe that's why?" Dale said.

Steve glanced across the table at his friend. The man had wrinkles on his forehead and his lips were stretched in a thin line as he stared at Tatum. Tension vibrated between them, the air crackling with some fight he wasn't privy to.

"Yes, you've made yourself clear about your opinion of my driving, Sheriff."

Everyone was silent. No one breathed as the two of them faced off. He didn't have a clue what was going on or why and he really didn't have time to worry about it. To his surprise, Tatum was the first to break their death stare.

"Thanks for a great breakfast, Kat." Tatum pushed her chair back and stood. "When you're ready, Doc, I'll be in the room I shared with Kat."

One by one his friends got up and followed Tatum to the kitchen with their plates. As he and Doc had been the last to sit down they were still eating when everyone else had gone.

"What's going on with Dale and Tatum?" he asked.

"I have no idea."

"But you knew she was coming back to the mountains."

"Yeah, she rang me early last month and asked if I was still looking for a nurse to help out part-time at the clinic." Doc took a sip of coffee. "It's hard to get anyone on account of them needing to be coyote so I told her anytime she turned up she had a job."

"Obviously she accepted."

"She told me she'd start mid-January."

"Did she also tell you she was pregnant?"

"Yes. Said she wanted to bring her babies into the world at home."

"What about the father? And it's not like this has been home for her in years."

"I don't know, Steve. All I know is I'd give my right arm for some help at the clinic and she's just what I'd wish for. I remember her coming to the clinic when Dad was still there. She had to be about ten and even then she knew she wanted to be a nurse."

"Seems strange that she'd stay away for so long and suddenly come back. Babies aside, it just doesn't seem right."

"I guess, but then look at Dale. He came back out of the blue and look how well that worked out."

"Yeah, it was a good thing for the pack."

"This will be too."

"I hope so."

They finished their meal in silence and Steve stacked their plates and mugs. He stood. "You go take a look at Tatum. I know you were thinking about it the whole time you ate breakfast."

She stood beside him and smiled. "Thanks. I am worried, especially now I know she drove her car into a ditch last night."

He kissed her forehead. "Go, I'll clear these away and meet you in the garage when you're done."

Steve found Kat alone in the kitchen loading the dishwasher and as much as he didn't want to have a conversation with her about her sister, he figured it was unavoidable and probably best to get it over and done with. He didn't need to start talking. She fired a question at him before he'd taken three steps into the room.

"You going to let her run you around for the next few years or will you man up and marry her?" She kept her back to him and didn't stop what she was doing.

He walked over to the sink and rinsed the plates and cups, handing them to her to stack in the dishwasher. When he was done he turned and leaned back against the counter, waited for her to look at him.

Kat put the final dish in the machine and straightened. She looked at him but before he could say a word she spoke again.

"I'm preaching to the choir, aren't I?" She sighed.

Steve smiled. "Yeah."

"She can't really give you the runaround now though, can she? I mean it's not like she can change what you did yesterday and everyone is going to smell you on her so whether she likes it or not she'll have to own up to it."

"I think she will. You know what Doc's like, once she makes up her mind it's full steam ahead."

"I can't believe she didn't say anything about that fucking dress."

The subject change threw him for a second but he soon caught up with her. "Did you notice anything odd at the house?"

"No. The only difference to any other night we've shared dinner was her wanting me to stay over."

"Nothing about the house seemed off? What about Doc?"

"She was a little tense but then she always is this time of year so I didn't think too much of it. In fact that's what I put her asking me to sleep there down to." Kat shrugged. "Figured she just wanted to know she wasn't alone."

He rubbed the back of his neck. "I'm moving her in here as of yesterday. We'll collect essentials today and leave the house locked up until after New Year or when your parents arrive, whichever comes first. Maybe you should think about staying out here with us."

"I was planning to spend the next week with Wendy. She isn't going home for Christmas this year and with Mom and Dad arriving sometime before New Year's Eve, I think it best I stay in town."

"You and Wendy could come out here."

Kat placed a hand on his arm. "Steve, I know you're just being the gentlemen you are but you don't really want me and Wendy underfoot for the next week. Besides, I think you and Gordie deserve to have this next week locked away in this house on the mountain. So I will gracefully consider your offer but regretfully decline it."

Steve laughed. "Was I that obvious?"

"No, but the sparks that fly between you two are sure to singe my hair if I stand too close." She grinned. "Go get the plow ready so we can get this show on the road."

He wasn't sure which one of them was more surprised when he pulled her into his arms for a hug. Kat remained stiff for a second before giving him one quick squeeze and breaking free.

"I'm glad you two finally got together. Gordie deserves to be happy and you're the one man I know who'll make sure she will be."

She strode from the room before he could comment. His chest tightened and his heart beat hard against his sternum. That Kat thought he was good for Doc pleased him way more than he thought it should. He'd never considered anyone's opinion important. The only person he'd ever set out to please was Doc and he'd screwed that up in so many ways he'd often thought he didn't deserve her. But Kat's faith in him made him feel worthy and Steve would do everything in his power to prove her right.

Steve headed for the garage. He found Brogan, Quinn and Dale already there, struggling to fit the snow plow to the front of his truck. Glancing through the open roller door he saw they'd already shoveled the driveway and turn-around so he could get the truck out.

"How the fuck does this thing go on?" Brogan asked.

"With great difficulty, but it shouldn't be too hard with all of us here. Normally it's just me that fits it," Steve said.

"Why isn't it on already? You usually have this thing on from late November or early December." Quinn stood straight. "I can't get that thing to lock in."

"We haven't had as much snow this year." Steve bent down to adjust a bracket on the front of his truck. "There, that should do it."

They worked together and quickly had the single-blade plow fitted for the trip to town. He'd leave it on now, until late February, that way he'd be able to get to and from town without much trouble. Since he'd moved into his house he no longer had direct access to the town plow, it was kept in a storage shed behind the community center and Harry was now in charge of clearing the main streets in Whispering Springs.

"Ready?" Dale asked.

"As I'll ever be," Steve answered.

"We'll all go to Doc's house. The women can help her get some things together to bring back here and we'll take a look around," Brogan said.

"Thanks."

"Don't thank me, Steve. I should have killed the bastard when we caught him. Instead I did the right thing and had him exiled." Brogan's fists clenched at his sides.

"You weren't the only one who had your hands on him that day. And remember I didn't rip his throat out even though I knew what had happened to Doc up here last May." Steve had almost given in to the need to hurt Marcus that day, but he hadn't.

"Water under the bridge. What if's will eat you alive if you let them, best to move on and learn from your mistakes." Dale walked over to the door to the house. "I'll tell the women we're ready to go whenever they are."

"So what's going on between our sheriff and Tatum?" Quinn asked.

"No idea. I asked Doc before and she's as clueless as I am," Steve said.

"She's a tough little thing, stood up to him without batting an eyelid." Brogan pulled his keys out of his pocket. "Never thought I'd see that. Most run a mile and it's not his size that frightens people, it's the *don't come near me* vibe he gives off."

"Yeah, I know what you mean. He's been like that all his life but it's worse since he returned from the city," Quinn added.

Steve could understand that. The thought of living in the city for years put him in a bad mood, never mind actually living there. "The city will do that to you."

"Not sure it was the city or what happened in it that made him worse." Quinn headed for the driveway. "I'm gonna warm up my truck, tell Rowan that's where I am when she finally gets her ass in gear."

"Hey, my ass is in gear." Rowan stepped out of the house into the garage. "Don't go getting all smart mouthed or Santa won't bring you any presents."

Brogan laughed. "Santa isn't likely to bring Quinn anything but coal in his sack. He's got bad boy ticks tallied up until eternity."

"Like you're any better." Rowan swatted her brother on the arm as she walked past.

"Hey." Brogan cradled his arm against his chest.

"Are those two at it again?" El asked.

"Quinn started it." Brogan and Rowan spoke together.

Quinn rolled his eyes and turned to head outside. "I'm leaving now, Rowan."

"I'm coming, I'm coming." She jogged after him.

"Come on, let's get this show on the road." Brogan offered his hand to El and led her from the garage.

Everyone else filed out of the house and Steve locked the door. Dale escorted Tatum with a hand on her elbow out to his squad car and Kat jumped in the back of Brogan's truck, which left him and Doc.

"Kat could have come with us," he said.

"I think she wanted to talk to Brogan about something."

"Oh?"

"Yeah, something about the new guide starting next year. She's supposed to do some training with him, I think. I can't remember exactly what she told me."

He helped Gordie into the truck and shut the door. Jumping over the plow, he skirted the front end and got in the driver's seat. In no time he'd reversed out and turned around. Steve drove through the unshoveled side of his driveway to the road. One by one the other vehicles fell in behind him and they headed for town.

5

Gordie jumped from Steve's truck when he pulled up to the curb in front of her childhood home. The place looked quiet, but a raw nerve twitched deep in her belly. She wasn't sure what it was but something felt wrong. Very wrong. Her instincts screamed run but she was done with running from Marcus and the fear he'd made her live with for months.

Steve stepped up beside her and grabbed her hand, entwining their fingers. He waited without saying a word while the others pulled up one car at a time and came to join them on the sidewalk. There wasn't as much snow on the ground here as there had been higher up the mountain at Steve's place, but there was enough to know nobody had walked up to the house from the street.

"Ready?" Steve gave her hand a gentle squeeze.

She sucked in a deep breath and blew it out through her mouth. "Yep. Let's do this."

They walked up the snow-covered path, their shoes sinking into the iced-over top with ease. Gordie wore a pair of boots Steve had loaned her, they were too big and her toes kept bashing into the steel-capped tips as her feet slid forward with each step. She'd have bruises if she didn't get out of them soon. Good thing hers were on the other side of that door.

Gordie froze on the bottom step. She hadn't even thought about her purse, never mind her keys. "I don't have—"

"Here." Steve held her keys out in his hand.

"Oh. Thank you." She gripped the key ring, reluctant to find the right key to open the front door. What was the warning bell going off in her head all about?

"What's wrong?" Dale came up behind them.

She turned her head and saw everyone else waiting back on the footpath. "I'm not sure."

"Want me to go in first?" Dale asked.

Gordie tilted her head and looked up at the second floor windows and stilled. There's no way she'd left her bedroom window open. "Yes." She handed over the keys.

Steve turned her to face him. "I'll go in with Dale. You go wait with the others while we take a look inside, okay?"

She thought about taking the easy way out, just going over and waiting for someone else to deal with whatever mischief Marcus had wrought in her house, but she couldn't do it. "No. I'm coming in with you."

"Doc."

"It's my house, my problem."

"Dale." Steve turned to the other man. "Tell her to wait outside."

"Can't. Technically this isn't an official call, otherwise I would." Dale looked at Gordie. "But if I tell you to move you move, got it?"

She nodded. Gordie might be brave enough to go in with them, but she wasn't about to question the authority of a sheriff who'd spent years on the mean streets of a big city.

"Right, let's go then." Dale walked to the door, key out. "Both of you stay behind me."

Steve shoved her behind him as they entered the house. The stench hit her full in the face like a brick wall. It was worse than a litter box. Gordie pinched her nose and breathed through her mouth until she got in the rhythm of breathing through her mouth only. Puddles of yellow fluid lined the walls and floor in the foyer and explained where the smell came from.

"Fuck." Steve pulled her with him into the living room. "I take it you didn't leave the place like that yesterday morning?"

"You take it right." Gordie quickly scanned the room. "There's none in here."

"No, it appears to just be in the entrance." Dale strode toward the dining area.

Gordie held tight to Steve's hand as they followed the sheriff through her house. There was another "marking of territory" section at her back door but nothing else on the lower level appeared to have been touched. At the stairs she took a deep breath through her mouth and tried to calm the nerves jumping around inside her. She knew whatever they found upstairs would be above and beyond the downstairs damage.

Kat's childhood bedroom was trashed. The furniture had been overturned and the bedding ripped from the bed. Gordie wanted to cry at the sight of her sister's prized collection of porcelain dolls—the clothes were in tatters and their pretty, painted faces smashed to smithereens.

"Jesus." Steve tugged on her hand. "Don't touch anything. Dale might be able to get fingerprints."

"I'll want photos too before you move anything, Gordie," Dale said.

She nodded and spun on her heel to leave the room but stopped when she saw the wall behind her. Gordie's chest ached when all the air was sucked from her lungs. Painted on the wall, in crude preschool skill, was a coyote, his eyes glowed un-naturally yellow, saliva dripped from its jaws and clamped between wicked-looking teeth was a cat. It didn't take a genius to work out what the message was.

"Get her off the street." Gordie took off at a run, a scream tearing from her throat. "*Kat!*"

"Gordie, wait."

She could hear Steve's boots hitting the hardwood flooring as he raced after her, but she couldn't stop. Had to reach Kat before anything happened. Her feet slid in the borrowed boots and she stumbled on the staircase. A hand gripped her forearm, fingers dug into her soft flesh and sent shards of pain slicing through her elbow and wrist. Gordie felt herself spin midair, her footing gone from underneath her completely but instead of landing on hard, wooden treads she slammed into the hot, hard wall of Steve's chest.

He held her close and they went down together. His body cushioned their fall and air expelled from his lungs as his back hit the stairs with a thud. Steve groaned in pain and Gordie had visions of snapping vertebrae before her breasts crushed against his ribs, sucking all breath from her. The front door burst open beneath them. Footfalls pounded the stairs above and below them, but she couldn't get past the look of agony on Steve's face.

Stars danced in her vision and pain lanced her chest. Gordie tried to suck in air, tried to move her arms and legs to get off him but nothing wanted to work properly. Her ears filled with a strange humming sound that she tried to shake loose but it didn't stop. Finally her lungs worked, lifesaving oxygen flowed through her veins bringing with it vital feeling and function.

She planted her hands on the step beside Steve's shoulders and pushed to lift her weight off him. He still hadn't spoken and the color of his skin was making her feel sick. She scrambled up, moved to the side and began to check his limbs for breakage.

"Where does it hurt? Can you feel your toes? Talk to me, Steve." She rambled on as she cleared one section of his body after another of any injury.

Steve tried to say something and she bent forward to listen but couldn't make out the words. She checked his pupils. Both reacted normally and Gordie breathed a sigh of relief that he didn't appear to have banged his head in the fall. His color was returning along with a harsh breath he dragged in through clenched teeth.

"Don't try to move. Let me check the rest of you." Gordie ran her hands under his head and another sigh left her chest when she found no lumps.

"Okay," he panted. "Catch. Breath."

"What?"

"Winded."

"Are you sure?"

He nodded.

"Okay, everyone back, give him room." She thrust out her hands to ward everyone off without taking her eyes off Steve's.

"I'm okay, Doc. You can relax now."

Relax? They just tumbled down half a flight of stairs and he wanted her to relax? "Not going to happen until you get up and walk and talk normally."

"Give me a second."

"Here, let me help you sit." Dale spoke from above them.

Dale shoved his hands under Steve's shoulders and lifted. Steve groaned but didn't change color or faint. That was a win as far as she was concerned. Gordie moved aside and helped him sit with an arm around his waist. He leaned in against her and she pushed back to keep them both from falling into everyone crammed onto the steps below them.

"What happened? Why were you screaming my name at the top of your lungs?" Kat asked.

Oh God. She'd forgotten about that. Gordie looked at her sister but couldn't come up with the words to explain.

"You old room is trashed and there's a nasty message on one of the walls," Dale told everyone.

Kat raised one eyebrow. "Really? What about the rest of the house?"

"Downstairs is clean except for the piss at the front and back doors. We only got as far as your room when Gordie panicked about you being out on the street."

"Let's check the rest of the house," Brogan said.

"Not without me you're not." Steve tried to stand.

"Hey, you can't get up yet." Gordie tightened her arm around him but only succeeded in getting pulled to her feet with him. "Okay, you can."

"I told you I was fine, just had the wind knocked out of me," he reassured her.

"At least let me check you over first."

"The only thing you're going to find is a few bruises. Honestly, Doc, I'm fine."

She wanted to believe him with every fiber of her being but her heart and her mind wanted proof before he did anything. Gordie checked his eyes again and found no change, just that penetrating gaze of his. He seemed all right so she conceded, but she'd be watching him closely for a while.

"Okay, but any dizziness or numbness or pain you tell me straight away."

"Yes, Doc." He grinned and leaned down to drop a kiss on her mouth. "Thank you for caring."

Gordie's cheeks burned. Everyone stood around them and even though they all knew she and Steve were together now she couldn't help the blush that stole over her skin.

Dale cleared his throat. "Let's get the rest of the upstairs looked at and then I can take some photos and dust for fingerprints."

"What good will that do? It's not like we don't know who's behind it," Kat said.

"We might know but we need proof because this time he's not getting exiled. I want him locked up," Dale said.

"How will you manage that seeing how he's not human?" El asked from over Brogan's shoulder.

"There are some jails that are shifter friendly." Dale grinned.

"So some humans know about shifters?"

"No, but there are shifters who live among humans and a few are in the correctional services so we have options when it comes to shifters who break the law. In the old days we'd have had to kill them," Dale explained.

"Oh." El wrapped her arms around Brogan's waist. "That's just horrible."

"It's the way it was, but there's been a lot of changes over the years and being able to lock up criminals whether they're human or not is just one of them." Dale turned and headed back up the stairs.

Gordie kept her arm around Steve's waist and walked beside him. He didn't need her support to stay upright but she needed to feel his warmth to reminder her he was fine.

S teve let Doc hold him steady. He could walk without her help but after seeing her trip on the stairs and the vision of her hitting bottom that had splashed across his mind in the split second before he'd caught her made him need her touch. She tucked nicely under his arm and he enjoyed the feel of her beside him.

They stopped at the door to Kat's room and everyone took a look inside. Kat whistled and then turned a shade lighter when she got a good look at the painting. She studied it for ages, stepped closer and touched the paint.

"It's dry and if I'm right it's paint like the sort we used in art class back in high school," Kat told them.

Doc reached out a hand and he let her go so the two sisters could hug. It was a brief squeeze and he soon found Doc cuddled back into his side.

"Okay, let's keep going," Doc said.

The bathroom was undisturbed, the tiled expanse clean and tidy. Steve and Doc followed Dale as he made his way along the hallway. Another door revealed a spare room furnished as a home office. This room looked worse than Kat's bedroom.

"Damn. That's a lot of paperwork," Quinn said.

"Yeah, it's the DNA records for my research on the coyote gene. It's not the first time I've found my papers trashed like this but at least it won't set me back months like the first time," Doc said.

"No? Why not?" Steve asked.

"I started keeping a computer record after the first break-in." Dale held up a shattered piece of her hard drive. "And I keep a copy of all my files at an offsite file storage company so my research is safe."

"Good. I doubt there's anything in here you can salvage," Dale said.

There were two rooms left and Steve turned to Doc. "Which one?"

"Mom and Dad's first. I have no doubt mine will be the worst so we'll save it for last."

Doctor and Mrs. Monroe's room was untouched. Like the bathroom not one thing had been moved, it was like the Monroes had gotten up this morning instead of months ago when they'd taken off on their latest cross-country adventure.

"Anyone else find it bizarre that this room is untouched?" Quinn asked.

"No. Downstairs is the same." Dale turned to leave the room. "He's not wasting energy on what won't get a reaction."

Damn, Dale was right. Everything that had been trashed caused an emotional reaction. Marcus was playing mind games with them. It wasn't just about fear either, the way he'd smashed Kat's doll collection held anger but was designed to provoke pain. And the painting, well that had everything to do with menacing Doc. He wanted her to worry about her sister, to fear for her well-being and the dolls played into that too. In his twisted way Marcus was letting Doc know he'd hurt her sister next.

Kat stood next to Dale as he opened the door to Doc's bedroom. All color drained from her face and she swayed.

"Dale." Steve broke his hold on Doc and lunged for her sister but Dale spun in time to catch her and lower her to the floor.

Doc dropped to her knees next to them and patted her sister's cheek. "Come on, Kat, don't faint on me. You're tougher than that."

Kat's eyes fluttered. "Jesus Christ. Steve, don't let them see."

Steve had no idea what she was talking about until he heard Rowan's cry of anguish. He turned and looked past Dale into Doc's room. "Fuck."

Quinn pulled Rowan into his arms and Brogan held El back away from the door. Steve got to his feet and quickly closed the door. He turned back to the group. "Take everyone downstairs. Doc and Dale stay here."

"Why? What's in there?" El's voice wobbled.

"I don't know and I don't care at the moment. Let's go down and wait for them to join us." Brogan steered her away down the hall.

Tatum and Dale helped Kat to her feet. She'd regained her color and her eyes sparked with heat of the angry kind. Linking her arm with Tatum, they followed the others. Quinn remained with a crying Rowan in his arms. Steve looked at his friend and neither of them had to speak to know what the other was thinking. Marcus would pay for this.

"We won't be long," Steve told him.

Quinn nodded and led Rowan away.

"What the hell is in that room, Steve?" Doc stood beside him. "What could be bad enough for Kat to almost pass out and to send Rowan, who has to be one of the toughest women I know, into a fit of tears?"

He turned to Dale. "One on either side of her?"

Dale nodded and together they bracketed Doc. Steve took a deep breath and cupped her elbow in his palm before opening the door. She surprised him, there was no gasp, no cry, nothing. Until the shaking started. Small tremors that turned into bone-rattling vibrations in seconds.

"Is that what I think it is?" she whispered.

"Yeah, if you think that's Rowan's wedding dress covered in blood."

"Oh God." She brought a trembling hand up to cover her mouth. "Wait, that's not just Rowan's dress."

Steve was unprepared for her to move so she got halfway across the room before he caught up with her. "What do you mean?"

She stood beside the bed gazing down at the red and white mess. Rowan's dress lay draped over the footboard and now that he was closer he could see what Doc was talking about. "El's dress, but whose is the other one?"

"My mother's." She reached out a hand but Dale grabbed it before she could touch anything.

"No, don't touch."

"Come on, we've seen enough. Let Dale do his job."

"I'm calling the station. I need a couple of men over here. Will you let them in and show them upstairs when they get here, Steve?" Dale had his phone to his ear already.

"Sure." Steve ushered Doc from the room.

"I know nothing Marcus has done makes sense but I can't help but wonder about the significance of the dresses. Regardless of his craziness there always seems to be a subliminal message in everything he does," Doc said.

"The message in Kat's room is clear, he's telling you he'll hurt her like the dolls. But I don't have a clue what the message in your room is. The one in your office is clear. Stop researching but why?"

"Stop researching?" She paused and looked at him. "I never made that connection."

"What did you think it was?"

"Just willful mischief."

"No, it's clear to me he's trying to destroy the research you've done so far, which means you'd either start again or give up."

"I'd never give up. What I'm doing will help generations to come."

"What exactly are you doing?"

"I'm tracking skills and bloodlines. Trying to work out if the coyote gene is thinned by breeding with humans or if there's no change to the DNA's strength."

"Found anything yet?"

"Yes, actually. The gene isn't diluted at all. And those that are turned may start with slightly less potent coyote traits but they grow stronger over the years. Depending on how young the individual is when they're turned, they could end up just as strong as a pure-bred coyote shifter."

"How would any of this affect Marcus?"

"I don't know. It was his father that was anti half-bloods and non-bloods but then the apple doesn't fall far from the tree."

"I think you could be right there. Malcolm was insane and it seems Marcus is following right in his footsteps." He slung his arm around her shoulders. "Come on, let's go meet the cavalry."

They'd reached the bottom step when a knock sounded on the front door. Gordie let Steve answer it, more than happy to allow him to take control for now. Suddenly exhausted, she leaned on the railing for the stairs. She wasn't touching any walls in the foyer. She nodded at the two deputies when they came inside.

"The Sheriff wants us to photograph the downstairs damage before going up, said you'd show us where, Mr. McKenna," the older of the two spoke.

"Here, and beside the back door through the kitchen. Someone has marked territory. Give us a yell when we can clean it up."

"Will do, Mr. McKenna."

Steve walked over and pulled her into his arms. The warmth radiating from his body helped remove the chill that had settled in her bones since she'd seen her room. She didn't want to remember those dresses covered in blood but the image was burned onto her memory like the ink of a tattoo. Gordie sighed and leaned into him.

"I'm not going to promise everything will be okay but I will guarantee I'll be standing beside you no matter what happens," he murmured in her ear, his lips brushing her skin, his breath warm and moist.

Gordie didn't answer him, there didn't seem to be anything but thank you to say and that felt like too little. She wrapped her arms around his waist and raising her head, stood on tippy toes. Her mouth met his in a quick peck. "It seems like too little but thank you."

"You don't need to thank me, Doc. You know I'd be here regardless of our current relationship standing." He grinned.

"What?"

"We're together."

"I know. So?"

"I've waited most of my life for this moment and with everything going on it's only just sunk in." Steve lifted her off the floor and spun around.

"Put me down."

"No." He stopped spinning and planted his mouth on hers.

This kiss was nothing like the chaste one she'd given him. It was wet and hot. He thrust his tongue through her lips. She opened wider and their tongues tangled, stroked and licked until she was breathless with want. Gordie curled her legs around his hips and pressed her sex to his. Her pussy clenched and moisture coated her panties. Steve groaned into her mouth and bucked his hips.

"Ahem."

She tore her mouth from his. Ragged breaths dragged over her teeth and along her raw throat. Her eyes wide, Gordie stared at Steve. They'd been seconds from taking the kiss to the next level and she'd totally forgotten where they were. Who was with them. There was a house full of people and she was moments away from stripping him bare.

"Sorry to interrupt, but could you show us where else down here needs photographing, please?"

The young deputy ducked his head but not before Gordie noticed the pink tinge on his cheeks. She looked at the other officer to find him staring back with a knowing smile. Her own cheeks flushed with heat, more than was already there from Steve's carnal kisses.

"This way." Steve turned and headed through the living room, Gordie still in his arms.

"Put me down," she whispered.

"No." He kept walking.

They passed everyone sitting at her dining table, mugs of coffee or tea in front of them. Gordie was glad to see her sister had played hostess. Steve stepped into the kitchen and indicated the door to the mudroom.

"In there."

Both men entered the small room but it soon became apparent the space wasn't large enough for the two of them. The older man came back into the kitchen and pulled a notebook from his shirt pocket.

"Got a second to answer some questions?" he asked as he licked the tip of a pen.

"The sheriff was with us when we came in," Steve said.

"Yep. And I'll ask him the same questions after I'm done with you."

Steve set Gordie on her feet. "Sure. Mind if we sit while you ask?"

"In here or out there?" The Deputy nodded at the small table and chairs in the far corner of the kitchen before lifting his chin to indicate the dining room behind them.

"In here." Gordie walked over and pulled out a chair.

"Did you see anyone when you got here?"

"No and the layer of snow on the front walk hadn't been disturbed either," Steve answered.

"Okay, so in your own words talk me through what happened." He sat opposite them, scribbling in his notebook.

Gordie let Steve tell him. She could have done it but she was tired and wasn't sure she wouldn't burst into tears if she had to say what had been done to the upstairs rooms. Resting her head on Steve's shoulder, she closed her eyes and let the sound of his voice soothe her.

She must have dozed off because next thing she knew Steve was lifting her into his arms and carrying her out of the kitchen. He headed upstairs and she tensed. The thought of seeing all that carnage again terrified her.

"It's okay, Kat changed the sheets on your parents' bed. We're just going to have a lie down."

"But—"

"Dale and the deputies are downstairs talking to the others and Kat, Rowan and El have already cleaned up the mess down there." He walked along the hall and she was relieved to see all the doors were shut tight.

"How long have I been asleep?"

"About thirty minutes but you need to rest and you need to

freshen up too. Kat is heading over to the café in a few minutes and everyone else will leave when she does." Steve nudged open the door to her mom and dad's room. "Dale said he'd be back later with some more equipment and until then we can't clean up here so I vote we take a nap while we can."

He lowered her to the bed and Gordie was surrounded by the smell of her mother. The bedding was fresh from the cupboard and the scent her mom always sprinkled to stop the linen from smelling moldy permeated every thread. She rubbed her cheek on the pillow and breathed deep. Steve tugged off her borrowed shoes and dropped them to the floor before toeing off his and climbing on the bed behind her.

Gordie snuggled into him, her back to his front, and relaxed. His warmth and the comfort of his arm draped over her waist calmed her in a way nothing in her life ever had. Even with the turmoil rolling around them she felt safe, secure and most of all loved. She probably wouldn't have taken that final step without yesterday's attack and for that she was thankful. He pressed his lips to her neck and a shiver raced over her skin.

"Go to sleep." His arm tightened around her, his hand splayed across her stomach and those talented fingers stroked her flesh in slow, easy circles.

"Mmm." Her eyelids drooped. "This is nice. Don't let go."

He chuckled. "Don't worry, I won't. You'll need a crowbar to remove me from your life now, Doc."

She smiled and drifted off with his heartbeat drumming against her spine.

Steve stared at the ceiling above him. Doc had turned and curled into his side about twenty minutes ago. He hadn't slept, couldn't with all the thoughts going round and round in his mind. Then there was the buzz bouncing from nerve ending to nerve ending currently making his coyote sit up. His instincts were screaming the shit was going to hit the fan. The question was what fan and what shit?

Doc stirred, mumbled something in her sleep and he pulled her closer, held her tighter. He figured they wouldn't be heading back up the mountain today. They would need to clean up once Dale gave them the okay and Steve didn't see that happening before later today. Kat said she'd send some food over from the café for their lunch and knowing her there'd be enough for their dinner plus breakfast and lunch tomorrow.

He should get up. There'd be no sleep for him and besides, he needed to use the bathroom. The sound of a truck pulling up out front made up his mind. Gently as he could, he slipped his arm out from under Doc. She snuggled into the bedding when he tucked it around her. Whatever she dreamed about put a smile on her face and he leaned forward to lightly brush his lips on hers.

Leaving her in that soft, warm bed was hard but he did. With as little noise as possible he picked up his boots, left the room and pulled the door closed behind him. He used the bathroom and had just stepped back into the hall when someone banged on the front door. Taking the stairs two at a time, he made it before whoever it was decided to make more of a racket than they already had. Steve swung the door open to find Dale leaning against the jamb.

"Hey." Steve stepped aside to let him in. "You're back early."

"I figured you'd want to get back up to your place before dark." Dale set down a heavy-looking black case and removed his jacket.

"No, I thought it might be best to stay in town tonight and head back tomorrow."

"Could be. There's supposed to be more snow this evening but not much. It's the big storm due in on Christmas morning that's got me worried." Dale looked at him. "You prepared to get snowed in for a few days up on that mountain of yours?"

"Always."

"Good. Let's grab a coffee before I get started." Dale walked to the kitchen without further invitation.

"Sure, why not?" Steve followed in his socked feet.

"Gordie still sleeping?" Dale was already filling a mug with the pot Kat had made earlier.

"Yes. That can't taste good." He nodded at the coffee in Dale's hand. "I'll put another pot on."

"This is fine. Anything is better than the sludge they try to pass off as coffee at the station. I really need to do something about who makes the coffee over there."

Steve laughed. It might be clichéd but it seemed TV shows were right, cops drank lousy coffee. "Get Kat to deliver some fresh every few hours."

"Now there's a thought." Dale finished and placed his cup in the sink. "Right, down to business."

Before Steve could say a word Dale had left the room. He'd never really been close to Dale when they were younger and since the other man had returned from the city they hadn't strengthened their friendship at all. Steve wasn't even sure if Brogan or Quinn knew him any better, but he wasn't about to let the sheriff's *don't get too close* vibe stop him from watching the man's every move.

He dumped the rest of the coffee from the pot and quickly set about making another one. Doc would want some when she woke up and no doubt they'd all want a few shots of caffeine as the day dragged on. Steve searched cupboards until he came up with coffee grounds and filters. Tossing the old filter in the bin, he dropped in the new one and added the rich-smelling blend. A rinse of the pot in hot water cleaned it enough for him. Once the water was poured in he put the pot on the heated pad under the drip nozzle and pressed the start button.

Heavy footsteps sounded above him. Dale had started in Doc's room. Kat had told him earlier that other than her doll collection there wasn't anything she'd left in her old room that couldn't be replaced easily. Doc's room on the other hand was a completely different story. Those three dresses were irreplaceable. He sucked in a breath and steeled himself to do what was necessary. They'd know in the next few minutes if anything could be done to save the delicate material from the blood soaking it but he wouldn't hold his breath wishing for a miracle.

Steve slipped into his boots and went upstairs to find Dale dusting the windowsill for fingerprints. The room was chilly due to the inch or so of open window. He could see where the lock had been jimmied off so he knew Doc hadn't left it cracked yesterday morning. Standing to the side, he tried to stay out of the way and still be able to see everything the sheriff was doing. When Dale barked an order over his shoulder Steve jumped.

"Bring that bag over here. If you're going to stand there you may as well be useful."

Striding over to the bag that was now open, Steve grabbed the handles and picked it up. He'd been right earlier, the damn thing weighed a ton. "What the hell is in this thing? Rocks?"

Dale laughed. "Rocks would be a lot cheaper."

"Yeah, but then they wouldn't help you get the job done." Steve moved over to the bed and stared at the white-splashed-with-red gowns. "So is this human or animal blood do you think?"

"I'd go with animal but only because I don't want to think about where human blood would come from." Dale finished dusting the window frame and with gloved hands, lowered the bottom section. "I'll be happier when the lab results come in though."

"I guess Marcus has really stepped over the line now."

"He'd stepped over it months ago but coming back after his supposed death has to be the dumbest thing he's ever done."

"So you believed Doc when she said it was him who attacked her yesterday?"

"Didn't you?"

"Well yeah, but there's no proof and you're a cop, you deal in evidence," Steve said.

"Maybe, but you're forgetting I'm also a coyote shifter and instinct is as much a part of my ability to solve crimes as the human skills of gathering information."

"I never thought of that. Guess that makes you better than the average cop."

"Not really, the courts still need hard evidence. Can't just turn up and say he did it because I can smell him all over the victim." Dale grinned.

Steve chuckled. "I can see how that might not work so well."

"Steve?"

He turned to see Doc standing in the doorway. She still wore his clothes and her feet were covered in a pair of his wooly socks. Steve walked over and gathered her in his arms. "I hoped you'd sleep longer."

"Probably best I don't or I won't be able to sleep tonight."

"After I'm through here do you mind if I go over to the clinic and see if I can pick up some prints?" Dale asked.

"No, that's fine. You still have the keys?" She pulled from Steve's embrace.

"Yes ma'am."

"Jeez, don't call me that. Sounds like you're talking to my mother." She grinned.

"Sorry, it's the job. I might not be wearing my uniform, but I'm here in an official capacity," Dale said.

"We'll leave you to finish up, Dale. We're going to get cleaned up so if someone comes by with lunch from Kat, can you let them in?" Steve asked as he ushered Gordie back through the door.

"Sure. I'll be at least another hour in here and then I'll go over Kat's room. Any chance Kat will send enough food for me?"

"Give her a ring and let her know you'll be eating with us," Gordie said. "Although knowing my sister it's probably not necessary."

"Okay."

"Come on, Doc, let's leave the Sheriff to it." Steve pulled her toward the room they'd slept in.

"Where are we going?"

"Back to bed?" he asked hopefully.

Her laughter echoed off the walls. "No way are we doing that in my parents' bed."

"Spoilsport." He pulled her close and whispered in her ear, "Then we'll jump in the shower and I'll help you wash your back."

Steve nipped her earlobe, sucked it into his mouth and flicked the delicate flesh with his tongue. She shivered against him, a moan gurgling in the back of her throat.

"Okay."

He laughed. "I love it when you're agreeable, Doc." Steve grabbed her hand and led her to the master bathroom.

6

Gordie couldn't catch her breath, her ragged gasps for air echoing off the bathroom walls. Steve was on his knees, his mouth doing wicked things to her sex. The tricks he did with his tongue were going to kill her. She'd die a blissful death with a smile on her face. Her pussy clenched when he sucked her clit between his lips and licked. Shudders of delight danced across every nerve and splintered into blinding pleasure the second he thrust his fingers inside her.

Her hips bucked, rode the wave of her orgasm as the sensations went on and on. Gordie muffled a cry with her hand, bit into the soft flesh to stifle more. The sting of pain combined with the bliss of satisfaction made her legs shake. If it weren't for the wall behind her, she'd fall. Steve kept pushing and pumped his fingers faster, stroked her clit harder. He rimmed her anus and sent her into orbit as he pressed on the tight ring of muscle.

Newly initiated nerve endings spasmed and her lower belly drew tighter and tighter until she thought she'd snap. He slid his finger deeper into her ass and she broke like a twig under a size-eleven boot. No resistance. She shattered into a thousand pieces, her legs going out from under her. Steve removed his mouth and hand, catching her in his arms as she collapsed into his lap. Gordie's mind and body were limp and he wasted no time in maneuvering her to straddle his thighs.

He thrust up, drove his cock deep into her still-contracting channel. She wrapped her arms around his neck and leaned into him. Steve gripped her hips, held her suspended a few inches above him so he could raise and lower his pelvis, impaling her over and over on his erection. Muscles, lax from post-orgasmic euphoria sparked to life as he dragged his length over sensitive, swollen flesh. Blood coursed through her veins, hot and heavy, to drown her in renewed need.

"That's it. Come for me again." He tilted her hips, drove his body into hers at a different angle.

"I can't."

"Yes, you can," he panted as he continued to pound into her. "Once more, Doc."

"Oh God."

With a speed that was mind numbing, he took her up to the peak again. He showed no mercy, driving his cock in and out, hard and fast. Harsh breaths echoed around them, the tiled walls bounced the sound back to drum in her ears. Steve's mouth found hers, his tongue demanding she give all. She couldn't breathe, couldn't think, could only feel. Rapture so savage it slashed and destroyed her. Forgetting they weren't in the house alone, Gordie pulled her lips from his and screamed as another release tore through her.

Steve arched and sank balls-deep in her convulsing core. His hips jerked twice before he went rigid beneath her. He came, her name a hoarse groan that sounded more like a prayer for help than a cry of relief. She slumped against him, their torsos sticky with sweat. Their skin clung and their chests heaved with the desperate need for air. Her heart hammered double time against her ribs and her lungs burned but she couldn't move. Not yet.

"Wow." Steve lowered his back to the floor, taking her with him. "That was..."

"Yeah. It was." Her fingers and toes tingled as feeling started to return.

"We didn't even make it into the shower."

"Good thing we didn't. I need one more than ever now." She sighed.

"I don't know. I'm kinda partial to having my scent all over you."

Gordie lifted her head and found his gaze with hers. "I don't mind either. It's the copious amounts of sweat and sex smell I'm objecting to."

Steve buried his face into her neck and sniffed. "Smells pretty damn good to me. Good enough to eat." He nibbled at her throat.

A shiver traveled down her spine. "Stop it." The teasing bites tickled her skin and Gordie wiggled on top of him. His softened cock slipped from her body and warm sparks of arousal danced around in her lower belly. It amazed her to think she could have any interest left after their last encounter but each time they came together the need wasn't quenched. Instead it grew stronger, deeper.

He sucked on her neck, pulled her flesh between his lips with increasing pressure and Gordie knew she'd be left with a love bite when he was done. A ribbon of excitement snaked through her. The idea of others seeing Steve's mark thrilled her in a way she'd never imagined. She tipped her head sideways, gave him better access and moaned with her delight of being his.

"Damn you taste good," he murmured against her throat. "I could spend the entire day nibbling on you."

"Oh God. I could let you." Gordie pressed into him. Her body plastered to the length of his, their legs in a tangle.

"When?"

She squirmed as his mouth trailed wet kisses along her jaw. "What?"

"When can I nibble on you all day?" He licked the shell of her ear. "It can't be today but it has to be soon."

Gordie couldn't think. He was licking and biting and kissing every erogenous zone on her head. "Umm..."

"Christmas." More kisses. "Can I have you for Christmas dinner?" He stroked his tongue down to her shoulder, along her collarbone. "Spread out on my table with all the trimmings."

Oh God. He would kill her. "Please."

"Please what, Doc?" His teeth scraped over the slope of her breast.

"Anything," she gasped. "Everything."

He smiled against her skin. "Mmm, I can't wait for Christmas dinner."

Steve rolled her beneath him and sucked her nipple into his mouth. The cold floor at her back made her shiver. The heat of his body covering her front made her melt. He thrust his hips, his hard cock pressing into her thigh. She parted her legs, wrapped them around his waist and dug her heels into his ass to pull him closer. A growl vibrated over her breast a second before his teeth pinched the puckered tip and his cock entered her in one plunge.

"Ah, yes." Gordie's head tossed from side to side, the hard cold tile going unheeded as a blazing fire devoured her. He drove into her pussy and his erection rubbed over inflamed walls, sending her into sensory overload. Pleasure and pain. Pain and pleasure. Raw nerves no longer able to distinguish the difference, no longer cared, only needed to be taken. To give him everything he demanded.

Steve buried his face against Doc's damp neck. He'd locked his elbows and braced his knees, but he struggled to keep his weight off her. His coyote was closer to breaking free than any other time they'd come together as satisfaction flowed through him. It amazed him that his wild side had been so quiet. The bizarre thing was he thought he understood why.

Doc had never run with any of the pack members that he knew of. Other than when Anthony had turned her and she'd run with the newly shifting teenagers of the pack, Steve couldn't recall her ever shifting. They'd change that over the next week. She needed to connect with that side of herself before his coyote could.

"When was the last time you shifted?" His lips brushed her skin and she shivered beneath him. "Shit. You're cold."

He rolled to the side and got to his feet. Reaching down he offered her his hand and pulled her from the floor. With her tucked into his side, he reached in and turned the shower on. In no time the water heated and steam billowed out to surround them. Gently, he nudged her in ahead of him.

"Come on, let's get clean and warm and then we can talk." He grabbed the soap and quickly lathered his hands.

Steve passed the bar to Doc and while she soaped up her hands he set to work washing her down. He didn't linger, couldn't afford to or his body would demand more of hers and neither of them needed that right now. If they weren't careful they'd wear each other out. A smile tipped his lips.

"What are you smiling at?" Her hands were busy cleaning his chest.

"Us. We're gonna kill each other with sex if we don't stop." Steve slid his hands over the curves of her hips.

"You started it."

"I didn't hear you complaining at all." He ran his hands up the inside of her thighs and she flinched. "Sore?"

"Tender. No, actually more sensitive, really, not sore."

Her delicate fingers trailed over his abs and he sucked in a breath, his cock pulsing with interest. "Jesus. We need to get some clothes on."

He stepped back out of temptation's touch and finished scrubbing himself down. Doc took the hint and did the same. Steve ignored the knowing smile on her lips and blanked out the wet, naked body in front of him. They really did need to head on back to his place where they'd have no interruptions and certainly no reason other than fatigue to keep their hands off each other.

Steve waited for Doc to step out and grab a towel. He couldn't stop his gaze from dropping to watch her sexy ass as she walked away from him. Mesmerized by the sight it took him a moment to realize she'd turned to offer him a towel and was in the process of covering up. With a sigh of disappointment he pulled it together and joined her on the bathmat.

"Why'd you ask about me shifting?" Doc had wrapped a second

towel around her head and was vigorously rubbing the water from her hair.

"Because just now my coyote was closer to the surface than any other time we've had sex and it got me thinking about how quiet that side of me has been." Dry, he reached for his clothes.

"I don't shift very much."

"Why?"

She shrugged. "It's hard to explain, but after Anthony I kind of shut that side of myself down. And I guess because I was so newly turned I hadn't made that big of a connection with my coyote."

"Understandable. And now?"

"Around you or because we're together?"

"Both."

"Being around you always stirs me up, human and coyote, that's why I stayed away for so long. But after you moved away my coyote wouldn't let me stay too far. Hence the walks up in the forest near your place. Just being close to you calms her."

"So your coyote side is making its presence known." He slipped into his pants. "When we get home I'd like to shift together. I think we need to do that."

Gordie stumbled as she stepped into the borrowed sweats, she couldn't wait to be given the all clear to get into her room so she could grab some of her own clothes to wear. "Why?"

"Because it's part of who we are and I want to see you in coyote form. I've never seen you." Steve reached over and cupped her face in his hands. "And because I think you need to fully connect with your coyote side. I don't think you ever really have and the more we're together, the more our coyotes are going to want to bond."

She stared at him, her gaze searching his. He could feel her pulse beating against the heels of his hands. Steve waited, breath held, until she nodded. Releasing his breath in a slow stream, he bent forward and planted his mouth on hers. The kiss was nothing more than skin on skin, but he felt it to his bones and knew she did too. Her eyelids lowered and he took them deeper.

Her arms slid around his neck and her body pressed to his. Steve ran his tongue over the seam of her lips, pushed until she opened and let him inside. He explored the moist depths, licked and stroked and tasted every part of her. Breathless, he backed off, slowed his caresses and eased them out of the lush mating of their mouths.

Pulling back, he laid his forehead on hers and breathed deep. Her breathing came as harsh as his and her eyes remained closed. When her lids lifted to reveal her brown eyes he could see she'd fortified her emotions.

"No. No holding back, Doc. We agreed, no more arm's length. Talk to me." He moved back, gave her room to breathe.

"I'm scared."

"Why? What could possibly be frightening about shifting together?"

"I've never done it before."

"What? Shifted in front of another coyote?" That couldn't be right, surely she and Anthony had run together.

"I'm not good at it. It takes me ages to make the change. And I haven't run with anyone since Anthony turned me and I ran with the coming-of-age coyotes."

"You never shifted and ran with him?"

She bit her lip and shook her head.

"Ah, Doc." He tugged her close, nestled her face against his chest and wrapped his arms around her. "It's not hard and I don't care if it takes all day for you to shift into coyote form. Don't worry about it now. We'll deal with that side of us when we don't have any distractions."

He smoothed his hands up and down her spine, waited until he felt her tense muscles soften under his touch. A shuddery breath rattled her chest and her arms gave his waist one hard squeeze before she slipped from his embrace.

"I know I'm being irrational. I'm an educated woman, probably too educated, but I can't help the feelings inside me. I've felt like an outcast in this town my whole life. I always knew I was different even when I didn't understand why." She held up her hand to stop the protest he would have made. "I get that no one tried to make me feel that way, even those against half-bloods and non-bloods didn't single me out any more than anyone else, but that clawing desperation to be like everyone around me is what led me to accept a proposal I had no right to. I can't help thinking every decision I've made in these mountains has been a bad one."

"You never did anything wrong, Doc."

"I know that, really I do, but it'll play on my mind forever regardless of what I or anyone else thinks and I can't stop that from affecting the way I relate to my coyote. I hated that side of myself for years when I was away from here. It took me a long time to come to terms with who and what I am. Neither of us can expect me to come to terms with us and what that means quickly, Steve." She gripped his hand, curled her fingers between his. "I guess I'm asking you to be patient and in return I promise to try harder to connect to both you and myself."

Steve brushed a fingertip down her cheek. "Gordie, I think once you come to accept yourself there'll be no stopping us. And I think that will be the easy part of all of this."

"Hey." Dale banged on the bathroom door. "You two coming out anytime soon? Tatum's here with our lunch."

Doc smiled at him. "This seems to be turning into a habit."

"Yeah, it looks that way," he spoke softly. "We'll be out in a second," he called out to Dale.

"We'll be in the dining room. Kat sent over a feast and I'm starving so we're starting without you in five minutes," Tatum yelled.

Holding Doc's hand, Steve stepped over to the door and pulled her with him. "Come on or they'll eat all the good stuff before we get downstairs."

She laughed. "This is Kat's food, it's *all* good stuff."

Steve had to agree. Kat might grate on his nerves but she could cook better than anyone he'd ever known and that made up for every other flaw the woman had. Plus she was Doc's sister and he'd put up with anything and anyone to be with her.

They found Tatum and Dale already seated and loading their plates. He pulled out a chair for Doc and sat next to her as he grabbed the first bowl of food. It only took a few minutes to fill their plates and start eating. Nobody spoke until most of the food was polished off and their hunger abated.

Tatum pushed her chair back and laid a hand on her huge belly. "Damn that was good."

"You sure you've had enough?" Dale asked.

"Yep. I already ate a piece of chicken pie with potato and gravy while I waited for Kat to put the food together."

"You ate twice what I ate just now. Where the hell do you put it all? Other than that beach ball under your sweater there's nothing to you," Doc said.

Tatum grinned. "I know. I'm hoping that means I'll be back to my normal size once these two are born."

"Here. Drink some more tea." Dale refilled Tatum's cup. "You need fluids as well as food."

"Thanks."

Steve eyed his friend and wondered what he'd missed. Not twenty-four hours ago Dale and Tatum had been at each other's throats and now here they were getting on like the best of friends. He glanced at Doc but she only shrugged and kept on eating.

"I finished upstairs, Gordie. You can clean it up whenever you're ready," Dale said.

"Oh. Okay, thanks." She reached for her drink and took a sip. "Find anything?"

"No, nothing more than I expected to anyway. Both rooms had prints all over them but they could belong to anyone who's been in here over the last few months. I'll need to wait for the lab results before I can tell you anything else."

"I've bundled up the dresses. I'll take them out to Gramps' and see if Grammy can do anything about the stains. If anyone can fix them, it's Grammy," Tatum said.

"Thank you, Tatum. I'll let Rowan and El know." Doc leaned back in her chair with a sigh. "I'll have to ring Mom and tell her too."

"You don't have to ring her. Wait until she gets here," Steve offered.

"I guess it won't matter either way, will it? It's still going to hurt."

Steve placed his hand on her thigh. "Yeah, it will and I'm sure she'd rather hear it in person than over the phone."

"You're right. I'll wait until she gets here." Doc stood and began stacking plates. "Tatum, are you staying out at your grandparent's now that you've moved back home?"

"Um, no, I can't exactly expect Grammy and Gramps to put me and the babies up. Besides, I'll need to be closer to the clinic for work. I'm living in town."

Dale stood suddenly. "I'll give you a lift to the garage so you can pick up your car, Tatum."

"Oh. Okay. Do you mind if we leave you with the dishes, Doc? It's just that Harry said he'd be closing up right after lunch and I don't want to be without my car or my bags."

"Sure, go on. Steve will help clean up."

He swallowed the bite he'd just taken. "Do I have a choice?"

"Not really, but go ahead and finish eating. I'll wait." Doc grinned at him.

"Very polite of you," he grumbled.

"I know. My manners are impeccable." She left the plates on the table, patted him on the shoulder and walked toward the front of the house. "Don't worry about getting up, Steve, I'll see our guests out."

Steve could hear the laughter in her voice but had no intention of calling her on her cheek because she'd called them *our* guests. She probably didn't realize what she'd done. Without thought Gordie had tied them together in front of their friends. As far as he was concerned it was one huge step in the right direction.

***

Gordie helped Tatum button up her coat and slip on her snow boots. "Did you want to start at the clinic after New Year? I know we said mid-to-late January but if you want to come in and get a feel for the place I'll be opening the doors again on the second."

"That would be great. I know a lot of the older generation but I'd like to meet everyone before I start taking over some of their care." Tatum took her handbag from Dale. "I've got your phone number so I'll ring you after Christmas and we can talk more about what it is you want and don't want."

"No need for that. We'll just get it all sorted when you start." She gave the other woman a hug. "Be sure to ring me if you have any concerns about your pregnancy. I worried about you changing doctors this far along but I'm thrilled that you feel safe enough to have these babies under my care."

"I'll be in touch if I get any lab results back but I doubt we'll hear anything before the New Year. There'll only be a skeleton staff on over the holidays." Dale opened the door and gestured for Tatum to precede him. "If anything else happens you know how to get hold of me."

"I do and thank you for everything you've done so far."

"It's my job, Gordie, but I'd be here even if it wasn't." He saluted and pulled the door closed as he stepped over the threshold.

"Alone at last."

Gordie jumped when Steve sneaked up behind her. "Jeez, don't do that."

"Sorry." He slid his arms around her waist. "We're not expecting any visitors for the rest of the day. It's a nice feeling having you all to myself."

She leaned back. "Yeah, but we'll be too busy cleaning to notice." Gordie sighed. "I don't know where to start."

"Kitchen. We'll tidy up the lunch dishes, check out what Kat sent over for dinner and breakfast before we tackle upstairs." Steve spun her to face him. "It won't take the two of us long and then we can start packing up some of your things."

"Are we still staying here tonight?"

"Did you not look outside when the others left? It's snowing again. The storm is supposed to be short lived but I doubt we'll be finished before dark so I thought we'd stick around here, have breakfast in the morning and then head over to The Den for lunch and then on home after that. Sound good?"

"Kat's expecting us to be at the dinner table on Christmas day."

"Not going to happen. The storm they're predicting for Christmas morning will keep everyone inside for a couple of days. That's why I thought we could appease her with lunch tomorrow."

"Okay." She sucked in a deep breath. "I guess we should get this over with."

Steve let her go. "Lead the way."

It didn't take them long in the kitchen and all too soon she had to deal with the mess upstairs. They started in Kat's room and Gordie cried the whole time she put piece after piece of her sister's doll collection into the garbage bags they were using. The wall would need repainting after she'd used a good paint stripper on it, although it might be worth ripping the drywall down and having new boards fitted.

She took a bag out of the room and went to get the vacuum. There were thousands of shards from the shattered porcelain embedded in the carpet. Gordie wasn't sure, but she wouldn't be surprised if the carpet would need to be replaced. Steve took the cord and plugged it in before shooing her out of the room.

"I'll do this. You go get clean sheets so you can make the bed when I'm done."

They'd stripped what was left of the bedding, the quilt had been an old one and rather than attempt to remove the slivers of ceramic she'd chosen to throw it out. She'd have to do the same with the one in her room. The thought made her cry all over again. Her Grandmother Monroe had made the quilt for her when she'd first come to live in Whispering Springs. Gordie had only gotten four years with her before she'd died, but Granny Roe had been the only grandparent she'd ever had.

Gordie pulled linen from the cupboard, the smell of her mother's favorite scent billowing out to surround her. It was a comfort, made her feel as though her mother was there with her, giving her a hug. Arms loaded up, she went back to Kat's old room and leaned against the doorjamb. Steve worked the vacuum as if he did it every day. Watching him do something so domestic gave her heart a jolt. He kept surprising her with his strength and his willingness to stand beside her no matter what.

The man plowed roads, built houses, did dishes and vacuumed floors. Her only experience living with a man other than her stepfather was Anthony and he'd been one of those men who firmly believed in women's work and men's work and never the twain shall meet. Steve was turning all she'd known and expected on its head but she wasn't upset. In fact she was thrilled to discover he thought of them as equals, both of them pitching in no matter what needed to be done.

"What are you smiling at?"

She hadn't realized he'd stopped the machine. Pushing off the wall, Gordie walked over and threw an arm around his neck. His height meant she had to stand on her toes but she planted her mouth on his for a quick kiss.

"Thank you," she said as she settled back on her feet.

"You're welcome but I'm not sure what I'm being thanked for." He smiled down at her.

"For being here. For standing beside me. For being you."

"All that huh?" His smile turned into a grin. "I guess you should be pretty thankful. Although, that kiss doesn't seem like enough payment for me being such a stand-up guy."

"Oh no you don't. You've had plenty of payment in the last twenty-four hours."

"I thought that was an even split of income. Seemed to me as though you were getting paid just as much."

Gordie's stomach fluttered and her pussy clenched, moisture dampened her panties. "We need to clean the house."

"We've been cleaning. I think we need to both get paid before we clean any more." He picked her up and stepped over the vacuum.

"Steve." Even to her own ears the protest held no strength.

"Gordie."

"We shouldn't."

Steve grinned down at her. "Yeah we should."

He lowered his head and kissed her. His tongue tangled with hers as they each sought to claim the other. They bumped their way into her parents' room and Steve put her down and started removing their clothes. Her shirt went, then his. He pulled the drawstring on her pants and pushed them down. She tugged his sweats over his hips. Each of them toed off their shoes and by the time they hit the mattress only their socks remained.

They hadn't bothered to pull the bedding back but neither of them noticed the wedding ring quilt beneath them. Engrossed in touching and tasting, they both took and gave with equal measure. Steve drove her to the peak quickly. Her orgasm broke over her in a tumble of sensation and need. But he wasn't done. With care he pushed her back up. This time slow and sensual led the way to the top. And when he finally came inside her they took the last steps together. He continued to thrust inside her until her release ebbed away. Spent but satisfied, she curled into his side and drifted off to sleep.

Steve let Doc sleep while he cleaned the rest of Kat's room. Too restless to sleep, he knew he'd be tempted to wake her up and have her again if he stayed in bed. Besides, he didn't want to be in the room when she worked out they'd broken the *not in my parents' bed* rule. The thought of how they'd smashed her rule made him smile as he hauled the last bag of garbage down the stairs.

The snow had stopped a few minutes ago but already the temperature was dropping inside the house. He walked around looking for the thermostat controls to check it was switched on. It wasn't until he'd walked the entire downstairs that he found the control box on the wall inside the little mudroom off the kitchen. Someone had the temp set too low so he turned the dial and waited for the furnace to kick in.

He waited several minutes but nothing happened and he was about to head down into the basement to check the heating system when Doc came into the kitchen.

"You finished off Kat's room."

"There wasn't much left to do and unlike you, I was awake."

"You should have woken me." She walked over to him. "What's wrong?"

"I was going to check the furnace. I turned up the heat but I haven't heard the unit start up yet." Steve pulled the door to the basement open.

"Hang on, the globe down there blew the other day, I'll grab a flashlight." She stepped into the mudroom and returned with a large flashlight.

"That looks more like a weapon than a light."

She grinned. "It's a two-for-one deal."

"A what?"

"Two-for-one. Two tools in one piece of equipment." Doc lifted the black stick above her head. "Anyone bothers me I can smash them over the head with it. Or I can switch it on and blind them before they get close enough to be any trouble."

"Wow." He ducked his head. "Remind me not to sneak up on you in a dark alley."

"I'm not about to find myself in a dark alley and I'd be concerned if I found you in one." She switched on the light and aimed it on the stairs. "I'll lead the way, I know where I'm going and I'd hate for you to fall down the stairs or trip over one of the million boxes Mom has stored down here."

They reached the furnace to find the pilot light had gone out. He was familiar with the unit so it only took a few minutes to ignite and have heat pumping through the venting pipes. As they turned to go back upstairs the flashlight hit on something to their right that made him reach out and grab Doc's hand to redirect the beam back to what he'd glimpsed.

Doc gasped and her hand trembled under his, the spotlight dancing over the plastic dry-cleaners bags. Steve plucked the flashlight from her grasp and quickly scanned the room. Nothing else looked out of place and other than the bags everything had a layer of dust to show how long they'd been down here. He entwined his fingers with Doc's and led the way back to the kitchen.

Once out of the dark he switched off the flashlight and placed it on the kitchen table on his way to the back door. He checked for signs of forced entry knowing full well that Dale had done that earlier but Steve had to see for himself. Next he checked windows, from one room to the next until he found himself at the front door. Doc followed behind, her hand still in his.

"What are we doing?" she asked.

"Checking for how the fucking bastard got inside."

"But Dale checked already."

"I know." He turned to look at her. "I need to see for myself."

"Okay."

They made their way upstairs and one by one he checked all the windows. There were no balconies so no outside doors and Steve was just about to concede defeat when he happened to glance up the hallway. At the far end from where they stood was a manhole in the ceiling and the square removable section appeared crooked.

"What type of roofing do you have?" he asked as he headed for the other end of the house.

"Type? Oh, you mean shingles or tin sheeting? Shingles, why?" She was right on his heels.

He stared up at the recently moved manhole and said, "Because I think I just worked out how he got into your house."

Steve pulled his phone out of his pocket and dialed the sheriff.

"Dale Turner."

"I know how he got in."

"How? I searched that house from top to bottom."

"I know. Also, we found dry-cleaning bags in the basement."

"Shit. Didn't the deputies look down there?"

"Yeah, but to be honest I doubt they would have realized what they were. I only recognized them because I picked up my suit last week and I knew where the dresses had gone missing from."

"Right. I'm still going to ream them a new one. Now tell me how you think Marcus is getting in that house."

"Through the roof."

"The roof?"

"Yep. I'm staring at the manhole in the upstairs hall. It's been moved recently and it hasn't been put back in the grooves properly so it's sitting lopsided."

"Give me five minutes to finish up here and I'll be over."

"Okay. See you in a few." Steve hung up and put the phone in his pocket.

"Do you really think he got in that way?" Doc asked.

He turned to look at her. "Yeah, it looks that way to me."

"So Dale's coming back?"

"Yep." He gripped her elbow and steered her toward the stairs. "Why don't we put a pot of coffee on and wait for him in the kitchen?"

"I'll make a pot but I'm boiling the kettle for some tea. I've had enough coffee for today."

Steve let Doc fuss over the tea and coffee making but it didn't escape his notice that her hands trembled. Maybe they shouldn't stay here tonight. She might feel safer back at his place or they could crash at Kat's.

"We're staying here." Her voice held a trace of anger. "I know what you're thinking and we're not letting him drive us out of here."

He glanced at the clock on the oven. "Well, it's too late to head up the mountain to my place and I guess Kat doesn't have room in that apartment of hers."

"No, she doesn't. We're staying put."

"Okay." Steve stood when the knock came on the front door. "I'll get it."

Steve opened the door and let Dale in. "Thanks for coming so quickly. Again."

"Anytime. Now where's the manhole?"

"Upstairs, end of the hall in front of the senior Monroe's bedroom."

"Okay, I'll go up and take a look. I'll give you a yell if I want to get up in the roof."

"Doc's making coffee so come on down for a cup when you've had a look and then we'll get up in the roof together. I'm not leaving it. I want to take a look up there to make sure none of the shingles have been moved."

"Will do." Dale turned and headed up the stairs two at a time.

Steve went back to the kitchen. Doc had poured a tea and sat at the table with a slice of what looked like chocolate cake.

"Is that what I think it is?" He pointed to her plate.

"If you think its Kat's special recipe, double-choc chocolate cake, then yes it is." She grinned and forked a piece of cake into her mouth. "Mmm..."

"Where is it?" He opened the fridge and peered inside. "I can't see it."

"Here."

Steve turned to find her placing a second plate with a slice of cake on the table. "That's not a very big bit," he complained.

"I know, but she only sent a small section of the cake, not the whole thing. I'm saving some for dessert."

He took the chair in front of the cake. "Quick, let's eat it before Dale gets down and wants some. I'm not sharing this with him if we don't have a whole cake."

"Don't worry, Kat packed some chocolate chip cookies so Dale can have those with his coffee."

"What?" Steve's fork paused halfway to his mouth. "Cookies? Damn, I'm gonna get fat at this rate."

Doc laughed. "Probably. I can't cook so I usually pick up dinner at the café before I head home every night."

Steve groaned. "Oh yeah, I'm gonna get fatter than Santa."

"Well as long as you have his cheery disposition we'll get along just fine."

"Having you sit on my lap and tell me your most secret desire is guaranteed to keep me in a cheery mood."

"Is that coffee I smell?" Dale asked as he entered the room. "No, don't get up, I'll pour my own."

Steve scraped up the last piece of cake and shoved it in his mouth. "There's cookies too."

Doc stood and went to the counter. "Here, let me get that for you, Dale."

"I'm fine, Gordie, sit back down so we can talk."

"You think I'm right?" Steve asked.

"Yeah." Dale brought his mug and plate to the table. "It looks like he came in through the roof to me too."

"Are you sure?" Doc asked.

"No, but we will be after we've had our coffee and gone up to look inside that manhole." Dale took a bite of cookie and closed his eyes.

"You're going up there?"

"Yes. We need to make sure all the shingles are in place or you'll get snow and water in the cavity and be in all sorts of trouble," Steve said.

"There's a step ladder in the mudroom. You can use that to reach the ceiling." Doc got up and disappeared into the small outer room. She came back carrying a five-rung, steel ladder. "The flashlight is on the counter. If you two don't mind I think I'll get started on cleaning my room."

"I'll be up in a second," Steve called after her. "Is it possible he got into the clinic the same way?" he asked Dale when he was sure she was out of earshot.

"Definitely. We'll take a look at that tomorrow, it's too late now."

"Okay. I'll take the ladder up. Finish your coffee and cookies, there's no rush unless you've got somewhere to be."

Dale looked startled for a moment but quickly masked the look with his usual, bland sheriff face. "Nope. Nowhere to be."

Gordie sat beside Tatum at the counter of The Den Café. Steve had dropped her here an hour ago to hang out with Kat before they headed up to his place for the rest of the week. Tatum had already been here and Doc's sister was busy bustling back and forth from the kitchen making all the meals that people would be picking up for the Christmas feast tomorrow. She'd explained to Kat about not spending the meal together and surprisingly Kat hadn't argued.

They'd spent the morning at the clinic with the sheriff. He'd insisted she walk through each of the rooms looking for anything that Marcus may have left behind. Unfortunately there was nothing new to discover and it seemed pointless to fingerprint when there must be hundreds of different prints throughout the building, but Dale did anyway. There was nothing in the roof space to suggest Marcus had been there either. After they'd finished Steve had wanted to go back to her parents house and check the roof in daylight to be sure there were no broken shingles or clues that may lead to Marcus' whereabouts. Rather than go with him she'd opted to stay here.

Kat came through the swinging timber half-doors from the kitchen and placed two steaming bowls of soup in front of Gordie and Tatum. She walked down the counter and pulled two fresh bread rolls from a basket and brought them back to them.

"Eat. It'll warm you up and fill your bellies." Kat eyed Tatum's nonexistent waist. "Not that your belly needs any more filling."

Tatum laughed. "You're right, but I expect to be filled out more before this pregnancy is over."

"How are you feeling? No cramping or sickness?" Gordie asked as she spooned up a mouthful of soup.

"No. Although, if you don't mind, can I pick up a blood pressure kit from the clinic before you leave town? My feet are a little swollen, but I think that's normal. And the usual backache but again, that's the same as it's been the whole pregnancy." Tatum dipped her roll into the bowl and took a bit. "Mmm..." She spoke around the mouthful. "This is delicious. Can I get some to take home with me?"

"Sure, I'll make you up a Christmas feast pack for three." Kat grinned and headed back to the kitchen again.

"God, your sister can cook."

"I know. She got all the domestic skills in the family."

"You can't cook?"

"I won't poison anyone but I can't make heaven the way Kat can."

"Damn. That sucks."

"Not really. I just stop by here every night I'm in the mood for something delicious."

"I think I'm going to be doing that. I can cook, not as well as this but I do all right. It's just lately I can't find the energy to walk, never mind stand around and cook. I fall asleep at the drop of a hat."

"That's to be expected, you are carrying twins."

"Yes, but I can't believe how easily I tire. Take the other night at Steve's. I'd walked from my car and by the time I reached the driveway I was exhausted. I could have literally slid to the ground asleep if I'd let myself. As it was, I knew I couldn't go any farther. Lucky Dale and Steve found me when they did. That never would have happened before I got pregnant." Tatum rubbed her belly. "I'm starting to get tired now so I'll need to head home soon. I'll finish this yummy soup first though, not passing this up for sleep, that's for sure."

"We'll walk over and grab that kit before you go."

"Thanks."

They finished their soup without another word spoken. Gordie let Kat know where they were going and what they were doing.

"Don't you want to wait for Steve to come back?" her sister asked.

"I don't know how much longer he'll be and Tatum needs to get home soon so she can rest. It's just across the road, Kat, and Steve and Dale went over the place this morning so I know there's no one lurking around. Besides, we'll only be a couple of minutes at the most."

"Okay, but if you're not back in ten minutes I'm coming after you." Kat came around the counter to walk them to the door.

Gordie helped Tatum into her coat before pulling on her own. Kat handed them their gloves and hats.

"Watch the sidewalk. It's bound to be icy."

Taking each step with care, Gordie held onto Tatum's arm as they traversed the slippery footpath. There was no traffic on the road so they crossed over at a leisurely stroll to be sure they didn't trip. Gordie led them around the rear of the building.

"We have to go in the back way. The front door has two slide bolts on the inside that you can't open from the street." Gordie pulled her keys from her pocket as they walked up the back lane. "Careful, there are a couple of potholes beneath the snow near that fence."

"I'm watching. Believe me, after the first few times of finding myself flat on my ass I take every step with care. I was never clumsy before I got pregnant."

"I won't ask because it's none of my business but you have to know everyone in town is going to be curious about the father. You ought to think about what you're going to tell everyone before the questions start."

"By the time I see the rest of the pack I'll have an answer ready. For now though I'd rather stay quiet on the subject."

"Okay." They reached the back door and Gordie slid the key into the padlock and then the two deadlocks. "Let's get in out of the cold."

The clinic was dark and freezing, no warmer than outside but at least they were out of the wind. Gordie flicked the light switch and the gloom vanished. She pushed the door closed behind them and led Tatum through the building, giving her a brief rundown of what each room was used for.

"I'll give you the full tour on your first day but for now let me grab that kit." Gordie started back to the storeroom.

"Mind if I just sit here for a minute? I'm suddenly tired enough for my legs to shake," Tatum said.

"No, that's fine. If it's okay with you I might just give you a quick once-over before we head back to the café."

"Sure." Tatum covered a yawn with her hand. She smiled. "Sorry, really tired."

"Why don't you come into the exam room and lie down for a bit?"

"No way. I do that and I won't get up until I've had at least an hour's nap."

"I've got nowhere to be in a hurry."

"Thanks, but no. I want to get home and curl up in a nice, warm bed."

"Okay. I'll be back in a second."

Gordie left Tatum to rest while she went to the supply room. She was occupied scanning the shelves for the new kit she'd recently ordered in preparation for her nurse starting work when the hair on the back of her neck stood on end as though a cold wind had blown across her skin. She'd shut the back door hadn't she? Locked it? Footsteps echoed behind her and her stomach clenched. Leaning out the door of the storeroom she glimpsed a flash of black disappearing into the reception area where she'd left Tatum.

A shiver rattled her spine and her heart sped up. Gordie stepped into the hall as Tatum's cry of distress reverberated off the walls. Her feet moved before the thought formed and she ran the length of the corridor.

"No!"

Gordie could hear Tatum's struggles before she entered the waiting room. She skidded to a halt at the sight of a familiar-looking man in black. Every hackle rose and sweat popped out of every pore as she remained frozen in place while the two figures fought.

"Gordie, run!" Tatum's shout got Gordie moving again.

Her heart pounded against her ribs and her lungs refused to take more than small gulps of air. She would not let him win this time. There wasn't much in the way of weapons in the clinic but she could improvise. Gordie picked up the bundle of magazines on the corner table and threw them at the mass of wrestling bodies. It was enough to draw the masked attacker's attention away from Tatum.

With a growl he shoved Tatum aside and came at Gordie. Spinning on her heel she ran toward the room most likely to hold some kind of weapon. The morgue. Moments ago the hallway had seemed short, now it appeared to go on forever before she reached her destination. Trays of sterile surgical implements sat to one side of the large room and Gordie headed straight for them. Scooping up a handful of plastic-covered steel, she darted around the end of an exam table, putting the slab of cold metal between her and Marcus.

She had no doubt who hid behind the ski mask. Gordie would never forget those eyes. He'd been wearing the same clothes two days ago so it was obvious who had returned. Tatum hadn't made a sound after he'd flung her against the wall and the doctor in Gordie wanted to go check to see if the other woman was all right but she couldn't afford to let her guard down or neither of them would be okay.

"You can't hide from me, non-blood bitch." His shout echoed down the hall.

Gordie crouched down behind the table and peered around the pedestal base to watch the doorway. If he kept going she could sneak out of the room and back to Tatum. His heavy footfalls grew closer.

"I'll kill you when I get my hands on you." He was moving from room to room, searching for her.

Fear sliced into her. He outweighed her by at least one hundred pounds, probably more, but Gordie knew the soft spots, knew where to strike to inflict the most damage if she had to.

"You can't hide and that bitch out front isn't going to save your sorry ass from what I've got planned."

His words chilled her blood, the venom in them unmistakable. She also couldn't miss the slight tinge of madness ringing in his voice. Gordie knew he'd checked most of the other rooms, knew it was only a matter of time before he reached this one and she needed a plan. Two plans. One for when he found her and one for if he passed on by.

"You're going to pay for all the trouble you've caused."

Trouble? What trouble? Gordie had no idea what he was talking about. She'd never had much to do with Marcus. He'd always considered her beneath him because she was human and then after Anthony had died he'd never even glanced her way. He hadn't even come to her for medical treatment once since she'd taken over the clinic from her stepfather.

"You think you're so smart hooking up with that McKenna bastard." He was in the next room, moving closer with every breath.

She fingered the plastic packets in her hands, glanced down quickly to see exactly what she had. Three scalpels, two sets of forceps and two pairs of scissors. What would she do with the forceps? A sound in the doorway drew her gaze. Black boots and jeans up to the knee were visible. She wasn't game to move for a better look. Gordie watched those boots intently. The second he came toward her or left she'd be ready.

He turned and went back into the hall. Air rushed from her chest, hissed through her teeth as relief filled her. Gordie carefully removed the plastic from the instruments and counted to one hundred before standing and tiptoeing toward the door. She couldn't hear anything and that worried her more than having him in the doorway in front of her would have. Soundlessly, she made her way across the room.

Her skin prickled and instinct made her jump back seconds before he charged into the room. He reached for her throat, his hands wrapping around her neck and hooking in her jacket as she tried to spin away. The zipper on her coat dug into her skin and she gagged as her airway was crushed. Gordie brought her hand up, scissors extended and drove them into the nearest body part. Cloth tore and skin broke as she pushed with all her strength. Marcus howled in pain and his grip loosened, allowing her to twist free of his hold.

"Bitch!" He'd removed his mask, his gaunt face skeletal in appearance and a mere impression of his former self.

Marcus lunged for her, the scissors protruding from between the fourth and fifth ribs near the center of his chest. His fingers caught her sleeve and he wrenched her back against him. The steal handles of the scissors dug into her shoulder and she applied pressure to drive them deeper. A curse filled her ears and he shoved her forward, sent her tumbling to the floor. Pain exploded in her back as she went down and she rolled away just before he kicked out a second time.

"Not so fucking tough now are you?" He lashed out with his foot again, grazing her hip with the toes.

Gordie grabbed at his pants, tangled her fingers in the fabric and pulled. He teetered above her so she gave the jeans another yank and sent him crashing to the ground beside her. She clambered for purchase but she slid on the slippery tile beneath her hands and feet. Steal glinted next to her and she realized she'd dropped her makeshift weapons in their struggle. Reaching out, she wrapped her fingers around the nearest one.

"Fucking bitch!" Marcus crawled after her.

With desperation she lashed out, but he dodged to the side and the blade of a scalpel glanced along his cheek, barely leaving a scratch. He kept coming, managed to pin her beneath him, his body crushing hers. She kicked and punched, bucked and thrashed in an attempt to dislodge him. Marcus tangled his fingers in her hair and used his grip to slam her head into the ground repeatedly. Stars burst before her eyes and Gordie's arms flailed about without purpose.

He was going to kill her. There was no way she could throw him off, he was too heavy. Tears burned her eyes and throat as he once again wrapped his hands around her neck and began to squeeze. The back of her head pounded but the pain had begun to go numb. Her arms and legs wouldn't work properly, their weight too much to move. Her vision blurred, blackness creeping in around the edges and she thought she heard someone call her name.

Steve.

"He's too late." Marcus laughed above her, his face a grotesque, distorted image. "You're dead, bitch, and he's next."

"No." The hoarse cry hurt her throat but she couldn't let him get Steve. With the last of her energy Gordie lifted her arm, the scalpel still in her hand, and slashed out at his face. At first she thought she'd missed. Marcus stopped squeezing and his mouth fell open. Everything happened in slow motion. For seconds neither of them breathed and then blood began to bead in a long line down the side of his neck. The beading quickly turned to a flow.

The flow increased rapidly until blood pumped from the slice in gushing waves. She'd hit his carotid artery. Marcus let go of her throat and grabbed his neck but he couldn't stop the surge. He fell to the side and Gordie used her hands and feet to scramble backward. She slipped and slid in the pool of blood forming on the floor, the slick warmth made her move quicker in a bid to get away. But it was all around her, over her. His hands fell from his body as he collapsed with the gurgle of his final breath in his throat.

Gordie stared at Marcus' lifeless body, the sea of red spreading out around him and began to tremble. Tears streamed down her cheeks as she curled into a ball and brought her hands up to cover her face. Sobs racked her chest, the heaving gasps compressing her ribs and stomach with pain. Wetness soaked into her clothes and she uncovered her eyes to see nothing but the blood she'd spilled surrounding her.

A cry of anguish echoed in the room, the sound vibrating in her ears as her scream of agony went on and on.

S teve walked into the café with Dale. They'd spent the morning combing the clinic and then the roof cavity at Doc's place but other than a few broken shingles they hadn't found any more clues.

He headed for the counter, searching the room for Doc as he went, but he couldn't see her anywhere. Kat was serving a customer so he slid onto a stool and waited for her to finish.

"Do you want to check the roof at the clinic again before you head home?" Dale asked.

"No. We'll do that before she opens up again though. I want it checked before she goes back there."

Kat put a couple of mugs down and filled them with coffee. "Can I get you something to eat?"

"No thanks, coffee's fine. Where's Doc?" he asked.

"She and Tatum walked over to the clinic to get something for Tatum."

Steve jumped from his seat. "Alone? You let them go alone?" He headed for the door at a run, dodging tables and chairs on the way.

"What's wrong? She said you'd checked it this morning. That it was safe," Kat protested behind him.

"We did," he yelled as he yanked the door open. "But I don't want her going there alone."

Dale was right behind him when he hit the sidewalk. They ran across the empty street and skidded to a stop at the front door. Steve tried the handle and finding it locked, began thumping on the door and calling out to Doc.

"Wait." Dale grabbed Steve's arm. "Listen."

He turned his head and held his breath. The murmured cry for help was barely audible through the thick timber panel. "That doesn't sound like Doc."

Dale put his ear to the door but he didn't need to, the next cry came through loud and clear. "What the fuck? Tatum!" Dale banged on the door.

Steve started down the sidewalk at a flat-out run as his stomach cramped with the fear that threatened to take him to his knees. *Where the hell was Gordie?*

"Where are you going?" Dale yelled behind him.

"Around the back." He breathed hard but kept running, Dale's footsteps pounding behind him. "We'll never break down the front door but there's a window above the back one."

Steve would smash through the timber wall if he had to. He ran past the clothing store, the small bookshop and slid sideways in the snow as he rounded the corner of the building. The alley was unplowed and he could see footprints where Doc and Tatum had walked. As he got closer to the back of the clinic he was hit by déjà vu. The back door stood ajar and his blood ran cold.

"Let me go in first." Dale had caught up to him and pulled his gun from its holster.

"Fine, but I'm right behind you."

They entered the building at a slower pace. Dale took the lead but Steve stayed right on his heels. No sounds came from the interior and he thought maybe they'd imagined the cry from Tatum. The sight that met them in the morgue almost crippled him. Doc lay curled on her side, covered in blood. A huge pool of the stuff lay between her and Marcus. Neither of them appeared to be breathing.

Steve dropped to the floor next to Doc and felt for a pulse. The hard, fast beat he found in her neck produced a gust of breath from his lungs. He tried to find her injuries but the blood was everywhere, he couldn't tell where any of it was coming from. "I can't find where she's bleeding."

Dale checked Marcus. "I'm not sure it's her blood. He's dead, looks like she slashed his throat."

"Jesus. What the fuck happened?" He tapped Doc's cheek. "Doc? Come on, Gordie, talk to me."

"I'll be back. I need to find Tatum." Dale left the room with his gun drawn.

"Come on, Gordie, don't do this to me. Not again." He turned to the doorway as people started pouring into the room. "Stay back," he yelled.

"Dad's here," Kat said as Doctor Monroe pushed past the cluster of bodies.

"Hey, Steve." The older man kneeled beside him. "What you got?"

"Don't know. She was out when we found her."

Doctor Monroe ignored the lifeless body not six feet away and went to work on his daughter. "Jackie, get over here and help me with our girl."

"I'll do it. What do you want?" Steve asked.

"Let's get her checked over for broken bones first then we'll get her up on one of those tables."

"Can we move her into another room?" Jackie asked as she crouched beside them.

"Yes, love, that might be a better idea." Doctor Monroe turned to yell over his shoulder. "Kat, go get one of the rooms ready."

"Okay, Dad."

"And the rest of you can get out," the older man said with an authoritative voice Steve remembered from his youth.

"Doctor Monroe?" Dale came in carrying an semi-conscious Tatum.

"Jesus, Mary and Joseph. What went on here?" He turned to his wife, his hands never leaving Gordie. "Jackie, go with Dale and see about that one for me. I'll bring Gordana in a minute."

The older man spent what felt like hours checking Doc over before speaking again.

"Young man, I'm gonna ask you to carry Gordie for me. These old bones aren't as strong as they used to be."

"Yes sir."

Steve waited for Doc's father to get up before pulling her limp body into his arms. He stepped across the wet floor with care and ignored the way his boots stuck to the tiles as he walked down the hall behind Doctor Monroe. They passed the first room where Dale and Jackie were talking to a now-awake Tatum and entered the next one. Kat waited for them, closing the door behind him as he cleared the threshold.

"Get her out of those clothes so I can clean her up," Doctor Monroe ordered as he went to the sink in the corner and scrubbed his hands.

Steve laid Doc on the table and helped Kat remove her bloody clothes. They threw them in the trash. Even if they were salvageable he was sure she wouldn't want them. He was relieved to find no visible wounds other than some bruising and the angry red ringing her neck. The thought of what those red marks meant boiled his blood and if Marcus wasn't already lying dead in the other room Steve would be out committing murder right now.

"Steve?" Doc's voice was a raw, gravelly whisper that hurt his ears, he could only imagine how it felt to her.

He finished tucking the blanket around her and leaned closer. "I'm here, Doc."

"Tatum?"

"She's in the next room. Your mother is looking after her."

"Mom's here?"

"Me too, sweet girl." Doctor Monroe stepped up beside the bed.

"Daddy?"

"Hey, sweetie, wanna tell me what hurts?"

"Everything." A slight smile curled her lips. "Nothing's broken. Took a kick in the back and hip, he bashed my head into the floor and tried to choke me." Her hand came up and brushed against her throat.

"I see that. You don't look so bad, considering." Doctor Monroe took the wet cloth Kat handed him. "We're just gonna clean you up a bit, you can take a shower back at the house later."

"What happened to Marcus?" she asked.

"He's dead." Doctor Monroe wiped the cloth over her face, removing the dried blood.

The color drained from Doc's face. "Dead?" She licked her lips. "I'm gonna be sick."

Steve grabbed the waste basket and shoved it under her as she leaned over the side of the bed and emptied out her stomach. Her father held her hair back and Kat handed Steve a clean cloth when Doc had finished vomiting.

"I want to go home." She slumped back against the pillow.

"Okay, I'll get your mother to take you while I check on our other patient."

"No."

"No?"

"I don't want to go back to the house." She turned away and curled into a ball.

Steve took pity on the older man. "Can I talk to you outside, sir? Kat, keep an eye on Doc."

They stepped into the hall as Mrs. Monroe came out of the other room, Dale and Tatum behind her.

"Hey, you okay?" Steve asked.

"Yeah, a little embarrassed at passing out and not helping Doc, but otherwise I'm good." Tatum leaned into Dale.

"I'll talk to you later, Steve. I'm taking Tatum home to rest. Brogan and Quinn arrived a little while ago. They're handling the Marcus issue with the help of my deputies."

"Need me to do anything?"

"No. Just take care of Doc."

Steve watched as Dale and Tatum headed for the back door.

"Want to tell us what's going on, son?" Doctor Monroe asked.

"I'll keep it short for now but the bare bones are this. Marcus has led a terror campaign against Doc, Gordie, for a few months. As usual, she's weathered it all on her own, but two days ago he stepped it up and the results are…" Steve tried to think of the best words to describe his and Doc's new relationship.

"You and my daughter are mated." Mrs. Monroe saved him the trouble.

He felt his cheeks heat. "Yes."

Doctor Monroe slapped him on the back. "About time you pulled your head out of your ass, boy."

"With all due respect, dear, I think it's Gordana who's had her head up her ass," Mrs. Monroe said.

Steve smiled. He'd forgotten how much he liked the Monroes. Being the town's only doctor and nurse, they'd been a huge part of his growing-up years. And now they'd be his in-laws.

"If it's okay with the two of you, I'd like to take Doc home with me tonight. I know we'll probably be stuck up the mountain for a few days with the storm due in tomorrow but I think she's going to need the time to recuperate."

"Son, I think her physical recovery will be far easier than the mental one. She took a life today. That won't sit well with her no matter how deserving the bastard was." Doctor Monroe held out his hand. "And I guess I should say welcome to the family."

Steve shook the other man's hand. "Thank you, sir."

"None of that *sir* business now, we're family after all." He turned to Mrs. Monroe. "Let's go get that girl of ours ready to go home."

He gave them a few minutes with their daughter. They hadn't seen each other in months and coming home to this couldn't be easy to deal with. The commotion at the other end of the hall drew his attention and he wandered down to see what was going on. Brogan and Quinn were making sure the deputies did their job, but Steve didn't think it really mattered. Marcus was dead and couldn't be punished for any of his crimes.

"Hey. How's Doc?" Brogan asked when he saw Steve standing in the doorway.

"Okay as she can be. She came out with minor physical damage, but I'm not sure about the emotional yet." Steve ran a hand over his head, dragged his fingers through his hair.

"You heading home?" Quinn asked.

"Yeah, Doctor and Mrs. Monroe are with her now. I'll let them have a few minutes and then we'll head out."

"Gordie's going with you? She isn't going home with the Monroes?" Brogan asked.

"She doesn't want to go home with them. Doctor Monroe seems to understand it better than I do though. I thought for sure she'd want to be with them."

"She needs her mate," Quinn said.

"I guess, but she's fought against it for so long I can't see that it would be this easy."

"It's not going to be easy, Steve." Kat came up beside him. "She's shutting down. She won't talk to any of us. Mom and Dad are just getting her dressed, where's your truck?"

"Shit. Down the street. I'll go get it, bring it around the back."

"Okay. I'll let Gordie know that's what you're doing." Kat walked back down the hall.

"I'll talk to you guys later." Steve waved as he headed out the back door.

Gordie allowed her mother and father to fuss over her. It must have been a shock for them to arrive home and find the mess she'd found herself in. They'd avoided the subject and while she was glad, she knew it meant rehashing the event later but right now she just wanted to forget everything that had happened in the last few days. The door opened and Steve came in. Well, maybe not everything.

"Ready to go home?" he asked.

Home. Such a simple word. One she thought she understood the meaning of until she'd taken that final step with Steve. Home wasn't a house to her anymore. Home was Steve.

"Yes. Take me home." She held her arms out and he stepped into her, lifting her off her feet for a full-body hug. Gordie buried her face in the warmth of his neck and bit her lip to stifle the tears threatening to fall. She refused to fall apart yet.

"We'll see you all in a few days," Steve said as he carried her from the room.

Gordie didn't look up or say goodbye to her parents or sister and she certainly didn't raise her head as Steve walked through the clinic. She didn't want to chance seeing anything again today. There'd be plenty of time in the coming weeks to deal with the clinic and the carnage Marcus had caused.

Steve placed her in the front seat and buckled her in. It wasn't the first time but she sure hoped it would be the last. She stared out the side window the whole time he drove up the mountain. He kept reaching over and patting her thigh but he needed two hands on the wheel for most of the treacherous drive.

They pulled into his driveway but he didn't go into the garage. The plow on the front had pushed a drift of snow up to the garage door. He hopped out and walked around to her side. She fell against him when he opened the door and unbuckled her seatbelt.

"Come on, let's get you inside and I'll come back out and deal with the truck in a minute." He picked her up in his arms and walked through the snow to the front door.

How he managed to get the door unlocked and open and both of them inside without dropping her she didn't know. She heard the door close behind them and sighed in relief. The warmth of the house surrounded her and she shuddered.

"Cold? Want me to turn the heat up?" He strode down the hall to his room.

"No, it's fine."

"I'll run a bath. The warm water will be good for your sore muscles."

Steve set her on the closed toilet and turned on the bath taps. The tub was huge, made for two and the nozzles around the sides tempted her beyond reason.

"Can I turn the Jacuzzi on?"

"Definitely."

He helped her undress and into the bath. The water was warm and she leaned back and let the heat seep into her skin and soothe her aches.

"I'll be back in five minutes. Don't let the water get above here." He pointed to the top of the jets.

"Okay."

Steve left and for the first time since she'd come to in the exam room she was completely alone. Her mind swirled with everything that had happened. She tried to retrace her steps, tried to work out if there was some other way things could have turned out. Gordie was relieved that Tatum and the babies were okay. There was no way she could have coped with that on her conscience.

She reached over to turn off the taps when the water rose above the silver jets. Lying back, she closed her eyes and willed herself to think of anything but today. Gordie hoped Steve returned soon or she'd fall to pieces. Startled by a noise behind her she sat up, her eyes opening wide.

"Sorry, should have made more noise coming through the bedroom. Didn't mean to frighten you." He stood next to the tub. Naked.

Gordie held up her hand. "Please." She didn't know what she was asking for but he seemed to understand what she needed.

He climbed in behind her and cradled her against his chest. When he pressed the button near his head the jets pulsed to life, the water and bubbles surging through them to pummel her from all sides. It was a gentle massage, rolling over aching muscles and tender bruises. Steve washed her with a soft, soapy cloth. Gentle strokes over sensitive skin.

When she was clean they lay back and enjoyed the spa bath. They stayed there until the water began to cool. The whole time he just held her close and drew small circles on her stomach with his fingertips. Suddenly the light touches weren't enough, she needed to feel him inside her, around her.

"Make love to me."

"Are you sure?" He stilled his movements. "You've been through a lot."

"I want to forget. Help me forget, Steve."

Steve stood, taking her with him. Water dripped from their bodies as he stepped out onto the mat. He didn't bother with towels, just strode out of the bathroom and over to the bed. Her back hit the soft quilt and Steve came down on top of her. She pulled his mouth to hers and thrust her tongue between his lips. Gordie tried to rush. Tried to dive deep into the mindless bliss being with him offered but he wouldn't let her.

He slowed her movements. Controlled her tongue with his and dragged her back to a leisurely pace. His hands stroked her body, soft, sweeping actions that nudged her closer and closer to the height of ecstasy. She tangled her fingers in the hair at his nape, ran her nails over his scalp and let him have his way.

They strolled up to the peak and when she fell from the edge he held her close and let her land in his waiting arms. He wedged his knee between hers and parted her legs. With a slow, easy glide, he slid inside her wet heat until he was buried deep. The ride was a gentle, calm journey back to the top. As they reached the summit he quickened the tempo, plunged harder, withdrew faster. Gordie gripped his shoulders, her fingers digging in to the tense muscles beneath his sweat-slick skin.

His mouth claimed hers in a kiss that mimicked the movements of their hips. Gordie lifted her legs and wrapped them around his waist, the change in angle allowing for deep penetration, more stimulation, and she was soon gasping for breath and rolling with the waves of her orgasm. Steve drove his cock to the hilt and came with her name on his lips.

They collapsed, exhausted, sweaty and well satisfied. He turned on his side, taking her with him, his softening length slipping from her body to rest between them. She waited to catch her breath, waited for the numbness to fade and real life to intrude once more but the day had taken a toll and she drifted to sleep before she could think about it anymore.

8

Gordie rolled over and flinched in pain. In seconds, memories from the day before came rushing back to drown her in fear, desperation, anger and guilt. Emotions bombarded her, clouding her brain and twisting her insides. Her stomach pitched and she jumped from the bed to race for the bathroom. She made it just in time to dry heave into the toilet bowl. Her hollow belly contracted again and again. Steve came in behind her.

"Go away." She didn't want him to see her like this, couldn't bear for him to watch her when she lost control. It was going to happen. She could feel herself unraveling.

"No."

A warm cloth wiped across the back of her neck, over her forehead and she shivered at the contact. Her whole body trembled and her tummy continued to convulse in a vain attempt to expel something that wasn't there. She couldn't remember the last meal she'd eaten. All she knew for sure was she'd eat again and Marcus wouldn't.

"Don't, Gordie."

"Don't what?" She struggled to her feet, stood on shaky legs and tried to push past him.

"Blame yourself for Marcus' death." He blocked the doorway with his body.

"Don't blame myself?" She laughed, the sound harsh and grating to her ears. "How do I do that when I'm the one who killed him?"

"He was on a path of self-destruction. It could have been any one of us he came after with murder on his mind."

"But it wasn't." Her voice grew louder. "It was me!"

"Gordie." He reached for her but she brushed his hand aside.

"Don't you see?" she screamed. "This isn't me! It isn't who I am or what I stand for. I'm trained to save lives, not take them."

Gut-wrenching sobs broke free. She bent double, the pain ripping her in two. Her body shook violently as what she'd done tore at her very soul. Her knees gave out and she tumbled to the floor, arms wrapped around her middle in a desperate attempt to hold it together. Why now? Why did she have to give in to the grief, *the guilt*, now? She didn't want to lose control and fall apart in front of the one person she couldn't hide anything from.

Steve slipped to the floor beside her and scooped her back against his chest. Turning her, he cradled her in his warm embrace and rocked her like a child. The gentle care, the understanding and love that he gave her no matter how much she fought it enveloped Gordie and she cried harder for all that she'd lost. They'd lost.

"I can't stay," she sobbed.

He stilled beneath her. "What do you mean?"

"I can't live here. Can't live through the whispers again." She shook her head. "I can't."

"What whispers?"

"The pack. They'll talk behind my back like last time, whisper behind their hands whenever I'm near." She hiccupped as she tried to stifle another sob. "I couldn't live with it when Anthony died. Barely coped when I came back. Oh God."

"Stop." Steve tipped her face up and looked into her eyes. "No one will whisper behind your back and if they do, stiff shit. Who cares what they think or say? Your friends, your family, *me*, none of us will ever judge you for what happened yesterday. And you can bet every one of those men is wishing he'd been there to protect you. To save you from going through what you did. Especially me."

He closed his eyes, rested his forehead on hers and took a deep breath. "Gordie, what you did yesterday would affect the toughest of men and I know beyond a doubt that if there had been any other way to stop Marcus you would have. Killing him was the last resort. The only choice when push came to shove and it'll haunt me to my dying day that I wasn't there to do it for you."

His eyelids lifted. Moisture pooled in his eyes and sadness so great she hurt for him swam in the dark depths of his gaze. "Steve—"

"No." He placed a finger over her lips. "Don't say anything. Come back to bed and let me hold you for a while. I need to know you're safe. That you're here."

Gordie couldn't hold out against his obvious need. He'd given so much of himself and not just in the last few days. He'd been there in the background for years and she doubted she could find the strength to get through this without him. When they were together she was stronger, it seemed logical he would feel the same. They'd only just begun to explore a future and the idea of one without Steve made her heart ache—her stomach cramp.

"Take me back to bed."

She wasn't sure how she'd cope with the events of yesterday but for now she'd put that aside and be what he needed. What they needed.

***

Steve held Doc while she slept. They'd been lying in the dark for hours but the first rays of sun were lighting up the sky now. The predicted storm had either missed them or not arrived yet. He glanced to the side, the digital readout on his clock showed six twenty-four. Too early to get up, too late to try for any more sleep. He sighed. Not that he'd been able to rest after she'd broken down.

Fear that she'd leave the mountains consumed him. Gnawed at his gut. He couldn't live without her. Not now that they'd connected.

But he didn't see himself living anywhere but here. Whispering Springs was his home, building this house had been his dream, a dream he wanted to share with Gordie. His arms tightened around her and she snuggled closer. Should he take her acceptance of him in her most unguarded moment as a sign?

He stared through the skylight seeing nothing but dark rolling clouds as the daylight did its best to break through. Snow began to fall, light flurries that slid down the curved sheet of glass. Steve had designed the skylight himself, had the panel of toughened glass specially made. The majority of the house around them was hand-crafted. From the timber beams supporting the roof and floors, to the furniture filling the rooms, he'd taken his dreams and turned them into reality.

"Why doesn't the snow stick to the glass?"

Steve hadn't realized Doc was awake. "The curved shape plus the house's heat rises to warm the panel from underneath. Small falls like this don't stick but if we get a good storm, more than a foot of snow on the ground, it'll cover the glass."

"You're not worried it will break?"

"No. That piece is specially designed, double glazed, you'd have to break it with a jackhammer."

"What else did you design?"

Her interest thrilled him but he didn't just want to tell her, he wanted to show. "Let's get dressed. We'll have something to eat and I'll give you the grand tour."

"Are you cooking?"

A niggle of fear pecked at his gut. Her voice was flat, devoid of any emotion and he wondered if it was an effect of the damage Marcus had done to her throat when he'd tried to choke the life out of her or if she'd clamped down on her feelings and shut him out again. "I'll cook."

He threw the covers back and rolled to the edge of the mattress. Sitting up, he scanned the floor for his pants before he remembered tossing the wet jeans in the wash last night. It suddenly dawned on him that Doc had no clothes. She'd come home in a hospital gown and the last thing on his mind had been to swing by her house to pick up the bag she'd packed. He hadn't washed in a week either, so the clothes she left the other day were still in the hamper.

"Damn." Steve stretched his back as he stood, glancing over his shoulder at Doc.

She'd pulled the quilt up under her armpits and leaned back on the headboard. "What's wrong?"

"I'm running out of clean clothes." He strode over to the dresser and rummaged around in the drawers. "I've got exactly three t-shirts, two pairs of jeans and one pair of sweatpants."

"I'll take a shirt and the sweatpants. I can put a load of washing on while you cook breakfast." She slipped from under the covers and got out of bed. With no regard for her nakedness, Doc walked toward him.

Steve groaned as he watched her breasts bounce with each step, his blood heated and his cock hardened. They'd made love twice during the night, the last time only a few hours ago and yet his body wanted more. He turned away, hoped "out of sight out of mind" worked. But it didn't stand a chance when her scent surrounded him and he could hear her pulling the shirt over her head, and picturing those gorgeous breasts being covered up did nothing to deflate his erection. He yanked on jeans and carefully pulled up the zipper.

"I take it you don't have any clean underwear either?" Doc pressed her lips to his back and slid her arms around his waist, her hands cool against his skin. "It's going to be awfully distracting knowing you've got nothing on under these things." She patted his cock through the thick denim.

"If you expect to eat any time soon you need to stop." Steve clenched his jaw and spoke through gritted teeth.

Gordie laughed and let go. "I need to use the bathroom. I'll meet you in the kitchen."

He turned his head, watched her walk away in his t-shirt, the sweatpants in her hand, and thought about following her. It wasn't as if they had to be anywhere. His stomach chose that moment to growl and remind him he hadn't eaten since yesterday morning. With a mental and physical shake, he cleared his mind of all sexy thoughts and finished getting dressed.

Steve detoured past the living room for a look at the deck. The snow continued to fall, growing heavier with each flake. Drifts collected on the north end and the wind picked up more snow and sent it flying in that direction as he watched. It looked as though the storm had arrived. A strong gust rattled the patio doors and it grew darker with every second.

He turned back to the room and searched for the remote so he could switch on the TV. Reception would be a problem soon but for now he should still be able to access the weather channel. What he saw didn't please him and he dropped the remote on the couch as he headed for the garage. He pulled out his snow gear and the tool he'd need to lower the snow guards fitted to the outside of each window. He stuck his head into the house and yelled for Gordie.

She came toward him at a run. Her feet were shoved into a pair of his work socks and she slid on the polished floor. "What? What's wrong?"

"Don't panic. I just wanted to let you know I'm heading outside to lower the window shutters. The storm is picking up and I don't want to risk a flying branch smashing any of them."

"Need help?"

"No, go on into the kitchen and put some coffee on. I'll only be a few minutes." He kissed her cheek. "I'll shut this door so the cold doesn't blow through when I open the roller door."

He closed the door and went to pull on his gear. With the wrench in his hand, he headed out into the growing storm. There had been no need to batten down the hatches before now so the shutters were still locked in their boxes. The guards were similar to a garage door but for windows, and once they were in place they'd keep out the cold as well as protect the glass.

It didn't take long and with all the boxes unlocked, he hurried back to the garage and the control pad that would lower all the shut-ters. Steve stripped out of his snowsuit and hung it up to dry. He double-checked the control panel before heading back inside the house.

Gordie had done more than make coffee. The scent of fried bacon and eggs greeted him when he opened the door between the garage and house. His mouth watered and he picked up the pace, his stomach rumbling with hunger. She was in front of the stove. His shirt covered her almost to her knees and the sweatpants had been rolled up so many times over her socked feet that she had to stand with her legs apart.

She shouldn't get him hot dressed like that. There was nothing sexy about her clothes or the way they hung off her body but Steve's cock had other ideas. His erection pressed against his fly, the cold metal zipper doing nothing to restrain its growth. With a moan he walked up behind her and wrapped her in his arms. He nibbled on her neck, licked at the red marks still visible on her skin and listened to the little whimpers of pleasure she made.

He hated knowing she'd been hurt. Hated being unable to take the pain away. But having her go soft in his arms went a long way to soothing his raw nerves. Steve rocked his hips, ground his throbbing cock against her lower back. She was a full head shorter than him and in this position he'd have to bend his knees to drive his length inside her. The idea made his blood surge, his pelvis buck and his balls ache. He'd like to take her in the kitchen, and every other room in the house, but first they needed to eat.

Steve groaned as he let her go and stepped back. He was gratified to hear a moan of need slip from her mouth. "Hold that thought, we'll get back to it." He patted her on the butt and headed for the coffee.

The spatula whacked him on the ass and he spilled coffee all over the counter as he yelped and spun around to face her. She held the utensil up, pointed at his chest.

"That was mean. You're a tease."

"A tease? I don't think so." He stepped toward her.

"Oh no you don't." She wagged the greasy spatula in his face. "The only thing you're getting now is breakfast."

He thought he heard her mumble "two can play that game" but he wasn't sure and when she picked up the frying pan he chose not to question her just in case she hit him on the head with it, eggs and all. "I'll set the table."

Making a hasty retreat, Steve grabbed plates and cutlery and took them to the table. He went back for coffee and found Gordie hefting a large platter of bacon, toast and eggs. "Here. Give me that. You grab the coffee."

Steve took the tray and waited for her to pick up their mugs. She led the way and his gaze dropped to her butt wiggling beneath the baggy layer of clothes.

"Stop looking at my ass."

Startled, he barely missed tripping over his own feet. "I wasn't—"

"Yeah, you were. I saw you."

He brought his gaze up to meet hers. "You did?"

She grinned. "Yep. Now put the plate down and let's eat. I'm starving."

Steve kept his hands off her while they ate. Although how he did when she made eating breakfast more erotic than a striptease was beyond him. He managed only the occasional touch as they cleaned up which was a miracle considering she kept offering him a view of that perfect heart-shaped butt each time she bent to put a plate in the dishwasher. He wasn't at all sure he'd be as successful during the tour of the house. The idea of christening every room with Doc zapped his blood as though he'd shoved his finger in an electric socket.

***

Gordie listened to Steve, the pride clearly evident in his voice when he talked about the specially designed aspects of his house. They'd started with the upstairs area and she had to admit he'd planned the layout well. The living areas were separate from the bedrooms with no common walls to help cut down on noise transfer. She'd always known he was talented with timber but as she admired the handmade furniture and built-in cupboards in each room, she had to admit he was a genius.

She held the handrail on the stairs as they headed to the lower level. The timber felt smooth as silk under her fingers. Each rung beneath the rail was carved with intricate patterns that required closer inspection. Gordie bent to study them more carefully. When the details started to take shape before her eyes they surprised a delighted laugh out of her.

"What?" He stopped a few steps below her.

"They're coyotes frolicking in the forest. But they're so tiny you have to get right up to them to see." She glanced up at him. "I want you to make something for the clinic."

He smiled. "Sure. What did you have in mind?"

"I don't know. I don't care." She trailed her fingertips over the tail of a coyote. "I just want something this beautiful there."

Steve laughed and leaned over to brush her mouth with his. To her disappointment, he pulled away before the kiss could lead anywhere.

"Come on, I want to know what you think about my plans for down here. It's a work in progress." He held her hand and walked through the open area. "This will have a pool table and the bar will be over there. I'm waiting on a special piece of timber for the top of that half wall."

Gordie could imagine the large space lined with comfy chairs and couches while the pool table took up center stage. "You'll need some plush seating around the edges. And the barstool seats should match the couches."

"Exactly." He pulled her over to a doorway on the wall next to the bar. "This will be a movie room. I've got one of those big screens in mind for that far wall and rows of seats back here. I figure this room will get a workout on days like today when the kids are snowed in and driving us nuts."

"Kids?"

"Sure. Don't you want any?"

"But I'm not—"

"Don't say it. Forget about leaving, forget yesterday. Think only of tomorrow and it's wide open. You're free to go after your heart's desire." He cupped her face, his thumbs stroking her cheeks. "What does your heart want, Gordie?"

Gordie's nose tingled with the tears she refused to shed. She could see a future with him. See their children running through the house, playing in the forest out back. His gaze searched hers and she couldn't hide what was in her heart from that all-seeing gaze of his.

"You want it, I know you do. It's yours for the taking, Gordie. All you have to do is stay."

"I can't." The first tear slipped from her lashes. "I couldn't handle the stares and whispers after Anthony died and I didn't kill him."

He rubbed his thumb over the moisture on her face. "I know it hurt before, but Gordie, you were grieving, you'd lost your husband, your baby, everything hurt. It wasn't the looks or the words that sent you running. It was your broken heart."

On some level she knew he was right, knew removing herself from her home had been the only way to cope with the loss she'd suffered. She'd distracted herself as best she could, immersed herself in her studies, had no life other than classes and books and then her internship. It took years to find the strength to come home but from the first day she arrived back in Whispering Springs she knew it had been the right time to return. The mountains were her home, had always been home and her coming back had never really been in question. How much of that had to do with this man?

Gordie wrapped her arms around his waist and buried her face in his chest. She cried silently, her tears soaking the front of his shirt, the salty taste coating her lips and tongue. He held her without speaking, let her take the time she needed and right there she knew she'd never be able to leave him and stay whole. No matter where she went or what she did he'd keep a piece of her with him and neither of them would ever find true happiness.

The crying jag slowed and she continued to lean against him, absorbing his warmth and strength. Gordie had no idea what would happen once word got out about Marcus, didn't want to speculate about the pack's reaction. Many were still loyal to the Connellys, and even with the events over the past year, they had allies. Whether they'd cause trouble was anyone's guess. She just hoped that now the last Connelly was gone, the pack could prosper.

She tilted her head back to look at Steve through tear-drenched eyes. "I'm worried about those sympathetic to Marcus."

He brushed the hair off her forehead. "I doubt any of them will be a problem. Most are old men and caught in a time long gone. Without a reminder they'll soon forget."

"God, I hope so."

"Even if they don't, Brogan isn't about to let the pack suffer and I'm certainly not going to let anyone hurt you if I can help it. I can't stop the talk but I can help you hold your head high and live here in peace."

"I'm not sure I'll ever find peace."

"You will. I'll make sure of it." He bent down and brushed her lips with his. "That's a promise."

Steve deepened the kiss. His tongue licked across her mouth and pushed inside. He tasted of bacon and coffee, and Gordie moaned as his tongue stroked over hers. She slipped her hands under the hem of his shirt and palmed his warm flesh. They pressed closer, their bodies touching, but the height difference proved awkward and restricted their contact. Frustrated, she pulled her mouth from his.

"More. I need more," she panted.

He picked her up, carried her out of the unfinished movie room and across to the stairs. With ease, he made the journey up to the main floor. His long strides ate up the distance to his bedroom quickly. In a second, he'd tossed her on the mattress and followed her down. She tore at his clothes, stretched his shirt to get him out of the barrier between her skin and his. Steve did the same to hers. With frenzied actions they stripped each other and were soon rolling naked on the bed.

Gordie ended up on top, straddling his thighs. Her fingers curled around his cock and she pumped her hand up and down in slow, loose strokes. His hips lifted, thrusting his rigid length into her grip.

"Harder." Steve wrapped his hand around hers and squeezed. "Tighter."

Guided by him, she dragged her hand over his silky shaft. Liquid beaded on the head and she leaned down to taste it. His scent filled her nostrils, his salty flavor coated her tongue and the need to take all of him gripped her. She opened her mouth, slipped her lips around the bulbous head and sucked. Gordie took him to the back of her throat and swirled her tongue along his shaft.

Steve groaned, the sound ended on a growl and his fingers twisted in her hair. He held her still and plunged his cock between her lips in short, sharp jabs. His hips jerked, his length pulsing against her tongue and more of his musky flavor filled her mouth. Gordie breathed through her nose and increased her suction. She gasped when he yanked her hair, pulled free of her mouth and tugged her up his body.

"Ride me."

She didn't need convincing. Gordie wanted to feel his length filling her core. Wanted his heat pounding into her until she saw stars. Steve held her waist and she used her hand to guide his cock to her opening. The crown rubbed over her clit, sending shards of fire into her pussy. Moisture covered her folds and he slid between them with ease, entering her in one smooth stroke.

Gordie tossed her head back and moaned. His flesh branded hers, the heat scorching a trail as it blazed out to invade every nerve, overpower ever sense. She surrendered, body and soul she gave herself up to the sensations of being joined with him. He jerked under her, his hips bucking off the bed to start the delicious friction that would drive them wild.

Time stood still as she rocked into him, slid her body over his in sensuous glides. She rose up, dropped down, rolled her pelvis and ground her clit against him. Each move delivered another blast of fire, turned her core into a molten mass desperate for release. He pulled her down and latched his mouth around her nipple. A jolt of electricity struck her, bowed her body and drove his cock deeper.

Gordie cried out, hung on the razor's edge of orgasm for what seemed like forever.

Steve sucked on her breast, drew on the peak before scraping the puckered bud with his teeth. He bit down. Pain and pleasure clashed and Gordie flew into the abyss. Her breath stalled in her lungs, her mind splintering in a million different directions as pure bliss saturated her senses. The world spun and she found herself beneath him, his body slamming into hers as muscles grasped greedily at his cock.

He rammed into her, pressed on her clit with every plunge and propelled her over a second peak. Her name burst from his lips as he came. His body bucked against hers, the spasms rolling from one to the other as their orgasms joined as effectively as their bodies. Wave after wave of heat and pleasure swamped her. She gasped for air and scratched at his back, desperate for solid ground.

Gordie slowly drifted back to earth. Caught between Steve and the mattress, she savored the feeling of satisfaction, contentment. He made her feel cherished, wanted, *loved*. And with all those came strength. Determination to have what should be hers. Take what should be theirs. She wouldn't walk away from him, couldn't if she were honest.

"I love you." The words surprised her. She hadn't even thought them and they'd tripped off her tongue as easily as her breath.

Waiting for a response just about killed her. He'd gone so still and she wasn't sure he'd taken a breath since she'd spoken. She pushed against his chest but he was as movable as a brick wall.

Gordie sighed and slumped into the bed. "Say something."

"I can't. I've waited forever to hear those words from you. Let me enjoy them a minute more."

She slapped his arm. "You idiot. It won't be the only time I say them."

"No, but this will always be the first time."

"At least one of us is getting a first today." Gordie couldn't believe the pouty voice she used. She sounded like a three-year-old sulking after being denied a cookie.

Steve lifted his head and stared at her. "You're pouting, Doc. It doesn't suit you. Besides, it's not necessary. I love you. I've always loved you. I will love you forever." He leaned down and kissed her.

They took it slow, lips meshing, tongues sliding, they rejoiced in the freedom of acceptance. When the kiss ended, Gordie opened her eyes and stared at the naked need in his gaze. A growl echoed from deep inside and she knew what she had to do. One final step.

"I want to run."

He reared back. "It's snowing."

"I know. But I need to run."

Rolling to his back, he took her with him. "You'll have to wait for the run but we could shift now. See what happens."

Gordie curled into his side. "Would you mind? It's been months since I changed and I feel her clawing to be free. I've never had that before."

"Want to do it now or later? I'm thinking a nap might be nice about now."

"It can wait. She's settled now that I've decided to run." Gordie yawned. "And a sleep would be good."

"Then sleep it is. We don't have to be anywhere and with the storm blowing like it is even if we did we wouldn't be going. Look up."

She glanced up at the skylight. The glass dome was completely covered in snow. "Oh. It's a bad one then."

"Yeah, I don't think we'll be driving out of here anytime soon, but if the snow stops falling we'll take a run in the forest."

Gordie yawned again. "Okay." She drifted to sleep in the comfort of his arms.

It took two days for the snow to stop falling long enough for Steve to be happy about going outside. He'd put her off as long as he could but he'd given in this afternoon. The sun was starting to dip toward the mountain and he wanted to be inside before it dropped behind the ridge and they lost daylight. They were in the garage. The house was locked up and he stripped out of his clothes and shifted quickly to escape the cold.

Doc stood near the door. She wrung her hands and he thought she'd changed her mind about running. She took a deep breath and grabbed the hem of the sweatshirt she wore. In a flash she had the top up and off, and was stepping out of her pants. It took her longer than him to shift, but not so long that he panicked. Her coat was a mix of grays and whites woven in a tapestry of thick strands.

Like her human form, her coyote was small, about half the size of his. He trotted over, nuzzled her face and nipped at her side. She danced away, danced back and he butted her with his head to get her moving. Her bark surprised him but he answered and took off out the garage door.

They ran. Sometimes he led, sometimes he followed. He chased her, wrestled her to the ground and let her go. The air was clear and crisp, the snow fresh and soft, and his heart pounded with the beat of his paws as they raced back to the house. Steve slowed down to a walk and took the last few feet to the garage at a stroll. Doc kept pace with him and they went inside together.

She shook, water and snow flying every which way and he quickly joined her. Even with their coats of fur, the cold was starting to settle in. It might have stopped snowing and the sun might be shining but it was still chilly enough to freeze them in moments if they didn't hurry. He shifted and reached for the towels he'd brought out before their run. Steve dried himself and waited for Doc to change.

"Hurry up. It's freezing out here." He held the second towel out for her to step into once she'd shifted to human form.

He watched her closely and realized something wasn't right. She'd lain down on her side and was panting heavily. Panic spiked but he reeled it in and went to her. Steve used the towel to pat her down and soak up some of the dampness. Her eyes drooped and it all fell into place.

Doc hadn't run in months, hadn't shifted in just as long and they'd been out in the winter air for a good hour. She was too tired to shift. He draped the towel over her and picked her up to carry her inside. Going straight to the bedroom, Steve laid her on the bed and finished drying her.

"Have a sleep. You'll be fine as soon as you've rested." The words were for his benefit as much as hers.

She yipped softly and licked his face. He tossed both towels at the bathroom and crawled onto the bed beside her. Her coat drew his fingers and he combed the fur behind her ears until her eyes closed and soft snores came from her throat. The thought of leaving her never entered his mind and he lay watching her sleep for long moments before drifting off himself.

The phone woke him. He sat up and reached for the bedside receiver. Obviously the lines had been repaired this afternoon. He'd checked before their run and found dead air. Steve glanced at the clock. Six thirty. They'd been asleep about an hour.

"Hello." He turned to look at Doc. At some point she'd shifted back to human form and lay on her stomach with her head buried in her pillow.

"Hey, Steve." Kat's voice came through crystal clear. "Just checking the two of you are still alive up there."

"We're fine." He sighed and leaned against his pillow.

"Thought you would be, but I promised Mom I'd call."

"Doc would have rung but the lines have been down since Christmas night," he said.

"The crews have been working like mad to get everything back up. Good thing I've got that generator out back or I'd have lost a truckload of food these past two days."

"The town lost power? Wow, it was a big storm."

"Not real bad, more bad luck, I think. The big old tree over near the substation came down, took out the power and they would have had it up and running quicker if the snow had stopped falling sooner."

"Anyone hurt?"

"No, nobody's stupid enough to go out in this weather."

He could hear someone talking in the background and Kat's whispered "give me a second".

"Are you at the café?" Steve asked.

"Yeah, Mom and Dad are here too. We were wondering if you guys would be able to head down here for dinner in the next few days."

"Probably be another day or two and that's only if the snow holds off."

"Well you'll be pleased to know they're not predicting another storm until after the first of the year. Hang on a sec, Steve."

There was some shuffling of the phone followed by what sounded like an argument and then Mrs. Monroe spoke.

"Steven McKenna, you get yourself and my daughter down here the minute you can. I want to see both of you within the next two days or I'll drive up there."

More shuffling and Kat was back. "Sorry." Her sigh sounded like wind blowing through the line. "I tried to hold her off. She's got some bee in her bonnet about you two getting married on New Year's Eve because she and Dad are planning to leave on the first."

"What?" He glanced at Doc, found her watching him intently. "Um, I'm not so sure about that, Kat."

"Not sure? That's not what you said the other day."

"No, that's not what I mean. I'm sure about the getting married part, it's the when that's uncertain."

Doc sat up and arched one eyebrow.

"Have you two even talked about a date?" Kat asked.

"Not specifically. Look, Kat, I'll talk to Doc, but no matter what your mother wants it won't happen if Doc's not ready."

"I get that but you'll have to tell it to Mom. The woman is driving both me and Dad batty." Kat dropped her voice to a whisper. "I think she's frightened Gordie will change her mind and run again."

He laughed. "Doc has never run from anything in her life."

"Yes, she has. She ran away after Anthony died and we didn't see her for months on end."

Steve sobered. "Kat, she wasn't running from anything. She was running *to* something. Doc needed to find herself and she couldn't do that here." He watched Doc as he spoke to her sister. Saw surprise cross her face, fill her eyes.

"But what's to stop her from doing that again?" Kat argued.

"Me." It was simple really, love and trust would keep her beside him. "Look, I've gotta go. We'll call and let you know when we're coming to town."

Steve leaned over and hung up the phone, never taking his eyes off Doc's. He couldn't read what she was thinking but he knew she was. That sexy over-thinking brain of hers was all but smoking as she tried to work her way through his half of the conversation.

"How did you know that?"

"What?"

"That I wasn't running away when I left here?"

He shrugged. "You're not a coward, Doc. Running would never occur to you."

"But *I* thought I was running."

"I never saw it that way. Before you married Anthony your plans were to go away to school, it seemed logical to go ahead with the plan after the accident. It gave you a focus, a dream you'd always had you could make come true." He reached over and threaded his fingers into the hair at her nape, tugged her closer. "What other dreams do you have, Doc?"

Steve leaned in and kissed her. He flicked his tongue along the seam of her mouth and applied pressure until she let him in. His caresses were feather soft, not demanding, just offering. She had all of him, held his heart—*his soul*—in the palm of her hand. Freely given, no strings. Take it or leave it, her decision wouldn't matter, he was hers until the day he died.

He rolled her beneath him. Took the kiss deeper and savored the feel of her body melting into his. Her breasts were crushed to his chest, her nipples hardening as he rubbed against her. She moaned into his mouth and he drew the sound in, swallowed it whole. They arched together, his sex pressed to hers and the give became take. Neither of them had put their clothes back on after their run so there was only skin on skin.

Heat and need rolled through him. Pulled his balls up tight and made his cock throb. He tilted his hips, slid his length along her slit and reveled in the moisture that coated his flesh. She writhed below him, her hot folds gripping his shaft, dragging him deeper into the maelstrom of sensations bombarding him.

Her mouth left his, her teeth nibbling a trail down his chin, his throat. "Love me."

"I do."

"No. Make love to me. Now." She bit his shoulder, her tongue soothing the sting with one long lick.

Steve leaned back, stared down at the woman under him and wondered if he could ever deny her a thing. "With pleasure."

She spread her legs, wrapped them around his waist and dug her heels into the backs of his thighs to pull him inside her. He flexed his hips, brought his cock to her entrance and thrust deep. Her walls gloved him, scorched him with liquid fire and drove him to the edge of sanity. Passion flared, exploded in a burst of wicked wanting that stole every other thought from his mind except claiming Gordie.

He drove into her again and again. Thrusting to the hilt and withdrawing to the crown on each stroke. She bucked and thrashed, her body meeting his in need and demand. Her teeth grazed his throat, sank into his shoulder and he nipped at her ear, licked and sucked and bit until she moaned against his skin.

"Steve." Harsh, hot breath coated his neck. "I want. *Need.*"

"What?" he panted. "What do you need, Gordie, what do you want?"

She arched under him and he sank deeper inside her, farther into the inferno consuming them. Her pussy squeezed him, gripped and released him in a punishing vise that stole his breath.

"*You,*" she screamed.

The orgasm detonated between them with such violence Steve

lost control. His hips jerked, his balls imploded and blasted shot after shot of cum through his shaft. Fire licked up his spine and erupted to shower him from head to toe in ecstasy. He collapsed on top of her, all energy incinerated by their joining.

"*Fuck.*"

Doc's lips curled on his shoulder. "Yeah, that fits."

"Jesus. Give me second."

"I want to stay."

He lifted his head, looked down at Doc's flushed face. "Was there ever any doubt?"

"For me, yes." She closed her eyes, took a deep breath that raised her chest, pressed her breasts against him. Her lids lifted to reveal tears. "I don't want to promise something I might not be able to give. I don't know if I can do it, but I want to."

"You don't have to know. Life doesn't hold guarantees, Gordie. All I ask is that you let me love you, love me in return and promise to never hold anything back again. No matter how trivial or how inconvenient something is, I want to know about it." He searched her gaze. "Can you give me that?"

"Yes." She kissed him quickly. "So you want to get married on New Year's Eve?"

Steve smiled. "I'll marry you whenever you want. I'd get dressed and plow our way to town now if you wanted."

"Really?"

"Yeah, really."

"Okay, let's go." She tried to push him off her.

He laughed, rolled to his side and pulled her with him. "New Year's Eve is good enough if that's what you really want. Besides, as far as I'm concerned we're as good as married now."

She laid her head on his chest, her fingers playing over his skin. "Steve?"

"Mmm."

"This is my dream."

EPILOGUE

The closer they got to town the harder her heart pounded. She could suck in no more than shallow gasps of air and sweat coated her skin, especially her palms. Her fingers trembled along with her stomach. Gordie just hoped she didn't embarrass herself and throw up the second she got out of the truck.

Steve's hand landed on her thigh. "Stop worrying. Everything will be fine."

"You can't know that."

"Yes, I can." He glanced her way, turned back to watch the road. "We have each other, don't we?"

"Yes, but—"

"See, everything is fine."

She took a deep breath. "That's not what has me nervous and you know it."

He patted her leg. "Gordie, you did what you had to, there was no other choice and those that matter to you, to us, know that."

They turned a bend and the town came into view. It looked exactly the same as it had every other time she'd traveled this road. On the surface nothing had changed. But on the inside, like her, nothing was the same. Steve drove through the center of town, found a spot across the street from the café and parked. He switched off the engine and turned toward her.

"If you don't want to do this now, would prefer to wait, we can."

"What?" She spun in her seat. "No. I want to get married. I've wanted it for days. What I don't want is to face the people waiting for us in there." She indicated her sister's café.

"The only people here are the ones we invited, our family and friends. None of them are going to judge you." He unbuckled both their belts and pulled her across the console as he opened his door. "Come on, let's go change your last name."

Gordie laughed. "Is that all we're doing?"

"Did I mention you'll be tied to me for life?"

She shook her head.

"Probably best to leave that until after we change your name then." He grinned and pulled her out of the truck behind him.

"What other secrets have you kept hidden?" They linked hands and checked for traffic before heading across the road.

"Oh, a lifetime of happiness, a houseful of children, getting old and wrinkly together." Steve put his hand on the door to Kat's place. "Ready?"

"And willing."

The noise from a party well underway greeted them. Kat came rushing over yelling above those already inside.

"They're here." She linked arms with each of them, separating them. "Let's get this show on the road."

Her sister led them to a small flower-festooned arch that had been place in front of the big stone fireplace at the back of the room. William Brant stood in a creaseless suit waiting to commence the ceremony.

"Gordie, Steve, lovely to see you both."

Steve shook the older man's hand. "Thanks for doing this on such short notice."

"Nonsense. It's my pleasure." William turned to Gordie. "Shall we start?"

"Yes."

They removed their coats and stood facing each other, their hands joined. Everyone moved in around them and a hush fell over the room. The vows were simple and in only a few sentences she was Dr. Gordana McKenna. Steve bent down to kiss her. A soft brush that was nowhere near enough. She wrapped her arms around his neck, pulled herself up on her toes and showed Steve what a real kiss should be like. Breathless, she gulped for air while whistles and applause rang in her ears.

He grinned at her. "Hello, Mrs. McKenna."

"That's Dr. McKenna to you."

His smile grew bigger. "Doc McKenna. Oh yeah, I like that even better."

Steve picked her up and spun around. Gordie tossed her head back and laughed. He put her down and they were surrounded.

Congratulatory hugs and kisses were delivered by all before Kat called an end to the ceremony and a beginning to the wedding feast.

Her mother cried. Silent, happy tears she reassured everyone but she continued to sniffle through the meal and Gordie sat beside her, holding her hand and talking. When everyone was stuffed full to the gills Brogan got up and made a speech. He kept it short but he did get in a dig at Steve for taking so long to chase her down. With the formal part of the wedding over a few people left but others stayed well into the afternoon and she sat back and enjoyed the rest of the day.

***

Steve watched his wife.

Jesus. His wife.

He'd wished and hoped and prayed for so long he still wasn't sure it was real. Doc laughed at something Rowan said. The women had been sitting together deep in conversation for well over an hour and he had a feeling most of the discussion centered on the coming babies. Tatum got up and headed over to Dale. She whispered in his ear and they both looked in his direction before she returned to the table.

He wasn't surprised when Dale walked over to stand beside him. The topic the sheriff brought up did shock him though.

"We went over the clinic with a fine-toothed comb. I know how he was getting in and out and where he's been hiding all these weeks."

Steve turned to look at Dale. "Marcus? Where?"

"It looks like he was hiding out in the roof cavity of the clothing shop next door. He removed some paneling to get into the clinic's roof space. From there he just had to drop in through the manhole like he did at the house."

"Son of a bitch."

"Doctor Monroe has organized to have the roofing checked and repaired. The deputies cleared out all the evidence and the rubbish so Gordie doesn't have to worry about that," Dale said.

"Why are you telling me this today?"

"Because I figured I'd rather you tell her about it before she opens up the clinic day after tomorrow."

"Coward."

"There's more."

"More? What more could there be?" Steve asked.

"His brother's coming home to claim the body."

"What?" Steve glanced around, dropped his voice so no one would hear. "Brady hasn't been seen in, shit, over ten years. Everyone figured old man Connelly killed him and Mrs. Connelly the year the Wilders were killed in that mountain accident."

"Well apparently the boy, man now I guess, is alive and well. And to make it even more interesting, Brogan hired him on as a wilderness guide and from what our sovereign says, Brady Connelly is definitely home to stay."

"Great. Just great."

Tatum walked toward them ending the conversation.

"Ready to go?" Dale asked her.

She covered a yawn with one hand while pressing the other into her back causing her pregnant belly to bulge even more. "We were ready an hour ago but we couldn't miss out on this special day."

Tatum waddled closer to him and tried to stretch up to kiss his cheek. "Jeez, help a girl out, Steve, bend down here." He leaned forward and she planted a kiss on him. "I'd say make her happy but I know you will so instead I'll say I hope the scientists work out how men can carry babies before you two decide to have children and you get to do this part."

He laughed and hugged her to his side. "If I haven't said it before now, Tatum, welcome home. I think having you around will lead to interesting times." He eyed Dale as the other man fidgeted beside them.

"Thank you. I'm really happy to be back. Come on, sheriff. Let's go home." She linked her arm with Dale's and ambled toward the door.

Doc came up next to him and slipped her arm around his waist. "Do you think we'll know what the deal is with those two anytime soon?"

"It's inevitable in this small town." Steve tugged her around in front of him. "So, are you ready to go home, Doc McKenna?"

"Yes," she sighed and laid her cheek on his chest. "I'm exhausted and I've done nothing but sit on my butt all day and talk."

"Well I'm sure flapping those sexy lips takes energy." He bent to plant a kiss on said lips. "You can nap in the truck because there's no way I'm letting you sleep through our wedding night. I've got plans for you, Dr. McKenna."

"Oh, sounds intriguing but I've got some plans of my own."

"Really?" He arched an eyebrow. "And just what might those be?"

She stood on tiptoes, put her mouth to his ear and whispered.

COYOTE LAW

COYOTE HUNGER BOOK 3.5

*For those who kept asking when the next coyote book was coming.
And to Tatum who turned up in Coyote Whispers and showed me who
Dale was.*

1

———

DECEMBER 22

Dale followed Tatum into Steve's home office and closed the door behind him. "You're not going to make this easy for me, are you?" he asked.

She turned to face him, one eyebrow arched in disbelief. "Should I?"

If he was honest, and he had to be for both their sakes, not to mention the babies she held safe inside her, he didn't deserve for her to make it easy for him. With a large measure of guilt and regret he shook his head. "No. You shouldn't."

Tatum sighed, her shoulders dropping a fraction as her chin lowered to her chest. "I didn't come home to cause you trouble."

"Fuck, Tay, you think I don't know that? You never cause trouble. Always the one smoothing things over, taking care of—"

"I didn't do a good job after Cade." Her gaze met his, her eyes glassy with unshed tears, and her chin wobbled. "Stupid hormones," she muttered as she used both hands to scrub at her eyes.

"Tay." He didn't know what to do. What to say. He'd gone back for her. To beg her to come to Whispering Springs with him, remind her what they were...

He'd fucked that up when he realized he wasn't as ready as he'd thought. And now she'd turned up here—pregnant.

"Why didn't you tell me?"

"Hard to speak to someone when they sneak out in the middle of the night."

He closed his eyes on a groan. Not his most shining moment, that's for sure. "I'm sorry. So, so sorry. I told you that over a hundred times in voice mails and texts. You never returned one of those messages." The last message he'd left only a few hours ago.

"I could probably accept an apology via phone if it was one time, Dale, but you left me twice. *Twice.*"

"I needed—"

"I don't care what you needed. You. Left. Me." She turned her face away. "I'd already lost Cade..."

Grief tightened his throat, yanked at his chest. "We both lost Cade."

She turned back, anger sparking in her eyes now. "Yes, *we* did. And when *we* should have pulled together, should have leaned on each other, *you* ran."

"I had to get my head on straight. I had to..." He tried to explain but words failed him. He'd been so lost in those first months after Cade. And watching Tatum's grief had only driven him deeper into the darkness choking him.

He'd taken leave from his job and returned to the mountains where he'd spent the early years of his life, more often than not with Cade by his side, and found some peace—hope.

"I'm sorry. I needed to be close to Cade."

"And I didn't?"

"I didn't say that. I just..." He shrugged. God. He was fucking this up. "I wasn't good for you. I couldn't help you if I couldn't help myself."

"So what, you came here, took a new job, and forgot about me!"

"No. Never!" Dale took a step toward her.

She held up a hand. "Don't."

He froze, muscles vibrating with the effort to hold back. He wanted—needed—to hold her, except he'd given up that right. Given up so much when he'd left her behind. He'd never meant for their separation to be permanent but he hadn't told her he was leaving, never mind why or that he'd be back.

Nodding, he murmured, "Okay."

She jerked, her hands going to her swollen belly and rubbing gentle circles. "Dammit. I need to sit down."

"You need to lie down." He risked her anger and moved closer. "Here. Let me help."

Tatum snorted. "Sure. *Now* you want to help."

"I never would have left if I'd known." And if he hadn't been up in his own head which happened to be shoved up his own ass, he would have known they'd finally managed to accomplish their greatest wish. He scooped her into his arms and walked to the couch.

"Jeez, Dale, put me down, I weigh a ton."

"You're light as a feather."

She thumped his chest. "Don't lie to me."

"Fine, you've got about twenty pounds extra on the last time I picked you up." He sank to his knees and lowered her to the couch sideways so she could lie back and stretch her legs out. His gaze was drawn to the mound of her belly. Swallowing hard, he lifted his gaze to hers and asked, "Can I...?"

"What?" she eyed him warily.

"Touch you," he said, tipping his chin toward her stomach.

"You just did. Without asking permission I might add."

"Tay. Please." He couldn't keep the emotions out of his voice, the slight edge of desperation that sliced through him like the deadliest blade.

"Fine." She reached out and grabbed his hand. "Here. Someone's having a hell of time attempting to kick their way out."

She placed his hand low on her right side, just above where her hipbone use to be before her belly grew round with his children. He'd barely made contact when he felt the first thump, a dull punch to his hand as though his palm had been injected with local anesthetic.

God. That was his child in there. Well, one of them anyway. Pressing closer, he cupped this new curve of her body with both hands and waited for more.

Dale had no idea how long they stayed that way, Tatum lying back, eyes closed, letting him feel their child—children—move within her. It wasn't until he heard the delicate snore he hadn't heard in months that he realized she'd fallen asleep. He didn't make a move or sound, just sat on the floor beside her and took her in.

She was beautiful. Even exhausted, with dark shadows beneath her eyes, fatigue etched into the edges of her mouth, she was gorgeous.

He remembered the first time he'd recognized her as his. Cade stood beside him; they'd returned from a run with the pack, when the newly shifted teens came bounding into the clearing. Within seconds everyone shifted to human form and Dale had taken one look at Tatum and lost his breath.

Cade had done the same.

He'd known Cade for as long as he could remember and sometimes Dale had thought they were one person. They weren't blood related but from the moment they'd met, they were inseparable. Always doing the same things—wanting the same things.

It had never been an issue until Tatum.

They'd been nineteen at the time, Tatum fourteen.

They'd known they were too old for her—that she was too young to be facing a mate, never mind two. Known they had to stay away, but when a coyote found its mate every instinct pushed to claim.

Two years they'd held off.

Two years of watching and waiting and slowly going out of their minds as every eligible boy in Whispering Springs tried to catch the eye of *their* Tatum. They hadn't known it then, but all that worry had been for nothing.

Tatum had set her sights on him and Cade long before her first change.

The death of her father had shaken them all and sent his life in a direction he'd never considered going.

Mrs. Brant—stricken with grief—had packed up and gone back to the city she'd grown up in, taking Tatum and her siblings with her. For Cade and Dale there had been no choice.

They had to follow.

Tatum was barely sixteen and they'd somehow convinced her mother to let them move in with the family—date Tatum. Mrs. Brant's crippling grief helped their cause. She hadn't cared what any of her children did and spent most of her time in her pjs, either in bed or lying on a couch in the living room.

It had fallen to Tatum, Cade, and Dale to see to the raising of Tatum's younger brother and sister.

On Tatum's eighteenth birthday, they'd gone to the local courthouse and acquired the necessary paperwork to make their union—his and Tatum's—legal. Dale couldn't remember how he and Cade had decided which one of them she'd marry. It didn't matter. It didn't change the fact they weren't a couple. They were a trio.

A trio that had fallen apart when a drug dealer—a stupid kid of fifteen—sent three bullets into Cade's chest in a dirty alley.

Dale lowered his head as tears of anger, frustration, guilt, and grief filled his eyes. They'd lost so much more than Cade that night. They'd lost each other. He'd lost himself—his way. He thought he'd finally found it again, but now, with Tatum and the babies...

He couldn't fuck this up. He couldn't lose Tatum and the family they'd always dreamed of.

"We have to work things out, Dale."

Head snapping up, his gaze collided with Tatum's. She reached out a hand and cupped his jaw. Her palm and fingers were soft and cool against his skin, rasping lightly over his stubble.

"Cade would kick both our asses if he was here."

One side of his mouth kicked up. "Yeah, he would."

A yawn big enough to crack her jaw escaped her.

Placing a hand over hers before she could pull it away, he said, "You should get to bed."

Her eyes searched his for long moments. Whatever she saw brought a small smile to her lips. "Okay. We'll leave it for now."

"We're not leaving anything. From now on, you and our babies are my priority."

"How do you know they're yours?" she asked, challenge in her gaze.

"Tay."

"Okay, fine. You've got me. It's not like I can lie about that."

He didn't want to know but he had to ask. "Do you wish they weren't?"

"No!" She pushed herself up, shoved him back with a hand to his shoulder. "Dumbass."

"Name calling?"

"Hey, you've been an ass and now you're being dumb. Ass. Dumb. Dumb—ass." She lifted both hands, palms flat, moving them up and down as though weighing each word as she spoke. Shrugging she added, "If the shoe fits."

Dale held in a smile and nodded. "You're right. I've been a total ass and that was the dumbest question ever asked."

Tatum frown, her eyes narrowing. "That was too easy."

"You haven't seen anything yet. I'm going to be the easiest man you ever met."

"Ah...okay, I have no idea what that means exactly but I'm too tired to work it out now." She swung her legs off the couch and Dale stood, holding out his hand. "I'll go see about that room Steve offered," she added as he pulled her to her feet.

He swallowed around the lump in his throat. "You could—"

Shaking her head, she said, "Don't say it. We're talking after months of not talking and for now that's enough."

"It'll never be enough."

"I'm not the one who walked away, Dale."

He hung his head. *Fuck.* He had so much to make up for. So much he'd missed. "I never intended to stay away," he murmured.

Tatum chuckled and patted her belly. "You didn't stay away."

"That's not what I mean."

"Dale. Please. I'm not mad enough to ignore you. Or keep you out of the babies' lives, but I need time to settle in here. Time to readjust to us living in the same place again." She sighed. "And right now I'm too tired to deal with any of this."

"Sorry." He put a hand on her lower back and urged her toward the door. "Let's get you settled for the night. We'll worry about everything else tomorrow."

"As long as you don't sneak out in the middle of the night," she muttered.

Dale smiled. "Not a chance."

"Humph."

"You might not believe me," he said as he steered her out of the office and back toward the living room. "But I was coming for you at the end of January."

"Really?" She glanced up, the hope in her eyes almost bringing him to his knees.

"Yeah."

"And by coming for me, you mean moving back to the city?" One eyebrow arched, her brow wrinkled as she glanced at his sheriff's badge.

"No. I was coming to bring you home."

Tatum rolled onto her back and blew out a breath.

She'd always slept on her stomach but since her stomach had been invaded by aliens who'd built a second story she'd been forced to find a different position. She'd tried her sides and her back. Even purchased one of those pregnancy body pillows in an attempt to get comfortable.

Ha!

Comfort was a thing of the past. She imagined one baby growing inside you would cause all kinds of discomfort, but two? Yeah, there was no chance she'd get more than a few minutes of sleep at a time. One or the other was always on the move. Or she had to pee. Good thing she'd found it easy to doze off anywhere, anytime. Those cat naps meant she made it through each day without collapsing in complete exhaustion.

"Can't sleep?" Kat's drowsy voice whispered through the dark room they shared.

She'd forgotten how dark nights were in the mountains. "Not since my belly extension."

After a small chuckle Kat was quiet, but Tatum could hear the questions all the same.

She wasn't ready to answer any of them and hoped she wouldn't have to. Not yet.

Not until she'd sorted things out with Dale.

Dale.

Her husband.

The father of her children.

The man who'd walked out when she'd needed him most.

Tatum wasn't sure how they'd find their way back to each other but she knew she wanted to. As much as she wanted to stay angry at Dale, she couldn't stop loving him or walk away.

She'd lost Cade. She'd be damned if she'd lose Dale too.

After Cade's death they'd bumbled their way through a couple of months until she'd woken one morning to find her husband gone. He'd taken nothing with him; his clothes remained in their closet. They were packed now—along with most of her own. On a truck arriving sometime after the first of the year.

In those months before he'd come home, Tatum had known exactly where he was. He'd taken at job in the sheriff's office in their hometown, his pay dropping into their account every other week. All she had to do was check their bank statement to see where he was and what he was buying.

At first she'd wanted to follow him. Especially when she'd realized he'd taken a job. But she'd given him space. Thought for sure he'd come home—call.

Six months later when he'd shown up on their doorstep, she'd welcomed him inside. Welcomed him into their bed.

They'd cried a lot that night. More than they had when Cade died.

She'd never seen Dale so vulnerable—so lost—out of control. They'd made love. Slow and desperate. And with their passion spent, they'd clung to each other in the dark until sleep came.

Waking to an empty bed the next morning gutted her as much as Cade's death had. She'd accepted Dale's visit as goodbye and would have let him go if she hadn't ended up pregnant.

The change had been obvious that first day but she'd chosen to ignore it until her sister had insisted she pee on a stick. By then she was over a month along and living in denial. Her sister's encouragement and that little plus sign had given her the slap in the face she needed—the motivation to pull herself together and go after what she wanted.

She'd lost one mate to circumstances beyond her control. She refused to lose the other if she could do something about it.

Of course it had taken her a few months to sort her life—*their* life —in the city out. She had to make sure her brother and sister would be okay without her. Had to decide what to ship to Whispering Springs, what to leave behind for Tavia and Tarak. When to give notice at her job and when to make the journey home.

Her plan had been to arrive the week after New Year but when the men arrived two days ago to pack their things, she couldn't ignore the need to be home. And by home she meant Dale's arms.

"I'm not going to ask any questions. Which if you ask anyone here they'll tell you is a miracle. But if you want to talk, I'm willing to listen," Kat murmured. "Although I have to admit I am *dying* to know what's up with you and our sexy, broody sheriff."

Tatum smiled.

"Anything you tell me would remain between us." Kat's hand found hers and squeezed. "I know we haven't seen each other in years and we weren't exactly BFFs before you moved away but I recognize someone who needs a friend when I see them."

"Thank you."

"You're welcome." Kat squeezed her hand again and let go.

They were both quiet for a few moments before Tatum whispered, "My last name isn't Brant."

"Oh?"

"It's Turner." Tatum sighed. "Sheriff Dale Turner is my husband."

2

DECEMBER 24

"**D**on't look at me like that," Dale growled, ripping off his latex gloves and tossing them in the bin.

Steve's expression became an emotionless mask but it was too late; he'd seen the look on his friend's face.

Frustration and anger tangled his nerves. He'd revealed far too much to Steve in the last few hours. He hadn't meant to but Steve had a way of 'not asking' that made you want to answer. He still wanted to.

"It was never about me liking guys." Dale dragged a hand down his face. 'Like' was too tame a word for what had been between him and Cade. He'd never touched Cade in a sexual way. Never wanted to. What they'd had wasn't about sex. Except in every other way that counted, their relationship was that of a mated couple.

"What was it about then?" Steve asked.

Dale sighed. "Tatum."

Steve frowned. "Tatum?"

"Yeah. Tatum."

"I don't—"

"I know you don't. And I can't explain it. Cade was...the other half of me. We couldn't have been closer if we were Siamese twins; we could finish each other's sentences, communicate without words. People joked about it when we were younger, how alike we were, always wanting the same things. Sometimes it seemed as though he was me and I was him, and I know he felt the same. And the second we laid eyes on Tatum, we knew she was ours. We waited years to claim her. Four years of waiting, of worrying about what people would say, knowing once we touched her there would be no going back." He paused his verbal diarrhea to suck in a breath.

It was so hard to explain what was between the three of them. It was something he'd never seen or heard of in coyote mates.

"Humans are so tolerant of alternate lifestyles nowadays that living together, the three of us, was easy in the city. Doing that here, especially with Connelly as sovereign..." Dale shook his head. The city had let them live as they were, without prejudice or persecution. And then it destroyed them.

"That's why you left so abruptly." It wasn't a question and Dale could see his friend joining the dots quickly. "You went after Tatum."

Dale smiled. Just a small curl of his lips. "Yeah."

"I never understood why William let his daughter-in-law take her children—his only grandchildren—to the city after his son died."

"Tatum's mother never fully embraced the mountains or coyote life—she never allowed Samuel to change her—and without her husband..." He shrugged. "She mourned Tatum's dad until her own death. Tatum thinks, and I agree, she died of a broken heart."

"And you and Tatum broke when Cade died."

Dale grimaced. They'd done more than break. They'd shattered into so many pieces he still couldn't find them all. Wasn't sure he'd ever be able to.

"I don't get what you've been through so I won't pretend I do, but I can imagine, and loving Doc makes that all the more realistic for me so I understand why you came home. What I don't understand is why you didn't bring Tatum with you in the first place. Why you went back only to leave her again."

"I never meant to leave a second time. And I was going back," he muttered.

"When?"

"Last week in January." Half his mouth kicked up when he thought about what he'd planned. "I was going to get her, drag her home kicking and screaming if I had to."

"I take it you didn't know about the babies before we found her crumpled in my driveway?"

"Fuck no! I'd have gone for her before now if I had." Dale shook his head, the surprise of seeing Tatum large with their children still a sucker punch to the gut. "We'd tried for years to have kids. From the moment she married me, Cade and I spent every minute we could trying to knock her up."

"I know it's no consolation, but sometimes things just aren't meant to happen when you want them to. Timing is everything."

Dale looked at Steve. If anyone knew about the right time, it was Steve. He'd watched his mate take another man as her husband only for Doc to leave the mountains for years after the man she'd married and her unborn child died. In some ways they'd been through similar experiences.

Steve clapped him on the shoulder. "C'mon. Let's finish up here and head over to the Den. Maybe a slice of Kat's double choc chocolate cake will make things better."

"Jesus. What are we? Teenage girls?" Dale grumbled. Although he wouldn't turn down a slice of Kat's legendary double choc cake. He just wasn't going to admit it out loud.

It took them another thirty minutes to wrap everything up at Doc's house. Dale sent his deputies to the station to log the evidence and file their reports. He'd do his later. After he got Tatum settled at home.

He'd listened to her arguments and let her stay in the apartment above the grocer's last night. She had no clue he'd slept in his car out front and he wasn't about to enlighten her. He wasn't telling her he had a key to her front door either.

When he'd first returned to town, he'd lived in the very apartment she'd organized to rent indefinitely. He'd only moved out when Steve had built his house up the mountain leaving his place in town open for new occupants. Since before he'd taken his trip to the city six months ago Dale had been redecorating rooms, adding touches he knew Tatum would like.

After almost a year of renovating old cabinets and installing new appliances. Months of ripping up threadbare carpet and replacing it or sanding hardwood floors, scraping walls and slapping on new paint. He finally had everything the way he thought she'd like and now he had to redo one of the rooms to accommodate their babies.

Dale smiled. He couldn't be mad about the extra work. Madly happy, yes, but angry mad? Definitely not.

He wanted to see her reaction to the things he'd done, the improvements he'd made so far. And now that she was here, she could guide him in outfitting the nursery.

Yep. Tonight she'd stay with him and if she still insisted on staying in her apartment he'd camp on her doorstep instead of freezing his ass off in his car if she wouldn't let him take the couch. From now on, they'd be living under the same roof. Like a husband and wife expecting their first children should be.

Parking behind Steve in front of the cafe, Dale hopped out and met the other man on the snow-dusted sidewalk. Rubbing his bare hands together, he blew on them and said, "Wow. It must have dropped ten degrees."

"Tomorrow's snowstorm is meant to drop temps to minus five," Steve said as he pushed the door to the Den open.

"They're predicting a bad one." Warm air enfolded him as he stepped inside. Dale scanned the tables but didn't see Tatum. "I've had my deputies making sure the older members of the community have all they need for a few days of being snowed in."

"I'll take getting snowed in as long as it's not as destructive as the series of storms we had two years ago."

"I'll second that. I wasn't here for the storm but I saw the aftermath and the repairs being carried out." Making their way to the counter, they took a couple of stools. "Do you want to check the roof at the clinic again before you head home?" he asked Steve.

"No. We'll do that before she opens up again though. I want it checked before she goes back there," Steve said.

Kat place a mug in front of each of them, and asked, "Can I get you something to eat?" as she filled the cups with steaming coffee.

"No, thanks, coffee's fine. Where's Doc?" Steve asked.

"She and Tatum walked over to the clinic to get something for Tatum."

Dale froze, mug halfway to his mouth, and stared at Kat.

Steve jumped from his seat and headed for the door, growling over his shoulder, "Alone? You let them go alone?"

"What's wrong? She said you'd checked it this morning. That it was safe," Kat protested.

"We did." Steve pulled the door open. "But I don't want her going there alone."

Dale didn't bother saying anything; he didn't want any of the women—especially Tatum—alone until Marcus Connelly was caught.

The trouble with Marcus should have stopped weeks ago when he'd driven his truck off Stattler Bridge. Kidnapping the sovereign's mate and leaving her to die alone in the mountains wasn't enough for the exiled pack member, no he had found a way to rise from the dead and terrorize their women once more.

That stopped now. Dale would see to it that Marcus left the pack for good if it was the last thing he did.

Determined to see to the safety of Doc and Tatum, Dale followed right behind Steve, his heart pounding in his chest, in his ears, as every worst-case scenario filled his head. They hit the sidewalk and sprinted across the street without looking.

Sliding to a stop at the clinic door, Steve yanked on the handle, thumped on the door, shouting, "Doc."

Call it instinct or whatever, but he grabbed Steve's arm. "Wait. Listen."

The door muffled the cry but Dale heard enough for every drop of blood in his veins to turn to ice.

"That doesn't sound like Doc," Steve said.

Dale pressed his ear to the door. Hoped he hadn't heard what his coyote was telling him he had. But the cry that came next was loud and clear.

"What the fuck? Tatum!" he yelled, hammering on the door with both fists.

Steve took off down the street.

"Where are you going?" Dale called out as he shook the doorknob in a vain attempt to get inside.

"Around the back."

Dale gave up on the front door and raced after Steve.

"We'll never break down the front door but there's a window above the back one," Steve yelled over his shoulder.

He knew the window. It was nowhere near big enough for either of them to get through but the back wall was timber. They could break that with a couple of well-placed kicks. He'd drive his squad car through it if he had to.

It turned out they didn't need the window or muscle or his car. The rear door was cracked a few inches.

Unholstering his gun, he moved around Steve, and said, "Let me go in first."

"Fine, but I'm right behind you."

He entered the dim hallway slowly. Listening intently, he tried to determine where in the clinic Tatum was. When they reached the morgue, Dale's gut clenched.

Doc lay curled on her side facing away from them, a huge pool of blood coating the floor around her and the man dressed head to toe in black lying on his stomach between her and the door.

Dale had no doubt who the man was.

Steve went to Doc while he checked Marcus.

"I can't find where she's bleeding," Steve choked, his hands frantically moving over Doc, his panic palpable.

"I'm not sure it's her blood." Dale took in the scene. "He's dead, looks like she slashed his throat."

"Jesus. What the fuck happened?" Steve tapped Doc's cheek. "Doc? Come on, Gordie, talk to me," he pleaded.

"I'll be back. I need to find Tatum." Dale held his gun in front of him even though his gut said he wouldn't need it. Instinct told him Marcus had worked alone.

Back in the hall, a few feet deeper into the clinic, a sound from behind had him spinning around, aiming his weapon. Registering old Doc Monroe and Mrs. Monroe, Dale lowered his gun and nodded toward the morgue. "In there."

Satisfied Steve would get the help he needed, Dale moved through the clinic toward the front door, checking each room as he went. Other than the morgue, nothing was disturbed and the only noise came from the rear of the clinic where Steven and the Monroes were taking care of Doc.

As he stepped into the reception area, the sight of Tatum crumpled against the far wall had Dale sprinting across the room and dropping to his knees. "Tay!" Placing his gun on the floor beside him, he searched for possible injuries.

"S-okay." She moaned, her head rolling toward him. "Fainted."

He pulled her up into his arms. "Fuck. Tay." Cradling her against his chest, he rocked, his heart pounding against his ribs—inside his skull—hard enough to hurt.

"Doc?" she mumbled.

"Steve's with her." He wasn't telling her anything else. Not that he knew Doc's condition, but Tatum didn't need to concern herself with that just yet. Not when she went limp in his arms and her head flopped to the side.

Holding her close, he climbed to his feet, and made his way back to the morgue and medical help. His basic first-aid training didn't feel sufficient for this situation.

Entering the room, Dale couldn't stop his voice from quivering when he spoke. "Doctor Monroe?"

"Jesus, Mary, and Joseph. What went on here?" The old man turned to his wife. "Jackie, go with Dale and see about that one for me. I'll bring Gordana in a minute."

Brogan and Quinn burst through the back door as Dale reentered the hallway.

"What do you need us to do, Sheriff?" Brogan asked, coming toward him.

Dale hadn't even thought about his role as sheriff and right now he didn't care if his lack of professionalism got him fired. All that mattered was the semi-conscious woman in his arms.

"A couple of deputies pulled up as we came inside," Quinn offered.

He needed to think... "They'll need to secure the scene...collect evidence." There was something else he needed to tell them... Except it was too hard to think of anything but Tatum. "Oh. My gun. It's on the floor where I found Tatum. Out front. In reception."

Quinn moved around them saying, "On it," as he passed.

Brogan gripped Dale's shoulder, gave him a squeeze. "Take care of Tatum. We'll take care of everything else."

He nodded and let Mrs. Monroe guide him into an exam room. Lowering Tatum to the bed in spite of every instinct screaming at him not to let her go, Dale reluctantly moved out of the way. He had to so she could get the attention she needed. But he didn't leave her side; he remained close, his hip pressed to the bed, his hands holding one of hers.

Mrs. Monroe seemed to understand his need to be near because she worked around him when she had to, checking Tatum's limbs for possible breaks, her head for bumps, her eyes with one of those tiny lights.

It seemed like years but was probably not even a minute before Tatum roused enough to talk to them. Mrs. Monroe asked questions and Tatum answered, her voice growing stronger with every word.

As Tatum revealed what had happened, he became more and more glad Marcus was dead. If he wasn't Dale couldn't be sure he'd be able to stop himself from grabbing his gun and shooting the man.

"How's Doc?" Tatum asked.

Mrs. Monroe's gaze met his. "Her dad is taking care of her." The non-answer seemed to appease Tatum.

"And..." She swallowed, licked her bottom lip. "Marcus?"

"Dead," Dale growled, his hands tightening around hers.

She glanced up at him, a world of emotion in those green eyes of hers. "Dead?"

Mrs. Monroe distracted Tatum from further questions by saying, "All right, let me check on that baby."

"Babies," they said in unison, their gazes locked together.

Dale stared down at his wife. It was a small thing, except they'd done that all the time in the past—spoken the exact same thing at the exact same time—back when they weren't this fractured version of themselves. The smile gracing Tatum's lips delivered another bubble of hope.

They could do this. They could find their way back to each other, could learn to be a duo instead of a trio.

He'd do anything—everything—to make it happen.

A *thump thump thump* beat broke into his thoughts and the silence of the room.

"There now, that's one..." Mrs. Monroe moved the instrument she pressed to Tatum's bare belly to the other side.

Thump thump thump.

The older woman smiled. "And there's two."

"They sound fine," Tatum said, her words filled with certainty.

"They do." Mrs. Monroe switched off the device and reached for another. "I'm going to take your blood pressure now you've had a chance to settle some. All that excitement is bound to have it a little high."

She went to work but Dale couldn't pay attention. All he could think about were those little beating hearts inside Tatum. He knew they were real. He'd felt them moving the other night except hearing them...

He closed his eyes and thanked the universe they were okay— that Tatum appeared to be okay.

"Dale?"

Opening his eyes, he found Mrs. Monroe looking at him with a knowing smile. "You can take Tatum home whenever you're ready. I'll have Doctor Monroe give you a call later but other than a couple of bruises, she and the babies are fine. Plus Tatum knows what to do if anything changes."

He swallowed, the lump in his throat all but choking him. "T-thank you."

She patted his arm, her smile growing wider. "You're welcome."

Together they helped Tatum to her feet and Dale wrapped an arm around her waist to be sure she stayed on them. She didn't argue and he hoped that meant she'd be as compliant when he took her home.

3

Tatum leaned into Dale as they left the exam room. She was a bit shaky on her legs but had nothing worse than a few aches and pains. Thankfully she hadn't slammed into the wall when Marcus had shoved her aside; she'd rolled along it before sliding to the floor and fainting.

"Hey, you okay?"

Glancing up, she saw Steve coming toward them; a frown furrowed his brow and pulled the edges of his mouth down. She had no idea what had happened after she'd passed out and the little information she'd received from Dale and Mrs. Monroe didn't set her mind to rest. She'd left poor Doc on her own to fight off a madman.

"Yeah, a little embarrassed at passing out and not helping Doc, but otherwise I'm good."

"I'll talk to you later, Steve," Dale said. "I'm taking Tatum home to rest. Brogan and Quinn arrived a little while ago. They're handling the Marcus issue with the help of my deputies."

"Need me to do anything?"

"No. Just take care of Doc."

Dale turned them toward the back door and ushered her outside. The cold air didn't bother her; her nerves, still in shock, were numb, and she couldn't feel much of anything except Dale's strong arm wrapped around her. And a sudden welling of relief to be out of the clinic.

"Shit," Dale muttered as he brought them to a stop a few feet from the door.

She looked up to see what the problem was but couldn't find anything to warrant his curse. "What?"

"My truck is parked in front of the Den."

"It's only around the corner."

"You're not walking that far."

Before she could protest she was fine and could walk the short distance around the buildings, he'd scooped her up in his arms, snuggled her against his chest as though she were a baby, and headed down the alley.

"*Dale.*"

"*Tatum,*" he mimicked her tone, his lips curled up on one side.

She rolled her eyes. "Put me down."

"No."

"You heard Mrs. Monroe, I'm fine. I can walk."

"Probably."

"Then put me down."

"I will." His stride didn't slow, if anything his steps got longer, faster.

"Now."

"Soon."

"For god's sake, Dale."

He chuckled. "God ain't gonna help you."

"Stubborn man."

"Yep."

"I really am okay."

"I know." He glanced down, his gaze awash with emotion. "Just give me this. Please."

It was the please that got her. And the look in his eyes. There was fear swirling in their caramel depths. "Fine. But don't get used to carrying me around."

"We'll see."

She huffed out a breath. "Stubborn."

"Yep."

Tatum didn't need to look at him to know he was smiling; it permeated every letter of that one word. With a sigh, she closed her eyes and laid her head on his shoulder. She'd let him have this moment.

Besides, she was tired. A permanent state lately, but she knew the drop in adrenaline from earlier had a hand in making her drowsy.

She must have dozed off because the next thing she knew, Dale was lifting her out of the passenger seat of his car. And they were inside an unfamiliar garage. "Where are we?"

"Home."

He didn't elaborate and when he moved through a doorway into the house he didn't point out anything. No tour for her. Instead he moved quickly along a dim hallway and into what had to be the master bedroom.

Lowering her to her feet, he said, "Let's get you out of your clothes and into a warm shower."

She was exhausted enough to let him take care of her. Without protest, Tatum allowed Dale to remove her clothes and usher her into the adjoining bathroom. He'd tended to her rarely in her life—she could count those times on one hand.

She'd missed his gruff care. He loved her, she knew that; he'd told her every day, shown her in little ways, except she'd always been so independent and self-sufficient that the times she needed him to care for her completely were few. She treasured them more because of how infrequent they were.

Until a year ago she'd been sure of their future. Now things were complicated, fractured, and even if they could pull it back together it wouldn't be the same. Nothing would be the same without Cade but they needed to find a way.

For the sake of their babies, they needed to work out how to be *now*.

How to be Dale and Tatum.

And they had to do it before the babies came.

***

Dale watched Tatum sleep. He'd managed to get her showered and into bed before she'd completely conked out.

That had been about thirty minutes ago.

She lay on her side, a little restless now, her legs moving around as though she were trying to find a comfortable position. He'd been tempted to leave the covers off her so he could see if the babies moved except the house was still on the chilly side. He'd turned the heat up and it would soon be warm enough for her to go without covers but for now, she lay beneath the quilt Grammy Brant had dropped off a few months ago.

He hadn't realized what the old lady was doing the first few times she'd appeared on his doorstep bearing a gift. She'd called by four times before he'd put the pieces together. It was the quilt that did it.

A hand-stitched wedding ring quilt.

As far as Dale knew, the senior Brants had never been told of their marriage or about the trio they'd formed with Cade. The old couple had visited them in the city a handful of times over the years, which had surprised Dale. He hadn't thought William would leave the mountains. But the old man made an exception for his only grandchildren.

Cade's funeral was the last time the senior Brants had made the trip down the mountain.

A few months later when Dale had turned up here, in Whispering Springs, without Tatum or her siblings, the old man had patted him on the back and told him everything would work out the way it was supposed to. William hadn't asked any questions, hadn't offered any further advice.

From that first day Grammy Brant—Dale had no idea what her first name was, for as long as he could remember everyone called her Grammy—had become a regular visitor, straightening things up if needed and leaving him food and a gift of some kind each time she showed up on his doorstep.

He'd felt uncomfortable around them at first. It didn't take long for that discomfort to disappear though. The Brants had always welcomed him. And they either didn't know about Tatum's pregnancy or...

"I need to ring Grammy," Tatum murmured.

Jesus, was she reading his mind? Had he been talking out loud?

"It can wait." He brushed the hair from her face. "Rest."

"She'll worry."

"Okay. You sleep. I'll call her." He pushed to his feet.

"They know."

Pausing, he gazed down at a sleepy-eyed Tatum. "Know what?"

She smiled. "Everything."

"Oh."

Closing her eyes, she said, "They've always known."

"*Always?*" He felt his eyes go wide and his eyebrows shoot up into his hair line as he stared down at her.

Smiling, she opened her eyes again. "I told them the year I turned thirteen that I'd found my mates. I think that was why Gramps was so upset when Mom took us away after Dad died."

A flash of memory. Of William coming to him and Cade, telling them his daughter-in-law was taking the children away. Jesus. The old man had encouraged them to follow. Had helped pack up their old truck. And Tatum's mother hadn't seemed surprised to find them at her door.

Shit. So much of the past began to make sense.

He brushed a finger down her cheek. "I'll call them now."

Her eyelids lowered and Dale watched for a few seconds, making sure she'd drifted off to sleep again before leaving the room to make the call.

The doorbell rang as he stepped into the kitchen. Thinking it would be Brogan or Quinn, he hurried to answer it. Except it wasn't the pack's sovereign or regal on his doorstep. It was the Brants.

Opening the door wide, he gestured them in out of the cold.

"She's okay," he reassured them. "Tired. A few bruises but she and the babies are fine."

Grammy enfolded him in a crushing hug and the full impact of his words finally hit him. He shuddered in her arms, relief and gratitude swamping him. Closing his eyes, he held the old woman close. She patted his back, rubbed soothing circles, and let him take comfort in her arms.

Gathering himself, Dale pulled back. "Sorry."

"Nonsense, boy. Nothing beats a good hug." She smiled up at him. "Now, let me get this soup on the stove. It's already made, only needs a little heating up."

Dale hadn't noticed the big pot William carried when he'd let them in, but with the other man's arms full, Dale didn't offer a hand to shake; instead he ushered them into the kitchen.

"I've spoken to Brogan," William said as he placed the huge pot on the cooktop. "With it being Christmas tomorrow and that big storm heading our way, we'll convene a council meeting after the New Year."

"I should—"

"Nonsense." Grammy lit the burner and took the lid off the pot. The room instantly filled with a delicious aroma and Dale's stomach growled. "You need to be here taking care of your wife. Your deputies are capable, and our sovereign and regal can take care of anything they can't for now."

He'd frozen at the word wife. Unsure whether to acknowledge the comment or not, he stood still, his mind swirling with a million possible things to say.

"William. Keep an eye on this while I go check on Tatum," Grammy ordered.

Dale watched her leave the kitchen and head straight for the master bedroom. She'd been here often enough she knew her way around so he didn't need to tell her or show her where to find Tatum.

"She's a force of nature that one. Not unlike our Tatum."

William's words had Dale turning back to the older man. "I..." He didn't know what to say. How to explain. *What* to explain. Rubbing a hand down his face, he sighed.

William chuckled. "Don't tie yourself in knots. I told you everything would work out the way it was supposed to."

"Not with any help from me," he muttered.

"Sometimes we have to take the long way round to get to where we're going."

Dale could understand that, but could they get to where they were going when one of them was gone?

Proving Dale was easy to read or William was a mind reader, the old man said, "You were never meant to get to the end together. As much as it pains me to say it, Cade wasn't meant to be with you here. Take comfort in the time you all had. It's better to have had than not."

"Doesn't feel that way."

"The children will help with that."

He groaned. "I've fucked up so much."

The old man grinned. "We all fuck up once in a while."

"But I hurt Tay. Over and over. And I left her to cope with her pregnancy on her own."

"You needed time. So did she." William gripped his shoulder and squeezed. "You're both in a better place now. And you're home. Where you were always meant to be."

Home.

The place Cade had refused to visit. He never would have moved back to Whispering Springs. Dale couldn't imagine living in the city forever, raising a family there. Hell, the only reason they'd stayed in the city after Tatum's mom died was because Cade wouldn't return to the mountains.

Cade had thrived in the city. Loved working the dark streets, being a cop in a large metropolis. He'd have been bored out of his brain working as a small town cop and yet Dale loved it. Loved knowing all the people in his territory. Cade would have hated that. He'd liked the anonymity of city life where Dale had found it disconnected—isolating.

Maybe they hadn't been so alike after all.

Tatum place her empty bowl on the timber chest masquerading as a coffee table and leaned back on the lumpy sofa with a sigh. She was so exhausted, she didn't care about the hard thing digging into her left butt cheek. "That was delicious."

"Do you want more? There's plenty." Dale picked up her bowl and climbed to his feet. "Grammy left us the whole pot."

"Maybe later." She watched as he made his way to the kitchen with their dirty dishes.

She'd woken a little while ago, the smell of Grammy's homemade chicken soup teasing her senses. Finding Dale, lying beside her, his head propped in his hand, his eyes glued to her face had momentarily given her pause. Then she'd smiled.

He used to watch her sleep all the time. Said he couldn't get enough of seeing her breathing whether asleep or awake.

Kat had been right in her description of Dale. He was broody, but only because he didn't waste words. If he didn't have anything to say, he didn't bother with small talk. That had been Cade's skill.

Out of the three of them, Cade had been the social one. Dale had been the tall, dark, and silent one. And she'd fallen somewhere in between the two.

It wasn't that she or Dale were anti-social. They just preferred to keep their circle small, close. Whereas Cade had never met anyone he hadn't treated like a lifelong friend. She had to wonder if that trait contributed to his death.

They'd never talked about what had happened. Dale hadn't wanted to burden her with the details. All she knew was Cade had been shot in the chest and bled out before help could arrive. She had no clue if he might have survived if that help had come sooner. Or if the kid who'd shot him hadn't kept police and paramedics out of that alley by firing at anyone who tried to get near.

Perhaps they needed to talk about what happened to Cade. Get everything out in the open so they could work their way through the grief, the incomprehensible events of that night, and finally put it behind them.

"Hey."

Glancing up she found Dale standing beside her, a frown on his face. She smiled and answered, "Hey, yourself."

"You okay? Want to talk about what happened?" he asked as he sat on the couch next to her.

She did want to talk, but not about what he thought. "Yes. I want to talk."

"All right." He turned so he was facing her head-on. "I'm listening."

"What happened the night Cade died?"

To his credit, Dale didn't flinch but she felt him stiffen, every muscle in his body going rigid, frozen in place. He sucked in a deep breath and let it out slowly. "He was shot three times."

"I know that. I want to know what happened. Why he was there, alone, without backup. Without *you*."

She'd never understood that part. Cade and Dale had been partners. They'd worked every case together, and if not, there was always another detective to go with them. It was a rule of their precinct—no officer went out alone.

Dale closed his eyes on a sigh. "He wouldn't wait. Said he knew the kid, he was harmless. Low man in the organization of the dealer we were after. Cade had been trying for weeks to turn the kid into an informant."

"But neither of you were on shift." Another thing she hadn't understood. Why had Cade gone out while off duty?

"No. We were home with you when he got the call from the kid. He told Cade he had some information he wanted." Dale opened his eyes. "I'll never forgive myself for letting him talk me into staying home."

"Do you think he knew something was off?" When it first happened, she'd wondered if Cade had been set up with the way the kid had barricaded the alley and kept everyone away.

"No. He honestly thought it was no big deal and perfectly safe."

"Then what went wrong? You know more than you've told me. I'm not fragile, Dale, and I need to understand so I can move forward." If he wouldn't tell her, she'd do the one thing she'd stopped herself from doing all this time. She'd go to their old precinct and ask.

"It was a setup of sorts. The kid was proving he had what it took to move up the ladder within the drug network. Of course he ended up dead as well. The network didn't want him snitching so they had someone shank him."

She knew the teenager had died in custody. Some sort of fight between inmates. She'd had no clue he'd been targeted by the people he'd worked for. "Such a waste."

"There was one good thing to come out of what happened."

"Oh?"

Dale nodded. "The kid's mother took her younger boys away from the city. Back to the small town she'd grown up in. Last time I checked, the three boys were proving that environment matters. They're all doing well in school and heading in the opposite direction of their dead brother."

"There's no father?"

He shook his head. "No. Hasn't been in the picture since the youngest was born."

"I can't imagine how that woman must feel." She smoothed a hand over her belly. Watching the child you raised succumb to a gang, deal drugs, murder a policeman... Tatum couldn't even begin to comprehend the emotions the woman was dealing with.

"She's as much a victim of her son's actions as Cade was. Luckily she has the opportunity to rebuild. Change the course of her other children's lives."

"Cade would like that. To know that she took her younger boys out of the city and away from the streets and the drug and gang culture that's so rampant."

"He would."

"Do you think we could help her? Maybe give her an anonymous donation of school supplies? A year of groceries or clothes for her growing boys? I haven't touched Cade's life insurance."

"If that's what you want to do with the money. But I thought you would want to use it for the babies."

"I'll put some aside for them but it's a lot of money, Dale. There's more than enough to go around."

The amount still astounded her. Even Dale hadn't known Cade had taken out such a large policy. When the lawyer had first contacted them about it, Tatum had thought it was a mistake. Except when all the paperwork and Cade's will had been finalized, they'd received a check for a million dollars.

Dale scrubbed a hand over his face. "I can't believe he never said he changed the payout on his insurance."

"I can't either, but when I think about it, it's such a Cade thing to do."

"Yeah, like going off on his own to meet a small-time drug dealer in an alley."

"He could be wildly reckless and super cautious depending on his mood." She smiled. "He did everything to the extreme, didn't he?"

"I never thought so before that night."

Tatum shrugged. "I guess we were so used to who he was that we didn't see it."

"Or overlooked it because we loved him," Dale murmured.

"We did love him."

Dale's hand slipped over hers, his fingers curling under to press into her palm. "We loved each other too," he whispered. "Cade might not be here but that doesn't mean the love is gone."

She turned to look at him. There was so much emotion in his gaze her tummy dipped. "The only thing that died was Cade. I still love him." Tatum smiled, her eyes filling, her bottom lip trembling. "I still love you, Dale."

4

───────

Dale sucked in a breath and held it as Tatum's words wrapped around his heart and squeezed. He didn't deserve her love. He'd abandoned her when he should have protected her—supported her. Instead of running away to get his head on straight, he should have held her close, leaned on her to help him through his grief.

"I'm sorry." He reached up and brushed a finger over her cheekbone. "I should never have left."

"No. You needed to get out of the city, I understand that, but you should have talked to me. Taken me with you."

He closed his eyes. "Yes. I should have."

"Next time."

His eyes shot open. "No. There won't be a next time. I'm never leaving you again, Tay. You have my word on that."

She smiled. "Just so you know, if you did go, I'd follow."

"You already did."

"Ha. Not at first."

"I don't think badly of you because you didn't come after me. Not with the way I left."

"I was mad about that in the beginning. But as the days passed and I thought about where you were, I knew you'd gone where you needed to be. When you came back then left again…well, I figured that was goodbye. I was really mad then. So angry I tried to ignore the changes in my body, to my scent, until Tavia said something. Her words and the pregnancy test she shoved into my hands helped me face reality. And then I knew I couldn't accept that as goodbye. If you were done with me, I needed to hear you say it."

"I'll never be done with you."

"Good."

"How about this? If either of us feels the need to go, for any reason, we say so. No more hiding how we feel or what we're thinking. I know that should be a given between mates but our mating was different than others and I think we, *I*, let that difference get in the way of what we are to each other. I hope you can forgive me, Tay, but I promise you, I'll spend every day for the rest of my life making it up to you."

"There's nothing to forgive. I know you; you didn't deliberately set out to hurt me. We were both in a bad place after Cade, struggling to find our way, not knowing how to reach each other. We let ourselves forget the most important thing we had. Each other. Instead we focused on what we'd lost."

"Cade."

A small smile curved her lips. "Yes. Cade."

"Come here." He pulled her into his arms and snuggled her against his chest. "I'll never forget what we have again," he promised.

"I don't love you because I loved Cade. I love you for you, Dale. My connection to each of you is separate and not reliant on the other."

"I didn't think it was. Except so much of myself was tied up in my connection to Cade. For so long I've thought of him as part of me. It took me a while to understand I'm still me without him. And recently I've discovered things weren't as I thought. We weren't exactly the same. If the situation had been reversed, he never would have come back here; the mountains would be the last place he'd seek solace."

"I never understood why he hated it here."

"It had something to do with when he was little, before I knew him, I think. He never told me how he came to live with the Bakers."

"They were a weird old couple. Gramps used to tell me to stay away from them. I think that's why he used to find work for you and Cade to do. So Cade wouldn't have to be at their house much."

"Your Gramps has a way of manipulating things. Did you know he encouraged us to follow you to the city? Even helped us pack our stuff, gave us gas money." Dale shook his head; he'd forgotten about the five hundred dollars William had pressed into his hand before they'd left Whispering Springs.

"He's a crafty old thing." Tatum yawned around her words.

"C'mon, let's get you back to bed." He pushed to his feet taking her with him. Snuggling her as close as he could with her belly in the way, he asked, "Do you need anything? A glass of water?"

"No. I'll be up all night peeing if I drink anything now." She went to move away from him and he tightened his grip.

"Let me help you."

"I'm fine, Dale."

"I know. I'd still like to help you." He wanted to carry her except he knew she'd argue against that. If all he could get was an arm around her shoulders, he'd take it.

"Don't coddle me."

"I'm not coddling you," he said as he steered her down the hallway to the bedroom. "I'm coddling me. I swear, seeing you crumpled on the floor stopped my heart. It might take me a few days to recover from that shock."

She glanced up at him. "I'm tough. If I wasn't harboring a couple of parasites I'd have given Marcus a run for his money."

Dale shuddered as ice drenched his veins. He had no doubt she would have. Just the thought of it took his breath and kicked his heart into overdrive. Tightening his arms around her, he muttered, "Thanks for putting those images in my head. I was already guaranteed nightmares; now I don't think I'm brave enough to close my eyes at all."

They entered the bedroom and Tatum headed for the bathroom. "I need to empty out before I lie down or I'll be up within the hour."

She didn't need to explain. He figured she'd want to use the bathroom before hopping into bed. While Tatum took care of things, Dale turned down the bedcovers. She'd made the bed when she'd woken. Smiling he remember the numerous arguments they'd had over the years about making the bed. He didn't see the point when you were only going to mess it up again.

"Aren't you coming to bed?" Tatum asked.

He hadn't heard her. She'd managed to get right behind him without him noticing. "I...um..." Glancing over his shoulder at her, he said, "You want me to sleep with you?"

She cocked her head to the side, her eyes narrowing. "Why wouldn't I?"

"Oh, well." He scratched his head. "I thought..."

Her laughter filled the room. "You should see your face. The last time I saw that look was our wedding night."

Memories bombarded him, his body instantly reacting to the vivid images. "I haven't felt this nervous around you and a bed since that night."

"Dale. I'm six months pregnant with your babies. I think we can sleep in the same bed without difficulty."

"Are you sure?"

Sighing, she muttered, "Dumbass," as she walked around him.

"Hey."

"Hey yourself." She climbed onto the mattress and pulled the covers over her belly. "We're either making this work or we're not."

"Of course we are."

"Then, *husband*, come to bed with your *wife*."

Dale stared at Tatum. She always managed to surprise him. "I didn't want to push."

"Push all you want—" a yawn cut off her words. "Jeez. I'm exhausted. You'd think I hadn't woken from a two hour nap less than an hour ago."

"Another reason I shouldn't—"

"Dale Turner, get your stubborn ass in this bed and hold me until I fall asleep, then you can climb out if sleeping with me is so repulsive."

"What? No! Fuck, Tay. I'd love nothing more than to crawl in beside you and hold you all night but I don't want to fuck this up any more than I already have."

"The only way you'll fuck things up further is if you don't get in here." She flipped back the covers and patted the bed beside her. "Promise I won't jump you."

He laughed. "Now that I'd love to see. You can barely walk straight with those two filling your belly."

Her lips stretch into a smile so blinding Dale had to blink. "See, nothing to fear from the ungainly pregnant woman."

"You're beautiful."

Tipping her head down, she fluttered her lashes, and said, "Flattery will get you everywhere."

Shucking his pants, he left his boxers and t-shirt on, and moved around the bed. He'd wanted to be under the same roof as her; being in the same bed was far more than he deserved. He hadn't begun to make amends for the pain he'd caused her. Dale wasn't about to refuse the invitation though. He might be a dumbass but he wasn't stupid.

He slipped under the covers and moved toward her. "Come here."

She wiggled over, burrowing into his side; her body curved around the babies, she pressed her face into the side of his neck the way she'd done so many times in the past. Arms wrapped around her, Dale took a deep breath and savored the woman in his arms.

He'd almost destroyed them by leaving her behind. He wouldn't make that mistake again. Now that she'd given him a chance to make things right he planned to make them so right she never thought about their time apart again.

5

———

DECEMBER 25

Tatum stared out at the storm, her insides churning in a mix of pleasure and fear. Pleasure because she hadn't been in the mountains for a snowstorm in years and fear because this was a doozy and Dale was out in it.

He'd gotten a call right after lunch. About ten minutes after the power had gone out. He'd already started the generator before being alerted to the storm damage by his deputy so she had heat and could use the lights. The stovetop was gas, so she'd rummaged around in the kitchen and found the ingredients to put on a batch of spaghetti sauce. It'd be ready no matter when Dale came home.

Home.

She glanced around. The tour he hadn't given her yesterday had happened this morning. With each room he took her through she could see the care he'd put into it. She could feel the love in every refurbished inch of the place.

That he'd done it for her—for them—well, she'd gotten a little teary over that. Pregnancy hormones hadn't just turned her into an exhausted blimp. They'd made her a leaky faucet. It didn't take much to bring her to tears nowadays, and Dale's care and thoughtfulness, the love he lavished on every inch of this place with her in mind, only cemented her belief in them.

He'd made them a home.

The house they'd had in the city had belonged to her mother and although the place had come to her and her siblings on her mother's death, no one had bothered to redecorate. Even the curtains were the same ones her mother had put up when they'd first moved in almost a decade ago.

This house was their first real home. Dale had told her he'd bought it from Steve and had planned to bring her here six months ago. He'd cut his words off at that; she wasn't sure what he hadn't wanted to tell her and wasn't sure if she should ask. Except she wanted to know.

Needed to know why he'd come back to her only to leave again.

It was the one thing they hadn't discussed yet. The last thing she needed to understand so they—*she*—could really move forward. Not that she was going anywhere.

Nope. She was here to stay.

She was fighting for what they had. Dale still loved her, had never stopped loving her, and she'd certainly never stopped loving him.

Light flashed through the falling snow and the sound of the garage door opening vibrated through the house. Pulling the blanket around her shoulders tighter, Tatum made her way to the connecting door and waited for Dale to come inside. She didn't want to open the door and let out all the warm air so she leaned against the wall opposite until he appeared.

"Hey." He stepped in from the garage, unzipping his thick jacket. "Tree took out the substation. No power 'til the snow lets up and the crews can get to it. Phone lines are down too." Hopping on each foot in turn, he yanked off his boots and dropped them on the floor.

He was fully clothed—jeans, sweater, scarf and beanie, thick socks, with one big toe poking out—and yet he may as well be naked for the way her body reacted. He hadn't done anything remotely sensual as he removed his outer layer but that didn't seem to matter. Every nerve quivered with excitement. It appeared him stripping out of his jacket and boots was enough to awaken her libido.

"You okay?" he asked as he stepped closer.

"Uh-huh."

He eyed her. "Tay?"

"It's just pregnancy hormones."

Frowning, he asked, "What is?"

"Anything, everything. It's always pregnancy hormones."

"O...kay." He moved even closer. "I want to wrap my arms around you except you're flushed with warmth and I'm cold. All the way to the bone cold. I'm gonna jump in a hot shower then I'll see about getting us some dinner."

"I made dinner."

"You did?" One dark eyebrow arched.

Nodding, she stepped into him and murmured, "Want me to wash your back?"

Dale froze, the look on his face making her laugh.

"Does it shock your delicate sensibilities that I want to get naked with you, Sheriff?"

"Ah..."

She trailed a finger down his chest until she reached his utility belt. "Why, Sheriff, is that a..." She patted his buckle. "Gun in your pocket or..." Glancing up through her lashes she saw Dale's throat work as he swallowed, his eyes dilate.

"Tay." The nickname was ground out through clenched teeth.

"Hmm."

"Don't tease me."

Giving up her coy act, she straightened and looked him in the eye. "Who's teasing?"

"Tay," he moaned.

"Sometimes a wife wants to wash her husband's back."

"You need to take it easy." He swallowed again, scrunched his eyes closed for a second as he took a deep breath. "After yesterday."

"Dale, after yesterday I want to make the most of every second. I *need* to make the most of every second." She planted both hands on his chest. "Please. Don't make me beg." She'd begged before. But not like this. Before it had been him driving her so out of her mind she couldn't do anything except beg him.

He eyed her for a few seconds and she thought he would deny her, making her wait until he'd gotten in the shower so she could sneak in behind him. Except he shook his head and blew out a breath. "My way."

"But—"

Two fingers pressed against her mouth. "No. I'm giving in on this; I won't give in on anything else."

"I don't understand," she murmured, her lips rubbing on the rough skin of his fingers.

"I know what you want. It's in your eyes, Tay. It's the look you gave me six months ago. It's one of the reasons I left."

"Oh." He didn't want her to want him?

"C'mon. I need to warm up." He grabbed her hand and tugged her behind him. "Although I'm pretty sure you taking your clothes off will do that if the fire in my groin is anything to go by," he grumbled as he ushered her into the bathroom ahead of him.

The hand on her lower back left her and she spun around to find Dale stripping out of his sweater and thermal. Next went the jeans, underwear, and socks. Jesus, he was a sight for the senses. Arousal shot through her and lit her up. Everything tightened and heated, and dampness slicked her panties.

Completely oblivious to the fire raging inside her, he leaned into the shower stall and flicked a couple of taps. Water poured from the ceiling shower-head as well as several nozzles positioned on one wall.

Without looking at her, he stepped beneath the spray, a shudder rippling down his body, a moan of pleasure rumbling in his throat.

Jesus. He was right. Stripping off clothes shot her temp up another ten degrees. She was sweating and the dampness in her panties became a flood.

"Get in here, Tay," he growled.

Her gaze darted up his body and connected with his. Fire blazed, scorched, and sizzled in his caramel eyes. A shiver worked its way down her spine. Goose bumps broke out on her skin. And muscles, unused in six months, contracted.

"I won't ask again."

She knew he wouldn't. He'd gone all alpha on her and she wasn't about to deny herself the pleasure his demands always brought her. Stripping out of her borrowed sweater and sweat pants, along with her soaking wet underwear—she'd forgone a bra—Tatum walked into the shower and into Dale's arms.

One of them moaned. Maybe both of them did. She couldn't be sure once his mouth crashed down on hers. Everything but the feel of him—wet and hot—pressed against her, invading her mouth, short circuited every synapse, zapped every nerve.

Hands slid over slick flesh. His. Hers. Both searching. Needing. Giving. Taking.

The last time they were together had been frantic—desperate— and now, as the frenzy of their first touches settled, their strokes turned sensual—worshipful.

"God, I missed you, Tay," he spoke against her lips. "I was such a fucking dumbass. Can you ever forgive me?"

"I'm here, Dale."

"Yes." His lips curved against hers. "Yes, you are."

She opened her mouth but the words she wanted to say were swallowed by his kiss. He took it deep, his tongue reaching in for hers, stroking, dueling, commanding. She surrendered willingly.

He'd never had to do more than kiss her to make her quiver with need. Except with her breasts extra sensitive and her hormones on overdrive thanks to her pregnancy, Tatum found herself on the verge of orgasm. His cock pressed into her belly, the huge mound stopping it from getting close to the throbbing need in her pussy.

"Dale," she gasped, tilting her hips toward him. "Please."

He worked out the problem quickly, his hand sweeping over her ass, around her thigh, and between her legs. His fingers stroked, pressed, dipped deeper to collect the slick arousal coating her folds. "You're so close."

"Yes." Panting, she rocked her hips, forced his fingers back and forth over her clit. "*Yes...*" she hissed as her climax detonated.

Pulling her closer with one arm, Dale continued to work her pussy until the pressure became too much and she jerked away. "Easy," he murmured, swirling his fingers lightly over her sensitized flesh. "Ride it out for me."

Following his demands, she let him take her through the final waves of pleasure.

"You're so beautiful when you come," he murmured into her hair. "So hard to resist."

The smile that curved her mouth was more post-orgasmic euphoria than pleasure at his words. She remained limp against him as he maneuvered them to the seat built into the side wall of the shower. He held her up while he positioned himself, then turning her around, he lowered her to his lap until he held her hovering over his cock.

"Put me inside you," he commanded.

She glanced over her shoulder. "Like this?"

"Yes. I can't take you against the wall like I want to on account of the babies."

"Oh." She hadn't thought of that. They hadn't been together for months. Hell, sex hadn't entered her head for months. She'd skimmed over those sections in the pregnancy books she'd bought.

"Tay," he groaned. "Hurry up. You're killing me."

Smiling, she reached down and wrapped her fingers around the base of his shaft. Holding him steady, she let him guide her.

The first touch drew a moan from both of them.

The first inch sucked the air from her lungs and left her insides quivering.

The first deep plunge took her right back up to the peak she'd just tumbled over.

Crying out, she gripped his hands where they cupped her hips and held on. He was strong enough to take control, to take them both on the ride her trembling body seemed to need once more. His teeth scraped over her shoulder, up the curve of her neck until he gripped her earlobe, flicking it with his tongue.

"Come for me again, Tay." His hands tightened. "I want to feel your hot pussy squeezing the cum out of my cock."

Tatum moaned, every muscle wrapped around his erection clenching. "Dale," she pleaded.

Finally he took command of her body and, raising her up slowly, he tortured them both. "Fast or slow?" he asked and pulled her back down hard. "Both."

He did it again. A slow glide up, hard crash down. Over and over he worked her body with his, drove her quickly to the edge but didn't let her tumble. He loved to hold her on that sharp peak. The razor slice of pleasure that bordered on pain.

"Dale. Please." She clamped her pussy walls around his length.

He grunted in her ear, nipped at her lobe, licked down her neck, and sank his teeth into the curve.

Air left her in a gush as pleasure filled her from head to toe when the sting of his bite set off her climax. Bucking on his lap, she held on, rode out each surge of ecstasy as Dale held her aloft and drove his hips up to slam his cock into her repeatedly.

Warmth flooded her. From the orgasm rolling over her and from the cum spilling inside her.

Dale gasped in her ear. "Tay." His hands left her hips and slid around her belly, cradling her against his chest as their breathing slowed, their heart rates lowering with every gasp.

They sat there, bodies cooling, for long moments. Steam drifted around them, water still flowing.

"Love you," he murmured into her neck.

"Love you too."

"I didn't mean for that to happen."

Tatum laughed. She'd always loved snapping his control. It rarely happened; not the sex, that happened whenever they got naked, but Dale's control was legendary. And she could break it. There was feminine power in that. Satisfaction—maybe a little smugness too—in knowing she could get to him so deeply he let go.

"We should get out." He was still hard inside her.

"Hmm…"

"Tay."

A smile curved her lips. "We're not done yet."

Dale had started with good intentions. Then again he *always* started with good intentions when it came to Tatum. He could pinpoint the moment things had gone off the rails today.

The second he'd looked up after dropping his boots.

Fire blazed in her eyes, her breath coming in shallow bursts, and she couldn't have hidden the twin beams pointing out from her chest.

He'd been helpless to resist her.

He always was with Tatum. She was his kryptonite.

Which made his retreat to the mountains confusing.

When he thought he could be all she wanted—needed—he'd gone for her only to fall back into the dark pit of his insecurity all over again.

Being with her without Cade didn't seem possible. He hadn't known how to love her on his own.

He did now.

Loving her was easy. She made it easy.

All he had to do was let it happen. There was no controlling love. They'd learned that when the three of them had discovered their connection all those years ago. Just because there were only two of them now didn't mean that love was any less. If anything, it was more for having loved Cade—been loved by Cade.

She stirred in his arms, making him smile.

She'd declared they weren't done and promptly fallen asleep. The hot water wouldn't run out. One thing he'd learned living in a house with six people. Instant hot water was the only way to go.

"Dale?" Her sleep-slurred confusion made him smile wider.

"Yeah."

"Oh, god." She tried to get off his lap. "I'm sorry. I didn't mean—"

He swiveled her around until she sat sideways and covered her mouth with a hand. "Nothing to be sorry about, Tay."

She smiled against his palm.

Removing his hand he said, "You obviously needed a nap after those two orgasms."

A flush that had nothing to do with the warm air around them filled her cheeks. He loved that she blushed when they talked about sex. Not all the time, but every now and then he could get a nice rosy flush out of her.

She tucked her face into the curve of his neck. "I hate that part of being pregnant."

"You're building little people in there. That's hard work. Plus I think it's the body's way of getting you ready for little to no sleep once they're here. Call it practice napping. You'll need to be an expert by the time they're born."

"I think I hit expert level in week five."

The reminder of all he'd missed—what he'd let her deal with alone—sat heavy in his chest. No more though. From now on, he'd be there every step of the way. Tightening his grip on Tatum, he rose to his feet. "Let's get cleaned up. You said you made dinner."

"Oh. I did."

He steadied her on her feet and reached for the soap. "You also said something about washing my back." Holding out the bar he waited until she took it before turning around.

"Why'd you leave the second time?"

Dale closed his eyes. He'd known she'd ask eventually. At least now he had an answer. Before she'd arrived in Whispering Springs, he couldn't have told her. As much as he was ready for her to come home, he still hadn't understood what sent him running six months ago.

"Dale?"

Turning around he cradled her face, tipping her head up as he leaned forward to rest his brow on hers. "I freaked out."

"Freaked out? Why?"

"That night. We were so...desperate, needy, and I know you came;

I did too but I didn't feel as though I was enough, if the two of us were enough. Cade wasn't there to soothe you after I'd taken—"

"Stop right there." She slammed her hands against his chest, pulled against his hold. "I never *needed* Cade to soothe me or you to take me. I only *needed* you to love me. And with every breath Cade took he did. I know you do too, Dale. It's all I ever need from you. However you want to do it. Demanding, soothing, both, whatever. All I want is for *you* to love me."

"I do. That never changed. Not for one second did that stop."

"Then you're enough. *We* are enough."

He brought her close and pressed his lips to her forehead. "I wish I could go back—"

"If wishes were horses, beggars would ride."

Laughing, he let her go and turned around. "Okay, time to get to work, wife."

In answer to his demand, she slapped his ass. Hard.

"Hey, payback's a bitch, Tay."

"Yeah." Pressing herself against him she muttered, "I'm counting on that."

Fuck. His body tightened. He remembered how much she loved playing. They didn't do it often, and honestly, it wasn't a kink he needed, but he did enjoy it. Tatum had too. And Cade had loved to watch them.

"We can do this without Cade," she whispered into his back.

"I know."

"He'd be really pissed if we didn't."

Dale chuckled then groaned when Tatum reached around and slid her soap-slick hand over his cock. "Yes."

Tatum giggled. "Was that yes to what I said or yes to what I'm doing?"

"Both. Jesus." He sucked in a breath when she quickened her strokes, squeezed him tighter. "Don't stop."

"I don't plan to."

Working her hand up and down, she drove him close to coming in an embarrassingly short amount of time. "Tay," he gasped.

She had two hands on him now. One cupped his balls, the other furiously stroking him from root to tip, with the extra squeeze at the head that he loved.

"I'm going to come," he growled.

"Wait." She moved around in front of him and dropped to her knees, pushed out her chest. "On me. Come on me."

His hands joined hers and together they jerked him off until he sprayed her tits with thick white streams of cum. Shuddering though each pulse, Dale wanted to get on his knees. Wanted to worship at her feet for all she'd put up with, for every wrong he'd ever done her.

6

DECEMBER 31

Six days.

Tatum couldn't wipe the smile off her face.

Six days of being with Dale and she knew they'd never be apart again. They'd worked their way through more of the past year and a half. Spoken of fears and hopes. She knew they were in a good place. Knew they were where they were supposed to be.

She also knew Cade never would have come here with them, and she could admit, and had done so out loud to Dale, that she never would have been happy raising their family in the city.

"You ready?" Dale slipped his arms around her from behind and stroked her belly.

He did that a lot. Stroked the babies. He talked to them too. He told them all about the mountains and how they were going to love growing up here. They'd made peace with being here—being without Cade. It still felt like something was missing but it didn't hurt like it had before.

"Tay?" He reached up with one hand and gripped her chin, turned her face away from the snow-covered street in front of their house so he could lean over and look at her. "You okay?"

The concern in his eyes made her smile. "Yeah, just thinking about everything."

"Are you happy?"

"Of course." She wiggled to loosen his hold and turned in his arms; sliding her hands up his chest and over his shoulders, she locked her fingers together behind his neck and stood on her tip-toes so she could press her lips to his before settling back on her heels and asking, "Why would you think I'm not? Isn't the smile I can't seem to wipe off my face a clue to how happy I am?"

"I want to be sure."

"Thank you."

"For?"

"Checking. But we promised we wouldn't hold anything back from now on. No hiding how we feel no matter what it is so you can bet your ass you'll know the second I'm not happy about something."

"Promise?"

"Pinky swear." She held up her hand, pinky cocked ready to link with his.

Smiling, he hooked his finger around hers. "Pinky swear."

Grinning, Tatum pushed to her toes again and kissed him. She'd meant for it to be a quick peck but Dale had other ideas. He thrust his tongue against her lips and forced his way inside. Not that she was objecting. Nope. She loved the way he demanded her response. He'd never truly force her but he'd push until she surrendered or said no. She couldn't imagine a time when she wouldn't surrender to him though. Everything he did was for pleasure. Hers and his.

When he finally let her go, they were both breathing hard and she could see the lust swirling in his eyes. She wanted to strip off her clothes and sate his hunger. Ease the answering need burning inside her.

Dale growled. "Fuck. We don't have time."

He snatched her closer. Slammed his mouth over hers once more. It wasn't enough. Would never be enough but they really had to leave. With a small growl of her own, she pulled away and slipped out of his arms.

"Hold that thought. We'll definitely get back to it. But for now, let's go to a wedding."

"Do you regret ours?"

"No, why would I?"

"We didn't have family or friends there. No celebratory dinner after."

"I had the two most important people there. You and Cade."

"If I haven't said it today, I love you."

"So you should." She hip-checked him and headed for the door before she changed her mind about leaving and dragged him to the floor. "Now come on. I want to get there before Doc and Steve."

"Are we out?"

Stopping, Tatum spun on her heel. "Out?"

"Yeah, you know. Are we telling everyone we're married? About Cade?"

"If it comes up." She paused. "Or do you think we should make an announcement or something?"

"I don't want to overshadow Steve and Doc."

"Oh, no. Definitely not. Okay, so we'll just answer questions if anyone asks."

"If that's what you want."

Smiling she moved back into his arms. "I want the whole world to know we're together."

"They'll know the minute they get a whiff of either of us." Dale laughed.

"Yes, they will." Grabbing a handful of his shirt front, Tatum pulled him down to her and kissed him.

EPILOGUE

FEBRUARY 26

"Dale!"

The scream from the bathroom had Dale falling over his chair in his haste to get to Tatum. Saving himself a busted nose by planting his hands on the floor, he scrambled on hands and feet to the wall and pulled himself upright. He sprinted down the hall and through the bedroom; skidding to a stop in the doorway of their en suite, he found her standing in a puddle in the middle of the room, her grey leggings soaked from the crotch down. "What the—"

"My water," she gasped. "My water broke."

He knew what that meant. And it wasn't that she'd peed herself. "But you're not due for weeks."

"There's two, remember? Twins are often early."

Now she told him. *Fuck.* He wasn't ready.

Sure the nursery was finished and they had everything they needed for when they brought the babies home but...

He wasn't ready!

They couldn't do this yet. "You have to stop it," he blurted out.

Tatum stared at him unblinking for a full minute before she burst out laughing.

"I don't see what's funny," he half yelled.

"I can't stop it. Not without drugs, and Doc and I decided at my last checkup that if I went into labor now it would be fine."

"Fine? Fine? It's not *fine*. The babies aren't due for weeks."

"Dale. I get that you're freaking out. Although with you having worked in law enforcement for as long as you have, I'd think you'd be cooler under pressure or when faced with unexpected circumstances—"

"Tay! You're having the babies early!"

"Yes, it would appear so."

"Early!" Why was she so calm? They were stuck up a mountain, the nearest hospital over an hour away and she was giving birth prematurely. This was not a stay calm or cool moment. "We need to get you to the hospital."

He spun on his heel and left the room only to swing back around and scoop Tatum into his arms. He completely ignored her wet pants. And her protests.

"Dale! Put me down."

"No. We need to get in the car."

"No, we don't. I'm having them at home."

That stopped him in his tracks. "You... Home... *What?*"

"I just need to ring Doc, then I want to get in a bath."

"You want to take a bath? Wouldn't it be better to rinse off in the shower than to take a bath?" He was having problems understanding. Or hearing. Surely he'd heard wrong. She couldn't possibly want—

"Yes. A bath. We're going to try a water birth."

"Water birth..." She wanted to... "Oh hell no. We're having these babies in a hospital where they can monitor every little thing. That's where you have premature babies, Tatum."

Smiling, she patted his cheek. "You're so sweet to worry."

"Sweet? I'd say smart—"

"Dale!" She waited for their gazes to connect and hold. "I'm having these babies in this house and there is nothing to worry about. I've had a textbook pregnancy which bodes well for a smooth labor. Please, put me down. I need to call Doc so she can get over here."

Dale stood there for a moment. He tried to get his panic under control. It wasn't easy but Tatum's calm helped him drag his mental state back from the chaotic swirl it had become.

She didn't appear to be in pain, and he knew what she looked like when she was anxious so he knew she wasn't worried at all in spite of the babies deciding they wanted out early. If anything she looked happy, excited. That alone had his breathing slowing, his muscles relaxing, and his mind calming.

"Okay. Home birth." Turning around he took her back to the bathroom. Placing her on her feet, he asked, "What do you need me to do?" Whatever she wanted—whatever she needed—he'd make it happen.

No matter what he wanted, they were having the babies. Now.

He could do this. He *would* do this.

Tatum leaned back against the pillows and cradled the precious bundle in her arms closer to her chest. Flynn William Turner had entered the world a full ten minutes before his sister. Caden Rose Turner was currently tucked up in her father's arms.

Seeing the big broody sheriff holding his daughter was worth every second of heartache over the last year. While she'd give anything to have Cade with them, she knew he'd never want to be here, in Whispering Springs, and after being back only a few months, she knew she wouldn't want to raise her children anywhere else.

She was even trying to convince her brother and sister to move back to the mountains after college. Tavia and Tarak had no family in the city and Gramps and Grammy weren't getting any younger. Plus Tatum really wanted her children to know their aunt and uncle, especially seeing how they had the twin thing in common.

Bending forward, she closed her eyes, pressed her nose to the top of Flynn's head, and took a deep breath. As a nurse she'd helped deliver babies and she'd always loved the smell of a newborn. At least with her own children she wouldn't be getting funny looks when she sniffed them. Being a shifter meant scent was an integral part of her nature and living among humans for the last decade, she'd had to resist the urge to smell a lot of things.

The bed beside her dipped and she opened her eyes to find Dale stretched out next to her. Smiling she leaned over and sniffed the little head peeking out of the baby blanket Grammy had made for the babies. She'd made two, of course, and Flynn was snuggled up inside his. Dale had wanted to wait until after they'd cleaned the babies but Tatum wanted her children to be wrapped in the love of family from the very beginning.

It was why she'd made the decision to return to the mountains.

To be closer to her mate, the family she'd been forced to leave behind, and to raise her children among their own kind.

And if she were honest, she'd admit to missing the home where she'd spent the first sixteen years of her life. It saddened her that Cade wasn't with them, that he'd never been happy here, but she knew he'd be happy she was happy, that Dale was happy. And he'd be thrilled to know they'd named their children after him.

Cade Flynn might not have been happy here but he would have been happy for them. He would want them to find their true home. He had only ever wanted her and Dale to be happy.

It would be hard to continue without him beside them but he'd always remain in their hearts. They'd make sure Flynn and Caden knew all about the man they were named for.

He'd live on in their children.

COYOTE LIES

COYOTE HUNGER BOOK 4

For everyone who has waited for the rest of the story.
To Fedora who stuck with me in times where I didn't want to stick with me.
To Tamara Y who was willing to dive in when I asked.
And for Mr.C because the person who loves you, who you love, is all that matters. Together forever, Babe.

1

JANUARY 15

Brady sucked in a breath when he rounded the bend and the first buildings came into view.

Whispering Springs.

The place he'd been born.

Eyes scanning, he eased off the gas, and took in the changes.

Here, on the outer edges of town, things looked the same. Mostly. There had definitely been changes, minor ones—new paint, some additions—but nothing stood out too much. He was sure he'd see more once he got to the middle of town but right here, on the outskirts of the town he'd grown up in, it was as though he hadn't spent over a decade living somewhere else.

A wave of comfort flowed over him.

Home.

He'd finally come home.

The years away didn't matter; in his heart he knew this was home.

Would always be home.

He'd sought out every piece of information he could before taking the job with Wild Encounters and making the journey here. The owners, Brogan Wilder and Quinn MacClellan, had intrigued him for a number of reasons. They'd managed to build a reputable company that offered wilderness adventures to shifters and humans unlike anything he'd come across in the region or the country for that matter.

Through discreet inquiries Brady also knew they were well on their way to bringing life back to an almost decimated coyote population. Both the natural packs that roamed this mountain range and the shifter pack who called Whispering Springs and surrounding mountains home.

As sovereign and regal of the Whispering Mountain coyote shifters, the two men had strengthened the pack Brady had always thought of as his in spite of not living within its midst these last thirteen years.

His chest ached, his stomach churned, bile rising up his throat, as he thought about his father's involvement in the near destruction of the once prosperous Whispering Mountain pack.

Thinking of his father always turned his insides. Brady couldn't remember much about the man from his early years, and his mother always insisted things hadn't been as bad as their final years living on the mountain, except it didn't seem to matter how much his mother said his father had once been a better man because Brady only remembered a man with a temper, a man whose anger simmered constantly and only took a small infraction—real or perceived—to set off.

Memories of the night they fled flashed through his mind.

His father's rage before he'd stormed out of the house leaving bruises behind. His mother throwing things in bags, racing from room to room taking very few of their possessions, before finally ushering them outside. Marcus, refusing to get in the car. The fear and desperation radiating from his mother as she frantically argued with her oldest son. Her vain attempts to drag Marcus into their beat-up old truck.

From what Brady could remember, his older brother had been stubborn and had idolized their father; his refusal to leave hadn't come as a surprise, but Marcus calling their mother a traitor and a whore had.

Brady had never wanted to hurt someone as badly as he had that night. He'd wanted to punch his brother in the face until he shut up and did what their mom wanted. Especially after she'd given up and climbed behind the wheel, her gaze fixed on the road ahead, never once looking back at the son she left behind.

She'd cried the whole fourteen hours she drove. Silent tears that streamed down her face and soaked her shirt.

He had never felt more useless or terrified in his life. At fourteen he'd been too young to defend her against his brute of a father but he had succeeded in avoiding confrontations during his early teens, protecting her as best he could by not setting off his father's rage. His efforts had never been enough.

Everything had come crashing down around them the night they left. The whole world had shifted beneath his feet with one act of violence his mother couldn't ignore.

Malcolm Connelly would stop at nothing to gain sovereign.

Not even murder.

Ironic how murder had driven Brady out of the mountains and murder brought him back.

A heavy sigh left his chest; the weight of all he faced sat on his shoulders like his favorite hiking pack. A burden he had no choice but to carry. Not if he wanted to stay. And he wanted to stay.

He didn't know what kind of reception he would receive from the pack members, especially after recent events, but he hadn't expected coming home to be easy. Not after the way he and his mother had fled. With a deep breath, he straightened his spine and focused on the town that as of today would be his home once more.

Punching the accelerator, he shot forward with a little more haste than necessary and drove toward his future.

In less than a minute he was driving down the town's main street. Slowing to walking pace, he scrutinized the shops lining the road, seeing familiar stores as he headed toward the Den Cafe. The cafe had been a fundamental part of life in Whispering Springs from before Brady was born. It didn't only serve great food, it served as a meeting point, a social outing, a place for pack members to congregate, to catch up, and, for the older generation, a place to gossip.

It wasn't surprising that Brogan had suggested Brady meet him and Quinn there. He remembered them both from before he left but he wasn't sure if they remembered him. They had to have recognized his name though.

No one had mentioned who he was—or the other reason for his return to the mountains—during his interview but they knew he'd grown up in Whispering Springs. They'd spoken on the phone several times over the last few weeks and Brady felt comfortable accepting the position with their adventure company even if returning to the mountain left him with a mix of anxiety and excitement.

Funny how something he'd longed for for years could bring such conflicting emotions.

On the one hand, he couldn't wait to return to the town he loved and missed. On the other, he feared the very people he'd thought of as family for the first fourteen years of his life. *Still* thought of that way if he were honest.

The cafe came into view and Brady quickly searched the street for a parking spot. Seeing one just beyond his destination, he sped up and slipped his truck between two off-road vehicles. He set the parking brake and turned the engine off except he didn't get out.

Muscles taut and chest heavy as though a weight pressed down on it, crushing the air from his lungs, he took a moment to get himself together. After several deep breaths, Brady grunted. With determination and a small amount of self-disgust, he yanked the keys from the ignition and popped his door.

Since the night his mother took him from his home, he'd vowed to never let fear stop him. And in the last thirteen years he'd kept that promise. He wasn't about to break it now.

He'd already broken the one he'd given his mother on her deathbed. Not that he could have done otherwise. He hadn't had anything to do with his brother in over decade and even he wasn't stupid enough to think he could have changed the outcome of his brother's life by making contact sooner.

No, his brother's destiny had been set in motion all those years ago when Marcus had chosen to stay with their father instead of leaving with their mother.

With more force than warranted, Brady shoved his door wide and climbed out. Slamming it shut behind him, he locked the truck and headed for the Den Cafe.

Encountering no one on the sidewalk, he breathed in and out, slow and steady, his stride becoming more relaxed with each breath of crisp mountain air and step he took.

Only a thin layer of snow crunched beneath his boots. It had been days since the last snowfall, but it was still the middle of winter in Whispering Springs and crisp was a polite way to say the air froze your nose hairs and cracked your lungs.

The temperature might be mild today, the sky a blinding winter-blue, but it was still bone-chillingly cold.

In spite of the cold and his apprehension, Brady felt the town—his home—seeping into his bones, embracing his soul, and warming his heart.

Glancing up and down the street, he smiled.

God, it was good to be home.

Not one to hide his head in the sand, he didn't think for a second that this was anything except the calm before the storm. There would be plenty to face the minute the townspeople realized who he was. He was prepared to meet whatever they threw at him; he'd come home for good, and no matter what his brother and father had done in the past, it wouldn't stop him from being here and claiming his place in the pack of his birth.

A bell jingled above his head as he pushed through the door. The sounds of people chatting, utensils scratching on plates, hit him like a brick wall, and he smiled at the homey feel of the cafe. Stepping inside, he shut the door, blocking out the cold, and scanned the tables for Brogan and Quinn.

As his gaze passed each group, silence followed as though an invisible soundproof blanket was being laid over the room. By the time he'd located the two men he sought in a back booth, you could hear a pin drop even without the added bonus of shifter hearing.

Brady stiffened his spine and returned the smiles of the men waving him over. With deliberate steps and head high, he moved in their direction; clamping down on the anxiety eating a hole in his gut, he kept the smile on his face and his gaze on target.

He'd made it halfway across the room when it hit him.

Raw, scraping need stole the breath from his lungs and snapped every muscle in his body rigid, tore at his nerves with razor sharp edges.

What the fuck?

His groin pulsed and his cock grew hard from one heartbeat to the next. He'd left his jacket in the truck and the sweater he wore barely skimmed his hips; his jeans, old favorites, hid nothing if someone were to look. God, he hoped nobody looked.

Clenching his jaw and eyes focused straight ahead, he moved as quick as his locked muscles allowed toward the far booth and the men he'd come to meet.

Reaching the table he held out a hand to the pack's sovereign and his new boss. "Brogan."

"Brady." Brogan's grip was strong, confident. "You made good time."

"I did." Turning to the other owner of Wild Encounters and the pack's regal, Brady offered his hand again. "Quinn."

"Brady, good to have you here," Quinn said with a quick shake.

Brogan motioned for Brady to take a seat and he slid into the booth as both men took the bench seat opposite.

"Did most of the driving at night. Plus I got away earlier than I'd planned from Nebraska," he explained. "Once I made up my mind to make the move, I wanted to get here. Get started."

He jerked in his seat as another wave of lust slammed into him. His gaze skimmed the room but he couldn't pinpoint the woman who had to be here.

"Something wrong?" Quinn asked.

"Huh?" He brought his gaze back to the men across the table. "No. No. Just taking the place in. It's not all that different from the last time I was here."

Brady hoped neither man saw through his lie. Not that the place had changed, that part wasn't the lie, but he hadn't lived in a pack since leaving Whispering Springs at fourteen; he couldn't tell if they were able to sense his deception—his discomfort.

He'd been around other shifters over the years and in spite of his mother's assertions not all coyote shifters were like his father, they had never joined another pack. She hadn't left his heritage in the past though; she'd told him about every aspect of being a coyote so he knew what was happening right now even if he wasn't sure what to do about it.

Never in a million years did he think he'd find his mate the first day he came back to town.

Except coyote instincts didn't lie, and right now his were screaming his mate was right here.

In the Den Cafe.

2

———

Jeez, Kat was tired. There were still hours left in the day and she was dragging her feet as though her boots were filled with concrete. Getting up at six to open the cafe hadn't bothered her until now. Then again, she was currently getting up at four and driving up to Steve McKenna's place where her sister was laid up with a busted arm.

They might be coyote shifters with quicker healing than humans but snapping the bones in your arm so they stuck out through your skin still required the help of human medical practices to repair. Besides, Gordie couldn't cook to save her life even with two arms so Kat had been going up each morning and making her and Steve breakfast, leaving pre-made lunch and dinner in their fridge too.

After today Gordie would still have to take it easy, but the cast would be off her arm. Both Steve and Gordie had protested for the last few weeks about Kat's hovering and she had to admit, if only to herself, that it had nothing to do with Gordie's busted arm or lack of cooking skills.

God. She hated thinking about what her sister had endured at the hands of that madman. It made her equal parts murderous and sick to her stomach. Kat would have killed Marcus herself if Gordie hadn't already taken care of that.

Closing her eyes for a moment, she drew in a deep breath to calm down. She'd hold it together. Like she had for weeks now. Since the moment she'd followed her parents into the clinic and seen her sister lying in a pool of blood.

The image would never leave her. It was as though it had been etched on the inside of her eyelids. Except it wasn't a black and white image. No. It was technicolor bright and all too real, right down to the metallic stench lining her nostrils.

No one knew Kat had been inside the clinic that day because she'd had to race outside and throw up in the dumpster behind the clothing store. By the time she'd pulled herself together the place had filled with people and Gordie had been checked out and allowed to go home with Steve.

It had taken more strength than Kat thought she possessed not to follow them up the mountain. If it wasn't for Dad's promise that Gordie only had bumps and bruises, she would have. The reassurance hadn't stopped her from going without sleep for a solid week though.

She'd finally gotten that anxiety under control when Gordie had tripped on the stairs and tumbled down, snapping her arm in two. One more sight Kat couldn't erase from her memory. Along with the terror of not being able to grab her sister before she fell.

As quick as her reflexes were, they hadn't helped when she'd been too far away from Gordie when she'd tripped.

Her sister had had far too much drama in her life and Kat hoped now that Gordie had admitted and accepted her mating with Steve, all the crap was behind her. She'd do everything in her power to make sure Gordie had nothing but happy days for the rest of her life.

She figured Steve had the same goal. That man had been trying to catch her sister's attention for years. Ever since Gordie had returned to Whispering Springs to take over from their father as the pack's doctor.

Thinking of her father made Kat smile. It was good to have their parents home for a while even if the circumstances for their extended stay weren't the best. Neither of them wanted to go traveling in their RV until they were sure Gordie was settled. Which meant Kat had to put up with a few reminders about being single but she could handle those for now.

Besides, she didn't think it would be long before Steve knocked Gordie up and that would take the pressure off by giving her parents something better than Kat's single status to occupy their minds.

Smiling, she headed into the storeroom. She'd grab a box of straws and restock before the lunch crowd got crazy. Not that she needed to worry; her staff were competent and capable. In fact, with Wendy in charge of the lunch shift, they didn't need Kat getting in the way and usually she didn't. After the morning rush, she'd normally head upstairs to her apartment for a few hours before coming back down to relieve Wendy and to handle the dinner shift.

Wendy had been around for as long as Kat could remember. Granny Roe had hired the young single mom before the doors to the Den had opened and the woman had proven her worth time and time again. Especially in the years between Granny Roe's death and Kat being ready to take control of the cafe she'd received as her inheritance. And while Wendy wasn't old or not able to do the job, now that she was in charge Kat preferred to open and close the doors each day. Just like Granny Roe had done before her.

She'd been four when Granny Roe died and while Kat's memories were few, they were all fresh, bright, and happy, and as clear as though they'd happened yesterday. She fondly remembered all the times she'd been here, in the kitchen and out the front, following Granny Roe around as she'd served drinks and food, chatting with customers.

Her granny had made this place into the heart of Whispering Springs without effort. It was just the way the woman was. She welcomed everyone with a wide smile and open arms.

Kat could only hope to emulate Granny. She'd be happy if she was a fifth as welcoming and nurturing as Granny Roe had been.

Crouching down she reached for a box on the bottom shelf. Her fingers brushed the side of the box when desire exploded in her belly, snapping her upright and dropping her back on her ass. Her pussy heated, pulsed, and dampened. Her breathing hitched, quickening and shallowing to raspy gasps, and perspiration broke out on her skin; goose bumps shimmered over her body as though invisible fingers tickled her flesh.

What the fuck?

Her gaze bounced around the storeroom. Alone. She was alone.

Squeezing her eyes tight, she took a deep breath and tried to focus, tried to work out what the hell was going on.

It was there, a scent, a connection—foreign and yet...somehow familiar.

Someone I know?

No man in Whispering Springs had called to her coyote. She'd lived here all her life, not setting foot off the mountain for more than a day or two, never wanting to. Kat, swallowed, a dry mouth and constricted throat making it difficult. Chills raced up and down her spine in spite of the heat blazing inside her.

Her head cocked to one side as a shiver of knowledge rolled through her. He knew she was here; she could feel him searching for her—his coyote reaching for hers. She jerked, muscles quivering with tension while her coyote tugged to be free.

She couldn't place who had her coyote clawing for release. Didn't readily recognize the scent or connection.

A stranger?

Another wave of heat and need rolled through her making her moan.

God. This couldn't be happening. She was sure she didn't know who had her inner animal wanting to burst free so she could roll over and submit. It had to be a stranger despite of the familiarity she felt.

A stranger in town wasn't necessarily a bad thing except she wasn't about to welcome her mate with open arms. Not until she knew who he was. Even then, mate or not, Kathren Joy Monroe would not allow her inner animal to dictate who she spent the rest of her life with. She was in charge of her own future and she wasn't about to let some *mate* change where she saw it going.

Shaking herself, Kat bent forward to retrieve the box of straws she'd come in for. There was no use putting it off, she'd just march out into the restaurant and see who her supposed mate was. Only when she pushed to her feet her legs wouldn't work properly, her knees shook, and when she left the storeroom she wobbled like she had after she'd shifted the first time.

Frustrated at her lack of control, she tossed the box on the countertop and leaned against the kitchen wall. She prided herself on her self-control and to lose it so quickly annoyed and angered her.

The anger was good. She could work with that, channel it and focus it on the problem. Clenching her fists she straightened her spine and steeled her resolve.

Nothing and no one made Kat's decisions for her, including her coyote half.

Gordie said she was a control freak but Kat just liked to make her own choices—decide her own path. She had a clear goal when it came to her life, and she was well on her way to achieving it; there was no way she would let some stranger—her supposed *mate*—derail her because their animals were meant to be together.

Fucking stupid fated-mate bullshit.

For the first time in her life she cursed her coyote genes.

"Hey, boss, you all right?"

Wendy's question broke Kat from her thoughts. Turning her head, she saw the older woman carrying a huge tray of dirty dishes just inside the door leading to the dining area.

Forcing a smile, she pushed off the wall. "Yeah, taking a moment to catch my breath. I've been run off my feet all day and that day started well before dawn."

"You still checking in with your sister each morning before work?" Wendy's voice was laced with concern, her forehead wrinkled in a frown as she made her way across the kitchen. "I can't believe she snapped her arm in half walking down a flight of stairs."

Kat couldn't either. Gordie had fought off a madman and come away with barely a scratch, then she'd slipped at the top of the stairs in the house she shared with her new husband, Steve, and tumbled to the bottom. Kat shook her head. Her sister had come out of that incident with a busted arm, a concussion, and a huge dose of embarrassment.

"Today was the last day. She got the cast off this morning so she'll be able to drive from now on. Not that she hasn't tried to already." Kat scowled, a grumble of displeasure leaving her throat at the thought of her sister attempting the treacherous snow-covered mountain roads with a cast on her arm.

Wendy laughed as she laid the heavy tray on the counter by the sink and opened the dishwasher. "Why does that not surprise me? Honestly, you Monroe women are all alike. Never let anything stop you from doing what you want. Stubborn to the core the lot of you," Wendy said as she glanced over her shoulder at Kat, her twinkling eyes and smile showing her words weren't meant as an insult.

Kat grinned. Wendy was right, although Kat preferred the word determined. Her friend's observations reminded her she didn't have to let the appearance of her *mate* interfere with her life.

Monroe females were independent, capable women who did what they set out to do, and they didn't need a man to get it done. She needed to remember that and continue to take her own path as Granny Roe, her mother, and sister had before her.

"I like to think we're determined." Kat walked over and reached for a stack of bowls. "And capable. There isn't anything a Monroe woman can't do."

"Being capable and determined doesn't mean you shouldn't accept help, young lady. There's greater strength in accepting help than there is in doing it alone. Take this place. You couldn't do it without all of us."

Kat's gaze jumped to Wendy's. "That's different."

Wendy shook her head. "No, it isn't, but I'm not arguing with you about it. We've got a full restaurant out there. Let's get this load in and started before we run out of clean plates."

In silence they packed the dishwasher and when the last plate was in Wendy closed the door and hit start.

"Right. Back to the trenches. Where you don't need me because you're capable but I'm helping anyway," Wendy said with a wink before striding across the room and slipping through the door to the restaurant.

Kat shook her head and pondered Wendy's words. The older woman made sense except Kat didn't think it applied to her current situation at all. Running the Den had nothing in common with finding your mate. It was two completely different things. This was a business. A mate was for life. She already had her life mapped out and nowhere on there was a mate mentioned.

Bracing herself, she followed Wendy's path and pushed through the swinging doors.

Time to face this new hurdle to the future she'd mapped out for herself and find a way over, under, around, or through it—*him*.

3

Brady's whole body tensed. Like a bowstring pulled tight ready to snap free when the arrow was released, every muscle strained to its breaking point.

Fuck.

He hadn't been prepared for this. His mother had told him what to expect when he met his mate, but *fuck*, this was way more than his imagination had conjured up.

Whoever his mate was, she moved closer. And closer.

His skin itched and his coyote howled, and it took everything he had not to shift in the middle of the cafe. With his hands clenched around the edge of his seat, he could only hope his claws didn't rip the material to shreds. He had to grind his back teeth to smother the growl rumbling up his throat and hold the shift at bay.

"You all right?" Quinn asked, a slight smirk tipping up one side of his mouth.

Nodding, Brady stretched his lips into what he hoped was a reassuring smile.

"Oh, hey, Kat, come over here and meet our newest Wild Encounters employee." Brogan waved at someone behind Brady.

Someone Brady was one hundred percent certain was his mate.

The sovereign's smile held genuine affection and Brady's coyote growled. He didn't like another man smiling at his mate. Knowing it was inevitable, Brady braced himself and turned to look at the woman Brogan waved over.

He grunted at the slam to his gut. He'd heard people talk about a metaphorical gut-punch but he'd never experienced it before and this was a one-two deal because *fuck,* he knew her. His mate.

Ren.

Jesus fucking Christ, it was *Ren.*

Brady hadn't seen her in thirteen years. Thirteen years of wondering what she was doing, what she looked like now, whether she would remember him...

"You!" Her arm shot out, finger pointed.

Okay, she remembered him.

"Get out!" That arm swung toward the door.

"Ah—" He glanced at Brogan before bringing his eyes back to Ren.

"Your kind isn't welcome here!" she yelled.

His kind? Coyote or Connelly? "Ren."

"Kat!"

The snap of authority had Brady jolting and Ren halting in her tracks. Brady pulled his gaze from Ren to find Brogan had risen to his feet, a scowl on his face that would cower the strongest of men. Only Ren didn't back down. If anything she straightened her spine and tipped her chin up.

"He's not welcome in my cafe." She crossed her arms, her defiant stand broadcasting loud and clear how she felt about him. The fact she was willing to go up against the pack sovereign said a lot about her dislike.

"It's okay." Brady got to his feet. "I should—"

"No." Brogan raised his arm, blocking Brady's way. "Kat, I understand this is difficult for you, but Brady has as much right to be here as any member of our pack."

She flinched, her gaze dropping slightly, but her anger didn't subside; she vibrated with it. "This is my business. I say who can and can't come in here. He can't."

Brogan sighed. "Kat."

"*My* business," Ren repeated.

"Fine. We'll take our meeting elsewhere." Brogan turned to Quinn. "Call Dale; we'll use the conference room at the station."

"Kathren Joy Monroe, you apologize to that young man right now."

Brady watched Ren's eyes close as she sucked in a breath, and the spectacular set of boobs she hadn't had last time he'd seen her thrust forward making his cock pulse, his coyote growl.

"Dad."

"Don't you *dad* me."

Brady looked beyond Ren to see Doc Monroe a few feet away, hands on hips. "It's okay, Doc," he reassured the older man. "I can—"

"No, it is not. There's no call for this kind of behavior. Kathren?"

"He's not welcome here," she said, a stubborn tilt to her chin as she spun to face her father.

"Here? On the mountain, in the town where he was born?" Doc took a step closer but didn't bother to lower his voice. Everyone in the room would hear him even if he whispered. "You weren't raised this way. Don't let your anger taint another with someone else's sins."

"Goddammit." Kat spun on her heel once more only this time she headed across the room to the door leading to the kitchen, calling over her shoulder, "Fine. But I don't have to be in the same room as *him*." She spat out the word 'him' as though it tasted foul on her tongue.

Brady's lips twitched with the urge to smile. He remembered Ren being full of blunt honesty. It was one of the things he'd liked most about her when they were kids. There were plenty of other reasons to like Ren Monroe—then and now if the curve of her ass and sway of her hips was any indication. Of course that could be because his mate was definitely in the cafe.

She fucking *owned* the place.

"I'm sorry, son." Doc Monroe's voice dragged his gaze off Ren's retreating ass. "It's been a rough few weeks. Still, that's no excuse for Kat's behavior."

"Why do you call her Kat?" Brady asked. "She was always Ren."

"She was..." Doc Monroe frowned, deep furrows forming on his brow and either side of his mouth. "That changed after you left."

Brady didn't know what to make of that. He had been the one to nickname her Ren when they were toddlers, unable to get his tongue around Kathren he'd shortened it. They'd spent so much time together over the years. His mother had been Doc Monroe's office manager and she'd taken care of Brady, his brother, Ren, and her sister, whenever they weren't in school while doing her job.

Shaking himself from the past, he held out his hand. "It's been a while. It's good to see a familiar face."

"I bet it is." Doc shook his hand, his other cupping their joined hands in a warm clasp that had Brady's hope for a smooth transition back into the pack growing. "When you're ready, come by the clinic and we'll deal with a few things so you can get settled at home without all that hanging over your head."

"Thank you. I'll head your way as soon as I finish with Brogan and Quinn."

"We're done, Brady. You're hired, all your paperwork is filed, you have the office address, the spring schedule, and a start date. We weren't planning on an official meeting, more a welcome to Wild Encounters lunch," Brogan explained.

"Oh."

Quinn laughed. "I'm not sure I'd eat here if I were you though." With a glance toward the kitchen, the regal murmured, "Who knows what Kat is up to back there."

"She'd better be putting the finishing touches on my lunch. Don't worry, Brady, she always packs too much, you won't go hungry." The older man patted his back. "Why don't you head on outside and wait for me? We'll walk across to the clinic together."

"Okay, sir. Thank you." Brady looked at Brogan. "Are you sure we've got everything sorted out?"

Nodding, Brogan said, "Yes. And don't worry about Kat. She'll come round."

Brady didn't think she'd be coming around any time soon. From what he knew, his brother had tried to kill her sister. He'd be lucky if Ren got over that by the time he was a hundred.

He shook hands with Brogan and Quinn, telling them to call if they needed anything between now and his first day of work. Making his way outside, he ignored the quiet that had fallen over the cafe during the confrontation with Ren.

Out on the sidewalk, he took a deep breath and once again studied the changes to downtown. Across the street the clinic and the clothing store appeared to have had facelifts. The bookshop on the other side of the clothes shop was new. He might duck in there before heading out to the house.

The house that was now his, according to the lawyer who'd called after Marcus's death. Brady could only assume their father had left the house they'd grown up in to Marcus because it was the same address.

He thought about the packet of information the lawyer had overnighted the first week of January. All Brady had been able to bring himself to do was read the letter from the lawyer. He'd have to deal with all the other papers eventually. According to his brother's lawyer, there was nothing pressing.

His gaze returned to the clinic across the street. Nothing pressing except dealing with his brother's body.

Before he could go down that dark road of thought, the door behind him opened and Doc Monroe came out carrying a bag of delicious smelling food.

"Come on, son, let's go tuck into this hearty lunch before we have to deal with the unpleasant stuff. No point spoiling our appetites."

If whatever was in the bag tasted as good as it smelled, Brady would work twice as hard to get Ren to forgive him. "Lead the way."

"I'll warn you in advance. Gordana is at the clinic today."

Brady's step hitched and he stumbled off the curb. "Is that going to be a problem?"

"Not for me. Not for Gordana either." Doc Monroe shook his head. "You aren't to blame for what your brother or father did, Brady."

He took the squeeze Doc Monroe gave his shoulder as a supportive gesture and soaked in the comfort of knowing this man and the woman his brother had tried to kill didn't hold a grudge. It was a shame Ren didn't follow their lead.

"I'm not sure what I'm supposed to do with Marcus," he mumbled as they crossed the street.

"You don't have to make a rush decision on that. We can continue to hold his body for as long as you need."

"That doesn't seem fair. Or right. Not after..." Slowing on the sidewalk in front of the clinic, Brady attempted to communicate his feelings. "You shouldn't have to deal with this at all."

"Not much choice. We deal with the dead as well as the living as the only two doctors in town. Life is full of unpleasantness that we must work our way through."

"But—"

"No buts." Doc Monroe opened the door to the clinic. "It is what it is, and we do what we have to when we have to."

Brady grabbed the door, held it open, and waved Doc Monroe in ahead of him. "Thank you. I'm still going to make this as painless for everyone as possible."

"Dad? That you?" The woman's voice could only belong to Gordana Monroe, and Brady took a deep breath and stopped just inside the reception area.

"Yep. I've got lunch and a visitor." Doc Monroe continued across the room toward the hallway that Brady assumed led to the back of the clinic.

The place had been renovated while he'd been gone. The reception desk now sat to the left instead of the right and the way to the exam rooms sat directly opposite the front door. To his right was an area filled with kids' toys and a small bookshelf loaded with books. Above that, on a wall mount, hung a flat-screen TV currently playing a cartoon.

Back when his mother ran the office, there had been a smaller children's area she'd made in one corner of the room where the reception desk now took up space. Gone was the timber wall paneling; in its place a coat of bright, crisp white paint and a couple of colorful posters with letters and numbers in the kids' area but otherwise the walls remained bare.

Strangely it didn't feel sterile and cold like other doctors' offices. He couldn't remember if it had in the past but he liked the welcoming feeling this room gave him.

"Brady?"

"Huh?" He stopped his study of the room and met Doc Monroe's gaze. "I like what you've done with the place."

"You can thank Gordana for that. When she took over, she spruced up the place and rearranged a few things, giving us a dedicated exam room for children. I have to admit, she's improved the place even when it was already functional and worked well enough. C'mon, let's take this food into the break room and chow down before it goes cold."

Following Doc Monroe, he entered the hallway as a woman stepped out of a room at the other end. Brady stopped. He hadn't seen Ren's sister in longer than he'd been gone but he'd recognize her anywhere. In spite of them only sharing a mother, the Monroe girls looked a lot alike.

Sucking in a breath, he let it out slowly before saying, "Hello, Gordie."

Her head snapped up from the sheet of paper she was studying, her gaze connecting with his. "Brady?" Her eyes widened before a smile stretched across her face. "Oh my god! Brady Connelly!"

He wasn't prepared for the warmth in her greeting and he definitely wasn't prepared for her to race down the corridor and launch herself into his arms.

Squeezing him tight, she said, "It's so good to see you."

Returning her hug and closing his eyes, he muttered, "It's really good to see you too."

And he meant it. The thought of his brother succeeding in

hurting this woman had him shuddering. The fact she'd hurt—killed—Marcus didn't cause him a flicker of animosity or anger. All he felt while he held Gordana Monroe close was relief.

Relief that his brother hadn't damaged this woman. It remained to be seen how much his brother and father had damaged the Whispering Mountain pack and Brady's chance of being accepted back into the fold.

4

Brady slowed down when he came to the turn that was familiar but not.

The trees along the drive had grown taller, their canopies thicker, and newer, smaller trees sprouted out of the ground between them. He couldn't tell if the flowers his mother had planted at the sides of the property entrance were still alive under the layer of snow covering everything or if the forest had reclaimed the flowerbeds she'd spent so much time tending.

One thing he could tell was the neglect of the driveway. Even with the snow he could see tall grass grew on what was once a gravel track. He'd have to fix that. It shouldn't be too hard but he'd need to wait until spring to do a proper job.

Having four-wheel drive helped navigate what amounted to off-road conditions but he still brought the truck to a crawl as he bumped along. Inch by inch he made his way toward the house he'd always thought of as home.

Even when it had resembled a war zone.

It had been all he'd known for his first fourteen years. Strange how almost as many years away couldn't change that deep sense of connection. The home Hank had given Brady and his mother had been a sanctuary compared to the house he slowly made his way toward and yet, this one would always be home in his heart.

Excitement and trepidation mixed together to make his nerves dance, his chest tighten.

He expected to find the place rundown, especially since no one had lived here for weeks, and he had no idea if his father or Marcus had looked after the place over the years. Throw in the storm that had swept across the mountain Christmas Day and he wouldn't be surprised to find snow had caved the roof in, and no doubt the pipes would be frozen.

Power would be an issue too. He had planned for the possibility of camping out. Good thing he didn't mind the cold and he'd come well equipped for both the freezing temperatures and being out in the open.

The back of his truck was packed with gear. He had everything he needed to spend a night or more outdoors. He would have to figure out what repairs he needed to do fast though. They were due to get another round of snowstorms next week.

Roof and pipes would be first. Windows, doors, walls. Probably should put a generator on that list too. He didn't think the one here would still run. Lots of work to do before spring arrived.

Two months.

Roughly two months to get his life in order before he took his first set of adventurers into the mountains. Brogan and Quinn shut their operation down through the winter months but everything fired up again the last week in March. Day treks, overnighters, and the longer camping trips happened March through October.

Brady had jumped at the chance to work at Wild Encounters. He'd heard a bit about them from people he'd guided at his old job. It wasn't until his mother had died last year that he'd even entertained the idea of coming home. But when he'd heard of the job opening and that his father was no longer sovereign, he couldn't apply fast enough.

He'd accepted the position only days before he received the call about his brother.

The news hadn't changed Brady's desire to come home. If anything, it had grown greater—more urgent.

There were so many ghosts that needed to be put to rest. Discovering his father's body lay in the cold-storage unit alongside Marcus had been a shock. He hadn't felt anything either way about the demise of the man who'd raised him. Probably because Malcolm Connelly had very little hand in making Brady the man he was. That had been all his mother's doing. And the man she'd sought refuge with all those years ago.

Brady smiled when he thought of Hank. He'd never met the man before that day, but the relief coming off his mother when they arrived on Hank's doorstep had been obvious. He knew they'd found someone they could trust.

Hank, according to Brady's mother, was an old friend. It took a few years for Brady to fully figure out what kind of old friend Hank was.

They'd been lovers before. And after.

In the years following their arrival, Hank had proven time and time again his love for Brady's mother as well as Brady. If he were honest, Brady would admit to wishing more than once that Hank *was* his father, that they'd always lived on the farm in Nebraska.

When Hank died in a freak accident out in the fields, Brady had felt as though part of himself had been ripped away. To say his mother had been devastated was understating it. She'd curled in on herself and left the work she'd once shared and enjoyed with Hank to their employees.

Brady still couldn't believe how much Hank's place was worth or that he'd left it all to him and his mom.

Things had been different after the accident; his mother barely talked, never smiled, and as her health deteriorated, Brady knew he'd be saying goodbye to her soon. On her death bed, she'd made him promise to find his brother. Make peace with Marcus.

He still wasn't sure what she'd hoped to achieve by extracting that promise but it was too late now to keep it. Then again, he stared through the windshield as his childhood home came into view;

maybe he could find peace for himself. Put some ghosts to rest and make a future here, in the house where he'd been born.

Surprise filled him when he pulled up in front of the house. The place wasn't nearly as rundown as he expected. If he didn't know better, he'd think someone still lived here. Except there was no smoke coming from either of the chimneys and if someone was here they'd have at least one fire roaring to warm the place up.

Turning off the truck, Brady climbed out and looked around. Other than the layer of snow covering everything, the whole area had a lived-in feeling. He supposed it had been lived in until a few weeks ago. From what Sheriff Turner had told him in their one brief phone call, Marcus had been here, teaching at the high school, until early December when he'd kidnapped the sovereign's mate and been exiled from the pack.

Brady didn't have all the information on that yet, but he planned to meet with the sheriff and find out exactly what had happened. He'd thought about asking the sovereign except Brogan was his boss and that didn't seem like the right thing to do this early in his new employment. He wanted to keep those areas of his life separate for now. They were bound to mix eventually but he wanted to make sure nothing got tangled in a way that could affect either his job or his place within the pack.

With a deep breath, Brady shook off his thoughts and moved toward the house. Shin-deep snow made the walk slow; not knowing what might lie beneath that layer of white slowed him further.

He paused at the bottom of the steps. It wasn't anxiety he felt, more a buzz of anticipation. These next steps were the first of his future.

Coming home had been the plan. Finding his mate here, in the mountains he'd spent years yearning for, to find she was someone he'd loved as a kid...

Ren.

Memories bombarded him.

She'd been his best friend—his everything—when they were younger. He'd let her boss him around, let her lead him into trouble.

Now that he'd seen her again, he couldn't fathom how he'd survived all these years without her.

It had cut him deep to leave and not look back, not try to contact her. The one time he had tried, his mother had nearly had a heart attack and made him promise to never do it again. Told him to forget about everything and everyone to do with Whispering Springs.

He'd tried to follow her wishes. He really had. Except forgetting Ren had been impossible and now he knew why. They might have been too young to understand their connection in their youth but they were both well aware of what it meant now.

The question was what they'd do about it.

She hated him.

He couldn't blame her.

Except...he couldn't accept that. Wouldn't. If it took him every breath until the day he died, Brady would work to change her mind.

He'd give her every reason to love him again.

But first he had a house to check and a list to make.

He bounded up the front steps and it wasn't until he reached the top that he thought about what a foolish move that was. The house might look lived it but that didn't mean it was sound. He could have broken a leg if one of the steps had given way under his weight.

With a little more care, Brady crossed the small porch and reached for the door. He wasn't sure why he expected it to be unlocked but he twisted the handle and pushed the door open anyway.

Frowning, he eyed the mechanism and realized it was a simple door handle without a lock at all. The back of the door didn't reveal a deadbolt either so there was no way of locking the front door. A glance down revealed something more unexpected. A metal plate with a hole at one side covered the threshold.

Brady stepped inside and pushed the door closed to inspect it more closely. What he discovered confused him a little. No deadbolt but there were two heavy duty slide bolts with padlocks. One at the bottom of the door that corresponded with the plate at his feet and another bolt at the top that fitted into a solid steel bar that spanned the doorframe.

A thought struck him and he opened the door again to recheck the outside. Frowning, he wondered how Marcus had locked the front door when he left the house. The only way to lock it was from the inside. And why would his brother need such heavy duty locks?

The door was the least of his worries though, and he headed into the living room to see what condition it was in. The fireplace was stacked ready for a match so he assumed the chimney was clear but he'd take a look when he climbed onto the roof to be sure.

Each room proved the same. While the furnishings were old and a little worse for wear, they'd do for now. Every window was nailed shut prompting more questions he didn't have a clue how to answer, and there was even some non-perishable food in the small pantry in the kitchen.

After living in the huge farm house Hank owned, Brady had some ideas of what he wanted to do with this place to improve it. First he needed to make sure the roof wouldn't collapse on his head.

Back in the kitchen he discovered where the deadbolt was. Marcus must have been coming and going through the backdoor, not the front. Although there was another set of steel bars and slide bolts with padlocks there as well.

Nailed shut windows, padlocked doors...

What the hell had Marcus been up to?

The answer to that question might not be something Brady wanted to know. Maybe the sheriff could give him a few answers.

He found the shed locked tight with yet another set of steel bars and padlocked slide bolts. He'd need to see about getting the keys or cutting them off. Catching sight of a ladder half buried beneath the snow alongside the shed, he dragged it out, and shouldering one end, continued to drag it through the snow to the back of the house where the roof was lowest.

Steadying the thing took time because he had to dig out snow to find solid ground but once he did, he was up the ladder and on the roof. He kicked snow off with his boot to see what condition the tiles were in.

"Damn." He gazed over the slope. "It's a fucking brand new roof?"

Down on his knees, Brady scraped away more snow and found the same thing. New shingles.

Marcus must have replaced it recently. His brother might not have updated any of the furniture or appliances but he'd made sure the roof held up. Which meant the chimneys were probably clear. Just in case an animal had found its way into one, Brady climbed to each and used the flashlight on his phone to check.

He wasn't a chimney sweep but he was smart enough to work out no animals had found homes inside them. Rubbing his cold hands together, he thought about starting the fire in the living room so he could defrost, then he remembered he needed to check the pipes and see if the old generator still worked.

It was going to be a long afternoon being wet and cold.

5

JANUARY 19

"He's the reason, isn't he?"

Kat swung away from the filing cabinet to find her sister standing inside the small office in the back of the Den. "What?"

"Brady. He's the reason you never followed through on all the talk about being a lawyer, about getting off the mountain?"

Sighing, Kat shook her head. "No. Not even close."

"But—"

"I never wanted to leave the mountain."

Gordie tilted her head, studied Kat as though she'd smeared her on one of those medical slides she was so fond of and pushed it under a microscope. "You're going to have to explain that to me. You never talked about staying here. Taking over the Den."

Kat laughed but there was no humor in it. "How could I? Why would I? What would you all have said if I'd voiced what I wanted? Jeez, you and Dad are doctors, Mom's a nurse. I barely made it out of high school and would have quit sooner if Mom and Dad had let me."

"What's that got to do with anything?"

"You wouldn't understand. All you ever wanted was to get away."

"No. All I ever wanted was to fit in!"

Kat eyed her sister. "Is that why you mated Anthony? To fit in?" God. How had she missed that?

Anthony had been an outsider who'd only lived in Whispering Springs a couple of years when Gordie accepted his mate claim.

Gordie glanced away. "We wanted the same thing."

God. So much of her sister's past began to make sense. "To belong."

"Yeah."

"But you did. You were, *are*, my sister. How could you think you didn't fit? I worshiped you. To the point I ignored what I wanted and said I wanted what you told me I should."

"What?"

Laughing, Kat asked, "You don't remember?" At Gordie's head shake she continued, "Jeez. We were arguing over something, I can't even remember what or when, and you said that I should be a lawyer. I would make a great lawyer because I could argue under water even when I was wrong."

"And you went with that? Jesus, Kat, you were born a nurturer. Running the Den fits you. Every time I see you I'm reminded of Granny Roe. The way you both always feed people, check they're okay. You might be bossy with it but your heart is behind it. I don't think you've met anyone you didn't want to *mother*, didn't love in some way."

"Love is not what I feel for the Connellys."

"Malcolm and Marcus."

"What?"

"It was Malcolm and Marcus. You can't tar Brady with the same brush, Kat. He was just a kid when he left here."

"He's one of them."

Gordie sighed and shook her head. "No. He was never like them; even as a kid he was different, and he hasn't been here for over a decade. Whatever it is you've got going on in your head about him, it's has nothing to do with what his father and brother did." Gordie moved closer, put her hand on Kat's arm. "What did Brady do, Kat?"

Kat's spine snapped straight. Was she so easy to read? "He's a Connelly."

"Yes. He is. But he's not the Connelly who tried to kill me. Or the one who tried to run Quinn down. Or the one who turned humans against their will and left them to suffer. Or the one who terrorized Rowen. Kidnapped El. Those and many more deeds were perpetrated by either Marcus or Malcolm Connelly. So tell me Kat. What has *Brady* ever done to us?"

"He left! Without a word. Up and gone when he'd promised!"

"Promised what?" Gordie prodded.

Sighing, Kat muttered, "He'd always be my friend. Always be there."

"When? When did he promise you that?"

"The year before he left."

"So when he was a kid, when he had no control over his life or what happened. Don't you think you owe him the opportunity to explain? Don't you want to know why he left, why he didn't come back until now?"

"No!" She yanked her arm out of her sister's grasp. "I don't care. He *lied* to me!"

Gordie grabbed her shoulders and shook her. "Stop. Stop thinking with a teenager's pain and think. Think about why, what could have made his mother pack up and leave in the middle of the night. Think about what Malcolm Connelly did to this pack while he was sovereign. Think about the things Marcus did, when he was a kid and when he was an adult. Think about those things, then think about what it must have been like to live with those two men. *Think, Kat.*" Gordie gave her another shake, harder enough to clack her teeth this time. "Think about what happened the day you asked Marcus about his brother."

Oh god.

She hadn't thought about that day in years. Brady had been gone nearly two years when she'd run into Marcus outside the cafe. She'd asked him about his brother and when he hadn't answered her, tried to brush past, she'd grabbed his arm and begged him to tell her where Brady was.

Unaware of the senior Connelly coming up behind her, she'd peppered Marcus with questions. He'd remained silent and only when his gaze drifted behind her did she turn and find an angry Malcolm staring down at her.

The sovereign had yanked her hand from Marcus's arm and bent over until his face was right in hers, his hand squeezing her forearm so hard she thought he'd break it, and yelled at her to never mention that name again.

There were more words spewed about betrayal, desertion, running away like a coward, but to this day Kat couldn't remember all that Malcolm Connelly had said because the pain in her arm had been too great. Her brain had screamed in agony, the internal screech ringing in her ears until she heard nothing else.

It was only when William Brant happened by that the sovereign let go and stepped back with a smile on his face. She definitely remembered his next words.

You be careful now, Kathren; a half-blood like yourself wouldn't want to have an accident like your sister.

It hadn't been a direct threat but the implication was there all the same. It was in his eyes too. Dark, evil eyes that made her skin crawl, made her shrink away in fear.

She hadn't said a word to anyone before sprinting away. She'd headed straight home and hadn't told anyone about it until Gordie had asked about the bruises on her arm. Swearing her sister to secrecy, she'd hidden the bruising under long sleeves until there wasn't a trace of them and never mentioned the incident again.

In fact, she'd all but wiped it from her mind.

"He's not to blame, Kat. You owe him an apology," Gordie said softly.

Kat took her sister's words for what they were. A suggestion as well as a reprimand. "I wouldn't go that far," she muttered.

"Well, maybe you could do something that would be a peace offering at least."

"Like what?"

"He's been out at the Connelly house for days. No one has seen him or heard from him and you know as well as I do if he'd been in town, you'd have heard about it at the Den from those old gossips."

"Maybe he left." Kat wasn't sure why that thought made her chest hurt and her coyote howl. Okay, fine, she knew.

Gordie arched one eyebrow but remained quiet.

"Fine. I'll see about getting some meals organized for him. I'm sure he's got work to do on the house and he's a guy so he probably can't cook anyway. He'll starve to death or freeze to death if he's left alone out there for too long."

Gordie's smile held a secret knowledge that Kat wasn't privy to.

"What? What's that smile?"

"Oh nothing. Be sure to tell him there's no rush on deciding what to do with the bodies."

"Bodies?" Kat thrust a hand up to stop her sister's reply as soon as her brain clicked. "Don't say it."

"It doesn't hurt me to say their names."

"No, but it will remind *me* and I don't need any more reminders than my memories, thanks."

"Are you ever going to admit you saw me?"

Kat's gaze locked with Gordie's. "How...?"

"Steve saw you. He told me because he thinks your constant hovering is because you're not dealing with seeing me covered in blood and thinking the worst."

"I'm dealing."

"No. You're coping."

Kat shrugged. "Same thing."

"No. It's not." Gordie reached for Kat's hand. "I'm here to talk any time you want."

"You don't need to talk about it."

"I don't now, but I did. And more importantly, I need you to know I've come to terms with what I did, Kat. I want you to accept it too."

"Accept it? Jesus, Gordie, I'd have killed him if you hadn't. The only regret I have is that *you* had to do it."

Smiling, Gordie murmured, "You sound like Steve."

"We both know you and love you, and with everything you believe in, we understand that taking a life isn't something you'd ever want to do." Unlike her. Kat still wanted to kill Marcus. If she could raise the dead she would, just so she could kill him all over again.

"No, I'd never want to but I'm comfortable with the fact I had to."

"Comfortable?"

"It was the right decision. For me and for the pack. If I had to live it again, I'd do it exactly the same."

"You would?" Kat studied her sister. Tried to gauge the truth in Gordie's words. She couldn't find any sign of a lie.

"In a heartbeat. And if I'm honest, I'd have to admit I'd tell everyone about the attack in the mountains all those months before, and all the little things that were happening at the clinic and the house, about my suspicions; I wouldn't keep those to myself so I guess I would do some of it differently."

"I was so angry with you when I found out you'd hidden all that. Especially Rowan's wedding dress. Christ, Gordie, I was *there*, in the house when you found it."

"I'm sorry. I wasn't ready to tell anyone and Steve has given me enough grief over it for everyone so you don't have to worry about my lack of disclosure going unpunished," she said with a cheeky little smile.

Kat held up a hand again. "Do not tell me about Steve's punishments."

Gordie's grin said it all. It thrilled Kat to see her so in love.

"I'm glad you're happy." She pulled her sister into a tight hug. "You deserve so much and I'm so glad you finally let Steve in. He'd give you the moon if you let him."

"I know." Gordie gave her a squeeze. "You deserve everything too. Don't do what I did. Don't let something pass you by because it's not in the *plan*."

"I'm not—"

"Don't lie to me. Lie to yourself if you have to, but you can't lie to me." Gordie let go and gripped Kat's shoulders, holding her at arm's length. "I know what it looks like, Kat. I stared at that lie in the mirror every day for years. It cost me years of happiness, almost cost me my life and it definitely came close to costing me the best future I could wish for because I refused to let Steve in. Don't be me. Let Brady in."

"It's not like that."

"Oh, really?" Gordie asked with a skeptical arch of her eyebrow and tilt of her head.

"Okay, fine." Kat pulled away and paced behind her desk, swung around, and took the three steps back again. "He's my mate."

"What?" Gordie's eyes popped wide, her mouth dropped open, then closed, opened, closed. "Mate," she whispered. "Are you sure?"

"Sure as I can be." She shrugged. "He has my coyote clawing to get out so she can roll over and offer her belly. She's never done that for a man before."

"Wow. Okay. Okay. So you really do need to apologize then."

Kat had to agree with her sister. Even if she hadn't decided to accept the mating bond with Brady, she needed to make peace with him. Needed to get to know him again. For her sake as well as his, she needed to forget his last name and all the trouble his family had caused hers.

6

JANUARY 20

Brady hated being idle so by the time he'd made sure the house was sturdy and not going to fall down around his ears, he'd started in on the renovations he'd planned out in his head.

It probably would have been better to get a builder's input but he'd worked on enough barns, sheds, and the occasional house over the years to know to check for structural support before tearing down a wall.

He'd been in the roof cavity and besides the boxes of junk and dust, he'd determined the wall between the two back bedrooms did nothing but divide the space. In his head he saw this whole rear area as a master suite.

Taking out the separating wall between the rooms would allow for a king bed and walk-in closet. He'd leave the bathroom as is for now but later he'd turn that space plus a section of the current master bedroom into an en suite and separate half-bath for guests.

That was a long way off though. He just couldn't stand doing nothing, and seeing how he had the skills, it made sense to get a start on what he wanted. It wasn't like he'd be putting anyone except himself out with the noise and mess.

He'd definitely have to engage a builder at some point in the future. He might be able to swing a hammer and throw up dry wall, but he wasn't dumb enough to tackle a second story addition without professional help, and he wanted to re-use the new roof if possible, which would definitely require an expert's opinion and know-how.

The rumble of an engine growing louder had Brady downing tools and gloves, brushing off the dust, and moving toward the front of the house. He wasn't expecting anyone although he wouldn't be averse to having a visitor. He'd always been content with his own company, but the last few days had worn on his nerves.

Then again, it could be the lingering sense of danger that seemed to permeate the house—hover in the air—that had him moving quietly around the place like he had as a kid, not staying still long enough to get in trouble.

Just this morning he'd dropped a mug in the kitchen, spilling hot coffee everywhere, and he'd flinched waiting for the slap to the back of his head his father would have delivered when Brady was younger.

Yeah, he might not be expecting anyone, but he could do with a little social interaction right now.

Stepping out on the porch, he squinted his eyes against the glare of sunlight off snow. The small windows in the back rooms didn't allow much light in. He'd have to think about replacing them with bigger ones or putting in one big one, instead of two, maybe some French doors that opened onto a small deck where he could add a hot tub.

Hmm...he really liked that idea. He'd have to pace it out later to be sure it wouldn't encroach on the yard too much.

He raised a hand to shield his eyes and focused on the direction the engine roar came from. It wasn't the driveway, whatever machine headed toward him—definitely a vehicle of some kind—came from the forest beyond the old crumbling half garage attached to the left of the house.

Brady frowned.

That had to come down. He'd build a full garage before next winter.

As he was contemplating the size of add-on needed, a large dark blur whipped around the outer edge of the lopsided building, spraying snow as it turned, and he blinked.

Was that a snowmobile towing a...

Rubbing a fist over each eye, he concentrated on the sight in front of him.

Yep. A snowmobile pulling a sled. He couldn't tell by looking who was driving but his coyote instincts certainly knew.

Ren.

Brady didn't know what to think. It had been five days since the scene in her cafe.

Five days of wondering if she'd ever come around. Wondering what he could do to help change her mind about him.

Seeing Gordie—now known as Doc—at the clinic when he'd followed Doc Monroe that first day had given him hope that he could regain Ren's favor. Neither Monroe had said a word against him. Or his brother, for that matter, and if anyone had the right to hold animosity, it was Gordana Monroe.

The only time any of his family were mentioned was when they'd asked him what he wanted to do with the bodies of his brother and father. He hadn't known they had kept his father on ice since last year. Gordie had explained their reluctance to bury him but also confessed to wanting to use his body for research.

Brady had no opinion on that. He actually didn't care what they did with his father. They'd never been close. The role of favorite son had gone to Marcus, and look what that had gotten him. Brady was more than happy to have been the forgotten one.

He watched Ren maneuver the snowmobile to position the sled close to the house. He'd offer to help, but at this point he couldn't be sure she wasn't here to kill him and load his body on that sled to be carted off into the mountains and buried, never to be found.

Grinning at the thought, Brady watched his mate carefully. Hoping for any clue that would indicate her mood or reason for being here.

When the engine switched off, Ren removed her goggles and

gloves, and remained sitting on the big machine while she gave him a once over.

"So you are alive then," she called out with a smirk.

"Was there doubt?" He walked down the steps to join her in the yard. A yard he'd spent two days clearing of as much snow as he could.

"Some." She glanced at the house behind him. "No one seemed to know what condition this place was in or whether you came with supplies, and you haven't been to town since you arrived."

He couldn't hold back a grin. "Checking up on me?"

"Hell no! Damn old codgers won't shut up about you. I can't serve a drink or meal without one of them telling me something about the *prodigal son*."

Brady frowned. "Prodigal doesn't seem the right word…"

"No, but those old coots think it is. I'm not going to point out their mistake. Besides, it would just keep them talking about you."

"Oh, and you can't have that." To avoid digging deeper into their —her—animosity, he tipped his chin toward the sled and asked, "What's all that?"

Ren hopped off the snowmobile and headed for her cargo. "I brought you a few things."

He was so shocked by her words that she had the straps off and the cover thrown back to reveal bags and boxes of supplies before he could get his brain to work and engage his mouth. At a complete loss for words, Brady stood there open-mouthed while Ren picked up a box and turned.

"Y-you brought me food?" he finally stammered, disbelief clear in his voice and no doubt on his face.

She shrugged, the box lifting in her arms. "Just a few things."

Grinning he stepped closer. "You were worried about me."

"No. There's a storm rolling in late tonight, early tomorrow. We're expecting a few days of solid snowfall, about two feet worth, and I don't want my sister to have to come out here to recover your body when you freeze or starve to death."

He moved closer, pressed his torso right up against her forearms, trapping them between his chest and the box. "You *were* worried about me," he whispered, the hope bursting to life inside him dripping from each word.

"No." She tilted her chin up a notch. "I'd be worried about anyone stuck out in the middle of nowhere."

"Really? So you've been dropping off supplies all over the mountain this morning?" Brady knew she hadn't. The flush in her cheeks wasn't only due to the cold. They'd gotten rosier the more he talked, the closer he'd gotten.

"No. Jeez. Here." She shoved into him making him take a step back and grab the box. "Just take that inside already."

A smile on his face, Brady did as directed. He wouldn't tell her he'd planned to make a trip into town this afternoon. He'd arrived with enough food and water to get him through two weeks but that had been more a precaution than necessity, and the trip to town was more about seeing Ren than picking up supplies.

He thought the house would be without running water or electricity when he arrived so he'd come prepared. It had been a pleasant surprise to find both still functioning once he'd fired up the generator that wasn't as old as he'd assumed it would be.

The supply of fuel he found in the garage would last at least a month and the fairly new furnace in the basement proved more than adequate to heat the three bedroom house once he'd fiddled with the thermostat.

"It's not as bad as I thought it would be," Ren observed behind him.

Glancing over his shoulder, he saw she had a second overloaded box in her arms. He ignored her comment and asked, "How much stuff did you bring me?"

Her cheeks blushed a deeper pink and she looked away before saying, "Just some staples."

Brady looked in the box he put on the kitchen table, then the one she placed beside it. "And by staples you mean the whole grocery store?" he asked with a raised brow.

It didn't look as though she'd forgotten anything; there was even a two-pack of toilet paper. Without a word, she spun on her heel and headed back out front.

Sighing, he followed. "Ren."

"It's Kat," she argued. "No one calls me Ren anymore."

The tone of her voice told him the subject of why was off limits. He'd get to the bottom of that though. After talking with Doc Monroe and Gordie—he couldn't get used to thinking of Gordie as Doc yet—the other day, he had a horrible suspicion that the name change was about him.

He couldn't imagine what it had been like for her when he'd disappeared. They'd been inseparable and he'd left without a word. Obviously he'd hurt her. If she'd felt anywhere near the level of pain he had over losing her, he could understand why she'd be so angry at him.

Why she'd not want anything to do with anyone named Connelly. In one way or another they'd all hurt her deeply.

Brady had a lot of making up to do. And he'd need to explain why he'd left, why he hadn't contacted her. He just hoped she could forgive him. For now he'd do everything he could to show her he was nothing like his brother or father and that he and his mother had been as much victims of their violence as the Whispering Mountain pack.

"Okay, Kathren, let me get that," he said, moving around her to pick up the box she reached for.

"Sure." She stepped back, her arms folded over her chest, eyes narrowed.

He scanned the sled as he grabbed the box and stopped. "Is all this for me?" Jesus. She really hadn't left anything out if this was all meant for him.

"Yes."

Brady could tell she didn't want to admit that, but what else could she do? She was here, with all these supplies; there was no denying she'd gotten them for him. Struck by a sudden thought, he asked, "How much do I owe you?"

"Nothing."

"Ren—" He froze at the look on her face.

"Nothing," she said with a stubborn tip of her chin.

"I can't let you—"

"You owe me nothing."

There was something playing in her eyes, something he thought he should know, except she pushed past him to grab more supplies before he could figure it out.

Leaving it for now, he headed into the house to unload. By the time they'd brought everything inside, he'd worked out his next step.

"Let me fix us some lunch. It's the least I can do after all this."

"Can you cook?" Ren inquired, one dark eyebrow arching.

He grinned. "I can open a tin of soup. Slap some cheese on bread."

"Ha." She unzipped her jacket, slipped it off her shoulders, and dropped it over the back of a chair before rummaging through a bag. "Good thing I brought a few ready meals then. I don't have time to whip something up."

Ready meals? Brady's smile spread as he set about emptying the bags and boxes and putting the food away while Ren organized lunch.

She might be saying one thing but she definitely meant another. The woman had brought pre-made food. She'd been more than worried about him. She'd thought about him for a while if all the containers of food ready to go in the freezer were an indication.

Maybe, like him, she hadn't been able to think about anything other than their connection since they'd laid eyes on each other five days ago.

He wasn't stupid though. He'd keep his mouth shut for now. One step at a time.

She was here. At his house. And she wasn't yelling at him or throwing him out. Progress.

The one thing that really gave him hope was all the supplies she'd brought with her.

She was taking care of him. She might not want to call it that, but he saw it for what it was.

Ren looked after those she cared about.

Brady wasn't sure what had happened or changed since he'd seen her last but he wasn't going to look a gift horse in the mouth. He'd take it as a good sign and not question it further.

As far as he was concerned they were heading in the right direction and he hadn't had to do a thing.

With effort, he'd have her loving him again in no time.

7

Kat was grateful that Brady hadn't pressed her about what she'd done. She couldn't really explain her actions to herself so telling him was out of the question.

She'd spent the last five days on tenterhooks waiting for him to show up at the Den. It had never entered her mind that he would take her at her word. She thought for sure he'd be there the next day. Or even after he'd dealt with the details of his brother's body that first day.

Instead he'd gone away and not come back. She couldn't explain the pain that brought her. She hadn't been surprised though. He'd left before. She'd expected him to leave again.

Why she'd thought that, she didn't know. It wasn't as though he'd made a habit of leaving exactly; he'd only ever done it once. Except he'd disappeared without a word. And not one since either. Her subconscious obviously thought he'd repeat that behavior even if her mind had started to see what little choice he would have had in the decision to leave Whispering Springs.

When Brady and his mother had first disappeared, his father had told everyone they'd gone to visit a sick relative and would be back. Days turned into weeks turned into months, and before she knew it, he'd been gone a year and no one seemed to acknowledge their absence. Least of all his brother and father.

Kat hadn't understood it as a teenager and in the years since, with an adult perspective, she still didn't understand.

She wanted to know why he'd gone. *Where* he'd gone. Why he never contacted her. Why he hadn't come home before now.

In the years since Brady disappeared, Kat thought she'd moved past the betrayal she'd felt when he left. The last few days—and lectures from her sister—had proven that a lie. In spite of the hurt he'd inflicted all those years ago, she still loved him.

She'd loved him with a young girl's heart, an innocent, naive love that hadn't died when Brady left. That young, fragile emotion had lain dormant, hidden in some recess of her heart only to be resurrected the minute he walked into her cafe.

Resurrected with the fiery blaze of a mates connection.

It explained a lot about her interactions with men, that was for sure.

She'd messed around with a few boys back in high school. Even dated a couple of men in the years since then, except none of them had inspired more than curiosity or a second date. There was no burn of desire. No urge to strip off clothes and get as close as possible like there was with Brady.

Jeez, more than once over the years, she'd entertained the idea she was frigid.

Brady had proven that notion wrong.

Her body had been in a state of simmering arousal since he'd arrived.

As she'd done for the last week, she ignored the demands of her body and coyote, and concentrated on getting lunch heated. She'd decided on beef stew. It would warm them up, and she'd been told by many it was one of her best meals.

Not that she was out to impress Brady with her cooking. Nope. She had no interest in dazzling him with her culinary skills.

He moved behind her where she stood at the ancient stove stirring the stew. "What is that?" he asked over her shoulder.

The kitchen was small, the stove in one corner where if someone wanted to see what she was cooking, they'd have to get up close. Real close. She tried to ignore the heat from his body, the warmth of his breath washing over the side of her face where he leaned forward.

The cool scent of forest and man overtook the smell of beef and vegetables warming in the saucepan and Kat's coyote stretched, rumbled a growl of pleasure at her mate's scent. Swallowing thickly, she managed, "Beef stew."

"Smells amazing. Sure beats canned soup."

"Canned soup?" She spun around, the breath sucking from her lungs at just how close he stood. If she breathed deeply, her breasts would touch his chest. They were almost eye-level. He had a couple of inches on her, and this close she could see the flecks of gold in his brown eyes. Licking her lips, she lowered her gaze to his chin and murmured, "Please tell me you've been eating something better than canned soup since you got here."

"I won't lie to you ever again, Ren." He trailed a fingertip down her cheek, over her jaw and, pressing under her chin, he applied pressure until she looked up and met his gaze. "I couldn't help breaking my promise before but I don't plan to ever break one again. So, yes, I've been living on canned soup."

Canned soup? What was he talking about? The only thing she understood was the fire blazing beneath her skin. The growl of her coyote as she clambered to be free. Free to take her mate. Be taken by him.

"Ren?" His finger left her skin.

"Huh?"

"The stew's boiling over."

"What? Oh!" Spinning around she switched off the heat and searched for steady ground. What the hell was that? He'd barely touched her and completely short circuited her brain.

She knew part of it was they were mates. The mating bond was sharp and fierce and hard to deny. Except she had to.

He needed to explain. She needed to understand.

No mating bond was going to dictate what happened in her life. If she was going to be with Brady—and right now she couldn't deny that was a probability—they needed to clear the air.

Jumping his bones, while appealing, wasn't why she'd come here today.

Kat needed to remember nothing and no one forced her hand. If she didn't want to mate Brady, she didn't have to. It was a shame she could no longer say with one hundred percent certainty she believed that.

Clearing her throat she asked, "Got clean plates?" while checking she hadn't burned the stew.

"Sure." Brady stepped away, taking his heat with him, leaving a chilled shiver racing over her skin in his absence.

Drawing in a deep breath, Kat tried to clear her mind of anything except putting food in front of them. She'd never had to deal with a raging libido before and wasn't sure she had the strength to deny their attraction.

That scared her.

The knowledge that Brady could distract her from anything and everything didn't sit well. For a woman used to being in control, having a man—a mate—snatch it away so easily was a terrifying prospect.

She might not know this grown-up Brady, but she'd loved the young Brady with her whole heart. If she couldn't trust him to be careful with her heart—and her heart would definitely be involved—they could hurt each other badly.

She cursed her lack of relationship skills. She'd never had a boyfriend, never let anyone as close as Brady had once been. Kat wasn't stupid enough to deny Brady's leaving was the reason for that. He'd cut her open, left her behind, and as far as she knew, he hadn't looked back. Except maybe he had. She wouldn't know until she asked him.

Biting her tongue, she filled the bowls Brady put on the counter beside her and held in all her questions.

There would be time to ask; she wasn't rushing into anything, not with the way her mind and heart and coyote were at war over what to do.

Her coyote wanted to lie down, roll over, and offer him her belly—her throat.

Her heart yearned for the love they'd once shared with the deeper adult connection their age hadn't allowed before.

Her head, well her head was screaming at her to run. Run far away because it knew once she let Brady in, she'd let him in completely, and this time, if he left she'd be slashed to ribbons and never recover.

Except had she? Had she ever recovered from the first time?

The roiling emotions she'd experienced when she'd seen him in the Den said she hadn't gotten over his betrayal at all. She needed closure on that part of their lives. Needed to understand why he'd left and why he'd never come back or contacted her in all these years.

"Ask me."

Kat's gaze snapped up to meet Brady's. "What?"

"I can all but hear your brain spinning with questions. Ask me, Ren."

"Okay." She put her spoon down, her stomach rolling at the thought of getting answers. "Why did you leave?"

"Because my mother told me to."

"Well, yeah, I guessed that, but why did she leave? Why did she take you away from here and never come back?"

"Do you remember the year Brogan and Rowen's parents died?"

"Yes. Their car slid off the road and they crashed into a tree. Dad said both of them died on impact."

"That was the night Mom packed up a few of our belongings and drove us off the mountain."

"Why? I don't understand. She left Marcus behind, and your father."

"Let me tell you what happened and then you can ask any other questions."

Kat nodded.

"Dad came home, smashed through the front door naked and yelling. At first I thought he was drunk. It wouldn't have been the first time he'd loaded up and gone off except that night was different. I didn't understand why until he mentioned the Wilders were dead. Yelled now that he was sovereign he could clear the pack of non-bloods and half-bloods, return the pack to being pure instead of tainted by human blood."

She opened her mouth but closed it when Brady shook his head.

"Mom ask him why he thought the Wilders were dead, and he looked at her like she was stupid. He backhanded her, sending her to the floor as he yelled he'd killed them. Shouted no self-respecting full-blood coyote should saddle himself with a human wife and half-blood children never mind be allowed to lead a pack with them by his side."

"But they crashed, went off the side of the road."

"I don't know the details of the crash, but if I know anything about my father I know he would have had supporters get rid of any evidence that pointed to the accident being anything except an accident."

"Oh." She could see Malcolm Connelly doing that. And she remembered when he first took over as sovereign he had a lot of supporters on the council and in the sheriff's department. That had changed during his reign of terror but before that, yeah, she could definitely see him getting someone to clean up after him.

"The look on your face tells me he could have covered it up."

Nodding, Kat said, "Yes, back then he had people on his side who would have helped."

"After more yelling, a few more smacks for Mom, a punch for me, and a smile for Marcus, he left. Everything moved quickly after that. Mom packed a couple of bags, left everything else, and told us to get in the truck. Marcus refused, called her all sorts of names, and said he was going to tell Dad we'd left. I think it was the last part that made Mom realize we had to go or we weren't going.

"She climbed into the driver's seat and drove. Hours and hours she drove and cried, and I couldn't do anything. Not then, not before, not after. We drove straight through to Nebraska and arrived at the house of a friend she'd known before she met Dad. A man she'd gone to school with; at one point they'd been a couple and I don't know how or why they separated and she ended up with Dad, but Mom and Hank were soul mates."

"Nebraska? How did she end up here?"

Brady shrugged. "I don't know. I wish I did. I still don't really understand why she wanted us to leave. I get Dad was abusive, but from what I remember, he'd always been that way, and that night wasn't any worse than all the others so why did she want to leave? Why did she forbid me from contacting anyone here?"

"Sounds like you have just as many questions as I do."

"I do. And I might have a way of finding some answers but I need help."

Kat didn't know how he could find answers when all the key players were dead, but if there was a way she'd help. "How? Help with what?"

"Mom left boxes. I haven't gone through them but I know there are journals in there. From the first day we arrived at Hank's she kept a journal. I have them all."

"Personal diaries? I'm not sure how I feel about reading someone's, your mother's, private thoughts."

"I'm not comfortable with it either except I think they hold the truth about that night and a lot more. I know we haven't seen each other in thirteen years, but if anyone besides me is going to read those journals, I want it to be you."

8

———

"How many more boxes?" Ren asked as he added two more to the pile against the wall in the living room.

"A couple. Why?"

"These aren't just filled with journals," she explained while rummaging through one. "There are keepsakes from when you and Marcus were little, personal papers, pictures, school reports, other stuff."

"Okay, so we need to go through everything before we start reading the journals then." He turned to head back out for the last load.

"Wait. You want me to help with that? Don't you want to decide what to keep and what to throw out?"

There were a dozen boxes of various sizes lined up against the wall. On his own it would take him days, but with Ren's help they could gather things into piles by priority and work their way through in one or less. "Let me grab the last two boxes, then we'll start piles and decide what we should look at first."

"It would be quicker to decide what to keep and not while we sort. If we sort then go through each pile, that's dealing with everything twice. Double handling is not an efficient way to do any job."

"Okay. We decide as we go. We'll need a throw, a keep, and a journal pile. We should keep those separate, right?"

Ren waved a hand toward the door. "Go get the rest, I'll grab a garbage bag for the stuff you want to get rid of, and once we empty a couple of boxes, we can store anything you want to keep in categories in separate boxes instead of having it all tossed in together like it is now. You might want to frame some of these pictures for the walls too so we should keep those separate from the other keepsakes your mother has in here."

Brady glanced around the room. The only thing filling the place was a worn couch and one chair; both items had been here when he was a kid. Everything else was stripped bare. Bare walls, bare mantle over the fireplace, bare shelves on the empty bookcase beneath the window.

He didn't recall his mother ever putting pictures up here. She'd filled Hank's house with them but here, in the mountain home she'd run from, she'd never displayed any. There had to be a reason for that.

Everything he'd learned in recent months pointed out he didn't know his mother as well as he thought he had. She had secrets. Secrets she'd taken to the grave if she hadn't written them down in one of the many journals scattered throughout these boxes.

It was a daunting task, going though all her things. He'd gotten rid of her clothes—and Hank's—before selling the farm, and Hank's estate paperwork had been dealt with by his lawyer. Hank hadn't had any family, which explained why he'd left the farm to Brady and his mom, so the decision on what to do with Hank's personal papers had fallen to them.

He'd kept the man's birth and death certificates as well as the original deed to the farm. Anything that dealt with the business of the farm went to the new owners. It had taken months to go through everything after Hank's death. Brady hoped these boxes didn't take him as long.

His mother had been of no use without Hank, and Brady hadn't really known what to do with most things so had relied on advice from Hank's lawyer. Luckily the lawyer had also been a friend and he'd been more than happy to lend a hand outside of his legal obligation, but that was more confirming Brady's decisions than helping him make them.

Now Brady had Ren. He might not have her the way he wanted to, but he had her. By his side to walk down this path that left him feeling gutted before they'd even started.

"Thank you." He leaned over and brushed his lips on top of her head. "I don't think I'd have the nerve to do this yet if you weren't helping."

"Why? It's just boxes of papers and photos from your mother's life."

"Actually, I think what we've got here is the family closet."

"Meaning?"

"There are skeletons in here I'm not sure I want to dig up."

"If you want answers, we're going to find them buried with those bones."

Brady sighed. "I know. I just can't help wondering if it would be better to not know. I have a bad feeling what we find here is going to be far worse than anything we already know about."

"It might be." Ren pushed to her feet and stepped into him, wrapping her arms around his waist as she rested her cheek on his shoulder. "But, Brady, you're not the only one affected by what we find. We need to know if your father really did have something to do with the Wilders' deaths and why your mother thought she had to leave the mountain in the middle of the night without a word to anyone before or after."

"And why Marcus stayed." Slipping his arms around her, he pulled her closer, lowered his head to rest his cheek on her hair. "I'll never forgive him for breaking her heart."

"I'm not sure we'll ever find the answer to why he stayed other than Marcus idolized your father. I saw it after you were gone. He was also terrified of him. Everyone was. And when Malcolm showed up after we all thought he was dead, Rowen said he looked unhinged to her. As though he'd lost touch with reality. From what Gordie discovered he'd been doing, I have to agree with Rowen; his actions definitely say he'd gone insane."

"Marcus?"

"No. Malcolm. But then with everything Marcus did in recent months, he appeared to have gone crazy too."

"We need to talk to the sheriff. I'm supposed to talk to him about Marcus anyway, so I guess we'll ask about the Wilders' accident and my dad at the same time."

Ren pulled back and looked up at him. They were close in height but she still needed to tilt her head back a little to make eye contact. "You want me to go with you to see Dale?"

"Yes, of course, you volunteered to help, remember?"

"I volunteered to help read journals which somehow turned into sorting through boxes of personal effects and now talking to the sheriff. I've got a life you know. I can't just drop everything to be at your beck and call, Brady."

"I'm not asking you to do that. It won't be for a few days. We'll have to wait until this storm front moves on. In the meantime we'll go through my mom's things and see what we can find."

"I need to leave soon, and if we get the snow they're predicting, I won't be able to come back for a few days."

"Stay."

"What?" She jerked in his arms, tried to pull free, but he held on.

"If we get snowed in, you won't be opening the Den, right, because no one will be out and about. Stay here, help me use the time we'll be trapped indoors to go through everything."

"I—"

"*Please.*" He'd beg if he had too. He wanted her close. Wanted to be able to convince her they could be more than childhood friends. He couldn't do that if she went home.

She searched his eyes, looking for something he wasn't sure he understood but desperately wanted to give her. "I'll need to make a phone call and check on things before I can say yes." She stayed in his arms, studying him.

"Make the call."

Neither of them moved; lost in their own thoughts, they remained still, wrapped in each other's arms.

Brady took the time to catalogue the changes in her face from when they were kids. She was still the same Ren; the girl he'd loved had grown into a beautiful woman, there was no denying that, except there were subtle changes. Small lines beside her eyes, her hair was shorter than she used to keep it, and her body had developed curves in interesting places.

Places his body was all too aware of.

All those changes had barely begun when he'd left and he had to wonder if he was the only man who noticed her. Now or in the years he'd been gone.

"You don't have a boyfriend, do you?" he blurted before the thought even registered in his head.

"What?" She pulled away from him; breaking out of his hold, she took a step back and slammed her hands on her hips. "What kind of question is that? Do you think I'd be here with you, in your arms, if I did?"

"You're not here *with me* though, are you? And that was just a comforting hug between old friends, right?"

Her mouth opened. Closed. The ends tipped down.

"Forget I asked. It's none of my business."

"None of your business." Palms flat on his chest, she gave him a shove. "Of course it's your business, Brady Connelly, you're my *mate*."

He sucked in a breath, every muscle snapping taut, his coyote howling with pleasure. Neither of them had voiced the mate thing out loud yet. Hearing her say it, admit it, had Brady's insides scrambling.

He wanted to throw her over his shoulder, find the nearest bed, and claim her.

Wanted to pick her up and spin her around.

Wanted to race outside and yell it for the mountain to hear.

"What are we going to do about that?" he asked instead.

"Nothing. Yet." She paced away from him. "I'm not ready for that.

I don't think you are either. There's too much"—she waved a hand at the boxes—"to deal with before we deal with us."

"Is there an us?" Brady mentally crossed his fingers.

"I might not be ready for there to be, but I'm not stupid and I refuse to live in denial. We're mates and even if I'm not happy about it, that's our reality. And I'm okay with it, as long as you don't pressure me to accept you. I get that neither of us really has a choice in this, but I'll be damned if we're forced to do anything before we get our heads around it and I'd like to get to know you again before jumping into a mating bond. So, yes, there is an us, but we'll deal with it in a way that suits *us*."

"Okay."

"Okay? Okay what? You're happy to wait until I'm ready?"

"Yes."

"Why do I not believe that?"

Brady laughed. "I'm not going to force you into anything, and I definitely won't be forcing myself on you. I will be honest about what I feel and the struggle I'm having waiting though. But you are right, there's far too much I need to deal with first. I want to put all of it behind us, put it in the past where it belongs, so when we are ready we'll be going forward with a clean slate."

"So we agree to put the mate thing aside and deal with all of this as friends."

"We're more than friends, Ren."

"Obviously. Still, we ignore all that for now."

"We can try. I don't know how successful we'll be. A mate connection is hard to ignore. It's the strongest connection there is, and we had it long before we knew what it was."

She tilted her head to the side, one eyebrow arching in question.

"You have to admit we were inseparable as kids. Our subconsciouses knew long before we did that we were meant to be together."

"I think our being mates explains a lot of things," she muttered.

"What?"

"Nothing." She gave his shoulder a push. "Go get the other boxes and I'll make that call."

"You didn't really answer my question."

"What question?"

"Do you have a boyfriend, Ren?"

She growled, her scowl cute in its fierceness. "*No.*"

"Good."

Before she could comment on his remark, he left the house and went to retrieve the last two boxes from the back of his truck. He hadn't bothered to bring them inside until now because he didn't want to deal with any of this. Except what he said to Ren was true. He—they—needed to put the past in the past and more forward with a clean slate. They deserved that.

And Whispering Springs deserved to know what his father had done.

Brady could only hope whatever his father had done hadn't left permanent scars.

Unfortunately, he thought those hopes would go unrealized. He had no idea what his father had been like outside of the house because Brady rarely spent time with him at home, never mind in town. Marcus truly had been the favored son and as bad as it was to think, he couldn't help but be grateful his brother had taken their father's affections.

Marcus had ended up dead, and Brady had to assume their father's influence had a lot to do with the outcome of his brother's life.

He'd struggled to understand how his mother could leave with only one son but maybe she knew something he didn't. Maybe there was something in her journals or papers that would explain everything.

"Hey, you bringing those boxes in? It's starting to snow."

Ren's words pulled him from his thoughts. He had no idea how long he'd stood there in a daze but she was right. The snow was coming down and it wasn't a light fall either. Glancing up, he scanned the sky. "The storm moved in early."

"Looks like it. Wendy said the sheriff was in to let all the out-oftowners know they should head on home before it got to the point they couldn't."

"Wendy?"

"My manager. She's keeping the Den open in case anyone gets stuck in town. She lives in one of the apartments above so she won't have to go out in the storm to get home."

"You're staying?"

Frowning, she turned her face up to look at the sky. "Yeah. Even if I hadn't decided to, I don't think I've got a choice now."

Brady turned to hide his smile. She might not be exactly happy to be staying with him but he'd work with what he could get. A lot had changed in just a few hours. With a day or two of snowed-in time he would have hours to convince her not only that their mating wasn't a bad thing, but it was something good.

9

Brady placed the last journal on the second stack and leaned back against the couch. "That's it. That's all of them?"

"I've got half a box to finish yet, but there aren't any more journals in here." Ren continued to pull things from the box in front of her.

It was dark out; then again, it had gone dark hours ago when the storm closed in on them. He'd started a fire and the furnace was pumping warm air through all the rooms to ward off the cold. The wind still managed to sneak in. Through cracks in the walls and floors. Brady had been mentally adding things to his list of improvements throughout the afternoon.

"We should take a break when you finish and have some dinner."

"I put lasagna in the oven when I went to the bathroom. It should be ready soon," Ren admitted without looking up, her gaze intent on the paper she'd just pulled from the box.

"You already put dinner on?" She blew his mind. He hadn't thought about dinner until he'd gotten through all his boxes and checked his watch to see they'd been at it for hours. It had been even longer since they'd eaten anything.

"Hmm..." She was focused on the paper in her hand, her brow

scrunching up, her lips moving as she silently read. "Brady, do you have another brother? Other than Marcus?"

"What? No, it was just me and Marcus." He straightened away from the couch. "Why?"

"This is a birth certificate for Jacob Connelly and if my math is right, he'd be about twenty-two."

"Four years *younger* than me?"

"Yeah. This is weird though. The mother is listed as Michelle Watson but the father is unknown. How can that be?"

What the fuck? His mother had another child? He couldn't remember her being pregnant or having a baby or there being any kids besides him and Marcus. And why would it list her maiden name? "I don't understand..."

"I'll put it with the journals. But it reminds me, did you find your birth certificate, or Marcus's?"

"No. They weren't in the boxes I went through. You didn't find them?"

Shaking her head, Ren kept studying the paper in her hand. "This is bizarre. I wonder if Dad would know about it? He would have taken care of your mom while she was pregnant. Probably attended the birth. He should have records of you and Marcus too."

"Does he keep records for that far back?"

"I think so. And I know Gordie scanned everything into a database when she took over the clinic so she'd have the information if it was recorded. Plus she's doing some kind of pack history thing where she's logging all members born in the pack, their family line, and where they are now."

"And if this Jacob wasn't recorded?" he asked, his gaze glued to the pile of journals. They looked innocent enough except they might hold an untold number of bombs within their pages.

"Then we hope the answers are in those books. Or maybe one of the older pack members would know. Possibly Grammy Brant."

"I'd have been four. You three. Gordie's the same age as Marcus, right? So they would have been nine? She might remember something. My mom being pregnant or a new baby."

"Maybe. But I don't remember all that much before I was around twelve."

"I guess I'm the same, but a baby is a significant event. And Gordie always struck me as super observant. She'd remember something like that. Especially seeing how all she ever wanted to do when we were little was play doctor."

"True. I'll send her a message after dinner."

Brady grabbed his phone. "We could call her now."

"It's not urgent. We'll have dinner and then I'll call. I know she doesn't hold a grudge against you but I'd like to handle this, if it's all right with you."

"You don't want me to talk to her? You think I'll upset her?"

"No. I know she doesn't blame you for what your brother and father did, and I'm glad for that. I just feel as though I should ask her this."

"Okay, but you know I have to talk to her about the bodies, right? It's not like I can avoid her forever. Not when we're..." He didn't say mates; he didn't have to. Ren might be ignoring it for now, but much like his mother's journals, their mate status affected more than them. Her family would have to accept their mating, and as far as he was concerned, the sooner the better. Of course he should probably wait until Ren accepted it. And agreed to the mating bond.

Sighing, she dropped the birth certificate next to the pile of journals. "You're right. I'm being stupid. Gordie might have moved on from the attack but it appears as if I'm still struggling with it."

"Wait. You were there? Did he hurt you?"

"What? Oh, no. I wasn't there until after. It might be easier to deal with if I had been there for the whole thing though. I'll never get over seeing Gordie lying in a pool of blood." She shuddered. "Even with the knowledge that it wasn't hers, I find it difficult to wipe that fear from my mind and heart."

"I'm sorry." If he'd packed up and moved back here right after his mother died instead of waiting months, he might have been able to get through to Marcus. Stop him from trying to kill Gordie.

"For what?"

"Marcus. If I'd been here maybe I could have—"

"No way." She sat up straight. "There is no way you could have done anything. God, we all knew he had been terrorizing Gordie and we still let her and a heavily pregnant woman go off alone. I'm just glad it turned out the way it did. Neither Gordie nor Tatum were badly hurt and they both seem to be doing well. Tatum and Dale have reconciled since then, so that was a good thing to come out of the attack."

"I just wish I'd been here."

"Why, so Marcus could have had another target? Don't for one minute think he would have welcomed you back with open arms. He'd isolated himself after your father died, well when we all thought he had, but I guess Marcus probably knew he wasn't dead the whole time. Then when Malcolm tried to run Quinn down and ended up really dead, your brother became even less sociable. Not that he ever was. From the time Malcolm became sovereign, Marcus acted as though everyone was beneath him and held himself apart from the rest of us."

"Dad's hatred of half-bloods and non-bloods would have influenced Marcus."

"Yes, they would have, and as much as I want to blame Marcus for that, I can't. Your father raised him, molded him." Ren shuffled on her knees until she knelt beside him. "And as much as I hated that you left, it probably saved you from a similar fate. I have to think your mother knew what would happen and tried to remove you both from Malcolm's orbit."

"I was never in his orbit. Marcus was always the favorite. Dad barely said two words to me most days. The only time he paid me any attention was when he needed someone to blame for something. And his fists did a lot of the talking then anyway."

"As much as I missed you, I'm thankful to your mother for taking you away from that. From him."

"I'm not sure I can be as generous. She cut away everything I'd ever known because of one man. I get that she felt it was her only option, and maybe it was, except she forbade me from contacting anyone here. She kept me from you and I can't forgive her for that."

"You will."

"I don't see how."

"She loved you enough to risk her life, Brady. If he'd caught you leaving…" A shudder wracked her. "She hurt you emotionally, and I have to believe she knew she would by insisting you not contact anyone. I know we don't know exactly what went on but I remember your mom, and what I remember is a woman who wasn't scared of facing Malcolm. I'd seen him get angry at her numerous times at the clinic when we were little. Something had to have happened for her to believe her only choice was to run and not look back."

"If what my father said about the Wilders is true, then I guess she thought he'd kill her if she stood in his way. I remember him yelling at her to keep her trap shut, something about not telling tales because accidents happened all the time."

Ren gasped, her hand reaching for his, gripping and squeezing tight. "He said something like that to me. It was after you were gone, after Gordie and Anthony had their accident."

"Anthony? What accident?"

"They were driving to the city for school when they were involved in a hit and run. Anthony died instantly and Gordie lost their baby while she was trapped in the wreck."

"When did this happen? After I left?"

"Yes, it was after that your dad made it clear I wasn't to mention you again."

"How? Why? You'll have to give it all to me, Ren. Why would he tell you not to mention me?"

"I asked Marcus about you but he wouldn't answer me, didn't say a word, and you know me, I don't give up so easily so I kept badgering him. Your father came up behind me, grabbed my arm, and told me not to mention you again. Then he warned me to be careful, that a half-blood like me didn't want to have an accident like my sister."

"Fucking hell." He reached over and pulled her against him. "I'm sorry he did that. Sorry I wasn't here to stop him."

Ren snuggled into his side, one hand pressed to his chest, her head resting on his shoulder. "You couldn't have stopped him. He was sovereign and he didn't directly threaten me."

"I wish he were alive so I could kill him," he growled. "I hope he died a painful death. He hurt so many people, tried to destroy so much... God. I can't believe I come from that."

"You're nothing like him."

"How do you know? You haven't seen me in a decade."

"I know you, Brady. I've always known you. Deep down where it matters."

She was right. And he could say the same about her. They might not know the little things like favorite color or food but they knew each other's heart. It was too soon to declare his love but it was there—had always been there—warming his chest and now giving him hope for a future with her.

It explained his lack of interest in any other woman. He'd always been in love with Ren. Had been waiting for the day he could come back to her.

Would she think him an idiot for waiting? For hoping she'd be his first?

Would she think less of him because of his inexperience?

He should tell her before they went any further. She might not want to be with him once she knew the truth.

Brady stared down at the top of Ren's head. How did he tell her...he swallowed, took a deep breath, and jumped right in. "I've never had sex with a woman."

Her head tipped back, her long lashes fluttering, her brows pulling in, a delicate wrinkle forming between them. "You're gay?" she asked in a whisper filled with disappointment and disbelief.

"No! Jesus, fuck no." He shook his head. "Why would you even think that?" Grabbing her hand, he placed it over his hard cock. "Have you not seen the way I react to you? Fuck, it doesn't matter how many times I jerk off, I can't get the damn thing to go down."

"But you just said..." Her eyes slowly widened, her fingers

twitching on his denim covered shaft, as the true meaning of his words registered. "Holy shit. You've never had sex?"

For a second she remained wide-eyed, incredulity written all over her face, and Brady felt his own face heat with embarrassment. Then her expression cracked, she pulled away, doubled over, and laughed her ass off.

For a stunned moment he remained silent, then emotion flooded him. "What the hell is funny about this?"

"Sorry," she gurgled, her laughter scrambling her words. "Give me. A sec."

Brady crossed his arms and waited for Ren to get herself under control. The embarrassment of moments ago was quickly overshadowed by anger. There wasn't anything funny about being a twenty-six year old virgin.

It hadn't been a conscious decision. His mother had been quite adamant that he not jump into sex when he was a teenager. She made it perfectly clear what the consequences of such an act could be and he'd heeded her warnings.

And if he were honest, he hadn't met anyone who made him want to change his decision because he wasn't looking. He knew who he wanted. Ren. He wanted the girl he'd been in love with all his life.

The one who was busting a gut laughing at him.

10

Kat pulled in a breath and tried to stop laughing.

Jesus. They were fucked.

Or not.

That thought had her snorting a giggle.

Shit. This was not going the way she thought it would. Neither of them had any practical experience and they were fighting a mating bond that amplified hormones.

Humans thought teenagers were horny; they had nothing on a coyote shifter in the middle of a mating dance.

"Damn. We're in trouble," she mumbled.

Brady frowned. "Well, someone is."

Kat stared at him as she pulled in deeper breaths and found some level of normalcy. He sat there with his arms crossed, face in a menacing scowl, and in spite of the anger rolling off him, she couldn't ignore the embarrassment and disappointment swirling in his eyes, or the arousal buzzing in her veins.

She had to clear the air. Make him understand she wasn't laughing at him. She was laughing at the situation they found themselves in.

"We both are."

He cocked one eyebrow but the scowl remained.

"We're on the same page."

"Huh?"

"We're starting this at the same place."

Shaking his head, he dropped his arms to his sides, and hands clenched, growled, "Stop talking in riddles. Why the fuck are we both in trouble?"

"Because neither of us knows what we're doing here."

"Of course not, we haven't found our mates until now."

Seemed she wasn't the only one slow on the uptake today. She couldn't believe for one second she'd thought he was trying to tell her he was gay. She'd spent most of the day trying to ignore the bulge in his pants, the hungry looks, the sensual brush of fingers when they'd passed things back and forth.

"No. We haven't. But it's the fact that neither of us have had sex before that means we're in trouble."

His mouth dropped open, snapped shut. Nostrils flaring, he dragged in a deep breath. "We're both virgins?" he asked in a strangled voice.

Kat nodded.

It was slow, but Brady's lips curled up and parted to reveal straight white teeth. She'd say the smile looked wolfish but he was a coyote and that would be an insult. Whatever she called it, that curve of his mouth telegraphed loud and clear that he was pleased by her revelation.

"You're happy about that?"

"Hell, yes. It means no one else will ever touch you. You're mine. Only mine."

"Ah, okay, that sounds a little too alpha for me." A shiver of excitement traveled over her skin, making her words a lie. She definitely liked his alpha vibe.

"The reverse applies."

"The reverse?"

"You'll be the only one to ever touch me."

"Oh." A curl of pleasure unfurled in her belly. The thought of being the first to touch Brady, to give him pleasure, had her coyote rumbling in approval.

"We get to explore together."

"Explore?" God, she sounded like a parrot. She'd never had her mind confused by lust before. Would it always be like this?

"Sex. We get to explore sex together."

"Explore sex..." Okay. She could get behind that. Now that she actually *wanted* sex, she could think of numerous things she wanted to try. Except... Sighing, she said, "We can't."

"What? Why not?"

"Because I'm not ready to be marked—mated."

"We can still fool around some."

"No. We can't." Shaking her head, she explained, "I've heard the mating connection amplifies our sensitivity. It's how Brogan marked El before she even knew coyote shifters existed."

"El? Brogan's mate?"

"Yes, she's the woman Rowen lived with when she left the mountains."

"Rowen left Whispering Springs?"

"Oh shit." She shook her head. "I forget you haven't been here. You don't know everything that happened since..."

"I want to know. I want you to share everything with me."

"Some of it involves Marcus and your dad. And those parts aren't good."

Brady took a deep breath. "Doesn't matter. I want to know it all."

"Why don't we start with all the mates? Brogan is mated to El. She's Australian and has a really cool accent. Then there are Rowen and Quinn. Everyone knew that would happen since they were younger, so when she came home, nobody was surprised they mated straight away. They're the reason El came here even though she was human and we don't usually let them this high on the mountain. Gordie and Steve—"

"Steve McKenna?"

"Yes. They're true mates unlike her and Anthony."

"Anthony?"

"He was a distant cousin to the Brants. Came to live here a few years before you left. You don't remember him?"

Shaking his head, he said, "No, but he doesn't matter, Gordie's with Steve now."

"Yes, they got together at Christmas but they've been doing the dance for years. Gordie was being stubborn."

"Runs in the family."

"What does?"

"Nothing." He did a rolling motion with his hand. "Go on."

"Right, Dale and Tatum would be next. He came home over a year ago and Tatum followed just this past Christmas. There's a huge story there but I don't know all the details. Something about them having a third mate who died. I'm not sure what that means, but I do remember Cade from when we were younger. He and Dale were best friends and always together, remember?"

"I think I remember them. And they both mated Tatum? Tatum Brant?"

"Apparently."

"Interesting. I remember Dad saying something about William Brant's half-blood granddaughter once. Before his hatred of non-bloods extended to half-bloods, he tried to talk Marcus into dating her but she was a few years younger than him; I think she's younger than us too. Anyway, Marcus said he wasn't into fucking little girls."

"Jesus. He said that?"

"If I'm remembering right, she hadn't shifted for the first time yet. So Marcus might have been crude but he was right."

"I'm not sure how much longer your dad pushed the Tatum thing because at some point Marcus turned his sights on Rowen. His obsession led him to attack her one day and she, like you, disappeared in the middle of the night. She stayed away six years. Long enough for Brogan and Quinn to take over as sovereign and regal."

"A lot has happened in thirteen years."

"It has. Let's leave the rest of the history lesson for later." She pushed to her feet and offered her hand. "Dinner, then I'll call Gordie about taking a look at those records."

"Okay, I'll take care of the dishes while you call your sister."

It didn't take them long to get dinner on the small, scarred table in the pokey little dining room. Most of the furniture was worn, old, and Kat wondered if Brady would want to replace it with his own things.

Brady ignored his food and looked around the room. "What do you think about taking down the walls between here and the kitchen and living room?" He pointed to the walls behind her and opposite.

Kat swallowed the bite of lasagna she'd just taken. "Me?"

"Yes, you. What do you think? The kitchen is too small as is and you'll want a bigger oven for starters, a bigger refrigerator too, so we should plan the space to accommodate larger appliances as well as an island counter I think."

"Me?" she squeaked. "Why would you need my opinion or preferences?"

His gaze returned to hers. "Because this will be our home and I want you to have input. The place needs renovating, bringing up to date, and I want you to have the things you like and need."

"Brady. I can't move in with you. You've just come back. Besides, I have my apartment above the Den—"

"You're my mate. We're going to eventually complete the bonding and I want you to live here. I don't care if it's tomorrow, next week, next year—okay, fine, next year better not be on option," he said with a grin. "But this place needs love and care and I want us both to give it that love and care. I want to give it to you, too, want you to give it to me."

"I." Kat closed her mouth. Swallowed. She had no idea what to say.

"Honestly, no pressure. I get that we need to work our way up to that point but I've got two months before I start work at Wild Encounters and I want to do some of the renovations before then. I already started knocking down the wall between the two back bedrooms in prep for the new master suite."

"You knocked down a wall? Do you even know how to do that?"

"Sure." He grinned. "You just take to it with a sledge hammer."

"Brady!" Was he crazy? "You can't just knock down walls. You have to check the roof won't cave in, make sure there aren't any electrical wires or water pipes..." She took in his smile, the twinkle in his eyes. "You know all that, don't you?"

"I may have done construction and demolition work before. I checked all those things. But don't worry. I plan to consult a builder about the second story addition."

"Second story..."

"Yes. I thought we'd put a second story on so we didn't take up any more yard space. I figured four bedrooms for the kids and possibly a fifth for guests."

"Four?"

"You don't want four?"

"Brady, I haven't even thought about having one, never mind four."

"We should probably talk about that. I'd like four. How many do you want?"

"I." She closed her eyes. He was doing her head in. She hadn't decided to accept their mating bond yet and he was planning their home and how many children they would have. "Brady, I can't," she sighed.

"Okay, forget about that. Tell me what your ideal kitchen would look like."

Opening her eyes, Kat stared at the man who'd been her childhood friend. He'd been her best friend. The one she told all her secrets too, the one who'd told her his. She remembered talking about what they wanted to do as adults. Brady had wanted to be a forest ranger so he could protect the mountains, and she'd wanted to run the Den.

She'd achieved her goal; had he?

"What will you be doing at Wild Encounters?"

"Taking treks into the mountain. Day treks and overnighters."

"Like a forest ranger?"

Brady laughed. "God, you remember that? Yeah, I guess in a way I'm like a forest ranger. Except I get to tell people what to do and what not to do on the treks. As a ranger, I wouldn't really have that much control over what people did, and I'd have to work within the constraints of a human government employer. At least working for Brogan and Quinn I can help other shifters as well as the forest and animals that call it home."

"You dreamed of being a ranger."

"I did. But this is better. And I get to be here in Whispering Springs. I finally got to come home."

Kat smiled. "I'm glad you're here."

He reached across the table and grabbed her hand. "In case you're wondering, when I say home, I don't just mean this house or the mountain. I mean you, Ren."

"I don't want to rush."

"I know."

"But I do want to move forward." What she really wanted was to kiss him but she wasn't sure they could stop at one.

"Okay."

"And I think we can explore sex without marking each other."

"Oh, how?" His hand tightened around hers.

"We can relieve some of this tension, make the whole thing less stressful."

"How? I can't be in a room with you and not want inside you," he said. The muscles in his arm where it rested on the table quivered, in fact his whole body vibrated in his seat. He was holding back. Letting her lead when clearly he wanted to take control.

"Okay, I get that. I want that too. Eventually, but... I'm not ready to close the deal. It feels like I'm on a runaway train and there's nothing I can do to stop it except slow it down a bit. Give myself—*us*—some time to think about this."

"I don't need time." Brady dropped her hand and stood; stepping around the table he moved toward her. "I know what I want. What I've always wanted. It's why I waited."

"Fuck, Brady, don't lay that on me. No pressure, right?"

"Sorry. I'm trying. Honestly. But this need for you is riding me harder than any mountain trek I've been on. I'm sweating and out of breath and shaking, and goddammit, I think I'm going to lose my mind if I don't get inside you soon."

She could see he was struggling, maybe more than she was because she wanted to hold back. He didn't. He wanted to barrel into this thing full speed, arms wide open. Kat didn't know if she could do that.

On some level, she trusted him. Believed he wouldn't leave again and yet... "I can't do it. Not now."

Sucking in a breath, he ran a hand down his face. "Okay. Okay. Tell me what you're thinking."

"We make ourselves come. In front of each other."

"You want to watch me jerk one off?"

"Yes. But I'll be doing the same." She glanced toward the bedrooms. "I can lie on the bed while you sit in a chair across the room."

"Christ." He scrubbed a hand down his face again. "You're trying to kill me."

"No. I'm not. This is just as hard for me but I need to be in control of this. I can't—won't—dive right in. It doesn't matter how much my coyote wants that."

"It might be better if you're in one room and I'm in another. I'll know what you're doing and I'll smell you but I won't be able to see you."

She smiled. "We could try phone sex."

A shudder wracked him, and he shoved both hands through his hair and yanked. "Jesus. You really are trying to kill me."

She laughed. "Pretty sure the killing is mutual."

And it was. But in spite of the struggle it would be to watch Brady get off, she needed to see it. Needed her own relief too. Kat feared if they didn't do something to relieve the tension winding them both tighter with every second they were together, it would snap. She wasn't sure that was the way to go with this whole mate thing.

Actually, she wasn't sure mutual masturbation was the right thing either, except now she'd voiced the suggestion, she couldn't stop the reel of images flickering through her head.

If they did this, took the pressure off, maybe she'd get her wish. Maybe they could kiss without the threat of ripping each other's clothes off.

11

They were quiet as they finished dinner, Brady didn't know about Ren but all he could think about was getting to see her naked, getting to watch... Shuddering, he picked up his plate and stood.

"I'll get started on the dishes." He turned his back and left the room. Hopefully being separated by walls would help relieve some of the tension twisting his insides.

His reprieve was short lived when Ren entered the kitchen and moved in beside him at the sink a moment later.

"The call wouldn't connect. The storm must have knocked service out," she explained, picking up the dish towel and reaching for the cutlery he'd washed.

"Maybe try again," he offered.

"Later."

The anticipation of what they planned hung in the air, making Brady twitchy, his pulse pound, his breathing shallow. His body had been on hyper alert since he'd sensed Ren in the cafe days ago and now that she was here, now that he'd spent hours with her, the slightest thing threatened to set him off.

He'd been aroused before; every teenage boy went through nights of wet dreams and days of ill-timed boners—coyote shifters were no different. Only this felt like he'd mainlined a gallon of coffee laced with crack. His heart raced like the winner of the Kentucky Derby; his breaths rasped in and out of lungs that felt as though they were being wrung dry, and his blood flooded his veins like lava spewing from a volcano.

And this volcano was about to blow.

He had some concerns about the plan. Mainly whether or not he could control himself once they got naked. The thought of Ren touching herself in front of him just about had his eyes crossing; it certainly had his cock hard as granite and leaking pre-cum. Fuck knows what would happen when it was a reality—within touching distance.

God. He couldn't be in the same room as her. He'd never keep his hands off her.

The bed in the master bedroom faced the door. He could stand in the hall, lean against the wall opposite; with the door open he'd have a clear view of her.

"Ready?"

Ren's voice snapped him straight, sent the pounding in his body to deafening decibels. He turned slowly, his gaze meeting hers. Relieved to see her twisting her hands in front of her and the way she chewed the side of her bottom lip, he swallowed around the lump in his throat and attempted to speak. When all he could manage was a croak reminiscent of a dying frog, he nodded and tried to offer a reassuring smile.

He was pretty sure he failed.

She eyed him for a few seconds then without a word, turned and left the kitchen. He could hear her footsteps as she made her way to the bedroom. Just the thought had his cock pulsing, his breathing ragged, and sweat popping out all over his skin.

Taking a couple of seconds to gain control and hopefully stop the trembling in his legs, Brady wished they hadn't spent over a decade apart. If he'd stayed in Whispering Springs, they would have reached this point long ago. It would have been simpler. They would have gone from being best friends to mates without too much trouble.

Now they were strangers but not. And he'd hurt Ren by not contacting her. With hindsight he knew if he'd tried and succeeded, she never would have revealed his whereabouts or that she was talking to him. He could—*should*—have trusted her with that.

He'd allowed his mother to separate him from the one person he'd been most connected to. Shaking his head, he cleared it of the past and focused on the now.

Nothing stood in the way of them being together except Ren's reluctance. And that was wearing down. Slowly, with each minute they spent together, she let down her guard a little more and he knew they were growing closer, could feel the connection they'd always had weaving into place, the threads stronger than before.

"Brady?"

Sucking in a breath, he called out, "Coming," as he stripped out of his clothes and dropped them on the floor at his feet. Quick strides had him down the short hallway and at the bedroom door.

The vision before him buckled his knees, and he had to grip the doorframe with both hands to keep from falling to the floor. "Fuck."

Pillows piled up behind her back, Ren reclined against the headboard. Her full breasts—and god did she have a first-class rack—were on display, their red-brown tips hard and pointing his way. She'd bent her knees, widened her feet, and opened her thighs until everything was on show. Every wet luscious inch.

"*Fuck*," he breathed out harshly. His fingers dug into the timber frame, and he was relieved to see his claws hadn't extended.

The smile she gave him said she knew the power she held over him. They might both be virgins but that didn't mean they were clueless, and Ren definitely wasn't clueless. She knew exactly what she was doing to him when she trailed her hands down her torso, up the inside of her thighs to her knees, then back down again.

Her fingertips skimmed either side of her pussy, back over her stomach, and finally across those sweetly puckered nipples he wanted to wrap his lips around.

And then she did it again. Stroked her fingers over her quivering belly, skimmed the wet flesh between her legs, down to her knees before reversing once more.

Slowly she touched herself. Taunted him with what he couldn't touch. What he wanted to touch more than he wanted to breathe. When she started her third round of caresses, the pounding in Brady's head began to sound like a chant.

Take her, take her, take her.

Blood surged, pulsing through his body and stretching his cock to bursting in a throbbing beat that echoed in his ears, accompanying the words in his head—his soul. He wanted to claim her. Needed to.

Sweat coated his skin and he could feel the fine hair all over his body thicken to fur as his coyote howled to take what was his. With a clenched jaw, Brady removed one hand from the doorframe and wrapped it around his pre-cum slicked shaft.

He'd dripped on the floor between his feet. The puddle grew as he stroked his flesh in a slow, light caress. He didn't want to go off too soon, and if he grabbed his dick and fucked his hand the way he longed to, it would be over in seconds. Already his balls were tucked up tight and the tingle of eminent release tickled his groin. They needed to get this party started or he'd be partying alone.

"*Ren.*" Brady squeezed the base of his cock in an attempt to stem the tide. "I can't... I need... *Please.*"

Her eyes were glued to his hand, to the thick shaft gripped tight in his fist. Watching her, Brady saw the shiver that rolled over her, saw the slick folds of her pussy grow plumper, redder, wetter.

Before he could beg more, she slid both hands between her legs. One set of fingers spread her pussy lips wide and the other delved between to swirl around her clit. He could see the bud standing tall at the top, could see the opening of her channel fluttering with each stroke of fingers on clit.

Breathing ragged in his ears, it took him a moment to realize Ren breathed just as harsh, that her heart pounded as hard as his. She might look relaxed lying back on the bed except for the flushed glistening skin, the taut peaks of her breast, the rapid rise and fall of her chest, the plump red flesh under her fingers...

Yeah, she was right on the edge with him.

He could smell her. The rich scent of her arousal intensifying with every second, every breath—every stroke. Her hips were moving now, lifting off the bed as she thrust a finger deep inside.

His cock pulsed, jerked, and he took a half-step forward before he could stop himself. He couldn't jump her. She'd offered him this and he'd take it no matter how much effort it took to stay by the door.

She hadn't said anything since she'd called him and he had to think she was as wound up as him and incapable of uttering a word.

Words might not be flowing from her lips but that didn't mean she was quiet. No. She made the most erotic sounds. Little whimpers and moans as she thrust a second finger deep while strumming her clit with her thumb; the whole time she held herself wide open for him to see every detail, every pulse of her folds as more blood rushed to the area.

Brady groaned, clenched his jaw, and fought to keep his eyes open and his orgasm from exploding. With the number of times he'd jacked off in the last few days, it was a wonder he could get it up, never mind come. It could be the mating bond or the woman on his bed; either or both could be responsible for his constant arousal and hair-trigger.

"Brady," she moaned, her hips undulating faster. "I'm going to..." Pulling her bottom lip between her teeth, she threw her head back and exposed her vulnerable neck, making his teeth drop.

On a gasping cry she went over the edge, her body shuddering and quivering, her back arching as the waves of her release took her under.

He held off as long as he could so he could watch every second of her orgasm except his coyote had other ideas, and as he own release exploded, it blew everything wide open. His coyote had never been this connected to his human side before.

It was as though finding his mate pulled that primitive part of him closer to the surface, gave them a shared goal, and right now that goal was to claim their mate.

Only he couldn't.

It didn't matter how much he wanted to or that he knew he could take her without a fight; he couldn't break her trust. He'd promised to hold back. Go at the pace she set.

And if he was going to do that, he had to leave.

Had to get away from the one thing he wanted most.

Pain sliced deep. Neither he nor his coyote wanted to go but if he didn't, he'd be on her. Marking her. Biting her. Claiming her.

With a roar, Brady emptied the last of his cum on the floor at his feet and spun around. Bouncing off the walls, he staggered back to the kitchen and the door that led outside.

"Brady!"

Ignoring Ren's call was the hardest thing he'd ever done, but he made it to the back door and flung it open. From one step to the next he shifted, let muscle and bone stretch and snap, reshaping him into the four-legged animal he was at his core.

Paws pounded on wood as he ran across the porch and launched himself into the snowy night.

"Brady!"

She'd followed him. With a quick glance over his back, he barked, growled a warning, before tearing off into the trees at the edge of the yard.

He hoped she wouldn't shift and follow him. He'd take her if she did. Neither of them would be happy about that. Their first time should be in human form. They could mate as coyotes after they'd sealed their bond, after their mating was complete and they'd claimed each other.

Pushing hard, he followed the trail he'd traveled over the last five days, winding his way through the trees until he reached the little creek at the base of the small incline the house had been built at the top of.

He'd done minimal exploring of the forest since he arrived. The house had taken most of his days but he'd made time to run every day. It settled him, to shift to his animal form and run free. Hopefully, running would calm the roiling hormones and urges of the mating bond.

Brady snorted.

Yeah, right. Nothing would soothe a mating bond except a mate. And his didn't want him.

No, that was a lie. She did want him; her body couldn't hide her true feelings, except she was reluctant to give in to their mating. Their history kept her guarded, more so than if they were strangers. He needed to give her time, needed to earn her trust and love once more.

As his muscles quivered and snow melted on his coat, Brady hoped it didn't take too long. He wasn't sure he could handle another session of exploring sex without touching her. If she wouldn't accept his mating claim, maybe he could convince her to accept his mark.

12

─────────

Kat watched Brady disappear into the night. She'd heard the warning in his bark; he didn't want her to follow, and she wouldn't. But she wasn't going to leave him out there alone.

Heading back to the bedroom, she redressed, then cleaned up the mess Brady left on the floor, before making her way to the front door to grab her coat and boots. Pulling her gloves from her coat pockets, she slipped them on as well as her beanie. Checking the slide bolts on the front door were locked, she went back to the kitchen and pulled out the ingredients for hot chocolate.

She'd need something to keep her warm while she waited and Brady would need warming up when he got back.

The kitchen was clean. They'd taken care of that before they'd... Kat shivered.

Jeez. She'd never felt anything like what they'd done. Sure, she'd taken care of herself over the years; it usually took far longer than it had just now, but still, she'd known she wasn't frigid in spite of her lack of arousal with any of the men or boys she'd messed around with in the past.

She'd heard a mating bond could be intense. Gordie had been honest about her mating with Anthony all those years ago but that hadn't been a true mating like she had with Brady. And Kat hadn't thought about asking her sister about the bond with Steve. Not with everything else going on in recent weeks.

Gordie would be honest with her though. She could trust her sister's thoughts and opinions because she'd never lie to Kat.

Glancing around, Kat spotted her phone on the counter, and grabbing it, shoved it in her pocket. She'd get a cup of hot chocolate, the quilt from the bedroom, and head out onto the back porch to wait for Brady.

Plan set, she made quick work of heating the milk, adding the cocoa, and stirring until the liquid was smooth. She filled a mug, left the rest in the pan, then ducked into the bedroom to grab the quilt.

Back in the kitchen, she picked up her cup and headed outside into the cold. Slipping out the back door, she shivered as the wind buffeted her. Small flakes of snow caught on the swirling wind wet her face and she looked for the most sheltered section of the porch.

The only place to sit was an old swing that didn't look as though it would hold her weight, except it was out of the flying snow, and unless she wanted to huddle on the floor, her only option. Walking over she put her mug down, and gingerly lowered herself, slowly letting the seat support her.

When the chains didn't creak or groan, she figured it was safe. Bending over, she lifted her mug and sat back. Slipping her phone out of her pocket, she draped the quilt over her legs and tucked it around her waist.

Three taps had Kat connecting to her sister.

"Hey, what's up?" Gordie answered on the second ring.

"Hey." Taking a deep breath, Kat dove right in. "What was your mating bond like with Steve?"

"Whoa. Whoa. Where did that come from?"

"I need to know if this is normal."

"If what's normal? Kat, where are you? What's going on? You sound like you're outside in the storm."

Sighing, Kat started at the beginning. "Brady's my mate."

"I know. You told me, remember?"

She'd forgotten that. So much had happened since Brady arrived in town. "I'm at his house."

"Oh. Did you mate?"

"No. I'm not ready for that. We haven't even kissed."

"Then what has you all worked up? I know you, you're freaking out over something. Is it because you can't control this?"

"Yeah, I guess that's part of it. I asked him to wait. I don't want to mark each other or mate yet and, well, I suggested we fool around with ourselves in front of each other and we did, except something happened and Brady ran, shifted, and took off into the forest."

"Slow down, slow down, one thing at a time. Let me get this straight, you masturbated in front of each other so you wouldn't be marked; is that right?"

"Yes."

"Okay, that sounds like a normal thing to do whether you're a mated pair or not, and it's probably sensible until you can come to terms with the hurt you both suffered when he left Whispering Springs. So what happened that made Brady run?"

"I don't know! That's why I'm calling you! God, Gordie, he couldn't get away quick enough and he growled at me when I followed, the message to stay put perfectly clear. Did I do something wrong? We both got off and I thought we both enjoyed it but maybe—"

"Hang on a sec, Kat," Gordie ordered before her voice muffled. She could hear her sister talking to someone and assumed it was Steve. Gordie's next words confirmed it. They also confirmed that Steve had heard every word of their conversation so far. "I'm putting you on speaker so Steve can talk."

Kat groaned as she closed her eyes and leaned her head back. The action made the swing rock beneath her and she straightened —braced—ready for the thing to collapse. Nothing happened though, so she eased back into her reclined position and took a sip of cocoa.

"Kat?"

"Hmm..."

"Sorry to interrupt but I think I can shed light on what went on," Steve explained.

"Okay."

"It's my opinion, and Doc agrees with me, that Brady came close to claiming you without your consent. Now I don't know him, didn't before, and I haven't even laid eyes on him since he returned so I can't make a judgement call on his character but I can tell you what it sounds like. Gordie has told me a little about him in the last few days, and I trust her assessment of him. He's taken the immediate danger, danger as he perceives it, away from his mate. From you."

"He took himself away because he thought he'd hurt me?" Kat didn't understand how Brady could hurt her; he'd never be physically violent with her and she was sure he loved her and wouldn't be emotionally abusive either. Gordie had been right to point out Brady was nothing like his father or brother because he wasn't. He'd only ever been kind, caring, and protective.

"By claiming you before you're ready, he'd be hurting you. And him."

Steve's words lit up all kinds of light bulbs. "Oh."

Jeez, she was such an idiot.

Brady would never try to control her. He'd value her opinions, her wants; he'd even pushed his own wants aside to give her hers.

"Kat?"

"Yeah."

"He'll come back," her sister said.

"Yeah, he will." Taking a deep breath, Kat asked the question she was pretty sure she knew the answer to, but wanted to hear the words from Gordie anyway. "Will this be a problem for you, Gordie?"

"What? You and Brady being mates? Why would that be a problem for me?"

"Because he's a Connelly. I'll be living in the Connelly home." Oh God, when had she made that decision? "He'll be a constant reminder of what happened."

"The only thing Brady will be is the man who makes you happy. Who helps you give me lots of nieces and nephews to spoil."

Kat laughed. "Jesus, you two need to give me nieces and nephews first."

"We could do it together," Gordie whispered. "Mum and Dad would be over the moon if we did."

"I'm not even mated yet. Shit. We haven't even kissed."

"Then when he gets back, kiss him."

Kat didn't think they were ready for that but couldn't deny the desire was strong. There was something else she needed to ask her sister. "Hey, Gordie, do you remember Mrs. Connelly being pregnant?"

"No. I didn't live here when Brady was born."

"I mean when you were about nine."

"Nine...? No, I don't remember her ever being pregnant. Kat, what's going on?"

"You transferred all Dad's old medical records to digital form, right?"

"Yes, you helped. Why?"

"So if there was another Connelly boy, it would be recorded in Dad's files and you'd have put them in your database."

"Kathren Joy Monroe, you tell me right this second what the hell this is about. There's only two Connelly children that I know of, and I'm pretty sure I would have remembered seeing a record showing Mrs. Connelly having another baby whether the baby lived or not, and I don't."

Kat could hear the frustration and curiosity in her sister's voice. She owed it to her to explain, especially seeing how she was going to ask to see those records. "We found a birth certificate for Jacob Connelly in Brady's mom's things."

"Jacob? It doesn't ring any bells. And I've got a good memory."

"Brady said that."

"So you want me to search the files?"

"I was going to ask to do it."

"I'd let you but patient confidentiality has to be considered."

"I'm only asking to see Michelle Connelly's records and she's dead. Believe me, I have no intention of gossiping about what I find at the Den or anywhere else."

"Okay, if Brady agrees, yes, you can go through her file. When?"

"After the snow lets up?"

"I'll be at the clinic as soon as that happens, so come in whenever, and I'll set you up in the office."

"Thanks, Gordie."

"What are you thinking?"

God, her sister knew her too well. "I'm not sure yet but something doesn't sit right with Brady's mom leaving Marcus behind. I can't pinpoint what, but it doesn't jive with the woman I remember."

"Yeah, I never understood that either and if I'm honest, I actually thought Malcolm had killed her and Brady, and hidden it. That was why I left after the accident. I don't remember it, anything, until I came to in the hospital but I always got a bad feeling around Malcolm and I had the nightmare where I was trapped and could hear him laughing."

"You never told me about that. But I know what you mean about Malcolm, he always gave me the creeps even before I had that run-in with him after Brady left." She didn't have the right to tell her sister Brady's revelation about the Wilders. He'd have to be the one to share that if it was going to get out. And she wasn't ready to voice her suspicion about her sister's accident either. So many things were clicking into place for her. For Brady's sake, Kat hoped she was wrong about most of them.

"Do you want to stay on the phone until Brady gets back?" Gordie asked.

"No. I'm good. I'll talk to you later."

"Message me every day."

Kat laughed. "I'm fine. I'll *be* fine."

"I know. I just worry with you being at the Connelly place."

"The threat the Connelly place held is long gone; you saw to that."

"I think there's more damage those men can do from the grave."

"What aren't you telling me?"

"Nothing."

"Bullshit."

"Right back at you."

"Fine. We'll keep our secrets for now."

"Secrets always find their way out into the open."

"They do, but these aren't mine to tell."

"Okay, let Brady know there's no rush on making a decision. He's got time."

"I think we should put that decision off indefinitely."

"Why?"

"You might want to do some research." God, she hoped she didn't give anything away. But her sister was good at reading between the lines, finding the pieces and putting the puzzle together. It was one of the many things they had in common. "Just don't do anything yet."

"All right."

Kat thought about the journals inside, the secrets they held, the one she thought might strip away everything Brady believed about himself and the family he'd been raised in.

"Call if you need me," Gordie said. "Any time. Day or night."

"Thanks. Give Steve a hug for me."

"Already on that," Gordie said with a laugh.

"'Night, Kat." Steve's deep voice reminded Kat she hadn't only been talking to her sister.

"'Night. And thank you."

"You're welcome. If he's not back in a couple of hours, give us a call. I'll head out and see if I can round him up."

"No need. I'm sure he'll be back when he's ready."

"Don't stay outside waiting too long, Kat; it's going to get cold fast," Gordie warned. "You can wait inside just as well as out there."

"How do you know I'm outside?"

"Do you even have to ask?"

Kat chuckled. "No. 'Night, you two."

"'Night," they chorused.

She disconnected and lowered the phone to her lap, her gaze on the dark shadow of the trees lining the yard.

She'd give Brady another ten minutes, then she'd go back inside. She doubted she'd be able to sleep until he returned but she could make herself useful while she waited. If the snow kept up, and it was supposed to, they'd be housebound for a few days, and nothing beat a nice pot of homemade soup on snow days.

She'd brought plenty of fresh vegetables with her earlier. The steak she'd brought would be better for stew but the whole chicken would make a nice accompaniment to all those veggies.

The wind howled through the trees, snow flying in every direction. Shivering, she tucked the quilt up under her chin.

It really was getting colder. Deciding Gordie had a point and not wanting to worry her or Brady if he came back and found her shivering on the back porch, Kat stood, gathered the quilt and mug, and headed inside.

13

Brady slipped in through the back door and cursed his own stupidity.

He'd left Ren alone. And she'd been forced to leave the door unlocked for him. He would have known if she were in danger but he should never have left her in such a vulnerable position.

Seeing his clothes folded neatly on the kitchen counter, he snatched up his underwear and t-shirt. He wouldn't need the jeans or sweater; it was long past time for bed, a bed he hoped he'd find Ren in.

Unless she'd risked the storm and gone back to town.

Making his way through the house, he checked everything was locked up and made sure the fire was banked before heading to the bedroom. He couldn't stop himself from crossing his fingers and whispering, "please be there, please be there," as he walked.

He hadn't abandoned her but couldn't—wouldn't—blame her if she saw his run into the forest as that. He'd barely held on to his control and he was ashamed he'd needed to, and proud he'd had the strength, to take himself away from her.

The mix of conflicting emotions he'd experienced since he'd arrived in Whispering Springs kept growing.

He hadn't expected his return to be easy but even those thoughts hadn't prepared him for the roller coaster of emotion he'd been on since he'd driven in to town. And if his worst fears were realized, the ride was far from over.

One thing kept him grounded, gave him a glimmer of hope that he'd make it through what was to come.

Ren.

And there she was. Curled on her side facing the door, snuggled beneath the quilt.

Brady took a moment to absorb the sight. In spite of his optimism, there had been a little niggle of doubt that he'd find her still here.

"Hey." Her sleepy voice brought his eyes to hers.

He smiled. "Hey."

She pulled the cover behind her back and murmured, "Come to bed. We can talk about it in the morning."

He walked closer but didn't climb in beside her. "I'm sorry."

"Nothing to be sorry about. You did the right thing. Now get in here and get warm. I doubt that cup of hot chocolate is still hot."

Brady spotted the mug on the side table. "You made me hot chocolate?"

"Hmm..." Her eyes drifted shut. "If you want I can reheat it."

"No." Brady circled the bed and slipped onto the mattress behind her. "I'd rather get warm by holding you."

"Can you do that without losing control?" she questioned with a sleepy slur.

He nestled in close. "Yeah, I think so. I'm more settled since we did what we did. Plus I'm exhausted."

"You've been gone for hours."

"Didn't go far."

"You could have locked yourself in the bathroom."

"No lock."

"Really?"

He grinned. "You didn't try to lock the door at all today?"

"No. Why would I. The door was closed."

Brady's grin widened. Yeah, she might not think she trusted him, but she did. It might not be a conscious thought but deep down she trusted he would respect her boundaries even if it were a simple closed door that she'd put between them.

Now he just needed her to trust him completely. He wanted everything with her and he knew he wouldn't get any of it until she believed in him—them—fully. "Go back to sleep. We'll talk in the morning."

After a few moments, she whispered, "I spoke to Gordie."

He hummed in answer. The long run and freezing temps he'd subjected himself to were catching up with him quickly.

"She doesn't remember your mom being pregnant or reading that she was in the files she transferred to the new database. She said we can take a look at your mom's file whenever we want."

"Mm'kay." Brady snuggled in behind Ren. "Sleep now."

"'Night." She wiggled back, her ass rubbing his groin, making his cock twitch.

Holding his breath, he concentrated on not getting another boner. Having her warm sleepy body in his arms had him at half-mast as it was and with the soft swell of her ass pressing against him, his body was reacting in the typical way. Blood rushed, his heart raced, and the half-mast headed towards full.

One arm beneath her waist, one draped over her hip, Brady kept his hands still and focused on her breathing, tried to match his to hers. Before long she drifted off, and eyes closed, he savored the feelings coursing through him.

This was what he'd waited for, why he'd never been tempted by any other woman; this one had laid claim to his heart—his soul— when neither of them were old enough to understand the depth or meaning of their connection.

He'd do anything to get them back to the pureness of their childhood friendship. He couldn't erase the mistakes, couldn't get back the time they'd missed, but he'd be damned if he didn't make the most of every second he had with her now.

With a sleeping Ren in his arms, he could finally relax, could think about the fact she hadn't run back to town after he'd disappeared into the forest. Could believe they'd find their way to the future they both deserved. The future his father and brother had tried their best to steal.

He'd had plenty of time to think while he'd been outside. He'd hit the small creek and followed the water for a few minutes before turning back. Racing up the incline he'd checked the house then returned to the creek. Over and over he'd run the course he'd set until the weather threatened to blind him.

Brady knew he'd been gone hours. His muscles ached, and his bones felt frozen to the marrow. Ren hadn't complained about the cold when he'd climbed in behind her, and with her warmth and the quilt tucked tight around them, his body temperature had already returned to normal.

One thing that had been in the forefront of his mind was the secrets he knew his mother's journals held. He'd face them, bring them into the open so they could find closure. And if they proved to be hurtful to someone else, they'd decide together—he and Ren— who needed to know.

He might hate the idea of keeping secrets, but he wouldn't hurt someone if they wouldn't benefit from the knowledge. Some things were best left buried.

Nuzzling his nose into the back of Ren's neck, Brady breathed deep and filled his lungs with the scent of her. They'd start going through the journals tomorrow. For now he'd hold his mate close and dream of their future.

———

The smell of bacon frying and coffee woke him. Reaching out, he slid his hand across the bed beside him.

Empty.

That explained the glorious scents flooding the house and making his mouth water and belly rumble.

Ren was up and in the kitchen.

How many nights had he dreamed of this? Or days. The want for her hadn't been confined to the darkness of night. He'd spent too many times to count thinking of her, wondering what she was doing, who she was with. She'd taken root in his head and heart, and the longer he'd spent away from her, the deeper his yearning went.

"Sleeping Beauty is awake." His gaze flew to the doorway where she leaned against the jamb, a smile on her face. "Hungry?"

"Definitely." Throwing off the covers, he swung his legs over the side of the bed. "Why didn't you wake me? I would have helped cook."

"Don't need help, and you got in late so I let you sleep late, but it's time to get up now. We've got books to read."

The reminder made him pause. He'd almost forgotten about the possible time bomb ticking in the living room.

Taking a deep breath, he stretched his arms above his head and relished the pull on his muscles. He should do a session of yoga to iron out the kinks his late-night run left in his body. Although he wasn't sure he wanted Ren to know he was into yoga. Most men lifted weights or ran miles; Brady preferred the flexibility and strength yoga delivered.

He'd taken plenty of ribbing over it in the past. He hadn't let the teasing get to him before except the thought of Ren thinking he was a wimp didn't sit well.

"What's that face?" she asked, pushing off the doorway and coming closer.

"Oh, I, um..."

"Spit it out. No lies, remember?"

With a sigh, he let his arms drop. "I was thinking about doing yoga to stretch after last night's run."

"Really? You do yoga?"

"Yes." He waited for the laughing to start.

"Cool. Mind if I join you or do you prefer to do it in solitude? Wendy likes to practice alone, says it breaks her concentration if she can hear someone else breathing, but I don't mind sharing space with someone else when I do it."

Okay. That wasn't what he'd expected. "I don't think I'd mind.

Never had anyone to do a session with so I guess we'll find out." Smiling, he pushed to his feet and moved in front of Ren.

Without asking, he pulled her in for a hug. She smelled like bacon and eggs and coffee. Three of his favorite things on his favorite person. Morning didn't get any better than this.

"We're snowed in."

"Yeah?" Brady couldn't find it in him to be upset by that.

"We've had a foot of snow overnight and it's still coming down, although it has eased off since I got up."

"This storm front is supposed to last a couple of days, right?" The idea of being trapped with Ren didn't feel confining at all; if anything it felt freeing. They would be free of outside influences and could make the most of the alone time to get reacquainted.

"Another forty-eight hours of snowfall according to the sheriff's department."

"Are you okay with that? Being stuck here?"

She leaned back and pressed a kiss to his chin. "Yes. C'mon, let's eat."

Pulling from his arms, she led the way out of the room. It was then he noticed she wore a pair of his sweatpants and one of his hoodies. Containing his grin was impossible, so he let it fly and followed behind her.

He found breakfast already on the table in the dark dining room. He really needed to knock out more walls, open up the entire area. Steam rose from their mugs and the platters of food. There was enough to feed an army. Good thing Brady had always had a healthy appetite. "Now this, a guy could get used to."

"Make the most of it. Normally by this time in the day I'd be at the Den serving this up to whoever wanders in."

"Well, count me in as a wanderer. I'll be there every morning." He dug into the pile of bacon and scooped more than half of the crispy meat onto his plate. He sighed. "And this is cooked exactly the way I like it."

"Wasn't sure if you would want sunny side up or over easy so I scrambled the eggs." Ren smiled at him. "Coffee is yours. It's a better roast than the one I brought with me."

"It was what my mother used. I'm not really a coffee snob. As long as it's hot, I don't care."

"Good to know."

"So what's a day in the life of Ren like?" he asked before shoveling a forkful of eggs between his lips. "Hmm...these are good," he praised through his mouthful. "Really good."

"It's the cheese."

Swallowing, he asked, "Cheese?"

"Yep. A sprinkle of grated cheese just before the liquid hardens and you need to stir."

"Well, whatever it is, they're delicious. Thank you."

"For?" Ren picked up her mug and brought it to her mouth.

"Cooking breakfast. You didn't have to. I don't expect you to take care of me."

She shrugged. "I like to cook."

"You also like to take care of people. But who takes care of you, Ren?"

Smiling, she put her cup down and leaned forward. "Apparently, you, *mate*."

"You want me to take care of you?" He had to tread carefully here. One wrong step and she'd back up again, and he knew they were on the verge of consenting to the mating bond.

"Isn't that what mates do? Take care of each other?" She cocked her head to the side, one eyebrow raised. "Did you change your mind after—"

"*Never*." He shot out of his chair and leaned over the table until his mouth was inches from hers. Fuck, he wanted to kiss her. Wanted to press his lips to hers. Wanted to lick his tongue along her plump lower one before pushing his way inside. "I'll never change my mind about you. About us."

"Okay. Well then. We should finish breakfast, then get started."

"Started?" He jerked upright. Jesus. Did she mean... His cock went rock hard, bulging the front of his underwear and poking out the top. He could feel pre-cum ooze from the tip.

"Oh, no, I don't mean we should"—she waved a hand between them—"you know. I meant we should get to reading those journals. You said you wanted all of that in the past before we mated."

Brady ground his teeth, clenched his jaw, his fists. "And you want that? To wait until after?"

"I." Her mouth snapped shut. She licked those lips he wanted to get his mouth on. "No. Yes. I want to go through the journals and see what happens. I'm not going to fight against our connection any more, but I don't want to jump in either."

"Okay." He held himself still. Breakfast forgotten in front of him. "Okay. I can do that."

"I'm asking too much, aren't I?"

"No. No, I, um, just need a second." He pulled in a few deep breaths, focused on getting his raging libido back under control. Strangely his coyote wasn't making a sound. Maybe because the bastard knew he'd get what he wanted soon enough.

Brady smiled.

Yeah, they could both relax. Because by the time their forced confinement ended, he'd be mated with Ren.

14

"Brady?"

"Yeah," he muttered while continuing to rummage through one of the boxes they'd pulled out of the attic. He wanted to be sure he had all the journals his mother wrote and thought she might have left some behind when she'd escaped the house years ago.

Kat waited for him to look up. It took a few minutes but she wanted to have his full attention when she told him what she'd just read.

He pulled out a string of tangled lights and sighed. "Why would they keep these? They're obviously useless." He tossed them aside to join the growing pile of trash and dug back into the box.

"Brady." She slapped her hand on the timber floor.

"What?" He glanced up, a scowl on his face.

Something in her expression must have given him a clue because he pushed the box away and moved on his knees across the floor to where she sat, one of his mother's journals in her hand, the rest spread around her in date order.

"What? What is it?" he asked, his eyes on hers.

"Have you ever read any of your mother's journals?"

He shook his head but his eyes never left hers. "No."

"Not even when you were little and found one?"

"No. She hid them. At least that's what she told me. I didn't even know she kept them until she got sick."

"Oh. Right. Yeah, I can see why she'd hide these," she muttered, glancing down at the open page.

"Why? What's in them?"

God. How did she tell him? Should she tell him or make him read the words in his mother's hand? "Um..."

"Kathren, please. Just tell me what has put that look on your face."

Taking a deep breath, she thought about the best way to upend his life. And it would upend it. What was written in these journals would change everything he knew about his mother and father. About the brother whose body he'd come home to claim.

"Ren?" Brady grabbed her forearm, his fingers curling around and squeezing. "Whatever it is can't be worse than your father trying to destroy a whole town."

She smiled. "Not the whole town. Only the non-bloods and half-bloods."

"See? What could possibly be worse?"

Fuck. It was worse. So much worse. "I think you should read this part." She turned the journal she'd been reading and held it out, open to the page that would probably be the hardest to read. At least it was what she thought was the most shocking of what she'd read so far. Her eyes scanned the rest of the journals.

God. What else was in them?

"You can't tell me?" he asked as he took the leather-bound book.

Remaining quiet, she kept her gaze on his face, waited for him to look down and read the words that had been like a punch to her gut and they weren't even about her.

"Fine. I'll read it." But he didn't. His eyes stayed locked with hers for a long time before he took a deep breath and blew it out in a rush. "You could just tell me..."

Kat rolled her lips between her teeth and tried to keep her

emotions at bay. It was hard though. This would hurt Brady. Hurt him in a way she wasn't sure he could recover from.

He hadn't given her the full details of the night his mother had taken him away or how it had affected him, but she'd got the impression it had scarred him deeply. This would open up those old wounds and deliver more.

Brady's voice cut through her thoughts.

> *"He brought the first child home the year I lost the fifth baby.*
> *I didn't ask any questions. I should have asked questions.*
> *The little boy was around two, barely talking or walking.*
> *He cried. Cried for a mother I knew nothing of.*
> *Malcolm told me to keep him quiet. To keep him out of sight.*
> *I wasn't sure what had happened or why this little boy was here.*
> *Matthew told me to be grateful. To mother the child as my own.*
> *And as much as it shames me to admit, I didn't argue. I accepted.*
> *That boy became mine.*
> *Became Marcus."*

Brady's gaze snapped to hers. "What the fuck?"

"I don't know." The confusion in his eyes matched her own. "I haven't read past that page. I didn't think I should..."

"You should. Jesus, I've got nothing to hide from you." He glanced down at the book in his hand. "But it appears as though my mother had something to hide."

"It sounds like your father and whoever Matthew is had a lot more to hide."

He took a deep breath and began to read again.

> *"In the first few years I kept to myself, to the house in the mountains.*
> *No one came to visit in all that time. And I never ventured into town.*

Not that Malcolm would have let me. He and Matthew brought supplies.
I was more a servant than wife and I was never the latter legally.
But that's a story for another time."

"Fuck." Brady dropped the book to the floor and dragged his fingers through his hair.

She gave him time. Let him get his thoughts together before asking the question burning on her tongue.

"Did you know Marcus wasn't your blood brother?"

He shook his head. "No." His gaze met hers. "And now I have to wonder if I'm blood related to my parents. Marcus clearly wasn't."

Kat could understand why he'd think that. She wanted to know the answer herself. But she wanted so much more than that, and Michelle's journals held the answers.

"I think someone needs to read everything your mother wrote. I think..." she licked her lips, swallowed. "I think we might find out why your father wanted to destroy this town and why Marcus helped him."

"Why? It's not like they can be punished for what they did or understanding their motives will make anything better."

"No, they can't be punished. Death did that. As for making things better... Brady, there are secrets here that could answer a lot of questions people have, could help the town recover from the years of terror your father and his supporters subjected us to."

"He's gone now. He can't hurt anyone from the grave."

"But he can. His actions have left a taint on this town. It's dark and insidious and will continue to eat at us until we put it to rest."

Brady laughed but there was no humor in the sound. "Sure. Why not blacken the Connelly name more?"

Kat bit her tongue except it wasn't enough to stop her from voicing the words swirling in her head. "You might not even be a Connelly. Marcus wasn't."

"Fuck." He dragged both hands through his hair again, tugged the ends. "How do we do this? Shit, we need to tell the sheriff. The sovereign and regal, the council."

"Not yet." She put a hand on his arm in the hope of grounding him. His need to run was written all over his face and while she could see the appeal, the weather didn't allow for it. "I think we should read as much of these as we can before we do anything, say anything."

"Okay, okay. We'll see what other shit the Connellys did." He snatched up the journal and flipped the pages to the beginning. "I'll read this one. You grab another one."

"I've read part of that one so let me keep going. Do you have a pen and paper? I'd like to make notes."

"We should try and put them in time order."

"I've done that already. Can you get a pen and paper?" He needed something to focus on besides the thoughts spiraling in his head.

She let go of his arm except before he could get up, she threw her arms around his neck and pulled him close. Neither of them spoke. They sat on the floor for long minutes while Brady calmed and Kat comforted.

"Thank you for doing this with me."

"It's what mates do, right? Support each other."

"You still want to be my mate after what we just read?" he asked, his lips brushing against her neck where he'd burrowed in. "I wouldn't hold it against you if you didn't."

"You know me better than that, Brady."

He sighed into her neck. "Yeah, I do."

"I'll be here no matter what."

"God, I hope so because I don't think that's the only rotten skeleton we're going to find."

Kat didn't agree with him verbally; she didn't have to. They both knew if Malcolm Connelly was capable of taking a child and passing it off as his own, he was capable of so much more. What, remained to be discover.

She only hoped it didn't break Brady.

Kat made notes about the last two pages she'd read. It had taken a couple of hours but she was pretty sure she now understood what Malcolm and Matthew had been doing. She also understood that Brady's mother had been brought to Whispering Springs against her will. Turned against her will. The woman had been trapped in a situation she had no clue how to get out of or where to go for help.

Michelle Watson had been taken off a street in Omaha, Nebraska, when she was barely eighteen. She'd been subjected to beatings and rape—because no one would argue otherwise—for years. All at the hands of a man who claimed to be her husband—her mate.

Kat still wasn't sure who Matthew was; Michelle hadn't mentioned a last name so far but she had mentioned him every time she wrote about the beatings. Up until this point he hadn't been involved in the rapes except the man had to have known what Malcolm was doing to his *mate*. Kat had no idea if Matthew was alive or not, but if he was she had every intention of hunting him down and putting him down.

No man deserved to live after what he'd done and allowed to be done to others.

It was the children that concerned Kat the most. They were under the age of three according to Michelle. So far Kat had a list of four names—names the men who'd kidnapped them had given them—and none of them were called Jacob.

Michelle knew nothing of where they'd come from before Malcolm arrived at the house with them. One thing Kat hadn't discovered, and what Michelle didn't seem to know up to this point in her journals, was where the children went after they spent a week locked in the shed out back.

The thought of going out to that shed had Kat's stomach clenching. Except she knew they would have to. Eventually. Maybe they would wait until they told the sheriff about what they'd uncovered.

Not that Brady had found much. He'd read half a journal before he dropped it to the floor and left the room. A few seconds later Kat heard banging from the back of the house. Wanting to be sure he was okay, she'd gone to check and found him taking out his anger on the wall dividing the back bedrooms.

She'd left him there. She knew someone who needed to be alone when she saw them.

That had been hours ago now.

Stretching her arms over her head, she dropped her chin to her chest then tipped it toward the ceiling, pulling on the kinks in her neck. It was time for a break. She'd make them lunch then decide what to do about the information she'd collected.

"Hey."

Turning her head, Kat found Brady in the doorway covered in dust and timber splinters. Smiling, she said, "You need to get cleaned up."

"Want some lunch? I'll wash up and make sandwiches."

"You wash up and I'll make something better than sandwiches." She'd brought a chicken pie with her yesterday that wouldn't take long to reheat.

"How'd it go?" Brady asked with a tip of his chin at the journals.

"Ah, I've gone through four so far. Do you know who Matthew is?"

"No. Should I?" His expression told her he didn't really want to know the answer to that.

"I don't know. He seems to be in every entry up to where I've read. You don't remember another man living here?"

He shook his head. "Was only ever Mom, Dad, Marcus, and me."

"Hmm..." Kat pushed to her feet. "Well, he's someone important in the early years of your mother's life here. I think he lived here too."

"Maybe you'll find why in a later journal." He eyed the leatherbound books warily. "I'll go wash up."

Kat watched him go with a heavy heart. Each thing she was discovering about Michelle Watson's past meant another scar for Brady. Not the physical kind, but the kind that were hidden, the kind that marked the heart and bled the soul. If what she was thinking was true, he'd be finding out he and Marcus had one thing in common.

Neither of them had been born with Connelly blood.

15

———————

By the time Brady cleaned up and reached the kitchen, the most amazing aroma filled the house, making his mouth water and his stomach rumble.

He loved Ren for many reasons but her skill with food might top the list. His mother had always said the way to his heart was through his stomach.

His *mother*.

God, was she even his mother?

He'd always thought he took after her but now that he was questioning it, their looks weren't enough alike for there to be no doubt about his parentage. They had the same shaped nose and color eyes except that could be dumb luck over genetics.

Their hair was similar, except now that he thought about it, his mother's hair had been white blond where his was more dirty creek water blond. And the man he had considered his father until today had been a blue-eyed redhead but his brother—who wasn't his brother at all—had dark hair and dark eyes to go with his dark personality.

The more Brady thought about the family he'd been raised in, the more he saw signs that all was not as it seemed. Marcus had never been happy. Even as a child, his brother had rarely smiled. And the number of dead animals he'd brought out of the forest over the years had to be excessive. Malcolm Connelly had always praised a kill, and Marcus had been pleased with both the praise and the spoils of the hunt.

Now Brady had to wonder if Marcus's need to kill hadn't been a big red flag his mother should have noticed. Then again, after recent revelations he didn't know or understand the woman anymore, so perhaps she'd been as pleased as her husband with their first son's efforts.

Except Marcus hadn't been their son.

And if Marcus wasn't, then what about him?

Hunting and killing had never appealed to Brady. Even in coyote form he didn't like to hunt. Maybe that was another sign he should take note of. So many things about his life he could no longer be certain of. So many questions and no one to answer them except a set of private journals left behind by the woman who'd raised him.

Shaking his head, Brady dispelled all thoughts of his family and the past, and brought his focus back to the woman in front of him. The one currently bent over at the stove.

She still wore his clothes and in spite of them being too big for her, the pants molded to the sweet curve of her ass as she leaned over and reached into the oven.

He opened his mouth to offer a hand but snapped it shut again. He didn't want to startle her in case she bumped into a hot surface. Instead he rested a shoulder on the doorframe and watched her lift a pie dish and place it on the counter. He couldn't help but admire her strength and ease as she worked. She was comfortable here, in the kitchen. He'd love to watch her at the Den.

It would be her place.

The one where she took control, held the reins, and directed others to do as she wanted.

"It's ready," she said without turning around. "Want to pour us coffee?"

Brady was one hundred percent sure he hadn't made a sound and she'd had her back to him the whole time; there was no way she would have seen him in her peripheral vision.

Frowning, he pushed off the doorjamb and asked, "How did you know I was here?" on his way to the coffee pot.

"I heard you leave the bedroom, could smell you when you came into the room." She glanced over her shoulder, her brow furrowed, her eyes squinting. "Actually, it was more that I sensed you than smelled you, but once I felt you behind me I could pick out your scent over the chicken pie."

"Mating bond." Grabbing the pot, he filled the two mugs she had placed on the counter beside the machine. "We might not have completed it or even marked each other but our connection is growing stronger."

"It is. Which is why I think we should mark each other after lunch," she casually tossed over her shoulder with a smile as if those words weren't the most significant of his life.

"Wh—" Saliva caught in his throat. "What?" he choked out. Coughing, he cleared his throat and asked, "You want to mark each other? After lunch?"

She'd fought against their bond long enough for Brady to believe it would be weeks before she would accept him and they could do anything about the connection strengthening between them with every second they were together, and now she was giving in? Just like that?

"What happened? What did you read in those books?" he demanded.

Something had to have triggered her acceptance. She'd said she wasn't going to fight their attraction—connection—but this was taking the reins and... *Ah.*

"You want to be in control, and to do that you say when and how," he guessed.

Ren turned and faced him fully. "Yes and no."

"Explain it to me because this one-eighty has my head spinning." And his heart racing. He crossed his arms over his chest even though every instinct screamed to cross the damn room and pull her into his arms and against his chest.

"I'd like us both to be in control, to make active choices instead of reactive, and I want you to know that those journals, whatever they reveal about you, or your family, make no difference to the way I see *you*. The way I *feel* about you."

"We were going to put the past in the past first."

"The past is already in the past; it doesn't change the fact we're mates or that I want to be your mate."

"You said you didn't want to."

"No. I said I wasn't happy about being forced to mate. But, Brady." She took a step toward him making every muscle in his body clench, his lungs seize. "If I had to choose, out of all the men I've known in my life, I'd choose you. Every time. I *chose* you before I knew what it meant to be mates, before I knew what love was I *loved* you. When you left, it hurt and I wanted to blame you for that, and for everything your family has done to mine, but you aren't to blame for any of it. Yes, you should have come back sooner. Yes, you should have tried to contact me at some point over the last thirteen years, but I under-stand why you didn't."

"Glad one of us does."

She smiled at him. "You know why you didn't."

"Yeah," he sighed. And he did.

He'd been trying to please the one person he still had in his life, the woman who'd raised him and now might not even be his mother.

A growl rumbled in his chest. "I hate all the secrets."

"Then let's make a rule right now, one we live by for the rest of our days. No secrets between us. *Ever*."

"I love you." He'd planned to hold back those words but if they weren't keeping secrets, then he needed to say them whether she reci-procated or not. He needed her to know he was all in.

Ren's smile grew as she closed the distance between them and placed her hands on his chest. "And I love you."

"Can we though? Love each other?" he wondered. "We haven't

seen each other in years and we've both changed, grown. We don't really know each other anymore."

"Are you doubting what you feel or what I feel?"

He shrugged. "Both?"

"Okay, then let's agree we have strong feelings of *like* to go along with our mates bond and we're prepared to build on those."

"Then we shouldn't mark each other." Fuck. He couldn't believe he was thinking it, never mind voicing it. "We should wait until we're sure."

"I'm sure I want to be marked by you. If you don't want me to mark you yet, that's fine. I'll wait."

"*No.* I want that. I just…"

She slipped her arms around his waist and laid her cheek on his shoulder, her face tucking in to the side of his neck. "Brady, I'm not going to change my mind."

"You already have," he argued. "Not a week ago you ordered me out of the Den, and now you're inviting me to make the most intimate connection two coyotes can make."

"That wasn't about you."

"How could it not have been about me?"

Behind him she gripped fistfuls of his shirt and tugged. "It was about everybody else. All the crazy shit that's gone on in recent weeks, months. Jeez, years."

"And me."

Ren sighed; her warm breath bathing his neck sent ripples of goose bumps across his skin. "Yeah, and you."

"Then we should wait." God, he was an idiot who should bang his head on the nearest wall.

He had the woman of his dreams asking him to mark her, and he was trying to change her mind, put her off.

Damn. He wasn't an idiot, he was fucking insane.

"Do you think we would wait if we'd just met?" she inquired with a smirk in her tone.

Damn her. She had him. He tightened his arms around her. "No, probably not."

Would it be so bad to mark each other? He knew there was nothing that could possibly change his mind about Ren. She was it for him, had been his whole life, but then she wasn't the one with all the rotting skeletons in her family closet.

Anything could come out of his mother's journals. They'd already discovered Marcus wasn't born a coyote, wasn't a Connelly by birth. Most likely Brady wasn't either.

She held tight to his shirt, her arms banded around his ribs, squeezing as though she knew he needed something to ground him, while his mind spun in circles going over the same things again and again.

Holding her close gave him strength; it also gave him thoughts of being in this position naked.

It would be so easy to take her up on the offer, to pick her up and carry her to the bedroom where he could spread her out on the bed and explore every inch of her body.

A shudder went through him. "I don't know if I could stop myself from claiming you once we started," he admitted.

"Is that why you're backpedaling? You think I'll be upset if we complete our mating bond while marking each other?" She leaned away, her arms remaining locked around him, a frown on her face. "Brady, I think you misunderstood what I'm asking. Or maybe I worded it wrong. I think we should claim each other. Mark, sex, bite, the whole bonding thing."

If he thought his body had clenched before, it was nothing compared to right now. He was so tight it wouldn't surprise him to find he'd lost inches in height and width; his skin felt like it had shrunk two sizes, compressing muscle and bone.

Dragging air into his lungs, he pushed it out through strangled vocal cords. "Did you turn the oven off?"

Ren's forehead wrinkled, her nose scrunched up. "Yes, why —hey!"

He couldn't stop a smile from stretching his lips as he scooped her off the floor into his arms and made for the bedroom. If they were doing this—and god help him, they abso-fucking-lutely were—he would do it right, do his best to make it good for Ren.

Which meant he had to get her naked and leave his own clothes on. To begin with.

If he let his cock out now, the damn thing would be shoved inside her before either of them blinked. And Brady wasn't about to embarrass himself like that. He'd be sure to make her come and if he managed not to come in his pants while doing so, he'd jerk off so he wouldn't be on edge when he took her the first time.

Fuck.

He was about to lose his virginity to the only woman he'd ever wanted. When did his life get so great?

Only days ago he thought he'd be run out of town by an angry mob, Ren leading the charge, and now he was lowering her to his bed, getting ready to sink inside her virgin body.

Double fuck.

There was no way he wasn't coming in his pants this first time.

16

Brady's hands curled around her waist, his grip sure—confident—before he skimmed them under her hoodie and up her ribcage. He hissed out a breath, his gaze darting to hers when he discovered what she wore beneath it.

"Fuck. No bra." His palms cupped and squeezed, fingers caressed and tweaked. "I need to see you."

He didn't have to ask twice. With a wiggle, she pulled the sweater up and bared her breasts.

"Jesus. Take it off." Slipping his hands behind her back, he lifted her up. "Take it all the way off."

Gripping the hem, Kat tugged the hoodie over her head and tossed it across the room where it landed in a heap on the floor.

"These too." Brady let her fall back to the bed and yanked on the waistband of her sweats, their fit so loose they were at her knees in one tug. "Jesus fucking Christ. No underwear at all? You've been walking around all day without anything under my clothes?"

"I didn't want to put my dirty—"

"Don't care." He slid the pants the rest of the way off and threw them in the direction of the hoodie. "New rule. No underwear at home."

His fingers came back to her waist, trailed over her skin as he explored the area, the slightly abrasive pads delivering a sensation between tickle and caress. She shivered beneath his touch as his strokes swept lower down her torso.

Grinning, he said, "Yeah, I really like that rule."

"Goes both ways." Her breathing hitched, her insides clenched, as he concentrated on a particularly sensitive spot on her belly right above her mound. "If I don't get to wear them, neither do you."

"Agreed. No underwear for either of us from now on."

Smiling, Kat reached for the button on Brady's jeans. "Let's get yours off then."

His hands covered hers. "No. Not yet. I want this to last and if I get naked now, it's not going to."

Her gaze caught his. She could see his coyote just beneath the surface, felt his fingers tremble on hers. "You're close to shifting."

"I know."

"Should we mate in coyote—"

"Fuck no! The first time I have you, I want my hands on you. Your hands on me."

"Then..." She didn't know. Had no clue how to navigate the need visibly coursing through Brady. Her own coyote was happy to be on her back, offering herself to her mate. "Tell me what to do."

"Lie back and enjoy."

"But—"

"Shh..." One finger covered her lips as he leaned over her. "Let me make this good for you."

"I want to touch you too." Kat ran her hands up his sides, over his chest, and around his neck. Locking her fingers together, she pulled his mouth to hers. "Kiss me, Brady."

Their lips met. A soft brush, back and forth. A little pressure. A lick of tongue.

They took their time, pressing, brushing, closed mouths learning the shape and feel of each other.

Kat had kissed boys. She'd kissed men. None of them kissed her the way Brady did. Like she was a treasure to be explored with a thoroughness that left her breathless.

His tongue stroked across her lips making them tremble, her breath sigh. He nipped at her top lip, bit into the bottom one with more force, and tugged before soothing the sting with the hot swipe of his tongue. He spent what felt like forever exploring her lips before pulling back enough to lock eyes with her.

"Open for me," he breathed against her mouth. "Let me taste you."

Parting her lips for him came as naturally as breathing. She wanted to let him in, wanted him to take whatever he wanted from her. To give him everything she was without fear or prejudice. It was just the two of them. No one else had a right to come between mates, and Kat vowed to make sure no one and nothing—past or future—did.

As his fated mate, her coyote had already bonded to his, but as a human she had the choice to give him her heart or guard it against any pain he could inflict. Except loving someone meant they could and would hurt you. That's what loving did.

It opened you up, bared you to the one you loved, and gave you the power to hurt and heal.

Kat intended to heal Brady.

"Take your clothes off."

Jerking away, he frowned at her. "I can't if I want to stay in control."

"I don't want you in control. I want all of you."

"You'll get me but I want to make it good for you first."

"Is this a macho-alpha coyote thing where you have to prove you can please your mate because I don't need that shit. Not between you and me."

"No. I don't want to hurt you, I want to make sure you're ready."

"I couldn't be any more ready, Brady. My thighs are slick with how ready I am. It's a wonder you can't feel how wet I am through your jeans."

"Ren. Please. I need to do it this way. Let me make you feel good then—"

"No. We do this together. I don't care if you get off quick because I can guarantee you I'll be right there with you." She cupped his face in both hands. "Brady, I need you inside me. And I don't mean your tongue in my mouth, although I'll take that too."

Air burst from his mouth and his eyes closed tight. "I'm afraid I'll go off the second I get inside you. That I'll be too quick for you to come."

"Then we won't stop. We'll keep going and from everything I know about a mating bond you'll stay hard. I'm not in heat, so I can't get pregnant, but I want to feel your cum inside me. I want to feel your warmth fill me up—"

"*Fuck!*" He dropped his chin, his breaths rushing in and out of his lungs in harsh explosions.

Before Kat could argue more, Brady levered up on his hands and sprang from the bed. At first she thought he would run like he had the night before but then he did what she'd asked and stripped.

And holy hell was she glad it was daylight and she could see every glorious inch of Brady Connelly in all his nakedness, because damn was he a sight to behold.

And hold.

She planned to do plenty of holding.

"Get back here," she demanded, spreading her legs wide in invitation.

A growl rumbled from his throat and his eyes lightened, his coyote showing through with the need to claim. "I don't want to mount you from behind in spite of everything in me demanding it. I want to see your face when I sink inside you."

"We can do the mounting thing next time."

Brady closed his eyes and shuddered. Pre-cum dripped from the tip of his engorged cock and Kat licked her lips.

What would he taste like? Would he let her lick him like an ice cream?

"*Kathren*," Brady growled, his voice rough and deep. "Eyes up here."

Dragging her gaze away from his groin, she found his hands clenched at his sides, the muscles and veins in his arms bulging. Further up, his chest heaved with each breath and his nipples pebbled within the light dusting of hair. The sharp angle of his jaw jutted forward, muscles clenching on both sides of his chin; his nostrils flared wide with each inhalation and his eyes blazed with a feral light that singed, caught fire beneath her skin.

Her coyote whined, whimpered in submission, and Kat had to fight the need to turn over, to offer him her back, turn her head, and offer her throat.

She could satisfy both her coyote and his if she gave him the latter so she twisted her head to the side, arched her neck to show him the tender sweep of her throat.

"Fuck. I'm done waiting." He lunged, caging her beneath him in one leap. "Open for me. Spread your legs and wrap them around my waist."

She was already lifting her feet, bending her knees, and curling her legs around him. Crossing her ankles, Kat locked her limbs around Brady's waist and raised her hips. "Don't wait. If there's any pain, get it over with quickly."

"No." He lowered his pelvis, pressed the length of his erection against her sensitive folds. "I won't hurt you."

"You might not be able to help it, Brady." She grabbed his face, made sure her gaze held his. "It won't last long and I doubt it'll be that bad. I've used a vibrator"—his eyes closed on a groan—"so it's not like I haven't had anything inside me before."

"Ren." His eyes snapped open, the fire in them scorching her from skin to bone. "Shut up. Stop talking. Let me think."

Rocking her hips up, she dragged her clit along his cock, over the tip, until the plump head rested at her opening. "Now. Brady."

"Ren."

His protest came too late. Using her thighs, Kat rose up and took him deep. A spike of pain shot through her, a fiery flash that was there and gone in less time than it took to suck in a breath.

"Ren?" Brady cradled her head, laid his forehead on hers, and pressed his lips to hers. "Shit. Ren," he breathed against her mouth. "I didn't want to hurt you."

Drawing in a deep breath, Kat concentrated on the sensations rolling through her. "I'm okay."

"I hurt you."

"*We* hurt me." She needed him to understand that the pain had been worth it. To be joined with him like this, to feel him inside her, stretching her with his heat, to know neither of them had done this before, that they'd only ever do this together. "Brady, I promise you, it's already gone and it was minor. I've survived worse."

"What?" His head jerked up. "What worse? How worse?"

"Relax." She stroked a hand down his back. "The last time I sliced a finger at the Den hurt ten times as much."

He frowned. "I don't like the idea of you being hurt."

"We have that in common."

"No, really. I don't think you should use knives anymore."

Kat rolled her eyes. How he could focus on something other than their current position was beyond her. "Brady. You need to move."

His gaze met hers, gold sparking as his body's impulses began to take over once more. With a short jerk he pulled back, the drag of flesh on flesh drawing a moan from each of them. "Promise me," he demanded.

"What?"

"Promise you'll tell me to stop if it hurts."

God, how could she ever think this man would hurt her—physically or emotionally? He wouldn't. It wasn't in him to do it. He'd sooner inflict pain on himself than her. "You won't hurt me."

"*Promise me.*"

"I promise." She gave him what he needed. "I'll never lie to you. And no matter what happens we're in this together."

"I couldn't live if I hurt you again."

Kat slapped her hands on either side of his face. "Stop. It wasn't your fault. You'd never intentionally hurt me, Brady, I know that to the depths of my soul."

He lowered his brow to hers. "It would kill me," he breathed against her mouth.

"I know."

His breath rushed out. "I can't believe we're here." His hips flexed, pumping his cock in and out in a quick, short thrust.

She couldn't hold in the moan, not when pleasure snapped through her, pulsing and sparking and making her insides clench around his hard length. "Again."

"That didn't hurt?"

"God, no."

The pain had been nothing. There and gone and all that was left in its wake was a different kind of pain. The kind that drove you mad until the man you loved drove himself inside you.

"I need..." She rocked her hips, squeezed internal muscles, and had them both moaning.

The movement had Brady bucking, flexing, thrusting. Had him lowering over her further, had his breath hot in her ear as he nuzzled into her neck. "Fuck. It's too good."

Kat took that as a compliment; she didn't worry about the fact he had no reference to compare it to. This was them, would always be them. No one and nothing would come between them ever again.

She curled her back, tilted her pelvis so her pussy was in perfect alignment for Brady's cock. He drove into her, over and over and as his breathing became more shallow, faster, so did his thrusts. His body ground against hers, the pressure on her clit with each plunge quickly taking her up toward the peak she'd only ever reached on her own.

Sure, she'd used Brady to get there yesterday but she'd been the one touching her body, pressing deep and plying her clit until the inevitable happened.

Now it was Brady. Her mate. The man she'd loved when he was no more than a boy. They might not know each other as well as they had but it didn't stop her heart from spreading wider than her legs and drawing him inside.

"I'm going to..." Brady panted.

Kat smiled. "Don't stop." She reached between them, slipped her fingers around one taut nipple and pinched.

Light burst, sensation exploded, and Kat went over the edge with a cry.

She wasn't aware of her teeth dropping, of leaning forward to suction her mouth to Brady's neck and sink them deep. Caught in the maelstrom of pleasure, she screamed around the flesh between her teeth when Brady reciprocated.

Warmth spread inside her core, muscles clenching and flexing and gripping. Spasm after spasm had them rocking together, Brady driving deep, deep, deeper, until a final wave of ecstasy took them under.

Panting for breath, Brady collapsed on Ren. Twisting to the side he took some of his weight off her but he couldn't bring himself to roll off completely.

He liked having her beneath him.

Her body cradled his in all the best ways and he loved how her pussy wrapped around his dick as though they'd been made to fit together forever.

He didn't have any idea what sex felt like with anyone except Ren and while that might not be every man's choice, Brady was extremely happy he'd waited. Ecstatic that she'd be his one and only. The fact he'd be hers only made that feeling multiply.

It wasn't as though he was some alpha asshole who wanted his woman pure or anything. He didn't. He wouldn't have been any less happy with his current situation if Ren had been with a hundred other men.

The thrill for him was in *her* being *his* only.

"Let's run."

"What?" Pulled from his thoughts, Brady raised his head and stared down at Ren. "You want to go for a run?"

"Yes." She pushed against his shoulders. "In coyote form."

"Um…"

"C'mon. Can't you feel it?"

Brady flexed his hips, his semi-hard cock still buried inside her. "Yeah, I feel it," he said with a chuckle.

Laughing she pushed at his chest this time. "Not that."

"You can't feel that?" He grinned down at her and rocked his pelvis back and forth. "Let me help you."

"Brady," she moaned. "I want to run with you."

The edge in her voice made him stop moving. "Why?"

"We never did before…" She pulled her bottom lip between her teeth, one lengthened canine showing. "I want to do this right."

"I don't think you have to worry about that. For a couple of virgins, I think we did it right."

"Not that!" she laughed, swatting at his arm with her hand.

Smiling, he lowered his forehead to hers. "Okay. You want to shift to coyote and run together. I get it. But Ren, it's still snowing."

"Oh." Her gaze moved to the window where the falling snow bumped against the glass.

"We should wait until after."

"After it stops?"

"No. After I take you again." He pulled his hips back then drove them forward. From root to tip, her pussy walls sucked at him, the slick heat making his half hard cock full to bursting in a single thrust.

He hadn't been worried, but when she arched up to meet him, when her walls clenched around him, Brady knew they weren't going for a run any time soon.

Lowering his head, he took her mouth in a hungry, wet kiss that had him breathing hard and thrusting harder. His chest pressed to hers, the lush curves of her breasts pillowing his body, their hardened tips poking him.

They spent forever licking and rocking. Mouths and sex joined in a slow sensual climb to the top. With each stroke, each slide of flesh on flesh, the tension tightened, the need increasing until Brady was driving in, plunging deep with tongue and cock. Panting into her mouth he let his body lead him. Lead her.

She worked with him, followed him, led him, in their search for satisfaction. He might have done this for the first time only moments ago but he knew what he wanted, what to do. Knew how to make her want, how to make her feel good.

And right now his instincts drove him to mount her.

Pulling from her body, he grabbed her hips and flipped her over. The squawk that left her mouth was part displeasure, part surprise. Except she didn't have time to protest further because he dragged her ass up, spread her legs with his, and plunged deep once more.

"*Brady*," she gasped, her pussy clamping down on his length hard enough to bruise.

Her back bowed, her shoulders and head dropping to the mattress, her ass pressing into him more.

He grinned in triumph and hammered into her harder. Deeper.

Arching over her back, he kept one hand on her hip and slid the other around beneath her in search of her clit. When he found his prize, he used their combined slickness to ease the glide of his fingers and stroked the rock-hard bundle of nerves until she was bucking under him.

Her gasps and moans, the wet slap of flesh on flesh, an accompanying soundtrack to their claiming. He might be the one taking her—claiming her—but she was claiming him in return. With every sound, every movement, she owned him. Heart. Soul. Coyote.

Bent the way he was, he had a perfect view of his mark on her neck. Neither of them had said a word about the bite they'd each delivered. About the mating mark that now sat on both their necks. He didn't remember sinking his teeth into her, didn't remember anything except the blinding pleasure Ren's fangs had delivered the moment he'd let go.

His orgasm had been powerful but when her teeth had punctured his skin it had just about blown his head off, and right now, looking at his own bite mark on Ren's smooth skin, he wanted to do it again. Wanted to take them both to oblivion once more.

He used his hand on her pussy to hold her close and slid the other up her waist, over one breast to her throat. Palming that delicate column, Brady applied a small amount of pressure, his arm across her torso supporting her weight, pulling her into him.

"I'm going to bite you," he whispered into her ear. "Just like before, I'll sink my teeth deep and claim you as mine."

She shuddered against him, her breath coming in harsh pants. "Brady."

His name on her lips in that breathy little way sent a shaft of lust through his groin, made his cock pulse, his balls draw up tight, and he knew he didn't have much time before he fell off the edge. He wouldn't go there alone.

"Ren," he murmured, then tongued her ear lobe, grazed it with his teeth.

Her body clenched around his thrusting length, her slick walls tightening with each retreat as though she couldn't bear for him to leave her. She needn't worry. Brady had no intention of going anywhere that wasn't with her. Nothing in his life from now on would be done without Ren.

He nipped the side of her neck. "Tell me," he growled needing to hear her acknowledge his claim on her.

"I'm yours." She turned her head as much as his hold on her throat would allow and locked her gaze with his. "I've always been yours."

"And you always will be." Gripping her tighter, he picked up the pace, pounded a little harder, dove a little deeper. "I'll never let you go now that I have you."

"I wouldn't let you."

Brady could see the truth of her words in her eyes. He might be attempting to mark her soul so she'd never be rid of him but she would do the same in return. She'd leave him with no doubts about their mates connection.

Her gaze softened as she stare at him, her body pinned in place by his. "I love you, Brady. I've always loved you."

His eyes closed, his lungs drawing in a deep breath while his body continued to rock into hers. "Love you too. Always," he whispered against her ear right before he dragged his teeth down her neck.

"Do it."

Gaze on hers once more, Brady smiled. "You can't bite me in this position."

"Don't care. I'll bite your ass later." She bucked her hips against him, drove her ass into his next thrust with brutal force. "Bite. Me."

Canines dropping, he lowered his head and pressed his lips to her neck and the mark already there. He licked at each of the puncture wounds. Breathing her in, he took his time playing his mouth over the bite that would forever mar her skin.

The whole time he drove his cock into her, stroked her clit, and held her in place. Tension rose; her need for release, his need to claim, coiled in an ever increasing swirl of desperation.

And when she writhed against him, when her breath came in panting bursts, her moans turning to whimpers and whines, he knew it was time to take them both over.

In unison, he drove deep inside her, bracketed her clit between his fingers and squeezed, and sank his fangs into his mating bite.

They exploded together.

A scream tore from Ren's throat, a hoarse groan from his, and their bodies thrashed and bucked with the waves of pleasure shooting through them.

Brady wasn't sure if they were both climaxing or if this was some kind of out-of-body thing because while he felt the ecstasy jolting through him, it didn't feel like his own; it felt like an echo of hers. His coyote howled in his head, the beast rippling beneath his skin, and his vision blurred, went white.

Flash lighting lit him up on the inside, scorched his veins and rose every hair on his body, the fine covering thickening with the shift threatening to take him over.

"Brady!"

Ren's cry brought him back to earth, her mad scramble beneath him snapping him out of his own mind and body to realize he wasn't the only one struggling against a shift.

He jerked back, ripping his body from hers in a brutal move that sent a shock of pain, a shaft of pleasure, through his groin. Disengaged, Brady sat back on his heels and watched Ren shift to coyote in front of him.

A grumbling whine echoed around them as she dropped to her belly, her tail curling around her hind leg, her muzzle flat on the bed, tongue out, breath panting.

"Fuck." Brady clenched his fists. His jaw. "Ren."

Her eyes met his, pleading. Confusion and pain swirled within the dark brown depths. He knew what he had to do.

Climbing from the bed, he ran for the back door and threw it wide; spinning around to get Ren, he found her behind him.

"Let's run." Shifting quickly, Brady led the way outside into the falling snow.

He shouldn't have ignored her earlier request. Shouldn't have taken her—bitten her—so soon after claiming her the first time.

Clueless as to the mating bond process, Brady should have known Ren's instincts were good. She'd wanted to run. He'd distracted her with more sex, another bite, and now they were in the woods, running between the trees at break-neck speed while snow drifted down around them.

Brady guided Ren down the slope to the creek then along the bank. They ran for long minutes, his coat wet from sweat and snow, before Ren barked and came to a stop. He didn't know why she'd stopped or what she had in mind, but he would let her lead on this.

She stood at the water's edge, her breathing labored, her coat shiny with dampness, and Brady had to struggle to pull air into his lungs. Not from their run. Physically fit, their dash from the house hadn't winded him, but the sight of Ren did.

Dark fur tipped with silver covered her coyote body. She wasn't small but she wasn't as big as him. It seemed strange that as humans they were around the same height but as coyotes he was at least a third bigger than her.

With a ripple of muscles, she shifted to human. "I'm sorry."

Changing quickly, on feet he stepped closer. "For what?"

"For losing control."

"Control?" he moved even closer. "You think I'm worried about you losing control with me? I want you to lose control. I want you to trust me enough to lose it but also to let it go. I need you to let me take care of you, and there isn't a more vulnerable state than when you give up or lose control."

"But—"

"No buts." He grabbed her hands, held them tight in his. "I want to be the person you're the most comfortable with, the one you trust to catch you if you fall, the one who makes sure you're not in danger. I want to love you and be loved by you, but most of all I want you to know that if you lose control, if you let it go, I'll be right there to make sure you're okay. I want you to trust me to be there—*here*—right beside you."

"I do trust you." She stepped into him bringing their now cold bodies flush together. "I trust you with every part of me. But, Brady, I could have hurt you by shifting when we were..."

He laughed when she couldn't finish her sentence, when a blush rose up her throat and filled her face. "The most that could have happened is a few scratches and the interesting predicament of being caught inside you."

Ren's face scrunched up, a clear look of distaste in her eyes. "Eww..."

Laughing harder, he pulled her hands around his back and held them there. "Yeah, maybe."

She tried to yank free. "Gross. Brady that's disgusting."

"Nothing about you and me together is disgusting. I'm not saying I want to take you that way but if we found ourselves in the position again and I wasn't fast enough to pull free, it wouldn't be disgusting. It would be us and anything between us is neither disgusting nor off limits. As long as we're both enjoying what we do, or find ourselves doing, I'll think it's the most wonderful thing in the world."

Rolling her eyes, she muttered, "Great. I've hooked up with a freak."

"Ren, I shift into a coyote. Ain't nothing freakier than that."

"That's not freaky."

He arched one brow.

"Fine, some may find it a little weird."

"I'd think anyone who wasn't a coyote shifter would find it weird."

"Pretty sure wolf shifters don't think it's weird."

"Oh no, wolves are weird. I've met a couple." He chuckled. "Definitely weird."

"Speaking of weird..."

He knew what she was getting at. "We should go back to the house and figure out what to do about the journals."

"I think you need to tell the sovereign and sheriff. I thought we could ask Gordie and Steve to invite everyone to their place so we're on neutral territory."

"Not a bad idea." He held her close and took a deep breath. The scent of her—them—filled his nose, almost distracting him from the question he needed to ask even if he didn't want to. "How much have you read? Do you know..."

"No. I've worked out what Malcolm and Matthew were doing but I'm not up to where you were born yet."

He breathed a sigh of relief. It would be short lived though; as much as he didn't want to know the answer to his parentage, he needed to.

In spite of Ren's protests, without that knowledge he couldn't move forward.

Not if he wanted them to have a worry-free future. With the secret hanging over his head, he'd always be waiting for it to come out. For her to realize his origins were something she couldn't live with.

"Stop it." She slapped his bare ass.

"Hey!"

"Nothing that is in those books can change this. *Us*."

"How can you be so sure?" he demanded, a harsh edge to his voice.

"Because I loved you in spite of the fact I hated you."

18

JANUARY 23

Because I loved you in spite of the fact I hated you.

Ren's words had been on repeat in his head for the last two days. And he still couldn't wrap his mind around them. Brady wasn't sure he ever would. All he could do was accept them.

"Stop going over it."

He turned his head for a second before refocusing on the snow-slick mountain road in front of them. "What?"

Her hand landed on his thigh. "You know what. If you leaving and not contacting me for thirteen years didn't affect it, nothing I find in your mother's books will change the way I feel."

"You don't know that."

"Actually, I do." Her fingers tightened on his leg momentarily. "You want me to trust you, Brady, but that goes both ways. You need to trust that what I say is the truth. That when I tell you I love you, I mean it, and when I say nothing can change that, you have to *believe* it."

He sighed. "I'm sorry. It's just…"

She squeezed his leg again. "I know. It's okay. We'll get through this and everything will be fine."

God, he wanted to believe that. With every breath he took he wanted to believe she'd stick by his side when all the rotting bones were uncovered because Brady was pretty sure those bones held decaying flesh—rotting, festering maggot-filled flesh.

"It's not far now, just around the next bend. Steve's place has a big driveway so if we're the last to arrive you can still pull in off the road," Ren instructed.

"Are we late?" The last thing he wanted was to be late when he'd asked to meet with everyone.

"No. No. Gordie invited everyone over for dinner. She promised to keep the true reason for getting together a secret until you were ready."

"*We*, until *we* were ready. This is about us now. I know it's my family, my past, but if we're mates that makes it your family, your past."

"Okay, then I'm ready whenever you are."

Brady could hear Ren's determination to stand by his side, her confidence that the people inside Steve and Gordie's house wouldn't run him out of town, and it had his spine straightening, his shoulders pulling back. Drawing in a deep breath, he let the anxiety rolling in his gut out as he exhaled.

"I think we should dive right in. No point dragging this out longer than we have to," he said. "It's not like putting it off gets us anything, and I'm ready to move on, to let all the secrets out so they're no longer hanging over my head."

"Our heads. It's hanging over *our* heads. And I agree. We get it done so we can move past it. I'll let Gordie know as soon as we get there."

He nodded, kept his gaze on the road, and sent up a silent wish that revealing what they'd discovered didn't mean he'd be finding a new place to live, that he'd be forced to take Ren away or worse, give her up.

Ren slapped his thigh. "Stop it! You're not going anywhere. *I'm* not going anywhere."

"What? Are you reading my mind now?"

"No, but I'm sensing your agitation; it's like the air thickened or something." She twisted in her seat, both hands now on his leg, her grip firm. "I get why you're worried but nothing we've uncovered was your doing. I know these people. They aren't about to blame you for something you never had a hand in."

Glancing quickly at Ren, he offered a small smile, before looking forward again. "I'll keep you to those words."

"You can. I promised I'd never lie to you and I won't, not even now when a lie might make you feel better."

Brady could hear the truth in her voice. She wouldn't lie. Not about this. She'd told him some of what she'd read in his mother's journals; he knew she hadn't found out if Michelle Watson was his birth mother yet. God. Michelle hadn't even been married to Malcolm Connelly. She'd been kidnapped and held captive until she'd lost the will—the desire—to escape.

Ren hadn't revealed the details of Michelle's early life in Whispering Springs although she'd given him enough to know the young woman his mother had been was subjected to isolation and brutal abuse. If Brady had to guess, he'd say at some point her kidnapper had become her savior.

Brady wasn't sure if he wanted to know all the details or keep his knowledge to a more general overview. What he did know was that they had to find out what Malcolm and this Matthew person had been doing with the children they brought to the mountains over the years.

"Here. Turn in here."

He took his foot off the accelerator and lightly touched the brake. The last thing he needed to do was put them in a ditch because he'd slammed on the brakes like some rookie driving in the snow for the first time.

Comfortable with his speed, Brady made the turn into the driveway of a huge log cabin. Only the house in front of them couldn't really be called a cabin. More like a mansion.

"Steve built this?" he asked as he brought the truck to a stop beside a sheriff's department SUV.

"I know, right?" Ren leaned forward in her seat, her gaze roaming over the beautiful house. "I knew Steve was good with his hands, a regular handyman around town, but I had no idea he was this good until he and Gordie got together and I came up here."

"I might have to talk to him about our place."

"He's good at the design aspect of a house too. According to Gordie, he designed and built this place himself with a little labor help here and there. Wait until you see the hand carved furnishings. I love the railing he did for the stairs leading to the bottom level."

"Are those the ones Gordie fell down?"

Between reading his mother's journals, Ren had told him what had happened in recent months, including her sister's accident at the beginning of the year. Brady was astonished to discover Gordie had walked away from her encounter with Marcus virtually unscratched but a tumble down a flight of stairs left her with a busted arm and an almost busted head.

Humming agreement, Ren tipped her chin up and said, "We've been spotted."

Brady's gaze zipped to the front door. Sure enough, two people stood in the open doorway. Gordie and Steve. "I met Gordie the other day so she's easy to place but I can't believe how recognizable Steve is. He hasn't changed at all."

"I know, I swear that man doesn't age. He looks the same as he did in high school."

"What, no wrinkles or gray hairs?" he asked with a smile.

"Not that I've seen. Although my sister would be to blame for those, not the years he's added to his life."

"Well, let's get this over with." Brady switched off the truck and unlatched his seatbelt. "No point delaying the inevitable."

Ren laughed as she undid her belt and opened her door. "You sound like you're going to the gallows."

"Feels like I might be," he muttered as he popped open his door. Brady barely had his feet on the ground and the door closed behind him when Ren threw herself at him. He had no choice but to catch her. "Hey!"

"Please stop it," she mumbled into his neck where she'd tucked her face after wrapping her arms and legs around him in a death-grip. "Everything is going to be fine."

Brady sighed. "I know. I just don't like being the bearer of bad news. Or the one whose family tried to destroy this town and the pack. And I don't want to even think about what Marcus tried to do to Gordie."

"I wouldn't either but I know nobody would blame me for what others did." She leaned back until their gazes locked. "No one will hold you responsible for Marcus's or Malcolm's actions. And if they do, they'll have to deal with me."

He grinned at the fierce look on Ren's face, the murderous glint in her eyes. His one-woman army defending him from the world.

Sliding a hand to the back of her head, he held her gaze with his as surely as he held her head. "Thank you. Thank you for defending me, for standing up for me when I'm not sure I should stand up for myself."

"You have nothing to defend against. You were a powerless kid before and then you weren't here. Nothing that happened while you were away can be laid at your feet and anything we discover in your mother's books isn't on you either. You haven't even read them. Only your mother and I know what's written on those pages."

Ren was right, his brain knew she was; it was just his heart, the one that ached to be accepted in the Whispering Mountains pack once more, felt heavy, like this could be the thing that turned the pack members against him.

She rested her forehead on his, her arms tightening around his neck. "We've got this."

Her words were a vow. Filled with strength and conviction and trust. Trust in *them*. Trust in *him*. "I love you."

Grinning, she smacked her mouth on his then jumped out of his arms, grabbed his hand, and tugged him toward the house. "Ditto. Now let's get this done."

With a smile, Brady let her pull him in spite of the fact he'd willingly follow her anywhere. They'd come a long way in such a short time. Only a few days and he'd lay his life down for hers. He had no doubt she'd do the same. And in that moment he realized she was right.

He had nothing to worry about from the members of the Whispering Mountains pack because all that really mattered was the woman with her hand in his. The woman who loved him no matter what had happened in the past.

Ren.

"Hey." He pulled her to a stop.

Looking over her shoulder, she arched an eyebrow.

"Why don't you go by Ren anymore?" He had wanted to know since old Doc Monroe had told him she'd stopped using it after he'd left.

With a sigh, she turned to face him. "You want to do this now?"

Brady nodded.

"Okay." She licked her lips, swallowed, then licked them again. "If I wasn't allowed to say your name or ask about you, I couldn't live with the reminder of you. You made me Ren and without you I couldn't bear to hold onto her."

Fuck. He closed his eyes, held her hand tighter.

She killed him. Slashed his heart wide open.

His fucking father had done that and Brady hadn't been here to protect her. With a quick tug, he yanked her into him and wrapped his arms around her.

Opening his eyes, he locked his gaze on hers. "You can't imagine how much it hurts me to know I didn't—couldn't—protect you from Malcolm or Marcus. But what hurts the most is that you felt as though you couldn't be Ren without me. You didn't, don't, need me to be her."

She shrugged. "It felt that way at the time."

"I'll never call you Kat." He grinned. "Seems a little weird to call a canine shifter Kat but that's not why I won't do it."

Brady palmed her face and brought his lips to hers. He didn't take the kiss deep, only pressed his lips to hers and absorbed the pleasure being able to do so gave him.

"I love you. I've always loved you, will always love you. No matter what you called yourself while I was gone, you are and always have been Ren. It's not my love or me that makes you her, it's who you are, and who you are makes me love you."

Ren rolled her lips inward, her eyes sparkling with moisture. "Brady," she breathed against his mouth.

He shook his head. "That didn't sound right. I mean—" She placed her fingers over his lips.

"No. It came out perfectly because it wasn't perfect. I know what you meant and I have to say it's the most wonderful thing anyone has ever said to me."

"Really?" Brady asked, skeptical that no one else had told her how important she was to them. "Your parents and sister have never said they love you?"

Smiling, Ren trailed her fingers along his jaw. "It's not the words of love that make what you said perfect, Brady; it's the reason you love me."

"The reason? Because you're you?" Now he was really confused. Didn't they love her for her?

She leaned in and brushed her mouth on his. "C'mon. Let's leave this particular talk for later and go have a different one."

Brady glanced over her shoulder toward the house where Gordie and Steve waited. He'd forgotten where they were, why they were here. "I'd prefer to keep this conversation going," he muttered.

"Me too." Ren laughed. "But considering I'd like to jump your bones right now and I don't think my sister would appreciate me doing that on her front lawn, we should really go have that other talk."

His gaze now back on Ren, a growl rumbling in his chest, he palmed her ass and lifted her against him so she could feel one bone in particular. "Do not tell me you want to jump my bones when I have to spend the next few hours with your family and friends."

"That bone. That's the one I want to jump."

Before Brady could drag her back to the truck and drive away, Ren pulled from his grip and ran for the door.

"Ren," he called as he took off after her.

Laughing she yelled, "Catch me if you can," and darted around her sister and into the house.

Faced with a smiling Steve and Gordie, he wasn't sure what to say or do. He was thankful for the longish sweater he wore though. At least they wouldn't be able to see the evidence of his lust.

Then again, coyote shifters, so they probably heard every word they'd spoken and could smell both his and Ren's arousal.

Ignore and distract. Brady held out his hand. "Hi, Gordie, nice to see you again."

Gordie eyed his offering then laughed. "I think we're beyond that, don't you?"

Confused, Brady almost didn't return the hug Gordie laid on him. "Oh. Right." When she let him go, Brady found Steve waiting with his hand out.

"I think we'll stick with handshakes," Steve said.

"Good. Yes. Handshakes." Brady slid his hand into Steve's.

"Welcome to the family," Steve added as they shook.

Caught off guard again, Brady glanced between the two of them. "Family?"

Gordie smiled and patted his cheek. "Yes. Welcome. Mom and Dad are going to be thrilled."

"Ah..."

Steve laughed and pulled him into the house.

Brady hadn't even realized he hadn't let go of the other man's hand. Rectifying that quickly, he glanced around and instantly found something to say.

"This place is amazing. Ren said you designed and built it yourself?" he asked as he turned to face Steve.

Steve gave him a smile that said he knew exactly what Brady was doing by bringing up the house. "Yes. I'll give you the grand tour—"

"We should get back to everyone first," Gordie interrupted.

Taking a deep breath, Brady nodded. "Yes. We should get the unpleasantness out of the way."

Steve motioned for Gordie to go first. "By all means, let's get this over with. Or started depending on your point of view."

Brady looked between his hosts; he wasn't sure because he hadn't seen either in years but he'd swear by the expressions on their faces he wasn't the only one going into this meeting with something hanging over his head.

19

———

Kat took a seat beside Brady. She hadn't had to tell Gordie to get straight to the reason they were here; apparently Brady had done that when he'd followed her inside after she'd teased him.

She probably shouldn't have done that, but she'd wanted him to think about something other than what they were about to reveal for just a few moments.

Her plan had worked. A little too well really, because now she was aroused and everyone in the room knew it. Damn stupid coyote senses. At least they didn't have to worry about announcing their recent mating bond.

Their mutual marks might be hidden by their clothes but for a room full of coyote shifters, seeing those bite marks wouldn't be necessary. Within seconds of them entering the house, their mated status would have been obvious.

They'd made quick work of the introductions and with Brady having grown up here, he didn't require in-depth details. Now that everyone had taken a seat, the room filled with tension, the air vibrating with anticipation.

Kat wanted to believe no one was looking at Brady as a threat but she couldn't deny that with the last name Connelly, his presence put everyone on edge.

She wasn't sure if Gordie or Steve had told anyone the real reason why they were here, not that it mattered. They'd all know soon enough.

"I know you all came here expecting a nice dinner with friends and to welcome our newest pack member, and we will get to that, I promise." Gordie smiled at her and Brady as she spoke. "Brady and my sister have some things to say, but *I* need to tell you all what I've discovered first, and while it's not the reason for this meeting, I feel it has something to do with what Brady and Kat are going to share."

"Just spit it out, Doc." Steve put an arm around his wife. "They're not going to shoot the messenger."

"I ran some tests. Before Brady came to town. I didn't know there was anyone to claim the bodies and I wanted to add to my research—"

"Doc, get to the point," Steve urged.

Kat glanced around the room; no one appeared to have a clue what Gordie was talking about but Kat's gut told her it wasn't going to be a surprise to her. Or Brady.

"It's okay, Gordie." Kat took Brady's hand in hers and gave it a reassuring squeeze. "Whatever you have to say isn't going to be worse than what we've discovered." She deliberately used "we" so everyone knew she stood beside Brady in this.

"Oh." Gordie sighed. "Okay. Well, anyway, as I said, I ran some tests. You all know I'm researching the coyote gene and whether it strengthens or weakens when mixed with human DNA. I acquired Malcolm's DNA when he was killed in his attempt to run Quinn over. It's how I determined the origin of the turned shifters who had shown up during that time period. That they were turned by Malcolm Connelly."

"The council blamed Malcolm for those and numerous other incidents, but I'm not sure some of it shouldn't fall on the younger Connelly's shoulders," Quinn said.

"It shouldn't. The shifters I mean. It was definitely Malcolm who turned the humans. It couldn't have been Marcus." Gordie looked at Brady, her hands twisting in front of her and Kat knew what she was going to say before she said it. "Marcus wasn't a Connelly by blood. My tests show he was a non-blood. And I don't have a record of the DNA line that he was turned by."

"What the fuck?" Brogan surged to his feet. "How the hell was Marcus non-blood? Connelly was full-blood; his son had to be at least half-blood."

"Malcolm brought Marcus to the mountains as a two-year-old and gave him to my mother." Brady said, drawing every eye in the room.

Kat held her breath. She'd let him lead this; she might be the one with the knowledge, the one who'd read Michelle's journals, but it was Brady's information to share.

"What did you say?" Dale asked, rising slowly to his feet. "Your father *gave* Marcus to your mother?"

"Ren and I have been going through my mother's things." Brady snorted. "That's if she even is my mother. She definitely wasn't Marcus's. At this point we don't know all the details. We're only partway through the journals she left. Ren has been taking notes. I don't think we should reveal everything we've discovered until we've finished reading all the entries and have a clearer view of what happened."

Dale strode forward, moving beside Brogan who stood in front of Brady, the sheriff's glower as fierce as the sovereign's. "I'm sure our sovereign agrees with me when I say I think you should explain your-self," he growled as he leaned in.

Kat moved closer to Brady on the couch. She straightened her spine, sat as tall as she could, and lifting her chin a notch, she raised her voice and commanded, "Sit down. Lording it over us from up there isn't going to get you answers."

"Ren. It's okay," Brady murmured, squeezing her hand. "I'm sure—"

"No, it's not okay. None of this is your fault, and we're in a position to explain what, until now, has been the unexplainable. If they don't play nice, neither will we." Kat tipped her chin up further and crossed her arms, her eyes daring either man to argue with her. "You want your answers, you sit down and listen, and only listen. You can ask questions after we finish telling you what we've discovered so far."

"Fair enough. But I want access to those journals," Brogan said taking his seat once more.

Dale took a moment to stare Brady down before glancing her way then following their sovereign's lead. The sheriff's gaze told Kat he wanted to make it clear while they weren't enemies, as sheriff he wouldn't let them get away with not answering.

"Kat is right. No one is going to blame you for anything your parents may have done, Brady."

Kat was glad for the sheriff's concession even if it sounded forced.

Ignoring Dale's words, Brady turned and addressed Gordie. "I'd like to come into the clinic and have you run tests on my blood. I think you'll find I'm not a Connelly either."

"Jesus. And the crazy just keeps on crazying," Quinn said, with a sigh. "I think you better explain why you think that."

"We've barely started with the journals. My mother seems to have written the majority of them after leaving the mountain. I don't know exactly what they cover. We know Marcus was brought here as a child and my mother was told to raise him."

"They're labeled by year and some have a name inside the front cover, but I think they might overlap timewise a bit too," Kat added. "Which is why I've been taking my own notes."

"According to the journals, Marcus was turned at the age of four by old man Baker." Brady revealed the one piece of information Gordie didn't seem to have.

Brady's words had Dale straightening in his chair, his hands clenching, his breath sucking in hard.

Tatum stiffened beside him. "Cade," she whispered, her hand finding one of Dale's.

Kat focused on Tatum, and whispered, "There's a book with the name Cade inside it. I haven't read it yet because I tried to put them into order before I started."

"Oh god." Tatum wrapped her arms around her expanded belly and bent forward. Dale reached over and scooping her up, placed her in his lap and cuddled her close.

"What year?" Dale ground out through clenched teeth.

"From what I've worked out, he would have been six," Kat offered in a louder voice.

Tatum buried her face in the side of Dale's neck and he held her tight, buried his nose in her hair, and whispered nonsense words Kat couldn't hear.

It took him a moment to get his emotions under control. When he did, Dale turned to Brogan. "I want that book."

Brogan nodded. "Once Brady and Kat have gone over everything, we'll make sure you get that one."

"How many other names are there?" Gordie asked, her gaze a mix of shock and curiosity. Kat could almost hear her sister's brain whirring around with possibilities.

Kat looked to Brady, tried to telegraph with her eyes it was up to him if he wanted to reveal that information now. He gave her a nod.

"Including Cade I found ten names written inside the covers."

"I don't recognize any of the names other than Cade. Those of you who are older and never left Whispering Springs may know them," Brady said. "I'd like this to remain between us until we know exactly what my mother's words reveal."

Brogan leaned forward in his chair, his arms resting on his knees. "Agreed. And if either of you want help going through the journals, let us know."

"Thank you, sovereign. I appreciate that but I'd prefer to know what else is in them before I share with you or anyone else."

"The offer stands." Brogan smiled grimly. "I thank you for your willingness to share this information. It can't be easy for you and I want to reiterate what Dale said earlier. No one will blame you for what Marcus, Malcolm, or Michelle Connelly did."

Brady tipped his chin in acknowledgement.

"Watson," Kat said. "Michelle Watson. She never married Malcolm."

Brady's gaze zipped to hers, his hand landing on her leg in a hard thump. "*Ren.*"

Too late she realized she'd revealed something she shouldn't have. They should have talked before coming here to be sure she knew what she could and couldn't say. "I'm sorry. I didn't mean—"

"It's okay. We should probably tell them that part anyway," Brady said with a sigh. Turning back to the room, he continued. "Michelle Watson was taken from a street in Omaha, Nebraska, and brought to Whispering Springs by Malcolm."

"Taken," Rowan gasped. It was the first time she'd spoken. "He *kidnapped* her? Kept her here all that time? But why didn't she—"

"Stockholm Syndrome," Gordie interrupted. "He had her long enough and isolated enough for it to develop. She didn't start working for Dad until a couple of years after Kat was born. Jesus, Kat would have been around four. She came in with burns to her hands and Dad offered her a job before he'd finished seeing to her wounds."

"Burns?" Brady asked.

"Yes. I remember because it was the first time Dad let me into an exam room while he worked on a patient. Well, he didn't exactly *let* me in. He was too busy seeing to your mom while our mom took care of you and Marcus."

"And he offered her a job?" Brady shook his head. "I don't remember her not working at the clinic. As far as I knew she worked there every day until..."

Kat stood. "I need to read the rest of those books. Maybe she tried to escape—"

"Ren." Brady stood and grabbed her hands. "They can wait. We'll get the answers and probably a whole bunch more questions we'll never find the answers to, but it can wait."

"But, Brady—"

He yanked her into his chest. Pressed her face into his neck. "No. Let's take the rest of today. Spend some time with your sister and

Steve. I know you missed seeing everyone the last few days while we were snowed in."

She smiled. Brady was right. She'd been pacing the floors with a journal in her hand, a notebook beneath it ready for her to jot anything significant down, for days now.

Claustrophobia had never been an issue for Kat but idleness had. Standing still, doing nothing, had never been her thing. She couldn't even stay still long enough to soak in a bath.

The only time she remained in one place was when she was in a kitchen. Except her mind and hands were so busy there she didn't notice the lack of movement.

"We've got plenty of time to read what my mother wrote." He squeezed her tighter. "Plenty of time to discover if she was my mother at all."

Shit. She'd forgotten to tell him. She was pages away from confirming that Michelle Watson was Brady's mother. In the journal Kat was currently reading, Michelle was pregnant. The joy in the woman could be felt in her words; she'd never made it this far into a pregnancy before and Kat couldn't deny the other woman's happiness had soaked into her words, into the pages of the book.

If she had the timeline right, Michelle was pregnant with Brady and he definitely wasn't a Connelly.

He was Matthew's son.

And she still didn't know who Matthew was or where he'd gone.

Before she had to bit her tongue to stop herself from revealing what she'd read this morning, her brother-in-law saved her.

"Okay, who's hungry?" Steve asked. "Thanks to the Den, we've got a feast waiting to be devoured."

Kat turned to her sister. "You got food from the Den?"

Gordie laughed. "You didn't expect me to cook, did you?"

Kat shook her head. "Jeez, no, but you could have asked me to bring food over."

Linking her arm through Kat's, Gordie tugged her away from Brady. "You did. Wendy sent the last of the beef stew you made before the storm and El brought along a batch of her grandmother's famous spaghetti sauce too."

"I brought bread," Tatum added as they made their way toward the kitchen.

"My contribution is clean up," Rowan added from behind them.

Glancing back, Kat found the men remained in the living room eyeing the newbie in their midst. She hoped they weren't too rough on Brady.

As if she could read her mind, Gordie said, "Don't worry. They're just going to grill him on his intentions toward you."

Kat laughed. "Only you would think telling me not to worry and then telling me what's about to happen means I won't."

"I think Brady's intentions are clear and I approve, but you know men, they have to thump their chests and grunt a few times before they give their approval," Rowan said as she moved past them with an armload of plates. "I'll get the table set."

"You approve?"

"I most certainly do. And I know what it's like to spend years away from your mate so I'm not about to judge you or him for giving off enough pheromones to slay a bull."

"Oh, but we weren't mates when—"

"Of course you were." Gordie patted Kat's arm. "You were just too young to know it but everyone else did."

"*What?*"

"Well, everyone who took the time to look." Gordie waved a hand in the air. "It doesn't matter. Water under the bridge. Now let's get the food on the table before it goes cold again."

Kat studied her sister. Had Gordie known Brady was Kat's mate all those years ago? She hadn't but Gordie was older by six years; she would have known what was building between her and Brady because she would have seen it in others. She'd also been close to Rowan before the accident, would have known about and understood the bond between their friend and Quinn.

Jeez. Kat closed her eyes and sucked in a breath. Why hadn't she been able to work out why Brady's disappearance had hurt so badly?

Hindsight. It was a brilliant thing. She hadn't only been in love with Brady all those years ago, she'd stayed in love with him. Through no contact and a furious hatred that was spawned by the actions of his father and brother—who weren't related to him at all.

She had to tell him what she'd read this morning; whether she knew for sure or not, he needed to know what she suspected.

And they needed to find out who Matthew was.

20

Brady stared at Ren. Surely he hadn't heard what he thought... "Say that again."

"Michelle is your mother. You're her biological child."

"And my father?" Every muscle in his body locked up.

"Matthew."

"Who the fuck is Matthew?"

"He's the man I asked you about before. The one who lived here. Are you sure you don't remember him?" Ren asked.

Shaking his head, Brady paced the living room. "No. I barely remember my—Malcolm—being here. I tried to stay out of his way, stuck close to Mom, or hid in my room." He dragged a hand down his face. "Are you sure she's my real mother?"

Ren confirmed with a simple nod.

God, he'd hoped. Prayed. And the relief rushing through him told him just how much he'd *needed* to be Michelle Watson's child. Anything else he could deal with, but obviously that would have been his breaking point. "Okay," he breathed out. "Okay."

"I want to skim through the rest of the journals, see if I can find out who Matthew is and where we might find him now."

"Find him?" Brady shook his head. "No. Absolutely not. He's

mentioned in the journals up until now. There's no way he didn't know what Malcolm had done—was doing—to Michelle. I don't want to find him. I want to kill him."

"But—"

He held up a hand. "No."

Before Ren could argue further, he left the room. The walls were closing in on him. His skin felt too tight. His bones itchy.

Knowing exactly what he needed, he headed for the back door, stripping along the way. Naked, he grabbed the handle and yanked the door open. Brady let the shift take him and bounded out of the house into the snow-covered yard.

His thought processes worked the same in coyote form except he always found they flowed more easily when he worked his canine body into a sweat. Doing it in human form never had quite the same result.

He ran between the trees, dodged around drifts of snow. Within a few minutes, his heart pumped as fast as his paws, and his mind worked in rhythmical circles until he felt calm enough to return to human form.

Return to Ren.

She waited for him on the back porch, his clothes clutched to her chest. "Better?" she asked as he crossed the yard toward her, his pace far slower than it had been moments ago.

From one step to the next, he changed to his human body, a smile curling his lips. "Yes. Sorry. I seem to run out on you a lot."

With a shrug she held out his jeans. "It's what clears your head. I cook. You run."

Smiling wider, Brady stepped one leg into his pants. "I seem to run more than you cook."

"I don't have as much weighing on my mind as you do right now."

Brady stopped with his jeans halfway up his thighs and frowned. "Not exactly a prized mate, am I?"

Ren's gaze traveled down his torso until she reached his groin; a smile kicked up one side of her mouth. "Oh, I don't know. You look like a prize to me."

"Oh?" He couldn't stop his body from reacting to her blatant stare of approval and he didn't bother to hide the fact either. Letting go of his pants he stood straight. "See something you want?"

"I see something I have." Her eyes met his once more.

Understanding, compassion, love, lust, so many emotions swirled in the dark brown orbs that Brady felt it like a kick to the gut. "You're not going anywhere, are you?"

Smiling, she shook her head. "Not on threat of death."

"I don't know what I did to deserve this complete devotion from you but I swear, I'll spend every second of my life making sure you don't regret giving it to me."

"All you have to do is give me the same."

"You have that already."

"Then we're good." She held out his shirt. "Want to finish getting dressed or do you want to take those jeans off again and come help me with mine?"

Brady didn't need to think about it. He shucked his pants and kicked them away before stalking toward her. "You want me to help you out here or inside? Because you have about two seconds before I make that decision for you," he growled.

When they returned home from her sister's house, Ren had gone straight to his mother's journals and not lifted her head until a few minutes ago when she had told him Michelle Watson was his biological mother.

He'd found it hard not to drag her off to their room the second they'd stepped foot in the house but he had done it. She hadn't seemed as wound up as he was or she'd been able to put it aside to focus on his mother's words.

He wasn't so lucky; she'd had him in a slow simmer of lust since the minute he'd entered the Den and after she'd teased him earlier, Brady had spent an uncomfortable few hours surrounded by people and with no hope of getting his mate alone and naked.

Of course once there was hope, Ren had other ideas.

It seemed as though he'd spent most of their recent relationship fighting to get close to her in one way or another.

At least now she was his and when he could get close, there was nothing stopping him from taking her. Claiming her.

"Ren?"

The smile she sent him had his balls tucking up tight. Her next move had his groin throbbing in a painful beat. And the next thing she did seized his lungs. Watching her strip out of her clothes just might kill him. Piece by piece, she discarded each article of clothing without taking her eyes from his.

Naked she stood tall, her shoulders back so her breasts thrust out, tempting him with their taut peaks. "Here."

"You want me to take you out here? In the cold?"

"On the swing." She pointed to the old seat he'd repaired the third day he was here. "I want you on the swing."

Arching an eyebrow he contemplated how best to do this without either of them suffering an injury.

"I'm not sure it will support us..."

And if it didn't, he wanted to be between her and the splintered remains of the chair.

Images flashed through his head, in a second he knew how he wanted to do this.

Striding over, he sat down and patted his thighs. "Climb on."

Ren walked toward him, an exaggerated sway to her hips. "You going to take me for a ride?"

"Think you can handle it?" he asked, knowing it would get her back up a little, which meant he was in for one hell of a ride because she'd be out to prove she could.

"Oh, Brady. Brady, Brady, Brady." She threw a leg over his, giving him a close look at the wet flesh between her legs. "You can't fool me. You know I'm up for it. The question is, are you?"

"I'm up for whatever you want, whenever and wherever you want and if I'm not"—breath hissed through his teeth when she wrapped her hand around his cock—"I'll die in my effort to keep up."

"No one's dying here. Unless we're talking about what the French refer to as the little death." Eyes on his, she rose, maneuvered his shaft into place, and held it tight. "Are you ready for a *little death*, Brady?"

"I'm ready for anything—everything—with you." Grabbing her hips, he lifted his own and drove his length deep then paused. "Only you."

Cupping one side of his face, Ren leaned in and brushed her lips on his. "Only you."

With a grin, Brady bucked his hips and said, "Let's ride off into the sunset together."

Ren groaned, rolled her eyes. "Jeez. Corny much?"

"You love me," he answered and rocked into her once more.

"Yeah, I do."

"Then marry me." It wasn't really a question and he accompanied the words with a tweak of her nipples.

"Yes." She moaned, her head falling back before it snapped back up. "Wait. What?"

Brady smiled. "We're doing this so let's do it right. Marry me."

"God. You're insane. We've only just—"

"Ren." He took his hands from her breasts and cradled her face. "I love you. You're my mate. I plan to spend my life with you. I want to do it with my ring on your finger and yes, we've moved fast but we know. We *know*."

Her eyes bounced between his, emotions tangling and tumbling in quick succession, and he saw it the moment she got it, got him. "Yes. Okay, yes, let's get married," she said with a laugh.

"There's my Ren." He loved seeing her sparkle with joy, and he hadn't realized until now he hadn't seen it this pure since before he left. Right then he vowed to make sure every day she felt this happy, smiled this brightly. "I missed you. Fuck, did I miss you."

Smiling, her eyes watery, she leaned in and pressed her mouth to his. "I missed you too. Don't leave me again, Brady."

"Never," he promised.

"Good." She rolled her hips. "Now, let's take that ride into the sunset."

21

———

JANUARY 29

Brady took a deep breath and addressed the four men in the room. "Thank you for coming out here. Ren and I are ready to tell you what my mother's journals reveal. Then if you wouldn't mind, I'd like all of you to accompany me when I open the shed out back."

He'd given Dale a rundown of what opening the shed was about, and he was glad to see the sheriff had arrived in uniform with a full kit for evidence collection. The other men were also here in their official capacities. Brogan Wilder, the pack sovereign, his regal Quinn MacClellan, and head councilman William Brant.

With a nod to Ren, Brady leaned back in his seat and let her take over.

"Like Brady said, thank you for coming and for your discretion. When I'm done explaining what we've learned, I'll hand everything over for you to go through and do with as you see fit."

"You don't want to keep the journals?" Brogan asked.

"Not particularly. I won't ever read them and I'm pretty sure Ren isn't interested in a re-read." They'd talked about it, he and Ren, and while it was his history, the history of his mother, Brady preferred to hold on to the good memories and keepsakes.

Plus he was pretty sure the sheriff's department would want to take them in as evidence along with whatever was left behind in the shed after all these years.

"Okay, then. When you're ready," Dale addressed Ren.

"I'll do this in point form, a timeline of sorts, and then you can ask questions or go over any of the books. I've labeled them by year and major event."

After receiving nods from everyone, Ren continued.

"Michelle Watson was snatched off a street in Omaha, Nebraska, and brought here. She was held captive, beaten, and sexually assaulted for a number of years before Malcolm allowed her to interact with other pack members. During those years Malcolm Connelly and a man known only as Matthew—"

"Caldwell. Matthew Caldwell. He lived with the Connellys from the time he was a child until he up and left without a word," William Brant explained. "Malcolm was always vague about where he'd gone and why."

"We'll get to where he went in a bit," Ren offered. "As I was saying, during those years, Malcolm and Matthew would take trips to the city and kidnap toddlers. From what Michelle knew, Malcolm would receive a call, leave here, and return with a child who they would keep in the shed out back for no more than a week before they took the child away never to be seen again."

"Except Marcus." Quinn interrupted. "Brady, you said Malcolm gave him to your mother."

"He did. From what my mother wrote, Marcus was the first child they brought here but we can't know that for sure. He might just be the first she knew about. We've compiled a list of names and other than Cade Flint, none of them are familiar," Brady answered. "And everything about Cade is different from the others. He was older and he remained here in Whispering Springs."

"In my opinion that happened because he was older. They couldn't convince him he wasn't Cade Flint in the days they held him in the shed," Ren added.

"Fuck." Dale shoved his fingers through his hair. "He never said a word."

"I think I know why." Ren's gaze connected with Brady's and he nodded. "Cade was given to the Bakers, and four years after he was brought to Whispering Springs, he returned to the Connelly property and the shed he was held in where he found Matthew and a newborn boy. According to Michelle's journal entry, Cade set fire to the shed with Matthew and the baby inside."

"Michelle managed to get the baby out but Matthew died when the roof collapsed on him. Malcolm buried his body beneath the shed before erecting a new one. We believe the body is still there," Brady added.

"That explains your request for me to be here in an official capacity," Dale muttered. "But I'm not sure I should be the one to oversee this with my connection to Cade."

"I don't think you'll compromise evidence or disregard it due to Cade's involvement. I have no objections to you taking lead on this. Anyone else?" Brogan asked.

"Sovereign is right, you're more likely to seek the truth due to Cade's involvement and at this point it's not as though he could be charged," William added.

"There isn't much information other than first names and dates on the children, but we do have something else significant that you might be interested in. The reason Michelle finally escaped Malcolm and left the mountain. The day she fled, she'd broken her silence and told Maggie Wilder about everything."

"Goddamn motherfucker." Brogan surged to his feet and pointed at William. "He killed them. I knew it wasn't an accident and you wouldn't do anything about it."

"I couldn't do anything even if the evidence that was presented suggested foul play," William argued. "Which it didn't."

Turning to Dale, Brogan commanded, "Reopen the case into my parents' deaths."

"Sovereign." Dale nodded.

Brady knew they needed to get to the final part of why they were here. Clearing his throat, he brought everyone's attention back to him and said, "The newborn caught in the shed with Matthew was registered as the child of Michelle, father unknown, but my mother's journals reveal the child was my full brother. Matthew fathered myself and the infant named Jacob. Both of us were given the last name Connelly because Malcolm didn't know Matthew and Michelle were sleeping together."

"What happened to the baby?" William asked.

"Michelle's journal entry for that day says after she'd gone to town to have the burns she received trying to rescue the baby and Matthew treated, she returned home and found the baby and Malcolm gone. When he returned—without Jacob—Malcolm handed her paperwork. A birth certificate and adoption papers. He'd forged her signature and given the baby away." Ren flipped through her notepad. "It's at this point that Malcolm began to show signs of mental instability. Michelle writes on a number of occasions that his moods become more and more volatile and his drinking increased."

"I tried a number of times to have him removed as sovereign due to his alcoholism," William added. "It wasn't until it got out of hand and he was drunk all day every day that the council started to realize he was no longer a good fit for the role. Of course it still took him attacking Brogan and challenging him to a fight for the position before they made any moves against him."

"Not that they needed to do anything when Malcolm disappeared over the ridge," Quinn growled.

"Anything else we need to discuss before we move outside? I'd like to start before the light fades," Dale explained as he stood, changing the direction of the discussion.

"Tell us what to do and we'll do it," Brogan said. "Anything your deputies would normally do."

"How are you with a shovel?" Dale asked, grinning.

Quinn flexed his arms. "All that snow shoveling is finally paying off."

Laughing, William pushed to his feet. "If it's okay with you youngsters, I'll sit the shoveling out."

"You can be in charge of the log," Dale said, handing the councilman a notepad and pen. "Write down everything we do. Also, I'll get you to label the evidence bags. Kat? Can you take pictures of the whole process?"

"Sure. Should I start before or after you cut the locks off?"

"Before. I want everything documented."

"Right, everyone has their jobs; let's get this done." Brogan headed toward the door where he picked up one of the shovels Brady had place there earlier in preparation.

He was relieved to have the subject of Malcolm Connelly out of the spotlight. Now they could concentrate on his father. Brady had been glad to discover he wasn't Malcolm's biological child except the unknown Matthew didn't appear to be a better option.

Both men had done horrible things according to his mother, and Brady hadn't come to terms with who his father was or his mother's apparent love for the man. And she had loved him. In some twisted way, Matthew had become Michelle's savior, the reason she hadn't tried to escape before the night Malcolm had gone on a murderous rampage.

Why Michelle hadn't left after Matthew's death still wasn't clear, but Ren had her theory on that. She thought Michelle had stayed in the hope of Malcolm revealing where he'd taken her youngest son. Whether Malcolm had worked out who'd fathered Jacob remained unknown but to Brady's mind it was clear. Malcolm had known.

It wouldn't surprise Brady to discover Malcolm had known he wasn't his child either.

"Hey." Ren slipped her arm through his. "You okay?"

"Hmm." Glancing down he offered a smile. "Yeah, I'm good. I'll be better when this is over, but now that we know everything we're going to from my mother's journals, we can move forward."

"You still happy to leave Jacob—"

"For now. Let's deal with the shed. Get married next week and enjoy some quiet before we rock the boat again."

"You're sure?"

God, he loved her. He'd made the mistake of telling her he didn't want to upset their wedding plans by looking for Jacob. Now she thought he was putting it off for her when really, he was doing it for himself. He needed to wrap his head around the fact he had another brother. One that was actually blood related. "It's been twenty-two years. A few more weeks won't make a difference."

"But—"

"Ren. I'm not ready."

"Oh. Okay." She frowned, studied him intently, her concern clear.

"I'm good, Ren. Honestly."

"Hey, you two, are we doing this or not?" Dale asked, half out the door.

"We should get this done. I want to sleep with you in my arms tonight, knowing there isn't a body buried in the backyard." Brady urged her after Dale.

"It's not exactly in the backyard."

"Close enough."

"I can't believe we're actually digging up a skeleton. We've been uncovering proverbial ones for days and now we're looking for a real one."

"Did you tell Gordie she could have whatever we find after the sheriff is done with it?" he asked, picking up the last shovel. He wouldn't ask his pack mates to do anything he wouldn't do, and that included digging up bodies.

"Yes. She wanted to be here but I convinced her it would be best to waited until Dale called. Once you find what we're after, he'll call her in to transport the body—bones, whatever—to town."

And that would be the point where the secret would get out. No way could they hope no one saw them wheeling a body into the clinic. He was ready for that. Had prepared for what he'd say. Until Dale concluded his investigation it would be a clear "no clue, I haven't lived here in years".

Brady figured that line would work for a while and until it didn't, it was all he'd disclose. Of course he'd avoid all conversation if possible.

"C'mon, Dale has the bolt cutters ready." Ren tugged on his hand. "He can't start until I've taken pictures."

He followed Ren and thought about all the changes to his life in the last two weeks.

Fourteen days.

Such a short time in the grand scheme of things and yet...

He'd come home.

Found his mate.

Bonded with his mate.

Discovered his father wasn't his father.

Uncovered a long lost brother.

And now he was digging up the bones of a man he'd never know but would be connected to for eternity.

It seemed to be far too much for fourteen days.

Overwhelming when he listed it all out.

The one bright spot was the woman walking in front of him. She held him up—held him together—just by breathing.

Kathren Joy Monroe was the light of his life and he couldn't wait to marry her next week and become Mr. Kathren Joy Monroe.

They'd spent the last few days talking about his last name. He wasn't a Connelly, and honestly, who would want to keep that or take that as a surname here in Whispering Springs?

Caldwell didn't fit either. So after asking Doc Monroe if he objected, Brady had decided to take Ren's name as his when they made their union legal.

It would remove the last of the dark cloud the Connelly name had put over the town and pack. And Brady wasn't attached to the name at all; in fact it left a bitter taste in his mouth.

Ren's father had suggested he take Hank's surname but that didn't feel as right to Brady as Monroe did.

Over the next few weeks they'd remove everything they could that tied this place to the past and start laying down new foundations for the future. He had Steve coming over later in the week to draw up plans and Brady hoped to get a start on those before next winter set in.

He wanted this place to become the Monroe place. And for Brady, the day he held Ren's hand and pledged his life to hers, took her name as his, would be the beginning of that. At that point they'd put the past and the Connelly name behind them for good.

EPILOGUE
FEBRUARY 15

Brady looked out over the yard at everyone who had come to help.

They were pulling down the shed. The one that had remained locked until a few weeks ago when the sheriff had broken the locks and gone over every inch of the building looking for evidence.

Not much was left after all these years, but the one thing they did find was Matthew Caldwell's body.

His father.

Jacob's father.

So much had happened in the last month.

Some good, some bad.

"Hey." Ren slid her arm around his waist. "What are you doing standing over here?"

Glancing down, Brady smiled. A whole bundle of good. He wrapped his arm around Ren's shoulders and pulled her in front of him. This right here outweighed all the bad. "I'm just taking one last look before we bury the past for good."

"You know I was thinking..." She looked over her shoulder to where everyone waited. "Do you really want to pull it down? I've got all the makings for s'mores and thought maybe we could burn it to the ground instead. A kind of exorcism, if you like."

"Burn it to the ground?" It was an intriguing idea. It would certainly solve the problem of what to do with all the junk inside. And they could toss on the timber from the old lean-to garage he'd left stacked at the side of the house after he'd ripped it down. "Should we get the fire truck out here?"

Ren patted his chest. "On the way," she said with a grin.

"You planned this?"

"Think of this as our phoenix moment."

"We'll rise from the ashes?"

"Our future."

He caught sight of Brogan and Quinn clearing a perimeter around the shed that had held so much of the bad.

It wasn't the shed Matthew had died in; that one had burned to the ground long ago, but Ren was right.

Exorcism by fire.

Burn away the past and leave the ground fresh for the future. Cleanse this place of all the lies, of all the pain, and allow new life, new memories to take hold.

Memories he'd make with his mate by his side.

Love small town romance?
Try my contemporary small town romance series *Winter Lake*.
Start reading Love Me Like You Do now.

If you enjoyed this book, please consider leaving a review. It only takes a few minutes and you'll be helping other readers find stories they'll enjoy, as well as supporting authors you love.

For what's coming next, latest releases, sales and more, join
Rhian's Royal Readers
http://www.rhiancahill.com/contact/newsletter/

ABOUT RHIAN CAHILL

Rhian Cahill is the alter ego of a former stay-at-home mother of four. With motherly duties rapidly dwindling, Rhian is able to make use of the fertile imagination she used to keep herself sane for all those years of slavery. Years spent living overseas and visiting tropical climates have helped inspire some steamy stories.

Multi-published in erotic romance, paranormal romance, and contemporary romance, Rhian, with the help of Mr. Muse, spends her days and nights writing.

When not glued to the keyboard you'll find her, book or knitting in hand, avoiding any and all housework as much as possible.

For more on Rhian –

Website – http://www.rhiancahill.com/
Newsletter signup – http://www.rhiancahill.com/contact/newsletter/
FaceBook – https://www.facebook.com/RhianCahillAuthor
Instagram – http://instagram.com/rhiancahill/
BookBub – https://www.bookbub.com/authors/rhian-cahill
Goodreads – https://www.goodreads.com/rhian_cahill

OTHER TITLES BY RHIAN CAHILL

CONTEMPORARY ROMANCE

Everyday Heroes World

Flashback

Flyboy

Fallout

Winter Lake Series

Love Me Like You Do

Love The Way You Are

When You Love Someone

Let Me Love You

Wild Rush Of Love

Party Games Series

Truth Or Dare

Spin The Bottle

Pass The Parcel (novella)

Are You Game? Series

7 Minutes In Heaven

Catch'n'Kiss

Red Light, Green Light

Hearts Are Wild Series

No More Talking (novella)

Dare You To (novella)

Mad Love

Boys Of Summer

Bondi Beach Boys

Sand, Surf And Sunnie

Only You Series

All Of You

For a full list of available books visit

http://www.rhiancahill.com/books/

For what's coming next, latest releases, sales and more, join

Rhian's Royal Readers

http://www.rhiancahill.com/contact/newsletter/